SHAMAN OF STONEWYLDE

SHAMAN
of
STONEWYLDE

The Fifth Novel of Stonewylde

KIT BERRY

GOLLANCZ
LONDON

Copyright © Kit Berry 2012

All rights reserved

The right of Kit Berry to be identified as the author of this work
has been asserted by her in accordance with the
Copyright, Designs and Patents Act 1988.

First published in Great Britain in 2012 by Gollancz
An imprint of the Orion Publishing Group
Orion House, 5 Upper St Martin's Lane, London WC2H 9EA
An Hachette UK Company

A CIP catalogue record for this book is available
from the British Library

ISBN 978 0 575 09893 0 (Cased)
ISBN 978 0 575 09894 7 (Export Trade Paperback)

1 3 5 7 9 10 8 6 4 2

Typeset by Input Data Services Ltd, Bridgwater, Somerset

Printed in Great Britain by Clays Ltd, St Ives plc

The Orion Publishing Group's policy is to use papers that
are natural, renewable and recyclable products and
made from wood grown in sustainable forests. The logging
and manufacturing processes are expected to conform to
the environmental regulations of the country of origin.

The Stonewylde Series
is dedicated to the memories of
Jean Guy, my best owl aunt
and
Debbie Gilbrook, my dearest friend.

The golden sliver of waning moon, almost in its dark phase, rose and set quickly. On the roof of the mediaeval tower stood a figure, alone and silent. She breathed deeply of the pure elixir that blew in from the sea and away to the hills beyond. The morning star dimmed further in the clear sky and Leveret closed her eyes, deep in reverie. The sounds of the Hall awakening, the cows lowing in the distance, the birds leaving their roosts to herald the dawn – all noise started to recede. In her mind's eye she saw a cleft between rocks, an entrance to another realm, and she stooped to enter.

Inside it was dark and dry and Leveret felt entombed. She reached out to touch the walls but the cave ballooned from the narrow entrance and she grasped only air. She could see nothing at all in the blackness, yet she was overwhelmed with a terrible sadness, sadness so powerful and so deep that everything else was stifled. A tiny light flickered up ahead, and shadows began to dance as the sound of sobbing filled the air. Suddenly she felt trapped, buried alive, and she turned to escape the ancient stone chamber ...

She was out, back on the roof again with the night dissolving around her and the birds singing their welcome to the Stonewylde dawn. Leveret wrapped her cloak tighter in the chill of the March half-light. She made her way back down the stone steps winding around the tower and, at ground level, slipped into the room that had been her sanctuary for the past seven weeks, since the disgrace at Imbolc. Today was Leveret's last day of seclusion; at the Spring Equinox tomorrow, this cocoon must split open and she must emerge and face the world again.

1

The taxi pulled up at the great wrought iron gates and she sat for a moment in the car, craning her neck to squint up at their height. Ornate and impenetrable, they guarded the prize that was Stonewylde, tucked safely inside away from prying eyes and those who would loot and desecrate her.

She saw the camera up above swivel around and knew she was being watched by the Gatehouse. With a chuckle she paid off the driver and, slamming the car door, hauled a bright woven bag onto her shoulder. As the car pulled away in a puff of diesel fumes, she hoped that her invitation was still good or else she'd be stuck here in Dorset, in the middle of nowhere, with no means of getting back to the station.

A little later, entrance through the massive gates having been successfully negotiated, she paused on the long and winding track leading down from the Gatehouse. She'd refused the offer of transport even though the walk would take ages. She wanted to approach the Hall gradually, on her own two feet, and really savour the moment when the outcrop of chimneys finally came into view. Having dreamed of the place for so long, that first glimpse must be taken slowly, in her own time. So she'd declined a car and set off alone, her bag slung over her shoulder. Her vivid skirts swirled around her calves in the breeze and the sun glittered with morning gold.

After striding along for some distance she stepped off the tarmac and into an open field. The lush grass was spangled with early wildflowers, and with a cry of joy she kicked off her shoes to wriggle her bare toes in the warm softness. It was a perfect spring day with blue, blue skies and tiny clouds. A buzzard soared high overhead, his mewing and keening cries mingling with the shrill lark-song. She heard the refrain of Stonewylde all around, the sacred music of nature that thrummed with the vigour and vitality of spring, the hum of growing, the rush of the wind.

In the field beyond, she saw several brown shapes moving around rapidly and before she knew it they'd passed through the hedge and were heading her way. The hares came into closer view, their long, white-tipped ears laid back and their huge hind legs bunched for speed as they raced through the grass. Then one caught up with another and they tumbled together in a fast and furious fight, rearing onto their back legs to stand upright, their front paws lashing out at each other, punching and batting. She smiled at the sight of the boxing hares as the female, having fended off the unwanted attention of the male, sped away into the distance with the other hares in close pursuit.

Her sea-blue eyes scanned the landscape rolling and undulating before her in a never-ending panorama of curves and hollows. The acres and acres of woodland were still light brown in their winter guise, the buds not yet begun to swell. Green velvet pasture stretched away into the far distance, dotted with white bobbles of sheep and lambs. Ploughed fields like square patches of dark brown corduroy were hemmed neatly with hedges. She took all this in, absorbing the shapes and the colours, the textures and the tones.

And the air! She breathed hugely, lungful after lungful of clean, fragrant air that seeped into her bloodstream and raced around her body, bringing that special energy to every part of her being. She tossed back her mane of wild tawny-blonde hair and laughed again. The chuckle turned to a whoop of pure joy as it truly hit her – she was actually here, right now, *in Stonewylde!* She'd done it; breached the Boundary Walls. She'd wriggled past those who'd stop her and every one of her kind, and finally made it back into the stronghold. Tomorrow was the Spring Equinox, the festival of the goddess of fertility and her sacred hares, and here she was with her feet on Stonewylde soil and her lungs full of heady Dorset air.

Gazing around at the bright beauty that was Stonewylde in the spring, Rainbow slipped her feet back into their shoes and set off again down the track. She stopped almost immediately to rummage around in the depths of her bag. Pulling out her phone she peered at it, a grin spreading across her lovely face once more.

'Still no signal!' she said happily, switching off the device and tossing it back in. Stepping forward, she entered a tunnel of starry blackthorn and began to sing with sheer delight. The exile was finally over and she was back in the place she'd always loved best in the world.

'You really do something with hares I've never seen afore,' said Merewen, eyes narrowed as she gazed at Magpie's finished creation. The great Stone Circle was alive with the creatures. After his wonderful idea at Imbolc, when he'd substituted a hare for the traditional arrow that flew from the bow of the crescent moon, Merewen had asked him to design the main pattern this Equinox. She'd expected to modify and improve whatever he came up with, but Magpie had created a design of leaping hares that took her breath away. He'd then drawn the template and every painter had copied the design onto each stone until the entire circle danced with his joyful hares.

Magpie was unable to answer but beamed his delight at her praise. His turquoise eyes sparkled, so very beautiful in their innocence and pleasure, and Merewen wondered again how such artistic talent had remained hidden for so many years. She'd even had the boy in a class up at the Hall School only last year – how had she missed it? But this was a different person from the filthy, dead-eyed creature who'd sat at the back of the Art Room sniffing and stinking in his own private hell. Magpie was a good-looking young man now, his rich golden hair glowing in the March sunlight and his strong, artist's hand now stained only with paint. He was still a child, despite his man's body and looks, but a happy and creative one who, unless Merewen was mistaken, had a truly tremendous gift.

'I'm very proud of you, boy,' she said gruffly, clapping him on the back. 'Your hares are so good that I'd like you to come down to the Pottery soon and work on a new design with me – something for this year's crockery. What do you think, David?'

The art teacher smiled, delighted that he'd been right to push Magpie forward. It was gratifying to know that his protégé found favour with Merewen, who was renowned for her blunt outspokenness and never gave praise lightly.

'I think that's an excellent idea,' he replied. 'Maybe after the Equinox is over? And of course, Rainbow will be here too. She's arriving today, I believe.'

'Ah yes, Rainbow!' exclaimed Merewen. 'Can't wait to see the girl again! There was a time when 'twere she who was my most promising pupil. I was sad to see her go with all the other Hallfolk. The only one I *was* sad about, mind you.'

'It's wonderful that she's been allowed back,' said David. 'I felt a little responsible and I was worried that—'

'Aye, I heard 'twas you as started the egg rolling,' said Merewen.

'It was actually thanks to Rainbow that I heard of Stonewylde,' said David. 'I met her at an exhibition and greatly admired her work. She represented nature in a way I'd never seen done before. She told me a little about Stonewylde, where she'd grown up, and I was intrigued. I got in touch, hoping to visit. I was really lucky that Miranda had just decided to recruit another art teacher – one of those wonderful instances of serendipity.'

'Aye, Rainbow'll be pleased to see you here, I reckon. Mind you, I'm not sure what sort of a welcome she'll get. Many folk are against her coming back to visit.'

David's face clouded.

'I really don't understand why. I've heard something of the awful business with the previous magus, but it was long ago and Rainbow must've been so young at the time. How can people resent her returning? None of it was her fault, surely?'

Merewen bent stiffly to pick up some paint pots lying by a standing stone.

'As an Outsider you'd never understand,' she said briskly. 'Feelings still run deep – she were Hallfolk and we were Villagers and many can't put that aside, even today. But still – I for one am looking forward to seeing the maid. I've heard great things of her work.'

'Oh yes, she's so talented! At least Dawn will be pleased to see her, I'm sure. This was really all thanks to her persuading the Council of Elders.' He turned to Magpie. 'I want to pop down to the Village School and have a word with Dawn. When Merewen's finished with you, can you go back to Marigold alone?'

Magpie nodded happily, staying by Merewen's side as they did a final circuit of the huge arena, checking that every detail painted on the stones was right. The bright March sunshine poured into the ancient circle, quickening the hares and spring flowers that adorned every stone, and gilding the great goddess Eostre painted on the largest stone behind the Altar. The other painters were clearing up their pots and brushes, and Greenbough's men had finished the bonfire-building and now swept all the stray twigs from the beaten earth floor.

At last the Stone Circle was clear and everyone had departed down the Long Walk, a good afternoon's work done. Magpie loitered behind, free for once of David's solicitous care. He crouched down with his back to one of the stones and simply gazed around. His wandering eyes took in everything: the stones, the bright paintings, the oak forest beyond, the blue sky and the shadows that moved across the arena as the small clouds raced in the breeze. He stared around in wonder, as a child might.

Leveret slipped between two massive stones into the Circle, coming up through the leafless oaks that fell away in a shallow descent on one side. Immediately she saw Magpie tucked into the base of a stone and her face lit up with a brilliant smile.

'Magpie!'

She raced over and dropped down next to him, taking his

paint-stained hand in hers and rubbing it against her cheek. He grinned back and leaned into her, nearly toppling her over. Their friendship was undiminished, although they'd seen little of each other in the past few weeks despite both living up at the Hall.

'I know these are your hares, Maggie,' she said happily. 'I recognise your style. They're the best that've ever been painted in the Circle. You're so clever!'

He squeezed her hand and they sat together in silence for a while, the sweet song of a robin filling the air. Then Leveret saw, in her mind's eye, a rainbow. It was richly hued, spanning the hills of Stonewylde, and she felt Magpie's confusion.

'A rainbow? Oh, Rainbow! Yes, she's a girl – woman now I suppose – who used to live here back in the old Magus' days. She was banished along with all the other Hallfolk but they say she's coming back soon for a stay. She's a famous artist in the Outside World so I guess she'll be interesting, and I'm sure she'll love your work, Maggie. Anyway, have you been well lately? Is everything alright?'

He continued to hold her hand and Leveret sensed a succession of images: Magpie eating at the table in Marigold and Cherry's cottage by the Hall, holding cutlery and using a napkin; Magpie lying in his own bed in the tiny bedroom with his clothes folded neatly in the drawers and his pictures pinned on every wall; Magpie digging manure into the trenched soil in the walled Kitchen Gardens; finally, Swift's secretive face peering into the Art Room as Magpie stood painting a huge canvas. He squeezed Leveret's hand then and she nodded.

'I know – I'm still not sure about Swift. I'd try to steer clear of him if you can, Magpie. And remember what I told you – never, ever eat anything that he or Jay or my brothers give you. It might be poisonous and you'd be very ill. You understand?'

He nodded emphatically and she sighed, releasing his hand and getting to her feet.

'I'd better go back now. Today's my last day of solitude – I'll be at the sunrise ceremony tomorrow and I'll have to face the community again. I'll look out for you, Magpie. And soon we must go to Mother Heggy's cottage together – will you help me clear it up? Clip's getting me a special new book and I'd love you to draw all the different plants for me. Would you do that?'

He nodded with a smile and Leveret thought for the hundredth time that whatever else had happened, the one good thing to come out of all the horrible events since Samhain was Magpie's new life.

Bluebell and Celandine skipped along by their mother's side as they left the Nursery in the centre of the Village, making their way across the cobbled area towards one of the lanes radiating out.

'If Granny Maizie isn't in, we'll see if she's up at the Hall,' said Sylvie, nodding to people as they passed by.

'Oh, I hope she has some honey biscuits in the pantry!' shouted Bluebell, the iron tips in the heels of her little leather boots clattering on the stones. Her white-blonde curls cascaded out from beneath the bright blue felt hat and her cheeks glowed. 'I love Granny Maizie's honey biscuits. And her oat-jacks! And her rosehip drink! And—'

'We get the idea, Blue,' said Celandine evenly. 'The whole Village doesn't need to know. Mum, why are we visiting Granny now? What's happened?'

Sylvie glanced down at her elder daughter, nearly seven years old and as perceptive as ever. The child's deep grey eyes, exactly like her father's, bored into her and forbade any platitudes.

'I'm going to ask if we can stay with her for a bit,' she answered quietly. 'We can keep her company now she's all alone in the cottage.'

'I thought Auntie Leveret was just living with Grandfather Clip for a little while until she was well again,' said Celandine. 'Isn't she going back to her cottage in the Village?'

'Is Auntie Leveret still poorly?' asked Bluebell, her hair tangling as she pulled off the hat.

'No, I think she's fine now,' said Sylvie, 'but she wants to stay in the tower. So, Granny—'

'So poor Grandfather Clip won't be lonely!' cried Bluebell. 'That's good. He always looks so sad and his face is all grey and patterned. Auntie Leveret will cheer him up. I wish she could live with us though!'

'But Granny Maizie will still be alone so we'll keep her company?' asked Celandine. 'Is that it?'

'Exactly,' said Sylvie thankfully.

'But what about Father?' Bluebell said. 'Then he'll be all on his alone!'

'He'll have Harold,' said Celandine drily. 'Oh Mum, I do hope Granny Maizie says yes. I'd really love to live in the Village with all my friends!'

'Yes, I always wanted to live in the Village too,' said Sylvie wistfully. 'It's fifteen years since I came to Stonewylde, almost to the very day – it was just before the Spring Equinox when I arrived – and I wanted to be a Villager then. So if Granny Maizie says yes, this will be perfect.'

Maizie was at home, but took some persuading to agree to them moving in with her, even temporarily. She gave the little girls a drink and biscuits, then shooed them out of the cottage and down into the long garden to see the chickens.

'I still think—'

'Please, Mother Maizie. I wouldn't ask if it wasn't important.'

Maizie shook her greying head and frowned at her daughter-in-law. Sylvie looked pale and drawn.

'What does Yul say?'

'I haven't told him yet,' Sylvie admitted. 'But Maizie, please – I can't spend another day in those apartments. It's not just that I need a break from Yul – it's the place too. I've never wanted to live in those rooms and the memories of Magus ...'

'Aye, but why now? You've lived there since you were hand-fasted – what ... eight years ago?'

'And I never wanted to live there! I said so from the start but you know how Yul always gets his own way! Honestly, I don't want to sound disloyal but he's awful at the moment. I simply can't take it any longer!'

Her face crumpled and she started to cry silently, haunted by the memories of Yul's increased drinking and aggression, and his regular insistence on her fulfilling her wifely duties. Maizie leaned over and hugged her, gazing sadly over her head at the white-washed wall that had once sported a nail and a dark, coiled whip. Her poor son – surely he deserved happiness? But she also knew that nobody loved Yul more than Sylvie and she wouldn't be asking this lightly.

'Right enough, you and the girls can come here for a while,' she said. 'But you must promise me it's just for a stay, not forever. You and Yul ...'

She stopped as sudden tears choked her throat too.

'I know, I know,' sobbed Sylvie, trying to pull herself together in case the girls burst back in. 'Believe me, I want things to be right between us. But it's been bad for a while now ... right back since Samhain I think. He's not my Yul any more. He's a different man – cold and cruel – and I can't bear to be with him when he's like that.'

'Dry your eyes,' said Maizie gently, stroking Sylvie's shoulder and feeling quite horrified at its angularity. ''Twill all work out in the end, that I do know. You and Yul were destined to be together – 'tis unthinkable for you to be apart for long. Nothing in this life runs smooth all the time and everything goes through darkness as well as brightness. By Beltane we'll have it all better again between the two o' you.'

'I do hope so,' Sylvie gulped, blowing her nose and brushing the tears from her eyes. 'I can't stand this – I just want my old Yul back again. And thank you, Mother Maizie. The girls will be so pleased – it's been difficult for them too.'

That evening in the Dining Hall, all talk was of the newcomer to Stonewylde. Most of the youngsters had little or no recollection of Rainbow or any other Hallfolk; amongst the adults, feelings were divided about her return. Hardly anyone had actually seen her arrive. Alerted by the Gatehouse, Martin had been waiting and had shown her straight to the bedroom he'd allocated her. Hazel had then taken her down to the Village to Dawn's cottage, next to the School House, and David had joined them for dinner. They were all still there, hence the excited speculation now in the Dining Hall.

'I met her,' said Swift quietly to some of the youngsters on his table.

'So what was she like? What did she say?'

The girls in particular were agog for details. Swift flicked back his long straight fringe and shrugged.

'She was okay, but not what I'd imagined. She just stared around her as if she couldn't believe it all.'

'What was she wearing?'

'Was she really beautiful?'

'Had she brought loads of paintings with her?'

The questions came thick and fast and Swift smiled, enjoying his moment of importance.

'She's pretty hot. She's got wild blonde hair all over the place. She was wearing a long bright skirt and she had bare legs and arms and loads of jewellery. And she can't have brought any paintings because she only had one bag. She can't have many clothes, in fact, if that's all she brought for three months.'

'Is that how long she's here for?'

Swift nodded.

'How come you know so much?'

He smiled again and tapped the side of his nose.

Upstairs in their apartments, Yul and Sylvie glared at each other across the dinner table. The girls were in bed, finally asleep. They'd spent the evening in great excitement packing their knitted animals and rag dolls into a big wicker hamper, along with their books, pencils and paper.

'You can't do this.'

'Yes I can. We're going tomorrow morning after the ceremony.'

'I won't let you. I'll speak to Mother.'

'It's too late – she's agreed. We'll be company for her now she's all alone without Leveret.'

'Nobody's even asked *me* about Leveret.'

'Why should they? It's not up to you. Clip and Maizie have agreed between themselves that the best place for Leveret is with him, in the tower. She'll be out of harm's way there and he's going to keep her really busy with her studies. Maizie's happy not to have the worry of her and Clip's happy to have a protégée. There's no need for you to be involved, is there, Yul?'

He frowned and Sylvie resisted the urge to lean across the table and stroke the lines from his forehead. His face was lean and angular, his hair long and rather unkempt. He looked desperate, and so vulnerable. She steeled herself; this had happened before and she'd regret it when he turned off the vulnerability and bit her hand with a snarl.

'Are you leaving me because of Rainbow?'

His voice had a different edge and Sylvie sighed and closed her eyes, shaking her head.

'That's it, isn't it, Sylvie?' His accusation sounded almost triumphant. 'You're annoyed because for once you're not getting your own way and—'

'*For once*? Yul, I *never* get my own way!'

'So because Rainbow's coming to stay for a few weeks to do some painting, you're leaving me and taking the children away from their home.'

'Oh for goodness' sake! I'm not exactly *leaving* you and it's certainly nothing to do with Rainbow.'

Yul stood up abruptly, making Sylvie jump. He abandoned the dinner table and took his glass and wine bottle over to the sofa. Sylvie loaded the dishes into the dumb waiter, realising with a jolt of pleasure that this would be the last time she'd do this for ages.

'Why are you so against her coming back? What is it about Rainbow that bothers you?'

'I don't want to discuss it, Yul,' she said wearily, closing the panel and pressing the button for the tray to descend. 'We've talked about it too much already and I'm sick of the subject. You know I hated the idea of her coming back. Yet you deliberately went against my wishes in public at the Elders' Meeting and humiliated me. Nothing we say now will make any difference.'

'And this is your revenge – moving out and taking my girls away from me.'

'No, it's—'

'It's your way of humiliating me in return! What's everyone going to say? The magus can't even keep his own wife by his side? What sort of a husband is he that she has to go running off to his mother? How do you think it'll make me feel?'

She looked down at him as he slumped in the sofa, glass in hand and his face mottled now with anger and self-pity.

'I don't know and to be honest, Yul, I don't really care. You haven't thought about my feelings much in the past few months and I need a break from you. I'm going to have a bath now and an early night. Don't drink too much – remember it's the sunrise ceremony tomorrow and you need to be on better form than you were at Imbolc and the Winter Solstice.'

'Yeah, stick the knife in, why don't you?' he muttered to her retreating back, pouring himself another drink. He glared at the ruby liquid, tormenting himself with the image of Sylvie undressing and slipping into the foaming water. He sighed and tossed back the wine. If this was to be their last night together for a while, he'd better make the most of it.

Clip stared into the flames burning in the hearth. He should really be up at the Dolmen now, spending the night in vigil ready to greet the sunrise at the Equinox. He'd half planned to go up earlier this evening but in the end decided against it. He stretched his thin frame, curling his bony toes in their felt slippers and making all his joints crack. Clip was really feeling his years now and looked older than he should. His wispy silver hair, now straggling down his back, added to the illusion of an old wizard but in fact he was only in his fifties.

He sighed heavily and, pulling on his reading glasses, once again picked up the wad of papers recently arrived from his lawyer prior to their intended meeting later in spring. It was all so complicated and made his head ache. He scanned the pages of closely-typed legal jargon and yawned. It was important to get the handover of the estate right. His gaze wandered easily from the paper as his thoughts drifted back to Sylvie's visit earlier on. She'd seemed jittery, but that was normal nowadays; even he could see that she was thinner and looking careworn. When she'd explained that she'd just seen Maizie and would be moving into the Village with the girls the next day, Clip had felt a strange sense of relief. He couldn't understand why, but knowing she'd be out of the Hall had made him glad. He didn't press her for an explanation although her stumbling excuse about wanting to keep Maizie company rang false to both of them.

'Is Leveret really happy living here with you?' she'd asked.

'She is – and so am I,' he'd replied. 'The situation after Imbolc was impossible and I couldn't let the poor child suffer any more. None of it was her fault, you know.'

She'd nodded at this and bowed her head.

'There are things going on ... I feel Leveret's got caught up in it all through no fault of her own. It's so good to know you're caring for her, Clip. She's a strange girl and I've never managed to get close to her, but ...'

'You should try!' said Clip. 'Really, Sylvie, she has a true heart beneath that difficult exterior.'

'I realised that when Celandine and Bluebell took to her,' said Sylvie. 'But she's never let me in. I did try just after Imbolc, when Yul was ranting and raving and Maizie was so upset and angry. I tried to tell her that I was on her side but she wouldn't open up to me.'

'I know,' he said sadly. 'She was in a bad way after what happened and she didn't know whom she could trust. I'm just glad that Maizie agreed to let her stay here with me. If Yul had had his way ...'

'Don't!' she said with a shudder. 'Thank Goddess you

intervened and took her under your wing. And I'm so pleased you've decided to keep her here. Originally it was only to be until the Equinox, wasn't it?'

'To be honest, I'd always hoped to keep her with me until I leave this autumn,' he replied. 'But I didn't say so at the time because I thought Maizie might baulk at that. She's so ambivalent towards the girl – she obviously loves her very much but she won't recognise Leveret's innocence in all this business.'

'I know Maizie's been very hurt by what she sees as Leveret betraying her trust,' said Sylvie. 'But at least this way she knows Leveret's being well cared for and she doesn't have to worry for her welfare. We must try to reunite them at some point – the whole situation's ridiculous.'

'It'll be good for Maizie to have you and the little ones living with her,' said Clip. 'It's a splendid idea. Will Yul be staying in the cottage too?'

Sylvie's face clouded. Her beautiful silver-grey eyes, darker ringed around the irises, met his.

'No, Clip – not for the foreseeable future. I think you know that things aren't good between us. I need to get away from here and think about it all.'

He'd nodded, not wishing to pry. And now, scanning the papers in his hand, he wondered about Sylvie and Yul's future together. They'd always seemed destined for each other, such a perfect pair. But something had changed. Yul was driven nowadays, brusque and aggressive. He reminded Clip more and more of his late brother Sol, which must be hard for poor Sylvie to cope with. She bore the brunt of her husband's mood-swings and ill-temper. Clip couldn't begin to imagine how it must feel to be married and forced to put up with another person's behaviour; in his opinion being single and celibate was one of the joys of being a shaman. He recalled the conversation he'd had about this very subject only recently.

'Can I really never be married or have children?' Leveret had asked as they warmed up a pot of soup over the fire in the Dolmen. Living with her made Clip pay more attention to the

16

need for food, which he guessed was probably a good thing. Stomach pains were still the bane of his life.

'It's not so much that you can't, as that you'll be a better shaman if you don't,' he'd replied. 'Having a partner and children takes an enormous amount of your time and energy, as well as your focus. You could of course have those things and go on to be a successful healer and seer – but I don't think you'd ever really achieve your full potential as Wise Woman or Shaman. But don't worry about it now, Leveret. You're only just fifteen and those decisions needn't be made yet.'

'No, but if I'm to be single and childless for the whole of my life, I think I should get used to the idea now, before the normal expectations really take hold,' she'd replied. And, as ever, Clip was struck by her wisdom.

Knowing that she was asleep downstairs in her room on the ground floor filled him with satisfaction. Clip relished the role of mentor and guide, especially as she was such a brilliant pupil. Hes thought of the workload he'd piled on her these last seven weeks since Imbolc. So many books, so much study, yet she'd kept up with it, reading and learning and – judging by her responses during their discussions – understanding and retaining everything she read.

Tomorrow, thought Clip, that must start to change as she had to reintegrate into Stonewylde society. He'd have a chat with Miranda, as head-teacher, and arrange for Leveret's classes to be cut significantly in areas where they wasn't vital. Miranda must understand the importance of what the girl was learning here in the tower and how this would benefit the whole community one day. And now the days would be getting appreciably longer and the weather warming up, Leveret must go out daily to learn more of the Goddess and her ever-changing robes. She must become a herbalist – a cunning woman – and begin to brew her remedies and treat minor ailments. Clip thought of Hazel – he must arrange for Leveret to spend time with her as well.

He gazed once more into the flames as they licked lovingly at the wood. Yes, he should be up in the Dolmen now, but more important was to be here in the tower whilst Leveret slept. Ever since Imbolc he'd been vigilant, fearing for her safety after she'd been fed poison by those who wished her harm. Clip knew there were evil forces at work in Stonewylde and until he fully understood them, he must guard his young ward as best he could. There were challenging times ahead but eventually all would be worth it. This was the year when he'd gain his freedom; the year when he'd finally escape the clutches of this place. Stonewylde had always clung to him like an unwanted and demanding wife; it was a marriage he'd never sought nor agreed to, but somehow he'd become firmly shackled. And now, at long last, he could hand over all the responsibility – the stewardship to Sylvie and the role of Shaman to Leveret. As for Yul ... hopefully he'd come to his senses and help share his wife's and his sister's burdens. This time next year, Clip thought gleefully, he'd be free, roaming the world wherever his spirit took him.

2

A crow flapped towards the oak woods beyond the Stone Circle, his bright eyes gazing down at the folk pouring into the arena. It was barely light with the sun not yet risen, and everyone was wrapped in warm cloaks and robes. By the Altar Stone stood the magus, bleary-eyed and pale, and beside him stood his tall, silver-haired wife in her green cloak. The crow circled and then landed on a standing stone in a flutter of black feathers.

More people swelled the crowds already there, murmuring quietly amongst themselves. At a nod from Yul, the drummers ranged around the perimeter began a low, insistent beat that bounced off the huge stones and filled the air. The atmosphere began to change, charging with energy that grew by the minute, amplifying throughout the vast circle and weaving in and around all the people. The amazing pattern of leaping hares painted above their heads on every stone, formed a carousel that seemed to spin with the sound until the hares were alive and dancing. The beautiful goddess of spring painted on the stone behind the altar, an egg in each hand, smiled down on the folk of Stonewylde as they stood, swaying and nodding to the ever-growing beat. Hearts thudded in unison with the deep reverberation of the drums, feet tapped in time, heads bobbed and souls synchronised until everyone present became attuned to the common purpose of welcoming in the Spring Equinox.

A large group of singers stood near the entrance, their voices joined in harmonious chant – which raised the energy still further. Yul's eyes scanned the crowds and he was glad he'd insisted that most of the chanting was now performed by a choir rather than remain his responsibility. They'd been practising since Imbolc and would now do this at every ceremony, leaving him only to contribute the odd verse or two. He hoped this would help him focus on what really mattered – the Green Magic.

Yul climbed up onto the Altar Stone, closed his eyes and concentrated hard. The drumbeats throbbed in and around him and the life-force of the folk packed into the arena shimmered. He tried, with all his might, to call up the earth energy that snaked underneath the soft earth floor of the ancient Stone Circle. He remembered lying here paralysed that Samhain, unable to move an eyelash but able to summon the energy to him. And now ... he felt a flicker, a glimmer, but it wasn't enough. He knew with a sinking heart that at the moment of sunrise, when the force should gather like a great dragon and pour up through the Altar Stone into his human frame – it would be merely a small, insignificant pulse.

He opened his eyes and looked straight into the eyes of the crow, perched unmoving on top of the stone. Just at the moment when the drumming stopped and the singers fell silent, the corvid opened its black beak and let out a mighty 'CAW'. People jumped and many made the sign of the pentangle; Yul scowled at the bird's inconsiderate timing but wondered if Mother Heggy were sending him a message. He scanned the moving lake of faces before him and noted with annoyance that two figures were hurrying down the Long Walk, late for the ceremony. One tall and one small – Clip and Leveret. They stood right by the mouth of the circle and Yul saw them both noting the crow standing sentinel. Sylvie frowned up at him and he realised he'd missed his cue for the chant. He scowled again and cleared his throat. The light was growing by the second and as the words began to fall from his lips, the sun appeared in the gap between the two stones where it rose every Spring Equinox.

Yul saw the bright golden sliver above the skyline and his soul cried out to it, cried out to the Goddess beneath him, begged for the gift of Green Magic to once more bless him. He felt a dart of energy fly up from the great stone under his feet, piercing him in pallid imitation of the massive thrust he used to feel. But, nevertheless, tears of gratitude welled and Yul raised his hands towards the fast-rising sun, the words now tumbling in a torrent of praise. It wasn't much – it wasn't enough – but it was something at least. The Goddess hadn't completely abandoned him.

During the communion part of the ceremony, when the Stonewylders came up to the Altar Stone to receive their cake and tot of mead, Yul decided not to share the little earth energy he'd been fortunate enough to receive. In the old days he'd been doused with magic and was happy to pass on a measure to each person in the community. But now, with so little for himself and certainly not enough to give everyone a taste, he realised his best course would be to store it within. He'd use it to put right some of the wrongs that beset Stonewylde.

The folk began to file up to the head of the circle where the tables were set up around the Altar Stone. One held the tiny cakes baked by Marigold and nowadays entirely free of the extra ingredients once added by Violet. The other was weighed down with casks of mead, again unlaced with the additives that used to bring an added dimension to the proceedings; this was now done only in the wicker dome at Samhain. Very young children were given fruit cordial and everyone present in the huge arena understood the significance of this communion; the fruits bestowed by the Goddess were shared by all. Over the years since Magus' demise, Yul had enjoyed sharing his own special gift with everyone and they'd now grown to expect the brief touch of magic.

But today, as people young and old shuffled up to receive their cake and mead, Yul stood back from the Altar Stone and merely greeted them. Instead of reaching out to clasp their hands and release a measure of earth energy, he picked up the ceremonial staff standing by the horizontal stone. He jabbed one end firmly into the soil at his feet and held the other end with both hands, as if channelling the energy back down into the waiting ground. Folk looked surprised, quickly dropping their hands when they realised their magus wasn't going to touch them. Sylvie's eyes scanned Yul's face when she saw what was happening and for an imperceptible moment their gazes met. Neither was fooled by the other's neutral expression; both knew exactly what the other was thinking.

The communion had been going on for some time when a group approached the Altar Stone and one in their midst, still hooded against the chill, came forward. She took the cake and ate it, tossed back her thimble of mead and then moved up to where Yul stood, splendid in his green Spring Equinox robes. His headdress for this festival was a wicker wreath woven with dog mercury, primroses and violets. He stood as straight and handsome as ever, the magus of Stonewylde and leader of the community.

The cowled woman stood before him and stopped, dramatically throwing back her hood to reveal a tangle of dark blonde hair that cascaded down her back. Nobody behind in the great crowd could see her face – but Yul could. His eyes widened and lips parted and in his hands, the staff twitched. Then he smiled and although the renewed drums and singing drowned his voice, he mouthed 'Welcome' to the woman before him.

Rainbow's beautiful sea-blue eyes met his and she gave a little bow. She stood still, holding up those behind her, and stared at him. Her gaze roamed over his face and missed nothing. She took in the hard planes of cheekbone and jaw, the strong nose and firm mouth. She noted the long hair, no different to when she'd last seen Yul as a sixteen year-old youth – a wild mass of dark curls that fell into his eyes. And the eyes; she remembered those so well. They were still deep and slanted, dark grey with long lashes. But now they were hard, no longer shining with hope and passion. There was something steely lurking behind them, something brittle and dulled. And Rainbow was surprised to see they were also somewhat bloodshot.

Sylvie stared at the woman who seemed to be transfixed by her husband. She felt her cheeks flush but Rainbow barely glanced her way. She'd always known Rainbow would be a beauty; the promise had been there in the thirteen year-old girl all those years ago. What she hadn't expected was the energy that danced around the younger woman. She exuded an animal aura like a sleek big cat; contained, assured and ready to pounce. Rainbow moved her head deliberately and the angle between her neck and jaw was perfect. Slowly she raised her eyes to Yul's, every beat counting. She twitched her beautifully curved lips into a cheeky grin that was both disarming and provocative. Rainbow radiated earthiness and an enveloping femaleness, and Sylvie felt every hackle in her body rise in antipathy.

Clip and Leveret, having arrived so late, were near the very end of the queue. Almost every other person had filed up to the Altar Stone and taken part in the sharing of cake and mead. Even the babies had their lips wetted with fruit juice in this ancient ritual that bound everyone together in an act of unity – giving thanks to the Goddess for the means of survival. Leveret had been nervous about attending the sunrise ceremony but it wasn't the cause of their lateness. That lay in a hedge awaiting their return.

Leveret, like most other people present, was bundled up in a cloak over her festival tunic. She still had almost a year to go until her Rite of Adulthood, which included the presentation of her own ceremonial robes. Her cloak was plain, the ordinary homespun dyed a muddy green, and her tunic underneath was similar, although a brighter green as befitted the calendar. A vast supply of tunics for all the children at Stonewylde was held in the central store in the Village, and as each garment was out-grown, it was returned and a larger size taken until adulthood was reached at sixteen. Leveret had realised that morning, as she pulled the linen tunic over her head and fastened the braided sash around her waist, that she'd had this same green tunic for at least a couple of years now. Clearly she'd stopped growing and would never be tall like Yul, Geoffrey or Gefrin. Gregory and Sweyn weren't particularly tall and neither was Rosie, but

Leveret was by far the smallest in size, with a slight frame that made her seem even younger than she was. She longed for stature such as Sylvie's, which would have made her feel more powerful and a force to be reckoned with.

She shuffled forward with Clip close by her side, her old brown leather boots made in the traditional Stonewylde style scuffing the ground. She didn't look around, reluctant to catch her mother's eye or the attention of her brothers and Jay. She and Maizie were locked in a silent, resigned truce. No further accusations were hurled, but neither was there evidence of any affection between them. So be it, Leveret had decided grimly, when she understood how it was to be. Trust nobody other than Clip, and learn, learn, learn. That was her mantra as she endured the days and nights, gradually distancing herself from the terrible disgrace of Imbolc. She'd barely set foot in the Village since her move up to the Hall, breaking with tradition and not joining the menstruating women in the Great Barn on the previous Dark Moons. Today too was a Dark Moon, but as it fell on the Spring Equinox nobody could gather in the Barn for crafting work and gossip.

Leveret felt many eyes on her although most people were gazing in open amazement at Rainbow. She still stood near the Altar Stone, for the crowd inside the Circle had to circulate in order to take part in the communion. Rainbow, however, rather than facing the Altar Stone and the goddess Eostre, had chosen to stand facing the throng, thus giving everyone the chance to gawp. Leveret too stared at Rainbow, now she was close enough to see her clearly. The woman glowed with golden ripeness, like a perfect sun-warmed peach, and Leveret was fascinated. Clip, by her side, was also gazing at the newcomer and as they edged forward, the last in line to receive a little cake and sip of mead, he nodded to her. Her pretty face split into a massive smile and Leveret was reminded of the tiny sundew plants that grew in the marsh; they too reacted instinctively but uncaringly to any stimulus.

Leveret had noticed that Yul wasn't bestowing the gift of

Green Magic to anyone and was glad she wouldn't have to put her hands in his. He was still glancing surreptitiously at Rainbow despite ostensibly greeting every communicant with a blessing, and then Leveret noticed Sylvie's face. It had shrunk back into a mask of dislike, her white, white skin unnaturally taut and her cheekbones and the tip of her nose delicate but very pronounced. Sylvie's strange eyes glittered in a way Leveret had never seen before. She looked like a silver snake and when her tongue darted out to moisten her white lips, the illusion was complete. Leveret shuddered and moved slightly closer to Clip.

They'd finally reached the table of cakes, almost empty now as Marigold knew the quantity required and didn't waste resources on baking extras. Clip ushered Leveret in front of him and she took her morsel of cake in both hands. She bowed and bent her head to take it into her mouth as Clip next to her held out his cupped hands. Martin, presiding over the Goddess' gifts, reached out to place a cake in Clip's waiting hands. At that moment, the crow on top of the stone jumped down in a noisy flapping of feathers and wings and landed on the table between the two men. Both jerked back in surprise and the crow immediately jabbed forward to snatch the cake from Martin's fingers. Its great black beak closed around the tiny golden cake and an eye swivelled to Clip. Hopping along the table it launched off, the prize still clasped in its beak, and then they saw its very strange tail. It had one long white feather amongst the mass of glossy black ones.

The crow's theft caused a ripple of surprise amongst everyone close enough to witness it. Clip smiled amiably and held out his hands for another cake, whilst Martin cursed its ill manners. Leveret felt a strange prickling and held onto the table as the two men, the painted stones and the crumb-covered table began to tilt and sway. She swallowed hard, trying to hang on to consciousness, and looked up at the nearby stone where the crow had taken refuge. As it gobbled down the morsel, pecking at stray fragments, it sidled round so that once more the startling white feather was visible. And then, sitting beside the crow on the megalith, she saw the shadowy outline of a tiny woman with long white hair, dressed in tatters and rags. The strange creature smiled and nodded to her, calling across the gap between them in a silvery voice, 'Leveret! Bright blessings, little one.'

'Will she still be there, do you think?' Leveret asked anxiously, as she and Clip hurried back along the Long Walk.

Everyone else was now making their way down to the Village for breakfast in the Great Barn. There'd be huge baskets of warm spiced buns awaiting them, their tops marked with a cross to denote the four fire festivals and the four seasons. There'd also be hard-boiled eggs with the shells dyed in pretty, natural hues, hunks of cheese and fresh milk. The Spring Equinox breakfast was always lovely, and Clip had thought this would be a good way of easing Leveret back into the community and in particular back into the Great Barn, the scene of her ignominy at the last festival.

After breakfast, the Village would be alive with activities: the display of exquisitely decorated eggs in hand-woven nests of spring flowers, the Spring Bonnet competition in which every child in the Nursery and Village School proudly took part, the drama and dance that the older children and young adults always presented, involving Eostre and her hares and the vanquishing of winter, and the men's hurdle-making competition. The day was packed full of events and of course the dance was held in the evening in the Great Barn, after the sunset ceremony. Despite her reluctance, Clip had imagined himself and Leveret spending at least some of the day with the community.

However this was not to be. They hurried back up the lane branching off from the Long Walk, and then forked off again onto a quiet, overgrown path that bordered open fields. They'd come along this circuitous route earlier as Clip had hoped to avoid bumping into the crowds of people walking down from the Hall. He hadn't wanted Leveret bolting back to the tower if anyone made an unpleasant comment.

'We're almost there,' said Leveret quietly. 'She crawled off to hide by that birch. I wonder if she's still about?'

Clip stood back as Leveret carefully picked her way through the dense undergrowth of heavy, wet grass, old brambles and new shoots of greenery. She paused and stood completely still, staring intently into the tangle. Then she bent, pushing the clinging brambles aside, and reaching into a thicket, she pulled out a tiny brown bundle. Lifting a corner of her cloak, she gently wrapped up the creature and, cradling it against her stomach, picked her way back out of the vicious thorns that clung to her cloak.

'She's still alive!' Leveret whispered, her green eyes shining with joy. 'Look!'

Carefully she peeled back the protective wrapping of her cloak to reveal a tiny leveret, a mere ball of fluff and ears. She stroked the flecked, baby-soft fur as the little animal's nose twitched in panic.

'See, Clip – it is her hind leg that's damaged. She seems to have lost half the paw.'

Leveret tried to examine the mess but the hare's leg was dark with dried blood and she was obviously in distress. Covering her up again within the warm material of the cloak, Leveret gazed up at Clip.

'We gave her the opportunity to disappear,' she said quietly. 'But she's obviously injured and won't survive in the wild. Even if her mother does return this evening to feed her, she wouldn't stand a chance of reaching adulthood with an injury like that. And if it were a fox that did this to her paw, maybe he's already finished off the mother?'

'I'm sure you're right,' he said.

'So we'll have to take her home, won't we? We can't leave her here for a predator to find.'

Clip nodded, knowing that Leveret was longing to tend and heal the tiny creature. They walked back to the tower steadily so as not to jolt the hare, all thoughts of joining the celebrations in the Village now forgotten. Leveret's head was teeming with how she should splint the leg if it were broken and which herbs would best speed the healing of the wound. Clip was wondering who to ask for some ewe's milk. Both were very happy to have found the tiny thing before it met almost certain death. And both were conscious of the significance of finding a hare on today of all days; it was as if Eostre herself had sent one of her creatures to them.

Down in the Village, folk were sitting at long trestles in the Barn eating breakfast. Yul had invited Rainbow to sit with him and Sylvie, and Dawn and David had joined them. The noise in the enormous barn was loud as everyone tucked into their hot crossed buns and cracked the prettily coloured hard-boiled eggs. Pitchers of milk were passed around and the atmosphere was buzzing.

Rainbow bit hungrily into a spiced bun and her gaze roamed the building, from the high vaulted ceiling with its massive rafters to the well-worn stones that formed the smooth floor. The rough trestle tables and benches, all made by the Stonewylde carpenters, were a far cry from what she was accustomed to nowadays. Her eyes were as round as the pendants that hung around every adult's neck. Every neck except her own.

'We're really looking forward to seeing your work,' Yul was saying, trying to compensate for his wife's lack of conversation.

'I haven't brought any with me,' laughed Rainbow. 'Most of my stuff's pretty big – I like a large canvas.'

'From what I've seen online, your paintings look very good.'

She smiled and laid her hand on his.

'Thank you! And I can't tell you how happy I am that your Council of Elders – or whatever it's called – decided to let me come,' she said. 'I'm very grateful indeed.'

'It wasn't unanimous,' said Yul a little awkwardly. 'You may encounter some hostility and—'

'Oh, don't worry about that!' she laughed again, tossing her tangle of hair. 'I'm quite capable of dealing with any opposition.'

Sylvie was talking to someone across the table but all the time trying to hear what was being said.

'What are you intending to work on first?' asked David eagerly. 'Have you brought materials?'

'Only sketch pads and pencils,' Rainbow replied. 'When I'm ready I'll have canvases and my paints and brushes sent down. I'm planning on spending the first week just roaming about and catching up with everything. There's so much to see!'

'You'll find it all very different now,' Sylvie said stiffly, leaning across Yul.

'Yes, I can see that,' said Rainbow. 'And it's been so long – over thirteen years. I keep expecting to bump into Magus around every corner.'

Sylvie was tight-lipped at this.

'You'll find that my husband is magus now and you won't bump into *him* at every corner,' she said.

'We'd really like you to do some work with the children,' said Dawn quickly. 'As I said in my e-mails, David's hoping to start a new project with—'

'Good grief, I'm useless with children!' Rainbow said with a throaty chuckle. 'Don't let me anywhere near kids – I can't stand 'em.'

Dawn frowned at this but David smiled encouragingly.

'You'll be great with them, Rainbow. And there's one I especially want you to meet. I think the boy is destined to be a great artist and I'd like your opinion.'

'Sure,' said Rainbow. 'But my real hope for this visit is to get a lot of sketching done and to start work on a series. I want to do an entire exhibition with the elements as the theme, and that's just for starters. And I also want to catch ordinary Villagers going about their business, dressed in their quaint clothes and practising their crafts.'

'We don't call anyone "Villager" any more,' said Yul sharply. 'That's all finished now.'

'So what are they called then, all these people?' She looked around artlessly. 'Have you promoted everyone to Hallfolk?'

'We're all the folk of Stonewylde,' said Sylvie, her heart thumping with annoyance. 'As I said, I think you'll find many things very different now. And you'd better be on your best behaviour too, because if there's any trouble you'll be asked to leave immediately.'

Rainbow leaned over and her blue gaze raked Sylvie's flushed face. Her eyes were wide with innocence but her lip curled derisively.

'Well, I'd be very grateful if you'd take me under your wing, Sylvie, and make sure I stay on the straight and narrow path. You know I always was a bad girl and trouble is what I do best.'

She scanned their affronted faces and threw back her head, roaring with laughter.

'Oh come on – I'm only joking! This is the festival of spring – when are we going to start having some fun? Since when did Stonewylde become so deadly serious?'

'Where's our little Harebrain today?' asked Gefrin later on, as he stood out on the Village Green with a tankard of cider in his hand. 'I thought Mother said she'd be coming down to the Village today?'

Sweyn shrugged. 'She were at the Stone Circle this morning but I ain't seen her since. Clip's got her well and truly guarded.'

'At least we don't have to put up with her any more,' said Gefrin, 'and she's not upsetting Mother.' He was busy watching a group of girls hanging around by the duck pond.

'Yeah, but she never did get her comeuppance after what she did at Imbolc,' growled Sweyn, his red face as belligerent as ever. 'We ain't letting her off the hook just 'cos Clip's keeping her under lock and key. We told her we'd get her and we will. Imbolc was just the start of it. And where's Jay today?'

'He went off to get the crones,' said Gefrin. 'He's got to help 'em down the lane. They want to join in the feast again like they did at Imbolc.'

Sweyn chuckled at the memory. 'Yeah, do you remember it? That were such a good day, especially when Yul asked us to take Lev off for a walk and get her to drink something! I'll never forget that. Pity she's not about today.'

'Maybe she'll come down later,' said Gefrin, nodding across at the girls who were staring his way. They burst into loud peals of laughter at this and he blushed scarlet. 'Do you think Meadowsweet likes me?'

'I don't know!' said Sweyn. 'She's as daft as the lot of 'em. What are they laughing about? Is it me?'

'No,' said Gefrin glumly. 'I think it's me. I don't understand. At the farm she's as nice as pie to me. It's all "Ooh Gefrin, this" and "Gefrin, that". She's always coming out to find me and talk to me. But now, when all her mates are with her ...'

'Who cares?' said Sweyn gruffly. 'They're all bloody stupid, the whole herd.'

'Not Meadowsweet!' said Gefrin. 'She's alright. I just wish they'd stop laughing at me.'

Later in the day, Martin stood in a corner of the Barn, his arms folded, surveying the scene. He'd always been a dour man, not given to smiles or softness, but lately he'd become even more grim. The ceremony in the Stone Circle last Samhain had been the start of a new regime, a turning point in the recent sorry history of Stonewylde. Since then things hadn't moved fast enough for his liking, but he recognised that changes were afoot and had been ever since that wild, terrifying night when he and the others had dared to meddle with the Otherworld.

Martin was a patient man and had bided his time. But this year would see the end of the travesty that Stonewylde had become. This year, the rightful leaders would take their place again and the dark-haired bastard-brat would be out, along with his shrew of a wife and her bossy ginger mother. Order would be restored, and Stonewylde would once again enter a golden age. Martin knew the part he must play in all this and relished it.

His slate-grey eyes darted about, missing nothing. There was Yul storming around and upsetting folk, in another of his foul tempers again. But Martin knew why and he chuckled to himself, his bitter mouth twisting with mirth. He had personally assisted the bitch-wife and her spawn in moving their things down to the Village, despite her protestations. He'd ordered the horse and cart from the stables and made a big show of getting youngsters to help carry downstairs the wicker baskets of children's toys and woven bags of clothes and shoes. If she'd hoped to sneak out quietly with her tail between her legs, he'd ruined that plan. Thanks to him, everyone had seen what she was up to – leaving her husband. And now she was out of his master's beautiful rooms that she'd destroyed with her stupid remodelling and redecorating, and down to the Village where she belonged. Or rather, didn't belong, because if Martin had his way she'd be out of Stonewylde in a flash. And those who rightfully should be in charge would finally take the reins.

Martin's face twisted further as he thought of the years of misrule they'd all had to endure. But not for much longer! As he thought this, he noticed his mother, aunt and cousin arriving in the Great Barn, accompanied by Jay. Where was Swift? He should be helping his grandmother too – no need for Jay to get all the perks that came with being favoured by Violet and Vetchling. For all his cleverness, Swift was getting a bit too high and mighty lately, Martin thought with a frown. In the old days he'd have given his son the strap and sorted him out in time-honoured fashion. That was all youngsters needed to bring them back to heel. But of course that sort of natural behaviour – a parent disciplining his child as he saw fit – was banned, thanks to Yul. And that was one of a very long list of reasons why Martin would be over the moon to see the end of the upstart's regime, and the start of the bright new era at Stonewylde.

3

Yul surveyed his little girls gravely. They sat together at the large scrubbed pine table in the parlour of the cottage where he'd grown up. Maizie and Sylvie were out and he had them to himself. The girls' pencils and paper were spread out, Maizie's tiny jar of violets pushed to one side.

'So you don't want to come back home to the Hall?' he asked.

Bluebell continued to draw her picture, tongue peeping from between her lips, whilst Celandine paused to regard him. Her deep grey eyes seemed to bore into him and suddenly he felt unworthy, wrong to try to manipulate his children like this.

'I'm sorry, Father,' she replied. 'You need to talk to Mummy about that, not us. But please don't worry because we're really enjoying staying here in the Village.'

He nodded, the lump in his throat making his eyes prickle.

'Are you alright, Father?' asked Bluebell. 'You must be a bit lonely and small in those big rooms. Are you scared?'

'Scared? Why would I be scared?'

Bluebell shrugged and continued drawing a faerie emerging from a flower.

''Cos I was scared there. That's why I had my nightmares and screaming. But I don't get it here, in Granny Maizie's cottage. It's safe here and nobody creeps about at night-time.'

Yul frowned at her.

'We're very busy here,' added Celandine. 'We have to do lots of jobs for Granny and it's just like when you and Auntie Rosie and Auntie Leveret and all the uncles were little.'

Yul smiled at this, just a little bitterly. Bluebell looked up and caught his eye. She carefully put down her pencil and, climbing down from the old chair, trotted round to be pulled up onto his lap. He buried his face in her curls and fought back the tears. He missed them so very much. Having spent so little time with them over the past few months, he'd never imagined it would be as painful as this.

'I miss you too, Father,' said Bluebell. 'Why don't you come and stay here as well? Then we could all be together.'

'I want us all to live together at the Hall in our rooms,' said Yul. 'That's our home, not here.'

Celandine looked at him steadily.

'I don't think Mummy feels that,' she said. 'She's been sleeping better here, and she's so busy and much happier. She weaves cloth every night and does knitting and quilting, and Granny's teaching her how to cook. She really loves it.'

'Yes, and we're in charge of all the chickens!' cried Bluebell. 'And we have to feed them and do the water and collect the eggs and tuck them in their bed at night-time nice and safe so the foxes don't get 'em!'

'We do lots more than that,' said Celandine. 'I'm learning to weave at the loom too, and Granny's teaching us all how to knit, even Blue. And we sweep the floor and bring in logs for the range and the fire.'

'And make our own beds! And we have to go to the Bath House for a proper bath but not every day 'cos we can just have a bowl of water and a cloth to wash here, Granny said. And guess what, Father – we all have to use a potty at night time if we need a wee!'

Celandine nodded at this.

'I don't really like the baths in the Bath House,' she said. 'They're not that clean and private. But if we're going to live in the Village we need to get used to it. The toilet in the garden isn't so bad, as it's like the one at Nursery. I don't mind throwing sawdust down the hole. And I don't mind not having lights here either. It's really cosy with the candles and oil lamps.'

'And if we're shivery cold we just put on another woolly like Granny told us to!' said Bluebell. She turned in Yul's arms and took his face in her chubby little hands, gazing intently into his eyes. 'But I miss you, Father, and I wish you were here too. Then it'd all be perfect for me.'

Clip left the tower through the door on the ground floor that led into the mediaeval part of the Hall. The silver-blue robes hung off his scarecrow frame as he strode through the Galleried Hall. His soft boots were silent on the ancient flagstones and he paused, gazing up at the gallery that ran along one side of the vaulted hall. Above his head, the carved Green Men and triple hare motifs went unnoticed as he remembered the time all those years ago when he and Miranda had announced to the world that it was he who'd fathered Sylvie. He'd never, as long as he lived, forget that moment of supreme joy as he saw his brother Sol's face turn dangerously white. All Sol's plans had come crashing down at that moment, whilst Sylvie's and Yul's lives had, in the space of those couple of minutes, soared from the depths of despair to the pinnacle of hope. Clip's lined face creased into a small smile at the memory and he shook his wispy white head ruefully. The emotion in this hall had been super-charged that day; he hoped there'd never be a repeat of that dreadful intensity.

Although not at quite the same level of passion, the Galleried Hall had seen many a struggle since then. He thought back to the last two Council meetings, held near the Moon Fullnesses of February and March, when things had become very heated. First there were all the terrible recriminations following the disastrous Imbolc. Maizie had been torn between anger and humiliation in equal measures, and Yul had made everything much worse with all the accusations and reproach aimed at Sylvie. Clip had been forced to intervene as his daughter was subjected to Yul's cruel bullying. Martin had added fuel to the fire throughout the whole meeting, making pointed remarks about the fact that it was Yul's sister who'd failed in her role as the Bright Maiden and who'd ruined the event for the entire community. He'd also brought up the issue about the computer network crash and Harold's failure to avert a crisis that had caused Stonewylde.com to disappear for the foreseeable future. Martin just wouldn't let it drop, and, as Yul's temper had risen, Clip had wondered what exactly was going on.

Then, at the last meeting barely three weeks ago, Yul had announced that Rainbow had been invited to spend the next few months at Stonewylde. At that point Sylvie had almost walked out of the meeting and Clip had been obliged to exercise his utmost skills in diplomacy to diffuse the situation. Again, Yul had launched an attack on Sylvie for her reluctance to allow Rainbow back into Stonewylde. When she'd dared to stand up to him and fight back, he'd hinted that her sanity was in question. Clip had been furious and had taken the unprecedented step of reprimanding Yul in full view of the whole Council, which had caused even more unpleasantness. He hated the politics and manipulations that riddled Stonewylde at present, and it was from all this that he longed to escape. If he were to leave by Samhain of this year as promised, he now had only seven months left. He was torn between euphoria and guilt at the prospect.

Clip left the ancient Galleried Hall and strode through the corridors and passages until he came to one of the wings at the back of the vast complex that was the Hall. The nurse he bumped into directed him to where Hazel sat, with a group of patients, in a bright and cheerful sitting room. All were busy with needlework or model-making, save one very elderly lady who was propped in a chair snoozing by the window. Hazel looked up from her conversation as Clip appeared in the doorway.

Soon they were drinking tea together in Hazel's office, and Clip felt at ease. He liked this woman; one of the original Hallfolk, she too had been enamoured with his brother, but it was Hazel who'd first recognised something in Sylvie and had brought her and Miranda to Stonewylde. She'd been an excellent doctor over the years and worked so hard. She'd managed somehow to integrate her up-to-date medical practice with the traditions of Stonewylde, and not upset too many people in the process.

'It's about Leveret,' he began, his silver-grey eyes twinkling at her.

'Is she in more trouble?' asked Hazel. 'I thought she was now tucked firmly under your wing.'

Clip chuckled at this.

'Very firmly. But there are two things I'd like to ask you to do for the girl, and you know I wouldn't ask if it weren't important.'

'Absolutely,' said Hazel, thinking how Clip looked rather haggard and wondering how to persuade him to have a check-up. He always managed to avoid the annual Stonewylde health-check that everyone else had. She respected Clip and had always sympathised with him in his predicament; he clearly had no wish to lead Stonewylde but battled to fulfil his duty.

'I'd like her to be allowed to come in and sit with the elderly patients and residents from time to time, and talk to them about their herbal knowledge,' he said, sipping his tea. 'Now you've had the go-ahead to start moving the more frail folk up to the Hall into their own special accommodation, I'd like her to record some of the old lore before it's forgotten.'

Hazel nodded at this, her blonde bobbed hair brushing the stethoscope around her neck. She knew that Clip had supported her idea to introduce a geriatric wing at the Hall in a bid to provide better care for the elderly, and also to free up cottages in the Village where space was at a premium. Many of the Council of Elders had strongly opposed the idea. It went completely against long-standing Stonewylde principles of living and eventually dying in your own cottage with your family caring for you until the end. Hazel knew too that the scheme would meet with a great deal of opposition amongst the old folk themselves, many of whom still thought of the Hall as somewhere out of their domain.

'Good idea, Clip, and the old folk will love it I'm sure. One of the things I'm concerned about is that they'll lose touch with the lifeblood of Stonewylde and feel themselves packed away up here. I want there to be lots of interaction between the elderly living here and the Village. Having our youngsters sit and chat with them regularly is a brilliant idea and I'll set that in motion from the start. I have no objection to there being another agenda in this case!'

Clip smiled at her and she thought again just how thin and almost desiccated his face had become.

'Forgive me, Clip, but I know you missed your check-up again. How are you feeling nowadays? If you're to leave us later this year we need to make sure you're completely fit and healthy, don't we?'

'Don't worry, I'm as fit as a fighting cock ... or a flea, or whatever the expression is,' he said blithely. 'And the other thing please, Hazel, is each week I'd like you to give an hour of your time – or more if you could – to teaching Leveret. No,' he said as she started to speak, 'this is nothing to do with what Miranda or Maizie or anyone else who controls the child's life wants for her. Please, Hazel, you must trust me in this.'

Hazel looked into his kindly, careworn face and nodded, having complete faith in him.

'Leveret is destined to become our Shaman, our Wise Woman and our healer,' he continued. 'It's a huge responsibility and she's so very young and so very powerless. There are a number of forces at work against her which manifest themselves in many ways – not least through her own mother. I'm talking deep Stonewylde magic here, Hazel. Do you understand?'

Again Hazel nodded.

'I remember,' she said slowly, 'when I first realised how hoodwinked I'd been by Magus, and how Sylvie was in such danger from him. I remember too that incredible sense of destiny that surrounded Yul and his plans to fulfil the old prophecy. Is that the sort of level we're talking about here?'

'Exactly so. Leveret needs support if she's going to win through and fulfil *her* destiny. She needs a sound medical knowledge as well as all the herbal and folklore remedies, and her magical understanding. She needs—'

'Yes, Maizie spoke to me a while ago about this. She's very keen for Leveret to become a doctor and she spoke of the girl's tremendous healing gifts.'

Clip took Hazel's hands between his and looked into her pretty brown eyes.

'Hazel, she'll never become a doctor, despite Maizie's dreams. Leveret can't leave Stonewylde and she'd never survive in the Outside World for all those years of study and training. She's under my tutelage at the moment and she's like a sponge, absorbing everything I'm putting her way. But what she really needs is to learn some of the underpinning principles of modern medicine. She'll never learn enough to become a doctor like you, but if you could teach her the very basics then she'll be better placed as a traditional healer at Stonewylde.'

Hazel squeezed his bony hands and gave him a warm smile.

'I'd be honoured to teach Leveret,' she said. 'She's a special girl and someone who's long been misunderstood. I'd be glad to help.'

'Thank you, Hazel. And I know you're busy, but just one more question. It's about what was said at the last Council meeting. Yul's wrong, isn't he? Sylvie isn't losing her sanity again?'

Hazel grimaced as she gathered their cups and stood up.

'It's Yul I'm concerned about, not Sylvie. She's fine, but he seems to have lost his reason. There's a look in his eyes sometimes ... I know he's like his father, but there are moments when I feel almost as if I'm dealing with the man himself again.'

Magpie trailed behind Leveret along an overgrown path by the stream. The sun shone down on them as they wandered under the bare branches of the trees, the buds still tight. A robin sang gloriously and Leveret paused, listening to the music. A smile spread across Magpie's face at the jubilant notes pouring from the small bird's throat. He pulled a sketchbook and soft pencil from his canvas bag and within a couple of minutes had created a vivacious little robin on the white page. Something about the angle of the bird's head and his open beak conveyed the intensity and beauty of his song even though he was simply marks on paper.

They continued for a while, Leveret with her wicker basket and Mother Heggy's gathering knife, and Magpie with his sketch book and pencil. Yellow celandine stars twinkled amongst the brilliant white wood anemones covering the damp leaf-mould underfoot. All around them the world was unfurling into spring.

'We're going to harvest some comfrey,' said Leveret to Magpie. 'I know it grows at the Hall but I want to gather some from up here, where it feels wild and free. It's to heal the hare, you see.'

Magpie nodded at this, having seen the wound.

'She's doing very well,' continued Leveret, 'and luckily she doesn't seem to have any broken bones. But it's a horrible wound and although I keep cleaning it with distilled witch hazel, I really want to put a nice poultice of comfrey on it. And I'd like to make some ointment too. Look, Magpie, I'll show you comfrey – I'm not sure if you remember it.'

She pulled a small battered book from the basket and flicked through the pages.

'Here – this one,' she said, pointing to the plant in question. 'Remember it in the Kitchen Garden? We really must do some work on the herb garden this spring. Clip has said he wants me to spend time in there cultivating, and you and I can do that together, can't we?'

He nodded happily.

'I'm sure there's a big patch of comfrey along here; I remember it from last year. Both the creamy white one and the lovely mauve-pink one too, I seem to recall. Comfrey's a great healer of wounds and makes the flesh knit together well. That will help our little hare, won't it?'

Since discovering the leveret at the Spring Equinox, Leveret had devoted herself to ensuring the tiny creature survived. She was kept warm and safe in Leveret's room in a nest of hay, with regular feeds of ewe's milk. Her damaged paw had been thoroughly cleaned and tended, but Leveret wasn't happy with the healing process and wanted to speed it up. The tiny bundle of soft fur no longer trembled but greedily guzzled at the milk she provided and sat contentedly in her lap whilst she read.

They came to the place she'd remembered and sure enough, there was a fine crop of comfrey growing thickly. It was too early in the season for the plants to be in flower, but it was the large hairy leaves and the roots that Leveret wanted anyway. Whilst she gathered leaves and dug up some pale roots, Magpie sat on a fallen log with Clip's old book of wildflowers and started drawing in his sketchbook.

'There, that's enough for now,' said Leveret after a while. 'We can always come back for more if we need to. I must dry some actually – there's so much I must do. Have you drawn the comfrey, Magpie? But there aren't any flowers yet, so – oh!'

She stared at the bold pencil strokes on the page, the drooping, pointed leaves with their down of fine hair. But what made her throat constrict in sudden excitement wasn't the exquisite botanical accuracy of the drawing – it was the marks underneath it. Magpie had written *"Comfrey"*. She gulped and stared at him. His eyes danced as he smiled at her.

'Magpie, you've written the word! Do you understand what you've done? You've copied it from the book, I know. But do you understand what that means?'

He simply gazed into her eyes and sighed.

'Magpie, listen! This is really important. Do you understand? Those marks, that word ...'

He pointed to the word he'd written, albeit a little clumsily as if the letters were part of a picture, and picked up a leaf from the basket.

'Maggie, I think you *do* understand!'

Leveret was suddenly beside herself with joy and hugged him fiercely, spilling half her leaves on the ground. The implications started to dawn: the prospect of Magpie learning to read and write, even if he couldn't speak, and what that could mean for his future.

'Come on, Maggie, let's get back to the tower so we can tell Clip! And Marigold and Cherry! Oh they're going to be so proud of you! I need to get my poultice going for Hare, and as soon as that's all bubbling away, we're going to see just what you can do. I'm so excited I might burst!'

Sylvie looked slightly incongruous in her mother's elegant little sitting room in the Tudor wing of the Hall. It was the weekend and there was no school today, so Miranda was still in her dressing gown and slippers. Sylvie was dressed like a Villager of old, a coarse linen skirt covering the tops of her traditional Stonewylde boots, a green knitted jacket over her plain blouse. She'd even arrived carrying a wicker basket. Rufus sat in his armchair engrossed in a book whilst his mother and sister chatted, his foot swinging repeatedly and kicking the table leg.

'So where are my little grand-daughters?' asked Miranda. 'I miss them now they're down in the Village all the time.'

'Come down later and see them,' said Sylvie. 'I was going to bring them up with me but they're playing with their friends on the Village Green and they didn't want to come. It's still such a novelty to be in the Village at the weekends when there's no Nursery.'

Miranda surveyed her daughter carefully; at least Sylvie's eyes were a little brighter now.

'And you're still enjoying being a Villager?' she asked. 'No problems living with Maizie in the cottage?'

Sylvie sighed heavily and met her mother's eye.

'You may recall, Mum, that I always wanted to be a Villager. Remember?'

Miranda nodded ruefully.

'Yes, I should have listened to you! And it's really okay with Maizie?'

'It's lovely. Obviously it's all very different and it's her home – I'm very aware of that. But the whole way of life is wonderful and I really love it. The busyness of it, the sense of purpose and

42

achievement. And of course now I'm starting the student coun-selling up here, I'll be really busy.'

'Yes, Martin said the room we wanted for you is available now, although I must say he's dragged his heels about it. He can be so very awkward at times. But it's ready now – do have a look in a minute – and we can start to timetable some sessions for the older students to come in and have a chat with you.'

'I'm really looking forward to that. Thanks for organising it all.'

'My pleasure – it's certainly much needed. I can't understand why Yul was so against it anyway.'

Sylvie's face darkened and she looked down at her hands.

'He's just being awkward too. I don't know what's wrong with them all. I just want to help and giving the students some careers advice isn't going to exhaust me, despite his worries. But it's more than that and we both know it.'

She glanced over to where Rufus sat, his bright red hair hang-ing over his eyes as he continued to read and kick. Miranda took the hint and nodded.

'And the girls? They're happy?'

'Oh yes! Maizie's working them quite hard really, considering they're so young, but they love it. She says they need to learn all the things that Village children do. Celandine loves weaving and little Bluebell adores the chickens. And soon, we're—'

'I wish I lived in the Village too!'

They both stared at Rufus in astonishment. He'd stopped kick-ing and glared at them both from beneath the red fringe. His jaw was stubborn but Sylvie noticed his mouth quivered.

'I don't want to lose you both!' laughed Miranda.

'I'm not joking, Mum,' he said gruffly. His voice was in the process of breaking and he had little control over it.

'But that's silly,' she said. 'You can't live in the Village, dar-ling. Who would you live with?'

'Sylvie and the girls,' he replied.

'But they're in Maizie's cottage, and she's no relation to you.'

'It's not fair!' he squeaked. 'I don't want to be stuck here. I

43

want to be a Villager too! Celandine and Bluebell are, so why can't I?'

'Come on, Rufus, you know—'

'Actually, there may be the perfect solution to this,' said Sylvie. 'I understand your feelings, Rufus, really I do. Everyone else at Stonewylde is busy and you feel so idle. That's how I've always felt. But even though you couldn't move down there like we have – or not now, anyway – I know that Maizie is quite desperate for some male help.'

'Is she?' His deep brown eyes were hopeful.

'Oh yes. She can't do the heavy stuff like chopping the wood and fetching the water, nor the deep digging in her garden. She was only complaining about it yesterday, saying how she wished she still had a young man about the place. Gefrin and Sweyn both live up here and they won't visit her every day to help. I'm sure she'd jump at the chance of having you down to help her out.'

'But he's not moving in there too!' protested Miranda. 'Really, I couldn't—'

'No, not move in, but he could come down at the weekends and maybe after school a couple of days a week? Honestly, Mum, it would do Rufus the world of good and I know Maizie would be so grateful. He wouldn't have to sleep there or anything – just spend a few hours helping her out, and maybe have supper with us sometimes. And it would build up those muscles, wouldn't it, Rufus?'

Their eyes met and he gave her a beautiful smile, his teeth very white in his freckly face.

'Please, Mum! I want to help and it would be great to be in Yul's old cottage as well – where he used to chop wood and stuff. Please?'

Miranda nodded slowly, seeing the merit of such an idea. She braced herself as he leapt up and almost knocked her out of her chair in a great hug.

Rainbow stood by the river bank watching the water rush by. She noticed the brilliant blue streak as a kingfisher darted downstream, and then saw it perch on a reed. She breathed deeply of the air, still very much aware of how precious it was. She wore her own long, brightly-coloured skirt with a pair of old Stonewylde boots and a linen smock that she'd found in the clothing store in the Village. She found it amusing that the prospect of wearing old Villager things should make her feel so happy. Her thick mane of hair had become even wilder since her arrival as she no longer bothered to tame it at all.

She accepted the mug of tea from Merewen who'd emerged from the Pottery, and together they sank down onto the bench on the riverbank. Merewen was covered in paint and her wiry hair sprang out around her face. She sipped her tea thoughtfully as they sat in companionable silence.

'So David and Dawn have got it on?' said Rainbow finally.

'They're walking together, if that's what you mean,' replied Merewen. 'Seem suited to me, more or less. He's an Outsider o' course, but not a bad 'un.'

'He's a nice guy, I believe,' said Rainbow. 'I don't know him well but he seems to be making Dawn happy.'

'Aye, she's content. Shouldn't wonder if they got handfasted.'

'Really? How lovely!'

Merewen drained her cup and threw the dregs to the ground.

'Come on, girl, there's work to be done. I'm firing tomorrow and the kiln needs to be prepared.'

'That was never part of the deal!' laughed Rainbow, following the older woman into the ancient building. 'I need to be out and about drawing. I want to see the children playing on the Green and I need to take some photos too.'

'Photos? I thought you were an artist. Why d'you need photos? I never liked the things much, what I seen o' them. Cold and flat, no life to 'em.'

Rainbow shrugged and picked up a bag containing her things.

'Just something I promised. Give me a couple of hours, Merewen, and I'll be back for some lunch and then I'll help with the kiln. And I want you to show me how you mix your paints. You never did get round to that all those years ago.'

'No, but I never realised you wouldn't be stopping here,' said Merewen. Her rather piercing eyes searched Rainbow's face. 'And I want to paint you, girl, afore you disappear from Stonewylde again.'

'Disappear?' laughed Rainbow. 'Not if I have my way! I'm planning on staying if I can wangle it, or at least keep the gates open for regular visits. This is my idea of paradise.'

'You're not a force that Stonewylde needs,' said Merewen slowly. The lines around her mouth deepened as she pursed her whiskery upper lip. She shook her grizzled head and sighed deeply. 'I may be wrong, but I don't think you'll be here very long. So all the more reason to get on with it now, afore it's too late.'

Rowan stood behind her daughter, seated at the dressing table, and rhythmically brushed the girl's blonde hair with a pure bristle hairbrush. Faun studied herself carefully in the mirror, slightly turning her face this way and that whilst her mother brushed and brushed. Soon the thick pale tresses were crackling with life, swarming down the girl's back and curling up on themselves at the end. Rowan's eyes softened with pride.

'There, one hundred strokes,' she said, laying down the brush.

'Are you going to do something with it or leave it loose?' asked Faun.

'Loose I think – we want her to see you and see pure Stonewylde, and of course recognise Magus' darling daughter too,' said Rowan.

She picked up the fine white blouse and started to dress her daughter as if she were a helpless child and not a tall and nubile teenager. Fastening the buttons for her whilst Faun stood impassively, Rowan then helped her into the filmy white skirt.

'Are you sure this is the best outfit, Mother? It's not very glamorous, is it?'

'That's the whole point, Faun. She's probably used to glamour. What we're going to impress her with is your pure, natural beauty and your Stonewylde roots.'

'And she'll really be interested in that?' Faun was doubtful.

'That's what Dawn was saying the other evening. I went round to the Village School for the weekly meeting and she told me all about Rainbow and why she's here. I knew some of it from the Council of Elders' Meeting of course, but Dawn told me a lot more.'

They clumped down the stairs to the parlour where Rowan's parents sat comfortably by the fire. Faun went across to the cupboard by the door to survey her choice of footwear, unsure what would come across as pure Stonewylde. All of it, she supposed, as she'd never had any clothes or shoes from the Outside World. Not yet, at least.

'Definitely the boots,' said Rowan. ''Tis what Stonewylde women wear in the winter and nothing else would look right. Pity though as you have lovely smooth legs and your feet are so pretty.'

Rowan's mother looked up from her needlework.

'You're going across to the Barn then?' she asked, not entirely approving of the mission. 'Make sure you stay warm, Faun. That wind has a chilly edge to it.'

Faun rolled her eyes at this and she and Rowan exchanged a conspiratorial smile.

'Mother, you know we're going to find Rainbow and why we're doing it,' Rowan said.

'Aye, but seems daft to me. O' course I'd love to have a painting done of our Faun, right enough. Nobody at Stonewylde is as beautiful as our precious girl. But 'tis the other plan I don't understand. Why would this Rainbow be so taken with our Faun as she'd want to—'

'Oh Granny, do stop fussing!' Faun was petulant, her deep brown eyes cold with irritation. 'She'll see me and want to paint me and then one day I'll be famous. That's all there is to it.'

'That's right! We know Rainbow's looking for people to paint. She's out and about looking for lovely things to sketch and interesting folk to draw. And our Faun is the loveliest thing here.'

Rowan pulled on her own boots and then tweaked at Faun's

waistband, tucking the blouse in more so it pulled tighter across her daughter's breasts.

'So 'tis natural her eyes will fall upon our girl and she'll be smitten! And she'll paint our Faun and put her in all the exhibitions she has up in London and somebody important will see our girl and realise that here, at last, they've found perfection. And she'll go on to—'

'Pah!' said Rowan's father, roused from his usual docility where the womenfolk were concerned. ''Tis a load o' nonsense, Rowan, and you know it! And besides – do you really want our Faun to be taken away from us? Seems to me all that there film and TV stuff is a pile o' horse-dung anyway, and I don't want my granddaughter mixed up in any o' that rubbish!'

Rowan wrapped Faun's soft mallow-pink shawl around her shoulders, tight-lipped with exasperation, then pulled the girl's hair free so it rippled in shining waves over her shoulders.

'Neither of you old 'uns has a clue!' she said hotly. 'I knew from the minute that Magus searched me out in the laundry fourteen years ago that one day, I'd achieve something great and special. I just knew it! And I done that – our Faun! And this now, 'tis our chance to push her forward at last and let her take the honour and praise that she deserves. She's our Magus' only daughter and she's a goddess. Look at her! She *should* be in films and TV – 'tis her rightful due! You wouldn't know as you don't ever watch anything, but *I* know. And nobody will ever say our Faun didn't achieve her potential 'cos her mother never bothered to push her to the front!'

4

Leveret entered the Village as dusk was falling. She carried a lantern to guide her home again later and was looking forward to the walk back. She enjoyed being out at night time with the owls calling and the foxes barking, though the bats were still in hibernation so no dark shapes flitted around as she walked briskly. She loved this freedom and thought how happy she was living with Clip, despite missing her mother. Every day was a kind of adventure for her, with books piled up by Clip for her to study, or a walk planned to look for certain plants, or a set of instructions to be carried out. She felt that Clip was enjoying teaching her as much as she enjoyed learning.

Luckily he'd overcome the head-teacher's objections about her missing school, promising she wouldn't neglect her course-work and would study everything she should under his super-vision. Leveret knew from Clip's expression that Miranda had been unhappy about the proposal, but there was little she could do in the face of Clip's determination. Leveret was also delighted about visiting the old folk so she could take notes. She was really excited and they'd discussed the Book of Shadows she needed. Clip had ordered it from a little shop he knew in the backstreets of London where they made books by hand, along with a special fountain pen and ink. He'd also promised her a great batch of equipment; bottles, flasks, corks, pans and everything she was likely to need to make herbal remedies for the community.

During their discussion Leveret had decided to tell him about

Mother Heggy's cottage. Much as she loved living with Clip in the tower, she knew that it was in the tumbledown cottage that the magic was strong. She'd always been drawn to the place ever since Yul had taken her there as a child and it was where she felt Mother Heggy's presence the strongest. She knew that Clip would never permit her to live there alone but that wasn't what she wanted, especially with the issue of her brothers and Jay still looming large. She wouldn't be safe alone up there. But she wanted to use the cottage for preparing and making medicine. In the tower she'd train to be a shaman, and in the cottage she'd learn how to be the Wise Woman. However they'd been sidetracked by choosing her book and Leveret resolved to speak to Clip soon about tidying up and possibly renovating the cottage. The winter had been mild but even so, the roof was leaking and the door was loose, and the range would never light unless the chimney was swept properly first.

Leveret walked into the Village and glanced down the lane leading to her cottage. She imagined Sylvie and her little nieces sitting with Maizie around the fire and her heart wrenched slightly. But she pushed those feelings aside and marched past the Jack in the Green and the merriment that spilled from its open door. She glanced into the Barn and saw it was as busy as ever, with groups of people her own age and younger engaged in activities or just sitting around chatting. She'd never been one to join in the craft and hobby groups in the evenings, preferring her own company or a good book. She wondered if her mother was in there but resisted the temptation to look inside properly; if Maizie were in there, what could they say to each other?

She continued on to the Village School and the cottage nestling against it like a shy child to its mother. Light glowed from the windows as she walked up the path, past the bright faces of the daffodils still visible in the fading daylight, and knocked on the front door. Dawn was surprised but gave her a welcoming smile and invited her in. Leveret was relieved that Dawn was alone and accepted a cup of rosehip tea. They sat in the comfy old armchairs by the fire and Leveret launched into the purpose of her visit.

'Yesterday I discovered that Magpie understands about writing,' she began.

'Magpie?' Dawn frowned. She hadn't had any dealings with him for years as he'd left the Village School long ago. She recalled the filthy little boy sitting mutely in the classrooms, unable to listen or engage with anything. She'd always felt that they'd failed Magpie. She'd done her best but he'd been born during the baby boom and there'd been no extra time or resources for a child such as him. The staff in the Nursery had warned her she'd get nowhere with him, and he was kept off school so often that in the end she'd given up trying. She recalled guiltily how relieved she'd felt when he finally moved up to the Hall School.

'Yes, Magpie!' said Leveret sharply. 'I know it's unbelievable but really, he understands that the marks on a page represent a word. Which proves that he's capable of learning to read and write.'

Dawn looked doubtful and Leveret scowled at her, even though she'd always liked Dawn. She remembered being taught by Dawn in the Village School and knew her to be both kind and patient. Leveret sighed.

'It doesn't matter if you believe me or not, but—'

'No, I haven't said that,' interrupted Dawn. 'Of course I remember poor Magpie as a youngster at school, and how he struggled with everything. I've also seen his almost miraculous transformation since he was taken out of his home and sent to live with Marigold and Cherry. I gather that was thanks to you?'

Leveret nodded, sipping her tea and studying Dawn carefully. Clip had told her she must learn to watch people, not leap in before she'd got their measure. A Wise Woman, he'd said, must bide her time, hold her tongue and allow others to reveal themselves. Leveret found this lesson a hard one to learn.

'And David has told me about Magpie's incredible artistic talent,' continued Dawn, and Leveret realised that in her haste to get help for Magpie, she'd forgotten about that connection. It was now common knowledge that David and Dawn were walking together, even though they were a little old to be canoodling on the Village Green or in the maze up at the Hall.

'That's right,' said Leveret.

'And you think he's capable of learning to read?'

'Yes I do. He copied the word *"Comfrey"* yesterday from a wild-flower book, when he was drawing the plant. I thought at first it was *just* copying, but he pointed to the plant and the word and honestly, Dawn, I really think he understood the link. Can you imagine the breakthrough for poor Magpie if he could learn to read and write? It wouldn't matter that he was mute if—'

'Hold on, Leveret!' said Dawn with a smile. 'We need to take it slowly. If that's all true, then it's really exciting. But we mustn't pin too much on it at this stage. Tell me, why did you come to me rather than Miranda? Surely if he's up at the Hall ...'

Leveret's face closed up at the mention of Miranda.

'You're used to teaching children to read and she's not. You've got resources here for that sort of thing.'

'Well, yes, but I don't think—'

'But anyway, I don't want *you* to teach him, Dawn. *I* want to. But I'd like your advice and maybe some books or something that I could use?'

Dawn was happy to help and they went through to the School House to find some suitable early learning books. Children weren't formally taught to read until they'd left the Nursery aged seven, though of course many learned long before then out of curiosity. Leveret couldn't remember a time when she hadn't been able to read as Yul had taught her at a very early age, anxious to share his skills.

When they returned to the cottage, Dawn gave Leveret a potted lesson in how to teach reading, explaining about the double-pronged attack of sounding out the letters and recognising the whole word. Leveret became very excited at the prospect of opening up Magpie's world, but Dawn urged caution.

'Remember, decoding and encoding – or reading and writing if you prefer – are two completely separate skills. And with

52

Magpie it's further complicated by the fact that he can't speak, so he can't sound out words. Nor can you check if he's read them correctly other than by picture matching. We have no idea of his conceptual abilities, so don't rush him, Leveret. His brain's obviously wired up differently from the norm and he may need a huge amount of patience.'

Leveret nodded; she'd spent all her life being patient with Magpie, giving him time and space to relax and express himself. If there was anyone in the world who could teach him to read and write, she knew it was her.

She stowed the books safely in her basket and was just thinking of leaving when they were interrupted. Rainbow came tumbling in from the dark, her hair like a ragged cape around her arms and her cheeks rosy from the night air.

'Well!' she exclaimed at the sight of Leveret. 'I can guess who you are!'

Leveret scowled up at her, shaking her hair over her eyes to obscure her face. She hated being the centre of attention, but more than that, she hated being likened to Yul. She muttered something incoherent and tried to get her shawl from the peg, but Rainbow took her arm and dragged her back into the light.

'Oh no, missy, I want a proper look at you.' She turned Leveret this way and that, scanning the girl's truculent face. 'If Yul were a girl he'd be you. Except for the green eyes. What's your name?'

'Leveret.'

'Ah yes, now I see. You're living with Clip in his tower, I've heard? How strange. And how old are you? You're tiny, but I don't think you're as young as you look.'

'I'm fifteen. And I'm leaving now.'

But they persuaded her to stay a little longer as Rainbow was quite fascinated by Yul's little sister.

'You know, Leveret, somewhere at home I have a sketch book from when I used to live here. I did a drawing of Yul standing on the Altar Stone as the sun rose, and it really could be you. He must've been fifteen at the time too, the same as you are now. I'll dig it out and show you when I next come to visit.'

'What? You're not leaving already?' Dawn wailed. 'You've only just got here, Rainbow, and after all the trouble I—'

'Hell, no! I'm planning on staying for the summer at least, and maybe longer. We'll see. Though I must find alternative accommodation – the room they've given me in the Hall is dreadful, all dark and poky and that miserable old git Martin won't change it. Don't suppose I could move in with you, Dawn?'

'Well, you could,' she said slowly, 'but with David popping by most evenings ...'

'I'd be playing gooseberry!' Rainbow laughed, and Leveret looked at her askance, having never heard the expression before. 'How about your tower, Leveret? I bet the light's wonderful on the top floor and you must have loads of room, just you and old Clip rattling around in there.'

'I don't think he'd want that,' said Leveret stiffly. 'You're much too ... noisy.'

Rainbow laughed again and sank back in the armchair with a groan of pleasure, wiggling her toes at the fire and stretching her arms luxuriously above her head. Leveret was quite mesmerised by her; she'd never seen anyone so naturally at ease and so overtly sensual. Rainbow was lithe and moved gracefully, and something about her made Leveret very wary.

'I'll tell you what,' Rainbow said, sitting forward and throwing another log onto the fire. 'I found somewhere perfect today that I want to make into my studio. It's a hovel but with a bit of renovation it would be wonderful.'

Leveret's heart started to thump in her chest.

'Really?' said Dawn. 'I can't think of anywhere in the Village that's—'

'No, it's out of the Village on the path up towards the cliffs.'

'Oh, you must mean old Mother Heggy's place? Goddess, I wouldn't want to go there! She was found dead in there, you know!'

'Really? How intriguing – so it's haunted as well. I wonder who I should ask about it?'

'But surely it would be too dark,' said Dawn. 'I've never been inside – nobody goes in there – but it looks so gloomy and the windows are tiny.'

'Well, I'd get a skylight put into the roof or something. And I—'

'NO!'

They both turned to stare at Leveret in astonishment.

'What? Why not? It's a tiny little place and it's in dreadful disrepair, but I'm happy to pay someone to do it up for me. And I'm not scared of ghosts!'

Leveret stood up and, grabbing her shawl, made for the door.

'Are you off? I'll come and visit you in your tower tomorrow, Leveret,' said Rainbow cheerily. 'I want to say hi to old Clip anyway.'

'We'll be busy,' mumbled Leveret, dreading the thought of this loud, pushy woman invading their space.

'Well, I'm sure Clip will spare me five minutes. I've got to see some boy tomorrow too – some half-wit who can't even talk. I can't say I'm wildly enthusiastic but David says he's brilliant and—'

'Half-wit?' Leveret's voice was shrill with fury. 'How *dare* you!'

And she stormed off into the darkness whilst Dawn explained to Rainbow just what a gaffe she'd made.

The air was thick with wreaths of smoke that hung overhead like sinister haloes. The three women sat as usual in their chairs around the fire, the two old ones rocking gently and the younger one with her massive legs propped up on a log. There was a stench of unwashed bodies and sour clothing only partially masked by the aromatic smoke. One of the crones started to cough, a deep croup that lasted for ages, but the others ignored it and continued to puff rhythmically on their clay pipes.

'I need some more o' your tincture,' croaked Vetchling eventually, when the cough had abated. 'This'll be the death of me, Violet.'

'Don't tempt the Dark Angel, Mother,' said Starling, making

the sign of the pentacle on her chest. ''Tis a nasty cough but it'll shift now that spring's here.'

'Aye, warmer weather is on its way,' said Violet. 'I know – we're in for a scorching summer, you mark my words. I seen all the signs.'

'That don't help me now,' said Vetchling. 'Feels like I'm coughing up my poor old lungs. Ain't you got none o' that special syrup left, Violet? The honeysuckle and poppy one? That one did me proud, right enough.'

'Aye, 'twas the poppy juice that done you proud, sister,' muttered Violet. 'You're a whisker too fond o' them poppies. One o' these mornings you won't wake up at all if you knock back too much of that one. I'll give you a dose of my mullein remedy – that'll help the phlegm come up.'

'I don't like that one,' whined Vetchling. 'It don't help me much and I'm already bringing up enough phlegm to put out the fire.'

'Stop your moaning, Mother,' said Starling irritably, tamping more herbs into her pipe. 'Auntie Violet knows best. She's the Wise Woman, not you.'

'Aye, I'm the Wise Woman, right enough,' muttered Violet. 'Though there's them that don't remember it.'

The logs crackled for a while as each woman sat, wrapped in their greasy shawls, ruminating on this fact.

'I seen the bitch-wife in the Village again today,' said Starling eventually. She shifted a buttock and let out a loud rumble of wind. 'She were dressed like an honest Villager and didn't it look daft, her with that hair. Who's she trying to fool?'

'Did you speak to her, daughter?' asked Vetchling.

'No, I spat on the ground and gave her the evils,' cackled Starling. 'She didn't like that. She don't look well, scraggy coney that she is. Just skin and bone.'

'Aye, just like when she first came here all them years ago,' agreed Violet. 'She were nought but a scarecrow then. What's she doing in the Village then? She don't belong there.'

'She don't belong anywhere at Stonewylde,' mumbled

Vetchling. 'Nor them brats o' hers. When's she to get her come-uppance, sister? You said at Samhain, when we was in the Circle, that her time here was over. Along with the dark-haired bastard. You said they'd be pushed out and our own dear ones would take their places.'

'Aye, and so 'twill be. Be patient, Vetch. 'Tis all a-coming just as I foretold. He's here now and 'tis all in motion, right enough.'

They sat in companionable silence for a little longer and then Starling sighed heavily, and with both hands lifted her great legs one at a time off the log. With a grunt and another explosion of wind, she heaved her bulk out of the chair and steadied herself as gravity redistributed her mounds of flesh. She shuffled over to the range and poured hot water into three filthy earthenware mugs, along with a generous pinch of herbal mixture and a good slug of something murky from a bottle.

'Night-caps are ready,' she said. 'Pity our Jay didn't come by this evening.'

'Aye, we need more wood chopped and more water,' said Violet crossly, rising from her chair. She tried to stand up straight but arthritis was taking hold. 'Who's supposed to look after us? If the boy don't come, we'll die o' cold and thirst.'

'Ain't his fault,' wheezed Vetchling. 'He has to live up at the Hall and he told me he can't come down every day. They work him hard in that school place he goes to in the Outside World and he has to do more o' that book-learning in the evenings.'

'Pah! Stupid notion, taking our young 'uns away,' muttered Violet for the hundredth time. 'We should have that idiot son o' yours back, Starling. You tell that sow Maizie we need him back here to do the heavy work.'

''Tis no use!' snapped Starling, sick of the complaints about their absent boys. 'Magpie ain't ours no longer. I seen him in the Village the other day with that Outside teacher, drawing some load o' rubbish. Hardly recognised me own son! His hair is gold, would you believe? He looks like an Outsider now, not one of us at all. All fancy clothes and airs and graces.' She spat accurately into the fire, making it hiss. 'I'd like to take the stick to him, so

57

I would, and beat him back into shape! He didn't even look my way – me, his own mother!'

'Don't you fret, my girl,' said Violet, picking up her mug with a twisted grip. 'All will be put straight soon enough. We summoned at Samhain and we done a good job. We know he's here amongst us. We know that by Samhain this year, all will be right at Stonewylde. All will be back in its proper place and the upstarts will be gone. 'Tis all happening. Remember what came about at Imbolc?'

'Aye – Imbolc were the best day!' cackled Vetchling, and then stopped as another cough erupted in her bony chest. She clutched the table and tried to steady her breathing. Starling threw more logs on the fire and pulled up the spark guard, oblivious to her mother's suffering.

'We could do with a man about the place,' she mused. 'How about it, Auntie Violet? Can you summon me a man? A nice little love spell? 'Tis been a long time and I could do with something to warm me up at nights, a woman in her prime like me.'

She leered at the crones, brown teeth gleaming in the flickering light.

'A man? Who needs a man? More trouble than they're worth,' said Violet bitterly, shuffling towards the stairs. 'We are three and we have the power. We don't need no man messing things up!'

'That's all right and good for you, Auntie,' said Starling, 'seeing as how you're the Wise Woman and solitary as you must be. But what about me? I have my needs and I ain't getting no younger. If we had a fine strapping man here to look after us, we'd have no worries about Jay turning up to chop our wood and fetch our water. We need the garden dug too, and lots o' jobs done around the cottage. You two are useless now and I can't do it all on my own. 'Tain't fair on me!'

'No, Starling, no man!' said Violet firmly. ''Twould spoil the balance and the harmony o' things. If you want your bed warmed, get yourself a cat.'

*

Harold's round glasses were bright with the reflected glare of his desk lamp as he gazed at the screen. Around him the bedroom was in near darkness and all the surfaces were piled high with plates and cups, legacy of too many meals taken in private away from the humiliation of the Dining Hall. Harold was not a popular member of the community right now and he found it much easier to bring his food up here and stay out of sight.

Muttering to himself, he sat tapping rapidly at the keyboard, entering data into the new system. He was attempting to repair the damage done at Imbolc but it was a daunting task. He'd spent ages building up the enterprise that was Stonewylde.com, but it had fallen in a matter of minutes, and would take a long time to resurrect. Harold was still mystified and more than a little frightened by what had happened that night, when his hopes and dreams for a great business empire had tumbled before his eyes and that strange message had flashed repeatedly on the screen.

He'd tried to hide the damage in a futile attempt to put it all right before anyone noticed. That had been stupid. Clearly the whole network had been hacked by someone who knew what they were doing. Yul had soon discovered that the system was down, as had all the students and teachers, Hazel and the medical staff and even Martin and the household staff – everyone, in fact, who used the network. Harold had prayed that it was only a few files infected but slowly it dawned on both him and Yul that the whole lot had gone. For a few days he'd tried everything he could possibly think of, with Yul raging at him constantly. But Harold was no computer wizard and had been forced to admit defeat. The final straw had been when he'd tried to reinstall the back-up and had reinfected the system. The virus had started up all over again; the backup was corrupted too and none of the data on it could ever be used. Everything had gone.

The expert called in to sort out the mess, at great expense, had been impressed by the sheer ingenuity of the virus. It was one he'd never seen before and extremely cleverly programmed. Much of his explanation and speculation had gone over Harold's head, but the bottom line was that Harold's data – his files and accounts, contacts and records, everything he'd worked so hard to build up – had all gone. As had the household accounts and records, the medical and dental files, everything to do with the farming and production of food, and all the school records too – lesson plans, student coursework and personal data. The system had to be wiped clean to destroy the virus that permeated the entire network; little bits of code, like poisonous seeds, were ingeniously tucked away inside the back-ups and programmes, and would suddenly bloom into deadly flower all over again at a hidden stimulus.

Perhaps the worst aspect was what had happened to all the customers' data. When Harold had launched his pre-Yule marketing campaign he'd succeeded beyond all expectation. The orders for goods had come flooding in during November and December, hundreds and hundreds of wealthy customers finding the unusual and exclusive Stonewylde products to be the perfect answer to their Christmas gift dilemmas. Harold had introduced a 'recommend a friend' reward scheme to bring more contacts to the mailing list, and this had resulted in a massive expansion of potential customers, whom he'd intended to contact in the New Year with a newsletter. But one of the nasty twists of the virus was to corrupt this database of contacts and send obscene spam to each e-mail address. There'd been a flood of complaints and Stonewylde's name had become sullied and blacklisted even though Harold had convinced the authorities of the company's innocence. Because of the collapse of the system, he couldn't even contact his customers to apologise.

A new network was almost up and running but Harold was worried that it would be hacked into again. The computer doctor had explained about Trojan viruses – ones concealed within apparently harmless data and links – and how some of the more sophisticated ones were very slow burn. They could lurk unnoticed for a long time before being detonated either by a pre-determined trigger, or by someone physically activating them. It terrified Harold that whoever had done this at Imbolc, or even before then if the slow-burn theory was correct, could and would do it again. There was a traitor in their midst and Harold had no idea who it could be.

In the meantime, everyone who'd responded to his January sales marketing drive was still waiting for their orders to be fulfilled, but Harold didn't know who they were. Their money had been taken but no goods could be sent out, and he couldn't even e-mail them to let them know. A few irate letters had arrived and luckily the orders could be dispatched to these, but other than that, the warehouse near the Gatehouse now sat idle. Yul had ordered a halt to all quota work as Harold had no idea what goods were required, and all the new schemes such as the llama herd and the range of toiletries were on hold.

Harold was devastated and took the disaster as a personal failure. He felt that he'd been targeted by the hacker. He constantly relived that dreadful moment when his temple of figures had crumbled and the red message had flashed before his eyes. He wondered almost obsessively who this Malus could be. And what did it mean? As soon as he was back online, he'd researched the meaning of Malus. Dismissing the crab apple links, he'd found references to an evil entity in a *Doctor Who* episode, and also a character linked to Dracula through a computer game. He dismissed these as well and decided that Malus must be a reference to an *'evil one'*, if Magus meant *'the wise one'*. So there was an evil one lurking in Stonewylde ready to cause mayhem, and the thought of that gave Harold nightmares.

One thing he knew for sure was that there was nobody within the community with the expertise to devise such a virus. The professional who'd assessed the damage was adamant that this was an extremely sophisticated bug and not the work of an amateur. Nobody living at Stonewylde could have created it, so the traitor was getting external help. Who could afford that? The thought crossed Harold's mind, much as he tried to dismiss it – was it actually Yul himself? He seemed the only person clever enough to come up with such an idea, but Harold couldn't see any possible motive. Yul had been delighted with Stonewylde.

com and the much-needed money pouring into Stonewylde's coffers. Why would he set out to destroy it?

Sitting now in his cold bedroom, for Yul's bad temper was such that it wasn't a good idea to spend any more time in the office than strictly necessary, Harold felt thoroughly depressed. Every scheme he'd dreamt up was now suspended, including the negotiations for supplying venison to a supermarket chain. In the furore after Imbolc when there'd been no Internet access for a good couple of weeks, and then with all his contacts lost, he'd missed the opportunity for that particular deal and the buyers had gone elsewhere. All his costings and research for schemes such as the bottled spring water had vanished and Harold was now far too despondent to start all over again, or at least not until he knew it was safe from sabotage.

There was only one bright hope on the horizon, one idea that had not gone down the pan on the night when this evil Malus had entered the heart of Stonewylde.com and wreaked such havoc. Harold, his thin face quite haggard with worry and stress, and his nervous tic even more jerky than usual, allowed a tiny hope to flare. This was the exciting proposal he'd been waiting to hear about on that terrible night. The e-mail never had come through because at that point the whole system had succumbed to the attack from Malus. But fortunately all had not been lost with this scheme. Harold was still scared of mentioning the idea to Yul in his present volatile state, but something must be decided soon, as time was of the essence. With a heavy sigh, Harold prepared to shut down his screen for the night and get some sleep. He knew this proposal could be the making of Stonewylde, the one thing that could get it back on its feet, but he was terrified of Yul's response. He must be brave and broach the subject with Yul; Buzz wouldn't wait forever for an answer.

5

Sylvie sat in her little office near the School Wing and gazed out of the window. It was almost Beltane and April had been bright and beautiful; the green haze that clothed many bare branches was already unfurling into leaves. Some of the older folk were shaking their heads and muttering about lack of rainfall and everything being far too early this year, but the younger ones were out and about, enjoying the warmth and that magical feeling of expectation when nature seems poised to explode.

She'd been sitting still for some time, lost in dreams, listening to the rooks noisily stealing each other's twigs up in the trees. This stirred a memory from years ago; standing on the terrace beside Magus and laughing together at the messy nests in the rookery. They'd been discussing her and Miranda's initiation into Stonewylde society and whether they wanted to permanently join the community. Sylvie suddenly had a very bizarre thought – suppose she were to open her eyes now and find herself back in that hospital ward with the pack of white-coated wolves still surrounding her. Suppose all of this had only been a dream?

A loud knock put paid to that idea and the door crashed open. Sylvie winced and glanced quickly at her list; this would be Jay, the last youngster she must see today. Taking a deep breath and trying to brighten her expression, she looked up to meet his piercing blue gaze. Sylvie felt herself spiralling in a weird vortex of time-slip, like a television programme she'd watched as a child where a figure spun around and around in a whirlwind of strange images. Surely this was Jackdaw?

The youth stomped across the polished floor, almost tripped over the edge of the Axminster rug, and approached her desk. She'd arranged the furniture so that visitors sat by her side rather than opposite, and she gestured for him to sit down.

'Hello, you must be Jay,' she began.

'Yeah.'

He wouldn't look at her but sat, enormous and awkward, slightly turned away so he didn't have to meet her eye again.

'I'm sorry, Jay, but I don't think we've ever had much to do with each other, have we? I do know a lot of youngsters here but I don't really know you at all.'

He grunted in reply, staring down at his dirty work boots. He wasn't wearing traditional Stonewylde clothes but had adopted Outside wear – jeans, a checked shirt and steel-toed boots. Only his heavy leather jacket was Stonewylde. Like his father, he had a large, bullet-shaped head with a massive neck, although unlike his father he hadn't shaved his head but, instead, kept his hair clipped very short. His eyes bulged in just the way Jackdaw's had, with a look of unhinged menace as if he were on the verge of losing his temper and becoming violent. Sylvie realised she'd tensed up and felt nervous of this youth, which was ridiculous.

'Right, Jay, just a few details first to establish things and then we'll have a chat about what you'd like to do with your future. Okay?'

He shrugged noncommittally and, picking up his papers, Sylvie sighed. This wasn't going to be an easy interview.

'You're living at the Hall, of course, and you're currently attending college in the Outside World? It seems … you're doing reasonably well, looking at your last exam results and college report …'

Jay shifted suddenly in his seat which made Sylvie jump.

'So … you don't have a family trade to follow. And—'

'No, I don't!' he said harshly, 'And that's because my dad was killed.'

'Er, yes. I do remember your father, and it—'

'Don't say nothing against him, I'm warning you!'

'I wouldn't dream of it!' replied Sylvie, shocked at his aggression.

'Yeah, well, there's them as bad-mouths my dad and it ain't right! He done nothing wrong but everyone hates him.'

Sylvie remembered Jackdaw's appalling treatment of Yul at the quarry. She recalled too the way he'd looked at her when Magus had dragged her there to visit – a kind of visual rape. She'd been terrified of the brute and knew that Yul had suffered again at his hands that Samhain, when he'd been captive in the stone byre after her moon-dancing on the cliff-top. Yul still bore some scars from the torture inflicted by Jackdaw. Besides which, he'd originally been banished for choking his young wife – Jay's mother and Marigold's daughter – to death. But she had no intention of bringing any of that up now.

'Jay, all we're doing today is talking a little about what you'd like to do when you finish college. We need to look at the options and see if you'd like to stay at Stonewylde or seek work in the Outside World. And—'

'I'll stay in Stonewylde o' course!' he said scornfully. '*I* belong here, unlike some.'

'What do you mean by that?'

She was astounded at his tone. He merely shrugged and looked pointedly out of the window. Sylvie considered asking him to leave the room, but that wasn't her remit and she must try to help him. He obviously had a dreadful chip on his shoulder.

'Alright, Jay, let's forget that and discuss what your interests are. What do you enjoy doing?'

He sniggered at this and Sylvie felt her skin crawl. He smelt horrible, not just unwashed teenage boy but another odour, rank and primitive. There was something about Jay that really made her uncomfortable.

'Do you have any idea what type of work you'd like to do at Stonewylde?' she asked, a little more sternly.

'Yeah. I want to work at Quarrycleave.'

Sylvie's jaw dropped open at this and her heart fluttered in her chest.

'But ... but Quarrycleave is closed! You know what happened there. Everyone knows. It's not a working quarry any more.'

'I want to learn about stone, and I want to work there,' he said stubbornly. 'My dad worked there – Granny Vetchling and Great-aunt Violet told me all about it, and my Auntie Starling. My dad done a good job there and he enjoyed the work. That's what I want to do.'

'But Jay, it's a terrible place. It's—'

'No it ain't! I been up there many a time and I love it. I feel ... I dunno ... it's where I want to be. That's what I'm gonna do – be a quarryman.'

Sylvie stared at him in disbelief, noting the way his greasy, slightly spotty face had broken out in a sweat. His bulbous eyes locked into hers and she shivered at the hostility and belligerence that emanated from him.

'Right,' she said, shuffling his papers and trying to make a note with a shaky hand. 'We'll look into apprenticeships in the quarrying industry. With both Portland and Purbeck close by, there must be some opportunities in that area. But Jay, I can tell you categorically – Quarrycleave will never be a working quarry again. And it's not a place you should be visiting.'

As the youth left her office, she felt immense relief and stood up to open the French window and blow away his lingering stench. She felt dizzy and strangely faint, and wondered whom she should talk to about Jay. He really didn't seem quite right.

Outside her office, Jay stormed down the corridor towards an outside door. He needed a smoke and knew just where to go. Shame he'd get roped into chopping wood, but it was a small price to pay. In his jacket pocket, his hand closed around the small chunk of pale, sparkling stone, about the size of a quail's egg. He'd recently found it at the base of the great serpent stone in Quarrycleave and it had strange carvings on it. Jay thought of it as a talisman; it came from his favourite place and, in the absence of any mementoes from his father, it served as such. He now carried it with him always. Quarrycleave was the place where he wanted to be, and no threats from that skinny bitch would stop him.

Sylvie knew she should be getting back to the cottage as the day was wearing on and evening was almost here. Maizie would be standing at the range in the kitchen, a delicious meal cooking and the table scrubbed and laid, ready for supper. The girls would have come back from Nursery a couple of hours ago. It was lovely that now they could just make their own way home together every day without waiting to be collected. Maizie would have greeted them, given them a drink and a snack, and then they'd either be out playing, doing jobs for her, or making something in the parlour. At the moment they were both enjoying knitting and felting, and were also writing more chapters in their book about hares and faeries. Sylvie smiled at the thought of her two precious daughters, but felt reluctant to go back to the cottage quite yet.

Instead she made her way through the corridors until she reached the Galleried Hall. She paused a moment, gazing up at the Green Men and the triple hares. The place held so many memories ... But resolutely, she went through a doorway with a pointed arch and into an even older passage. And then she'd reached the heavy oak door to Clip's tower. Studded with iron rivets and nowadays locked on the inside, it wasn't inviting. Sylvie lifted the heavy iron knocker and rapped hard. She repeated this and eventually heard the bolt being drawn back on the other side; there'd been no sound of footsteps, but when she saw Clip's felt slippers she knew why.

Sylvie gave her father a brief hug – two tall, thin people not designed for soft bosom cuddling – and followed him up the spiral staircase. They passed Leveret's bedroom on the ground floor, and Sylvie glimpsed a small almost monastic cell, the little bed neatly made and on the floor next to it, piles of books of all shapes and sizes. The next floor saw a similar room that was Clip's, again very simple, and a shared bathroom. But the top floor was the place of comfort and comparative luxury and Sylvie felt a thrill of pleasure as they climbed the last few stairs and emerged into the large, circular room.

It always smelled good here; incense or herbs or plain wood-smoke. A fire crackled in the hearth and a kettle sat on the hearth-stone ready to be boiled at a moment's notice. All around lay Clip's wonderful collection of sacred objects, and yet the great room felt uncluttered. He ushered Sylvie to one of the old leather sofas, and she sank gratefully into its depths surrounded by bright patchwork cushions. Clip made them both a cup of tea and came to sit down opposite her. Sylvie was just taking a sip, finally relaxing after the unpleasant encounter with Jay, when a sudden movement across the room made her jump and almost spill her tea.

'*What?*' she cried, and Clip laughed as the young hare left its nest in the alcove and loped over to her inquisitively.

'Don't worry, it's Leveret's hare,' he said. 'She's hand-reared the creature, and very successfully too.'

Sylvie stared at the little hare in amazement. It was beautiful, with rich golden fur dusted with darker tips and long ears that swivelled as it listened to the different voice. Its eyes were a dark gold and its nose constantly twitched, sniffing Sylvie's foot and then her hand as she tentatively stroked it. It seemed completely unfazed by her, and then stood up on its hind paws and placed its front ones on her leg. With a push it jumped off the floor and onto her lap, and Sylvie laughed with delight. The creature set-tled comfortably on her lap and laid back its ears, enjoying the touch of her gentle hand.

'It's adorable!' she breathed. 'I didn't know Leveret had a pet hare. What's it called?'

'It's a she, and Leveret won't name her, but simply calls her Hare. We found her, strangely enough, on Eostre's day. She'd been quite badly injured – see her hind paw? We think she was probably only a couple of days old when we found her. To be honest, I really didn't think she'd survive. But she's doing very well – Leveret's been amazing with her – and I think we now have a friend for life. Certainly she couldn't be released into the wild. She's imprinted on us and besides which, she limps quite badly and would never escape her predators.'

'She's so soft!' said Sylvie in wonder. 'Oh Clip, please can I bring the girls to see her? They'd absolutely love her.'

'Of course, and it would do Leveret good to see them too. Bring them soon. How are they settling into Village life? And how are you?'

Sylvie nodded, trying to smile.

'Tell me, Sylvie. What is it?'

Clip's gentleness was her undoing and to her chagrin, Sylvie burst into tears. He put down his tea and moved to sit next to her, holding her close and letting her cry. Eventually she'd shed enough tears and blew her nose in a handkerchief. The leveret still sat in her lap, its eyes closed.

'Sorry,' she said. 'I wasn't intending to do that.'

Clip patted her hand.

'So tell me, then.'

Sylvie tried to explain her feelings; her disappointment and sadness at the way her marriage was deteriorating. She missed Yul dreadfully and longed for things to be right between them. But the man who thundered around the Hall bullying people and rode down to the Village in a foul mood to find fault with everything – that wasn't her Yul. He'd become a different man, not one she knew or liked, and she didn't know how to talk to him any more. Clip sighed – he was hardly the person to give advice on marital relations and didn't know what to say to help her.

'Sorry – I know you have a million better things to do than listen to my tales of woe,' she said, with an attempt at a smile.

'I have nothing more important to do than be here to listen to my beloved daughter,' he replied gently. 'I just wish I could give you some good advice and make it all better. Sadly I can't.'

'I know. But rather no advice than bad advice,' she said. 'It's just good to talk to someone non-judgemental. Poor Maizie does her best and she's so kind to me, but you know what she's like about Yul. She can't see anything wrong with him at all, and try as she might to be impartial, she's always so defensive about his behaviour.'

'Is she happy for you to be staying with her?'

'Oh yes, she loves it. She'd be so lonely otherwise, with Leveret up here. And she's a wonderful grandmother – the girls really adore her. She's fine with me but she firmly believes that a woman's place is by her husband's side. She can't understand why Yul and I don't just patch up our differences and get on with it.'

'Maizie only sees what she wants to see,' said Clip, and Sylvie nodded.

'Can you see a change in Yul?' she asked. 'It's not just me imagining it, is it?'

'No, there's something amiss,' he agreed. 'He hasn't been right for a while now. I'm sorry, I've been so caught up in preparing myself for leaving this year and teaching Leveret – I've neglected you in the process. And Sylvie, there are things I must tell you about Stonewylde.'

'Yes, of course.'

'I've been corresponding with my lawyer and soon I must go Outside to sign the papers. It's about handing over to you when I leave.'

She looked at him warily, scared of the responsibility but not wanting Yul to take over as he planned to do.

'It's complicated and I'll explain it fully to you when I understand it properly myself. But my lawyer and I – after much debate, we've decided to change things. I knew you'd be happy not to have quite so much weight on your shoulders, so rather than simply sign the whole estate over to you, I'm intending to create a type of Trust and register the place as a charity. There'll be a Board of Trustees, of which you'll be chairperson, but it means that Stonewylde won't actually belong to you – or to any one person. I feel this is the right way forward, if you're agreeable.'

Sylvie's throat had constricted at his words and she could barely speak. She felt as if suddenly a huge dark cloud had lifted and a ray of sunshine had penetrated the gloom of her life. She'd never have imagined that learning she was not to inherit Stonewylde would have such an effect on her.

'Sylvie? What do you think? Of course if you're not happy about it, I—'

She turned and in a completely uncharacteristic gesture, planted a kiss on his thin cheek.

'Thank you!' she cried. 'Thank you, darling Clip!'

'That's a relief!' he smiled. 'I had thought it would meet with your approval but you worried me there for a minute. I don't intend to say a word to Yul until it's a *fait accompli*. I know he wants ownership, through you, and I'm really not up to a battle with him.'

'Exactly!' she agreed. 'That's why I'm living in the Village. I'm not up to doing battle with Yul any longer either.'

Marigold looked fondly at the pair of bent heads at her table – one gold and one dark. Magpie's finger was jumping along the page, following the words as Leveret slowly read the text to him. When they got to the end, she then made him go back and tested him on what she'd read.

'Magpie, which word says *"nest"*? N-e-s-t.'

He looked carefully and pointed.

'That's right! And which word says *"robin"*? R-o-b-i-n.'

Again he pointed, and again he was right.

'So can you write the word *"nest"* for me? N-e-s-t. Don't look at the book, do it from your head. Remember how the word looked, and think of the sounds of the letters. Write them down here for me, Maggie. Two more words and then we'll stop.'

Marigold shook her head in amazement. The little maid was a natural teacher, so patient and so very good at keeping Magpie on task, and she always sensed when he'd had enough. Marigold herself, along with most people on the estate, had only learned to read and write comparatively recently and she wasn't as fluent as the youngsters who'd been doing it all their lives.

She watched Leveret with her boy – for she now thought of Magpie as her grandson – and her heart swelled with pride. All around the cluttered cottage were labels. Leveret had made labels for almost every object so that Magpie was surrounded with words to help him make sense of the world around him. His early years had been so very deprived that not only was he unable to speak, but he lacked a lot of basic vocabulary as well and didn't have the means to ask. Discovering this had been a breakthrough in understanding Magpie's problem. Leveret was now giving everything in his world a name and writing each word down so he learned to read it and spell it at the same time. Marigold found it helped her spelling too, and she and Cherry agreed that at this rate, their Magpie might well learn to read and write properly.

Leveret started packing away the books and pencils; she wanted to get back to the tower to see Clip and Hare. She must pop out at some point before dark and gather more cowslip flowers whilst they were still young and fresh, and the moon was on the wax. She was making an ointment for treating sunburn and skin blemishes, which would come in useful if the weather continued so warm. She needed to build up a supply of useful remedies so that folk would start to come to her. There was also some schoolwork to be finished and handed in, and she had exams coming up in June too, so needed to revise for those. Miranda had agreed to her taking many subjects a year early, which was great as far as Leveret was concerned as it got them out of the way. She didn't give a fig for her results as she had no intention of ever using them in the Outside World, and what use were silly bits of paper here? But she needed to do reasonably well or else Miranda may insist she return to school full time.

Leveret stepped out onto the cobbled area outside the row of terraced cottages where Magpie lived. Tucked into the shadow of the Hall, they overlooked the great courtyard outside the kitchen that led into the Kitchen Gardens where Magpie worked most days. These were the homes of people who, in the old days, had been senior members of staff at the Hall. Two doors down from Marigold and Cherry's cottage was Martin's home, and as she walked past it on her way back to the tower, Leveret glanced up to see Martin standing in the window of his parlour.

She nodded politely to him but then did a double take. She was horrified to see his thin, pale face, so very like Clip's, had twisted into a grimace of hatred. Her heart jumped as she felt the force of his loathing, an almost tangible entity that hovered in the air around his contorted face. She stopped dead, caught in the moment, and felt the world prickling and fizzing around her as she slipped into that other place.

There was the man, tall and silver haired, not unattractive but rather dissolute, with a weak mouth and chin. He rode a horse that clattered on the cobbles and he surveyed the two young women carrying his babies in their swollen bellies. One girl was tiny, with wild silver hair and sharp teeth which she bared at him, almost growling in feral hatred. He looked at her sadly and Leveret felt his pain and longing for her, and also his sharp animal lust. The other young woman pushed forward and, grabbing the bridle, looked up at him as he sat there astride the horse, a fine figure of a man in his prime. She was dirty and unkempt with dark, greasy hair and a filthy shawl around her shoulders. She leered at him and rubbed her great belly in an almost obscene gesture. He turned away, feeling disgust both for her and with himself. But he also felt a lure, and against his will he throbbed in remembrance as she taunted him.

Leveret swallowed and shook her head, trying to clear it of the strange vision. She stared at Martin, still in the window, and understood he was the second baby, born of that dirty woman who'd imagined her son destined for great things. The tiny silver-haired one must be Raven, already familiar to Leveret. Poor Clip, to have been born of such hatred. And poor Martin too, for the dirty woman had evil in her heart. Leveret knew she'd seen Old Violet as a youngster and Basil, the lord of Stonewylde, who'd sown his seed so irresponsibly.

Leveret knew the family history for her mother had spoken of it often enough. Basil had met with a sudden end, wasting away rapidly, and everyone in the community suspected foul play. It was common speculation that Elm, Basil's brother, had engaged Violet's services in despatching his rival, and all because he too wanted the tiny Raven and her moongaziness. Why had Violet turned against Basil? Had he rejected her for Raven? He'd obviously favoured Raven's baby over hers, bringing little Clip to live in the Hall as his son and heir, whilst presumably Violet's baby Martin was raised in the filthy cottage on the edge of the Village.

She continued on her way, anxious to be out of Martin's sight, but then heard a door open behind her. She hoped it wasn't him, for the expression on his face had been frightening. Why did he hate her so much?

'Hey, Leveret! Wait a moment!'

It was Swift, hurrying out of his father's front door and quickly catching her up. Her heart sank, but he smiled charmingly and chattered away as if they were the best of friends.

'Are you going back to the tower? I might join you and pay my Uncle Clip a visit. How's it all going? I hear you've been let off school – why's that?'

Leveret shrugged; she really didn't want to say too much to Swift in case he was in league with Jay and her brothers, and given the blind hatred she'd just seen on his father's face, Swift mustn't be trusted at all.

'I'm still doing my schoolwork, but Clip's tutoring me now. And I'm taking some exams too, when you take yours.'

'Really? Taking them a year early? You must be even cleverer than I'd heard.'

Leveret scowled at this clumsy flattery.

'I don't think Clip will want a visit at this time of evening,' she said. 'We have lots of work to do tonight.'

'I won't stay long. And how's our Magpie? I assume you've

just been visiting him? Father said you're in that cottage most days.'

'That's right. He's my friend.'

'And he's my cousin. Or second cousin or something. My father is cousin to his mother Starling. Though between you and me, that's a connection he tries to ignore. Have you seen her lately? What a disgusting woman!'

Leveret ignored his chumminess and entered the Hall through the massive kitchen door. Swift followed close behind, happy to see that he was almost a head taller than her now.

'Are you walking with anyone, Leveret?' he asked innocently, well aware of the answer.

She stopped and turned on him, her scornful gaze raking his face. He flicked his straight, silver fringe in a gesture he knew girls found attractive, and smiled disarmingly.

'No, I'm not!' she said. 'And I don't intend to either.'

'That's a shame,' he said. 'You looked so good at the Outsiders' Dance at Yule, and at Imbolc when you were Bright Maiden.'

She glared at him and then continued impatiently across the flagstones of the kitchen. The huge table which ran down the centre of the room was empty, ready for the preparation of breakfast the following day. All the youngsters on kitchen work detail had finished their tasks and returned either to the communal sitting room or their dormitories. The copper pans on the wall gleamed as Leveret made for the door.

'Why don't you want to walk with a boy?' he pressed. 'What if one were to ask you – perhaps at Beltane? I've heard there're to be several handfastings at the Moon Fullness after Beltane so there'll certainly be romance in the air. How would you feel about that?'

'I'm not interested in boys!' she retorted, flinging open the door and entering the corridor. She turned and headed for the Galleried Hall and the tower, regretting that she hadn't gone home the outside way even though it took longer. She'd have avoided going past Martin's cottage and all this pestering.

'Now you've broken my heart!' he laughed. 'Why ever not?'

'Because the Wise Woman is solitary!' she snapped, and then wished she could snatch the words back.

'*The Wise Woman*?' He grabbed her arm and spun her round, staring into her eyes. 'Oh Leveret, you're making a big mistake if you think you're destined to be the Wise Woman. Does Clip know? Oh, of course, I understand – he's trying to teach you!'

Swift laughed sharply, ignoring her struggle to free her arm from his grip. He might be small compared to other sixteen-year-old Stonewylde boys, but he was strong.

'Listen to me! My Granny Violet is Stonewylde's Wise Woman. Traditionally the role's passed on from one to the next – there isn't room for two of them. You've no idea what you're messing with here. Wait till she hears of this!'

'I don't care about that!' retorted Leveret. 'It's nothing to do with Old Violet. She's not the Wise Woman – she doesn't help people. Nobody comes to her for healing.'

'Some still do, and she has the power and knows the Old Ways. And *you* couldn't heal a headache! You're useless – you even got the wrong mushrooms when you tried to top yourself at Quarrycleave! What a joke – no wonder your brothers call you Harebrain! On second thoughts, I won't come to see Clip after all – I'll go and visit my grandmother instead. Won't she have a laugh when she hears this piece of news!'

Up in the Art Room in the School Wing, Rainbow sat on one of the long tables swinging her legs. David was sorting the trays of watercolours, trying to bring about some semblance of order to his classroom after a day's teaching. He still felt somewhat in awe of the rather exotic Rainbow, only knowing her as an acclaimed artist. He was a little shocked at how most of the Stonewylde community regarded her as an unwanted exile being given a second chance. She made him jumpy and she knew it, teasing him all the more.

'Not long till the big day,' she said. 'Fancy you and old Dawn getting handfasted! I feel like a proper matchmaker as it was me who first told you of Stonewylde, wasn't it?'

'Yes, and thank Goddess you did!' he said. 'The thought of living in the Outside World now ...'

'Do you appreciate just how honoured you are?' asked Rainbow. 'You'll be the first Outsider to gain permanent residence since ... oh, I guess since Sylvie and Miranda arrived.'

'I know – I can't believe how lucky I am,' agreed David. 'I never thought I'd find a woman like Dawn, nor a home like this. It's not even a dream come true because I'd never dreamed of such a life.'

Rainbow rolled her eyes and pretended to vomit.

'Come on, David, spare me the sentimental bollocks. You've fallen on your feet though, no mistake about that. Do you come across much hostility here?'

He thought about that for a moment.

'I think there is amongst some of the older folk. But nobody's said anything outright.'

'You're lucky! The other day an old boy bumped into me in the Village and he glared at me and muttered, "Scout!" like it was an insult. And when I told Dawn she laughed and said that at one of their stupid Elder meetings, some old fool had said I was the scout ant, sent in ahead of all the others! And soon Stonewylde would be swarming with ants.'

David regarded her steadily.

'Yes, I heard that theory too. And are you the scout?'

Rainbow chuckled and launched herself off the table. She padded around the big Art Room, fiddling with things.

'Now that would be telling, wouldn't it? But anyway, I guess you'll be bringing guests into Stonewylde, won't you? Both for the handfasting and afterwards, if you're to live here permanently. I mean, people to stay for the weekend or whatever.'

'That's true, but they'll all be my Druid friends and relations and they'll understand what it's all about here. I spoke to Yul first, obviously, and he's very happy for me to bring visitors in. I think he's hoping to attract more of my kind, if truth be told.'

'Fresh breeding stock!' laughed Rainbow. 'Well, at least Sylvie likes you. She hates me.'

'Surely not? I don't think she—'

'Oh, there's no doubt about it,' said Rainbow drily. 'She's not the first woman to take an irrational dislike to me of course – I should be used to it. But who cares – she's not in charge here, luckily. As long as I keep Yul sweet, I can stay.'

'But Yul isn't actually in charge, is he?' asked David.

'Maybe not officially, but to all intents and purposes. Just like his father. You never met Magus of course, but believe me, Yul is exactly like him in every single way bar one.'

'What's that?'

'His colouring – Magus had the Hallfolk silvery blond hair and very dark eyes. It's really quite uncanny, the likeness between them both in looks and their ways. And of course, I know Magus' other son, Buzz. Now he really is nothing like Magus, not as I remember him anyway.'

'And there's Rufus too, isn't there? Magus' other son, I believe,' said David. 'He's a nice lad, always works hard in class though he's not especially artistic.'

'Haven't spoken to him yet. He's ginger isn't he, like Miranda?'

'I'd hardly call Miranda ginger! That deep auburn hair ...'

'True. And I met Magus' other child a while ago – the Princess Faun. What a little madam! But she's very picturesque and she has Magus' colouring. Her mother was keen for me to paint her and I probably will, as she's certainly got something.'

'Have you started any painting yet?' asked David, giving the room a final sweep of his gaze before shutting up for the night. He was longing to get down to the Village and see Dawn, who must be wondering where he'd got to.

'No, not yet, though I've filled several sketch books and taken lots of photos. I want to meet that boy you talked about, David. Now I've seen some of his work I'm fascinated. I think you're right – he's a total natural and I really love his style. I was thinking I may be able to include some of his stuff in my exhibition perhaps, as complementary to my work. What do you think?'

Privately David thought this was a brave suggestion, for in his opinion – and much as he admired Rainbow's art – Magpie's work was superior. Or if it wasn't now, by the time the boy reached maturity it certainly would be. Magpie had the makings of a truly great artist, and every time David heard talk of Stonewylde's dire financial situation, he smiled. What no-one seemed to realise was that they had a potential goldmine in Magpie, the boy that everyone derided.

He nodded at Rainbow, thinking that he must beware of her. She wasn't quite the woman he'd thought she was. He wouldn't put it past her to exploit or even plagiarise Magpie, and David had no intention of allowing that to happen. Magpie was his protégé and he personally would protect him from predators such as Rainbow. Or, for that matter, Yul.

6

Clip watched Leveret, knowing that something was troubling her. She'd been quiet ever since Sylvie and the girls had left. She was feeding Hare, who was now around six weeks old and weaned from the ewe's milk that she'd thrived on. Leveret fed her on greens and Hare sat at her feet, eagerly taking leaves from her hand. The young hare was beautiful, growing steadily but still fluffy, with soft fur. She was very tame and particularly loved Leveret, whom she followed around the tower like a little shadow. Leveret had yet to take her outside, although she'd carried her up onto the roof, blocking off the gap leading to the outside stairs, and they'd sat basking together in the sunshine and fresh air.

Celandine and Bluebell had visited several times recently and were besotted with the young hare. On their first visit they'd sat completely spellbound, hardly daring to breathe, whilst the creature sniffed their shoes and then their hands, before allowing them to stroke her. They'd squabbled over whose turn it was to have her on their lap, and were disappointed when she'd hopped off both laps and chosen Leveret's instead. They'd missed seeing her being fed with a teat, which Leveret had stopped as early as possible, as she'd read of the danger of milk inhalation. But they'd loved watching Hare lapping at her little bowl of milk, and they always arrived with handfuls of young dandelions and purple clover which Leveret had said were Hare's favourites.

Clip was delighted, as he adored his two granddaughters and

had always longed for more contact with them. They in turn had become very at home in the tower, which they both found fascinating.

'Grandfather Clip, why do you have so many strange things?' asked Celandine in wonder when they'd visited the tower earlier in the day with Sylvie.

'Because I travelled all over the world in my younger days and collected them.'

'Are they all magic?' asked Bluebell, her eyes round as full moons.

'Oh yes, lots of these things are magical,' said Clip with a smile.

'I remember when I first came to Stonewylde,' said Sylvie, 'and I was a little younger than Auntie Leveret is now, and Grandfather Clip held a Story Web in the Great Barn. He made magic then – he told us the story of the Rainbow Snake and he turned his ash staff into a real snake!'

Both little girls gasped in amazement, gazing at their grandfather with renewed respect. Clip chuckled at this and nodded.

'Your father was only a lad then, and he came up onto the stage and held the snake for me,' he said. 'And you should've seen his face when it changed back into my staff at the end of the story.'

'Wow!' breathed Celandine. 'That must've been so wonderful!'

Both children stared hard at the old ash staff propped against the wall.

'Can you do it now?' asked Bluebell, trotting over to Clip and earnestly gazing up into his silvery wolf eyes. 'Please, Grandfather? Magic your stick and turn it into the Rainbow Snake just for us?'

'I think some of my powers aren't quite as strong any more,' he said ruefully.

'I bet they're just as strong!' said Celandine loyally. 'Maybe you just need a bit of practice?'

'Why don't you do another Story Web?' asked Sylvie. 'They

used to be so very special and everyone loved them. You haven't done one for ages.'

'No, I haven't. I'm not sure why – they didn't really seem appropriate any more, not now everyone reads books and watches television and films in the Hall. Do you think folk would like a Story Web?'

Leveret, sitting silently by a window, looked across at him, so thin and earnest in his old robes with battered felt slippers on his feet. He'd been such a lonely man for many years, yet here he was now with her, his daughter and his granddaughters all together in his tower, the centre of attention. She was so glad for him, even though she wasn't particularly keen on Sylvie being here. Leveret really loved Clip and the closer they became, the more she respected him for his wealth of knowledge and kind wisdom.

'I think everyone would love a Story Web,' she said. 'I can barely remember the last one you did. Maybe you could do one at Beltane?'

'That doesn't really give me much time to prepare,' he said. 'I think perhaps the Midsummer Holiday would be better, at the Solstice. I could do it in honour of your birthday, Sylvie!'

'That would be lovely,' Sylvie said. 'But don't drag me into it, please. I'd be so embarrassed.'

'I'll tell you all what,' said Clip, beaming at his granddaughters. 'I'll prepare a very magical Story Web especially for all the children at the Solstice.'

'Ooh yes, yes!' squealed Celandine and Bluebell, and then Clip looked across at Leveret.

'But only on one condition. Leveret must assist me with the story and the magic.'

'What?' she gasped. 'Oh no, not me, Clip! I couldn't, and especially after what happened at Imbolc.'

'That was entirely different,' he said. 'And anyway, Leveret, if you're to be the next Shaman of Stonewylde, you need to learn how to keep everyone spellbound, don't you?'

After a bit of cajoling from Clip and the girls, Leveret had accepted the challenge. Sylvie kept out of the discussion as she knew Leveret was still rather hostile towards her, as she'd always been. It was a shame and she wanted to make things right between them. Maybe now, with everything so changed around, it was time to try and build a better understanding between them. Sylvie knew it wouldn't come from Leveret so it was up to her. Clip was showing the girls some tiny mommets he'd brought back from Russia many years before, and telling them the story of the terrifying old witch, Baba Yaga, with her iron pestle and mortar, and her house built on chicken legs. They were engrossed, so Sylvie plucked up courage and asked Leveret for a private word outside on the roof top where she knew they'd be alone. The girl's reluctance was obvious but Sylvie was determined.

'Sorry, Leveret, but we really do need to have a chat,' she said, once they were outside. Leveret stood by the crenellated edge, gazing out at the trees bursting into bud in the parkland. The birds were singing their hearts out and the late afternoon sun was warm. Sylvie watched her, struck again by her likeness to Yul. Leveret was blossoming and had lost her air of haunted desperation. She no longer looked like a grubby little urchin who sidled around trying to avoid contact with people. She hadn't grown physically, yet her stature had changed. She held her head up, looked people in the eye and moved with far more assurance and confidence now. But, Sylvie noted wryly, her scowl was the same.

'What do you want, then?'

'I just thought maybe we should try to talk.'

Leveret shrugged, continuing to gaze out over the landscape.

'So, we're talking. What did you want to say?'

Sylvie sighed. Maybe this hadn't been such a good idea. Leveret had always been difficult with her; prickly and unwilling to establish any kind of channel between them. She really didn't know where to start, as it wasn't as if they'd had an argument that they could patch up.

'Are you happy living up here?'

83

'Well, obviously I am. Anything's better than my life was before.'

She hadn't changed that much after all, Sylvie decided; still rude and hostile.

'I wondered if you'd be coming down to the Village soon to visit your mother?'

Leveret turned and glared at Sylvie, her angry eyes taking in every detail of the pale woman's face. Sylvie wasn't looking good these days, her eyes strained and weary, her mouth sad. Leveret felt an inkling of pity, despite herself. Sylvie had always been so perfect and beautiful, but somewhere along the line that had disappeared. Her serenity had been punctured, and with it her beauty. Leveret found her fierce dislike starting to dissolve and a reluctant sympathy seeping.

'Has Mother asked you to invite me to visit?' she asked, a little more harshly than she intended. 'Was this her idea?'

Sylvie shook her head, her long silver hair rippling as she did so. She drooped like a wilting flower, thought Leveret, as if all her vitality and energy had been sapped.

'No, Leveret, she hasn't asked me to do anything. But I know that she misses you and—'

'That's not really the point, though. You can miss someone but still not want to see them.'

'True,' agreed Sylvie, thinking of Yul. 'But I'm sure Maizie does want to see you.'

'Well, I'm not sure!' said Leveret bitterly, all the feelings that she'd kept at bay now flooding back. 'And until I am, and she asks me directly herself, I won't see her. And just for future reference, you needn't take it on yourself to try and make things better between me and my mother, thank you Sylvie. It's none of your business!'

'Oh, Leveret!' Sylvie stared at her in dismay. 'There's really no need to be so antagonistic towards me.'

'I'm not antagonistic – I just don't want you interfering. It really is nothing to do with you, despite the fact that you're now so happy living in *my* home with *my* mother ...'

84

Leveret's voice tailed off and she felt alarmingly close to tears, which made her angry; she'd done with crying at Imbolc. But Sylvie's cheeks had flushed.

'Don't be jealous, please!' she snapped. 'I'm not happy at all, believe me! I'm only living there because your brother has become such a brute and I have nowhere else to go. And besides, it works both ways, Leveret. How do you think *I* feel about *you* living so cosily with my father? That's a privilege I've never had!'

They stared at each other, quite aghast at the lacerating emotion that had flared up seemingly out of nowhere. Green gaze met silver one and something strange happened as they looked, for the first time ever, deep into each other's eyes. Empathy bloomed and both of them crumbled, their mouths quivering and tears welling. Leveret was suddenly overwhelmed with compassion. Rapidly crossing the flagstones of the roof, she reached up and put her arms around her sobbing sister-in-law. Sylvie grabbed hold of the smaller, younger girl and held on tightly, the sobs choking her.

'I'm so sorry, Sylvie,' said Leveret through her tears. Her throat ached with sadness for this poor woman who'd done no harm to anyone. 'I've always disliked you and it's so stupid. I really don't know why, because you're a lovely person and you've always been kind to me. I'm sorry!'

Sylvie couldn't speak but gradually her sobs subsided, although she still clung to Leveret. She found it strangely comforting; there was something strong and vibrant within Leveret. Eventually her tears stopped altogether and Leveret gave her a final hug.

'We'd better go back inside,' she said gently. 'Shall we get together soon and have a proper talk?'

Sylvie had nodded, blowing her nose and managing a shaky smile.

'And Sylvie, I'm sorry how I've always behaved towards you. That's over now, I promise.'

*

That had been earlier, and Clip, having watched Leveret and sensing some of her inner turmoil, insisted on them making a journey that evening.

'I think you need to ask some questions, Leveret. It's Beltane the day after tomorrow and, for that, we need to join in the celebrations and everything up at the Stone Circle and in the Village. So I'd like us to go up to the Dolmen this evening and journey from there. Remember I said to you we'd do that when the weather became warmer?'

Sitting together in the entrance to the ancient cave, a small fire now burning amongst the ring of stones and aromatic smoke filling their nostrils, Clip looked carefully at Leveret.

'Things are happening, Leveret, and there are big changes on their way. I don't know why, but I'm just not getting any answers, try as I might. Maybe that's because you're on the wax and I'm on the wane. Have you had any of your other visions lately?'

Leveret shook her head.

'No, not really. I felt something the other day when Martin was watching me ... but nothing that really helps. Right now I feel ... confused. Sylvie and I had a talk earlier and it's preying on my mind. I'm not sure how successful a journey I'll have this evening.'

'I'm sure you'll be given the answers you need if the time is right,' he said, stoking up the fire and passing her some water. 'And I have something here, something I've made for you.'

Clip reached into the bag he always carried and pulled out a parcel wrapped in cloth. He solemnly handed it to Leveret with both hands and made a little bow.

'I found her lying on the path when I visited Mother Heggy's cottage recently, after our conversation,' he said. 'I've preserved this for you – tanned it all myself, so there's a lot of my intent and energy in it. It's for you to wear sometimes when you're journeying. All the ancient shamans would've had something similar.'

Mystified, Leveret opened up the cloth and stared at the thing in her lap. It was – had been – a hare, and a large one at that. The head was intact, presumably stuffed, and the enormously long ears lay back flat. Golden glass eyes stared at her in the flickering firelight and Leveret shuddered as something fleeting touched her memory, something from long, long ago in a different era. The fur pelt was beautiful, a speckled golden brown, and fully opened up so that it stretched out in a great piece of material with four paws still attached, and a tuft of a tail at the bottom. There were long leather laces attached on either side, near the head. Leveret's hand moved to touch it and she received a jolt that sizzled through her body. She cried out and turned to Clip in wonder, her eyes shining.

'Clip, I ... I—'

He smiled and patted her arm in understanding.

'No need to say anything, it's alright. I'm assuming she died of natural causes, as there wasn't a mark on her, no wounds of any kind. She was lying right in my path, on the ground near Mother Heggy's cottage and she was still warm – what could I do but cure her skin for you? I've long thought you should have a shaman's headdress or magical costume of some kind. You may recall my cloak of black bird feathers? That will be yours when I leave Stonewylde, but I realised that you should also have your own totem garment. You must put the hare's head here, over your forehead, so she looks out from your inner eye chakra and her ears lie back over your head and crown. Tie the laces here, under your chin ...'

Leveret looked up at him and now it was Clip's turn to shiver. The hare headdress was perfect. The hare's sightless eyes gazed out from the girl's forehead and the soft fur, with the fine leather inside so carefully tanned over the past two weeks, fell in a kind of heavy veil from it, reaching right down her back. Leveret's wild dark curls and the hare's front paws framed her pointed face, whilst the rest of the skin hung down over her shoulders with the hind paws level with her breasts. She had become hare-woman; even her green eyes had changed.

Clip picked up his large frame-drum and beater, and settled

more comfortably on the cushion, a recent concession to comfort. Leveret, magical and bizarre in the hare headdress, pulled her warm cloak around herself and gazed into the flames of the fire. The soft April light outside the stone cave began to fade unnoticed as the deep-voiced shamanic drumbeats summoned, insistent and throbbing. The flames crackled brightly in the hearth, and outside a crow called across the landscape ...

Raven drew her into the entrance; not her usual one, but a tree tunnel of sorts, long and stretching away beneath an arch of beech trees. Leveret recognised it as the Long Walk leading into the Stone Circle, although in this Middle World landscape everything was slightly different. The trees breathed, their green-lichened trunks expanding and contracting with each breath, and their delicate twigs and unfurling leaves trembled with life-force. They sparkled a brilliant lime-green, giving out light and energy. As usual, the way was lined with waist-high stones all carved and hewn into shape. And in the dreamscape, the stones themselves had life, each grain and molecule pulsating with being. The worms in the earth by the side of the pathway were visible, beautiful and perfectly designed for their role in the great web of life. The sky through the branches above was pure, forget-me-not blue and so limitless it made Leveret want to cry.

Raven strutted alongside and turned its glossy head to fix her with a knowing eye.

'Everything is connected, everything is true,' it said, with the beak that never opened.

The Long Walk stretched ahead and Leveret walked its length peacefully, sniffing the air and the scent of nature all around, like a perfume more subtle and sublime than any other. The bird song was a symphony greater than any that man had, or ever would, compose. Leveret felt perfectly, completely happy in such a place. Of Clip and his silver wolf, there was no sign.

They reached at last the entrance to the Stone Circle, and over the two stones there was a woven archway of hawthorn boughs smothered in starry blossom. Inside the Circle it was different again, and at first Leveret thought the great arena was empty. Each megalith was painted as usual, but instead of the normal patterns and motifs, the stones were painted all over with leaves. If was like walking into a woodland grove rather than a stone henge. Real boughs of many different types of tree lay on the tops of the stones and stood propped between them, so that all was green and leafy.

Then Leveret noticed a couple standing over by the Altar Stone. He was dressed as the Green Man – or maybe he was the Green Man – in a robe of leaves and a massive headdress of hawthorn blossom. His skin was green and his grey eyes bright in his face, and as Leveret stared at his mass of dark curls she realised it was Yul, but a very young Yul, not much older than she was now. By his side stood the May Queen, his Maiden of Beltane and of course it was Sylvie. She was a young, exquisite girl with skin like pearl and hair like silver corn-silk, dressed in the traditional white dress with a wreath of blue-bells and white blossom on her head.

The Green Man was merry and bright and he glowed with a strange green light that danced all over him. The May Queen glowed silver as if washed with moonbeams and sprinkled with stardust. Silver threads chased all over her pale limbs as if alive. As Leveret watched, the Green Man began a dance upon the earth floor and, as if by magic, the green energy began to awaken beneath his feet. She could see it clearly, like a great coiled snake under the ground slowly coming to life, moving as the boy's dancing feet marked out the sacred pattern that quickened it. And the Maiden too began to dance, trailing silver moonbeams and magic as she moved, her light feet caressing the earth and the waiting serpent so it flexed with pleasure and delight.

And her vision expanding suddenly, as it did in the dreamscape, Leveret saw this great serpent of Stonewylde, this life-force and magi-cal being, curled beneath the land all around, stretching out along the ridgeway and beneath the riverbed and below the Village and around the Hall. It writhed below the Wildwood and the cliffs, the hills and the valleys, the wells and the springs. Everywhere the snake spread its coils and its length, and then, with her vision expanded even further, like a lens pulling back and back, Leveret saw that the serpent was simply one aspect of the great Goddess in the Landscape that was Stonewylde, her life force and her life energy.

The boy and the girl in the Stone Circle, their dance now done, fell into each other's arms. And Leveret saw such complete love, such absolute tenderness in their embrace and their kiss that she could not breathe for the tears that choked her throat. Such perfect harmony – the darkness and the light, the green and the silver, the male and the female. And Raven turned to her and spoke softly.

'This is what has been lost and must be found.'

'But how?' asked Leveret.

'The Circle must be free of taint,' Raven replied.

'But how?' she asked again but there was no response, for the vision was fading and now they were somewhere else completely.

They were at the entrance to a cave where boulders were heaped around the mouth. Carefully they picked their way through and into a long, dark passage. They walked slowly along, noting the carvings of snakes all over the walls and roof, until they were inside a great tomb. Leveret looked around in wonder at the rock-lined chamber. It was dry, the air strange with the scent of earth, herbs and incense. Tiny oil-lamps, little more than primitive finger-pots filled with oil and a burning wick, were dotted all around the edges of the stone-lined floor. A long stone table lay in the centre, and off the chamber were several dark portals leading into blackness. Leveret was scared of what might lie in them and looked to Raven for reassurance. Raven bobbed its head and said, 'You are right not to look beyond this chamber. That is not for you to know just now.'

'Where are we?' she asked in wonder. 'Is this the Lower World? Is it a tomb?'

'Tomb and womb, death and birth, earth and breath – 'tis all the dance of life.'

And then, as the vision began to fade, Leveret saw a staff with a snake entwined around it and recognised the Asklepian, the ancient symbol of healing and medicine, the wand of life and death.

It was strange for Leveret, only two days later, to be walking down the Long Walk into the Stone Circle for Beltane sunrise. She glanced at the beech trees and stones lining the way with slightly different eyes, aware of their alternative reality. By her side, as ever, was Clip, ash staff in hand. He no longer conducted any of the ceremonies, having told the Council that this was part of the leaving process and necessary for everyone concerned; a gradual release rather than an abrupt departure.

Inside the Stone Circle the usual Green Men were painted all around and Leveret wondered again about her last journey and what hidden messages it may have contained. She recognised Magpie's handiwork in the clever design of blossom and birds that chased around the upper parts of the stones, and the enormous and wild Green Man gracing the largest stone behind the Altar Stone was definitely his. She saw Magpie in the crowd, his butterscotch-coloured hair gleaming, and sent her love to him. It didn't always work, but sometimes they picked up each other's thoughts from a distance. He turned, and immediately locating her in the shadowy circle, beamed her way.

It was a shock to many when Yul appeared, not in resplendent leafy attire, but dressed in a general green cloak and headdress, with Sylvie by his side in plain white robes. Then a small Green Man and a pretty May Queen emerged from behind the stones and stood on the Altar Stone whilst Yul led the ceremony, with help from the choir. Leveret wondered if this had anything to do with the fact that he wasn't receiving any Green Magic, and presumably not sharing marital relations with his wife either. Both seemed requisite for him to perform his usual Green Man function at Beltane, so perhaps the break with tradition was due to that. It meant that when the sun rose from behind the May Sister and the Bel Fire was lit, the rays fell on a member of the community other than the magus. There was a swell of discontented muttering that made Leveret cringe on Yul and Sylvie's behalf.

It wasn't till later in the ceremony when she was up nearer the front that Leveret realised with a shock who was playing the part of the Green Man; none other than Swift. Yul and Sylvie stood handing out the mead and the cakes, making Martin superfluous other than as a pair of hands to top up the tots of mead. But the expression of pride on his face as he stood by the Altar Stone where his son was splendid in costume was obvious to all. As Leveret took the thimbleful of mead from Sylvie's hand, their eyes met.

'Beltane blessings, dear Leveret,' she murmured.

'Bright blessings to you, Sister Sylvie,' Leveret replied and was rewarded with a grateful smile.

In contrast, Yul refused to look at her properly, and mumbled his blessing almost inaudibly as he handed her the cake. Leveret thought again of her vision and that beautiful, vibrant boy who hadn't just dressed up in a leafy costume – he'd actually transformed into the Green Man. She recalled the dancing green light around him, the sheer magic that emanated from him. Leveret understood then that her healing skills would not only involve herbs and medicines for the sick, but also spiritual reparation for the dreadful illness that was infecting so many at Stonewylde. And not least her oldest brother.

The first dance on the Village Green had taken place – the glorious Maypole Dance, with the unique carved and painted tree trunk, and the host of maidens dressed in white. Leveret was glad she'd avoided getting roped into this humiliating event, where in the past she'd invariably got herself tangled up in the bright ribbons and cords, or tripped someone over by skipping to the wrong side. She watched from the crowd and was amused to see Faun doing her utmost to be the centre of attention. At thirteen this was Faun's first dance – it was for maidens from thirteen up to sixteen – and the way she behaved, thought Leveret, it was as if Faun were May Queen herself.

She and Clip also watched the young men's Dance of the Staves, which, this year, was particularly athletic. Leveret saw that neither her brothers nor Jay were taking part, and this didn't surprise her as none of them were light on their feet. Being the Green Man, Swift couldn't participate; he and his May Queen stood close to Yul and Sylvie, and Leveret guessed that this had all been planned to smooth away any awkwardness about the magus and his wife living apart. Leveret didn't have access to any gossip now she lived in the tower with only Clip for company, but she could guess how tongues must be wagging about the unheard-of separation.

Rainbow had been busy all morning with a sketchbook and pencil, wandering around the Green and stopping to draw rapidly as something caught her eye. Now Leveret noticed her standing in the great circle of spectators and watched her pull out a camera and start taking photos. Leveret thought she seemed so busy snapping away that she was missing the dance completely.

The Jack in the Green, his face blacked up and his jaunty feathers and colourful tatters bright in the sunshine, gradually disappeared inside the cage of wooden staves, whilst the young men, all dressed in green with white ribbons fluttering and bells jingling, leapt around him. Leveret noticed Rufus dancing, his red hair so distinctive, and she caught sight of Miranda's proud face watching her son leap and dip. Clip, standing close beside her, chuckled unexpectedly.

'Do you know it was at Beltane I said to Miranda that she'd be having a baby soon and she laughed at me. And all these years later, here that baby is, taking part in the young men's dance. And even funnier, in a way – at the same time as that, Sylvie asked me if I had any children and I said no, I'd never been blessed. And that was to my own daughter! What a strange and beautiful world it is.'

Leveret glanced up at him and squeezed his hand.

'Sylvie's lucky to have a father like you, Clip,' she said. 'I never knew my father, but I've heard he was a terrible man.'

'Yes, he was,' agreed Clip with a twisted smile. 'But nobody can help their parents. In fact it's all the more admirable if you turn out to be a decent person despite your bloodline, don't you think? Talking of parents, have you seen or spoken to Maizie yet?'

'No,' said Leveret quietly.

'Maybe you should try to—'

'Not yet, Clip – unless I can't avoid it. I just don't feel ready yet.'

He nodded and then they both jumped as the fiddles, flutes and drums reached a crescendo and, in sudden silence, the dancers leapt up together and shouted, 'Jack – ho!'

During the Naming of the Babies ceremony, Hazel edged up to Dawn and gave her a playful prod in the belly.

'Are you intending to take part in this next year?' she asked.

Dawn smiled happily and nodded.

'I hope so, if you've taken out my hormone implant in good time and everything's in working order,' she said.

'Well, the handfasting's next week, isn't it? The Hare Moon's a week away, so come up any time and we'll remove it. Does David want to start a family straight away?'

'Yes, he certainly does. We're both longing for children. We're neither of us getting any younger and this isn't something we'd ever thought would happen.'

'Oh Dawn! You're still a young woman – and he's not exactly over the hill either. Wait till you get to my age – that's when you realise that you'll probably never be taking part in the Naming of the Babies.'

Her voice was wistful and Dawn sighed in sympathy.

'You never know, Hazel. The Goddess moves in mysterious ways ...'

Swift and Valerian, his May Queen, stood behind Yul and Sylvie as they sat on their thrones on the dais announcing the babies' names, welcoming them into the community and handing out the silver charms to each mother.

'I wanted the Green Man hisself to bless little Badger,' muttered one of the mothers processing round the circle with her baby boy all dressed up in his finery. ''Twon't be the same if 'tis just Yul with that Swift all greened up behind him.'

'I know,' said the mother next to her. 'I feel the same. 'Tis a disappointment and no mistake. And look at Sylvie's face! She looks like the skies have fallen in on her. What a shame, on our babies' special day.'

'I remember when I were a youngster, this ceremony was a real occasion. There'd be a huge crowd o' mothers lined up with their little 'uns all bedecked and beribboned. 'Tis as if now there are only a few of us, they can't be bothered to do it proper.'

The last woman came up with her baby all dressed in white to be presented with her silver charm.

'Bright blessings to Poppy!' said Yul, flicking a glance at his list. 'She's a fine Lammas baby and we welcome her into Stonewylde. Beltane blessings to Poppy and all her family!'

He took the chubby little girl, already sporting a couple of teeth and a ribbon in her top curl, and hugged her. Her face screwed up and she started to howl. Yul hastily returned the screaming child to her mother, who moved along to Sylvie.

'We present Poppy with her ear of corn, the symbol of Lammas, and wish her a happy and healthy childhood,' shouted Sylvie over the bawling.

The mother snatched the charm on its ribbon, knowing it would only upset her baby more to have something dangled round her neck, and stomped off from the dais. In the audience, Starling let out a bellow of raucous laughter.

'I'd scream if Yul kissed me and all!' she shouted. 'The grumpy git's enough to make anyone cry!'

There was some stifled laughter at this, and then the crowd broke up and all went into the Barn for lunch. Sylvie immediately turned on Yul, who'd decided to ignore Starling's heckling.

'You must stop Rainbow now!' she hissed. 'Don't keep brushing me aside over this – she's been doing it all morning and it wasn't agreed on!'

Surreptitiously Swift leaned forward to adjust some of the leaves around his hem.

'And neither was it forbidden!' snapped Yul. 'Stop being hysterical and leave the girl be.'

'I'm not hysterical, Yul, and you know it. She's overstepping the mark and we never said she could wander around taking hundreds of photos of everyone in the community. It's an invasion of people's privacy and I want it stopped. Would you prefer me to tell her?'

'No, no, I'll have a word with her,' he said with exaggerated weariness. 'I don't want you flaying her with your sharp tongue, when she's done nothing wrong.'

Sylvie glared at him, longing to challenge him, but knowing that this was certainly not the place. She noticed Swift close behind eavesdropping, and turned on him.

'You should be in the Barn, Green Man!' she said sharply. 'Take your Queen and get in there to say the thanksgiving before lunch.'

Yul rolled his eyes at the green youth in sympathy, and, slightly unsteadily, climbed down from the dais. Swift hid a smile as he took Valerian's arm and led her down the steps. It seemed that Yul had taken his advice after all and had a good swig of mead to get him through the morning.

Yul found Rainbow sitting on her shawl spread on the grass, with her back against a chestnut tree. She was wearing the customary white dress, worn by all the girls and women in the community at Beltane. She'd woven some bluebells into the long, wild tresses of hair that fell almost to her waist and her feet were bare. She grinned at him as he approached across the Green and put down her sketchbook and pencil.

'Bright Beltane blessings, Yul!' she said, patting the shawl next to her. 'Come and sit with me for a while. You look totally pissed off.'

'I am,' he said ruefully. 'Totally.'

He flung himself down next to her, sharing the tree trunk and clasping his knees up to his chest, just as he'd always sat. Their shoulders weren't touching and he was careful to keep apart. She turned her head to grin at him again, and he was struck by the light dancing in her sea-blue eyes, so bright and knowing.

'I'm disappointed you're not the Green Man,' she said. 'I imagined you'd be splendid.'

'It's the first year I haven't been,' he said. 'We thought ... we thought it best this year to give some youngsters a chance at taking the lead roles for a change.'

'Shame – I bet you look gorgeous. And fancy foregoing that rollicking around in the bluebells all night!'

'That was in Magus' time,' he said. 'We've changed the customs quite a bit. Sylvie's always the May Queen and the Lammas Queen. She does everything except the Bright Maiden.'

'How very greedy of her,' mused Rainbow. 'Fancy taking all the main parts. But she decided not to bother this year – maybe she's bored of it.'

Yul grunted noncommittally and sighed.

'I wanted a word with you about the camera,' he began and Rainbow laughed.

'And there I was thinking you'd sought me out for an intimate conversation, Yul! What a disappointment. Do you realise you've been avoiding me ever since I arrived?'

'No, I haven't! I've spoken to you many times.'

'Not alone. I've been here six weeks, yet this is the first time we've been alone together. Why is that, I wonder?'

He frowned, not sure how to handle Rainbow.

'Anyway, we've finally got a moment of privacy,' she continued, 'so let's just enjoy it while it lasts. I've been so looking forward to this. I wanted to tell you that you grew up into all I'd imagined you would.'

He gave her a sidelong glance. Nobody at Stonewylde ever spoke to him in this way.

'Yes,' she sighed, 'you really are one hell of a man. It's just as well I left Stonewylde when I did, because I was developing a dreadful crush on you, just like all the other Hallfolk girls. We all had the hots for you – did you know that? Lucky old Sylvie – I hope she appreciates just how fortunate she is.'

Yul couldn't stop the bitter laugh that escaped his lips. Rainbow sighed again and leaned her shoulder against his.

'Though I heard that you no longer live together as man and wife. How dreadful!'

A strand of her tawny blonde hair, glinting with strands of gold, blew across his arm. He stared down at it.

'Rainbow, come on ...' he said helplessly.

But she only chuckled in her husky, inviting way and leaned into him just a little more. Where her golden hair brushed his skin, he began to tingle.

7

Dawn smoothed her dress and gave herself a final once-over. She caught her own terrified eyes in the mirror and made a face.

'Honestly, I feel like a teenager,' she laughed shakily. 'I'm in my thirties but I'm so ridiculously nervous!'

'You look lovely,' said Rainbow, flicking a glance at the bride before resuming her own grooming. Rainbow wore a dress of turquoise silk shot with a deeper blue which changed colour as it caught the light, perfectly matching her eyes. She'd had it sent down the minute she'd been given the honour of attending Dawn at her handfasting, knowing Stonewylde had never seen the like of such a dress. Both women wore a circlet of bluebells and wood anemones on their heads; Rainbow's wild hair cascaded down in tawny blonde tresses that put Dawn's rather wiry fair hair to shame. But, like many a bride before her, Dawn had a light in her eye that refused to be outshone by a prettier face.

'Are you sure you remember what to do?' asked Dawn anxiously, wishing that Rainbow would spare her just a little more attention. 'It's all very different nowadays, Rainbow.'

'Yes, I'll be fine,' said Rainbow. 'I'll just follow the others if I don't know.'

'You have my ring for David? And my vow? And the cord? Oh no, what about—'

'Stop fretting, Dawn,' Rainbow laughed. 'Honestly, it's all here safely in my little basket. And your flowers too.'

'I think we should join the other brides now,' said Dawn.

'We're all meeting up in the School House as usual. It's strange – usually it's me in there keeping everyone calm and checking they've all got their bits and pieces ready. I never thought I'd actually be a bride myself!'

'So, who's in charge of keeping the peace today?'

'It's Rosie – remember her? Yul's sister. It has to be someone who's not related to any of the brides, so they don't get too caught up in all the giggly nerves. And the men will be in the Jack, of course, with all their attendants. I hope David's feeling alright.'

'Of course he is! I saw his family and friends coming down from the Hall earlier. I gather they're very impressed by everything here.'

'I'm just so glad it's Clip who's officiating today, with Sylvie. It was good of him to agree to do the handfastings one last time. I feel very honoured.'

'I can't believe they're only held once a year now,' said Rainbow. 'Seems a bit weird to me. We always had them at every festival up in the Stone Circle, didn't we? Why on earth change something that works well?'

'Oh, it's much better like this, really. The Village Green is more ... open, more friendly somehow, and if it rains we just go into the Barn. It's lovely, you'll see. Having all the handfastings together just once a year at Hare Moon make it more of a big, special occasion than just a little ceremony tacked on to the end of a festival celebration. Now come on, let's get to the School House. They'll be calling us very soon.'

On the Village Green, David's guests stood out like a cellophane-wrapped bouquet of bright, hothouse flowers placed in a wild-flower meadow. All were either pagan or at least familiar with the customs and therefore comfortable with the proceedings, although David had warned them that nothing would prepare them for Stonewylde. They'd imagined they'd blend in well amongst a pagan community, and yet they looked outlandish. What most hadn't appreciated was that every garment worn at

Stonewylde was not only hand sewn but also home grown. The linen was woven on hand-looms from flax and hemp grown in the fields, dyed with plants grown especially for the purpose, embroidered and appliquéd by hand. Leather was made from the skins of animals bred, reared, slaughtered and tanned here. Wool came from the Stonewylde flocks and was hand spun and dyed, before being felted, knitted or crocheted into garments. Nothing was artificial or imported, which made the Outsiders' outfits, however carefully chosen for the occasion, seem rather garish and synthetic.

But the Outsiders had been made welcome by most, for David was a popular member of the community and had been at Stonewylde for well over a year now. Dawn was highly thought of too, despite her Hallfolk origins, and the children and teen-agers she'd taught were particularly excited today. They raced around outside the circle of people whilst everyone waited for the ceremony to begin. There was a great deal of happy laughter and chatter amongst the folk, who were all dressed in their finest robes and tunics. Girls and women had blossom and flowers in their hair and the men and boys wore bits of greenery. Many of the older ones had brought along their staves, beribboned for the occasion, and others had a wand decorated with ribbons or wool. Many families too had brought their bell, the one that normally lived over the hearth of the house to summon the woodland sprites and elves at Yule.

'This is absolutely beautiful!' murmured David's mother, resplendent in a long velvet dress of bright emerald green with gold silk inserts, an elaborate wreath on her head and a great deal of heavy jewellery at her neck, wrists and ears. 'I'd never have guessed somewhere like this existed in our modern world.'

'Stunning,' agreed his father, equally fine-robed in rich scarlet and brilliant white, and sporting a large dragon on his back. 'I'm so happy for our lad. I wonder if parents of the groom are allowed to move in here too?'

David's sister Sarah laughed at this, keeping hold of her children in case they did something frowned upon. The Stonewylde children running around like puppies were all a little wild and boisterous. Her husband wished he'd brought his camera even though David had warned them it wouldn't be a good idea.

'I'm going to ask him if we can all come and stay in the school holidays,' said Sarah. 'The kids would have a wonderful time here and it's just what I've always dreamed of, a community like this. It's perfect!'

They stopped talking as Clip raised his ash staff for silence. The crowd gradually quietened and the children were all gathered in from outside the circle. There were several concentric rings to keep the circle a reasonable size, and everyone now joined hands. At a sign from Clip, a group of drummers began a soft rhythm like a heartbeat, and a youngster with panpipes played a gentle, meandering tune that hung in the warm air and mingled with the birdsong. A handful of girls began a joyful dance in the centre of the circle, leaping and twirling, stretching their supple limbs and delicate hands, tossing their hair and whirling their skirts.

After a while, Clip raised his staff again; the dancers and musicians stilled and silence descended.

'Folk of Stonewylde, we're gathered today on our sacred Village Green to witness the handfasting of seven couples. And today is made more special by having Outsiders in our midst! Let us welcome David's guests to Stonewylde.'

Everyone cried, 'Welcome!', to which the small band of Outsiders smiled their thanks and gave little bows.

'And now we call on the seven couples and their attendants to join us on the Village Green!'

A man with a great cow horn climbed onto the dais and blew, long and hard. The strange, low sound wailed around the circle of people and then wended out, around the circle of trees and beyond. He gave the summons five times, and then the drummers began to play, an excited rhythm that quickened everyone's pulse. From out of the trees on one side of the Green came the seven men to be handfasted, each accompanied by his chosen attendant, and from the other side, the women and their friends. The two groups approached the great circle of Stonewylders and stood outside.

'Who comes to our circle today to be joined to their true-love in marriage?' called Clip.

The attendants called out the names, one by one, and when all fourteen names had been called, Clip spoke again.

'Does anyone in our community know any reason why any of these fourteen should not be handfasted today?'

'No!' roared the people in one great voice.

'Shall we open the circle to welcome them inside?'

'Yes!' came the reply.

At a signal, the circle parted in two places and the two groups entered and faced each other across the circle. All the brides wore circlets of flowers on their heads and the grooms wreaths of leaves, and each carried a small bunch of flowers. The attendants stood modestly behind them, ready to assist. Rainbow, however, upstaged every bride by the sheer vivacity of her shimmering silk gown, and Sylvie, stepping forward on the dais to speak, swallowed a throb of irritation.

'First, we must invoke the spirit of Stonewylde and awaken the energy and magic. We call on the five elements and the Green Magic of Stonewylde!'

'We call on the Goddess in the Landscape, she who is the earth beneath our feet, the air we breathe, the warmth in our veins and the water that flows around and within; she who quickens our souls with the life-force and gives energy to every living thing,' cried Clip.

'We call on you, Goddess, and invite you to bless our ceremony,' called Sylvie. 'We honour all your creations and feel your divine spirit within, around, above and below. Everything is born of you, and to you everything will return. We honour the beauty of the living world around us! Folk of Stonewylde, we will take a few heartbeats to give thanks for all creation.'

The drums throbbed very quietly now, as Clip led the gratitudes. He invoked thoughts in everyone's minds of the trees, flowers, bushes, birds, fish, animals, rocks, hills, valleys, woodlands, heaths, beaches, the river, streams, marshes, insects – every part of the great beauty around them that was Stonewylde, their own piece of nature, their own corner of creation. Soon everyone's heads were full of the wonder and glory of the natural world.

'And tonight is Hare Moon,' cried Sylvie. 'We honour the Bright Lady and invite her to join our ceremony! She who brings her silver magic to Stonewylde – welcome! We ask that you bless the couples with romance, true love and fertility!'

'They haven't called the quarters!' hissed David's grandmother. 'Don't they realise how to do it?'

'Ssh, Ma!' whispered David's father. 'I think they've called not only the quarters, but just about every other energy and element known to mankind! Yes, yes, and womankind.'

'I thought they'd do it properly here,' she said, disappointed. 'From what David told us, I thought they'd get it right. They haven't even cast and consecrated the circle!'

'They don't need to,' said David's father, gazing around the Village Green at the encircling trees now in bursting leaf. 'Can't you feel this is a sacred grove, Ma? Why bother with theatricals when the place already throbs with the Goddess' magic?'

She frowned at him and, closing her eyes, began to make her own private invocations. David's parents' eyes met and they both grinned; she was such a stickler for ritual. Meanwhile, the attendants had been asked to bring forward the seven pairs of rings. Each pair was placed in its own tiny basket, like a little nest, and a chosen child for each couple proudly paraded the rings around the entire circle, whilst Clip continued his words.

'These rings represent eternity, the full circle, the journey with no beginning and no end. They represent completeness and wholeness, and this is what we wish for each couple being joined today. May you love each other for eternity, and find completeness in each other.'

When the rings had travelled the circuit, the seven couples came forward into the middle of the circle and faced each other, with their attendants behind them. Dawn looked into David's eyes and saw her nervousness and joy mirrored there. And then something else – something deep and everlasting that made all other emotions tumble away as they joined in that special, timeless place where their souls connected. Dawn felt her lips tremble and her eyes fill with tears, and thanked the Goddess that against all odds, she'd found this love in her lifetime. She'd realised all those years ago, when begging to be allowed to stay at Stonewylde, that the chances of ever finding a partner were remote. Yet David had arrived and almost instantly they'd both known, both felt the pieces of jigsaw slide into place and realised just how their lives had always been patterned to bring them together one day, to this point. Dawn saw that same under-standing in his eyes and her heart sang.

'And now, before you exchange your rings and make your private vows to one another, repeat after me these binding promises ...'

Each couple clasped hands, facing each other, as they repeated the old words. Dawn was glad she was speaking in unison with the thirteen others, for her voice trembled.

'I came to this circle as one alone, but I leave as half of a pair. I offer myself to you as your helper, your friend, your lover and your guardian. I give you my love, my heart and all that I am. I stand before you and hope that I am enough. Will you wed me?'

Sylvie found her throat aching as her father said the words in short bursts, repeated by the seven couples as they held hands and gazed into each other's eyes. She couldn't bear to locate Yul in the circle and catch his eye as she normally did during the handfastings every year, silently renewing their promises and reaffirming their love through eye contact. This year it was too painful. What had happened to them both? She remembered so clearly making these vows herself, meaning every single word and feeling so sure that she and her beloved would feel as they did at that moment, forever. As the couples now all chorused, 'I will!' she took a deep breath, for she had to speak the next words.

'Love is friendship that has caught fire and will not be doused or checked,' she said, using every grain of self-control to keep her voice strong. 'You have chosen to be handfasted, to make a commitment to stay together and perpetuate that love. Marriage means never again being alone in the darkness, never again being on the outside looking in. Marriage means coming into the brightness and warmth of the hearth, and never wanting for love and companionship. Marriage means loving and being loved with all your heart, all your soul and all your body, for evermore. Are you ready now to bind your hands in sacred union, to be wed together as a couple?'

'I am!' came the fourteen replies.

The attendants came forward and, whilst the drums played a lively beat, the complicated business of the handfastings began. The specially woven cords had been plaited ceremoniously by the couples the day before, the resulting braided piece being knotted at either end, one knot by each family. And now the attendants proceeded to fasten their couple together at the wrist – the man's right hand and the woman's left, in a figure of eight binding which represented eternity. Finally each pair was bound fast, and Clip moved down the line to tie the loose ends into knots.

'May the Goddess keep your marriage strong, like these cords that bind you in wedlock,' he murmured to each couple as he tied their knot. 'May love warm your hearts here in this world and continue to the Otherworld.'

'These ties of hemp will not be broken until the Hare Moon has set!' declared Sylvie. 'And may the ties that bind your hearts and souls never be broken.'

Next was the exchanging of rings. These were placed on each other's ring finger on the bound hand, as a permanent reminder of the cord that now circled their wrists. Then the couple faced each other again to make their private vows, whispered only to each other. Simplicity was the key. Dawn's eyes sparkled with tears when David began to whisper the words of John Donne, knowing how she loved the poet.

'I wonder, by my troth, what thou and I didst till we lov'd?'

When he'd finished the poem she swallowed, and looking deep into his kind, loving eyes, she softly spoke the words she'd written especially for him.

> *'If you feel a little strange when walking high in the hills,*
> *And sense a presence in the woods but never turn around,*
> *If your spirit soars with the larks on a bright summer's day,*
> *And you thrill with quicksilver when Lady Moon walks the night,*
> *If your soul cries out at the beauty of our world,*
> *And you feel a reverence so deep and so old,*
> *Then take my hand, take my heart, take my love*
> *And stay with me forever in Stonewylde.'*

The final part of the ceremony could now begin, and from the dais the attendants brought down the seven brooms. There was an excited buzz from the crowd; the brooms had been made by each couple together, a piece of wood chosen, seasoned and finished for the broomstick, and then either carved, painted or scorched in whatever pattern they chose. Together they'd gathered their choice of twigs and made the brush part, tying it with willow and reed. The brooms had stood in the Barn overnight and everyone had had the chance to tie a small ribbon of linen to the handle, with a message or symbol written on it, or simply a wish made over it. The brooms now fluttered with colourful ribbons and were lovely to behold. The handles were all different; while some of the other couples had chosen oak or holly, Dawn and David had chosen the traditional, magical ash. They'd also decided on the customary birch twigs for the brush as they were desperately hoping to have children soon.

'Jumping your own broomstick is the final symbolic act in our ceremony this afternoon,' said Clip. 'As you leap over the broom, you leave behind your old lives and hearths, and cross the threshold into your new wedded lives together.'

The brightly decorated brooms were held at each end by the two attendants, and the couples were called. The crowd cheered and rang their hearth bells frantically. Bound at the wrists, one by one the couples took a run and leapt over their broom.

Rainbow had bent down opposite David's brother as they both held the broomstick for their couple. She gave him a wicked grin, knowing her silk dress was gaping and revealing her cleavage.

'How high shall we hold it then?' she laughed, a mischievous glint in her eye.

'Only low, I was told,' he replied. 'We don't want them tripping over.'

David and Dawn started to make their run, she desperately holding up her skirts and hoping her headdress wouldn't fall off. At the last moment Rainbow tried to raise the broom higher but it was David jumping on her side and he tucked his feet up and managed to clear it. Flushed, he spun round to see Rainbow laughing at his brother.

'Oh, come on!' she cried. 'It's only a bit of fun! You're all so damn serious.'

Once all the couples had jumped, Clip raised his staff again.

'You are now officially married! We wish you joy in your new lives together, and many years of love and happiness.'

'May the fecundity of the Hare Moon bless your wedding union tonight, and the Bright Lady dust you with her magic. Bright blessings!' cried Sylvie.

'Bright blessings!' echoed everyone in the circle.

The musicians struck up a lively tune and the seven couples, joined at the wrists and carrying their broomsticks before them, processed all the way around the circle and then out through a gap that opened towards the Great Barn and the feast that awaited them all. By common consensus, Dawn and David led the way, and then the seven pairs of attendants fell into step too, followed by the rest of the community. Gradually everyone trooped out of the circle and into the Barn, taking their seats at the rows and rows of trestle tables. The tables were laden with food and drink, and David's family and friends were quite overwhelmed by the hospitality.

On the large table at the head of the Barn sat the seven couples, and there was great hilarity as they attempted to eat and drink with their hands tied together. As was the custom, each couple shared a cup and ate from the same plate, helping each other and even using cutlery together. Dawn was brimming with happiness, her rather plain face alight with joy. David felt a strange bubbling excitement deep inside and still couldn't believe that he was married – not only to the woman of his dreams, but also to Stonewylde. He looked across at his family and hoped they'd all visit him, as the Council of Elders had promised they could. He noticed his grandmother looking rather sour, which surprised him as she was the one who'd brought his father up in the pagan tradition and always insisted on the old ways being followed to the letter. The rest of his group seemed to be having a wonderful time, although his brother had left Rainbow and the other attendants to return to their table and sit with them all.

Rainbow herself wasn't joining in the feast. She now leant against a wall with a glass of wine in her hand, watching everything. She'd left her camera in her room at the Council's request, though it irritated her that they'd imposed such a petty restriction. Taking photos was hardly a crime, after all. She glanced at the table of brides and grooms where everyone seemed to be having a splendid time, and then her gaze roamed to David's family party. She'd dismissed his brother as being unworthy of any effort; in fact, the whole bunch was pretty boring.

She watched Yul for a while, sitting next to his wife and knocking back the cider like a youngster. His face had that dark, closed expression that she remembered from the old days – say the wrong thing and he'd bite your head off. Yul was clearly a troubled man, despite having got everything he'd ever wanted. Rainbow still found it difficult to accept that Yul had once been a mere Village boy, a complete yokel unable to read or write, with no education or status whatsoever – yet here he was now, in effect the lord and master of Stonewylde. It just went to show what could be achieved with a little perseverance and determination. Although right now, he didn't seem very happy with his lot.

Rainbow stared at Sylvie, seated by his side. She really didn't look good. The ethereal beauty and magical promise she'd possessed as a girl, that moongazy quality of perfect alabaster skin, silver silken hair and dreamy grey eyes, now looked pinched and washed out. She was far too thin and it wasn't attractive at all, especially for a woman approaching her thirties. Everything about Sylvie was sharp and edgy. She looked up suddenly and caught Rainbow's gaze. Instead of looking away, Rainbow raised her glass in a silent salute, which Sylvie pointedly ignored.

Sylvie was ignoring Yul too, and instead spoke to Clip on her other side. Clip was so like her, right down to the thinness and pallor. His special handfasting robes hung off his angular shoulders and his cheeks were gaunt. He was very animated, discussing something of great import with his daughter. On his other side sat Leveret, small and dark, silently sipping from her glass, watching everyone. Something about her made Rainbow feel a little uncomfortable, although she was itching to sketch her and capture that strange, otherworldly aura. What Dawn had told her about the girl was intriguing and she was certainly one to watch.

Rainbow followed Leveret's gaze and saw that it was now fixed on Magpie, sitting across the Barn near the door to the kitchens. Rainbow brightened at the thought of Magpie – there was something promising! His golden hair glinted in the light and his unusual, rather handsome face was devoid of expression. He ate slowly and carefully, only his extraordinary eyes showing any liveliness. She wanted to paint him too, but more than that, she wanted to get inside his head. Rainbow knew David was right; Magpie had a really special talent. She'd watched the boy when he hadn't realised she'd been there, and the way he worked was incredible. He rarely looked up from the paper or canvas; it was as if he'd taken a mental snapshot of his subject earlier and referred to that. He worked fast and what he created had fluidity, movement and perfect rhythm.

Rainbow was fascinated by him and wished he could talk. She'd love to discuss his way of working and discover if there was something she could learn from it. She felt he was a raw and untrained genius and she wanted to be part of his success. David had become increasingly cagey about Magpie, almost suspicious of her interest, which made Rainbow all the more determined to get involved. She'd briefly considered a liaison with him – and hadn't entirely ruled it out as an option – but he was very young and more to the point, as gormless as an egg. So she'd bide her time and try to fathom out just what made Magpie tick. And, in the meantime, she was very keen to paint him. There was something classical about his face and posture that she longed to capture.

'Blessings, Rainbow!'

Rainbow swung round to stare into the dark eyes of Faun. The girl was tall, almost the same height despite her youth, and obviously in her best party frock. Rainbow noted the excessive ringlets in her hair and the lip-gloss – lip-gloss at Stonewylde? She was shocked, but after a moment's thought realised it might only be some kind of natural product; beeswax, perhaps? Faun was preening and pouting which made Rainbow smile. She'd already been targeted by the girl's mother, Rowan, whom Rainbow recalled as the beautiful May Queen all those years ago. Faun shared some of her qualities, not least her fine, creamy complexion and statuesque posture, but her colouring was pure Magus. As Rainbow looked into the velvety dark brown eyes, she shivered.

'Mother wondered if you'd like to sit on our table over there? If you're all alone?'

'No, not really, thanks. I'm not hungry and I'm just enjoying people-watching.'

The girl looked crestfallen and returned to her table. Then Rainbow noticed a rather gorgeous young man further up, and wondered how she'd missed him up until now. He had light brown hair, slightly curly, and lovely blue eyes. His face was clean-cut and very masculine, and his physique an absolute joy.

Rainbow's stance changed imperceptibly, her body insinuating itself into a more provocative pose as she leant against the wall. She knew the turquoise silk glimmered around her curves, and she shook out her mane of hair so it hung more artfully. Soon enough her intense stare worked its magic and the young man looked up from the table and straight into her eyes. She raised her glass to him and gave a small, enigmatic smile. Yes, he'd do very nicely indeed, whoever he was.

8

'Why is she sitting up there next to Clip, with Yul and Sylvie and everyone?' demanded Rosie of her mother as they replenished dishes in the kitchen. Both had bright cheeks and looked so alike; hot, bothered and busy. Maizie shook her head, deftly transferring tiny beef tartlets to one larger dish.

'She lives with him, don't she? Who else would she sit with?' replied Maizie briskly. 'Truth be told, Rosie, I don't really care just so long as she's being properly looked after and not getting into any mischief.'

'Aye, but Clip! Why *him*? He's not even our kin – who's he to be taking such an interest in our Leveret? Besides, nothing ever were done about that Imbolc business. She let us down, Mother, and yet she never got punished or—'

'Rosie, you sound just like your brothers! Only today Sweyn were saying the self same thing.'

'Well, that's because you're our mother and we don't like to see you made a goose of by that little madam! You brung us up to believe in just punishment where 'tis due – and that's here!'

Rosie's dark curls bobbed indignantly as she lined up a row of little jugs to be filled with cream. Maizie stopped a moment and laid her hand on her eldest daughter's arm.

'You're a good girl, Rosie, and I'm proud of you. Always have been – you never once let me down. Our Leveret's a different jar o' jam altogether.'

'Aye well, I think you should have a word with her today. 'Tis the perfect opportunity. She needs to—'

'No, I don't want to get meself upset about it all today. D'you know, she were conceived at the Hare Moon? 'Tis why I named her Leveret.'

'For Goddess' sake, Mother! You're still soft on her! She always does this – wraps you round her finger and gets away with it! You've been soppy over Leveret from the day she were born, and because of that she's turned out a bad 'un. Look what she did at Imbolc, when she were Bright Maiden!'

'All that happened at Imbolc … I don't know, I don't think 'twere entirely the maid's fault. No—' she raised a hand to silence Rosie's protests, 'I know what you, Sweyn and Gefrin, and Yul hisself all think. But I can't in my heart believe that Leveret would've deliberately messed it all up like that. There were something afoot that day, but I don't know what, and to be honest, I've had my fill o' the whole business. All I want to do is put it behind me. Leveret's a difficult child and she always were a challenge, from a suckling babe-in-arms. In fact, right back to her conception, now I think on it. So I just want to leave be. She's happy at the Hall and off my hands, so please – no more about it, Rosie.'

Leveret's brothers were less forgiving, and, as the warm afternoon wore on, they became more vociferous in their grudge towards the youngest member of their family. They stood together by the bar watching their sister as she left her place by Clip's side and picked her way around all the tables towards the kitchen area. Magpie sat near the door to be close to Marigold, who'd been bustling in and out throughout the feast. Magpie gazed around in silence and Leveret settled herself next to him. The tables had been mostly cleared of food and the men had begun to pack them away, or push them to the sides of the Barn ready for the dancing later on.

'She's still friends with old Rabbit-gob then,' said Gefrin, and Sweyn let out a shout of laughter at this.

'Yeah, Hare-brain and Rabbit-gob – they make a good pair. Next thing we know they'll be handfasted and have a litter o' long-eared babies with bob-tails! Ugh!'

They eyed Leveret malignantly as she sat talking to Magpie.

'Look – what's the point in that? He can't bloody talk and he's as thick as horse-dung! Why does she act like they're having a chat together? She's so embarrassing!'

'I wish we could get her like we planned. But there's never a chance, is there? She's always with Clip.'

'She must be on her own sometimes. We just need to keep our eyes open and be ready.'

'I think we need Old Violet and Vetchling, like Jay said. Imbolc was so good, and that were thanks to them. Let's do it properly and get their help again.'

'Good idea. Let's find Jay – where is he?'

Sweyn curled his lip and sneered.

'He's trying to get Tansy to go up the quarry with him tonight for the Hare Moon.'

'So long as it's Tansy. He better not bloody try it with my Meadowsweet!'

'She ain't your Meadowsweet, is she, Gef? And anyway—'

'She will be – I'm going to ask her to walk with me. I'm waiting to do it proper at Lammas with a corn-favour.'

'Lammas – that's months away! Some other bugger will've had her by then,' laughed Sweyn. 'And she's not interested in you anyway. Why d'you want to bother with girls? Bloody waste o' time, if you ask me.'

Gefrin flushed, his thin, spotty face miserable.

'I just like her, that's all. She's alright. I see her every day at the farm and I think about her a bit and ... you're sure Jay ain't interested in her? It's definitely Tansy?'

'Yeah, it's Tansy, though it ain't her Rite until the Summer Solstice, so it's a risk. And why he wants to take her up the quarry I don't know. He'll have to nick one o' the cars to get up there and if he gets caught, there'll be big trouble.'

'Quarrycleave ain't a good place to go anyway,' said Gefrin.

'Remember when we went up there with him once? After he'd gone on and on about it? Goddess knows why he likes it there so much. That place gives me the creeps and I wouldn't want to go there in the dark even at the Moon Fullness.'

'Nor me. Good luck to him, if he does get Tansy up there.'

'Shame he ain't here, though. Then we could've planned what to do about our little sis and how she'll get her comeuppance.'

Leveret and Magpie left the Barn, as many were now doing, to get some fresh air outside before the music and dancing started. It was late afternoon, warm and drowsy with that soft expectancy of May, when all is growing and unfurling and summer only a whisper away. The Village Green was clustered with folk in their finery, including the seven handfasted couples. Leveret and Magpie wandered over to the large pond, where the ducks were busy dabbling and froglets swarmed in the mud. They sat on one of the log benches and gazed about them, happy in each other's company.

'Isn't it lovely to see David and Dawn like this?' she said. 'They're so in love.'

Magpie held an image of a pair of pretty blue and yellow blue-tits, fluttering around each other in a courtship dance. Leveret laughed.

'Exactly! They're like a pair of love-birds.'

Then she looked at Magpie strangely. She could see the word *"bird"* very clearly in her head, in bold black ink on creamy parchment.

'Are you sending me the word, Maggie?'

He looked at her and grinned, his turquoise eyes dancing and his face flushed with pleasure.

'You can actually send me a word? Honestly, what's happened to you? You're so clever!'

He squeezed her hand, and she sensed his simple joy. His world was a million times better than it had ever been before and he brimmed with happiness. She felt all this in that squeeze of the hand.

116

'Oh Maggie, do you think you'll ever be able to talk? Can you try?'

Instantly his face darkened and he looked away, all vivacity dead.

'What? What is it, Maggie? I'm sorry – what's wrong?'

And then it came to her in a stomach-wrenching, heart-stopping deluge that made her want to vomit.

Screaming, screaming with hunger and discomfort, sore and cold, hungry, hungry, cold and wet, screaming, screaming, screaming ... and a red, angry shout and a shake and hatred, so much hatred, and a slap, another violent shake, and then a dirty rag into the mouth, stuffed in, rammed in so hard that breath was almost impossible ... then bundled away in a small dark place for a long, long time ... no more screaming, no noise, no sound ever again ...

'Oh my Goddess!' cried Leveret, her eyes popping with peppery tears. 'Is that what she did to you? Is that why? Oh my poor darling Magpie!'

She leant against his shoulder, still holding his hand tightly, hot tears dripping from her cheeks onto her knees.

'Maggie, forget that. Put all that away, back wherever it was, and never ever think of it again. You and me – we can tell each other things without talking and now you can write and read you have enough words. I'm so very sorry, Magpie.'

She sat sadly now, trying to put the horrendous image out of her mind and feeling guilt-stricken for dredging it up out of his. If Starling were to walk past now, she thought fiercely ... but instead, two little girls came tumbling across the grass towards her, bubbling with excitement and laughter.

'Auntie Leveret! How's Hare? Have you got her here with you?'

Leveret smiled as Bluebell climbed up onto her lap and Celandine pressed against her knees. It was impossible to resist their affection – nor did she want to.

'No, I don't think she's ready to come out with me yet,' she replied, wiping her cheeks briskly. 'She'd be scared of all the people and noise. Maybe one day I'll bring her.'

'You could make her a special basket to carry her in,' said Celandine.

'Yes, like a little nest!' cried Bluebell. 'With a lid so if she's scared you could make her all safe.'

'I expect she'll be quite heavy when she's fully grown,' said Leveret. 'Have you ever seen a grown-up hare? They're actually very big, especially the females. I don't know if I fancy carrying her around.'

'Then make her a little buggy!' said Celandine. 'Like the babies have – those wicker ones with wheels and a handle.'

Bluebell shrieked at this and Magpie covered his ears with his hands.

'Oh Auntie Leveret! Hare tucked up in a buggy! With a bonnet and all!'

'Bluebell, ssh – not so loud. Poor Magpie doesn't like that shrieking noise.'

The little girl stared at him in consternation, then guiltily put her thumb in her mouth to silence herself.

'Is this your friend, Auntie Leveret?' asked Celandine, smiling shyly at him.

'Yes, this is Magpie. Magpie, these are my two nieces, Bluebell and Celandine. You know them of course, but I don't think you've ever really met them, have you?'

'I like your goldy hair, Magpie,' said Bluebell, removing her wet thumb. 'It's like Granny's toffee that she makes.'

'Magpie can't talk back,' Leveret said, 'though he understands what you're saying to him. Magpie is a very clever artist and his drawings are magical.'

'Really?' asked Celandine, her eyes gleaming. 'Would he do some pictures for our book, do you think? You know, the one about the faeries and the hares?'

Leveret smiled at her and nodded.

'That's a very good idea,' she said. 'Magpie's only just learning to read and write himself. He's probably about the same stage as you, Bluebell. We could let him read your story for himself, and

118

then maybe he'd draw some pictures for it. Would you do that, Maggie?'

He nodded, smiling a little uncertainly at the girls. He'd never had anything to do with children, having always been the butt of derision in the Village.

'Why is Magpie only learning to read and write now, when he's a grown-up?' asked Celandine with a frown. 'Didn't he go to school like everyone else?'

'He had a very sad and difficult time when he was a little boy,' said Leveret. 'It wasn't his fault, but he was too unhappy and scared to learn.'

'That's horrible!' said Bluebell. 'Poor Magpie – the teachers should've made him better.'

'Yes,' said Leveret. 'Everyone should have. But still, Magpie's happy now and I think he'll enjoy your book.'

They were then joined by Sylvie, who'd changed out of her special handfasting robes and now wore a pretty dress. She sat on the bench next to Leveret, smiling at them all. Leveret felt a shiver of pleasure at her company and greeted her warmly.

'Why don't you girls see if the faeries are dancing under the rowan trees today?' she said. 'I wouldn't mind a chat with Auntie Leveret myself.'

'Can we take Magpie?' asked Bluebell, wriggling down from Leveret's lap. She reached up and took his hand, giving him a little tug. He stared at her awkwardly and Leveret glanced quickly at Sylvie.

'Would that be alright? He's as gentle as a lamb, I promise.'

Sylvie only hesitated for a fraction of a second before nodding, and Leveret beamed.

'Magpie, go with the girls and help them look for faeries, but stay away from anyone else. And be careful, won't you?'

She still had memories of Magpie in the woods, rabbit blood glistening on his face. Surely with Yul's children by his side he'd be safe from the tormentors?

When they'd gone, Sylvie sighed heavily, gazing out at the Green and all the joyful people. She was just a sliver of ice inside.

'Leveret ... I don't know where to start, really, but ... I need some help. Or at least someone to talk to. I don't know where to turn, but I thought maybe you'd understand?'

'Yes, yes of course! I want to help – what can I do?'

Sylvie shook her head despairingly.

'I just don't know! I don't even know what's wrong, let alone how to put it right. I'm so very, very depressed and sad.'

'Maybe that'd be a way to start – focus on getting rid of the depression? Perhaps everything else would be easier if you're feeling more positive.'

'That might help. I just can't raise myself above this thick, heavy fog that hangs over me every day, all the time. I feel there's a demon on my back, turning everything grey and bad. I'm really just going through the motions of coping. If it weren't for your mother ...'

Leveret smiled at this.

'I'm glad she's helping you,' she said gently. 'She can be so kind and loving.'

'She looks after me and the girls, takes away all the struggle of getting through each day. But above all, she's given me the chance to be away from Yul.'

'Have you tried any medication for your depression?' asked Leveret. 'I've been spending time most days with Hazel and if you were to tell her about this —'

'No,' said Sylvie firmly. 'I really don't want any drugs. There's stuff ... things from when I was really ill a few years ago ... I don't want to go down that route.'

'Okay, but how about a natural remedy? Would you feel more comfortable taking something herbal, the sort of thing Mother Heggy would've brewed?'

Sylvie turned to look at her closely. Leveret's clear green eyes shone, so lovely in her dark face. This girl – Sylvie had always been rather scared of her. But she was wonderful; how had they never got on before?

'I remember Mother Heggy's remedies,' she said. 'They looked foul but they certainly worked. That's not the same thing as taking an anti-depressant, is it? Natural medicine is very different. But I'm not going to Old Violet, if that's what you're thinking!'

'No, I can help you!' said Leveret excitedly. 'I'm studying all the old folk medicines and I can make you a remedy. What you need for depression and chasing away those dragons is Hypericum – St. John's Wort. It's entirely natural, Sylvie, and it's been used for a long time to cure depression.'

'Alright,' she said. 'If you're sure.'

'Yes! Honestly, it's perfect for your needs. It's started flowering nice and early this year because it's been so warm and I'm actually in the process of steeping a tincture right now, as a general pick-me-up tonic. But that won't be ready for another week, so I'll make you up infusions in the meantime. I'm afraid it won't seem to have any effect for about four weeks, but you must stick with it.'

'Thanks, Leveret. I'll give it a go as long as there are no side effects.'

'You may get slightly more sunburned that usual – I've read it can cause photosensitivity. But I'm sure you're careful about that anyway with your pale skin.'

'That's really kind of you. I feel better already!'

They smiled a little shyly at each other.

'Actually, Leveret, I've just thought of something else you could do, if you wouldn't mind? It's about moondancing ...'

She stopped and Leveret glanced at her, noting the sadness in her eyes and the droop of her mouth and her shoulders. The younger girl longed so much to heal Sylvie, to make her happy and whole.

'Yes? I'll help in any way ...'

'Last year I promised the girls I'd take them up to Hare Stone one Moon Fullness so they could watch the Bright Lady rise over the hills and maybe dance with me around the stone. They remembered, and now of course they're pestering me. I thought maybe tonight, at Hare Moon ...'

'That sounds like a wonderful idea!' said Leveret. 'Just what you need, and lovely for them to be part of it too. What can I do?'

'Just come with us, and be there if you're needed.' Sylvie wasn't going to mention anything about voices or ghosts. 'I used to get so moongazy and strange. And although I don't any more, I'd like to have you there with us just in case. It's quite a long walk for the girls, especially Bluebell, and another adult would make me feel happier about taking them along.'

'I'd be honoured!' said Leveret, flattered to be asked, and even more flattered to be considered an adult.

Much later, with the party going strong in the Great Barn and the seven couples leading the dancing and merriment, the little group slipped out and began the long walk up to Hare Stone. On Leveret's suggestion, Magpie was accompanying them in case Bluebell's legs gave out. Both children had taken immediately to the silent young lad and now skipped along the path leading through the woods. It was still light as the birds sang their joyous evensong, flitting amongst the trees in a flurry of activity before nightfall. The birdsong was amazingly loud, reverberating through the twilight in a cascade of different calls and trills. Many of the trees were already in full leaf, their trunks rising from a deep blue lake of perfumed bluebells. Leveret felt the magic of the place all around her as they walked through the enchanted landscape. She agreed with her nieces that the woodland elves and the bluebell faeries were surely hiding amongst the trees watching them as they passed through.

Sylvie was wrapped in her own thoughts, remembering all the times she'd walked this path with Yul by her side; she almost felt his presence now. She wondered if he were still in the Barn drinking or whether he'd gone outside to watch the moon rise. Was he thinking of her, she wondered? Had he noticed her leaving? Did he care at all?

The light was fading as they finally left the wood, ducking through the archway of boughs and out into the field beyond.

The hill loomed large above them and Bluebell regarded it with a sigh.

'I wish I could fly,' she muttered, but began to climb determinedly through the tussocks of grass and outcrops of stone, up towards the great monolith that stood in lonely glory at the top. Magpie understood that he was there to help the little girl and stayed close by her, holding her hand and helping her along. Celandine walked between Sylvie and Leveret and was very excited at finally fulfilling her wish to dance for the Bright Lady.

'Will you be moondancing tonight, Mum?' she asked.

'I really don't know,' said Sylvie. 'I'm not sure how I'll feel when the moon rises. I may just sit by the Hare Stone and moongaze.'

'Like Father used to do.'

'Yes, like he used to do.'

'Do you think the barn owl will visit and the hares'll come?'

Leveret looked slightly askance at this.

'Is that what used to happen?'

'Oh yes,' nodded Sylvie. 'Every month. I was your age when I started coming here, Leveret. I was frantic to dance and then I'd go into a trance.'

'But not anymore, Mum.'

'I still feel something,' Sylvie said quietly. 'But somehow life has got in the way ...'

They paused to get their breath at the outcrop of large boulders, almost at the top, and Sylvie recalled her scare several months ago when she'd been convinced that Magus was there with her. Leveret was also recalling her strange experience at the place and looked around a little apprehensively, though having company made her feel less uncomfortable. Magpie stood gazing up the hill, wrapped in his own world, and Leveret knew he was thinking about a painting. Nobody managed to capture the essence of Stonewylde in the way Magpie did. Celandine and Bluebell chased each other around the huge rocks, their tiredness forgotten.

'Mummy! I've found a load of paper snakes!' cried Bluebell suddenly, as Celandine squealed in horror.

'What?'

Sylvie was there in a flash, snatching her child away from the object of fascination on the ground. When they all looked, they saw her description was very apt; caught up in a patch of thistles were several tissue-like snake-skins of varying lengths.

'Oh wow!' said Leveret. 'Look how many have been shed!'

'Shed?' asked Bluebell, struggling to get free and have a proper look.

'Snakes get too big for their skins so they push them off, like an old dress they've grown out of,' explained Leveret.

Bluebell giggled at this.

'Are they bare underneath?'

'No, they've already got a lovely new skin on.'

'So are these their old dresses?' asked Celandine.

'That's right, and they use a spiky thing – like these thistles – to help pull the old skin off. Isn't it clever? These are adder skins – see the V by the head, and these zigzag patterns?'

'Adders are poisonous!' cried Sylvie. 'Are they still about?'

'No, not at this time of evening,' said Leveret. 'They'll be curled up asleep now.'

'We must be careful though,' said Sylvie. 'Girls, look where you're treading and keep your shoes on. No bare feet tonight.'

Leveret was carefully extricating the tangled skins from the thistle and putting them into her bag. Magpie examined one minutely, stroking the rustling softness with a gentle finger.

'Why are you taking them, Auntie Leveret?' asked Celandine.

'I like them,' she replied. 'They'll only break up into nothing out here in the open, and I'd like to keep them.'

'You're just like Grandfather Clip!' said Celandine with a smile. 'Collecting strange things to put in the tower.'

'Why on earth are there so many all together?' said Sylvie. 'Don't they shed their skins when they come out of hibernation? I remember years ago we had a plague of adders one summer and we all had to be so careful.'

'I think they can do it several times in a year,' said Leveret, 'but I'm not sure. I'll have to do some research. I'd imagine with so many together like this there's a hibernaculum somewhere around here.' She turned to the girls. 'That's like a big dormitory where all the vipers huddle up together for the winter and go to sleep. They keep each other warm.'

'Oh yuk!' said Celandine. 'That sounds horrid. I don't like snakes.'

'Well, I do! Can I have one of the old dresses please, Auntie Leveret? To keep in my room?' asked Bluebell.

Leveret smiled at her and nodded.

'Of course you can. Just keep it away from Granny Maizie – she doesn't like snakes either.'

Magpie had left them and continued up the hill as dusk closed in. The sun had set whilst they were in the woods and the sky to the west was a rich apricot, streaked with bright gold. From the woods below, the birds still sang. Avoiding the thistles and old sheep dung, they left the rocks and climbed the final slope to the hill's summit.

At the top of the hill they stood by the massive Hare Stone feeling its energy and the soft heat it gave out where the sun had warmed it all day. Bluebell laid her cheek against its rough, lichened surface and spread her little arms to embrace it. She was tiny compared to its vast bulk and she sighed with pleasure at the feel of it. Celandine stared out towards the coast where the moon would rise, a slight breeze lifting her tumble of curls. Sylvie stood by her and took her hand, and Leveret was struck by their likeness. Magpie sat down with his back to the great stone, watching the horizon. Leveret joined him and Bluebell wriggled in between them, patting them both as if they were the arms of her chair.

Gradually the birds stopped singing and the evening darkened. The first star twinkled timidly, then grew bolder and brighter in the lavender-blue sky that deepened to indigo. Other stars appeared slowly, one by one, and the hush descended. Then – at last – a bright pink sliver slid up from the misty bed, growing by the second into a slice and then a dome of pure, flamingo-pink moon. Leveret's breath caught in her throat and she felt little Bluebell's trembling wonder. Magpie was alive with the magic and Leveret could feel the colours through him; their telepathy enabled her to experience the beauty in an almost visceral way far beyond her own normal appreciation. Sylvie and Celandine were now silhouettes as they stood together, gazing at the moon as she rose from her slumber to walk the night.

Leveret thought she saw something pale shimmer over Sylvie and frowned as, dropping Celandine's hand, her arms rose from her sides to form wings above her head. She stood perfectly still, her long, slim arms outstretched, her silver hair in a swathe down her back, her entire body yearning towards the brilliant pink moon that had now cleared the horizon and was climbing steadily in the night sky. By her side Celandine did the same, her arms rising skyward. Leveret stared harder; Sylvie *was* shimmering. There were very faint silver threads on her skin and in her hair as if she were alive with tiny filaments of light. A strange cry came from her mouth, and Leveret put a reassuring hand on Bluebell's arm as she felt the child stiffen. And then Sylvie was off, her feet skimming the short grass as she skipped and danced in a great spiral around the hilltop and the marker stone. Celandine stood for a moment longer, then with a pirouette she joined her mother, leaping into graceful arabesques.

Leveret exhaled sharply and squeezed Bluebell's arm.

'We'll just sit very, very quietly, Blue, and watch them dance,' she whispered. 'We mustn't say a word or break the spell.'

The child nodded, and then jerked in surprise. From below, where field met dark woods, a pale barn-owl came flapping towards them. Its massive wings were silent as it approached, to circle around the hill top and the moondancers. Bluebell let out a long and shaky breath and Leveret felt tears prickling behind her eyes at the sheer magic of the Hare Moon. She sensed Magpie's complete bewilderment at the scene he was witnessing; his attempts to make sense of it so that he could interpret it onto canvas. And then out of the darkness came the hares, their long ears laid back and their bodies lithe and muscular. They joined the moongazy mother and maiden in their graceful dance to honour the Bright Lady and bring down the moon magic to feed the soul of Stonewylde.

The moon shone down not only on the sacred hill but also on the Place of Bones and Death. Her rose-gold face had now turned to a brilliant, diamond-bright silver as she tiptoed through the canyons of stone. She could not banish the shadows and darkness there, nor scare away the creeping terror that stalked the quarry looking for new prey. The spirits of the many, many folk who over the centuries had lost their lives at this place, stirred in restless slumber. For them the Otherworld was a place of cruelty and entrapment from which there was no escape. Bones and treasures lay buried here, crushed beneath stone, abandoned here as sacrifice, huddled in forgotten, walled-off caves. Menace and death walked the corridors between the ivy-clad rock-faces. On the platform of the great Serpent Stone, writhing with carved snakes and gouged with empty sockets for moon eggs, a strange figure capered. He was made of shadow and moonlight, terror and moonlust. His hair was silver and his eyes were black, but he was not of this world.

A girl sobbed convulsively into her hands as the youth tried to jam the keys into the ignition and start the engine. His hands shook so much that he kept missing, and then the key-ring dropped to the floor.

'Bloody well SHUT UP, you stupid bitch!' he yelled, his voice shaking. He stank of fresh sweat and his eyes bulged from his head.

Finally his scrabbling hands found the key on the floor of the Landrover and shoved it into the ignition. He turned it sharply and the engine fired into life; relief flooded through him and brought a new wave of rank perspiration. The girl was huddled up in the passenger seat, her tears flowing freely, trying to keep her sobs quiet for fear of angering him further. He forced the vehicle into gear and yanked the steering wheel round as he let out the clutch too sharply. They almost stalled, but at the last second the engine held and they were off, bouncing down the track towards safety. Behind them, in the moonlit darkness, Quarrycleave sighed with disappointment.

9

Yul's eyes drooped and he pulled himself up quickly, imagining the humiliation of actually nodding off as Tom, Greenbough and even Cherry had all done in the past. He tried very hard to stifle his impatience as the meeting continued into its third hour. Outside the sun was scorching and, in the Galleried Hall where the stained glass windows were so high, this created a blaze of brilliant colour up near the vaulted roof, and bright patterns on the floor and the people below. Every door was pushed wide open to bring in a draught. Though none led directly outside, Yul could smell one of his favourite fragrances in the world – the scent of freshly cut hay. It was the eve of the Mead Moon, which some liked to call the Honey Moon, and the Summer Solstice was only a couple of weeks away. The warm, dry weather of April and May had continued into June, bringing everything on very early and causing a great deal of worry about irrigation.

This was the subject under discussion at present, and Yul had to admit that he'd stopped listening quite a while ago. What he wanted now was a ride on Skydancer; a hard gallop along Dragon's Back under the arching blue skies in the searing heat until both he and the stallion were drenched with sweat. And then a swim in the sea, plunging into the cool water, swimming fast through the lagoon to haul himself up onto the long rock that guarded the beach, and lie there as the water evaporated and the salt crusted his skin. He sighed so heavily that it sounded like a groan, and those closest to him in the circle glanced in surprise.

With a scowl, Yul dragged his attention back to the stifling room and the stifling people in it. Edward was droning on and on about the state of the crops. Yul knew he should care – he did care – but the endless discussion of every single matter was driving him crazy.

'We'll pump water from the river, as we've done in the past,' he interjected suddenly, 'and if that gets too low, we'll sink bore holes outside the Village. We'll concentrate on the fields nearest to water, work out the minimum yield we can survive on for the harvest, and just forget the rest. It's happened before and it'll happen again. Drought is drought and we're not going to starve.'

Everyone stared at Yul as he cut across Edward's monologue, and he thought how closely they resembled a herd of cattle.

'Right then,' said Edward, nodding slowly. 'So we'll—'

'For Goddess' sake, Edward – you're the farming manager! You're in charge of the farms – make a decision and then implement it. It doesn't need to be discussed here with people like ... Cherry, and Rowan ... and Sylvie – people who know nothing about farming. That's your area of expertise, so get on with it, man!'

Edward clamped his mouth shut and his ears burned red. Yul exhaled sharply and looked at the agenda in front of him. It was interminable today and he couldn't bear much more.

'We're a council, Yul, a committee,' said Sylvie evenly. 'We need to make major decisions by majority vote. Edward was only following procedure. Sinking bore holes isn't something we do lightly and he was right to bring it up here, for open discussion.'

'Aye, I only thought—'

'You thought absolutely right, Edward,' she said firmly. 'So, are we all agreed on Yul's recommendations? Calculate the minimum crop yield required and irrigate accordingly? Good! And the next item—'

'The next item is Stonewylde.com,' said Yul irritably, furious with Sylvie for her efficient put-down. 'Harold will now report on this.'

''Tis a bloody disaster!' said Martin. 'Several months down the line and I still can't find my files. I never wanted the stupid computer in the first place and if it's not back to working order soon, I tell you all now, I'm not using it again!'

He glared round the circle, his thin face pinched with anger, his slate-grey eyes brooking no argument.

'It would be good to have access to all the medical records soon,' agreed Hazel. 'I'm managing without them, but it's not good practice.'

'Same for the schools,' said Miranda. 'We're struggling. What news, Harold?'

The poor young man, who'd lost weight since the system failure at Imbolc and was even more jerky and nervous than ever, cleared his throat.

'Well, it seems—'

'And when I think o' the work I did on organising all the information we need to get a price for a new boiler in the Hall,' interrupted Martin, 'it makes my blood boil!'

'I'm sorry, but I'm afraid all the data is gone,' stuttered Harold.

'What do you mean, *gone*?' barked Martin. 'Surely you can find the old files, now we paid a fortune for that computer solutions man to fix it all?'

Harold shook his head miserably and felt as if he were collapsing under a hail of stones. He was the victim of his own success in persuading people to use the network for everything.

'And what about the quotas?' asked Maizie. 'The Village folk asked me last Dark Moon if they still need to do them quotas or what. What's happening, Harold?'

He twitched and threw a beseeching look at Yul, who stared stonily ahead.

'I'm sorry to say ... Stonewylde.com has been forced to cease trading,' Harold said. 'Permanently.'

'So we're not getting any revenue from it at all now?' asked Miranda. 'I thought that things were pretty desperate. Why—'

'They are,' whispered Harold. 'All the reserves we'd built up have gone.'

'But I don't understand,' said Dawn. 'Why has Stonewylde. com ceased trading? I thought it was all doing so well. I know we lost the customer database, but surely—'

'I heard it were on account o' some nasty photos,' said Tom. 'I never did like photos. That Rainbow, she were clicking away at Beltane, and—'

'Shall I tell them, Harold?' said Yul in a clipped voice, not pausing for an answer. 'Basically, after Imbolc and the crash, Stonewylde.com apparently sent out a marketing e-mail to every customer on the database asking if they'd like to buy the new Stonewylde calendar at a reduced rate, as it was already February. These beautiful calendars, at a bargain price, featured animals from Stonewylde in idyllic country settings. But, when the customers clicked the link to actually see these calendars ... let's just say, it was definitely a case of "four legs bad".'

'That's not funny, Yul!' said Sylvie. 'The photos on the link were obscene and illegal, and many of the recipients complained to the police. They'd trusted Stonewylde and now our name is dirt. We can never sell our products again, or at least, not under the Stonewylde brand name.'

There was shocked silence, broken only by Martin's angry breathing.

'Whole place is falling to rack and ruin, as I always said it would!' he muttered.

'On a lighter note, I'd like to thank everyone for the wonderful handfasting last month,' said Dawn, brightly. 'We had the most perfect day and we do appreciate everything everyone did, especially as David was an Outsider.'

'Still is!'

'We'll ignore that remark, Martin,' said Miranda, 'and concentrate instead on what we can do to put things right again here.'

She flicked a glance at Clip, who'd said very little so far

today. His face was grey and she wondered if he were ill.

'There's only one thing as can put all to rights at Stonewylde,' Martin said, 'and that's—'

'I think maybe I should tell everyone now!' burst in Harold unexpectedly. Blushing and fidgeting, he looked down at his notes. 'I been pondering a long while about when best to mention this, and I'm not sure . . .'

'What?' snapped Yul. 'Just spit it out, Harold, so we can bring this tedious meeting to an end!'

'I don't know . . . I weren't sure whether to say about it to just you privately, Yul, or what . . .'

'We've already mentioned the need to discuss things as a committee,' said Sylvie gently. 'So you're right to raise any issues now, Harold, with everyone here. You must remember that Yul isn't actually in charge of Stonewylde – we all are.'

'Well, 'tis about an e-mail I got a while back, before the system were infected with the virus. And since then I've had more e-mails, once I'd got a new address up and running, and I've had a letter and even a phone call . . .'

'The suspense is killing us!' said Miranda, as fed up as Yul about the length of the meeting. She had students taking exams and couldn't waste time on banalities. 'What? What about an e-mail? Is this something that'll help get Stonewylde out of the current financial crisis?'

All eyes were on Harold as he flushed scarlet and jerked his wrists.

'Yes!' he said. 'Yes, it will! Or it could, if we agree to it.'

'If 'tis another o' your daft schemes about selling off our spring water or our deer—'

'I've been talking with someone who wants to help us. Someone who loves Stonewylde as much as we do and—'

'Harold!' Yul's voice was like a whip-crack. 'Who have you been talking to? It had better not be—'

''Tis Buzz!'

There were several gasps but other than that, complete silence. Yul's face had turned scarlet but now all the blood drained from it. He was dangerously white, his lips thin and pale, and his eyes flashing fire.

'You traitor!' he hissed. 'How *could* you, Harold? I trusted you!'

'No, no!' protested Harold, 'I done nothing, Yul! *He* contacted *me* – and I haven't done nothing at all, only read of his ideas and proposals. And honest, he's got such good ideas about how we can—'

'How *dare* you discuss Stonewylde with Buzz!' shouted Yul, quivering with fury. 'The one person in the world who will never, *ever*—'

'The one person who rightfully should be here leading Stonewylde!' said Martin. 'About time he came back where he belongs.'

Yul jerked in his seat and looked as if he might leap across the circle and punch Martin, but Clip stood up and held out his arms in a soothing, placatory gesture.

'Alright, alright,' he said softly. 'Enough of this. Martin – you're being deliberately inflammatory and if you continue, you will have to leave the meeting.'

'No, I only—'

'Enough, Martin!' Clip's voice was like steel and he fixed the other man, so like him in appearance, with an unbending gaze. Martin lowered his eyes and muttered, but fell silent as Clip continued to stare at him. 'We'll discuss this in a calm, rational manner. Harold, we appreciate you're not to blame – if that's the right word – for being in contact with Buzz. You've clearly been targeted as someone who may have influence and who's in touch with the financial situation here.'

'Yes, and if Harold has been blabbing—'

'No, Yul, Harold's loyalty is not in question. Now, Harold, tell us what Buzz has proposed.'

'Well, I think he wants—'

'NO!' shouted Yul, shockingly loud. His deep voice echoed around the stone walls of the Galleried Hall and carried up to the vaulted ceiling where the Green Men gaped. He scanned the ring of stunned faces and, for a second, had a vivid flashback to

134

a scene so long ago in this same place: countless faces staring at him, shocked and frightened, as he confronted Magus. His beloved Sylvie, tightly laced into an amethyst dress with diamonds at her wrists and tears in her eyes, and Magus' cruel, pale face twisted in hatred, deliberately tormenting him ...

'Buzz can never come back here and must never be part of Stonewylde,' said Yul, his voice low and shaking with emotion. 'I vowed once to kill him and that still stands. I will not – could not – live in the same place as him and not fulfil my vow. So, if you decide as a "committee" to bring Buzz back here, then I shall be forced to leave Stonewylde for good.'

'Oh Yul, there's no need for such talk!' said Maizie in consternation. 'Surely after all this—'

'Mother, you of all people should understand why I could never tolerate Buzz returning,' he said. 'You must recall what he did to me as a child, what he did to our Rosie, and then what he did to Sylvie. How can I ever allow a person like that to contaminate Stonewylde? My father banished him and, in this instance, he acted rightly.'

'I think Buzz should come back and help put us right.'

Everyone in the room turned incredulously to stare at Rowan. She very rarely spoke at any meeting and never said anything controversial. Her creamy skin was flushed, and her chest rose and fell sharply.

'Rowan, surely you don't want— ' began Dawn, but Rowan interrupted, her mouth trembling and words tumbling out in a rush.

'Buzz is our Magus' eldest son and 'tis his rightful place, leading us. He were born and bred to do it, unlike some, and 'twere never right that he were banished and not allowed back. When our Magus were murdered, Buzz should've come back then to take over the running of Stonewylde.'

'Well said!' agreed Martin. ''Tis exactly what I think, and many o' the folk too.'

'Rubbish!' said Cherry hotly. 'Nobody would want that nasty piece o' work back here.'

135

'No, they wouldn't!' agreed Tom. 'Goddess knows what Buzz's turned out like, but if he's anything like the cocky bugger he used to be ...'

'He must never come back,' said Sylvie quietly. 'Yul's absolutely right and I support him entirely. I for one would never want to be at Stonewylde if Buzz were here—'

'Now we see your true colours!' spat Martin. 'Is this about winning and losing, or is it about saving Stonewylde from ruin? Because if anyone here really cared about Stonewylde, they'd welcome Buzz and his money with open arms!'

'Not at all,' said Clip firmly. 'There are other ways of saving Stonewylde from ruin, Martin – and besides, it hasn't yet reached that point. We do need money, but we're not on the brink of financial collapse. I suggest we close this meeting now, as tempers are running high, and all think of how to generate an income for Stonewylde. That will be top of our agenda next month. Harold, I suggest you e-mail Buzz and thank him for his kind offer of help, but tell him we have other courses of action to provide for our financial needs and don't need his assistance.'

He grimaced sharply and sat down again in the great carved chair. Sylvie thought how wonderful a man Clip was, to be able to diffuse such a volatile situation. But it was old Greenbough, as gnarled now as the trees he'd tended all his life, who had the final word.

'See? I said that maid were just the scout, and now she's bringing 'em all in. You mark my words – there'll be more coming afore long. Stonewylde will be crawling with Hallfolk all over again if we don't be on our guard against 'un.'

The Council of Elders had dispersed, everyone returning to their work for what was left of the afternoon. Sylvie had no career counselling appointments today, so had dropped in to see Hazel. The doctor was concerned about Sylvie's pallor and wanted to give her a check-up, but Sylvie had dismissed her fears and assured her she was feeling a little better. She decided not to mention Leveret's natural remedies, not wishing Hazel to feel sidelined in any way. After some discussion they'd agreed to wait until the autumn, when Sylvie was due for her annual medical and to have her implant replaced. Hazel had also voiced her concerns about Clip, and Sylvie had promised to try to persuade him to have some tests.

Sylvie crossed the great entrance hall, stepping around the teenagers on work detail who were half-heartedly dusting the oak panelling and replacing the roses in the huge vases. She wanted to get back to the Village, or at least get onto the track leading down there, before the younger students who still lived at home left the Hall School. She was never sure whether to walk with any of their groups or not and it always felt a little awkward. Only a couple of days ago the same thing had happened and she'd ended up tagging along with a group which included Faun.

Faun had been almost rude to her in front of the others in the group, and Sylvie found herself disliking the girl, who was loudly opinionated and ridiculously self-absorbed. Sylvie hoped her own daughters wouldn't end up like that, although it was clear that Faun had been spoiled by her adoring mother and grandparents, and now had an inflated idea of her own worth.

Rushing across the hall to get ahead of the youngsters before they set off, she was surprised when Yul appeared, as if he'd been waiting for her.

'May I walk back down to the Village with you?' he asked. 'I'd like to see the girls and I'd like to talk to you in private rather than a public arena.'

'Er, yes, of course. The girls love it when you come down to the cottage.'

'And you don't?'

'Oh Yul! That's not what I meant.'

They passed through the entrance porch where the riveted oak door stood open, and stepped outside into the hot June afternoon. It was blindingly bright after the cavernous gloom indoors, the sky a bleached-out blue and the gravel circle and surrounding grass vivid in the sunlight. The smell of new-mown hay was strong, mingling with velvet scent from the heavy-headed roses that arched over the porch and scrambled up the stone wall. Their feet crunched on the gravel as they crossed the turning circle and headed off through the stone pillars and onto the long, tree-lined drive.

It was cool and soothing in the shade after the searing brightness, and Sylvie breathed deeply of the refreshing air, feeling the energy of the trees all around her, their magic prickling at her skin. She sighed heavily and was surprised to feel Yul's hand slip into hers.

'That was a hell of a meeting,' he said.

'Dreadful!' she agreed. 'And, as for the business about Buzz ...'

'I'm so glad you backed me on that,' he said. 'I wasn't sure if you would.'

'Well, of course I would! I feel the same about him as you do.'

'I doubt that,' he said wryly. 'I know he pestered you that summer and then attacked you in the maze, but *I'd* put up with a lifetime of his bullying and abuse.'

'True,' she said, thinking of the awful incident at the ballet when Buzz's hand had rested so intimately on her leg for the entire performance. And even worse, the assault when she'd been strapped to the bed and helpless in the private clinic; she still couldn't bear to think of that. But Yul must never know of those things. He'd only today mentioned his former threat to kill Buzz and this could perhaps tip him over the edge.

'I can't believe that Harold betrayed me – us – like that,' he mused.

'Honestly, Yul, I think Clip's right. Harold has been manipulated – there isn't any question of betrayal.'

He glanced at her as they walked along, still loosely holding hands but both aware of just how awkward it felt, when before it had always been so natural.

'You always back your father, don't you?' he said. 'Never me.'

'Please let's not argue,' she sighed, 'I don't want to contradict you and start another squabble, but you should know by now that I always back whoever I think is right, regardless of who it is. And, lately, that happens to be Clip rather than you. But I agree with you totally about Buzz – he must never return here.'

'No, the bastard!' said Yul bitterly. 'Can you imagine him trying to take over Stonewylde and reinventing himself as Magus?'

Sylvie refrained from the obvious comment, managing to remove her hand from his in order to find a handkerchief in her bag.

'I was shocked at Martin's unpleasantness,' she said. 'And his rudeness.'

'He's a real viper in the nest and I've always wondered about him,' agreed Yul. 'I know Clip wanted to keep him on and give him a special place at Stonewylde so he felt valued, but I wish we'd got rid of him from the start.'

'Remember how he used to be with Magus? All that fawning and obsequiousness?' said Sylvie. 'He obviously never changed – just hid his true feelings from us all these years.'

'Yes, but what worries me is why he now feels able to show them. What's happened to make him feel he can now safely reveal where his loyalties lie?'

'There's something going on,' said Sylvie. 'I've felt it for some time now ... some kind of undercurrent. Can you feel it?'

'Yes ... but what I feel more is this chasm between us,' he said.

They'd reached the fork and could now turn off for the track down to the Village, or take the path that would lead to the Long Walk and the Stone Circle. Yul stopped and touched her arm. His grey eyes were clear today, and full of longing.

'Please? Can we just visit the Stone Circle together?'

She nodded, feeling sorry for the unnatural way he now had to behave. This humility and his tentative request – it wasn't Yul at all. He was a man of action and decision, and having to tread so carefully around her was alien to him. She regretted that she'd forced him to adopt these tactics, but the alternative was the rampant arrogance and bullying which she would no longer accept. If only he could find a happy medium; be himself but respect her autonomy too.

Soon they reached the end of the shady Long Walk and were at the entrance to the sunlit arena. Even though the afternoon was now well under way, the heat was tremendous. The birds were almost silent and the bees had ceased their activity; all slumbered in the baking, drowsy gold of the June afternoon. Only woodpigeons called lazily from the oak trees that fell away from the henge, and barely a whisper of air stirred.

They entered the blindingly bright sacred space and were at once blasted by heat bouncing off the great stones. The beaten earth floor was a scorching carpet that burned through the soles of their shoes. Everything shimmered in the haze and Sylvie felt slightly unreal. For a second she thought she saw movement by one of the stones, but when she blinked there was nothing. They stood together surveying the empty circle, almost reluctant to walk any further into the searing dustbowl.

'Let's go over there and sit in the shade of the stones,' said Yul, taking her arm and guiding her to the welcome black shadows. The relief was instant the moment they stepped out of the blazing sun. They sat down, their backs to the stone and their legs out before them. Yul took Sylvie's hand in his and rubbed it against his cheek.

'I love you,' he said simply. 'I love you the same now as I've always done. Without you my life is pointless.'

His words touched her heart in their directness and brought tears to her eyes. She longed for nothing more than things to be right between them, back to how it had once been. Could they start again, with a new consideration for each other? Maybe Yul understood now how hurt she'd been by his bullying and put-downs. Perhaps now he was ready to treat her how he'd always used to: with gentleness and respect, but as an equal.

'I love you too, Yul,' she said, her mouth dry and head slightly spinning. Hope for true reconciliation flared inside her.

'Really?' His eagerness was poignant. 'Do you really still love me? I thought perhaps not.'

'Oh Yul, how could I not love you? We're the darkness and the brightness, remember? We belong together and we made vows.

140

That handfasting ceremony last month …'

Tears strangled her words.

'I know,' he said and put his arm around her, pulling her close. It felt so good; like an enclosure of comfort holding her safe. He buried his face in her silky hair as he'd always loved to do. 'I kept thinking of us – of the vows we made to each other at our hand-fasting, and how it had all fallen apart. It broke my heart, Sylvie. And then you disappeared in the evening, at the Moon Fullness. I stood alone and watched the moon rise, and I thought you'd gone off with one of those Outsiders.'

'Oh Yul – don't ever think that! You really are the only one for me, ever. I was up at Hare Stone, moondancing. It was abso-lutely magical.'

'At Hare Stone?' His voice sounded a little odd and there was a pause. 'You went moondancing again without me?'

'Yes, I'd promised—'

'But why didn't you ask me to come? I'd have loved that, like the old days, just you and me. Didn't you want me there?'

'I didn't think you'd want to come, Yul. And besides, you'd ignored me all day.'

'Ignored you? No, *you'd* ignored *me*! And you'd managed the whole handfasting ceremony quite well without me. I felt use-less and unnecessary all day.'

She felt how tense he'd become, his body rigid beside hers.

'Oh Yul, I—'

'But that's not the point. To be honest, I'm shocked that you went moondancing without me after what happened last time. You shouldn't have gone up there alone – that was a crazy thing to do. Why—'

'But I wasn't alone. I took the girls, and Celandine was—'

'*The girls*? You took our little girls up there without informing me, after you'd had hysterics the previous time? Oh for Goddess' sake, Sylvie, how *stupid*! You should've thought—'

Abruptly Sylvie pulled away from his arm, which suddenly felt as restrictive as an iron coop. She launched herself to her feet and the world tilted at the suddenness of movement.

'How *dare* you?' she responded bitterly, feeling more angry with herself than him. Why had she imagined he'd be different today? 'Who are you to call me stupid?'

She brushed the dust from her skirt and, with a final glare at his flushed face, turned away, and headed off towards the Long Walk.

'Sylvie!' cried Yul, scrambling to his feet. 'Hold on! I only meant—'

'No you didn't! You haven't changed at all, have you?' she retorted over her shoulder. 'And until you do, we have no future together.'

Maizie looked fondly at the red-haired boy splitting logs out in the back garden. He was a lovely lad, so willing and helpful, if a little shy. After the day's fiasco at the Council of Elders' meeting it was good to return to normality. She thought back to the tension in the Galleried Hall and her son's outburst at the mention of Buzz. Not that she blamed him, of course. It was funny to·think that Buzz, Yul and this boy, Rufus, were fathered by the same man; all three were so very different in colouring and temperament.

She made the boy a cool drink of elderflower cordial, for it looked as if Rufus had nearly finished chopping the wood. It was only for the range, of course, and in this heat-wave, she wished she could dispense with that altogether. She looked sadly at the vegetables wilting in their beds outside, all suffering from the drought. Every drop of water used in the Bath House was piped into tanks, to be used for irrigating the cottage gardens. She'd send Rufus along there to collect some in a minute. There was still half an hour before suppertime and Sylvie was down the end of the garden picking strawberries with the girls. Sylvie had come back from the Hall later than her and in a strange mood; Maizie had no idea what was going on, but she knew that Sylvie was deeply unhappy.

She tutted to herself as she began scrubbing some new potatoes. A woman's place was by her husband's side, not living with his mother. Poor Yul – she'd felt so sorry for him today when Sylvie had put him in his place. The girl was right, of course, but that didn't make it any easier to see her boy put down like that. She wished that they'd patch things up. Nobody expected marriage to be easy, and there were bound to be difficult spells – droughts and floods, along with perfect weather. Trouble was, Yul and Sylvie had been basking in the perfect weather for too long and had no idea how to cope with this storm. She recalled her years of marriage to Alwyn, then quickly cast that thought aside as she put the potatoes on to boil. There was a nice piece of ham ready to carve, and salad from the garden already washed. If Sylvie had picked enough strawberries, they'd have them with some cream. She hoped Rufus would stay for supper – he was a good boy and the little girls enjoyed his company no end.

The front door banged opened and she peered through from the kitchen, thinking it must be Sweyn or Gefrin come by for a visit. They didn't come very often now that Sylvie and the girls were staying – in fact they'd only come once and hadn't been back since. It wouldn't be Geoffrey or Gregory; they were busy with their own young families, as was Rosie. And then Yul appeared, so tall and dark, and as always, Maizie's heart leaped with love for him. He was her special son and always would be, however he behaved. Yul had good reason to act the way he did; after all those years of misery and being treated worse than a dog, she'd forgive him anything. She beamed her welcome, even though they'd only seen each other that afternoon in the Galleried Hall, and then stood on tiptoes to kiss his cheek. His mood didn't seem to have improved, for his mouth was hard and eyes cloudy.

'I just came by to see the girls,' he said. 'Are they about?'

Maizie nodded towards the back garden and Yul glanced out through the open door into the brightness beyond. The rhythmic thud of an axe blade on wood was loud and Yul frowned.

'Who's chopping the wood, Mother?' He hoped it wasn't Sweyn, who always made him feel aggressive. Gefrin was marginally more bearable.

''Tis our Rufus,' she said.

'Rufus?' he barked. 'What the hell's *he* doing here?'

'Chopping wood, as you can hear! He's such a good lad, so helpful, and—'

'But why Rufus?'

Yul was surprised at just how much he resented the thought of that boy in *his* old back garden doing jobs for *his* mother. He'd even have preferred gingery, porcine Sweyn. Rufus irritated him with that deep red hair and freckles, and those dark, soulful eyes; he didn't belong here.

'Oh Yul, don't be silly. He's a good boy and he offered to help me. Sylvie arranged it all, seeing as how I have no man about to do the heavy work.'

Yul stood there, dominating the kitchen, his anger and jealousy seething around him with no place to go. He saw the cold drink sitting on the table ready for the boy, and from the garden could now hear his daughters' voices calling to Rufus.

Resentment bubbled inside him like a bellyful of acid.

'So not only has she left me and moved in here, to my old home – she's now arranging for her bloody brother to take over—'

'Her brother? Oh yes, o' course! I always think of him as *your* brother, Yul – Magus' son. Well, I need someone to chop the wood and bring in the water – and the lad has no kin of his own to do it for. 'Tis all part of growing up at Stonewylde and he's never had to do it afore. Hard work's good for a growing boy – surely you don't mind me making use o' him?'

Yul frowned, ashamed of his jealousy and annoyed with himself for being so petty. Then he let out a shout of laughter, took his plump mother in his arms and gave her a great hug.

'Goodness, boy – don't break me in half! What is it now?'

'I've been a fool for getting so upset – the irony of the situation just hit me!' he laughed. 'Magus punished me as a young lad by sending me to Miranda and Sylvie's cottage to chop wood and do the heavy work for them. And fourteen years later – here's Magus' and Miranda's own son chopping wood in my mother's cottage in the Village! Who'd ever have thought it?'

10

They stood before the ancient door which now hung on strong iron hinges. Leveret pulled out the key from where it dangled on a cord round her neck, and, unlocking the heavy padlock, she lifted the latch. It clunked up and she pushed the door open. No longer did it stick, or squeak alarmingly. Instead, it swung easily and they stood on the threshold and peered inside.

Leveret turned to Clip, her eyes shining with joy.

'Thank you!' she breathed. 'Thank you for arranging this, Clip.'

He looked down at her barely up to his chest, and smiled.

'My pleasure. Tom was very happy to supervise the renovations and at least the cottage is secure now. The door's been mended and re-hung, the windows open and shut and don't let in the draughts, and the roof's been repaired and re-thatched. They swept the chimney too and fixed the hearth so you can light a fire safely. All it needs now is a bit of a clean.'

Leveret was almost reluctant to step inside but, with a deep breath, she entered Mother Heggy's cottage. All traces of the plants and fungi she'd collected, the notebooks and bottles, and most importantly, the Book of Shadows, had been safely moved to the tower before the repairs began. The hovel was now empty except for the few bits of ancient furniture: the scrubbed table and chair, the large dresser, the settle along the wall and, of course, the battered rocking chair. But it no longer seemed a hovel, and today Leveret had brought with her a broom, cloths and beeswax. The other necessities would have to wait until Magpie could help her carry them up here. She hoped the little spring hidden in the hill nearby was still trickling so she could collect water.

Clip eased himself slowly onto the chair and indicated the rocking chair.

'Please be seated, Wise Woman,' he said with a twinkle in his eye.

Solemnly she put down the basket and broom and sat in the chair, sliding herself back until she was comfortable, and closed her eyes.

The sounds of summer coming through the open door – the squeal of seagulls, the piping of larks and pipits, the drone of bees – receded and in their place came a rustle of old leaves, blowing slightly in the doorway.

'Time to take the besom and sweep the place clean!' came a voice, as dry as the leaves themselves. 'Time to take your rightful place, my little hare. You've work to do and now it can begin. Only you can save our Stonewylde.'

A breath of wind blew in from the door and touched her face, and then came a great 'CAW' and a wheezy chuckle.

Leveret's eyes flew open and met Clip's wolf-grey gaze. He smiled at her and gave a chuckle himself.

'Old Mother Heggy's feet didn't reach the ground either,' he said. 'I have no idea what she was like as a girl, but I'll bet she was very similar to you.'

'Did you hear the crow?' she asked, her heart racing.

'The crow? No, I don't think I—'

There was a scuttering noise from above and they both peered into the rafters. Leveret wriggled out of the chair and hurried outside, looking up on the roof. The new thatch gleamed in the sunlight, clean and straight like a combed head of thick hair. Scrabbling about by the chimney was a crow, and, as it turned, they saw a white tail feather. The bird paused and regarded them steadily. Leveret shivered and Clip laid a hand on her arm reassuringly. The crow then opened its huge beak and emitted a stream of loud, insistent *CAWs* that at first shocked her, but after a while made her giggle.

'Alright!' she laughed. 'Enough, Crow – I get the message! Please, make yourself at home whenever you wish.'

They were about to return inside but Leveret stopped.

'Why don't you wait outside whilst I sweep the place? It won't take long and I don't want the dust to irritate your lungs.'

'Alright, that's kind of you,' he said. 'But my cough has gone, in case you hadn't noticed. I said it was just a winter thing.'

'Maybe so, but I've heard your breathing at night time, Clip, and I don't want to make it worse.'

'That's not a cough!' he said. 'That's just old man snoring. But yes, I'll stay and make Crow's acquaintance if you like.'

When the cottage floor had been thoroughly swept, Leveret called Clip in excitedly and pointed to the pentagram revealed on the flagstones. He nodded, not liking to tell her that this was the spot – in the centre of the pentagram – where Mother Heggy had been found at the Winter Solstice all those years ago. She'd probably hear it at some point, but no need to spoil her pleasure now.

'I think I may come up here this evening for the Mead Moon,' she said.

'Would you like me to come too?' he asked. 'I had intended to go to the Dolmen, but—'

'No, thanks – I think I should be alone for the first Moon Fullness I celebrate here,' she said.

'And you're not scared? What about Mother Heggy's ghost?'

Leveret laughed at this.

'She's haunted me all my life,' she replied. 'Maybe once I start doing what she wants, she'll leave me in peace.'

'Alright, just so long as you feel safe.'

'Mother Heggy is with me,' said Leveret, 'and I really believe she watches over me. I'll bring her magical things back tonight – the things I told you I found hidden in the chimney alcove. Much as I love having them with me in the tower, they belong here. I shall cast a spell of protection around the cottage tonight and then they'll be safe here.'

'A good idea,' he agreed. 'And I shall do the same from the Dolmen. Don't forget to bring your new headdress for the Moon Fullness, will you?'

She smiled, her green eyes brilliant with excitement.

'*I shall go into a hare* ...' she said softly.

'May I see what he's working on at the moment?' asked Rainbow, impatiently watching the last of David's class troop out of the Art Room for lunch.

David rapidly scrolled through the slides ready for the afternoon's class, ensuring all was ready and the screen correctly linked to his device. He too had been affected by the Imbolc Crash, as it was now referred to, and was trying to be very careful how he stored his lessons.

'If he gives permission,' he replied, wishing she'd leave him alone.

Rainbow wandered nonchalantly around the room, picking up things and examining them, slowly making her way to the side room where she knew David stored the portfolios and canvases in progress. Today she wore a very thin cotton dress in a soft shade of coral pink. Her golden skin was tanned more deeply from the relentless sunshine, making her blue eyes appear even bluer. Her tawny hair was several shades lighter and wilder than ever, glinting with gold threads and falling in a great tangle down her back. She was beautiful and she knew it, moving with graceful, sinuous ease between the long art tables towards the side room.

'Rainbow, no!' said David sharply, realising her intent. He tried to head her off, dodging around the tables and colliding with her by the door. She looked deep into his angry eyes and raised her golden eyebrows.

'No, David? Really? Are you going to stop me?'

She moved towards the door and he tried to block her. She leaned forward to grasp the door handle and he grabbed her bare wrist. She was only centimetres from him and he could smell her heady scent. Her hair brushed his hand and she shook back her mane, laughing.

'Do you want a tussle on the floor? No? Come on, David, I only want to see what Magpie's up to at the moment. Why so secretive?'

She wriggled forward, her wrist still in his grip, and her hip brushed against his. Angrily he flung her away and turned his back on her, defeated. She laughed again, a deep throaty laugh that mocked and yet invited.

'Oh, don't be so silly,' she said. 'And look what you've done to me, you brute!'

His fingers had left marks on her wrist, which she rubbed hard.

'We can't have Dawn thinking you've been manhandling me, can we? Not quite the sort of thing a newly-wed man should be getting up to in the classroom.'

She opened the door and stepped inside, looking around the room. She sniffed the oil paint fumes appreciatively and smiled, flicking through a rack of canvases. But then she stopped, and David heard her small cry. He scowled – she could hardly have missed the huge canvas propped against the far wall. He heard her whistle of delight and she summoned him to join her.

'Oh don't be so stuffy, David!' she called. 'I'm not going to pounce on you. Come in here and tell me about this.'

Reluctantly, he entered the small room and stood beside her to gaze at the canvas that stood drying.

'What's to tell? You can see for yourself, surely.'

'It's ... well, words fail me. Certainly his best work, and he's so young! Makes you sick, doesn't it? How long has this taken him?'

'He started it just after Hare Moon – obviously – so less than a month. He's almost done, but I have to stop him and make him slow down. I think if I let him, he'd just paint, with no food or sleep, until it was completed.'

'Maybe you should let him do that and see what happens.'

'Magpie needs caring for, Rainbow. Despite this extraordinary talent, mentally, he's just a child.'

'And has Sylvie seen it yet?'

'No, and it's a surprise, so please don't breathe a word. Dawn says it's her birthday at the Solstice and we thought maybe it could be presented to her then, during the celebrations.'

'So, was Magpie actually there? I mean, is this a real scene or is it his imagination? I know that as a girl Sylvie used to be what was termed "moongazy", whatever that meant, and it was supposedly the reason that Magus was so obsessed with her. Is this Magpie's interpretation of moongaziness or what?'

David shrugged.

'Who knows? He can't tell us, can he? I tried to find out when this had happened, and all he did was point to the moon and the hares, so I assume it happened at Hare Moon – and certainly that's the theme here. But the figures – Sylvie and her little girl, the moon goddess as Mother, the hare in the moon and the owl – honestly, the whole thing is just breathtaking. And this strange bit under here, hidden deep inside the hill – what's that all about? That's one of the attractions of course – Magpie is a complete enigma and probably always will be.'

Rainbow stood gazing and shaking her head. Then she took a deep breath and patted David's arm.

'Thanks, David. Sorry about the underhand tactics. No hard feelings, I hope? I promise I won't spoil the surprise. I wonder if she'll be up there again tonight, for the full moon? I recognise the place of course – we used to call it Hill Stone. Maybe I'll wander up there this evening with a sketch pad and hope I get lucky.'

'You coming down the Village to see the crones tonight?' asked Jay as he shovelled shepherd's pie down his throat.

'Yeah, let's do that,' said Sweyn. 'We want to ask them about our sister and see if they have any good notions about what we can do.'

Gefrin was about to mention his need for some help with Meadowsweet, but then thought better of it. He didn't want Jay getting ideas.

'So you're not going with Tansy again?' he asked, scraping his plate clean and looking hopefully towards the serving table. In a minute they'd shout the call for seconds and he was ravenous.

'Are you taking the piss?' growled Jay.

'No! Why?'

'I thought I told you that weren't going to happen again!'

'No, Jay, all you said was Tansy—'

'I don't want to talk about it,' Jay snapped. 'If you want to come I'll be leaving as soon as we're done here. I need a drink and a smoke tonight.'

Sweyn and Gefrin's eyes met and they both grimaced, but subtly. Jay was quite volatile enough without angering him further.

'Mum, *why* can't we go there again? Please? It's the best, best thing ever!'

'If you carry on like this, Celandine, you won't come with me at all.'

'But Mum, the Village Green isn't where we should dance for the Bright Lady,' said Celandine. 'You know that – why are you pretending you want to go there? I don't understand.'

'Exactly! You're too young to understand, and maybe that proves to me you're too young to come moondancing at all.'

Celandine was close to tears, plucking at the tablecloth hem compulsively.

'For Goddess' sake, child, don't unpick that!' said Maizie sharply. 'What's got into you? Any more o' this nonsense and you'll be sent to bed!'

Celandine jumped up from her place and ran up to her bedroom, slamming the door.

'She's a bit young for that sort o' moodiness, surely?' said Maizie, pouring Bluebell another glass of milk.

'Actually, I think I understand what's wrong with her,' said Sylvie. 'I wish I could take her to Hare Stone again, but I think Yul may go up there tonight. He was angry I'd taken the girls there last month and he'll probably try to check up on me.'

'Why would he be angry, Mummy?' asked Bluebell.

'Oh Blue! I don't know – I suppose he thought you were both too young.'

'Silly Father! Course we aren't too young. Can I come to the Village Green with you and Celandine tonight?'

Sylvie sighed and shook her head.

'We've already discussed this, Bluebell. If Celandine and I need to dance, then you'd be all on your own watching and you'd maybe feel a bit scared in the dark. Stay here nice and cosy with Granny this month and help her with the honeycombs. Another time, when Auntie Leveret can join us again to look after you – then maybe you can come.'

'So why's our Leveret not joining you tonight?' asked Maizie. 'There was a time I couldn't keep the girl in at the Moon Fullness, try as I might. She'd be sneaking off, picking things and harvesting things and – oh!'

Without warning she burst into tears. Bluebell jumped down from her chair and flung her arms around her grandmother, and Sylvie also gave her a hug.

'Oh Maizie, it's alright! She's doing something with Clip I believe. You know all the magical stuff they get up to. Don't worry, she'll be safe.'

''Tisn't that!' sniffed Maizie. 'I don't like all that dabbling but I know she's safe with him looking over her.'

'What is it then, darling Granny Maizie? Why are you crying?'

Maizie blew her nose.

''Tis just that I miss her so much.'

Later, as the moon rose over Stonewylde and flooded the land with silver, Dawn and David lay in each other's arms amongst the oak trees near the Stone Circle and smiled contentedly in the darkness. Dawn placed hers and David's hands on her belly and whispered the words she'd heard as a child, words that seemed to work for others.

'Make a wish and make a child,
A seed to grow at fair Stonewylde,

At Honey Moon we wish tonight
For one new life, O Lady Bright.'

David chuckled and kissed her tenderly, thinking that no child could wish for a more magical or sacred conception than this.

In the cottage at the edge of the Village, six were crowded in the stinking parlour. It was a very warm night and the fire was out, but the windows were shut fast and the air was rank. Smoke hung in a pall over everyone's heads as they sat drinking, the boys their cider and the women a concoction of mead laced with something stronger. They weren't wasting that on the young ones, not that the murky liquid appealed to the lads anyway. Only Vetchling was without a pipe, as her cough hadn't improved with the warmer weather. Try as she might to have a good smoke, it only made her cough until she was sick, and left her gasping like a landed fish. She'd given up trying now, and sat wheezing and muttering complaints.

'Remember we're casting tonight, and you promised me a man,' said Starling, in her usual reclining position, not even having to stir to feed the fire now.

'I told you, that's daft!' said Violet crossly. 'I ain't doing it.'

'You promised, Auntie, and if you don't I'll go and find one myself, and leave you two old biddies on your own. How would you manage then? That bitch doctor would have you up the Hall like a shot!'

'Aye, she would that,' croaked Vetchling. 'We'd be up there in the Hall in nasty rooms all starched and bare, with none of our things about us. Oh no, you get her a man, sister. As long as he moves in here, he won't be no trouble. And he can chop the wood for us then.'

Violet regarded her balefully and leant forward to spit into the cold hearth. Jay drew hard on his pipe and took another swig of the strong cider. He knew his Uncle Martin arranged for supplies of the best stuff to be sent down here, which was good of the old man. He was never quite sure what his uncle – or second cousin or whatever he was – felt about him. Martin was always polite to him, but he'd noticed some strange looks. Certainly he was a force to be reckoned with, and Jay wouldn't want to be on his wrong side.

Sweyn and Gefrin were now thoroughly befuddled with the drink and pipes, and both were beginning to wonder why they'd come here. The crones weren't interested in plotting wickedness aimed at their sister. They seemed bad-tempered and out of sorts with each other tonight, like a trio of edgy cats, and neither brother wanted to be on the receiving end of any of their nastiness. They weren't sure how they could make an exit without causing offence, so they sat on the logs swigging more cider and feeling the worse for it.

'She got a creature, so I hear,' muttered Violet.

'Aye, and now she has a creature, there'll be no stopping her!' whined Vetchling. 'As ever, trying to take what's rightfully ours.'

The boys looked at each other helplessly, having no idea what they were on about.

'But this Solstice ... we know what'll come about! 'Twill be the start o' the ending for the whole nest of 'em.'

'Aye, sister, you speak right as ever. The hare-girl's magic shall be shown for what it is – puny, sickly stuff that ain't got a spit o' power to it! This Solstice, 'tis time enough.'

'And after that ... after the Solstice, all will begin to fail as we always said 'twould. We know what will come around, for who could resist the lure?'

Starling shifted uncomfortably in her huge chair and let out a sharp belch.

'Shall we start casting soon?' she said. 'You two old 'uns can barely keep your eyes open after dark nowadays, and I don't want to miss this night. A love-spell cast at the Mead Moon – none can escape that!'

'Reckon we better get going then,' said Jay, knocking out his pipe.

Sweyn and Gefrin stood up quickly, anxious to be gone.

Gefrin stumbled as the blood rushed to his head and he grabbed at his younger, heavier brother to steady himself. Sweyn was caught off balance and crashed into the empty hearth, knocking his head hard on the lintel. All three women squawked at this, unable to get up, and Jay ducked out of the way as Sweyn toppled over, narrowly missing him. The whole incident happened fast, leaving the young man groaning on the filthy floor, a huge blue lump on his temple.

'Bloody hell, Sweyn!' cried Gefrin, trying to bend over his brother and almost falling headlong into the greasy ashes in the hearth himself. 'I'm sorry – are you alright?'

Sweyn groaned and Jay bent to take a look.

'Silly bugger's almost knocked himself out,' he said.

''Twas to be expected,' cried Vetchling, but broke off as the cough took hold of her.

Violet tried to make herself heard over the awful lung-wrenching sound of her sister's suffering.

'Put a cold compress on it,' she screeched, waving a gnarled hand at the boys. 'We ain't got nothing here, but do that when you get back. Now take him out of here! I don't want no poking about in my cottage asking questions! Get out!'

Gefrin managed to heave Sweyn into a sitting position, and then with Jay's help, get him up on his feet. The heavy youth stood swaying between them, still unable to speak.

'Off you go, lads,' cried Starling. 'Shut the door behind you – we got work to do tonight!'

Yul sat with his back to the Hare Stone. He'd watched the sun setting and had, to his surprise, felt a thrill of earth energy in his veins as it disappeared behind the hills. Swifts sliced above his head in a breathtaking aerial display as they devoured gnats in the warm, still air. Gradually the birds' high-pitched twittering stopped and the skies darkened. Yul tipped his head back, his knees hugged to his chest, and gazed up at the dome of night above his head. Sylvie wasn't coming – of that he was sure. She'd have been here by now.

He felt a hard knot of disappointment in his chest. Why had he criticised her in the Stone Circle? Why couldn't he just hold back for once? He was desperate to heal the rift between them and make it right again. If only she'd come tonight, he could have shown her just how much he loved her. He imagined her spread out on the grass beside him, her hair like a great silver fan, her slim arms reaching out and pulling him down as their lips found each other ...

His eyes flew open as he heard the sound of someone approaching. His heart hammered in his chest – he'd try so hard to get it right tonight. His eyes prickled with tears as he thought just how much he loved Sylvie – his beautiful moon-angel. He longed to watch her spread her wings and dance, with the moonbeams caressing her white skin and the starlight sparkling in her silver eyes. She was his magical, moongazy girl and—

A blonde head appeared and instantly he knew it wasn't Sylvie. His hopes and excitement deflated like a punctured balloon and he hung his head bitterly. In the near darkness, the figure came further into view, climbing the steep hill. Just as he recognised who it was, she called out to him.

'There you are!' she cried. 'What happened to you?'

She was a little out of breath and threw herself down on the short grass in front of him.

'What?' He didn't want to engage with her at all tonight – he just couldn't be bothered. She wasn't Sylvie and that's all that mattered.

'One minute you were greeting me and the next you'd vanished!' she said.

'What are you talking about?' he said crossly. 'I haven't greeted you.'

'Don't be ridiculous – you just called me by name a minute ago! Down there, by the rocks just now. I've been looking all over the place for you – I thought you were playing some kind of silly hide-and-seek amongst the boulders when you vanished like that. Anyway, here you are and – oh!'

As they were speaking, the moon had risen and was now a

great golden disc floating on the horizon, the heat in the atmosphere making its edges appear jagged.

'Goddess but that's beautiful!' breathed Rainbow. 'So very beautiful.'

She sat up and spun round to face the rising moon, glad she'd found Yul at least, though it was a pity Sylvie wasn't here. Magpie had captured something so magical, and she was intrigued to see how much was real and how much his imagination.

Rainbow and Yul sat for some time in silence. They watched the diagonal path of the moon as she rose stealthily in the warm night, stars twinkling around her in the dark velvet sky. The scent of cut hay was strong, and above their heads bats took over where the swifts had left off, as moths fluttered in the darkness all around them. But Sylvie wasn't here and they both felt her absence. Rainbow reached across and patted his leg.

'Were you waiting for her too?'

When he didn't answer, she sighed and wriggled herself backwards to rest against the monolith next to him. The stone warmed her back and she closed her eyes, thinking that life couldn't really be more perfect than this. A warm summer's evening at Stonewylde, the full moon overhead and Yul by her side with nobody to disturb them. But his next words smashed her fantasy.

'You've been at Stonewylde long enough, Rainbow – since the Equinox. It's the Solstice in two weeks' time and after that I want you to leave.'

'*What?* Why?'

'This was only ever meant to be a short visit for you to do some sketching. It's been three months now and that's enough. We can't have you thinking you live here.'

'But ... why not? Why can't I live here?'

'Because you don't belong here.'

'Why not? I have as much right to be here as you, or Sylvie, or anyone else. I spent large chunks of my childhood here and I love Stonewylde. I think that—'

'You don't have any right to be here. Folk here don't like you being around – you make them feel uncomfortable.'

'Do I make *you* feel uncomfortable, Yul?'

'No, of course not! Only in so far as you don't belong here and don't share our common ethos.'

'If I go quietly after the Solstice, will you allow me back again for another visit?'

He thought about this for a moment.

'To be honest, Rainbow – it's unlikely. Sylvie never wanted—'

'Sod what bloody Sylvie wanted! How can you be so damn *cruel*? I absolutely *love* Stonewylde and it's not fair that you can just send me away. I *do* belong here and I know that if I could stay, I'd become a great asset to the community. I'd bring in revenue, and—'

'We don't want Hallfolk money,' said Yul coldly, stretching out his legs ready to stand. Rainbow put her hand on his thigh and stroked it, feeling hard muscle through the thin material.

'Yul, you know how I feel. Please ... don't send me away. I'll do anything to stay, anything at all. I could make you very happy, and—'

He brushed her hand away and stood up quickly, ignoring the unbidden throb of desire.

'I already am happy, thank you very much, and nothing you could—'

'No, you're not!' she cried angrily. 'You're as miserable as sin and I know why! A man like you – a real, red-blooded man – needs a woman by his side. Your beloved wife has chosen to leave you and move out – how can you say you're happy? I don't think you know the meaning of the word any more. And—'

But he'd gone, striding off down the hill without a backward glance. The hares sitting upright in the long grass gazing at the moon slid down onto their bellies or scattered as he approached. Rainbow was left on her own on the hilltop in the silvery darkness.

In the moonlit cottage, Leveret sat in the rocking chair with Hare in her lap. Her eyes were shut and she stroked the soft fur, fondling Hare's velvet ears with a gentle touch. She felt at peace; earlier in the evening she'd put on her hare headdress and cast a spell of protection around the whole cottage. At the last minute she'd abandoned the formal ritual she'd memorised. Doing what felt right was often better than doing something by the book, and Leveret had decided to trust her own instinct tonight.

As the moon rose she'd been ready outside the cottage with Hare on the ground beside her. The creature's paw had mended cleanly, and, although she'd never run like others of her kind, she could lope about quite happily. Leveret had a shoulder bag full of lavender gathered earlier in the day and now, with Mother Heggy's athame in her hand pointing skywards, she shuffled slowly around the cottage in a widdershins direction strewing the herbs on the ground with the other hand. She called on the power and magic of the Bright Lady, the Triple Goddess as Mother, to protect the hallowed cottage. Hare lolloped along by her side until they'd completed a circle around the building.

'I ask you to protect this little house from all harm, to keep away those with ill intent, and to welcome all who come with an open heart!' Leveret said softly. 'I ask you to make it a place of healing and magic, for me as it was for Mother Heggy. I ask for her spirit to bless the place, and help me become as wise as she was.'

Hare sat down and raised her long ears. There was a flurry of wings and the crow landed on the roof. His one white feather glowed in the moonlight and his beady eye gleamed. He perched on the new thatch and began to *CAW* very loudly in the darkness.

'Five, always five!' came a rustling whisper, so Leveret continued to circle the building, bringing down the moon magic through the athame and her own body, casting a ring of protection and energy around the tiny cottage. She didn't stop until she'd made five circuits, and then the crow fluttered down from the roof and stood at the threshold looking in through the open door.

Leveret watched, holding her breath, hoping desperately that the bird would enter the cottage. But it let out another mighty

CAW and, with a clumsy flapping of wings, flew off into the silver night. Disappointed, Leveret went inside with Hare at her heels and poured herself a small measure of mead. She sat in the centre of the pentagram, the hare headdress still draped over her head, and drank the mead and ate a little cake, honouring the bounty of Stonewylde and the Earth Mother.

She tried hard to focus on Mother Heggy and call the spirit of the Wise Woman into the pentagram. She hoped for another vision, something that would offer guidance and advice. But nothing came and, after a while of sitting in the darkness, Leveret rose and moved across to the rocking chair. Now she sat here, gently rocking, with Hare in her lap.

Gradually her eyes drooped shut and her hand stilled. Girl and creature dozed whilst the Lady Moon climbed higher, peering into the silvery thatch and through the shadowy casements, brushing an outline of moonlight onto the tiny bent figure in battered hat and ancient boots who stood in the centre of the pentagram watching.

11

Leveret and Magpie, in their battered straw hats, were hard at work in the walled Kitchen Garden. Earlier in the year, Clip had negotiated with Thorn, the head gardener, and they'd agreed on a good-sized plot where Leveret could create a medicinal herb garden. Many of the plants, fungi and bark needed for natural remedies would be foraged from the hedgerows and woods, but some plants must be specially cultivated in larger quantities. Magpie had been assigned to work permanently in Leveret's garden as he'd proved himself worthy of the responsibility, and Marigold and Cherry were delighted at this acknowledgement of his progress.

The piece of ground that Leveret had been given was slightly tucked away from the busier parts of the enormous Kitchen Garden, in a warm and sheltered spot. Leveret had studied designs of old herb gardens and then planned hers carefully, using every available bit of the rich soil. Many plants were already flourishing thanks to the very warm weather, and Magpie now hoed away the weeds whilst Leveret harvested some bright orange heads of calendula into her wicker basket. In the shade of the high brick wall lay Hare, snoozing in the heat; she was never far from Leveret's side. Bees hummed busily, their bodies fuzzy with pollen, and butterflies danced in the bright sunshine. In the air hung the aroma of many scented plants – lavender and lemon balm, catmint and clary sage – layer upon layer of fragrance rising from the profusion of Leveret's medicinal plants.

By the brick arch leading into the walled Kitchen Garden, next to an espaliered peach tree, stood Rainbow, silently watching the pair at work. With their coarse work-clothes and battered straw hats, they could have been from another century. Leveret was chattering away to Magpie and Rainbow drew a couple of sketches, then took her tiny camera from her shoulder bag and quickly snapped the boy and girl as they worked. Magpie looked up and spotted her, and immediately Leveret's head shot up too. It was very strange, Rainbow thought; as if he'd warned her they were being watched, which of course was impossible.

Now that she'd been spied, Rainbow sauntered over to where they worked, ignoring the other gardeners and a couple of students on work detail. She wore a cornflower blue dress today and Stonewylde sandals and a pretty straw hat, finely made and decorated with ribbons and a flower.

'Hi!' she said. 'You two look so happy working here together. I wondered, Leveret – are you and Magpie going out? I mean walking together?'

Leveret shot her a withering look and shook her head. Then Rainbow noticed Hare and went over to stroke her, marvelling at the creature's huge amber eyes and finding her twitching nose adorable. This was the perfect introduction to the subject she wished to broach, although she was unsure whether to address Leveret alone or include Magpie as well.

'I've seen Magpie's beautiful painting of Sylvie up by Hill Stone at the last full moon,' she said. 'It's absolutely stunning.'

Leveret nodded, not wanting to encourage the woman to stay any longer than necessary. She'd ruined the peace and sense of purpose they'd been enjoying.

'When I leave Stonewylde to go back into the Outside World for a while, I wondered if I might take a few of Magpie's smaller paintings with me? I'd like to show them around, maybe hang a few in my next exhibition. Would that be alright?'

Leveret frowned, knowing it was certainly not alright.

'Magpie would hate his paintings to be taken away,' she said. 'So no, you can't.'

'That's a pity. He's so talented and I think he has a great future as an artist. I'd like to be the one to introduce him to the main players in the Outside World.'

'Magpie isn't interested in the Outside World.'

'But he deserves public recognition! He could be famous and—'

'Why? How would that make his life any better? Recognition here at Stonewylde, where people have mocked and abused him all his life – that would be good and he deserves that. But the Outside World ...'

Leveret made the dismissive flick sign and resumed her picking. Rainbow shrugged and bent to examine some huge opium poppy-heads. She pulled out her sketchbook and, with a few pencil strokes, the poppies were on her page forever, caught in perfect full bloom before time could ravage them. Magpie was watching her carefully, his turquoise eyes examining her face. She smiled at him and he smiled back.

'Magpie, I really love your painting of Sylvie in the moonlight with the hares. It's absolute magic.'

His grin widened and he nodded eagerly. Tentatively he reached out for her sketchbook, which she passed to him. He leafed through it slowly, pausing over some of her fanciful interpretations which seemed to interest him more than the technical reproductions.

'Would you like to see some of my work?' she asked, touching his arm. 'It's all in Merewen's studio down at the Pottery. Would you like to come down with me and have a look?'

He nodded, but Leveret intervened crossly.

'We're working!' she said. 'Stonewylders do have to work, you know, not just swan around all day.'

'In that case I'll arrange it through David, when Magpie's working at his art,' replied Rainbow smoothly. 'I won't take your boyfriend away from scratching around in the dirt with you, missy. We'll do it later, when he's engaged in more creative activities. See you later, Magpie!'

Leveret watched Rainbow's retreating back with a scowl. She disliked everything about the woman, from the golden down on her arms and legs to the calculated coquetry of her smile. She was so artful and false, and Leveret couldn't stand it.

'If you go down to the Village with her, Maggie, make sure David's with you. Be very, very careful of that woman, won't you?'

He nodded, and she sensed from him the image of a rainbow in the sky and dark clouds blowing in to obliterate it. That made her laugh and they resumed their work with renewed enthusiasm.

Later in the day with the calendula picked and ready to be infused, Leveret went up to Mother Heggy's cottage to begin work. She and Magpie had lugged up all the things that she'd need to make the cottage a working Wise Woman's place. There was ample firewood, a bucket for collecting water and a cauldron for boiling it, bottles, flasks and jugs, Leveret's pestle and mortar, chopping knives and mixing spoons, ladles and pipettes, paper, muslin and labels. They'd also brought up a few creature comforts, and the old hovel was now clean and bright, with colourful crochet-patch cushions and blankets on the settle, a small rag-rug on the stone floor and gleaming bottles on the dresser. A jar of flowers sat on the table and a small fire burned in the hearth.

Leveret had found the trickling spring hidden in the bracken and half filled the bucket. This spring-water was now in the cauldron over the fire, and, while waiting for it to boil, Leveret lined up the bottles and laid out all the tools she'd need to make a calendula tincture. She was making an ointment for general skin conditions too, but the tincture was for Clip. He never spoke of it, but she was sure he was suffering from some kind of digestive problem. Calendula was known to be effective for this and she hoped it would detoxify and cleanse his system, and maybe help his body to repair any internal damage. She also had a large basket of lavender flowers for distilling their essential oil; this was good for relieving stomach cramps and colic, and she'd seen poor Clip double up when he thought she wasn't looking. She'd tried to broach the subject and persuade him to visit Hazel but he simply denied any pain and laughed it off; too much fasting, too much food – anything but admit he had a problem. Leveret hoped that her remedies may help, and she poured out a measure of alcohol ready to add to the pile of brilliant orange petals.

Hare was the first to hear the intruder. She was lying on the flagstones by the doorway in a patch of sunlight but suddenly raised her head and lifted her great ears. Immediately Leveret felt defensive; few knew that she had staked her claim to Mother Heggy's cottage. She thought of the spell of protection she'd cast around the place and hoped it would be enough to repel people like Jay and her brothers. Her glance flicked around the tiny room – the old Book of Shadows was lying on the dresser, the athame was wrapped inside a cloth in a drawer, and the gathering knife was on the table.

Just as Leveret was thinking that she couldn't hide everything precious every time someone came to the door, she heard a familiar voice call her name and was flooded with relief. She had great faith in the ceremony she'd performed here at the last Moon Fullness, but how the spell would physically stop unwanted visitors she wasn't quite sure. Hare loped outside to inspect the visitor, and the doorway darkened as Sylvie stood on the threshold and peered inside.

'May I come in?'

'Come in and welcome!' said Leveret, and her sister-in-law came over to give her a quick hug. Their new-found closeness was still recent enough for this to feel slightly awkward, but both were anxious to strengthen the bond.

'I popped into the tower earlier and Clip said you were up here. Wow – what a transformation! Do you know, I haven't been here since ... oh. Oh dear, I wish I hadn't said that.'

'It was you and Yul who found her dead, wasn't it?' said Leveret gently. 'He told me about it once, long ago. He used to bring me up here when I was a little girl.'

Sylvie shook her head sadly, and sat down on the chair at the table. Hare came over and Sylvie picked her up. She crouched down in Sylvie's lap and laid her ears along her back while Sylvie stroked her velvet fur.

'Yes, we came up here at the Winter Solstice, still in our ceremony robes, to tell her that finally her prophecy had been fulfilled. Poor Yul – he was absolutely devastated when we found her. She was sitting rigid on the floor – oh, it was horrible, really upsetting. I loved Mother Heggy too.'

'I hadn't realised you'd known her that well,' said Leveret.

'I didn't really, but she took such an interest in me. She thought I was the girl she'd once adopted, Raven, because of my hair and my moongaziness. I'm not sure quite how much her mind wandered, but she was a truly wise old thing and she supported me and Yul long before anyone else did. In those days, any liaison between Hallfolk and Villagers was completely against the law.'

'I can't imagine how difficult it all must have been back then,' said Leveret.

'It was wonderful in some ways, of course, but very different. Mostly it was just unfair. Poor Yul – he suffered so much. I really must remember that. He had to fight so fiercely just to survive, let alone find happiness ... Maybe I'm being too hard on him now. It was that steeliness and strength that first attracted me. I shouldn't knock it now.'

'Yes, I suppose so,' agreed Leveret. 'But Sylvie, it's not just that. He really has changed. He used to be so kind, so loving – and now he's mean and cruel. I once loved Yul so much, but I don't now. He isn't the same person.'

'It's very sad,' said Sylvie. 'I honestly feel at times that it's Magus looking out through Yul's eyes. He's always been dominating but, as you say, he's almost become a different person.'

Leveret thought back to the journey where she'd seen Yul and Sylvie in the Stone Circle together as youngsters, so in love. Something had happened to blight their love and harmony, creating dislike and discord in its place. She recalled the words about taint, and wondered if there were something she could do to remove it and set everything to rights again. She sighed

– making calendula tincture and distilling lavender oil was challenging enough for now.

'I'm sorry I can't offer you anything other than spring water to drink,' she said.

Sylvie laughed and accepted a ladleful in a cold stone mug.

'If this drought continues,' she said, 'your private spring water could be in great demand. I don't know if you've heard, but in the Village the Bath House has been shut – no baths or showers at all. We're all washing with a bowl of water – and pouring the slops onto the fruit bushes and vegetables. And once a week we can wash our hair using a jug of water! The Laundry's really rationing water too and they're saying not to change clothes so often – make things last a few days if possible. Poor Celandine is quite beside herself. You know what a particular little thing she is.'

'Well, tell her it's no better at the Hall,' said Leveret. 'Bowls to wash in and we must keep the waste for the Kitchen Garden. Martin patrols the corridors apparently listening out for the sound of running water! Marigold bakes everything now rather than boiling it to save a bit of water. Next we'll be asked to lick our plates clean!'

'It can't go on forever though,' said Sylvie. 'It'll have to rain soon. The river's so low and an awful lot of the crops are just withering and dying. It's very sad.'

'How are you feeling?' asked Leveret, changing the subject. 'That Hypericum should be starting to work now, as it's been a few weeks, hasn't it?'

'Yes, I've been taking the tincture three times a day like you said, although I think I preferred the infusion. But I know the tincture's more powerful and actually, I do think it may be working. I feel stronger in myself now, not so panicky and tearful. And certainly I don't feel as depressed as I was. It may not be only the St John's Wort of course …'

'No, it may be a number of things, but I'm so glad you're feeling less depressed. I think you should continue to take it every day in case it is the remedy that's helping – it certainly won't do any harm. My next batch is almost ready and I'll add some honey to this lot to make it taste better.'

'Thank you, Leveret. I appreciate your care.'

'It's what I want to do,' said Leveret. 'I've been making quite a few things, and Hazel's started using some of my cough remedy for the old folk in the Hall, which is such an honour. Marigold has my calendula ointment in the kitchen for burns, and the witch hazel water for cuts. There's loads more I've started to make.'

'You're turning into a proper healer, aren't you?' said Sylvie, gazing around the tiny cottage. 'You've made it really cosy in here. I bet when Mother Heggy was a young woman, it looked just like this; all bright and welcoming. I even saw a crow sitting on the roof as I came up!'

'You mean the one with a white tail feather?'

'Yes, most unusual. He watched me coming up the path.'

'He seems to have adopted me, which is wonderful.'

'Very unusual to have that white feather ...' Sylvie glanced around. 'Raven grew up in this cottage too – I wonder where she slept?'

'Mother Heggy slept on the settle and Raven had a cot by her side. When she grew too big for that, she had a pallet on the floor.'

Sylvie looked at her in surprise.

'Really? How on earth do you know that?'

'I just know it – I'm not sure how. Just as I know that things will work out between you and Yul.'

'Will they? Are you sure? Oh, Leveret, that's what I want more than anything in the world! What's going to happen?'

Leveret frowned. She'd had dreams and seen things in her head, but was never quite sure what was simply her imagination and what was a shamanic vision.

'I've seen a fiery phoenix,' she said slowly. 'A phoenix rising from its own ashes. That makes sense, I guess. And ... a dry, dark place – I think it's the yew on the Village Green.'

Sylvie nodded excitedly.

'That's our special place!' she said. 'What else?'

But Leveret could say no more. How could she tell Sylvie of the very strange sight she'd seen with her inner eye: a tiny toad crawling out of a small bag to sit on the grass at Hare Stone, his golden eyes staring out unblinking? What on earth was the significance of that?

The Summer Solstice sunrise ceremony was over and people were trooping back to the Hall or the Village. As it was still so early, many slipped back to bed for an hour, for a long and busy day lay ahead. Others went off for breakfast, but Yul stood behind the Altar Stone as the glittering sun rose higher and higher in the bright blue sky. Another glorious day, although for once everyone wished it had been cloudy and pouring with rain. Sylvie was helping to clear up the remains of the cakes, beautiful in her gold Solstice robes, and Yul stood watching her. He wore the huge robe that Magus had always worn, with the high collar framing his face and hundreds of embroidered golden suns glinting in the sunlight. His dark face was closed, his deep grey eyes narrowed as he watched his wife gracefully clearing the Altar Stone.

As he watched her, his mouth bitter, he felt a huge throb of desire for her. How long was it since they'd made love? And how long since they'd made love properly, with their old abandonment and passion? Today was her birthday and with it the anniversary of their magical union under the yew tree. He almost groaned at the thought of it. Why had she left him? Yul hadn't accepted their separation in any way; they belonged together and this was all so wrong.

Earlier this morning he'd flown into a rage as he prepared for the sunrise ceremony. It upset him that he must get ready in the Hall, in that great bedroom, all on his own. He and Sylvie had always helped each other dress for the ceremonies, and some of the robes and headdresses were difficult to manage alone. It had been depressing and lonely waking up yet again in the enormous bed without her there, washing without her flitting in and out of the bathroom. Even pulling on the heavy robes that Cherry had laid out for him the night before without Sylvie there felt wrong. They should have been laughing together and reminiscing about previous festivals. The Summer Solstice was always especially poignant – why wasn't she with him, by his side?

Today, Yul vowed to himself, would be the day that he and Sylvie were reunited. This ridiculous estrangement had gone on for too long – since the Equinox in fact. He missed her and the children dreadfully, and he missed their intimacy too. He was a man in his prime; it was torture to have his desirable wife always so close at hand, reminding him of all he was going without. The whole situation was wrong and today it would be put right. Tonight was the Dark Moon and Yul made a solemn promise that by tonight, he'd have his gorgeous wife back in his arms, where she belonged.

The Green Magic had come to him a little today, snaking around the arena until, at the moment of sunrise when the Herald lit the spark to set the fire alight, it had shot up through the Altar Stone into his waiting body. He'd felt his hands tingle and his hair stir slightly – it was an improvement on last time, and at this rate it may even be near normal by Lammas, especially if he and Sylvie were reconciled. She straightened up and turned around, her silver hair flowing down like a heavy veil from beneath the golden headdress, her body so tall and elegant in the shimmering robes. He longed to grab her, to twist her hair around his wrist and kiss her, very hard and very long, over the Altar Stone. But ... that sort of behaviour had got him into trouble and now he must tread so carefully and act so correctly. He scowled and turned away, missing the way her eyes had softened and her lips had parted as she'd looked at him, also feeling echoes of that glorious Summer Solstice so many years before.

Down on the Village Green, the celebrations were in full flow. Everyone wore their straw sunhats in the blazing sun, and many sat under the trees around the Green in the shade. Inside the

Great Barn every door was wide open in an attempt to catch a draught. It was cooler in here than outside and Starling was enjoying herself. Life in the cottage had become difficult lately and it was good to get away from the old ones. Even Starling now found the stink in the stifling cottage unpleasant; the two crones were superstitious about open windows and doors and, as the hot weather continued, the stench increased. Vetchling's cough was worse than ever and kept them all awake at night, and she complained constantly about the heavy pipe smoke in the air. Violet could no longer stand up straight and was finding it difficult to hold even a spoon or mug in her twisted hands, let alone make it to the privy at the end of the garden. She moaned bitterly about her aches and pains and was becoming more help-less with each passing day. So Starling now had to bear the brunt of running the place and caring for them both, and with Jay visiting less and less, her life was no longer easy.

Starling waddled around the Barn, dark compared to the bleached-out brightness visible through the massive doors that stood open, looking for any left-overs. Lunch had finished a while ago and, although most of the dishes had been cleared away, some remained on the trestle tables. Due to the extreme heat, the food had been served in here rather than outside, though many had taken their laden plates and sat under the shady trees. Starling had eaten well at lunchtime but the lure of left-over pas-tries and sausages was too strong. She knew she should put some in a bag to take home to the two old ones. They'd be rocking by the dead fireplace, grey and grumbling in their discomfort, with the foul odour of dirty plates, rotting scraps and incontinence all around them. Starling really couldn't face them, so instead of stuffing food in her bag, she stuffed it into her mouth.

She let out a bellow of indignation like a startled heifer when someone came up from behind and gave her a resounding whack on the rump. The flesh wobbled and undulated, sending shock waves all around her body. She turned, her greasy hair flicking into the plate of sausage rolls, to find an enormous gingery man standing behind her with a grin on his face. It was Cledwyn, younger brother of the late Alwyn, and Starling leered at him in delight.

'Cheeky bugger!' she said through a mouthful of meat and pastry.

'You got an arse and a half there, girl!' he exclaimed, rubbing his tingling hand. 'A man could drown in that there slurry o' fat.'

'Oi! That ain't very nice,' she said. 'I could say the same about you, Cledwyn! I seen less meat on a prize bull!'

'That's not all you seen less of on a prize bull, my maid,' he replied with an obscene gesture, and they both roared with laughter.

He sidled up even closer and laid his hand on the giant shelf of her bottom. He smelt high but then so did many people in this heatwave with the restrictions on washing and laundry, and Starling wasn't so sweet herself. She rubbed herself against his bulk, delighted at this unexpected attention from a man she'd long admired. Cledwyn shared his deceased brother's looks and colouring, right down to the ginger bristles on his fat fingers. He had a ruddy face and the same pugnacious under-bite, and Starling wiped her greasy fingers in the folds of her dress and gave him her full attention.

'Don't you let your goodwife see you getting up to tricks with me,' she said. 'I had a run-in with her once and she's never liked me since, miserable old cow.'

'Aye, you're right there, m'dear,' he muttered, running his hand over the never-ending expanse of her backside, as a farmer might examine potential stock. 'She is a miserable old cow and I'm well done with her. She ain't my goodwife no more.'

'What?' Starling almost screeched. 'I never heard! Nobody in this bloody Village tells me nothing!'

'We was hand-loosed a good six-month ago,' he said. 'She kicked me out and now she's with that old goat Woodruff, in my cottage and all! Most o' the brats are gone up the Hall now, only two left at home, but she got to stay in the cottage because of it and I'm back with my old ma.'

'Never!' exclaimed Starling. 'Why hadn't I heard? So you're a free man?'

'I am that, my little birdie,' he chuckled, ignoring the sausage-grease that glistened on her chins. 'So if you fancy a trot round the Green, and maybe a wander into the woods ...'

At this, Starling abandoned all thoughts of more food and favoured him with an alluring look that promised much. She smoothed down her stained and crumpled dress and gave a little provocative wriggle.

'Can't think of nothing I'd like better,' she said. Her heart thumped with pleasure at her good fortune. 'I'll just use the privy and then I'm all yours.'

12

Sylvie sat under the shade of a great horse-chestnut tree on the Village Green sharing a rug with Maizie, her daughters, her mother and Rufus. They'd enjoyed the picnic, bringing plates of food and drink out from the Barn, and were now relaxing in the drowsy afternoon heat. Although the usual Summer Solstice games were scheduled, nobody had much enthusiasm for them this year as it was so very hot. The tug-of-war over the river had been a waste of time as there was now only a trickle of water down the middle, and the mud banks had baked solid, fissured with great cracks. Instead, most of the young people had gone down to the beach to swim in the sea, leaving those still on the Green and under the shady riverbank willows in peace and quiet.

Nearby, on their own picnic rugs, were other members of Maizie's family: Rosie and Robin with their children, and Geoffrey and Gregory with their wives and babies. Sylvie was thoroughly enjoying herself and feeling, for the first time, like a true Villager amongst her family. Celandine and Bluebell played with other children, including their cousins Snowdrop and Edrun, Rosie's pair, and Rufus was good-naturedly giving piggy backs and lifting children up into the trees to perch in the branches. He too was having a lovely time as a Villager; like Sylvie he'd always lived at the Hall and had missed out on this experience. His and Miranda's deep red hair shone out amongst the other heads, but for once he didn't feel like an Outsider.

Miranda was relaxed too, lying on the rug with her eyes shut, listening to the happy sounds all around her and unwinding after the mad bout of exams. There were still a few to go, but mostly the students had finished and she could now have a break from the relentless duty of being headteacher at Stonewylde.

Sylvie looked lovely in her dress saved specially for this occasion – one that she'd made by herself almost from start to finish. With Maizie's guidance, she'd woven the thread into fine linen and then prepared dye from sorrel, which had coloured the cloth the softest of pink. She'd cut out the dress from the length of material and had sewn it herself in a simple sleeveless Village style, then attempted a little embroidery around the neck. The result was a pretty dress that perfectly complemented her silver hair and fair skin, bringing out her natural delicate colouring and showing off her slimness to best advantage. She was extremely proud to have made it herself, though aware that most women in the Village did this all the time for themselves and every member of their family. She'd decided to make similar dresses for the girls next, and then maybe she'd make something special for Leveret.

Sylvie wondered where Leveret was today; surely not down at the noisy beach with all the other teenagers. She'd find this difficult of course, not sitting with her mother and family, so Sylvie thought she was probably out somewhere with Clip, who was also nowhere to be seen. He'd never enjoyed the heat and was perhaps up in the Dolmen, always cool and dark, or else in his tower. Sylvie was just speculating where Yul could be when he appeared down by the Jack in the Green, emerging from the low-ceilinged pub with a group of young men. She hoped he wasn't the worse for cider; they'd barely spoken yet today, although after the sunrise ceremony he'd wished her a happy birthday and said he'd join her later. She knew he tried to mix with everyone at the festivals, and, given all the recent difficulties, it was more important than ever for him to do so.

He stood in the bright sunlight and was clearly trying to get his bearings, gazing around at the crowds of families all tucked under the trees. The browning grass of the Green was almost deserted save for a few green woodpeckers searching for ants. Sylvie had been really looking forward to spending the day with him after his promise earlier in the Stone Circle. She'd been thinking lately that she must try to make more allowances for his need to be in control. It was only in reaction to his terrible upbringing and all that he'd gone through to reach manhood; recently she'd forgotten why he'd had to develop those hard and dominating qualities. She knew there was a wonderful, loving and gentle side to Yul as well, and it was up to her to bring this to the fore and help him to get the balance right.

But now she found herself hoping he wouldn't join them after all. He seemed to be swaying slightly and she didn't want him spoiling this lovely family occasion with drunkenness. He'd either be belligerent or maudlin, and both were unappealing. Just as she was wondering how best to avoid him, Dawn and David approached. They wore the newly-wed aura of bliss, strolling hand in hand across the grass. David had long abandoned Outside clothes and he and Dawn made a lovely Stonewylde couple in their plain outfits and straw hats. They greeted many people as they passed; Dawn was a key figure in the community because of the Village School, and David had been accepted now that he was properly handfasted and had moved into her cottage next to the school.

'Bright Solstice blessings, everyone!' Dawn said to Sylvie's group. Everyone smiled up in greeting and Maizie invited the couple to join them on the large rug. Dawn shook her head and explained.

'Actually, we came to invite you all up to the Hall for a surprise. Some of the folk have prepared Sylvie a special birthday tea-party, and there's something else for her. Something she'll love.'

Sylvie flushed at this, a little embarrassed.

'That's very kind! But why? We don't normally celebrate birthdays much, and it's not my thirtieth till next year.'

But Dawn and David only smiled enigmatically and said that

this was something unplanned, but important nevertheless. So the group gathered themselves up to begin a slow walk to the Hall. Geoffrey, Gregory and their families declined as it was a trek with the babies in the heat, but Rosie and Robin were persuaded to come, and walked together whilst Rufus went on ahead with the four children. Celandine and Bluebell adored him and had recently grown really close to him. They treated him like the big brother they'd always wanted, although he was really their uncle on both sides. Snowdrop and Edrun barely knew Rufus, but had taken to him straight away and he was now quite the centre of attention. Maizie and Miranda walked either side of Sylvie, and David and Dawn brought up the rear.

They crossed the Village Green and the children ran straight over to Yul, who was still on the cobbles outside the pub with another tankard of cider in his hand. His daughters flung themselves at him and he tried to hug them and balance his drink too, spilling some of it and cursing. He looked up to see Rufus staring at him with those dark, velvet-black eyes and was shocked to see how tall the boy had grown.

'Father, will you come up with us?' asked Bluebell. 'Please?'

'Come up where? Are you off to the beach?'

'No, we're going to the Hall for a special birthday tea for Mummy and a surprise,' said Celandine.

By now the rest of the group had caught up and all stood a little awkwardly outside the Jack in the Green. Sylvie smiled tentatively at Yul, feeling slightly embarrassed on his behalf – he should really be part of the group. He saw her standing there with that half-hearted smile on her face and his family all around her, and felt the anger fizz in his chest. When Bluebell let go of him and clutched onto Rufus instead, begging for a piggy back, something snapped.

'I haven't been invited,' he said coldly. 'It seems it's all been planned and nobody bothered to tell me. So, no thanks, I don't think so.'

'Oh Yul, don't be so silly!' said Maizie. 'We none of us knew about it!'

'Do come, Yul. We're all intrigued by the surprise and it would be lovely to have you with us,' said Miranda tactfully.

Yul glanced at Sylvie, wearing a new dress, and with a daisy chain in her hair that the children had made her. He suddenly felt completely superfluous to her life, certain that they'd never be reconciled. Why should she need him? She had the children, she had all his family and hers, and the support and approbation of the Council of Elders. She had everything. If he were dead she'd manage fine without him. In fact, Stonewylde would manage fine without him. His face darkened and he turned away from the group, almost in tears.

'No thanks,' he muttered. 'I'd rather stay here.'

Marigold and Cherry fussed around in the kitchen preparing the birthday tea. With Magpie and Clip's help, they'd put up trestle tables in the large courtyard outside the kitchen, which by this time of day was in shadow. The tables had been laid with snowy white cloths and jars of white moon-daisies and pink rose-buds, and the two women now stood back to admire their handiwork.

'There, 'tis done. And so pretty too,' said Cherry, sweating in the heat.

'Aye, and no more than she deserves. Goddess knows why she feels she must live down in the Village away from the Hall, but things must be bad if she has to do that, the poor maid,' agreed Marigold.

Both women had a soft spot for Sylvie, and, once Leveret had suggested the idea of a little birthday tea before presenting Sylvie with Magpie's painting, they'd jumped at the chance to make a fuss of her. As these things do, it had grown from a simple tea with a bit of cake into this rather grand event.

Martin looked out sourly from his upstairs window overlooking the courtyard, his face grim. He knew what was happening – the women had made no secret of it – and heartily disapproved. His wife Mallow, a meek and almost invisible creature, tried to draw him away from the window but to no avail. He stood with his arms folded and uttered a continuous stream of invective and criticism. Mallow wished that Swift were there to distract Martin, but of course the boy was off having fun with his friends and wouldn't be back for a long time, if he bothered to visit at all.

Martin watched the two plump women bustling about setting out the plates and cups. Magpie and Leveret appeared and his tirade increased. That stupid, half-witted mute – who did he think he was, dressed up in his finery capering about like a fool? Martin's wife cringed in the corner, wishing he'd say she could go back downstairs now. She'd been summoned upstairs to look at what was happening outside their window, and she hoped desperately that she wouldn't, as happened so often, bear the brunt of his cruel ill-temper. Then Hazel arrived at the party, and the torrent of abuse continued, directed now against jumped-up doctors who thought they ran the place and forced old folk out of their homes. The final straw was Clip's arrival, as he planted a kiss on the rosy cheeks of both Marigold and Cherry. Martin's wife closed her eyes in despair, for nobody riled Martin more than Clip. Her husband had turned an alarming shade of red and his hands shook with rage.

There was a flurry of activity and then suddenly the court-yard was teeming with people. Martin watched as Sylvie put her hands to her face and opened her mouth wide in surprise at the lovely table laid out for her. He saw the children, excited at this exclusive party which was almost unprecedented at Stonewylde. He watched Rufus, awkward and standing close to his mother. He saw Magpie hopping around, not sure where he should sit or how he should behave. And he saw Maizie and Leveret carefully nod to each other and then find seats at opposite ends of the table as if that were perfectly natural. Rosie of course stuck close to her mother and glared at Leveret, which made Martin smile. Not all quite so "rosy" then, he thought malevolently.

But what really pleased him was the fact that Yul wasn't present. There was no sign of him, and, as Marigold and Cherry added extra plates and cups, having been unsure how many would turn up, he noticed that there wasn't a place laid for Yul. Good – that meant they were still apart and, with any luck, would stay that way.

The food was brought out by the two kitchen women – he always thought of the sisters in those terms – helped by Leveret. So much food! What a waste of Stonewylde's resources. What was wrong with the good food served down in the Great Barn? Finally they were all seated, so many of them, and Martin felt the angry thumping of his heart begin to calm a little. He'd watched long enough and now with a twisted smile, he turned to his white-faced wife.

Yul stomped up the track leading to the Hall, a bitter after-taste of cider in his mouth and desperate for a drink of cool water. He felt hot and sticky, and longed for a shower, which was out of the question at the moment, even for the magus. He thought about going down to the beach for a quick swim and was very tempted, but he'd made the decision to attend Sylvie's party and knew it was the right thing to do.

His white linen shirt clung to his chest and back, the waist-band of his trousers was wet with sweat and his long damp curls stuck to his face. The track to the Hall was empty, as most folk were either down in the Village or on the beach, and certainly not walking any distance in the very hot afternoon. The sun beat down mercilessly and Yul found himself hurrying towards each patch of shade along the track. He thought, in a slightly befuddled way, about this party for Sylvie and why the very mention of it had upset him so much. He was honest enough to admit he was jealous; everyone loved Sylvie and made such a fuss of her, but they'd never have done this for him. He was also jealous that they were all in on it together and had left him out. He wished he'd thought of a lovely surprise for her, something to make her want him back again. He recalled his vow at sunrise this morning – if he didn't do something drastic, she'd never be in his arms by nightfall.

He then saw a sight coming towards him that made his heart

sink. Rainbow looked cool and fresh in a thin dress and straw hat, her hair twisted up out of sight.

'Why Yul!' she exclaimed. 'Whatever are you doing here?'

'I'm going to have a birthday tea with my wife,' he said irritably. 'And I can't stop because I'm late.'

'You're looking incredibly hot and bothered,' Rainbow laughed. 'Though still a sight for sore eyes, I must say. There's something about a curly-haired man in a damp shirt ...'

'Stop it, Rainbow,' he said. 'This stupid teasing and flirting will be your downfall one day – nobody'll ever take you seriously.'

'Oh, I don't know – it's served me quite well up till now. So, why a birthday party for Sylvie? That's not very Stonewylde, is it? Oh! Of course – it's the painting!'

'What? What painting?'

'It's a surprise,' she said. 'So don't tell her.'

'How come *you* know? Bloody hell, it seems everyone's in on this except me!'

'Oh, stop being so cross and grumpy. Why not come with me for a quick swim before the party? I've just been back to collect my swimming things and I'm heading for the beach now.'

'I can't,' he said, wishing that he could. 'I'm late already.'

'Come down later then,' she said, her blue eyes sweeping his face and lingering on his lips. 'You know how good that cool water will feel on your hot, sweaty skin. I'm planning on staying the evening there and forgetting about the Barn and all that dancing. It's much too hot for that. See – I have a picnic here.'

She showed him her basket and he noticed the bottle of water. His throat was parched and although he was reluctant to ask any favours, he couldn't stop himself. She laughed huskily and handed it to him, watching his throat as he gulped and gulped, drips of water running down onto his chest.

'Sorry!' he gasped. 'I've almost drunk it all.'

'Never mind, I'll fill up at the Village,' she said. 'Though you owe me now, Yul. Seriously – I'm leaving soon, as you told me I must. It would be great to have a swim and a proper chat with you before I go. If you can get away at all, come and join me. Tonight's the perfect time with everyone else busy in the Village.'

The tea was over and Leveret was jittery with anticipation. It had been David's idea to present Magpie's beautiful moondance picture to Sylvie, and, as soon as he'd suggested it, she'd known he was right. She'd talked about it to Magpie and once he'd fully understood, he was very excited too. He'd never in his life given anyone a gift – he'd never had anything to give – and the whole concept of it was thrilling. Marigold and Cherry were simply bursting with pride, and Dawn was dying to see Sylvie's reaction to the stunning painting that currently took up almost half the wall in the Art Room where it was propped. They hadn't been sure where to hang it, with Sylvie living down in the Village at the moment, so they'd decided to let her make that choice. The painting would never fit in Maizie's cottage even if Sylvie did want it there.

Marigold began to stack the tea plates but David stood up at the long table and asked for silence, so she sat down again. The courtyard was lovely in the shade, and there was a slight breeze blowing through. Everyone had enjoyed the delicious tea and Sylvie was happy. Clip smiled at her with love in his eyes, and she looked across and caught Miranda's eye too, seeing the same expression there. It was a poignant moment for her – both her parents together – and she felt a lump in her throat. Leveret was beaming at her, a true sister at last. Her beloved daughters now stood one on each side of her, holding her hands and as curious and excited as she was. Rufus grinned, happy to see the sister he'd finally got to know better looking so radiant, and Maizie felt proud that she'd helped Sylvie get back on her feet again. This woman sitting at the head of the table was a different one from the poor bedraggled creature at the Equinox, who'd begged to be allowed to move in. Sylvie looked around the table as David waited for silence, and she realised just how lucky she was to have all these people here who loved her. If only Yul had come . . .

'I'm not one for long speeches,' said David, 'and it's not really my place to do this. But as Magpie can't speak and Leveret says she's too shy, it's down to me, I'm afraid.'

Everyone nodded at this and looked at Magpie and Leveret, sitting next to each other grinning so joyfully. Maizie suddenly had a dreadful notion that David was going to announce they were to be handfasted or something – though they were too young of course. Why were they looking so excited? Maizie hadn't seen Leveret properly for a while now – only brief glimpses in the distance – and was amazed at how much the girl had changed. She'd lost her haunted, hunted look and had filled out a bit; she looked happy and Maizie was shocked to realise she'd never actually seen Leveret look truly happy since she was a small child.

'We all know that Magpie has led a difficult life, but thanks to certain people at this table – and most especially Leveret and Marigold – his life is now filled with happiness. He still can't speak, but he's learning to read and write, which will open up his world completely. That's all thanks to Leveret's hard work. Dawn says she's a natural teacher and is amazed at what she's achieved with our Magpie.'

He raised his glass to Leveret and everyone joined him. She sat blushing with pride as David continued.

'When Magpie's transformation began, I noticed his extraordinary talent in the Art Room. Over the months since the Winter Solstice – and unbelievably it is only six months since he came to live with Marigold and Cherry – he's become a different young man. His talent has not only blossomed, it's positively flourished. Magpie is an extremely gifted artist. I've never before seen the like, and I've seen a lot of artists in my time.'

Magpie sat beaming at this, his ears pink. Leveret was blinking back tears – all those years of protecting him, striving to get justice for him, fighting his battles and desperately trying to keep him safe – and now this. Her eyes brimmed and she glanced up to find her mother staring at her intently. Maizie's look said everything and no words would now be needed on the subject, no apology or justification. In that one look Maizie acknowledged her own huge share of the blame for poor Magpie's continued and unnecessary suffering, and also acknowledged that Leveret had been right all along. The look lingered between mother and daughter and then Leveret gave her a tiny smile. Maizie knew she'd been forgiven and her own eyes filled with tears. She lowered her head, searching for a handkerchief in her pocket.

'Sylvie,' continued David, 'Magpie has created something very special which he'd like to give to you for your birthday. He can't tell you what he felt at the Hare Moon when you allowed him to accompany you, your children and Leveret to the stone on the hill to watch you dance. He can never thank you in words for the profoundly moving experience. But he can paint his thanks and his awe. He can show you just how moved and overwhelmed he was that night. He's painted you something so beautiful that words can't do it justice ... So now I'll shut up, and we can all go across to the Art Room to see Magpie's gift that's awaiting you.'

Everyone clapped at this splendid speech and pushed back their chairs. David gestured for Magpie to lead the way, and Leveret found she could no longer hold back her tears. She stood to one side as Magpie proudly led Sylvie, flanked by her daughters, towards the Art Room, followed by everyone else. Leveret felt two plump, familiar arms enfold her and then her face was against her mother's bosom and both were crying their eyes out.

By the time Yul arrived at the Hall, there was nobody in sight. He looked in the Dining Hall and even raced up to his apartments, but the birthday party was nowhere to be found. He went back to the kitchen again and then realised it had taken place outside in the courtyard, but was now over. He gazed at the long table, still pretty with the daisies and roses, and the remains of the birthday tea. He took a used glass, poured himself some elderflower cordial from the jug, and picked up a left-over slice of cake. So now where were they all?

There was a sharp rapping on a window and he looked along to the row of house-staff's cottages. He saw Martin in the window gesticulating at him, and then a minute later, the man appeared in his doorway.

'The party's over!' he cried. 'They didn't wait for you, Master Yul!'

'So I see,' said Yul. 'Do you know where they've all gone?'

Martin's thin face grimaced and he waved his hand dismissively at the Hall in general.

'They've gone to look at some painting in the Art Room. 'Tis meant to be done by that half-wit Magpie, but I reckon 'tis the Outsider's handiwork myself. I can't see my slut-cousin Starling's bastard brat being able to paint something of any merit.'

Yul had no idea what Martin was on about, but headed towards the School Wing. Before he got there he heard their voices – so many of them. They were all crammed into the room, standing in a small area so they could get a proper look. He noted all the people present, including Clip and Hazel, and felt a jab of bitterness. It seemed everyone close to Sylvie had come to the party except him – even Rosie's children. Why wasn't he in on this? Why had nobody thought to invite him?

Then he noticed Leveret and his mother standing close together, Maizie with her arm around the girl, and this made him really mad. What about the Imbolc fiasco? Maizie had vowed to wash her hands of Leveret, and only Clip's intervention had saved his sister from the fate he'd planned for her: boarding school in the Outside World. Yet now here they were cosied up again as if none of that mattered.

He located Sylvie at the front of the crowd but her face was turned away from him. Everyone was staring at something that he couldn't see. He pushed his way into the stuffy, packed room and reached the front of the group, right next to Sylvie. His girls looked up and saw him and Bluebell clutched his leg in delight. But he couldn't drag his eyes from the great canvas that dominated the room. It stood on the floor leaning up against the wall as it was too big to be hung in here. The breath caught in his throat at the sheer magic of it – this was his moongazy girl, this was the one he'd fallen in love with all those years ago and had suffered so much for, to save her from Magus and to win her for himself. This was the sight he'd craved – Sylvie as a moon angel, dancing around Hare Stone with her creatures.

All this hit him right in the chest, as if someone had punched him very hard. This was their beautiful, intimate scene of pure magic at Hare Stone and it had been his special privilege to be both witness to it and part of it. Yet here was a room full of people gawping and commenting, violating his and Sylvie's privacy, their magical and very personal time alone, their wonderful secret. He felt as if Sylvie had betrayed him, cuckolded him, by allowing everyone to see her moondancing. He'd believed this to be for his eyes alone, but no longer. This was just the start, this private viewing; soon every single person at Stonewylde would be able to look at the painting and share the mystical experience.

And even more – there was his darling Celandine dancing too, like a tiny replica of her mother, leaping with the hares, the silver moonbeams brushing her hair and the star-fire in her eyes. So she too was moongazy? And this boy Magpie – he'd been up there that night with Yul's family watching and memorising it all, whilst Yul himself had been down in the Village worrying about where Sylvie was, thinking maybe she'd gone off with one of the Outsiders from the handfasting.

Without a word he turned on his heel and left the room, his heart aching. He heard Rosie call after him and then his mother, but he didn't stop. He strode to the stables and grabbed his saddle, and within ten minutes was cantering out of the stable yard towards Dragon's Back.

The sun set over the hills to the west, burning like a huge golden wheel as it sank lower and lower, unwilling to admit defeat and submit to darkness. Yul was miles away from the Hall, near the western edge of Stonewylde. He should be up in the Stone Circle now, leading the sunset ceremony, but found that he no longer

186

cared. Somebody else would've done it – perhaps Clip, or maybe even Martin. It really didn't matter. He received the earth energy as the sun blazed into fiery oblivion behind the horizon. He felt the serpent energy beneath his feet as he stood, staring at the hills, poor Skydancer's reins loosely held as the exhausted horse drooped beside him. He smiled bitterly as the Green Magic flickered into him – too late now to share with the folk. Too late and, as ever, too little.

He recalled his vow at sunrise this morning to have his wife in his arms by nightfall, and for a minute it felt as if someone had stabbed him through the heart. He tried not to relive the acute sense of betrayal that had sliced through him in the Art Room. He tried not to think of Sylvie at all; it was simply too painful. Ever since his first glimpse of her in the woods that Spring Equinox when she'd come to Stonewylde – ever since that moment, all he'd wanted in his life was her. She was his entire reason for being and yet now, somehow, he'd lost her. He couldn't bear it.

The sun had gone and yet the sky was light on this, the longest day of the year. And tonight was the Dark Moon. The Dark Moon at the Summer Solstice – the opposite of that night when he'd seen his father die. That had been the Moon Fullness at the Winter Solstice – the brightness in the darkness. Tonight it was the darkness in the brightness and he felt that tremor of old, that feeling of power deep within which always came to him at the Dark Moon. He felt very old, very strong, and beyond any normal, everyday consideration.

Yul swung back in the saddle, his thighs protesting at yet more punishment. Skydancer needed a drink and a rubdown but, for once, Yul simply didn't care. He rode back the way he'd come, though not at the same breakneck pace for the horse was spent; along the great ridge of land, the spine of the Goddess in the Landscape, the Dragon's Back ridgeway. The light faded a little more from the pure blue sky, leaving an orange ribbon along the south western horizon where the sun had set on this, its furthest point south. No moon rose tonight. Yul's fury pounded in his veins as he galloped back to where he knew he must go, the place where he must be tonight.

He rode straight down towards the Village and from a long way off, heard the merriment and music. Tiny lanterns were strung out in the trees around the Green, and people were outside, dancing and laughing, eating and drinking. Where was Sylvie? Was she out on the grass, dancing with bare feet and flying hair? He skirted behind the Barn by the dried-up river, along the bank where the willows hung their heads in sorrow. He crossed the bridge, the one where he'd sat with Sylvie all those years before when his soul cried out, so alone in the darkness. Skydancer's hooves clattered on the bridge and then he was on the other side, trotting down the path, heading for the place that called to him whilst this darkness was in him and the anger so deep and strong.

Past the reeds, past the spot where fresh water normally met sea water, though now the fresh water was exhausted and had been overwhelmed. Onto the sand where the spiky grass grew in tufts and the pebbles began. He forced Skydancer onto the shingle, knowing the horse didn't like the beach. The breeze coming off the sea, salty and warm, stirred his stiff curls and dried the latest sweat that saturated his shirt and sheened his body. He reined in the stallion and sat for a moment, sniffing the air appreciatively. The sound of the waves breaking gently on the shore was soothing, calming. The thumping in his veins eased a little and he took a deep breath.

The beach seemed deserted. The sun had finally moved far enough away to claim the golden ribbon on the horizon, yet the sky was still blue and full of light. White pebbles gleamed in the strange midsummer night's twilight; the water was a shimmering mass with tiny curling peaks where the waves broke softly on the shore. Then he saw her further down the beach, waiting as he knew she'd be. She'd known he would come to her tonight, at the darkness in the brightness, at the Dark Moon. She'd known that this night – this one time – he'd be unable to resist her lure.

Slowly he urged Skydancer along the shingle and onto the sand, where the water lapped at the reluctant stallion's hooves. At last they reached the woman reclining on the shore amongst the pebbles and the shells. Her hair was loose and wild over her bare breasts, her legs were wrapped in a sarong. Yul stopped and looked down at her. He felt a massive, overwhelming surge of desire like nothing he'd ever experienced before. This was not tempered with love or adoration or tenderness, nor even with normal lust. This was pure animal instinct and it obliterated everything in its path. He dismounted, his legs trembling and the shirt still sticking to him.

Dropping the reins and letting the horse free – he wouldn't go far – Yul ripped the limp white linen from his torso then removed everything else. She stood up and the shimmering sarong fell to the stones. Naked, she stepped into the waves. Her wild hair fell about her shoulders and curled at her waist, and she looked back at him enticingly. He watched her plunge sleekly into the gleaming water. As she swam, lithe as a fish, a trail of phosphorous glowed behind her like a bright tail. He waded into the sea to follow, ensnared by the promise.

When he reached the rock, gasping for breath, she was already lying on it, recumbent and glistening. The strange twilight danced off the water droplets that shimmered like silver scales on her skin. Her body was perfect, curvy and smooth, and her hair hung over her breasts like long strands of floating seaweed. Her eyes and teeth glinted slightly as she moved her head. He hauled himself out of the water to sit beside her. She laughed softly, a soothing sound like the whisper and murmur of the sea, and shook back the long tails of hair to reveal all her beautiful curves and inviting hollows.

He stared down at her in stupefied wonder. In a fluid movement she sank back onto the hard rock and lay supine, gazing up at him. She raised a languid arm and he felt her cool touch trail down his chest. He shuddered and she opened her arms to him. With a groan of despair he fell upon her gleaming smoothness, drowning in the depths of her welcome. She wrapped herself around him in a salty-wet embrace and dug her fingernails of shell into his back. As the rhythm of the waves licked and lapped against the great rock, Yul plunged deeply, irrevocably, into her world of betrayal.

13

The children of Stonewylde were seated in tiers on battered old benching, and their fidgeting and chattering became noisier and noisier as anticipation grew. Finally the enormous doors of the Great Barn were closed to the bright and sunny afternoon, and it became dark and quiet inside. Everyone hushed as a slow, deep drumbeat reverberated through the cavernous building. Then came the sound of panpipes, haunting and wild, weaving through the air. A spotlight onto the circular stage made a pool of light in the gloom and illuminated a small fire-cauldron and some large logs scattered around like seats in a forest.

Clip stepped onto the stage dressed in the old rainbow-coloured cloak, his silvery hair long and ash staff in hand. He began to weave words, images, magic and symbols into a wild tale of strange people who lived in a landscape of forest and mountains where a wicked spell had been cast to blight the land. The children were completely silent as the tall, gaunt man whirled around like a flash of the spectrum and the Barn filled with the sweet aroma of burnt herbs.

He told of a magical hare that had come into the land to cure all evil and heal all wounds. The light dimmed further and the music changed, sounding like faerie chimes. Suddenly, on the stage there appeared a Hare Woman, small but with real hare's ears, who loped into the centre. In her hand she carried a short staff and around it writhed a carved snake, from bottom to top. The Hare Woman told of her quest to break the wicked spell and put right all the terrible wrongs of the land. She stood and spoke of her magic, and the children sat with open mouths.

Then Hare Woman brandished her staff, an Asklepian rod, and whispered to the children to beware of the snake that curled around it, for if they stared for too long, or looked at it too carefully, the snake might come to life. There was a mass intake of breath. Celandine and Bluebell were beside themselves with suppressed excitement, having immediately forgotten that Hare Woman was their Auntie Leveret dressed up. Every child tried not to stare at the snake but couldn't resist, and slowly, one vertebra at a time, the snake quickened into life.

'I do hope that there are no children here staring at the snake, seeing how it has begun to wriggle,' admonished Clip in his softest, most sing-song voice. 'Because once the snake comes to life, only the magical Hare Woman can turn it back to wood again. Oh dear – I saw the tail wriggle. And now ... yes, I can see the rainbow colours appearing on its scales.'

He threw a handful of herbs onto the fire burning in the little cauldron and brightly-coloured sweet-smelling smoke obscured the stage for a moment.

'The snake has changed,' he sang, 'and now he writhes around the staff like a rainbow. Hare Woman, can you break the wicked spell that blights the land? Can you use your magic wand, with the snake as your helper?'

'Only if the children all promise to help me too,' she replied.

At this the children became even more excited, and the story web continued with the young audience joining in. Finally, after battling with evil goblins and bad faeries, Hare Woman broke the wicked spell and the land returned once more to peace and harmony. Clip then picked up his own staff and began to whirl it around his head.

'And so Hare Woman has saved the land! Now she must return to her tiny cottage where she spends her days brewing remedies to help the folk with their ordinary ailments,' he cried.

He turned, the rainbow tatters on his cloak flying out as he spun around, faster and faster, and the drums beat wildly. All eyes were on him as the Hare Woman transformed back into an ordinary young girl, sitting on one of the logs with a carved stick by her side. Clip slowed and the drums beat slower too – until they stopped.

'And behold!' said Clip. 'The magical Hare Woman has vanished, and in her place is a simple, ordinary Stonewylde maiden called Leveret. But look, children – what's this in her lap?'

Everyone craned forward in their seats and there was another collective gasp.

'It's Hare!' shrieked Bluebell, unable to stop herself. 'I know Hare!'

And everyone clapped like mad as Clip took a bow, and Leveret stood up, holding the hare in her arms with the creature's head looking over her shoulder and her ears lying flat. Leveret bowed too and the applause was wild. She grinned at Clip and he beamed back at her.

'And that is the other role of the shaman,' he said to her over the noise. 'To bring magic to the folk's lives and break any wicked spells that might be hanging about!'

'I don't want you to go in the morning,' he said petulantly, lying on his side and stroking her smooth belly with a dried stalk. 'Stay a bit longer – until the autumn, when I go off to university.'

'I'll be back long before then!' she laughed, stretching with a sigh of pleasure on the fragrant hay. The late afternoon sun poured in above them through the open shutters of the hay loft, and the air was thick with dancing motes.

'But when? When will you be back? How will I survive without you?'

'Oh Kestrel, don't be silly. This was only ever a bit of fun,' she teased. 'Anyone would think you'd fallen in love with me!'

'I have fallen in love with you,' he said quietly. 'I can't bear the thought of you leaving tomorrow. Please, Rainbow, please—'

'Stop it, Kes. Really, it's not funny. This was only ever a game.'

'Not to me,' he said bitterly. He'd swum and worked in the fields every day, and the sun had tanned him a deep golden brown and bleached his curly hair a bright hazelnut-gold. Rainbow smiled up at him, tracing the definition of muscle on his naked torso. He'd certainly helped her while away the rather boring evenings at Stonewylde on many an occasion; she hoped he wasn't going to prove too difficult now.

'Kes, you're a grown man and always knew the score,' she said. 'I'll be back long before the autumn when you leave for uni, so don't worry. And there are plenty of lovely girls at Stonewylde to keep you busy.'

'I've already had most of them,' he said moodily, 'and I don't want any of them anyway. They're not a patch on you.'

She shook her head in exasperation and rolled over onto her front, revealing her lithe back with the ribs just nudging at her golden, downy skin. Her hair was spread over the hay, a tangle of tawny tresses glinting gold. Kestrel traced the whorls of blonde down that furred her back, so fine and soft, with the gentlest of touches.

'Mmn, that's nice,' she purred, closing her eyes and flexing a little.

He gazed down at her and his eyes filled with tears.

'Rainbow, if you really must leave, please say I can visit you? Or could I come to London with you tomorrow? I won't be any trouble, I promise.'

She chuckled drowsily and wriggled in the hay; a shaft of sunlight now fell onto her skin and she glowed gold, like an idol.

'Kes, you have no idea of my lifestyle in London,' she murmured sleepily. 'I'd be a laughing stock if I came back with an eighteen year old country lad on my arm, however gorgeous he might be.'

'I'm almost nineteen!' he protested. 'And I've been at college for two years now – I know all about the Outside World!'

This really made her laugh and she rolled over again and gazed up at him, her sea-blue eyes heavy.

'Kes, shut up. See if you can please me all over again, there's a good boy. And no more whingeing about me leaving in the morning or I'll ignore you when I do come back. You're not the only good lay at Stonewylde, you know – there are plenty more fish in the sea.'

Yul and David, meanwhile, struggled up the great staircase with the canvas. They had to carry it over their heads to clear the newel post and balustrade, and then negotiate the half-landing very carefully. For a terrible moment Yul thought it wouldn't fit through the huge doorway, but by using the highest point of the arch it just squeezed through.

'Which wall will you hang it on?' asked David, looking around the grand apartments with interest.

'I have no idea!' snapped Yul. 'Just prop it up here for now.'

'It would fit over there,' said David, pointing behind the desk, 'if you moved that other painting. Or perhaps if you hung the mirror somewhere else, it could go over the fireplace? That would—'

'It doesn't matter,' said Yul. 'Anywhere other than downstairs for all the world to see!'

David gazed at him in bemusement. Yul looked really rough today; blood-shot eyes, a crumpled shirt and he stank of alcohol. David realised he hadn't seen Yul about at all since Sylvie's birthday party at the Solstice, when he'd suddenly appeared in the Art Room. Had he been holed up in here ever since? It certainly smelled like it.

'Where would Sylvie want it hung, I wonder? As it's her birthday present,' he said mildly and the look Yul gave him would have withered a lesser man.

'I don't give a damn where she wants it hung!' he thundered. 'It's not to go on public display ever! How dare that boy paint my wife like this?'

'Yul, I'm sorry,' said David gently. 'I had no idea you felt like that about it. I'm sure Magpie meant no harm. He didn't realise that—'

'I know that – but it's not the point!' Yul spat. 'This moon-dancing at Hare Stone – it was something private, something precious between me and my wife. And now ... just go, David!

Thanks for helping me carry it up here, but just go!'

'Yul, please – I'm sorry. Can I get you something? You're not looking too good, and—'

'Get out!'

Hazel had persuaded Yul to join her outside in the maze for a stroll in the late afternoon sunshine. He'd refused point blank to come to the hospital wing and didn't want her in his rooms. Alerted by David, she realised as soon as she saw the wildness in his eyes that something was really wrong.

They walked now around the gravelled paths of the maze, surrounded by walls of deep green clipped yew. It was warm and peaceful, and Hazel glanced sideways at the tall man by her side. David had said he was in a mess, but he looked as if he'd just had a still forbidden shower and was wearing clean, fresh clothes. This made it harder for her to broach the subject of his health.

'Hazel, I know you mean well but I'm fine,' he said wearily, sensing her hesitation. 'I haven't been sleeping properly in this heat and I miss Sylvie. That's all. And I was very upset by that damn painting and this afternoon I lost my rag with David a little.'

'Okay,' she said gently. 'He was concerned about you. So how are you now?'

'Absolutely fine other than, as I said, missing my wife and children.'

'It must be hard. But it's not permanent, is it? I thought they'd just gone down to stay with Maizie to keep her company for a while, now that Leveret's left home and she's all alone.'

'Between you and me, Hazel, that's only the half of it. I don't want to discuss it, but there's more to it than that and I want her back. How do you think she is herself, health-wise?'

'Actually, Yul, I really think she's a lot better than she was. She'd lost weight and was looking very careworn, but in the past month or so she seems to have perked up no end. I know that doesn't sound a very professional diagnosis and I haven't given her a check-up yet, but that's how it seems to me. She's brighter and chirpier and putting on some much-needed weight. Obviously Village life and Maizie's cooking agrees with her.'

He nodded at this.

'I thought the same. She looks a lot better lately and although I'm very pleased, I can't help but think it means she won't want to come back to the Hall.'

'Why don't you go down to the Village then, just temporarily? If you were staying in the cottage too ... ?'

He gestured towards a bench tucked into an alcove and they sat down. A tiny wren soon appeared and hopped around on the gravel before them, flicking her wings and tipping her tail. Hazel glanced at Yul and saw the dejection and despair on his face. He gazed at the little bird without seeing her and his face was hollowed, full of angles and shadows. His dark curls were long, having dried in the sun in a tangle around his face. Hazel felt a twist of sympathy for him. Whatever their problems were, Yul's love for Sylvie wasn't in doubt.

'I don't think she'd have me.'

'But you don't know that, Yul. You must try, if you're to be reconciled. I can't speak for Sylvie of course, but I do know that she loves you more than anything. She's found you ... over-dominating in the recent past. And you know this, I'm sure. So start again – woo her, bring some romance into your marriage, win her back. I don't think you'd find her unreceptive.'

He leant forward and put his head in his hands.

'Oh Hazel ... if only it were that simple.'

The pert little wren had flitted over the wall of yew into the alcove behind, and perched on the bench arm. She didn't notice someone already seated there, silent and completely still, listening to the private conversation. A smile spread over the boy's handsome young face and as Yul and the doctor stood up to leave, he flicked the blond fringe from his eyes and quickly rose too.

Swift knew the maze better than anyone at Stonewylde, for he'd grown up nearby and had spent many an hour playing in here whilst his mother wore herself out trying to get the cottage up to his father's exacting standards. As he sped out of the maze ahead of Yul and Hazel, he thought about all he'd just heard and filed it away in his archive of eavesdropped information. Nobody knew for sure why Sylvie was living in Maizie's cottage, although speculation had been rife. But now, Swift felt, he knew more than anyone else. It also explained why only the night before, when he'd just been casually passing Yul's rooms, he'd heard harsh sobbing.

Leveret lay on a sofa in the tower with Hare on her lap, and Clip sat opposite in his chair.

'We need to get back down to the Village in a minute,' he said. 'We must be in very good time for this evening's Story Web. It really doesn't do to arrive late or in a fret about the time.'

'I'm ready to go when you are,' said Leveret. 'I've got the outfit and everything ready.'

Clip smiled at her fondly.

'You were very good this afternoon,' he said. 'The children loved you and you have a natural gift for performance. The adults this evening will love you too.'

She wrinkled her nose at this.

'That's kind of you, Clip, but honestly I don't have a gift in that area. I was terrified the whole time and I was shaking terribly.'

'Well, it didn't show and you handled it all beautifully.'

'And as for my wonderful Asklepian wand – wow! That was such a lovely surprise.'

'I had it carved for you a while back. Every magician needs a wand, and every healer needs a Rod of Asklepius. You know it's the ancient symbol of medicine, don't you?'

She nodded.

'This Asklepian was carved from rowan, the tree of healing, and it's your medicine wand. Before I leave, I'll have a shaman's staff made for you too. That will be ash, like mine, as it's the tree that links our realm to the other realms.'

'Clip, I hate it when you talk of leaving. You don't *have* to leave this autumn, do you? I mean, if you could stay a little—'

But he shook his head.

'Leveret, we both know that I have to.'

'But I won't be ready! I don't know enough!'

'What you don't know, you'll learn. We spend our entire lives learning, Leveret, and you'll never feel that you know enough. Now, let's prepare ourselves for this evening. We'll need all our strength and concentration if we're to lead the whole community in a story. Magic takes its toll and we need to be both strong and at peace with ourselves.'

They closed their eyes and Leveret stroked the hare in her lap, her own magical creature, sent to her at the Spring Equinox when light and darkness are balanced. She tried to attune herself to the energy all around, and also align her spirit with Clip's. He'd already told her they'd be working very closely together tonight and must trust each other completely. Leveret just hoped she'd be worthy of assisting him in this Story Web for the community. She had no idea what he'd planned.

When they arrived in the Village the Great Barn was empty but for a couple of musicians; everyone else was at home eating supper. Clip rearranged the stage a little, re-laying the fire-cauldron with fresh wood and replenishing the supplies. Leveret was despatched to a small side room to get changed into her costume, which included her shaman's headdress that had so delighted the children earlier in the day. Hare was safely nesting in her closed basket on a bed of hay, happy to snooze quietly.

Leveret slipped on the outfit of short brown tunic and brown leggings with pointy toes. Clip had told her she was echoing a famous illustration, published in a book in Antwerp in the early 1600s, of a Saxon hare goddess. She found it a little bizarre, but he insisted that she adopt this style of dress, saying it had important cultural and mystical significance. She covered up the outfit with a plain brown cloak, and for now kept her headdress tucked into the big pocket inside. Her other prop was a large pewter plate that had been burnished until it shone – Clip said this represented the moon and was also part of the magical illustration she must recreate.

When Leveret re-emerged into the main body of the Barn, she found Clip fiddling about with bags of herbs which he strapped to his belt.

'You understand why and how we use herbs for effect,' he said. 'But it's important that they're to hand, and that you don't muddle them up. Otherwise they can't be used properly and could actually be counter-productive. So, when you do this alone for the first time, keep it simple.'

She nodded, terrified at the very thought of standing on this stage with Clip, let alone by herself.

'I don't *have* to do Story Webs though, do I?' she asked. 'Shamans can just be there to consult on an individual basis, can't they?'

'Yes, but putting on a performance to a crowd – nothing beats that,' he said. 'The Shaman is the only one who can travel easily between the realms. People want to be led to places they can't reach themselves. They want to be shown truths they couldn't see alone. A really successful shaman can hold the entire community spell-bound and take them on a magical journey to other places. This is what we'll do this evening, my Leveret. We haven't had a Story Web for so very long and I don't suppose you even remember the last one.'

'No, I don't. I wish I knew exactly what we're going to do tonight,' she said, quaking inside. Despite the afternoon's success in front of the children, she was now suffering from stage fright. She also couldn't help but remember the last time she'd stood in the centre of the Great Barn in front of the entire community.

'I don't really know myself,' Clip replied, and putting his arm around her shoulders gave her a hug. 'But don't worry – it will be wonderful, I'm sure. I've never had a disaster yet.'

*

The air was hot and heavy with the scent of so many people crammed in tightly together. The tiers were packed solid and even the aisles were full. The musicians sitting cross-legged near the stage had been drumming for a while and the magical sound of the flute drifted around. Leveret sat on one of the logs on stage, small and hunched up in her brown cloak with the hood pulled up over her headdress. Hare lay quietly inside her covered basket on the floor; she seemed to sense when she must stay still.

Clip wore his cloak of black feathers and held his staff. The fire crackled and flared different colours as he added various herbs. He spoke in the language of the storyteller, his resonant voice soft but compelling as he carried the audience away on a magic carpet of words and images. Again, he spoke of a land that had been put under a spell, but now his story was more complex and much darker. The audience shivered and trembled as he conjured images of evil and death, and nameless beasts that stalked the realm.

'But behold, there came amongst the people a hare goddess. No ordinary hare, no ordinary goddess, but a strange and powerful mix of the two.'

The drums had started to beat again and Clip moved around the stage with the staff pointing into the audience and attracting all the attention to himself. This bit they had agreed on, and Leveret knew she must now climb onto the highest of the up-ended logs, which she managed without mishap. The headdress was secure under the hood, and in her hand she clutched the huge polished pewter plate. At a signal from Clip, she undid the ties at the neck and the cloak fell to the floor. It revealed her standing motionless, dressed in the hare headdress, brown tunic and leggings, and holding the silvery plate in front of her stomach. Clip looked up at her and shuddered; she was an exact replica of that famous alchemical woodcut depicting the goddess – it was uncanny and felt almost archetypal.

The story progressed as he told of how the hare goddess had come, with the full moon rising in her belly, to break the wicked spell. The drum was insistent and she heard the change in Clip's voice – the moment when he stopped merely telling the story and started to weave the magic. He spoke of the hare goddess and her powers, her ability to heal and cure and make whole again that which was broken.

He created more coloured and aromatic smoke and began once again to circle, whirling so that the black-feathered cloak flew out around him. This was Leveret's cue to climb down from the tree trunk, where she'd surely lose her balance eventually, and start to engage with the audience. Carefully she stepped down and looked out at the rows and rows of faces all around her, the firelight flickering on those near the front, all of them glistening with sweat. She could see they were spellbound, their eyes fixed on Clip as he moved and spoke. Nobody seemed to notice her at all, as if she were invisible now she'd climbed down from the stump.

But then the drumbeat changed again as Clip signalled to the drummers to stop. He'd picked up his own shaman's frame-drum and now created a single, insistent beat that calmed the nerves and soothed the senses. He stood still, at the side of the stage, and seemed to melt away into the shadows so only his voice remained.

'Behold!' he cried again, 'The Hare Woman of Stonewylde is come in our midst. She is here to heal, here to cure, here to work her magic. She will lead us all now into a magical, faraway realm ...'

He stopped speaking, but the drum continued its monotonous, compelling beat. He nodded to Leveret and she realised with a sharp jab of terror that this was her cue. She must now perform. She took a deep breath and felt the fear tingling in her fingertips and her heart thumping in her chest. Still the drum beat: boom, boom, boom. It called, it summoned the people to follow ...

'Come close, my folk of Stonewylde! Come follow me towards the wood,' she said in a soft, clear voice. 'We are ready to travel on a journey, a journey that will take us far and deep, to a place not of our normal realm but to another, magical realm. I take your hands and lead you there safely. I will let nothing harm you. No fire-breathing dragon, nor flesh-eating vulture will come close, for I, the Hare Woman, will protect you. Come, come with me through the archway of trees, through the archway into a new and strange land ...'

And there was Raven, huge and glossy black, waiting for her in the bright place. They greeted one another. He told her to climb on his back, for first he was taking her to the Upperworld, a place of clouds and dreams. And when she told him of all the folk who were with her tonight he opened his great beak and let out a mighty *CRUK!* of welcome.

They flew through a crack in the clouds, to a place of great beauty and possibility. They flew up to where all was soft and sparkling, where colours were brighter and everything seemed to be newly washed. In this beautiful place they wandered a while, exploring the wonderful land and marvelling at the fantastical creatures that roamed there. And when it was time to leave, they spoke with the queen. She was old and wise but still beautiful, with sky-blue robes dusted with stars and long white hair that reached her waist. She touched each traveller with a wand of crystal, telling each that they might take back with them one small token from her lands.

And then the queen turned to the Hare Woman and said that, as Shaman of Stonewylde, she might ask one question. Although nobody else would hear what that question was, they would all hear the answer. When Hare Woman had asked her question, the old queen nodded and replied that yes, there certainly *was* reason to fear and they must all beware of the snake that sheds its skin only to return in a different one. With that, they flew back down through the crack in the clouds, and Raven said they must now enter the Underworld, the place of darkness and laby-rinthine passages.

They found a tiny cave mouth, like a foxhole, in a bank of earth. Above it grew purple foxgloves, their little trumpets freck-led inside with deep magenta spots. By the side of the foxhole was a great oak tree, and looking up they saw mistletoe growing thickly where the branches met the trunk. On the other side was a slender rowan tree with delicate leaves that seemed to wave them on, into the dark hole that awaited them.

They passed through the earthy entrance, avoiding the roots of trees and plants that hung all around them like vines, ignoring the stones that pattered from above, down onto the path. After a while, it grew brighter ahead and they were out of the tunnel and had entered the Underworld. It was a strange place, and the folk gathered closer together behind Hare Woman, fearing what might come. Raven led them all along, telling everyone to beware where they trod, for there were dangers underfoot.

After a while, they came to a clearing in a great forest where the moss grew emerald green and was rippled with faerie rings. There were brilliant red and white Fly Agaric toadstools around, and on one of these sat a strange little creature, part elf, part moth. He told them all to eat of the tiny mushrooms in the faerie rings if they were hungry, and they fell upon the sweet golden fungi, devouring the lot. Frowning, he offered them acorn cups of fresh dew, which they gulped down. He frowned again and told them that they were greedy folk, who should take care not to destroy with grasping avarice the bounty they had.

'Only take a little – just what you need, and no more,' he said. 'For when everything has been consumed, you will wish you'd shown restraint.'

And, like the wise queen before, he told the folk they might each take one token back to their land. Whilst they chose this, he whispered to the Hare Woman that she may ask one question. When she had done so, he pondered for a while.

'That is a hard question to answer,' he replied. 'But here are my thoughts: in autumn you see the leaves dying and falling, and you think the world is ending. In the dead of winter, everything is grey and bleak and it seems this will last forever. But then comes the spring and all is renewed. The leaves grow again – not the same leaves as before, but new ones, just as beautiful, from the same source. So take heed of this, and never try to stop that which you cannot change.'

With that, he disappeared and a wind blew up. Hare Woman gathered them together quickly to retrace their steps back to the long earthy tunnel. They hurried along behind her and, as they popped out underneath the foxgloves, Raven said that he must be gone. All around the land seemed to fade and then grow bright, and the white light was everywhere, flooding their blinking eyes ...

She opened her eyes and the rows of faces were all blinking owlishly at her, dazed and confused. The fire was low, the drum still beat, the air was close and dark around them. There was a movement across the floor and the lid to the basket was pushed open. Hare lifted up her head and then hopped out, loping across to Leveret who bent to pick her up. She stood in the centre of the Great Barn, still in her brown tunic and leggings, with the shaman's headdress on her head, holding the soft golden hare in her arms. All eyes were upon her.

There was a sudden *CAW* audible over the single drum beats. From up high in the barn's rafters, a crow sailed down, a crow with a white tail feather. He landed on the stump where she'd stood earlier and began to preen himself. Leveret took a deep breath.

'So now, folk of Stonewylde, take back with you tonight the two gifts you've been given, and ponder on the two answers. Sleep well in your beds and know that the magic is safe and guarded. For I, the Hare Woman, am here amongst you and the magic is in me.'

Clip stopped drumming and there was sudden silence. Leveret bowed. The audience erupted into wild applause that made the crow take off back into the rafters again, and Hare flatten her ears. Leveret gave a small smile and her eyes found Clip's. She could do it – she was worthy of the new title she would inherit when he'd gone.

14

Sitting in her office in the School Wing leafing through the files of students still to be interviewed, Sylvie realised that she was one of the lucky ones. Because of Yul's reluctance to let her take on the role of Student Counsellor, she hadn't had any data to lose when the virus had hit Stonewylde's network. All the youngsters finishing Hall School this summer had been interviewed and she was now working through the year group below, as they'd soon be making their choices for higher education or apprenticeships. Sylvie had found the role rewarding so far, and Miranda had assured her it would make a great deal of difference in the community.

She was disturbed by a knock on the door and surprised to see Harold. He entered nervously and was persuaded to sit down beside her, more jittery than even the shyest student she'd had in for a chat. The Imbolc Crash had taken away his already shaky self-confidence and her heart went out to him; he'd always worked so hard, even when it made him unpopular, and his loyalty to Stonewylde was unquestionable.

'Relax, Harold,' she said gently. 'You know me well enough – I don't bite.'

He smiled and pushed his round glasses back up his nose.

'I'm sorry to bother you, Sylvie, but I'm not sure where Yul is at the moment, and even if I was ...'

She nodded at this; Yul had been like a bear with a sore head since her birthday. He'd disappeared for a few days and had missed the Story Web. He'd re-emerged after that but since then he'd been more absent than present. He wasn't getting any work done and she'd heard he was out riding even more than usual. Sylvie knew she should try to speak to him. He was obviously still very upset about the beautiful moondance picture she'd been given, and she really didn't know what to do to make it all better. It was such a shame, as the painting was truly wonderful; David had told her Yul had hidden it away in his apartments.

'I know, Harold – he's not in the best of spirits at the moment, is he? But please speak to me instead. You know that's fine, though if it's a business thing I don't know how much I'll be able to help.'

'It is! Oh Sylvie, 'tis amazing news but I got to give an answer today because it's all last minute and rushed.'

His words came tumbling out and she smiled encouragingly.

''Tis thanks to Rainbow, I think – she e-mailed me after she'd gone and said she'd been talking to some friends who're in the "fashion industry".'

He said these last two words as if referring to some alien planet, which made Sylvie smile, although the mention of Rainbow didn't. She'd been heartily glad to see the back of the woman and had vowed she'd never return to Stonewylde.

'Okay – I don't know much about the fashion industry, but—'

'No, well, neither do I but that don't matter. Basically 'tis the fashion label called Aitch – you may've heard of 'em? I hadn't, but I've done some research now, and they're really big and grand. And there's this here fashion collection thing – oh really, Sylvie, I don't know nothing about it but I been trying to find out and I think it could be brilliant! The first thing is they want some things from us very quick for some show they got on in Paris. I got a list – stuff like wicker baskets, some felt hats, boots – that sort o' thing. "Accessories", they call 'em. And then if that's all alright, they want to place a big order for stuff for their next collection and they might even want to come here to do some photographs and suchlike.'

He paused for breath and Sylvie stared at him in bemusement.

'So ... you say this has come from Rainbow?'

'No, 'tis not her that's ordered it all, but she said she knows people in the industry. I think she knows lots o' people in London. She showed 'em some o' the photos she took when she were here and they loved all the Stonewylde stuff. They said 'tis like back to nature and all that. So, what I need to know is this: is it alright to say yes to them?'

'Oh goodness, Harold! You need to know now?'

'I need to let 'em know today. 'Cos if we can't, then they need to find another supplier. But they say they want to buy British and not get in cheap imported stuff that's been made in China or the like. They want the "authentic country look" – and that's us, they say. 'Tis all very sudden but that's thanks to Rainbow.'

'But she's not directly involved in this, is she?' asked Sylvie. The last thing she wanted was that woman thinking she could come back.

'No, all she done was show 'em the photos and they loved 'em. And she gave my e-mail address. Seriously, Sylvie – go and look at Aitch on the Internet. Then you'll see how big they are and you'll be as excited as me. I think this could really be the making of us, and they're offering so much money!'

Sylvie sat at the kitchen table talking to Maizie whilst the girls were out in the garden picking raspberries and redcurrants.

'I'd like to ask him, Mother Maizie, but I have no idea where he is. Since the Solstice he's been behaving very strangely, and—'

'He were upset by that painting, that's why!' said Maizie stoutly.

'I know, but there's no need to just disappear, surely?'

'You know what Yul's like. If he takes it into his head to disappear ...'

'Anyway, I can't ask his opinion because nobody knows where he is. I've asked Clip and he just said to do what I think best, which is no help. I mentioned it to my mum, and she said much the same. Nobody's that fussed, but, as Harold says, it's a great opportunity and it'll bring in some much-needed cash.'

'Well in that case, we better say yes,' said Maizie, picking up her sewing. 'We need money bad, don't we?'

Sylvie nodded.

'The thing is, Mother Maizie, and you'll know the answer to this better than most – can we make the stuff they need for this Haute Couture Fashion Show thing in time? We've got just a few days to do it, but if we can, they'll pay so well! Then maybe they'll put in a big order with a much longer deadline, so we can organise the workforce properly to get that done. What do you think? Harold needs to let them know by this evening.'

'Let me see the list,' said Maizie, and slowly worked down it. Sylvie almost offered to read it for her but then thought better of it. She waited, and eventually Maizie nodded.

'I reckon if we start work tomorrow morning and get everyone involved, we could do it. 'Tis just a few baskets, some boots and some felt hats, all said and done. Oh – and them scarves too. But we could do it if we gathered everyone together for a big effort.'

'Could you organise that, Maizie? You know best about the resources we have and who's fastest at making these things. It goes without saying that they must be perfect.'

'Aye, I'll do that. 'Twill get us out of a little bit of the mess with money, won't it? But long term ...'

'I know, Maizie. Long term we need a proper solution to our financial problems. Thank you – that's great. I'll nip into the Barn and phone up to the Hall and tell Harold to say yes. Goodness knows what Yul will say but—'

'Truth be told, my dear – if he ain't here, he's got no right to say anything, has he?'

Leveret stood on the roof of the tower gazing out at the sinking sun. The crow had appeared, as he so often did now, and was sitting watching her from the crenellated stonework. She turned and cast her eye over the massed chimneys, some so ornate and others plain. The Hall was such a vast building and Leveret was pleased she was in a separate part of it and not in one of the big dormitories with other girls. She realised how very lucky and privileged she was to be living in the tower with Clip.

The crow started to make a racket – he was a noisy creature – and then she looked down and saw the cause of it. Gefrin stood a distance away in the parkland and was staring up towards her. Leveret's heart lurched in alarm. She'd managed to avoid Jay and her brothers since Imbolc, but it was now almost July and the situation couldn't go on forever. Why on earth was he out there watching her? Surely he wouldn't do anything with Clip around? She was just about to go downstairs off the roof to get out of his sight when he waved at her and began walking towards the tower.

Leveret watched him approach, noting that he was no longer quite so skinny and lanky. His long, rather rat-like, face still filled her with loathing, bringing back memories of so many incidents over the years, but she despised him marginally less than Sweyn. She knew that at some point she'd have to face her tormentors and deal with the situation, and this was as good a time as any to make a start – indeed better than most, as she was on her own territory and had Clip close to hand.

Gefrin stopped several metres away from the foot of the tower and stood gazing up at her. He saw the crow sitting on the battlements and shivered, almost turning tail at the last moment. But Lammas was approaching and he needed help, so plucking up his courage, he called up to her.

'Hey, Lev! I wanted to talk to you!'

She wasn't going to make this easy for him.

'Yes?'

'Can you come down a minute?'

'No!'

He thought about this for a moment.

'Can I ... can I come up then?'

Now she paused, enjoying the power after a lifetime of having none where her brothers were concerned.

'You can, but Clip's downstairs in the tower and if you even think about being nasty, he'll—'

'No! No, really, Lev. I'm not like that now.'

She laughed at this and watched him climb the stone staircase that helter-skeltered up round the tower from the ground. When he'd almost reached the top, the crow gave a mighty *CAW* and flapped away, showing his white tail feather. Gefrin stared at the crow, then climbed the last few steps.

'I ain't never seen a crow with a white tail,' he said. 'Is he yours? He were there at the Story Web too, weren't he?'

Leveret nodded. She'd wondered if her brothers had been present. So far many people had commented on what a special evening it had been and she'd noticed that people were treating her differently now – far more respectfully and carefully. This certainly seemed to be the case with Gefrin who would by now, under normal circumstances, have twisted her arm or pulled her hair, or at least insulted her.

'So ... you're living with Clip now?'

'You know I am. Since Imbolc when I was Bright Maiden.'

He had the grace to blush at this and look away. She noticed how bad his skin was; covered with big pustules and greasy like his hair. It wasn't easy with the water being rationed, but Gefrin had never been too fond of washing even when the rain fell every day.

He fidgeted, but she wasn't going to put him at ease. She realised that they'd never stood together like this before, just talking like normal people. No wonder he found it difficult.

'I ... I thought you was very ... very magical the other night,' he stammered.

'Thank you.'

'I were surprised because ... you seemed different. Not like you been in the past.'

She glared up at him from behind her mass of dark hair. It had escaped Maizie's scissors since moving here and now cascaded wildly down her back. He saw her green eyes blaze and actually cringed at her stare. She almost laughed out loud at his discomfort but managed to maintain the fierce expression. He blushed again and stared at his hands.

211

'The thing is, Lev, that ...'

'Leveret! My name's Leveret. Or Hare Woman of course.'

'Sorry, yes. It's just that I wanted to ask for your help, seeing as how you can do magic.'

'How do you know I can do magic?'

'The other night ... I never knew you were like that. When I found the things in my pocket afterwards I went all cold.'

'What things? What are you talking about?'

He looked at her in consternation.

'You said about taking something back from the Upperworld and the Underworld. We could all take just one token? I couldn't believe it when I found 'em in my pocket, and neither could anyone else.'

'What did you find?' she asked, thinking this was some kind of joke. Everyone knew the objects found in other realms weren't real, merely symbolic.

'Same as everyone else,' he replied earnestly. 'A feather and a stone. I couldn't believe it. Jay was mad and he threw his away. Sweyn said he were going to but he ain't – I think he's too scared. We talked to lots o' the others and everyone had the same. It made me realise that you really are magic.'

Leveret gave a tight smile at this and nodded in what she hoped was a wise and serious way. Inside she was alive with curiosity and disbelief – how had everyone chosen the same objects? And more to the point, how had they ended up as real items in people's pockets?

'So what I wanted to ask you please, Lev ... I mean Leveret, is ... could you help me get Meadowsweet at Lammas? I'm going to ask her to walk with me but I think she'll say no.'

'I don't blame her! Why would she want *you*?'

Gefrin's face fell and he looked miserably at his feet, shaking his head.

'She don't. That's why I wanted to ask for some help. What can I do?'

Leveret regarded him steadily, wondering how she could turn this to her advantage.

'If you're asking to consult me as the Wise Woman, you'll need to come back tomorrow morning.'

'I can't – I'm at work from just after dawn. I get back around tea-time – can I come to see you then?'

'Yes, in the tower. Come through the Galleried Hall and knock at the door. I shall be waiting for you. And you'll need to do some preparation.'

'Yes? I'll do anything – I really like Meadowsweet and I want to walk with her so much. I want to be handfasted with her one day if she'd have me.'

'You *are* serious about her,' said Leveret. 'I shall need you to do two things before tomorrow, and you'd better do them right. The first is that you must make a list of the five things you like most about Meadowsweet. The second is a list of five things that she may *not* like about you. Do you understand? Bring the two lists tomorrow, written in your very best hand, and maybe I'll help you.'

'Thanks, Lev! Leveret!' His spotty face broke into a grin. 'If anyone can make it happen it's you.'

'We'll see,' she said dourly. 'I may decide not to make it happen of course. Don't assume anything.'

Not long after sunrise the next day, Maizie used her network of communication at the Village Pump to spread the word about the new quota. Everyone was asked to gather in the Great Barn once the children were at school and the household necessities done, and to pass the request around. There was grumbling at first, but Maizie and Sylvie both stood on the dais and explained to the women why this needed to be done, and why so fast. Harold and Yul weren't mentioned – it became a woman's thing, and, as Maizie had known would happen, everyone agreed to cooperate.

The possibility of future work came up too, and the women agreed that they were more than happy to do their bit to help bring in money to Stonewylde. They liked the idea that the men at the Hall had messed up with their stupid computers and quotas and that now it was up to the women of the Village to sort out the mess.

The list of what was required for this rush order for the fashion label Aitch was discussed and the items shared out, people volunteering to their strengths. It was agreed that, if everyone worked at it, two days would be enough to complete all the items, though the Stonewylde boots were trickier. Old Larch the cobbler was called in and consulted, and, as it was only ten pairs required for this order, he agreed that he'd pull out all the stops, get all his men onto the job, and promised to have them done in the two days. Sylvie was delighted at the positive attitude amongst the folk. There was a real buzz in the air that she hadn't felt for a long time, and she wondered if it were anything to do with the recent Story Web. She'd sensed a new pulling together afterwards as everyone had left the Great Barn chattering excitedly. It was as if the magical experience had reunited people into a community again.

She made her way up to the Hall a little later and went to Yul's office to find Harold and give him the good news: they'd only need two days to complete this order. She was glad Yul wasn't there. Harold was delighted and said he'd notify the fashion people immediately. He explained how happy they'd been that their order had been accepted and thought they'd be really impressed at how quickly it could be turned around. Sylvie sat down at Yul's desk and used his computer to take a look at the fashion company.

Their logo was designed with the capital A very large compared to the rest of the word, so it looked like "A itch", which she found a bit silly. She was completely in the dark about the fashion industry, having come to Stonewylde at the age of fourteen, penniless, and with no inclination for fashion. Even whilst at college in the Outside World she'd had no interest in designer labels. So now she took a good look at the website and grimaced at some of the styles and the models' emaciation. Had she made a mistake in agreeing to this? Was this really the type of industry that Stonewylde should be associated with? She began to have doubts, but then read a piece about the forthcoming collection which cheered her up.

'Did you see this, Harold?' she asked. 'They're saying that the new collection for next winter will be something entirely different, and they're calling it Earth Ethics. That sounds good, doesn't it? They want to use organic, natural materials and source their suppliers ethically – I guess that's where we come in. And they're also saying that they support the national campaign to use normal-sized women as models rather than "Size Zero" super-waifs. I like that.'

Harold looked across from his desk and gave her a nervous smile.

'Yes, that's what they said in the e-mail – 'tis for this Earth Ethics thing. I just hope Yul don't mind when he finds out.'

'Still no news where he is?'

Harold shook his head.

'Tom says he took his horse and went off somewhere.'

Sylvie turned back to read more about Aitch and their pledge to redress past wrongs perpetrated by the fashion giants. Looking at the glamorous photos and exotic clothes, it gave her a thrill to think that soon Stonewylde could be linked to all this, and perhaps doing its bit towards bringing higher principles to what many would see as a very shallow business.

Leveret realised that she needed to make some suitable clothes for her new roles; people would expect to see her dressed properly as befitted her station and Gefrin's request had reinforced this. She thought it would be good to actually weave, dye and sew the Wise Woman costume herself, and in doing so imbue it with her magical intent. She was aware of the irony of the situation; Maizie had spent years trying to interest her in these traditional skills, and now she wished she'd taken notice and learned them better. For now, a traditional Stonewylde robe from the Village store would have to do.

Gefrin returned late in the afternoon, jumpy with nerves and looking over his shoulder as if terrified that someone would see him visiting Leveret. He followed her up the interior spiral staircase to the great circular room at the top. Clip was out rambling over the hills but Leveret didn't tell Gefrin that. He looked around in wonder, and she indicated for him to sit on a small wooden stool which didn't allow much room for his long legs. He looked both sheepish and scared, and again she had to hold herself back from smiling and spoiling the illusion.

She sat on an ornate carved chair, looking very old-fashioned in the traditional robe, and stared down at him gravely. He almost jumped out of his skin when suddenly Hare came loping across the floor. Even though he'd seen her at the Story Web, he gawped at the hare as she put her front paws onto Leveret's knee and pricked up her great ears. Leveret lifted her onto her lap and Gefrin could only stare in amazement – she was so big and tame.

'Now you must read me the two lists you've made,' she said. 'And then we'll talk about how to increase your chances of success in wooing Meadowsweet. But first you need to convince me that you're worthy of walking with a girl. I shan't help you if your intentions are dishonourable.'

By the time she'd finished with him, Gefrin's humiliation was complete. His character defects had been examined in detail and he'd been forced to acknowledge all his failings. Leveret sent him on his way with a large bottle of watercress and witch hazel astringent cleansing lotion, a jar of comfrey cream for the worst of the boils, and a decoction of burdock and dandelion roots to be taken daily to tackle any internal toxicity that might be causing his skin to erupt. Leveret didn't know Meadowsweet well, but she knew that Gefrin's acne probably didn't help his cause. He'd hesitated when it was time to leave, and she wondered if he was going to apologise for the way he'd treated her all her life. She had no idea how she'd react to that; forgiveness just wasn't possible so soon. But she needn't have feared, for all he did was request that she didn't tell Sweyn about his visit.

A couple of days later came the encounter that she'd long dreaded. Leveret was up at Mother Heggy's cottage making a batch of remedies: some antiseptic ointments, pain killers and cough medicines for general use, and further supplies of Sylvie's tincture that appeared to be working so well. It was late afternoon, the sun was golden and warm and the swifts were riding high, twittering and squealing. Leveret had her tools and equipment laid out on the table and the water in the cauldron had just started to bubble. Hare lay in a corner asleep on the cool flagstone floor.

At one end of the ancient table sat Magpie, bent over the pages of a large book; he was making fine pen and ink drawings on the creamy page. This was their own Book of Shadows, arrived a while ago from London, and now its pages were filling with recipes for Leveret's remedies and Magpie's illustrations of the plants, barks and herbs required. They were both enjoying creating the book, which also featured observations and instructions about all sorts of other aspects of nature.

They heard the crow causing a commotion and Leveret went outside to investigate. Her heart started to thump as she recognised Sweyn's gingery head further down the path. She rushed back inside and picked up her Asklepian wand, not entirely sure what she'd do with it but wanting something in the way of support. Magpie looked up at her and she smiled reassuringly at him.

'No need to worry, Magpie – it's just that stupid Sweyn come to pay us a visit. I'll soon see him off, and anyway, we're protected by the spell I cast around the cottage. You just stay in here out of his sight.'

She stood outside the door of the cottage, the rowan wand in her hand and the white-tailed crow on the thatched roof behind her. Her eyes narrowed as she watched Sweyn toiling up the hill, sweating profusely. He looked up, his breathing laboured, and his red face darkened further at the sight of her. She stepped forward and held the snake-carved wand before her. He reached the final approach on the path and she pointed the wand at him, raising her other hand to point to the sky.

'Stop!' she cried in an authoritative voice. 'Come no farther or you'll step into the enchanted circle that's been cast around this cottage!'

He stopped and glared at her, the sweat running in rivulets down his fat cheeks.

'You don't fool me with that crap!' he huffed, trying to regain his breath.

'I'm not trying to fool anyone,' she replied. 'I'm only trying to warn you. There's a spell of protection around this cottage and if you attempt to break through it, I can't vouch for your safety. I'm talking about powerful magical forces, Sweyn. Be it on your own head if you decide to ignore them.'

He glared at her, his heart still pounding from the strenuous climb in the heat, and tried to decide whether or not to come any further. He wasn't scared of her, but on the other hand ... At that point, the great golden hare appeared in the doorway and lolloped outside to stand next to her, its massive ears upright and alert. The Hare Woman, Clip had called her the other night, and here she was with her creature again. Despite the beating sun he shivered, and then stepped back with a cry of surprise as the crow that had been strutting about on the thatched roof suddenly opened its wings and cawed. It took off and sailed down, landing on Leveret's shoulder. He noticed the way her green eyes lit up at this and shivered again.

'You really are a mad bitch!' he hissed. 'I hate you!'

She stood there, her wand in her hand with the snake's head pointing at him, the hare by her side and the crow on her shoulder, and stared at him intently. Her green gaze was unwavering and his sweaty skin started to prickle with fear.

'What's that lump on your forehead?' she asked. 'How did you get that?'

'None of your bloody business!' he retorted.

She continued to stare and involuntarily he rubbed the bump that was still there after almost a month. It ached and throbbed quite a bit but he tried to ignore it.

'You must put a cold compress on it morning and night,' she

said. 'I'm warning you – go to the hospital wing and ask them to help. If you don't ...'

'Are you hexing me now?' he cried. 'Because if you are—'

'I don't hex people,' she replied evenly. 'But I see things – as you know. I am the Wise Woman of Stonewylde and I'm warning you.'

'Sod your stupid bloody prophecies!' he yelled, very disturbed. 'You're a stupid, crazy—'

At that point, a huge magpie landed on the path almost next to Sweyn and he glanced at it nervously. The blue, black and white bird hopped towards him making loud chattering cries, and he took a step back. The bird began to peck at his shoe, still squawking noisily and repeatedly, and he took several steps backwards. It made a run at his feet then and when he tried to kick it the magpie flapped its heavy wings and took off, flying closely over him. As it crossed above his head, it let out a great blob of white and slimy dropping that landed in his hair. With a yell of disgust Sweyn tried to rub it off and the thick, gooey mess smeared over his hand.

'You bloody revolting *bitch!*' he screamed at Leveret. 'You won't get away with this!'

'Don't come here again,' she called out, 'or next time I'll summon a whole tiding of magpies. Be it on your head! Be gone, and don't come back!'

Sweyn turned and stumbled back down the path. The magpie continued to harass him, dropping more slimy bombs with accuracy. Leveret stood for a while longer, watching his retreating back and smiling with glee. So that's how the spell worked, she mused. She had no idea why he'd decided to pay her a visit but she didn't care; he'd be unlikely to return in a hurry. Chuckling to herself, she went back inside to continue brewing.

'Why did nobody think to ask me?' shouted Yul furiously.

All eyes in the Galleried Hall watched him apprehensively as he shifted in his chair, unable to contain himself. It was so very hot already and the Hay Moon meeting had only just begun.

219

'Yul, we had to decide straight away – there weren't time to wait till you came back again,' said Maizie in a placatory voice. 'You'd disappeared and—'

'Hardly disappeared! I was out riding for a day or so! You could've waited till I got back.'

'We didn't know when you'd be back,' said Sylvie firmly, sick of his tantrums at these meetings. 'And we didn't know where you'd gone, so don't blame us for getting on with the job of running Stonewylde. Anyway, enough of us decided that it was a good idea so even if you had been around and had objected, you'd have been over-ruled.'

He glared at her, grey eyes startling in his deeply tanned face. His hair was wild and longer than ever; if it weren't for the lines around his mouth and the stubble on his jaw, he could have been a boy again.

'When are they coming to do the photography shooting? Is that going to be soon?' asked Rowan, a gleam of excitement in her eye.

'The photoshoot isn't definite,' said Sylvie, who'd somehow become the champion of the Aitch project even though it was really Harold's thing. He was keeping very quiet and she guessed he was terrified of Yul's wrath. 'As I explained, we've sent the goods off to them for the fashion week, and when that's over, we'll hear if they do want to go ahead and place a proper order. We'll need to negotiate that, not just jump at anything they offer, and also make sure we can fulfil their demands without putting our own people out.'

'We seemed to manage this initial order very quickly,' said Miranda. 'All credit to Maizie for organising that so well.'

Maizie smiled at her in thanks and nodded.

'Aye, but 'twere the folk, not just me – they worked hard to get it done quick. They're willing to work on a regular order if needs be, now I explained it all to 'em.'

'But we must get this right,' said Sylvie, 'so it doesn't end up with everyone upset like they were with Stonewylde.com. I'm thinking of the boots – they ordered ten pairs of our special brown leather boots for the show, and Old Larch managed to get his team to make them in only two days. But that was exceptional and we certainly couldn't supply Aitch with anything like the volume of boots they'd probably need for the shops. We couldn't cope with an order for several hundred pairs, could we? So, we must think the whole thing through carefully.'

'Yes, but what about this photoshoot where they want to use our girls for models?' said Rowan. 'When will we know if they're doing that? How will they choose which girls they want?'

Sylvie shrugged at this, guessing the reason behind Rowan's interest.

'I have no idea, although if it's for their new season's range I imagine it would be very soon. No reason why it should just be girls – it could be boys too, as Aitch do both men's and women's fashion. But honestly, I don't really know any more than I've already told you all. And I'd like to point out that this is all thanks to Harold and his negotiations.'

All eyes turned to him and he blushed, jerking his wrists in his jumpy way. Yul sighed elaborately and squirmed in his seat. The stifling heat could only get worse as the sun climbed higher.

'What do you think of this mad scheme?' he asked Martin, who'd sat in grim silence so far, with his arms folded and a sour look on his face.

Martin shrugged and turned his face from Yul, as if the very sight of him was more than he could bear.

'Makes no difference to this Council what *I* think, does it? Folk know my thoughts on how Stonewylde has fallen back into the mire and how we should put it right again. I made myself clear many a time.'

'Well, I want to make it known now how I feel about this fashion thing and supplying them with goods,' said Yul firmly. 'I don't like the idea of it and if I'd been consulted, I'd have said no.'

'But why?' asked Sylvie. 'We all know how desperate the financial situation is and they're paying good money. Why are you so against it?'

'Because it's mixed up with Rainbow,' he replied. 'And you of all people, Sylvie, should understand my unease. You were the one who didn't want her here at all.'

'Yes, and I was over-ridden on that. And this isn't mixed up with Rainbow, so there's no need to worry on that score. We were just very lucky that she knows some people in the fashion world and happened to show them some photos of Stonewylde. I never wanted Rainbow here – you did. But now, with this Aitch business, at least one good thing will have come out of her visit after all.'

She glared at Yul and he looked down at his hands, his face hidden by his hair. She was glad he had the grace to look guilty.

15

Sylvie was surprised when Miranda ushered her upstairs into her rooms in the Tudor Wing later in the day. She'd been about to leave the Hall for the Village for a quick supper and to collect Celandine, having promised her eldest daughter that they'd moondance up at Hare Stone tonight for the Hay Moon of July. This year it fell very early in the month, which meant that there'd be a Blue Moon right at the end, on Lammas Eve. Sylvie had arranged with Leveret to take Bluebell up to the tower for the evening so she wouldn't feel quite so left out, as there'd been tears at the breakfast table that morning. Sylvie had no idea whether Yul would turn up at Hare Hill or not, but she was determined it wouldn't make any difference to her plans either way. He'd been avoiding her since the Solstice and she wished he'd get over this silly sulking about the painting. It had got to the point where if he bumped into her, he'd actually avoid looking her in the eye. She thought sadly of her hopes for reconciliation; this seemed further away than ever.

'I can't stay too long, Mum,' she said as Miranda sat her down in an armchair and quickly made a pot of tea.

'Just a cup of tea and a brief chat,' promised Miranda. 'Rufus is down with Maizie and the girls I believe, so at last I've got you to myself.'

'They do love his visits – it's funny how they've all become so much closer since we moved down there, isn't it?'

'Sylvie, I need to tell you something,' said Miranda, pouring their tea and setting the two cups and saucers on a little table between them. She looked across at her daughter and thought how much better she seemed recently – brighter eyed and in much higher spirits.

'Sounds intriguing!' laughed Sylvie.

Miranda hesitated and almost decided not to proceed.

'I want to ask your advice. It's ... the thing is, I've received a letter from my mother.'

Sylvie's eyes widened with shock and she carefully placed her cup back on the saucer.

'*Your mother?*'

Miranda nodded, and Sylvie saw the strange conflict of emotions in her eyes.

'After all these years, she's got in touch with me. I can't believe it either.'

'But you haven't had any contact with her since ... I don't know when. My birth? How did she know where to find you?'

'When we lived in the flat in London, she – both my parents – had that address. We moved there when you were tiny and I made sure they knew where I was. Not that I wanted to see them, but from a sense of duty really. Stupidly, I thought that one day they may want to apologise. I'd hoped to give them the means to make it possible.'

'But they never did.'

Miranda shook her head, and Sylvie saw very clearly the bitterness in her expression, even after all this time.

'I've neither seen nor spoken to them since they told me in the hospital, in no uncertain terms, that unless I gave you up for adoption and pretended to all their friends that you'd never even been born, they'd never see me again.'

'It really is unbelievable,' said Sylvie sadly. 'How anyone could treat their daughter that way ...'

'Well, they were the sort of people who cared more about their standing in society than they did about a sixteen-year-old daughter who'd been unlucky enough to get pregnant. It was the sort of scandal that would've been so humiliating – they'd never have been able to hold their heads up again in their social circle.'

'I don't know how they could sleep at night, kicking you out like that with a newborn baby.'

'They supported me financially until I was eighteen, all arranged through their lawyer so they need have no direct contact. I suppose they thought by giving me money – and it wasn't much – until I reached adulthood, they'd done their duty.'

'As if you were able to cope alone at eighteen with a toddler!'

'I know, but they were completely unrelenting. I remember in the hospital when I said that I couldn't give you up, my father saying that I'd made my bed and now I could lie in it. I can picture his face now, as he said that ...'

'So you told them we were moving here?'

'Yes, I thought I should. By then, of course, I knew they'd never want to be reconciled and I didn't want that either, so many years on. But I thought they should know where I was ...'

'Have they ever been in touch?'

'No, and they don't even know Rufus exists. Nor their great-granddaughters. But that's their loss – and now it's too late.'

She gazed out of the window and sighed.

'What's happened, Mum?' Sylvie asked gently.

'My father's dead. He died a couple of years ago apparently, and now my mother's been told she doesn't have long to live. And guess what? She wants to see me! I expect she's terrified of the reception she'll get at those pearly gates she believes in so fervently.'

'Oh, Mum!'

Sylvie rose and sat next to her mother on the sofa, putting her arms around her. Miranda's deep red hair, now a little silver at the temples, fell onto her chest and Sylvie felt her shudder with silent sobs.

'Don't be upset, Mum,' she said. 'It's just not worth it.'

'I know,' whispered Miranda. 'Why it still hurts, even after twenty-nine years, is beyond me. But it does. It's the thought that all those shallow, braying friends of theirs, all the philanthropic charity dinners and lunches and cocktail parties and golf tournaments – all that ghastly social life and their holier-than-thou friends meant more to them than I did. Stupid, I know.'

Sylvie held Miranda close for a moment, and then released her to look into her face.

'So are you going to see her?'

Miranda shrugged and took a deep breath. She picked up her tea, sipping it thoughtfully.

'I just don't know, Sylvie. I don't know what to do. I wanted to tell you and get your reaction. I'm completely torn. I'd love to just ignore the letter as she's ignored me since I was sixteen. But this is probably my last chance to see her again. What if one day I regretted not having made up with her? I just don't know ...'

'I need to think about it,' said Sylvie. 'I can't give you any advice until I've had a think. There's nothing else is there? No hidden agenda? She's not about to leave you a fortune or anything?'

'No!' smiled Miranda. 'The letter was short and formal, and actually came from her lawyer. He sounds like some stuffy old codger – just the sort of family lawyer they'd have. He said he was writing on behalf of my mother, at her instruction – that my father had died almost three years ago and my mother had been diagnosed with a terminal illness and was anxious to make her peace with me before she died. He made a point of saying that their Wills and Estate had been successfully tied up long ago, and I should be under no misapprehension that I'd be a beneficiary. It was only on that understanding that my mother wished to see me. In other words, if I were just gold-digging, forget it!'

'How very rude!' said Sylvie. 'As if you'd want their money anyway.'

'Exactly! But that's the sort of people they are, always imagining the worst of everyone. So, my dilemma is – do I go to London and see my mother, or don't I?'

Whilst Celandine and Sylvie prepared to go up to Hare Stone to dance with the hares, Leveret spent a lovely evening with

Bluebell and Magpie. Clip had gone to the Dolmen as usual, but had been particularly quiet for the past few days. Leveret was worried about him as his appetite seemed to have withered to nothing, but as ever he brushed her concerns aside. He took the remedy she'd prepared for him with good grace, but she knew he was only humouring her.

During the warm evening Leveret had taken rugs, cushions and a little picnic up to the roof of the tower, wanting to make it special for Bluebell. Sylvie had explained that she was feeling very hard done by at being excluded from the moondancing. The three of them sat on the roof, watching the swifts and the swallows arcing in the soft blue skies, and drinking "magic" strawberry elixir. Leveret told Bluebell she'd made it so that they'd all be able to see the moonbeam faeries later on, when they walked back to the Village. The three ate some little white-currant tartlets that Marigold had baked when she'd been told about Bluebell and Magpie coming for the evening – they were meant to look like little full moons, and Leveret explained that they helped your magic wings to grow new feathers so that your moondream flying would be better.

Hare lay on the rugs with them and Bluebell wriggled happily against her cushion, trying to feed a bit of her tartlet to the unreceptive creature. She hoped that perhaps Hare would grow magic wings too, and they could fly together in their moondreams.

'Actually, Auntie Leveret, this is better than going to Hare Stone,' she said, sipping at the sweet strawberry drink and licking her lips in delight. 'Poor Celandine's only got dancing and all that long walking. I've got this magic feast and Hare too!'

Leveret smiled at her and patted her little arm. Bluebell laid her blonde curly head against Leveret and sighed.

'And I don't like the man up there.'

Leveret frowned at this and glanced down at her niece, who was picking white-currants out of the tartlet.

'What man?'

'The one who was watching us last time.'

'There wasn't a man there, Blue. Only Magpie.'

227

'Oh Auntie Leveret! You know who I mean. He's the same man from our rooms in the Hall and I don't like him. I don't like his eyes and his staring at Mummy.'

'Is Starling coming back tonight?' whined Vetchling.

Both crones sat in their chairs by the dead hearth. In the kitchen the range was out so they couldn't even make a hot drink, but they had a bottle of mead and shared this in their filthy mugs.

''Tis not likely, sister. She were here earlier when you was sleeping and she's left us some bread and cheese, but 'tis Hay Moon tonight.'

'Dratted girl don't care for us no more,' said Vetchling. 'Now she's got her man, she can't be doing with us old 'uns. How will we live, Violet?'

Violet took out her pipe and tamped a pinch of her herbal mixture into the bowl. Vetchling glared at her, the seams and wrinkles in her gaunt face black with grime. Violet ignored the look and, before lighting the pipe, hawked into the fireplace that bore evidence of much previous throat clearing.

'I ain't stopping me pipe just 'cos you have,' she muttered. She drew on the pipe and took a toothless sip from the mug, smacking her lips in appreciation. 'Aye, that Starling o' yours is no good. I told you a man were a bad idea.'

'Aye, you did, sister,' said Vetchling sadly, her voice rasping horribly.

'Can you fetch the bread and cheese, my dear?' said Violet. 'I dropped the bread yesterday on account o' my poor back. I just can't stand straight no more.'

''Tis your old bones all bent up,' said Vetchling sympathetically. 'You're like a sea-blown hawthorn, sister. Aye, I'll get the supper in a minute when I got my breath. But I wish 'twere a nice, soft rabbit stew. I can't eat that bread and cheese much with my sore mouth and no teeth.'

'Aye, but that lazy good-for-nothing Starling can't be bothered to cook for us no more,' Violet mumbled. 'She don't care about

228

us, now she's with that Cledwyn and his kin. Forgot us she has, leaving us to rot.'

'Maybe your Martin'll drop by to help us?' wheezed Vetchling. 'He's always been a good man, your Martin. Soon be his time, right enough.'

'Aye, sister, you speak true. Time enough soon for our Martin. But not that Starling – oh no! She'll rue the day she made me cast for her, you mark my words. Starling'll be squawking loud by and by, and we'll just laugh, you and me, for 'tis her own fault. Always was greedy as a weaned pig, that one, and now she's got herself more than even she can swallow.'

In a corner of the Jack in the Green, tucked into the ancient wooden settles with their tankards on the battered table between them, sat Kestrel and a group of friends. They'd long finished their exams for the summer and many had now finished college altogether. The freedom from study meant that they now worked on the farms and in the Village industries, even students such as Kestrel, who'd be leaving in the autumn for higher education.

The talk was ribald, as it so often was at the Moon Fullness, and most of the lads were now drinking up ready to go for a stroll around the Village Green with a likely girl. The girls themselves were in huddle in the Great Barn, shrieking and giggling as they discussed the boys. They all could have stayed up at the Hall, and often did for the winter months when it was too cold for dalliances outside. But this very warm weather made the Village Green and surrounding woods, fields and haylofts a much more attractive option.

'Are you coming then, Kes?' asked Lapwing, a good-looking lad who'd recently turned sixteen. He had laughing blue eyes and a nice smile, and this, combined with his long legs and prowess at sport, made him popular with the girls.

Kes regarded him moodily and downed his tankard of cider to the dregs, banging it down on the table. He let out a loud belch and stood up. Lapwing and a few others headed for the door. Old George watched them fondly, reminiscing to the group of old men playing dice that they reminded him of his younger self, all that moonlust and laughter.

The wide wooden door stood open to the night and the lads ducked under the low lintel. But Kestrel hesitated and then turned back towards the table.

'Kes!' called Lapwing from outside. 'Aren't you coming?'

'No,' he muttered, 'I can't be bothered.'

He got another tankard of cider and sat down again, staring at nothing, his shoulders drooping. Jay and Sweyn appeared in the doorway and were surprised to see their mate there. Soon all three were sitting together drowning their sorrows.

'I can't stop thinking about her,' said Kestrel. 'I wonder what she's doing right now? Do you reckon she's thinking of me?'

'I doubt it,' said Jay gloomily. 'Why would she be? Living up in London with all them smart people and paintings and stuff. Why would she be thinking of you?'

'I heard they're coming to do a fashion photoshoot maybe,' said Kestrel. 'My dad was talking about it. She's bound to be with them, isn't she?'

Sweyn shrugged and drank steadily from his tankard. The Moon Fullness was one of the times when Old George turned a bit of a blind eye to drunkenness, and didn't chuck the younger ones out so early. Sweyn just wanted to forget everything. His recent encounter with Leveret had shaken him more than he admitted; she'd changed so much and he no longer felt he had the upper hand. He hated her more than ever, but could see no way of regaining his superiority over her. The lump on his head throbbed and he thought of what she'd said about getting it looked at. Much as he disliked the thought of taking her advice, he realised that perhaps he should.

'Where's Gefrin tonight?' asked Jay.

Sweyn shrugged again.

'He's up at the Hall watching a film,' he said. 'He don't want to drink 'cos he says it's bad for his skin.'

Jay roared with laughter at this.

'Bloody hell! How daft is that? Who cares about his skin?'

'He's trying to sort it out before Lammas,' said Sweyn and then suddenly remembered he was sworn to secrecy about this.

'Lammas? Why?'

'I dunno. Are you seeing Tansy tonight, Jay?'

'Yeah, what happened to Tansy?' asked Kestrel. 'I thought you'd had a date with her a while back.'

Jay scowled and looked at the table.

'Didn't work out.'

'But you took her up the quarry, didn't you?' asked Kestrel. 'How did that go? Did you crack the nut?'

'It weren't that simple. There was something ... I hadn't really planned it proper and we went to the wrong part o' the quarry I think. I ain't been back there since, but soon I'll go there in daylight and really explore the place. Then I'll know where exactly to take a girl at the Moon Fullness.'

'Will you take Tansy again?'

Jay shook his head and laughed harshly.

'She'd never go there again. She were shit scared. It *is* scary there, I'll give you that, but it's a good sort of feeling. Deep, exciting. I ain't never felt like that before. She were so spooked that it ended up spooking me. But I will go there again at the Moon Fullness, I tell you. It's the sort of place I'd take a girl for a good seeing to. Not a girl I liked – a girl I wanted to put in her place. A girl who'd been too clever for her own good and needed bringing down to earth again with a bang.'

He laughed at this and took a long draught of cider, then stood up to get another round in.

'You sound like you've got someone in mind, Jay,' said Kestrel.

'Oh yes,' he grinned, his eyes bulging. 'I have just the girl in mind. The time ain't quite right yet, but as soon as it is I'll know, and I'll have her up there like a shot. And she'll never be the same again, after I've done with her at Quarrycleave.'

Harold sat at his lonely screen in near darkness, reading through the e-mail and attachments for the umpteenth time. He wished it had come through earlier so he could've shared it with Sylvie.

Ideally he'd have shared it with Yul, but he'd seen him disappear upstairs earlier with some bottles, and Harold had enough sense not to disturb him now. It was the Moon Fullness tonight, of course, so the whole of Stonewylde was in mild upheaval as it always was on such a night; the old ways ran deep.

Harold remembered back to when he was a lad, and Magus was the ruler. Then the Moon Fullnesses had held even more significance. All the girls in the servants' quarters would be in a flutter about who he'd choose to spend the evening with, who was going to get lucky that month. And of course often it wasn't one of them at all, but a Hallfolk woman or someone from the Village. Harold recalled laying the fire in the master's rooms and how terrified he'd been of the man.

Lately he'd found himself thinking of Magus often; the sinister flashing red message on all the computer screens at Imbolc had had a profound effect on him. Many a time Harold found himself looking over his shoulder, feeling the hair on the back of his neck prickle for no apparent reason. He didn't really believe in ghosts but, like most members of the community, he had a healthy respect for the Otherworld and its inhabitants. The possibility that perhaps Magus had somehow returned – as implied in that flashing message – was something he tried not to think about too much, especially at times such as now, when he was alone in Magus' old office almost in the darkness. He shuddered at the thought.

Scrolling up again, he looked at the attachments. The office at Aitch had written that in view of the impressive quality of the items received, the company had decided to go ahead and use Stonewylde goods within their new Ethical Earth range for the winter collection. The attachment was a contract between Aitch and Stonewylde and the terms and conditions were extensive. Presumably Sylvie would have them checked over by a lawyer before they could be accepted. The other attachment was the order for goods for their new autumn and winter range and it was large – a huge number of felt hats, slippers and bags, wicker baskets, hemp scarves and a lot of Stonewylde leather boots and belts. It was an order worth a considerable amount of money.

Harold better than anyone understood why Stonewylde was in such desperate need of money. The community might appear to be self-sufficient, and in terms of food and most clothing, it was. But there were so many other things that must be paid for with hard cash, not least the farm vehicles and fuel to run them, and the agricultural equipment needed for food production and processing. The hardware for the computer network and all that entailed, funding for the students who attended college and university, medical supplies and equipment and items such as glasses and dentures – all these must be paid for somehow. And then there were even larger demands such as a new heating system and roof renovations for the Hall, glass for windows, solar panels and machinery for the wind farm. Much of the infrastructure at Stonewylde was in need of replacement and there was no money to pay for it; a source of income was now an urgent necessity, although few people in the community really understood the gravity of the situation.

In their e-mail, Aitch had said that once the contract was signed they'd arrange for the photoshoot to take place. There'd be preliminary auditions for suitable Stonewylde models to work alongside their professional ones, and they'd send their scout down at the earliest opportunity. Harold let out a deep breath; if this worked out it would kick-start the recovery after the disaster of Stonewylde.com. He had hoped that Yul would be amenable to Buzz's offer, but had known in his heart Yul would never accept him back at Stonewylde. Even years later, Harold vividly recalled searching for Yul in the woods, the day after Buzz and his Hallfolk gang had beaten him up during the Spring Equinox celebrations. He remembered Yul's fear at his summons to Magus' presence in the Galleried Hall, and his sympathy with Yul's sense of injustice. Harold remembered many incidents from their childhood at the Village School, when Yul was just a skinny little Village boy and big, sturdy Buzz had swaggered around bullying him with impunity. No wonder Yul had rejected Buzz's offer of help now. But, perhaps this new initiative with Aitch would start to put Stonewylde's financial affairs back on an even keel, and then maybe Yul would come round to the idea. Despite Yul's difficult behaviour in recent months, Harold felt infinite respect for him and would never willingly let him down – which made the accusations of treachery all the more painful.

In the massive sitting room upstairs, Yul sat on the sofa and tried to drink himself into oblivion. The television blared inanity in the corner and a near empty bottle of mead sat on the small table. But stupor evaded him tonight, however hard he tried. Instead, his eyes were constantly drawn to the enormous painting still propped against a wall. There was his source of despair – his quicksilver angel, blessed with moonbeams and surrounded by her sacred hares, bringing down the moon magic bestowed by the Bright Lady, dancing it deep into the spirals of Stonewylde.

Yul gazed at the painting as he'd done constantly since the Solstice, and marvelled at Magpie's insight. Somehow the boy had captured the very essence of the moondance, not only depicting his beautiful Sylvie, their daughter and the hares, but somehow making perfect sense of what was happening. Yul wondered yet again what must go on inside Magpie's head. Despite being mute and his apparent lack of wit, the lad instinctively understood the mystical moondance and then, even more impressive, had the talent to recreate it on canvas for others to appreciate.

Now, in the aftermath of the debacle that was this summer's longest day of the year, Yul couldn't quite recall exactly why the painting had upset him so much when he'd stumbled into the Art Room. He still felt a sense of betrayal at having his secret and intimate relationship with his moongazy girl laid bare and public. But in reality, he understood that what had truly upset him that day wasn't the painting at all. It was the sense of not belonging, of being excluded, of being on the outside looking in. That had hurt him in a place he hadn't realised was still so raw, touching on emotions not felt for many years. And because of this …

Yul hung his head and began to sob. Deep, noisy sobs that he didn't care if anyone heard, for he deserved the humiliation. He'd betrayed Sylvie. She was the reason he was here on this Earth, and nothing would ever be the same again. He felt such guilt that he wanted to drown himself in a lake of tears. He was stabbed by his awful, inexcusable treachery and infidelity, and wallowed in a pool of deep-red guilt. He could never go back, never undo what he'd done, never make it all perfect and beautiful again. He felt his deceit written all over his face and marvelled that none could see it. It was writ so large, so boldly, in letters of lurid, indelible, stinking fluid that could never be washed away. Sooner or later someone would actually look at him properly and notice it.

And as for Sylvie – she was walking around Stonewylde, eating, sleeping, caring for their daughters – and oblivious to his treason. She'd spoken to him and smiled at him, she'd looked at him in consternation and perplexity, felt annoyance and irritation – he'd been unable to respond to her because *UNTRUE* was on his shirt and in his heart and he was incapable of behaving normally. How could she not see his guilt? How did she not smell the stench of Rainbow all over him, oozing from every pore? How could he ever go near his beloved wife again, knowing that he was smeared with the unspeakable taint of that siren?

The mead at long last took its toll and his hand dropped the empty glass to the floor. His head sunk to his chest and merciful oblivion was finally his. As the small bright Hay Moon traversed the starry skies, the magus of Stonewylde slipped into drunken slumber.

16

Sylvie and Clip stood together on the roof of the tower, some-where private where they wouldn't be overheard. They gazed at the rolling parkland stretching away to the distance on one side, the magnificent trees in full July robes. But the searing weather had taken its toll and not only was the grass ochre-gold, but the horse chestnuts were starting to brown already.

'Surely it must rain soon,' said Sylvie. 'This summer has been unbelievably dry.'

'Of course it will, and then there'll be too much and every-where will be flooded because the earth's as hard as rock,' Clip replied. 'Sylvie, I have those papers here, signed as you asked.'

'Thanks,' she smiled. 'That's great – we can get the ball rolling then with this Aitch business. Do you think it's a good idea?'

He shrugged, his lined face looking so drawn that she wanted to hug him. As usual, she held back.

'I realise Stonewylde needs revenue,' he said. 'I suppose this is as good a means as any, although ... there's something about the fashion industry that somehow leaves a bad taste in my mouth. And my lawyer said this contract I've now signed is drawn up rather more in their favour than ours. If things don't work out, we're still bound to honour it, with no exceptions – there's no get out clause. But if that's okay with you ...'

'We don't really have much choice right now,' she said. 'But we'll have to come up with something else lucrative, I know. I agree with your reservations about the fashion trade – despite their "Earth Ethics" label, I'm not convinced the business is ethical at all. Still, better to have our folk working honestly and in lovely conditions, than to have some poor exploited workers in an illegal sweatshop lining their boss's pockets with Aitch's business.'

'True.'

'I do wish though ... I have a kind of fantasy, a dream that I've thought about over the years ...'

Clip watched her profile as her eyes roamed the parched landscape. His daughter was so beautiful, and he could never look at her without feeling a jolt of pride and love. To think he'd created her – the surprise of it never lessened. Her classical features, her long silver hair, the delicate fineness of her; Clip adored Sylvie and wished he were better able to show it.

'What do you dream?' he asked gently.

'That Stonewylde could become a place of healing,' she said hesitantly. 'I read somewhere of a new theory about the purpose of the most famous stone circle, Stonehenge. They say now that perhaps it was a place where people came to be healed, a kind of sacred hospital where the earth energy was so powerful that people made pilgrimages there.'

'Yes, I can see that,' said Clip. 'I must say I've felt very potent forces inside that great henge.'

'Well, I feel it's the same with Stonewylde,' said Sylvie. 'Not just our Stone Circle, wonderful though that is. There's Green Magic at Hare Stone, and on the Village Green, in the woods, up on Dragon's Back – so many places at Stonewylde where you can sense the energy and healing. Remember when I came here all those years ago? I was so very ill, and probably would've died if we'd stayed in London, but my cure here was miraculous.'

'It was amazingly fast,' agreed Clip, still finding it uncomfortable to reminisce about Sylvie's early days – and her exploitation – at Stonewylde.

'So, my dream is to make Stonewylde a place of healing. I'd love to offer the experience I had here to others,' she said. 'And if their illness were too far progressed for a cure, at least they'd die in a beautiful place with the Goddess in the Landscape all around them. Imagine if the last thing you saw as you passed on was the view from Hare Stone, or feeling the sun's rays on your face in the Stone Circle? That's the one thing that consoled me about poor Professor Siskin's death – at least he died on the Village Green, the place he loved most in the whole world, with the stars overhead and the trees all around him.'

She paused and swallowed hard. Tentatively, Clip put his arm around her and was rewarded with her head on his shoulder as she nestled against him.

'I don't tell you often enough,' he said softly, 'but I love you so much, Sylvie.'

She smiled at this.

'I feel the same, Clip. I'm honoured to have a father such as you.'

'As for your dream,' he said, 'I don't see why that couldn't happen. I've been talking with my lawyer recently about tying Stonewylde up safely – remember we discussed it before? She recommends that the estate becomes a charity, and that would sit well with your idea.

Sylvie turned and looked into his grey wolf eyes, her own shining with joy.

'Really? Could we *really* do this?'

'I don't see why not. There's yet more paperwork so we're talking about the future, not the present, but I think it could be done.

'I don't believe it!'

'Well, we have our wonderful Hazel, and Leveret's destined to become an exceptional healer too. We can recruit more staff if necessary or best of all, train our youngsters in health care. We could offer all types of therapies and our own natural remedies. It's a very exciting thought.'

'Though I guess we still need a source of revenue,' said Sylvie.

'That's true, but as a charity we can fund-raise. And our patients may be able to donate.'

'Maybe ... but it's really important that Stonewylde is for

everyone, not just the wealthy,' she said firmly. 'I'd never have been able to come here if we'd have had to pay, would I? Despite all the awful things he did, that's something I'll always be grateful to Magus for. He took us in when we were penniless, and it's thanks to his invitation that I was healed. And that I found you.'

The couple from Aitch who'd come to find suitable models and possible locations were overwhelmed by Stonewylde. Sylvie had instructed Harold to look after them, and a meeting had been called in the Great Barn for anyone interested in modelling during the proposed fashion shoot later in the month. Many of the girls and some of the boys from the Hall turned up bright and early, and Sylvie thought perhaps she should pop over there to keep an eye on things. Harold walked down with the photographer and her assistant who were slightly bemused to find themselves having to use their legs, and upset that their phones were unusable. When they arrived in the Barn, they were greeted by a crowd of eager youngsters all anxious not to waste their entire Saturday hanging about.

The photographer, a bright young thing named Chelsi, stood up and explained that she and Benjy were only assistants to the main photographer Finn, who'd be doing the actual photoshoot himself within the next couple of weeks. Today they'd take shots of anyone interested in joining the professional models as extras. Sylvie watched from the sidelines, noticing how helpful Harold was. They went outside and the youngsters formed a queue to have their photos taken. Meanwhile, Celandine and Bluebell and many other children ran around the Green as they always did at the weekends, whilst their mothers collected bread from the Bakery, meat from the Butcher, milk from the Dairy Store and water from the Village Pump.

Standing in the queue were Faun and Rowan, and Sylvie was amused to see Faun showing off so blatantly. She looked lovely and Sylvie was sure they'd choose her anyway, without the dramatics.

'Mother, why do we have to stand in this stupid queue?' Faun demanded, and Rowan replied to her quietly. Sylvie thought again what a spoiled child she was; everyone else was waiting patiently. Miranda had persuaded Rufus to take part and, as he and Faun were fairly close together in the line, she had a chance to compare them. Rufus had suddenly grown very tall and thin, and his arms and legs seemed far too long for his body. His gleaming auburn hair hung over his eyes, which were the same dark-chocolate brown as Faun's, and he was covered with freckles. He was a striking boy and complemented his half-sister Faun perfectly. They ignored each other and Sylvie thought what a shame that was, although Yul as the other half-brother hadn't been a good role model for sibling bonding.

'But Mother, Rainbow said I'd definitely be able to model for Aitch, so why do I have to do this audition thing? They should just put my name down,' Faun whined, and Sylvie itched to give her a good telling off. Instead, she walked away. Noticing Yul standing in the shadows of one of the Barn's buttresses, discreetly watching the proceedings, she went over to him. It was about time they patched things up, at least superficially. Yet, once again, he wouldn't even look her in the face.

'Can we please have a talk?' she asked him, a little more tersely than she'd intended.

'I was just about to leave, actually,' he replied, gazing across the Green at the spectacle of the Outsiders taking photos of the youngsters, one by one. Anything rather than look her in the eye.

'We *need* to talk, Yul. You've been so cold and distant lately and I—'

'Have I? I'm sorry, Sylvie – I didn't mean to be.'

'That's good. I thought you were ignoring me deliberately. Could we go for a walk and have a chat?'

He hesitated and she felt cut to the quick. Why was he so reluctant to have any contact with her?

'I suppose so ...'

'Good. Let's go down to the beach, shall we? Then—'

'NO!' he shouted, and Sylvie stared at him. He really was behaving oddly.

'Shall we just take a stroll around the Village Green instead?' she suggested. 'Maybe it'll do all those wagging tongues good to actually see us together.'

They walked, like a courting couple, around the huge circle of trees. Yul seemed to relax a little as she chatted easily, telling him about the girls and how they were getting on. Eventually she broached the subject that she knew was causing him distress.

'Yul, about my birthday ... I hope you know that—'

'I'd really rather not talk about it, if you don't mind,' he said stiffly.

'But Yul, the whole thing was a complete surprise to me. And—'

'Really, Sylvie, please can we leave it? I only want to forget that day ever happened.'

'But you're still upset – I can see it! I know you too well, Yul. You can't hide things from me. I know what's going on in your head.'

'Do you really? I don't think so, Sylvie.'

They'd come, finally, to the great yew tree. They stopped and both gazed at it. Their sadness was almost tangible as both were assaulted by memories.

'Oh Yul! What's happened to us? I never wanted it to be like this.'

'Neither did I. But it seems that what we once had has gone ...'

His words cut into her and shredded her heart.

'No, it's not gone!' she said shakily. 'And as far as I'm concerned, it'll never be gone.'

But Yul shrugged and turned away before she could see the tell-tale expression on his face, and the tears that yet again clouded his vision.

A couple of weeks later, Chelsi and Benjy returned to Stonewylde with a gaggle of models and a crew of assistants. They were to settle in and sort out the locations, and then Finn the photographer would arrive the next day to do the photoshoot. By this time, with all the fuss that surrounded their arrival, Sylvie was beginning to regret ever championing the stupid scheme. But the folk had already started work on the large order for goods and so far everyone had shown willing.

Yul had eventually been persuaded to allow the visitors from Aitch to use his apartments for their stay. He'd refused Sylvie's request at first but had then capitulated with bad grace; even he could see it was ridiculous for such a large suite of the very best rooms in the entire place to be used by just one person who wasn't even around half the time. The master bedroom, the children's room and several other rooms further along the corridor were given over to the visitors, whilst the great sitting room with the dumb waiter was their designated head-quarters for the weekend.

At the Hall, everyone was agog to see the minibus pull up and an assortment of glamorous people emerge, mostly grumbling, as the journey had been long and cramped. A second vehicle followed behind, crammed with the clothes, accessories and all the equipment needed for the photo-shoot in the morning. Assistants, make-up artists, hair-dressers and the models themselves were greeted by Harold and taken straight up to Yul and Sylvie's apartments.

Benjy emerged from the rooms later on with the list of Stonewylde people they wanted to use in the photo-shoot. Many youngsters were disappointed, upset to find they hadn't been included. Kestrel was chosen, but could barely speak from frustration at discovering Rainbow hadn't arrived with the other visitors. Miranda was delighted that Rufus had been chosen, although he wasn't so pleased. Faun wasn't in the least bit surprised to find herself on the list and made sure everyone knew about her success.

Sylvie sat in the office with Harold, going over the paperwork for the orders again. She wished that Yul would sort himself out and take part in this business arrangement. She and Harold were trying to organise the labour fairly and make sure there was a proper production schedule for the goods required. This was much more Yul's forte, but since the Solstice he kept disappearing on his horse, sometimes taking off for days. This meant Sylvie must be constantly available in case some decision was required.

There was a knock on the door and Chelsi appeared, looking rather fierce in a pair of heavy-framed glasses and wearing what Sylvie assumed to be a very fashionable combination of Aitch clothes.

'Hi there! I just wanted to run through everything that's happening tomorrow,' she said, a clipboard clutched to her chest. 'This is really Benjy's job, but he's sorting out a couple of the girls. He's so much better with them than I am. They're all having tantrums because their phones don't work. But there's no signal at all here, is there?'

Sylvie smiled a little incredulously, finding it hard to appreciate just how much difference this made to people's lives in the Outside World.

'Harold's your contact point and he'll stay with you all day tomorrow,' she replied. 'What time's the photographer arriving, by the way?'

'Finn said he'll get here first thing in the morning,' said Chelsi. 'And apparently there's a chance that Aitch may come too, which is a real honour. That doesn't happen very often.'

Sylvie wondered if she were supposed to be impressed by this. Presumably Aitch was incredibly famous and glamorous, but she was determined not to act star-struck.

'We'll arrange for breakfast to be sent up to your rooms tomorrow morning,' she said, 'although it would be easier for us if you could all come downstairs for supper this evening.'

'Fabulous!' said Chelsi. 'I don't know who I have to speak to about dietary requirements, but some of our girls are a little fussy in their eating habits. I have a list here.'

'I'm sure Marigold will do her best,' said Sylvie. 'Though we won't have anything exotic, I'm afraid. We grow all our own food at Stonewylde and we eat what's in season. But tell your girls that everything's organic at least.'

'I will, though it's the calorific value that bothers them, not the chemicals. To change the subject completely – I don't suppose you'd like to take part yourself tomorrow?' asked Chelsi, her glance appraising Sylvie from head to toe.

'Me? Oh no, I don't think so!' laughed Sylvie.

'Pity – obviously you're much older than most of our models, but Paige is a wizard with cosmetics,' said Chelsi.

'I'm sure she is,' said Sylvie, 'but it's not my sort of thing at all.'

'You weren't a model when you were younger then?' asked Chelsi.

Sylvie suddenly recalled Magus' remarks when he'd held her captive in his rooms, starving her into submission and dressing her like a doll in costly designer clothes. She shook her head with a chuckle.

'I only wondered,' said Chelsi, 'because I'm a scout and you've got that look about you ... What's your connection with Aitch then? I thought perhaps you'd had dealings in the past, maybe on the catwalk or something.'

'There's no connection whatsoever,' said Sylvie. 'Now I must get back to the Village and my children. I'll leave you in Harold's capable hands.'

That night Sylvie lay in her bed trying to get to sleep. She could hear the owls calling outside and then the cry of a fox, and she hoped the girls had shut the chickens in properly. She imagined Yul on the sofa in his office, where she assumed he was sleeping whilst the Aitch crew were in the grand apartments. It was a strange thought knowing that their private rooms were full of other people, but Sylvie found that she didn't mind at all. She'd never felt comfortable in those rooms and she realised then that she wanted to stay in the Village permanently. She wondered if Yul could be persuaded to move back here? If only they could have their own little cottage in the Village, just her, Yul, Celandine and Bluebell ...

Sylvie slowly drifted towards sleep with that delightful thought growing in her imagination. She pictured herself working at the loom with a casserole bubbling on the range, whilst Yul chopped wood in the back garden and the children weeded the vegetable beds. But then, something that had been tugging at her mind all day suddenly re-emerged and dragged her back from the brink of sleep. It was to do with Faun and her success at being chosen as one of the very few Stonewylders to join the photo-shoot in the morning.

Benjy had brought the list to Harold, who'd tried to find the half dozen youngsters on it to tell them the news. They were scattered around, some, like Kestrel, working in the fields and others in class. Sylvie had been in the School Wing when Harold had located Faun in the corridor. She'd witnessed the girl's smug lack of surprise at being chosen, in such sharp contrast to her friends' disappointment at being passed over. Sylvie had wished then that, despite her prettiness, Faun had been rejected too. It would have done her inflated self-esteem no harm at all. But now, lying in the darkness and half asleep, the thing that had been bothering her all day popped into her head.

She thought of the day when the scouts were doing the mug-shots in the Village, and Faun had been making a fuss about having to queue up. She recalled Faun's words, which suddenly didn't make sense. Previously, Harold had said that someone from Aitch had e-mailed him about supplying goods for their fashion show *after* Rainbow had returned to London; she'd shown her Stonewylde photos to friends in the fashion industry, who'd been impressed. And yet ... on the audition day Faun had complained about wasting her time having to queue because Rainbow had *already* promised her a modelling part in the photoshoot. Had Harold lied to her and the whole thing been a setup all along?

*

'Have a lovely day, my darlings!' said Sylvie to her daughters as she left them at the Nursery gate.

Both girls kissed their mother goodbye, skipping up the path and into the building with all their friends. Bluebell turned at the door and waved again, and Sylvie stood for a moment in thought. Should she pop in and ask Rowan about Faun's strange remark? Maybe she'd misheard, but it was bothering her, making her worry that there was some kind of subterfuge going on. But when she asked one of the women inside for Rowan, she was met with a laugh.

'She's not in today!' said the Nursery teacher. ''Tis the photo thing with them photographers and Rowan's off.'

'Really? Why?'

'On account o' Faun being a model.'

The woman rolled her eyes at Sylvie and smiled.

'But surely Rowan doesn't need to be there? I'm sure none of the other mothers will be.'

''Tis the girl's big day and Rowan wanted to look after her. That girl's the apple of her eye and don't we all know it!'

Sylvie queued in the Bakery with a wicker basket over her arm, chatting to other women waiting their turn. The aroma of fresh bread was wonderful, and Sylvie took her loaf with a grateful smile. She stopped off at the Butcher's next, as Maizie had asked her to pick up some beef for tonight's supper. She also wanted to pop into the General Store and get some more candles as she'd noticed Maizie only had a couple left in the drawer. When she'd finished these errands, she'd have a quick cup of tea and then go up to the Hall to see if Finn had arrived yet.

Chelsi had explained they'd be doing the models' hair and make-up in the Hall, and having a photo-session up there first. They liked the exterior of the Hall and the courtyard with its ancient cobbled yard and old water-butts, with the walled Kitchen Garden in the background. Later they'd be setting up in the Village for a longer session around the Green, outside the Barn and the Jack in the Green. Sylvie hoped that Rufus would

246

enjoy it – she was surprised he'd been chosen, given his freckles and gangly limbs, but he was a good looking boy and perhaps his unusual colouring and skinny height were what they wanted.

It would be strange seeing the minibuses and all the equipment down in the Village, and a whole group of Outsiders too. Sylvie had a moment of doubt – had she made the right decision encouraging this? It had only really gone ahead because she'd supported it so whole-heartedly; certainly Yul had made no secret of his distaste for the entire venture. But the money was desperately needed; apart from the revenue from the boots, clothes and accessories they'd ordered, Aitch were paying handsomely for using Stonewylde as a location for this shoot. Really, there hadn't been a choice.

With her basket over her arm, Sylvie walked back from the General Store across the cobbles and started off up the lane leading to Maizie's cottage. She knew Maizie was out and about today, liaising with the people working on the goods for the Aitch order, and making a couple of her welfare calls. She'd have left the cottage beautifully tidy, with the floor swept, the tops dusted, the kitchen scrubbed and the beds made

Sylvie walked up the path and opened the front door, stepping into the shady parlour which smelt strongly of lavender. Maizie had put jam jars of it in every window sill as it was good for keeping the flies away, a necessity in this heat. Sylvie put the beef and bread in the cool pantry and made sure the catch on the old wooden meat-safe was secure before shutting the door. If any insects got into Maizie's pantry there'd be trouble. The tiny room was immaculate, with rows and rows of preserves lined up, all neatly labelled in Maizie's careful writing.

Sylvie decided against a cup of tea after all – it was just too hot. Instead, she poured herself a glass of precious water and stood at the kitchen window gazing out over the long back garden. The sun blazed down and everything looked so dry. The chickens were scratching around in their enclosure and Bluebell's favourite, which she'd named Lucky Clucky, was enjoying a good dust bath. The pig lay on its side in the shade panting, and the bees were busy. Sylvie tried to imagine Yul here as a little boy, out in the garden helping Maizie grow the vegetables and tend the animals. She loved the fact that the girls were now doing the same. Even though she and Yul hadn't had a son, at least Rufus was enjoying his time here. She must try and work on bringing him and Yul closer, as Miranda had asked her last year.

She'd turned away from the garden to put the new candles in the dresser drawer, when there was a frantic knocking at the front door. She was surprised to see one of the young women whom she'd noticed earlier going into the Barn to begin work on the felt hats.

'Oh Sylvie, there's a message for you! You got to go up to the Hall – 'tis very urgent.'

'What's happened? What's the matter?' said Sylvie, grabbing her sun-hat.

'I don't rightly know the details,' said the woman, hurrying alongside Sylvie as they headed back into the Village. 'I were just starting on the felt with the others when the phone rang. 'Twas Harold, and he sounds in a right state!'

'Harold? Oh dear, I hope it's not some issue with this photoshoot!'

'Aye, I think it is! He said there were trouble and you must come quick as you can. He sounded terrible!'

'Nobody's been hurt, have they? I hope it isn't some horrible accident!'

Leaving the woman at the Barn, Sylvie dashed up the track, wishing for once that there was some form of transport available. The old painted cart still brought old folk down from the Hall to the Village and back, but it wasn't in use today. Why hadn't Harold sent down the models' minibus to collect her if it was such an emergency? She hurried along, clutching onto her floppy straw hat as her thin cotton skirts flew out. Where on earth was Yul when he was needed? This galloping off into the sunset on Skydancer would have to stop. She knew Clip was away for a couple of days, sorting out the estate with the lawyer. But Miranda and Hazel were up at the Hall, not to mention

Martin. There were people already around who could make decisions in an emergency.

As her sandaled feet sped along the dusty way, Sylvie became more and more concerned, imagining the worst. Why had Harold sounded terrible? What sort of trouble meant she must come up so quickly? Had anything happened to Yul or Miranda? Perhaps the woman had got it wrong and it was nothing to do with the photoshoot. She knew that her girls were safe in Nursery – who else could it be? Leveret? Or had some call come through about Clip? Maybe he'd been taken ill in the town or the lawyer's office.

At last the long, tree-lined drive came to an end, and she rushed between the huge stone pillars to the enormous gravel turning circle in front of the Hall. Its beautiful facade glowed in the sun, the hundreds of mullioned windows glinting. The minibus and transit van sat parked outside, looking completely out of place; since Magus' demise the only vehicles here were old, work-related ones. Then she saw a vehicle even more incongruous – a large and very aggressive-looking red sports car. Sylvie had no idea about cars, but this one looked very expensive indeed – all jutting angles and big shiny bits. She grimaced; this must belong to Finn, the photographer that Chelsi and Benjy had been going on about. Or maybe even Aitch, the owner of the fashion label. The last thing she needed, if there was an emergency, was to be worrying about being hospitable towards them; they'd all just have to get on without her.

Feeling hot and sticky, her bare legs dusty and her hair falling all over her flushed face under the straw hat, Sylvie hurried across the gravel and into the dark entrance porch. She heard the raised voices immediately, and Harold's voice the loudest.

'No! We must wait till Sylvie gets here! She's in charge, not you!'

She dashed across the stone flagstones of the porch, so worn and shiny, towards the open door. Then came Martin's voice.

'*She's* not in charge, you fool! And besides, you're nothing but a jumped-up pot-boy! I tell you, we—'

Sylvie walked in, blinded for a moment by the shadows after the brilliance of sunshine outside. She heard the arrogant drawl even before her eyes had adjusted to the dark interior, and smelled the alien stench of cigarette smoke.

'Do stop your squabbling, the pair of you. Really, I have no problem waiting for Sylvie to arrive. Aha! Here she is at last!'

Sylvie stopped dead in her tracks and her mouth went completely dry. Before her stood Finn the photographer and Aitch the fashionista. Sylvie realised that they themselves were the emergency that poor Harold had been unable to cope with. She stood and stared in absolute shock, unable to speak but finally understanding what Aitch actually stood for.

17

After all those years, it was bizarre to find Holly and Fennel in the entrance hall behaving as if they belonged at Stonewylde. Flushed, sweaty and covered in dust, Sylvie slipped straight back into her old role of gauche misfit and stood there awkward and tongue-tied. Holly, in contrast, had fulfilled her early promise and transformed into the soignée, sophisticated "Aitch".

'Sylvie, I never knew!' Harold squeaked. 'I'm so sorry! If I—'

'Hold your tongue, boy!' snapped Martin, looking as if he might actually strike Harold. ''Tis not your place to speak, and besides, why should anyone apologise for Hallfolk taking their rightful place again!'

This galvanised Sylvie into action. She turned on Martin and gave him a withering stare.

'Neither is it your place to speak to Harold like that, or use the term *Hallfolk* in that context. I suggest you get back to whatever you were doing, Martin, and leave me to speak to our visitors.'

Without giving him a chance to respond, she turned her back on him and smiled at Holly and Fennel. Holly was draped on a carved settle by the great fireplace, smoking a cigarette and flicking her ash towards the flower arrangement placed in the empty hearth. Fennel lounged against the mantelpiece over the fireplace, and both stared at her in bemusement.

'Welcome back to Stonewylde!' said Sylvie brightly. 'This is a surprise, as you knew it would be, and I can't pretend I'm not shocked. But let's go into the office and have some coffee, shall we? Martin – would you please arrange that with Cherry right now. Harold, do join us.'

She gave nobody time to demur but swept off towards the office, snatching the straw hat off her head. But then she turned and spoke over her shoulder.

'And Holly – absolutely no smoking anywhere in the building, if you please. That's one rule that'll certainly result in your early expulsion, should you break it again.'

There was complete uproar in the kitchen and Martin walked in to virtual mutiny. Cherry and Marigold were both a-quiver with indignation and outrage, which made Martin's championing of the visitors even stauncher.

'They got NO right to be here, not after all that happened!'

'How *dare* you say such a thing!'

'Bloody Hallfolk! Old Greenbough were right all along – let one in and they'll all be flooding back!'

The three older Villagers stood glaring at each other, the women's faces bright red with explosive anger, and Martin's grizzled face very white and grim. Finally, Martin broke the silence.

'Sylvie said to bring coffee for them all. So you better get to it, Cherry.'

Marigold clattered the kettle on the range and searched in a high cupboard for the best silver coffee pot.

'Aye, and they better not upset our Sylvie neither. Is she safe with 'em? Where's Yul when you need him? He should be here now supporting his goodwife!'

'Aye, sister! Nowhere in sight, and Clip's away too! Should we go in there and lend a hand, d'you reckon?'

'You'll do no such thing!' roared Martin.

'What about Miranda?' suggested Marigold.

'Aye, I'll see the lie o' the land when I take that coffee in. And what about Dawn and Hazel? Mind you, they were once Hallfolk and maybe—'

'Aye, Cherry, and now they're Stonewylde folk through and through.'

'True, my dear. Ugh, I never did like that Holly – nasty little madam!'

In the study, the atmosphere was tense but reasonably civilised. Harold had retreated to silence, the arrogance of the two visitors relegating him to pot-boy all over again, just as Martin had suggested. He perched miserably on the furthest corner of the sofa with his hands between his knees to stop them trembling. Sylvie had regained some of her composure and, although still dusty, now sat with her legs elegantly crossed and her hair smoothed, trying to maintain her dignity. She stared at Holly in fascination; it was nearly fourteen years since they'd seen each other, yet she'd have immediately recognised Holly in a crowd.

The feline face hadn't changed other than to become sharper and more brittle, losing the fluidity of youth. Holly's skin bore witness to her smoking habit; despite her immaculate cosmetics, it looked dried out and creased into tiny lines around the mouth and eyes. Her fine blonde hair fell in a beautifully cut bob and shone with expensive products. She was still small and lithe, thin but well-muscled, as if she worked out every day and ate very little. Holly looked like an expensive but jaded doll and her brown eyes were reptilian in their coldness. Naturally, she was dressed in the most fashionable and chic of outfits, which made Sylvie's faded linen dress and old leather sandals seem even more rustic by contrast.

Fennel was tall, slim and very much the dandy. He had a slight look of his sister Rainbow about him, but was nowhere near as beautiful. His hair was artfully long and distressed, and his rather weak chin and jaw sported blond stubble. He too was immaculately dressed and moved gracefully in his casually crumpled clothes.

'So ... why did Fennel become Finn?' asked Sylvie.

The pair of them sat opposite her on the other sofa and Fennel shrugged eloquently.

'Finn is cool, Fennel not so much. Somewhere along the line Fen became Finn. Simple.'

'And you're a photographer rather than an artist? I remember you always liked art.'

He laughed a little falsely at that.

'I leave the painting to my sister, who does it rather better than me. Photography is a far more exciting medium.'

'So where's Yul?' asked Holly abruptly.

Sylvie was annoyed that she couldn't answer this with any conviction, but she waved her hand airily.

'Oh, out and about on the estate.'

There was a knock on the door and Cherry came in bearing a large tray with the coffee. She glared at the two visitors and crashed the tray down on the low coffee table.

'Shall I pour for you, Sylvie?' she puffed, her cheeks scarlet with resentment and everything about her bristling hostility.

'No, that's fine thank you, Cherry,' Sylvie smiled. 'But if anyone can locate Yul, wherever he is on the estate, that would be wonderful. Thanks.'

Cherry stomped from the room and Harold twitched in his corner and stood up abruptly.

'I'll see if I can find him, Sylvie!' he gabbled and almost ran from the room.

Sylvie leaned forward and poured the coffee with as much poise as she could muster, very aware of the two pairs of eyes watching her every move and taking in every detail. She felt so scruffy compared to the two of them, although even if forewarned, she'd never have achieved their pinnacle of sophistication and style.

'So, Sylvie – you're the mistress of Stonewylde, just as you'd planned all those years ago,' said Holly, taking a cup of black coffee and refusing sugar. She sipped and grimaced, putting the cup back down on the tray with a delicate shudder.

'Indeed!' said Sylvie. 'My coup paid off and Stonewylde gained a new dictator!'

They gaped at her and she couldn't help but laugh.

'Oh come on! I'm certainly not the mistress of Stonewylde – we run the place democratically with a Council of Elders nowadays.'

'Magus would turn in his grave,' said Fennel, which made Sylvie shiver. He drank his coffee quickly and looked at his watch. 'Well, we'd better be getting on with the photoshoot. My time is valuable and I haven't come all the way down here for nothing.'

'You go on, darling,' said Holly, dismissing him with a wave of the hand. 'I'll stay and chat to Sylvie. We've a lot of catching up to do.'

'Hold on a second!' said Sylvie. 'I'm not sure that we'll want to continue with this whole venture. You've tricked us into it, and—'

'Oh no you don't!' said Holly sharply. 'You were given a bona fide contract and Clip signed it. It's legally binding and, whether you feel tricked or not, the deal will go ahead. I'd give in gracefully if I were you, Sylvie, because you won't win this one.'

Starling could barely push open the rotted gate as the dried-out riot of dead plants had flopped across the path and blocked access. Brambles scratched her dirty feet and swollen ankles as she waddled up to the front door and lifted the latch, bracing herself for the stench. All was quiet as she entered save for the frantic buzz of bluebottles, and for a terrible moment she thought she'd find two corpses. But then she saw the faint rocking motion of Old Violet's chair and breathed a gasp of relief.

''Tis only me come with some provisions!' she called, using the wicker basket to push things aside on the table and make a space.

''Tis the starling hopped back into the old nest,' muttered Violet from her chair. 'Found your way back then, my girl?'

'Aye, you know I won't forget you, Auntie Violet,' said Starling. 'Where's my ma then? Oh – she's asleep!'

'She's always asleep,' said Violet bitterly, glancing at the shrivelled up woman in the rocking chair next to her. 'I'm on me own most o' the time, it seems. You bought us some food then?'

'Just a loaf and some milk, Auntie,' said Starling blithely. 'The pair o' you don't eat enough to keep a sparrow alive. Here, I'll soak you some bread in the milk now.'

'I ain't a weanling!' said Violet. 'I could do with a nice rabbit stew. You got the makings for that? A tasty bit o' soft rabbit – mmn.'

'No, I ain't got time to build up the range and cook a stew,' said Starling. 'Last time you said to bring bread and milk and not bother with other stuff as it only spoils.'

'Pah! *You* can't be bothered is more like it. Just 'cos it won't be filling *your* belly, you can't be bothered to cook us something tasty. Come here, girl, and let me look at you.'

Reluctantly Starling sidled round the chairs and plumped herself down in her old throne with the log for a foot rest. The hearth was covered in ash since the grate had never been cleaned from the fire back in spring, and it bore evidence of the crones clearing their throats. Starling reflected briefly on all that she'd given up in her quest to find herself a man.

'You still enjoying your new nest then, Starling?'

Vetchling had opened her eyes a crack and gazed at her daughter with dislike. She'd shrunk in on herself so much that she was almost part of the chair, like a battered, filthy old cushion lining the wooden frame.

'Aye, he's a good man,' she sighed.

'If he's that good, why've you got a blackberry lip?'

''Twas my fault,' said Starling. 'He told me to shut up and I didn't. I got to learn new ways now and it ain't easy.'

Violet tutted in disgust and reached for her pipe, then discarded it when she remembered her pouch of dried herbs was almost empty.

'I never let a man do that to me,' she said. 'You're a fool if you let him beat you.'

Starling shrugged and patted the great mound of her stomach miserably.

'I don't mind that so much, though he is a bit handy with his belt. But he don't let me eat enough neither. Always him and his old ma first and then I have what's left, and only then if he says so. I need my food, a big girl like me.'

Violet chuckled at this.

'Not so big no more. I can see you lost some o' that fat and you've a sight more to go. So old Cledwyn's got you held down tight, has he? He'll be putting a bridle on you next! But you don't have to stay there, mind. You can come back to us.'

'But I love him, Auntie! He's a hard man and a mite heavy-handed, but I want him. I got a big itch and he's the only man to scratch it. He'd come and get me anyway if I moved back here – he already told me that. Said he'd drag me back by my hair and keep me tethered to the bedpost if I tried to leave him!'

She giggled excitedly at the thought of this, fiddling with her long greasy hair like a young girl preening.

'So who's to take care of us?' whined Vetchling. 'I need some-one to look after me with my poorly chest.'

'I'll tell Martin to come and see to you,' said Starling. 'He won't let you both rot.'

'No, our Martin won't,' said Violet. 'He's a good boy, right enough, and he won't let his old ma rot.'

'Aye, you speak right, sister,' wheezed Vetchling. 'He always were a good boy – better than my nasty pair o' brats.'

'Well, thank you for that!' said Starling indignantly. 'Who's the one who looked after you both all these years? Ungrateful old cow!'

She heaved herself up from the chair and took the little churn of milk and the loaf out from her basket. She located their filthy bowls on the floor beside their chairs and, as there was no water to rinse them out, she simply tore up some chunks of bread into each encrusted bowl and covered them with milk. Their spoons were wiped hastily on her skirt and she stomped over with the brimming bowls.

'There you are, nice dish o' milk sops each, just what you asked for. I'm off now and I don't rightly know when I'll be back. Cledwyn don't like me being out for too long.'

'He ain't there in the daytime,' mumbled Violet through a

mouthful of soft, slimy bread. 'He's at work in the Tannery all day.'

'Aye, but his ma watches me like a barn cat. She got me down on me hands and knees scrubbing the floors and weeding the vegetable beds,' said Starling. 'And if she says I ain't worked hard enough, I get it from Cled when he comes home – and I don't get no supper neither! So it's hard for me coming here and I reckon I done my bit, right enough. Our Martin can take care o' you both now.'

Without a backward glance she snatched up her basket and hurried out of the filthy cottage, leaving the door standing open.

'Stupid girl's left us in a draught!' rasped Vetchling. 'Get up and close the door, sister.'

'I can't!' said Violet. 'I can barely stand no more – 'tis my poor old back. You shut the door, Vetch.'

'In a minute, when I got my breath. She's given me too much o' these slops – I can't eat all this! I'll just put it down here on the floor for later ...'

They both dozed off in the warm morning, the flies buzzing around them.

The Aitch crew had taken over the Barn as their headquarters whilst shooting in the Village. The make-up artists and hair stylists had spread out the tools of their trades all along the trestle tables, with extension leads trailing from wall sockets for the hair-dryers, hair-straighteners and curling tongs. Covered racks of the brand new collection of clothes had been brought down in the large van and wheeled inside the Barn. Fortunately, there was plenty of room, so the scene wasn't quite as chaotic as it could have been.

Despite the bright sunlight, the photographic assistants were juggling large white umbrellas and light panels out onto the Green, and Chelsi and Benjy were in top gear marshalling and bullying, liaising between the different factions. Finn, as everyone knew him, was outside on the Green choosing his exact locations. This was the autumn-winter range, but the vegetation clearly showed it to be the height of a very dry summer, so he had to be careful. Inside the Barn the models were in various stages of dress and undress, and all heavily made up to look very natural.

As the youngest on the photo-shoot, Faun and Rufus struggled with the logistics of getting changed and seeing others do so. The scarecrow-thin models had been pulling outfits on and off up at the Hall all morning without a second thought, but Faun and Rufus both found this impossible and battled with modesty. Rufus had turned out to be the darling of the event and everyone made a huge fuss of him. They all found his freckles "adorable" and the silky red hair that fell into his beautiful dark eyes was much admired. Being so gangly himself, he was the perfect foil for the tall, skinny professional girls, and his shyness meant that he just stood still and smiled without fidgeting or trying to pose. Finn found him delightful to work with and talked of getting him on other shoots in the future.

Faun was finding it all rather heavy going. She was bitterly disappointed to find herself used as an extra, rather than starring as the main model of Stonewylde with the Outsiders as her attendants. She was reasonably tall with a slim but curvaceous figure; next to the models she looked fat and dumpy. She had a heated argument with the hair stylist who refused to curl her hair into ringlets; this wasn't the natural look they were aiming for at all. Rowan had been obliged to return to the Nursery to deal with a crisis involving one of the children, and Faun had to fend for herself. She had the horrible feeling they were all laughing at her. Kestrel and Lapwing, the other boys chosen as extras, were having a good time, although Kestrel was still upset by Rainbow's absence. His only consolation was in learning that Finn was her brother, and that she'd apparently mentioned Kestrel to him. The lad felt flattered and found Finn to be very friendly. Skipper and Betony, the other Stonewylde girls chosen, spent most of the time giggling together.

The folk in the Village were wary of the Outsiders who'd invaded their territory, and distrustful of all the equipment.

Finn behaved as if the entire Village had been put there for the sole purpose of providing a backdrop for his art, and Chelsi and Benjy were constantly engaged in smoothing ruffled feathers. Swift had tagged along to the group when they'd been up in the Hall and had made himself the indispensable go-between. Harold still smarted at Holly and Fennel's attitude towards him and found the situation difficult; Swift, being unaware of the old Hallfolk/Villager distinctions and blessed with silvery-blond hair anyway, was in his element. Finn kept referring to him as a poppet, and Chelsi and Benjy were happy to have someone so quick-thinking around to assist.

Holly had stayed up in the Hall after the morning's session. She was enjoying wandering around the building looking into everything and making loud remarks about just how much it had all changed from "the good old days". Sylvie decided she'd better stay with her, unsure what mischief Holly may get up to if left alone. She really wished that Yul was around to help and phoned down to Tom in the stables again.

'Still no news,' he said glumly. 'I'm sorry, Sylvie – I just don't know where he goes off to on Skydancer. I never liked to ask.'

'Could you send some people out on horses to search for him?'

'Aye, but 'tis the old thimble in the hayrick thing. He could be anywhere and Stonewylde's a big place.'

'You're right – it's a silly idea. Well, when he does come back, tell him we need him straight away, won't you? He's not going to be happy about Holly's ruse and I really could do with some support.'

Just then Leveret came into the kitchen from the Kitchen Garden where she and Magpie had been working all morning, trying to ignore the noise and commotion caused by the Aitch people. She'd kept herself out of sight, hiding behind the taller plants, as she really didn't want to engage with the Outsiders at all. Her senses felt assaulted by them; they were so noisy and bright and she couldn't bear it. Magpie felt the same, so they'd kept their heads down and got on with their work, and hadn't been noticed. But now she came in to get some food for them both, and bumped into Sylvie who was looking for Marigold. Holly had refused to eat the lunch provided and had requested a plain green salad with shredded chicken breast for her supper.

'Oh Leveret! Isn't this awful?' said Sylvie. 'I feel we've been invaded.'

'We have,' agreed Leveret. 'I hate them being at Stonewylde.'

'I wish Yul were here,' said Sylvie. 'I know he'll say, "I told you so" but I'd still like his support. Holly's a nightmare – she always was as a girl and she's ten times worse now.'

'Where is Yul anyway? Why isn't he here?'

'I don't know! Nobody's seen him for a couple of days now and I asked Tom to send out a search party, but as he rightly pointed out, Yul could be anywhere. It's too big a place to do that.'

Leveret was silent at this. She gazed out of the window for a moment and then went very still. Sylvie watched her in consternation.

'Leveret?'

The girl turned to her, green eyes still far away.

'He's up at the Dolmen.'

'How on earth do you know that?'

Leveret shrugged and gave her a little smile.

'I can see him.'

'You're amazing!' breathed Sylvie. 'You really are magic, aren't you? I wasn't sure at the Story Web – whether it was all some kind of very clever trickery. But it's not – you really are Clip's natural heir.'

'Thank you! He's up there, Sylvie, and he has no idea what's going on down here. Shall I go and get him for you?'

'Oh Leveret, would you? I'd be so grateful. I don't like to leave Holly to her own devices for long. I just don't trust her, and with Martin back to his old "Hallfolk are my masters" ways, I dread to think what she may get up to. Could you tell him what's happened and bring him back straight away? If you can persuade him to come, of course.'

*

261

Leveret contemplated taking Magpie along, but knowing how upset Yul had been about his painting, she decided against it. She dreaded being alone with her brother but also knew he must be fetched back to deal with this situation. He'd be furious and might well decide to shoot the messenger, but there was no choice.

She hurried up the dry track leading into the hills, where the earth was pale grey and laddered with roots from the silver birches that sprung up in profusion in this heathland area. The gorse all around smelled sweetly of coconut and Leveret noticed several adders amongst the heather as she climbed the track. There'd been many sightings of adders this year, perhaps because it was so hot, and she remembered the old skins they'd found that night near the boulders at Hare Stone.

That got her thinking of the Moon Fullness; soon it would be the Blue Moon on Lammas Eve, and Leveret wanted to spend the evening in Mother Heggy's cottage with Hare and Crow. The moon magic at the Blue Moon was especially potent and she must tap into that. She also had many plants to gather and harvest whilst the Bright Lady wore her blue robes, and would ask Magpie to help.

All these thoughts jostled in her mind as she crossed the edge of the heath and headed away from it, further up into the hills. Soon the Dolmen would be in sight and she must face Yul. He'd doubtless be livid at being disturbed, and especially by her. They hadn't really spoken since the early days after Imbolc. She knew he'd wanted to send her away from Stonewylde altogether, to attend boarding school in the Outside World. If Clip hadn't intervened she'd be there now; Yul hadn't liked to be over-ridden by his father-in-law and consequently had ignored Leveret ever since.

She focused on Yul for a moment, trying to visualise him. What hit her was a maelstrom of seething, unrelenting misery. At that moment the distinctive stone portal of the ancient edifice came into view and she saw Skydancer tethered in the shade of a nearby rowan tree. Of Yul himself there was no sight, but as she approached the tomb she saw it was clearly occupied. It was littered with Yul's paraphernalia: a bedding roll, a big stone water jar, the remains of a fire and a pile of books.

She called his name but there was no answer, so she went over to Skydancer. The great horse dipped and shook his head, allowing her to stroke his soft nose. Leveret didn't share Yul's affinity with horses but she'd known Skydancer since her childhood, when he'd been a beautiful foal. She was standing under the rowan tree with him nuzzling her chest as she stroked him when Yul appeared. His heart leapt with shock to see an intruder in his territory; this subsided to irritation when he realised it was Leveret, looking very grubby in her old work clothes.

She looked up and their eyes met, and for just a second he felt a jolt of affection for his little sister. He recognised the apprehension in her expression and knew that his scowl was fierce and unwelcoming. But the flicker of affection was soon smothered by exasperation; why had she come when it was obvious from his choice of bolt-hole that he wanted to be left undisturbed? He had no desire whatsoever to start mending his relationship with her, so if she'd come for that she'd be disappointed. She gave him a tentative smile and stepped forward.

'Blessings, Yul,' she said softly. Her green eyes sought his and held him in a luminous gaze. He felt something tugging at his mind and was instantly taken back to the time in Mother Heggy's cottage when the crone had ransacked him with her soul-searching. Surely Leveret couldn't do that? He broke eye contact immediately.

'Blessings,' he said tersely. 'Why are you here? If you think that—'

'You're needed urgently at the Hall. Sylvie sent me.'

His face changed, losing the closed hardness and softening into concern.

'Sylvie needs me? Right – hold on just a moment!'

He strode to the entrance of the Dolmen and gathered up all his bits and pieces, shoving them into the back of the cave then covering them with dried bracken. Leveret noticed it with a pang; Samhain and her first journey. Then he unhitched Skydancer and began to lead the horse down the path. Leveret had to run to catch up.

'Aren't you going to ride down?'

'No, I'll walk with you, so you can tell me what the problem is. I'm assuming it's nothing mundane or Sylvie wouldn't have sent for me, but nor is it life and death or you'd be more agitated. Are Sylvie and the girls alright?'

'Yes, they're all fine – it's nothing to do with them but it's pretty bad. Aitch and all the fashion people are here.'

'Yes, that's one of the reasons I chose to absent myself. I made it very clear to everyone that I didn't think we should do any kind of deal with them.'

'Yes, I felt the same,' agreed Leveret. 'I couldn't believe it when Clip signed that contract.'

They'd now reached the laddered path and started to pick their way down, trying not to trip over the roots that became more exposed as the dusty earth eroded further under their feet. Leveret went first, and Yul, leading Skydancer, followed.

'It was a stupid thing to agree to!' he said vehemently. 'We do need money urgently, but not by these means. I can just imagine the type of people they are – shallow and commercial and totally at odds with Stonewylde and all our principles. I'm sure they see us as anachronistic and quaint, and—'

'Yul, we've been duped.'

'Duped? What do you mean?'

'Aitch stands for Holly.'

'*What? Bloody hell!*'

'She runs her own fashion label and Finn the photographer is actually Fen. Or Fennel.'

'I don't believe it! The bastards!'

'They're horrible,' said Leveret.

'I know they're horrible! Bloody Hallfolk and their damn sly, sneaky, underhand, deceitful ... Oh, it makes my blood boil to think they finally managed to worm their way in by the back door – how bloody *clever!* Goddess, this is *awful!*'

'You can imagine what it's been like at the Hall since the two of them arrived this morning.'

'Holly and Fennel back in Stonewylde ... I just can't believe it!'

'It was bad enough yesterday, when the models and crew descended on us. But today when the pair of them arrived—'

'Didn't anyone think to throw them all out? Clip? Sylvie?'

'Clip's away for a couple of days.'

'Away? Where?'

'Seeing a lawyer, I believe.'

'Really? Not about this matter?'

'No – he'd already done that before signing the contract. He's seeing his lawyer about something different and, like you, he wanted to be away during the photoshoot. He said he couldn't bear the thought of Outsiders crawling all over the place.'

'Pity he didn't think of that before he signed the damned contract!' spat Yul.

Leveret glanced back over her shoulder at him. He was dirty and his hair a wild mess, and now his face was thunderous. She shivered; if anyone could get rid of these unwanted Hallfolk, it was her big brother.

'Sylvie did try to throw them out,' she explained, 'but it seems the contract Clip signed is legally binding. We have to go through with the photoshoot and fulfil their order or else we're in breach of it, and apparently Holly says she'd definitely sue.'

'The bitch! That sounds just like her. How come you know so much, Leveret?'

'Sylvie told me.'

'Since when have you been Sylvie's confidante? I thought you didn't like her?'

Leveret glanced at him.

'Sylvie and I have become much closer recently. We get on very well now.'

'Well lucky old you!' he said bitterly. 'I wish I could say the same of my relationship with her.'

*

Yul dropped Skydancer quickly into the stables, pre-empting Tom's attempts to pass on Sylvie's message with a dismissive wave of the hand. He was about to dash upstairs to his apartments to clean up when he remembered they'd been requisitioned by the Aitch crowd. Cursing, he flew into his office to have a quick forbidden shower and change of clothes before confronting the intruders, only to be greeted by Sylvie and Holly sitting in there on opposite sofas.

'Ah, the wandering hero returns!' cried Holly, jumping up. 'Good to see you at last, Yul!'

She went to kiss him, a charming smile on her face, but he glared at her and pulled back.

'Forgive me for the dirty clothes and stink of the outdoors,' he said abruptly, 'but I've been camping out and wasn't expecting visitors.'

'And we've commandeered your bathroom, poor thing,' she laughed. 'Not to mention your bed. When I saw—'

'Yul, I'm so glad Leveret found you!' said Sylvie. 'I've been entertaining our surprise guest all day and I'd hoped you'd come back to help me.'

Yul shot her a look of sympathy and then crossed to sit by her side on the sofa. He took her hand in his and squeezed it.

'Sorry I'm so dirty,' he apologised to her. Turning to Holly, he spoke smoothly. 'You must be feeling very pleased with yourself to have fooled us so completely. That was one hell of a trick, Holly.'

'Trick? There's been no trick, I assure you.'

Yul rolled his eyes.

'Let's not play games, please.'

Her thin, pointy face broke into a smile, revealing perfectly shaped teeth and razor-sharp lines around her mouth.

'But I love playing games, Yul. You should remember that. And as for fooling you ...' She shrugged nonchalantly and drummed her long fingernails on the arm of the sofa. 'Well, I must say I was pretty sure we'd be rumbled before arriving here, and I knew you'd never agree to the deal if you discovered who you were doing business with. Not after you'd rejected Buzz's offer of help.'

'Such powers of deduction!' said Yul. 'But you took the risk anyway.'

'My only hope was to get the contract signed before you realised who actually owned Aitch. I honestly thought you'd find out – it's not exactly a secret. A search at Companies House, not to mention a good dig on our website, would've given the game away.'

'We clearly didn't do our homework very thoroughly, did we?' he said mildly, and Sylvie was amazed at his restraint. Holly's smug satisfaction was unbearable.

'Well, no disrespect, but I don't imagine homework's ever been your strongest point, Yul,' she said, her brown eyes roaming over him insolently. Sylvie longed to jump across the coffee table that divided them and slap her hard around her nasty little face.

'True,' said Yul ruefully. 'I didn't even know my alphabet till I was sixteen, poor Villager that I was. And here you and Fennel are now, having completely hoodwinked us.'

'Yes, here we are and very lovely it is to be back,' said Holly, stretching like a little cat. Her scrawny arms showed off great muscle definition and the elegant shift dress she wore, boldly patterned in caramel, black and white, rode up slightly to reveal her trim legs, tanned and smooth, and shod in dainty black patent high heels. Her body was perfectly toned and expensively maintained and as she stretched, showing as much thigh as was decent, her eyes watched Yul very carefully.

He yawned hugely and turned to Sylvie.

'Shall we ring for tea? I'd like to see a copy of this contract. I'm sure it is watertight, but there may be something Clip's lawyer missed. Perhaps there's some loophole meaning we can legally eject these undesirables from the premises at the earliest opportunity.'

'Why *Yul!*' squealed Holly, her sinuous pose abandoned. 'There's no need to be so aggressive! We—'

'You were all asked to leave Stonewylde nearly fourteen years ago,' he said in a voice as cold and hard as black ice. 'Nothing has changed, Holly. You're not welcome here and the sooner you leave, the better.'

18

Fennel was having a tantrum as Yul, still dirty and wild, rode into the Village on his stallion. The models were posed around the water pump wearing Earth Ethics creations: voluminous skirts of woven material, little knitted jackets and Stonewylde felt hats and leather boots. Kestrel and Lapwing, wearing the male version of the new collection, stood behind them as if in deep conversation; both brandished pitch-forks. Rufus held a scythe and was in the centre of the scene, and the three Stonewylde girls stood in the background with wicker baskets on their arms.

Chelsi, Benjy and all the stylists were to hand, darting in and out of the tableau to tweak strands of hair and folds of skirts. Lighting assistants hovered just out of shot with the big white panels carefully angled to bounce light back up from below, and Fennel stood with a large camera getting more and more irate as the afternoon wore on.

'Why isn't *anyone* listening?' he cried. 'Sabrina – chin up there, towards the Barn. Jojo – *point* that foot, I want to *see* the boot! All to me, to *me*!'

He leapt around, twisting and turning, as the camera shutter whirred continuously. Village folk stood on the sidelines staring in bemusement, although many had grown bored as the shoot had been in progress for some time. Muttering and sniggering could be heard, which made Fennel spin round and glare at the culprits, only to find that someone on set had moved the second his back was turned.

'For Christ's sake, let's *lose* the damned yokels!' he hissed. 'Chelsi – sort them out!'

The girl with the fierce glasses and clipboard moved towards the gaggle of Stonewylders who lounged against the stone wall making wry comments. Just as she was about to remonstrate, the Nursery opened its doors and children began to pour out, laughing and shouting.

'What?' Chelsi, Benjy – deal with this! I *cannot* work under these conditions!'

Fennel ran a hand through his long, tousled hair and actually stamped a foot in distress. Benjy set off towards the swarm of tiny children heading their way, and two of the models began to sneeze violently.

A large woman in an apron came out from the Barn and walked straight across the set. She stopped in front of Fennel, planting her hands on her hips.

'Maizie sent me to say that tea's ready in the Barn,' she said. 'So come and get 'un now.'

The Stonewylde teenagers immediately unfroze from their positions and turned hungrily towards the Barn, causing Fennel to shriek at them all.

'*Did* I say the shoot is done? *Did* I say anyone could move?'

Into this chaotic scene came Yul. He sat astride Skydancer and held him on a tight rein as the grey stallion clattered over the cobbles. The horse was spooked by the strangers and particularly disliked the reflective panels. Yul had come straight from meeting Holly and was still dishevelled and unwashed, his clothes rough and his boots dusty. None of the Aitch team had seen him before and everyone stared up at the dark man in fascination.

Yul regarded the crowd and located Fennel, still recognisable as the youth of Yul's memory. His immediate thought was to jump off his horse and punch Fennel on the nose, as he'd always longed to do as a boy. But now ... he had an example to set, but more to the point – what had Rainbow told her brother and Holly? This was a terrifying thought, but he'd just have to assume that Rainbow had been discreet.

'Tea in the Barn?' he said loudly. 'What are you all waiting for?'

The six Stonewylde teenagers, all bored and tired with standing around for hours on end, gave him grateful looks and immediately trooped off to the Barn. Fennel was furious at having his shoot disbanded like this, but couldn't take his eyes off Yul. So this was how the Village boy had turned out. He still looked rough and ready, but no less attractive for that. The set emptied until only Fennel and Chelsi remained. She stared at the dark and authoritative man with open admiration.

'Go and keep an eye on them all, Chelsi,' said Fennel, putting the camera carefully into its lined bag. 'Make sure the clothes are covered if they're stuffing their faces, and don't let anyone wander off. We'll be regrouping over by that yew tree in twenty minutes.'

'Okay, Finn. With the Russet Rustics range?'

He nodded.

'Yes, but nobody's to get changed until I've come in and spoken to them all. It's like herding cats today and I need everyone together when I talk to them.'

She smiled up at Yul, who was still engaged in keeping Skydancer under control, and then she walked briskly towards the Barn. Fennel snapped the camera bag shut and then turned to Yul.

'You haven't changed much.'

'Neither have you,' Yul retorted.

'Have you seen Holly yet?'

'Yes, and she's on her way down with Sylvie.'

'We were wondering when you'd stop skulking in the shadows and actually make an appearance.'

'I'd hoped to avoid you altogether, but Sylvie asked me to come.'

'Why avoid us? You didn't even know it *was* us, surely?'

'True – it was a clever ruse. But let me tell you, Fennel – as soon as this photoshoot's finished, you're out. Gone – and not coming back again.'

Fennel gazed up at him, his eyes narrow with dislike.

'Well, we'd better make sure we take our time, hadn't we?'

Martin looked around in horror, a handkerchief held to his face. He'd grown up here in squalor, but that was many years ago; the scene around him brought back memories of the worst aspects of his childhood and made his heart beat faster in panic.

'Mother, you must move up with me,' he said. 'This is no good.'

'Never!'

'And Aunt Vetchling – she needs treatment. She's not looking well at all.'

'Are you saying your own mother, the Wise Woman o' Stonewylde, ain't good enough to treat her sister?'

Old Violet regarded her son balefully. Despite the heat, she clutched her greasy shawl around herself. Her face was dark with grime, and the smell emanating from her bent-up body was indescribable.

'No, Mother, 'tis just that—'

'I want rabbit stew!' she muttered. 'Me and Vetch, we ain't had proper food for a long time. That feckless Starling ... the girl's cursed and she'll get her come uppance, right enough.'

'When did she last visit? She told me she'd been yesterday and brought you food.'

'I don't remember ... 'Twas a while back. Food – pah! Milk sops is all she brung us, and curdling as soon as she'd gone. We need meat to keep our strength up.'

Martin stared at her in dismay, noting the stringy arms beneath her shawl and the scrawniness of her neck. He could barely force himself to look at Vetchling, who slept in her chair in a grey heap, her emaciated face withered and skull-like. He wondered if it was too late for her altogether, for her breath rattled and bubbled and she'd shrivelled to nothing.

'I'm going back to my cottage now,' he said firmly, 'and I'll send the goodwife here straight away with food and provisions for you. She can also start to clean the place up.'

Old Violet grumbled a bit at this, rocking in her chair.

'Aye, but I don't want her poking into things,' she muttered. 'Never did like that woman.'

'Mallow will do exactly as she's told, Mother, so don't fret. But we can't have this, can we? The flies ...'

'I need more baccy and more mead,' said Violet querulously. 'Send them down with her. And a nice bit o' rabbit.'

'We'll see,' said Martin grimly, his face still pale with disgust. 'When Mallow's scrubbed the place up a little we'll decide what's to be done. I don't see that you and Aunt Vetchling can look after yourselves any more.'

'No, we're old and feeble now!' said Violet. 'We need to be coddled. But we ain't moving and that's rock-sure, so your Mallow can come down every day, and you can get that Jay to chop wood for us again, lazy lout that he is. Smoked our pipes but never lifted a hand to helping us old 'uns.'

'And Swift – my boy can do his bit too,' said Martin. 'I'll not have it said that my son shirked his duty. And Magpie as well – there are three boys who should be down here helping out.'

'Aye, right enough. You're a good lad, Martin. I said you'd not let us rot.'

'No, o' course not, Mother. I still can't believe Starling just walked out like that! I never knew.'

'Starling – pah! She'll rue the day she cast for a man. Mark my word, son. That Cledwyn's a nasty piece o' work and she'll be sorry, just as I told her. I don't want her back here no more neither. Look at poor old Vetch! Starling just turned her back on her mother and me and left – never even shut the door, and we all know what *that* means!'

Holly had changed into more casual attire but was still very chic next to Sylvie and the other Stonewylde women.

'We need an evergreen!' said Fennel. 'Everything else screams of summer, and this is the autumn/winter collection.'

Sylvie caught Yul's eye. He stood with Bluebell in his arms watching the scene with dismay.

'But you can't ...'

Sylvie stopped, not knowing what to say. The yew was there for all to enjoy of course, in full view on the Village Green. But somehow it was their private, special place, and the thought of Aitch invading it was horrible.

'What's the matter?' asked Holly in mock concern. 'Why not the yew? Oh! I've just remembered!'

She let out a bray of laughter and her eyes danced with malice.

'Remembered what?' asked Fennel irritably. The models and stylists were in the Great Barn changing into a new batch of clothes whilst he and the assistants set up the next location.

'I saw them kissing under this tree all those years ago! Kissing and God knows what else. Oh, how very sweet! She doesn't want us using their special tree!'

'Why is that lady laughing, Father?' asked Bluebell. She lowered her voice to a loud whisper. '*I don't like her very much.*'

Yul squeezed her tight and chuckled.

'*Neither do I!*' he whispered into her soft curls.

'Please, Holly – our child is here,' said Sylvie, casting an agonised glance at Yul.

'Don't worry, darling – your secret's safe with me,' Holly laughed, eyeing them slyly. Yul stared at her, wondering what she meant by that. 'And what a pretty child she is!' she added

'Thank you,' said Sylvie, edging a little closer to Yul and Bluebell.

'Could we possible include the three of you in this next set? Purely as extras of course. You all look so wonderfully bucolic.'

'Absolutely not!' snapped Yul.

Fennel glanced up from his viewer to look at them.

'You're right, Aitch,' he said. 'They'd be perfect.'

At that point, the Village School opened its doors and an even larger flock of children poured out through the gate, like a murmuration of starlings.

'No!' he cried. 'This is bloody *ridiculous*!'

Benjy was leading some of the models and extras across the Village Green from the Barn, and they became surrounded by children dancing around excitedly on the cobbles and dead grass. The stylists and remaining models emerged, also getting tangled up with children and Fennel groaned, raking his hand through his hair again and looking wildly about him. He lifted the end of a branch of the yew – a massive branch clothed in the dark green barbs – and tried to peer into the gloom under the tree.

'Aha! This looks interesting in here – and a lot more private.'

Sylvie jerked in horror.

'Oh Yul, please! Don't let them take photos under our yew.'

He still had Bluebell in his arms but he turned to look at Sylvie. Their eyes locked into each other's, pale silver-grey into deep smoky-grey. His guilt still hung heavily in his heart but, stronger than that, his love for his beautiful wife flared brightly. As they stared deep into one another's souls, the mutual memory shimmered between them. He tore his glance away to move quickly towards Fennel, and Bluebell had to cling on tightly.

'No!' he said sharply. 'You mustn't take photos under there.'

'Why ever not?' asked Fennel, pulling the branch aside even further. 'Actually, it looks perfect. That trunk is incredible and it looks almost wintry, it's so dark.'

'Let me see,' said Holly, coming forward.

'You can't take all those people in there!' said Yul.

'Why? We—'

'Because the yew tree is heavily toxic, and someone might get poisoned,' came a clear voice, and all turned round to stare at Leveret.

'Who on earth are *you*?' asked Fennel, eyeing her speculatively. 'And why didn't you audition as an extra?'

Leveret ignored this and stepped forward to join the group, with Celandine by her side.

'Auntie Leveret!' cried Bluebell happily.

'Hello, Celandine!' said Sylvie, bending to kiss her other daughter.

'Look, I really don't have all day,' snapped Fennel. 'The light's changing and I need to get these outfits shot.'

The group of models, extras and stylists were now milling around on the grass waiting to be instructed, and the assistants stood with their panels, umbrellas and lights.

'Just do it, darling,' said Holly, lighting a cigarette.

'No! You mustn't take these people under the yew tree,' said Leveret firmly. 'It's extremely toxic – not just the berry seeds, leaves and bark, but the air itself can be affected too. Surely you don't want to risk anyone falling seriously ill?'

'How do you know about this?' asked Fennel sceptically.

'Because I'm studying medicine and yew is one of the best known poisons. *Taxus baccata* – some say it's linked to the word "toxic",' Leveret replied. 'If your professional models were to be taken ill ...'

'Alright, alright!' muttered Fennel, dropping the branch and turning from the tree. 'We'll do the shots outside the Jack in the Green instead. I'll just have to find somewhere else to shoot a non-seasonal exterior that looks natural. Where's Rufus, by the way? Don't tell me he's disappeared!'

'He's round the back of the Barn,' said Benjy. 'That big horse is tied up there and Rufus went to see it. I'll go get him now.'

As the crowd moved off towards the pub, Yul and Sylvie gazed at each other again and he felt a surge of love. She did still love him, that was for sure. He'd been wrong to think she'd left him for good; it was obvious her feelings still ran deep. Maybe, just maybe – if he could put the terrible guilt to one side and Rainbow kept her mouth shut – there was hope for them yet. He smiled at her and she smiled back. Setting Bluebell onto her feet, he held out a hand to her.

'Sylvie ...'

She took it and he felt her longing.

'Mummy, did Auntie Leveret just save the day?' asked Celandine, tugging at her other hand. She'd learnt the new expression at Nursery and was anxious to try it out. Dragging her gaze from Yul's, Sylvie smiled down at her daughter.

'She most certainly did! Thank you so much, Leveret.'

Leveret had been hanging back, not wanting to intrude nor

276

wishing to join the photographic group. She came forward and smiled, her green eyes glowing.

'A pleasure! The yew is sacred – we don't want that bunch of idiots messing up the magic, do we?'

Marigold stood in the cavernous kitchens at the Hall, hands on ample hips, facing Martin.

'Our Magpie is *not* going down to that cottage nor ever will!'

''Tis only right, woman! He's a grandson too, just the same as Jay and Swift, and he should be helping out as well. It's only fair that—'

'Only *fair*?' Marigold's voice was almost a screech. 'From what I heard, our poor boy spent most o' his young life working like a slave for them three women. And—'

'And so he should, just like any other young Stonewylde Villager. 'Tis part of our way o' living, that the young should help the old.'

'Aye, but not to be beaten and starved as he were. I can tell you now, Martin – Magpie will never set foot in that filthy hovel again. By all means send your boy and Jay in, but leave our Magpie out of it!'

'Finn and I are staying down in the Village for a while,' said Holly to Chelsi. 'There's an old chum of mine who's still here and we're popping in to visit her.'

'Okay, Aitch,' said Chelsi brightly, supervising the loading of the clothes racks back into the transit van. 'We'll see you at tea-time.'

'We've had tea already,' said Holly. 'But we'll be back for dinner. God I hope they've sorted out something edible for me. That lunch was disgusting.'

'Don't you start,' said Fennel. 'The girls have done nothing but moan about the food, which is ridiculous considering they only ever eat a forkful of anything anyway.'

'Do you want me to send the minibus down for you later?'

asked Chelsi, watching the models, stylists and assistants climbing aboard.

'No, we'll walk. In the absence of a gym, I need some form of exercise,' said Holly, drawing on her cigarette.

'Speak for yourself!' said Fennel. 'I don't want to walk all the way back to the Hall. We had to do that far too often as youngsters.'

'It'll do you good, you flabby old thing!' said Holly with a sharp jab at his stomach. 'Just keep an eye on all the girls, won't you, Chelsi? We don't want anyone wandering off and getting lost in the Hall – it's so vast.'

She tossed her cigarette to the cobbles and ground it out, then, with a quick look around, kicked the butt out of sight.

The minibus and transit van drove slowly out of the Village, avoiding a line of ducks waddling across the track and an old man who glared fiercely and took his time moving out of the way. Holly and Fennel headed for the Village School; Swift had told them that Dawn would be found either there or in the cottage next door.

From the school windows she'd watched the crowd on the Village Green and had been fascinated to see Fennel and Holly in action. She'd kept well out of sight though, and her heart sank when she heard a loud voice calling through the open school door.

'Coo-eee! Are you here, Dawn?'

She put aside the lessons she was preparing for the next day with a sigh, and quickly smoothed down her hair and dress. Like Sylvie, she felt very frumpy next to the immaculate Holly, especially after a long day teaching in the heat. She'd hoped to finish her lesson prep quickly and get back into the cottage to start supper before David came home from the Hall School.

'Holly, Fennel! What a surprise!'

The pair of them looked completely out of place in the Village School, even though they'd both once been pupils here. They looked around in wonder, and at Dawn with incredulity.

'Goodness, Dawn – you've changed! Whatever's happened to you?' exclaimed Holly thoughtlessly.

Dawn swallowed her retort and reminded herself that civility was the better way. Holly closed in on her and tiptoed to air-kiss both cheeks, as did Fennel.

'I'm the head-teacher here now,' Dawn replied with a smile. 'And I've recently been handfasted too. So my life is quite hectic.'

'Indeed,' said Holly, gazing around but not even noticing the bright paintings and pictures that covered every wall. 'God, this takes me back. I remember sitting on that very same bench there, flicking beetles at Yul one autumn when there was a plague of the things.'

'Can I get you a cup of tea?' asked Dawn. 'Presumably you're on your way back to the Hall?'

She led them both into her cottage and they sat in the tiny parlour where Rainbow had also sat only a matter of weeks before. Sipping his tea, Fennel closed his eyes wearily.

'What a day!' he said. 'It's not been the best of shoots so far.'

'So, tell me everything,' said Dawn with polite enthusiasm. 'I can't believe you're in the fashion industry and so successful. It's all so glamorous! And you're a photographer, Fennel! Well done both of you. Are you two married?'

They both shouted with laughter at the notion.

'I'm divorced,' said Holly. 'It only lasted eighteen months, the bastard. But he was worth a fortune, so I got to keep Aitch as my settlement and we're doing very well. I studied fashion design of course, and I've worked for all sorts of fashion houses. But nothing beats having your own label.'

'What about you, Fennel?'

'It's Finn now,' he said. 'I went to art school but I realised that wasn't what I wanted, and photography was. I freelance of course, but I'm also Aitch's house photographer and artistic director for the shows.'

'That does all sound impressive! And what news of Buzz? Rainbow didn't mention any of you when I asked her. She implied she wasn't really in touch with any of the old crowd, other than you of course, Fenn – Finn. How's Buzz?'

Holly and Fennel exchanged a look and Holly laughed.

'Oh, you know old Buzz – always a bit of a lad, wasn't he? He's married, with two young kids. Wife's a wimp, but Buzz can be a naughty boy of course. Doing well in business last I heard.'

'So he—'

'Do tell us about your husband!'

But when Dawn started to tell them about David it was obvious they weren't interested. Instead they started to ply her with questions about Stonewylde, the Council of Elders, Sylvie and Yul, Clip and his plans. They seemed to know quite a lot already, but Dawn couldn't be sure exactly how far their knowledge went, as they were very guarded. She began by answering fairly openly, but after a while their relentless interrogation irritated her.

'Look,' she said abruptly after a particularly personal question about Yul and Sylvie's marriage, 'I can see this isn't a social call at all. You've just come to find out as much as you can and you're trading on the fact that I used to be Hallfolk with you in the old days.'

'Oh Dawn!' said Holly, 'of course it's a social call! Nobody else at Stonewylde will speak to us – you're the only friendly face here.'

'We're just interested in what's happened to the old place over the years,' said Fennel. 'You're lucky – you weren't kicked out like we were.'

'Actually I was,' said Dawn. 'And it took me a long time and a lot of effort to be allowed back in. I'm not going to jeopardise that by appearing to be your mole. It was bad enough that Rainbow used me as a way to get back into Stonewylde.'

'What's poor Rainbow done wrong?' asked Holly sharply. 'No need to be hard on her. All she wanted was a sabbatical.'

'Maybe,' said Dawn, 'but seeing her again made me realise that I just don't share her – or your – values. I'm sorry if this appears rude, but I think you'd better leave now, before people start thinking I've been fraternising with the old Hallfolk and that my loyalties lie with you.'

'My God, she's gone native!' said Holly rudely, standing up. 'Well, good luck to you, Dawn, if it's what makes you happy.'

'It does,' said Dawn quietly. 'It makes me very happy.'

Holly's scathing gaze swept the small, simple parlour and then brushed over Dawn's untidy hair, and creased skirt and blouse. Her lip curled and she tugged at Fennel to get him up out of the chair.

'Come on, Finn. Let's leave Dawn to her idyllic lifestyle. Hubby'll be home soon, and there's tea to cook and housework to be done.'

Dawn watched their retreating backs, noticing how Swift appeared from nowhere to escort them. She felt upset at their nastiness but overriding that was a profound sense of relief that she was not, and never would be, one of them.

'Well this has made my day!' beamed Maizie at the sight of Sylvie and the girls returning to the cottage with not only Leveret, but also Yul in tow. 'What a turn up! Lucky there's a big beef pie in the oven for supper. I can do some extra potatoes, and—'

'I hope it's alright, Mother Maizie, but I've invited Rufus too,' said Sylvie. 'Yul's tethered Skydancer down by the orchards where there's still some grass, and Rufus is getting him some water. He'll be along soon – is that okay?'

'Course 'tis!' laughed Maizie, bustling back into the kitchen. 'More folks, more jokes, I always say. Do you all want tea, or a drop o' cider to celebrate this lovely family get-together? I got a nice little barrel in the pantry. Leveret, can you sort that out for me, my love?'

The little cottage was full and Maizie was in her element. Rufus returned shyly from the orchard, where he'd given Skydancer a bucket of water and made sure the stallion was comfortable. He was so honoured that Yul had entrusted him with this chore. When he'd seen his older brother approaching earlier, he'd been terrified of Yul's wrath at finding him round the back of the

Barn with Skydancer. He'd abandoned the stupid photoshoot as soon as he'd realised that Yul's beautiful horse had been left unattended.

But Yul had smiled at him – it seemed to Rufus this was the first time ever – and thanked him for keeping Skydancer happy. Then Sylvie and the girls had appeared and she'd suggested Rufus join them for supper, and Yul had actually smiled again and said it was a good idea. Rufus was almost beside himself with joy, but felt awkward walking in as, technically, he wasn't one of the family by blood or marriage. Although Yul was his half-brother and Sylvie his half-sister, and the girls his half-nieces, he wasn't related to Maizie at all, and it was her cottage and her family reunion.

But as soon as he arrived, the little girls were all over him as usual. Maizie told him to wash his hands as he smelt of Yul's horse, and Yul grinned in a conspiratorial way. Leveret gave him a really big smile too, and when he sat next to her, as there was nowhere else to sit, she whispered how glad she was that he was there as this was her first time home since February, and she was feeling very awkward. Yul poured him a small tankard of cider and said that Rufus was so tall now it was hard to imagine him still a child, and Maizie asked if he'd be kind enough to chop a few more logs for the range during the week. Rufus sat there, his ears burning red and his auburn hair falling into his eyes, and thought this was the very best moment of his whole life, to be part of such a family gathering.

'I need neutral external backdrops,' Fennel said as he, Holly and Swift trudged up the track to the Hall. Despite his offer, Holly had refused to let Swift phone up from the Barn to request a vehicle to fetch them.

'So the shots against the Great Barn ...' said Swift, flicking his silvery blond hair aside.

'Yes, they're okay, but most of the stuff on the Village Green will be no good,' said Fennel. 'It shows the trees in full leaf – I know the horse chestnuts are going brown already, but it's pretty obvious we're in the midst of a very hot summer, and autumn and winter clothes just seem incongruous.'

'There must be somewhere more neutral,' said Holly. 'Chelsi and Benjy should've sorted this out for us but they haven't. Come on, Swift – you're about as bright as they get in this place. Think of something!'

'There's the maze,' suggested Swift, very flattered at Holly's compliment, particularly as she'd only said earlier that he looked exactly like the Hallfolk of old. Walking with them now, both of them with blond hair, Swift felt he really was one of them. 'That's clipped yew, so it's evergreen and it wouldn't necessarily look like summer.'

'Mmn – possibly,' said Fennel.

'There's the beach?' said Swift. 'No trees there.'

'No – beach equals summer in most people's minds, unless it's grey and windswept.'

'Mooncliffe? That's pretty desolate in terms of trees, although there's the sea again in the background ...'

And then it hit him and he yelled out loud, grabbing Fennel's arm.

'I know, I know!' he cried. 'I've thought of the perfect place! There are no trees, so no giveaways about the season. It's very desolate and atmospheric, and it would show off the collection beautifully!'

'Where?' asked Holly. 'Come on, Swift. Where is this perfect place?'

'Quarrycleave!'

19

Rufus sat miserably crammed into the very back corner of the minibus as it jolted slowly up the track. He didn't want to be here and wished he'd had the courage to leave. It had all started so well this morning, with great memories of the evening before in the Village with Sylvie and the girls, Maizie and Leveret, and best of all, Yul. His brother had joked with him throughout the evening, and then, unbelievably, had allowed him to ride home on Skydancer. Admittedly, Yul had held onto the reins and walked alongside, but Yul had said he had a good seat and a good way with him. This morning Rufus had eaten breakfast on a complete high, reliving every wonderful minute of the night before as he gulped down his porridge.

But the bad stuff had started not long afterwards. They'd all gathered in the grand sitting room of Yul's apartments as instructed, and Holly and Finn had stood up and explained about the problem with the parched landscape and getting the seasons to look right in the photos. Rufus had been surprised when not only had Swift turned up at the meeting, but also Jay. Rufus was frightened of Jay and, whenever the large, bullet-headed youth was around, tried very hard to keep well out of his way. Surely Jay wasn't taking part in the photoshoot?

When Finn announced that they were all going up to Quarrycleave, the Stonewylde extras had been shocked. They had all been brought up to avoid the place; it was known to be dangerous. But Finn had explained that Jay was coming along to show them around as he knew the place better than any.

'It's where my father died!' whispered Faun dramatically, and Skipper and Betony rolled their eyes sympathetically.

'And mine,' muttered Rufus, though nobody heard that.

Finn then said that this was not how he liked to work and wished the location had been checked out first, but hopefully they'd get some exciting shots. Aitch reminded them that the quarry would be dusty and everyone must take great care not to get the clothes ruined. Then there'd been a knock at the door, and into the crowded, untidy room had stumbled Leveret. Rufus had been even more surprised to see her there, looking so out of place. The room was packed full with the models, stylists, assistants and Stonewylde extras all sitting around on every available seat, and she'd looked terrified and very small as she'd stood just inside the door.

Rufus had been embarrassed to realise that he wanted to put his arm round her and protect her from the laughter and jeering that greeted her announcement. It made him squirm now just to think of how everyone had humiliated her.

'I'm sorry to interrupt,' she'd stammered, 'but I had an awful nightmare last night and I knew I must warn you all. Something really terrible is going to happen at Quarrycleave and you mustn't go there today.'

Martin regarded his pale wife sternly. His wintry eyes bored into her, making her tremble all the more.

'You'll stay there all day,' he said, 'and only return this evening to cook for me. And yes, I realise 'twill take some time to get the place straight, but you have time.'

'But the range ...'

'Swift and Jay will have stocked up the wood and brought down some water by now,' he said coldly. 'Get the range lit first so you've got hot water, and then start scrubbing, woman. You'll need the range to heat up their food every day, even though you'll be preparing it here.'

'I'm not sure as I can manage the ...'

He took a step towards her and she flinched as he reached out to close his hand around her wrist. He yanked her closer so her terrified eyes met his.

'I shall visit the cottage myself later today. You're not to stop work or leave before then. We'll go round it together, so you can show me just what you've achieved.'

She nodded, standing on tiptoe as he held her in an unyielding grip. He wrenched her wrist just a little, not wanting to incapacitate her.

'Mallow – we both know that cleaning is not your strong point. Goddess knows I've had to bring you up to scratch on many an occasion, with your slovenly ways and downright laziness. So just make sure you work really, really hard today. You understand me?'

'Yes, Martin,' she squeaked, blinking back the tears that always angered him further.

Every child in the Nursery and the Village School trooped into the Great Barn and sat on the floor facing the dais, little ones at the front. The other children were lined behind them in age order, finishing with a row of twelve year olds at the back. All the teachers, assistants and helpers, and many of the young mothers and babies stood at the sides, whilst Dawn, Rowan and Hazel stood on the raised platform. Eventually everyone was present and Dawn began to speak.

The children's faces became more serious and round-eyed as she progressed. She was talking slowly and clearly so everyone, even the tiniest child in Nursery, could understand. Then Hazel spoke, taking her cue from Dawn as to how best to address an audience of such tender age.

'So, do we all understand what happened to Barley yesterday? Who'd like to tell me?'

A forest of hands shot up and she chose a small child at the front.

'Please, Doctor Hazel, he were playing in the bushes and then a giant monster snake jumped up and bited him hard and—'

'No, it wasn't a giant monster snake and it didn't jump! Who can tell me properly?'

This time she chose an older child, who explained with a little more accuracy how poor Barley had accidentally uncovered a coiled adder in the bushes, which had bitten him when he tried to put the undergrowth back to cover it up, and he was now very poorly in hospital in the Outside World. Hazel then reminded them again about the risks of going near adders, and what to do if they thought they might have been bitten.

'In your rooms in the Nursery and the School, we're putting up pictures of what adders look like,' she said. 'Remember males and females – boys and girls – are different colours. If you see a plain snake without the chevron zigzag pattern, it's probably a grass snake or a smooth snake, or maybe even a slow-worm. But just to be on the safe side, don't ever touch any snake at all. What must we always, always remember?'

And everyone chorused together in a great chant, the rhyme that Dawn had quickly penned to reinforce the message:

'Never ever touch an adder
That will only make it madder
Venom from a zigzag adder
Makes you ill and makes you sadder.'

As Hazel watched the children troop out again into the arid sunshine, she smiled at Dawn.

'Let's hope that's done the trick,' she said. 'We don't want any more bites.'

'Barley will be alright, won't he?' asked Dawn. 'He's only five, and—'

'He'll be fine,' said Hazel. 'He's a strong chap and the Nursery staff called me quickly.'

'When's he coming home?'

'The hospital's keeping him in for another day, just to be on the safe side. Sometimes the effects of envenoming can take several hours or even a couple of days to appear, so they've got him under observation. But they want to avoid giving him anti-venom if possible, as that itself can be dangerous.'

'Poor little boy,' said Rowan. 'I couldn't believe it when they called me back in from the photoshoot to say he'd been bit. 'Twas frightening.'

Hazel nodded, picking up her bag to return to the Hall.

'It's usually only young children or the very elderly who're in any danger from the venom.'

'So older children and adults would be alright?'

'Yes, usually, although some people are affected badly and go into anaphylactic shock if they're bitten.'

'We've been lucky so far,' said Dawn. 'There's such a plague of adders this year.'

'I've been reading up on it and I talked to the staff at the hospital,' said Hazel. 'Dorset's been especially hard hit this year and they reckon it's because of the heat. Usually the worst time is earlier, in April and May when they're coming out of hibernation and mating. Apparently they're fuller of venom then, and are more likely to release it all in a bite.'

'Ugh!' shuddered Rowan. 'I really hate 'em!'

'We must all be extra vigilant,' said Hazel. 'I can get in a stock of anti-venom, but I'd rather take any victim out of Stonewylde and into the nearest hospital, just to be on the safe side. It's really not my area of expertise. One of the doctors was telling me about this man who'd been bitten a couple of weeks ago – she showed me the photos. It was horrendous! The venom had spread right up his leg – he was bitten on the ankle – and his leg had turned black! It's bruising – the venom contains an anti-clotting agent, and this poor man had an allergic reaction as well. I'd never have believed it if she hadn't shown me the photos.'

'Poor little Barley could've died,' said Dawn. 'Thank Goddess he'll be alright.'

'Let's get the adder pictures put up in the classrooms now,' said Hazel. 'Keep them all chanting that poem – it's silly, but great if it works!'

Rufus was feeling sick, bearing the brunt of the bumps on the track as he was squashed behind the seats into the rear of the minibus. The transit van containing the clothes and equipment was following behind, and Aitch and Finn had taken a couple of the models with them in a borrowed Landrover. In front of him sat Faun, the other Stonewylde girls, and two of the stylists, all chattering about hair and cosmetics.

In the next row of seats sat the Stonewylde boys, and Kestrel and Lapwing were regaling Swift and Jay with tales of exactly how boring the whole photoshoot had been so far.

'Just about the only good thing is that we'll be in loads of magazine and we might be famous,' said Lapwing, who'd be starting college in the Outside World in the autumn and was excited at the prospect of advance popularity.

'It's much more interesting behind the scenes,' said Swift. 'I'm well in with Aitch and she says I can visit them in London and maybe get some work experience next year.'

'Really? Would you go?' asked Lapwing, a little nervous at the thought of attending local college, let alone a trip to London.

'Yes! You would too, wouldn't you Kes?'

'Like a shot! I want to go and live with Rainbow,' said Kestrel.

'You're all bloody mad!' growled Jay. 'I hate this whole bloody thing.'

'Not really into the glamour, are you, Jay?' laughed Kestrel.

'No I ain't! I can't believe you roped me into this, Swift.'

'But I thought you'd like the idea of Quarrycleave getting some good attention,' said Swift. 'You're always on about the place, but most people hate it – they won't even talk about it.'

'That's 'cos they don't understand it,' said Jay. 'It's special and it scares 'em. But it'll be okay today in the sunlight – it's only night-time it's a bit weird there.'

'That's not what Leveret said earlier,' Lapwing laughed. 'That was so funny when she came in like that!'

Rufus felt his face burn hot as they all burst into raucous laughter. Although Leveret was no relation to him, they shared the same half-brother, Yul, and through that link he felt an affinity with her. He also remembered her kindness to him the previous evening, when he'd been nervous in Maizie's cottage.

'She is crazy, isn't she?' said Swift. 'It made me think of that time at Imbolc when—'

'Shut up!' cried Kestrel. 'Don't even mention that! It was one of the worst days of my life!'

'She's a nasty little bitch and I can't stand her!' spat Jay. 'I'd really like to—'

'She's alright,' said Lapwing. 'She's just batty. But do you think she's right about Quarrycleave? What she said about something terrible happening?'

Jay chuckled harshly at this.

'Yeah, she may well be right about that, but it ain't today. She's got her timings wrong.'

'I know Aitch is really worried about the clothes getting ruined there,' said Swift. 'But I think Leveret meant the old legends about the quarry. The Place of Bones and Death – remember?'

'My mother used to threaten us with that when we were little,' said Lapwing. '"*If you don't behave you'll go up to the Place of Bones and Death and the Beast that stalks will eat you alive*' – that's what she used to say. We were well scared.'

'Yeah – that's 'cos you're all just a bunch o' little girls!' said Jay. 'And that half-wit Leveret is the worst of the lot with her stupid prophecies. She just likes showing off.'

'But she is magic,' said Betony, butting in from the seat behind them. 'Remember her Story Web? My mother says she'll be Shaman of Stonewylde when Clip leaves in the autumn.'

'Over my dead body,' muttered Jay.

Yul knocked on the door of Sylvie's office and her face lit up at the sight of him. He smiled and came to sit beside her at her desk.

'You're looking very efficient,' he said, acknowledging all her papers, filing cabinets and trays of brochures and leaflets.

'I have to be,' she said. 'If all else fails, I'll get a job in the Outside World as a Careers Advisor!'

Yul sat silently for a minute, savouring the closeness of her. To be near her like this, to smell her scent and feel her presence, was a joy.

'Sylvie, it was lovely last night at the cottage,' he said gently. 'I can't tell you how happy I felt after all that we've been through recently.'

She smiled at him and tentatively reached across to take his hand. It was so brown next to her pale one, and she stroked the calluses he always developed when he'd been riding more than usual.

'I enjoyed it too,' she said. 'And so did the girls. And Maizie. And Leveret and Rufus too – it was a wonderful evening, all together like that. I've missed you.'

'Have you really? Do you think, maybe ...'

She tilted her head to one side and her swathe of silky hair hung even lower, pooling on her lap and falling over to brush his arm.

'Yul, I never wanted us to be apart, not permanently. I only went down to stay with Maizie because I needed some breathing space from you, and a chance to think about it all. But I miss you and I want to be with you.'

'So when our rooms are empty of all these damn visitors ...'

He looked hopefully at her, his deep grey eyes blazing with want and need. But Sylvie frowned and shook her head.

'I really don't like living in those rooms. I'm sorry – I don't want to be difficult but when you and I get back together again, which we will, I'm not sure that I can go back there. That's one of the things we need to sort out.'

'Okay ... I love you, Sylvie, and I want you to be happy. I've changed and I do realise now what a complete bastard I'd become towards you.'

'That's maybe a little strong,' she laughed, 'but you've been incredibly difficult to live with.'

'So, where do we go from here? I want you to lead this and not be bullied into anything by me this time.'

'The Aitch lot are leaving tomorrow morning aren't they?' she asked.

'Yes – or maybe tonight. I think it depends on when they finish the bloody photoshoot. I can't wait to get rid of them, fulfil the contract for the goods they've ordered and be done with them.'

'I'm really sorry about it – it was entirely my fault,' she said ruefully.

'No, it wasn't,' he said, squeezing her hand. 'I'd have fallen for it too – they were pretty cunning. There's no blame for you – you were only trying to help.'

'But I feel such a fool. Anyway, what I was going to say was that it's the Moon Fullness tomorrow night at Lammas Eve, and it's a Blue Moon too. I've already promised Celandine I'll take her up to Hare Stone to moondance, but I wondered if you'd like to come too?'

The look in his eyes was all the answer she needed.

David and Magpie were standing in Merewen's studio by the dried up river, drinking tea and looking around with great interest. Merewen herself was perched on a tall stool at her work bench, her smock as filthy as ever with old paint and clay, and her grey hair a wild and wiry halo around her head. Before her she had a number of sketches on pieces of parchment, and several patterned plates were laid out too.

'You see, Magpie?' she said in her deep voice. 'These are some of the original designs, and this is how they ended up on the actual pottery. Take a close look, my lad.'

He picked up a sketch and stared at it, then looked carefully at all the plates.

He smiled at Merewen and nodded enthusiastically.

'So do you have any ideas, Magpie? We use a new design each year, usually around harvest time. There's no hurry but I wanted to get you involved this year. David, what do you think?'

David nodded and looked at Magpie.

'I'm sure Magpie will come up with some excellent designs, Merewen. We both know what a talent he has.'

'I wanted to come and see this moondance picture he's done,' said Merewen. 'Rainbow told me about it, but now I heard 'tis gone?'

'That's right, Yul wanted it taken from public display. But Magpie's done lots of other work and you're welcome to come up and take a look.'

'Aye, I'll do that,' she said. 'You alright with that, boy?'

He grinned and nodded at her.

'I heard you're learning to read and write, Magpie. Is that true?'

He nodded again, and picking up a stub of pencil, he pulled one of the old bits of parchment towards him and started to write. His letters were strange; not like a small child's learning to write. They looked more like hieroglyphics or cuneiform script, neat and carefully written. He wrote "I am Magpie" and when Merewen praised him, he wrote another word "ptri". This had them stumped for a minute until, with a bit of sign language, Magpie explained he'd written "pottery". David laughed and clapped him on the back.

'I remember now – Dawn told me that he has trouble with sounding out words and putting in vowels. She reckons it's linked to his inability to speak. So he writes the consonants only, unless the vowel is very obvious. But actually, you can see that "ptri" is almost right.'

'Well I never,' said Merewen, not entirely sure what David was on about. 'Who'd have thought it? 'Tis thanks to our Leveret, I heard. She always did have a special link to the lad.'

'Somehow she understands Magpie better than anyone,' said David. 'It's a pity she's not here to interpret, because I'd hoped to talk to you and Magpie together about Rainbow – I wanted to ask what you thought of her. I know you remember her from her childhood here, and you were looking forward to seeing her again. So was I, but once she was here ... I don't know, I changed my mind a little.'

Merewen nodded at this.

'Aye, she weren't quite the person I'd thought she was,' she said. 'I were disappointed, to tell the truth. Her art is good, but I don't think her heart is.'

'That's the perfect description!' said David. 'Good art, bad heart!'

They both looked round to see Magpie having what appeared to be a kind of fit, and David clutched him in alarm. The boy was bent over and shaking horribly, making a strange choking noise. But when he straightened up and they saw the look on his red face, they realised he'd been laughing.

'I've never seen you laugh before, Magpie!' said David.

'Don't suppose the lad's had much to laugh about,' said Merewen.

'I want to ask your opinion, Merewen, because Rainbow's keen to help promote Magpie's work in the Outside World. She wanted to take some of his pieces with her, which I refused. But she also offered to help in any way she could to get him exhibited, and obviously she has a lot of contacts in the art world. What do you think?'

He regarded Merewen's grizzled old face. She'd recently gained a pair of heavy glasses which helped her no end, but only added to her rather grim demeanour. It occurred to him that she'd know nothing of the art world at all, having as far as he knew, never left Stonewylde.

'I know Stonewylde is struggling for money,' she said. 'If Magpie's work could help that, I reckon 'twould be a good thing. The boy loves to draw and paint. If he really understood, I'm sure he'd be happy if the community could do well from his skills.'

'That's just what I thought,' said David. 'I wondered about limited edition prints maybe – that way his art isn't being lost, which may upset him, but simply being replicated. Maybe I should ask Marigold?'

'Aye, that's best. O' course, Starling is his mother ...'

David shuddered.

'I'm not asking *her*! Not after the way I've heard she abused the poor lad.'

Merewen nodded her agreement.

'Aye, but from all accounts, she's getting her justice now. Seems she's cottaged with Big Cledwyn, who's the brother of Alwyn. He's the one who treated Yul so bad all those years, and the whole family are a wormy barrel of apples. 'Tis all the talk in the Village, the state o' Starling.'

She glanced at Magpie, not wanting to distress him, but he was busy sketching a running design of yew slips, decorated with berries and a tiny wren.

'I've heard something of this,' said David. 'Dawn tends to get all the gossip.'

'Aye, they say Starling's no better than a drudge to Cledwyn and his mother. They work her like a carthorse and barely feed her. The weight's dropping off her, what with no food and all that hard work. He beats her most evenings out in their wood-shed, after he's had his cider, just for a bit o' fun.'

David grimaced at this.

'That isn't right.'

Merewen shrugged.

''Tis no more than she deserves. She's free to leave him but she don't. When she comes into the Bakery and the Butcher every day she keeps her head down and nobody talks to her for she's a right old mess, worse than ever before. And she's left Old Violet and her ma Vetchling to their own ends. Martin's poor little goodwife has been down there and nobody knows what's to come o' them. But nobody likes to visit for they're nasty crones, the pair of them. For so long, folk feared the three women in that cottage at the end o' the lane. But now ... seems they all got what they deserved in the end.'

'What goes around, comes around – that's what they say in the Outside World. Oh well, if you think it's a good idea I'll go ahead and see if I can arrange for some limited editions of a few of Magpie's pieces. We'll see how those sell and then we'll take it from there. It would be great if our Magpie could earn some money to help Stonewylde, wouldn't it?'

*

The men in the Gatehouse watched as the bright red sports car roared up the track towards them. The horn blared loudly and insistently and they grinned at each other, ignoring it. The gates remained shut, and Holly jumped out of the passenger seat and stomped over to the Gatehouse. She banged on the door and yelled at them to open up at once.

'Sorry, missus,' said one of them, ambling out to stand on the doorstep. 'Was you wanting to leave?'

'Too damn right!' she snapped. 'Open the gates immediately! And the minibus and van will be following soon, just as soon as they've got everything loaded.'

'Finished your business at Stonewylde then, have you?' asked the other man, appearing behind him.

'Yes we have – not that it's anything to do with you!'

'Right enough.'

Holly marched back to where Fennel sat revving the engine.

'Bloody hell! I never thought I'd say it but I'm pleased to see the back of Stonewylde!' she said as the gates swung slowly open.

Fennel shot the car through the gap and waited as a couple of other cars whizzed past the turning, going much too fast for the narrow road. He pulled out quickly and slammed up through the gears until he too was roaring along the road, with the very high boundary wall a huge presence by their side. Holly lit a cigarette and inhaled deeply, shutting her eyes.

'Feeling a little stressed, darling?' asked Fennel, turning up the air conditioning to deal with her tobacco smoke.

'That was a hellish day!' said Holly. 'A nightmare! We should never have gone to Quarrycleave – that girl was absolutely right.'

'It's the strangest place I've ever seen,' Fennel said. 'And I don't think any of the shots will be remotely usable. A complete bloody waste of time. We'll just have to use the exteriors from the Village and the Hall.'

'Was it the lighting? Or the expressions on everyone's faces?'

He laughed mirthlessly.

'Both. The light was crap – so much bouncing off the white rock. I should've thought of that. No – scrub that – Chelsi and Benjy should've done their work properly and checked it out first. Those two are in big trouble.'

'But it wasn't just the light?'

'No, it felt ... uncomfortable, didn't it? And that showed on everyone's faces. What with that damn bird appearing and making all that noise so everybody kept craning their neck round to see it. Was it a crow?'

'I have no idea. It was huge and I kept thinking it was going to attack us.'

'And once Minky had seen that bloody snake – forget the whole photoshoot! Nobody would concentrate and they were all over the place.'

'Did you see it?'

'A glimpse – it certainly was huge.'

'I got a good look and it was quite terrifying. Annoying though all the squealing was, I don't blame them for being so frightened. After that we were all scared to tread anywhere for fear of giant adders rearing up like cobras. As for the rock-fall ...'

'Hardly a rock-fall, darling! It was just a few stones falling from above and nobody was hurt.'

'But they could've been. Why did they fall like that? There was absolutely nobody up there. Honestly, Finn – the whole place was profoundly creepy and I really didn't like it. I was glad when that silly Faun girl fell off the rock and we decided to call it a day.'

'Didn't she make a fuss? All the shrieking and dramatics – I thought *I* was a drama queen but she puts me to shame.'

'Rainbow did warn us about her. But the mother's loyal – she's that girl Rowan, the old May Queen – and we need all the Stonewylde friends we can get. So putting up with Fabulous Faun was a necessary evil, and she is a pretty girl. Definitely got Magus' eyes, hasn't she? But oh – the state of the collection! Everything's covered in that beastly rock dust just as I thought it would be.'

'I'm looking forward to getting back to civilisation again,' said Fennel, taking a corner far too fast. 'Stonewylde's all very well, but unless the old regime were reinstated, I'm not sure that I'd want to spend much time there. It used to be fun as Hallfolk, when we were treated properly, but this time everyone was so hostile towards us. Hostile and plain rude.'

'And we know whose fault that is!' said Holly grimly. 'Yul's as handsome and Heathcliff-like as ever, and he certainly has his bite!'

Cherry looked in on the grand apartments that ran along the very front of the first storey of the Hall; the best rooms in the entire place. A wave of cloying scent assailed her as soon as the opened the arched door. Body spray, deodorant, hair products, cosmetics – chemicals filled the room with their pungent odour. All traces of clothes had been packed and removed, but as the mini-bus full of people and the loaded van pulled away from the gravel circle outside, Cherry stood shaking her head at the aftermath.

Magazines, dirty tissues, used cups and glasses littered every surface. The spacious sitting room was a complete shambles. She flung open the leaded windows which for some inexplicable reason had been kept shut, and went through to the other rooms. The bathrooms were terrible: plastic bottles abandoned with half their lurid contents unused, spilled cosmetics, soiled tissues, all types of hair, and even some underwear. Cherry's plump face darkened and she exclaimed out loud at the sheer awfulness of the selfish guests.

But what really made her angry was entering the beautiful master bedroom, and finding a mess on the dressing table mirror. Someone had scrawled, in bright red lipstick, xxx H xxx. Cherry hated the thought of that nasty little woman sleeping in here, in Yul and Sylvie's bed, and being so bold as to write on their mirror. Cherry understood exactly what was in the woman's mind as she'd left her mark, and before summoning all the students on work detail to help her clean the apartments, she picked up one of the alien tissues and scrubbed off the lipstick. If the dear couple were ever to patch up their differences and make their marriage whole again, the last thing they needed were barbs such as that.

20

Martin sat next to his mother in Starling's newly-scrubbed chair. Vetchling was asleep, curled into her rocking chair with an old blanket covering her wasted body. She snored noisily, the breath soggy in her lungs, and Martin found it difficult to ignore the painful sounds. He couldn't hear his wife working upstairs; she knew better than to disturb him with any noise.

The cottage was still filthy but, nevertheless, the transformation was astounding. Mallow had worked very hard indeed, although there were weeks of labour ahead of her to bring the old cottage into a clean, habitable state. Violet had eaten two dishes of rabbit stew today, cooked until it was mush, and was now smoking her pipe contentedly with a clean glass of mead to hand.

''Tis the Blue Moon,' she ruminated, rocking slightly. ''Tis a special night and I feel it in my bones, but I ain't seen aught. Something's afoot, that's for sure.'

'All the young 'uns will be out tonight,' said Martin, with distaste. 'I've told Swift he's not to get involved with all that until he's walking with a girl. 'Tis Lammas tomorrow and I don't know if he's intending to ask anyone.'

'Aye, he were here yesterday for a while with Jay,' said Violet. 'Neither of them were too happy about it. Moaning and grumbling, they was.'

Martin frowned at this.

'They should do their duty, right enough,' he said. 'And my goodwife?'

'Aye, she done her bit, little mouse that she is.'

They sat quietly for a while with only the harsh sound of Vetchling's breathing disturbing the silence.

'There's something afoot tonight,' muttered Violet crossly. 'I need my scrying bowl. Fetch it for me, Martin, and fill it with water. I need to see ...'

Clip and Leveret had reached the Dolmen, and Clip was surprised to see Yul's belongings in evidence.

'I don't suppose he's had a chance yet to come back and tidy up,' Leveret said, 'but at least he's left us some firewood. I'll lay the fire, shall I? Though it's so warm tonight ...'

'It is, but we need the flames for the journeying,' said Clip. 'I'm glad you've come up here with me for the Blue Moon. We don't have many Moon Fullnesses left before I'll be gone, and we must journey together.'

'I don't want to think about you going,' she said quietly, laying the sticks in the fire-circle and poking in some kindling.

'When we're done here, you can still go up to Mother Heggy's cottage as you wanted.'

'I do so want to make contact with her,' said Leveret.

'I know,' said Clip, 'but truly, Leveret, it'll happen when the time's right. If Mother Heggy wished to speak to you, she'd find a way. She doesn't need the Blue Moon to make it happen.'

'I know,' said Leveret. 'I just wish she'd hurry up.'

Clip found their cushions from the back of the cave, where the capstone and the stones that made up the side walls diverged into the hill. He and Leveret had fasted all day and he'd brought along a little bottle of mead and a cake each, for after their journey. He set these on a stone and tightened the skin of the frame-drum slightly. Leveret sat with him in the entrance watching the sky. It was a very warm evening indeed, the last day of July. The sky was full of diving swifts and the air smelt almost metallic.

'There'll be a storm soon,' said Clip. 'Can you feel it? Not yet, maybe a day or so, but it's on its way. Too late for the crops though.'

'It'll be really sad tomorrow at Lammas,' said Leveret. 'We'll all be giving thanks for the harvest and celebrating the start of bringing in the grain, but it's so poor this year! I was listening to Edward and some of the farmers earlier, and they said it's one of the worst years they've ever seen.'

'I fear it may be even worse than we imagine,' said Clip sadly. 'Because if I'm right, and there are storms on the way, they'll flatten what crops we do have.'

'When we journey tonight, I hope we're given answers about the future,' said Leveret. 'It seems to me that the shadows at Stonewylde are as deep and dark as ever. If I'm to be the Shaman of Stonewylde, I must know what to do to make things better for folk.'

'Our guides will help,' said Clip. 'Your raven and my wolf.'

'Shall I let Hare out of her basket, do you think?' asked Leveret? 'Will she wander off whilst we're in a trance?'

'I think she should be free,' said Clip. 'Let her out now, and put on your headdress too, so you start awakening the magic.'

Hare was glad to be liberated; she was very docile in her basket when the lid was on, but as soon as it was removed her ears would stand up, she'd sit up in the hay nest and look all around, before hopping out to sniff and explore. She seemed happy to stay within the Dolmen, much to Leveret's relief, twitching her nose and whiskers, and examining the dried bracken at the back of the cave.

'I wonder if our ancestors brought their totem animals here,' mused Leveret, watching Hare in her new surroundings.

'Depends on what it was,' said Clip. 'I don't suppose a bear or wolf would have been such a good idea!'

They both laughed at this, and Clip decided to light the fire to give it a chance to establish before the moon rose.

'Clip, I've looked on the Internet and in books, but I've never really found the answer to this – were dolmens built as caves for the Shaman or as tombs for the dead?'

'Nobody knows why they were built, Leveret, and I doubt we ever will. Most are Neolithic, as you've doubtless discovered, around five to six thousand years old, and you find them all over the world. I've visited some really stunning ones, and I've always been so glad we have our very own Dolmen at Stonewylde. I've been coming up here since I was a child. But as to what their original purpose was ...'

'What do *you* think though, Clip? In your heart, not your scholar's cap – tomb or magical cave?'

'We have no concept of what life was like for our ancestors all that time ago so it's impossible to speculate. To be honest, *how* they actually managed to build a dolmen amazes me, let alone *why*. But it was obviously something really important to them, to go all that trouble. Some have had human remains excavated nearby but that doesn't mean they were built as tombs – the bones could've come later. So ... in my heart, I think they were a Shaman's cave, perhaps representing the womb, the place of darkness from where we all come. They could have played a part in funerary rites too – as in representing the womb for rebirth into the Otherworld or wherever. But one thing's for sure – they were built for magic and trance. You can feel it so strongly in here.'

Leveret nodded at this, her small dark face serious beneath her Shaman's headdress. She stroked the fur that hung down over her shoulders and covered her breasts.

'I think so too. When you've left Stonewylde, Clip, I'll come up here regularly to journey at the Moon Fullnesses and the festivals. Wherever in the world you are, maybe our spirits can join together in the other realms.'

He smiled at her over the flames that crackled brightly between them. Her green eyes sparked with magic and he felt a rush of love for this very special girl who'd enriched his life so unexpectedly.

Yul, Sylvie and their two daughters were on the bone dry grass at Hare Stone, the remains of their supper spread out on a cloth.

Maizie had packed them a little picnic basket and they'd been up here for some time. The girls had run around playing, being very careful to look out for adders, whilst their parents had sat side by side with their backs to the great monolith and talked. They'd been physically apart since the Spring Equinox, over four months ago, but had been emotionally distant for much longer than that. Tonight felt very special to both of them.

Yul glanced at Sylvie, admiring her exquisite profile and the way her hair fell over her slim, pale arms. She was his moon-gazy girl, so beautiful and strange. Nobody would ever compare to her. He thought of Holly who'd left yesterday in a flurry of gravel and insults. He thought too – reluctantly – of Rainbow, who'd also left in a cloud of bad temper. Sylvie was so kind, so calm, so loving. She shared none of their attributes; the spiteful-ness and nastiness. Everyone at Stonewylde loved her for her shining spirit, but he'd trampled on that. He'd bullied her, taken her gentleness for weakness and had ridden rough-shod over her. He imagined what it would be like to be handfasted to a dif-ficult, selfish woman such as Holly or Rainbow and shuddered at the thought.

Sylvie was acutely aware of her husband sitting by her side, his body not quite touching hers. The heat he gave off pulsed at her skin. His long legs were bent up with his bare arms clasped around them, the strong sinews visible under his brown skin – she found herself craving physical contact with him and was quite shocked at these feelings. It was the Moon Fullness of course, but since the advent of the hormonal implants at Stonewylde, moonlust wasn't what it used to be. Yet Sylvie felt on fire for him. She longed to kiss the base of his throat – that small hollow she loved. She wanted to feel the silkiness of his thick, dark curls that tumbled so profusely over the neck of his jerkin and onto his shoulders. She wanted to take his strong, lean face between her hands and gaze into his smouldering grey eyes. And most of all, she wanted to feel the weight of his body on hers.

The little girls had grown tired of chasing around and had flopped onto the hard ground on their backs, staring up at the blue sky above. The sun was going down in the south-west – a big, coppery ball, and the swifts still swooped in great arcs over the hill.

'You may feel too tired to dance tonight, Celandine,' said Sylvie, tracing her daughter's shin bone. This girl was going to be tall and slim like her; already her limbs were so long and slender.

'I think I'll be fine, Mum,' she replied, and turned her serious eyes to Yul. 'Father, this will be the first time you've seen me moondance. I hope it won't spoil Mum's dancing for you. She told me how you always loved to watch her.'

Yul felt a sudden lump in his throat at his daughter's insight. It made his stupid outburst on Sylvie's birthday, when he'd lost his temper over the surprise painting and tea, seem so churlish and selfish. His seven-year-old daughter's emotional maturity shamed him.

'I feel very honoured to be here to watch both of you,' he said. 'And I'm so blessed to have not one, but two moongazy girls in the family. Bluebell and I will cuddle up together and look out for the barn owl, if he comes, and see if we can spot the hares creeping up the hill. Won't we, Blue?'

She nodded, patting his shoe from where she lay staring in wonder at the infinite sky.

'I'm so happy you came too, Father,' she said. 'I feel safe with you here.'

'Of course you're safe, Bluebell,' laughed Sylvie. 'Hare Stone is a magical place.'

'It is magical, Mummy,' said Bluebell, 'but it's not safe at all.'

Old George eyed the gang of lads in the corner of the Jack in the Green indulgently. They were getting a little raucous, but it was Lammas Eve and the Moon Fullness and the Blue Moon all rolled into one. They'd a long day ahead tomorrow, reaping and stooking up in the Lammas Field, and then the threshing competition back in the Barn later. Better to get a bit tipsy now and sleep it off early, he thought, resuming his conversation with

Tom and a few of the other older men. All were bemoaning the recent invasion by Holly and Fennel, not to mention Rainbow a few weeks before, and they were speculating how long it would be before Buzz tried to make an appearance.

'Remember that Lammas cricket match when Yul bowled him out?' said a grizzled old man. 'We celebrated that night, right enough!'

'Aye, and 'twere not long after that he were banished, cocky little bastard!' growled another.

'I don't like 'em coming back like this,' said Tom. 'Makes me feel uneasy. Sylvie and Yul have promised that's it, no more Hallfolk visits. We just got to finish making them boots and suchlike, and take their money, and then we're done with 'em.'

'Daft, them all going up Quarrycleave yesterday.'

'Aye, any fool knows to leave well alone up there,' agreed George.

'The Beast that stalks – will they've awakened 'un, d'you reckon?'

'Weren't no blood spilt. But even so ...'

They eyed the youths in the corner, singling out the four who'd been amongst those to visit the quarry the previous day. The men lowered their voices and huddled closer.

'They do say that Jay – son o' Jackdaw as was – is the one who's drawn to the place. He been up there a few times, I heard tell.'

'More fool him! He don't know what he's stirring up.'

'Should we warn him?'

'No son o' Jackdaw's going to listen to us! He's growing into a nasty piece o' work by all accounts.'

'Aye, if he's daft enough to go up there, be it on his own head.'

Old Violet peered into the dark bowl half filled with spring water. She twisted and tipped it gently, so the liquid moved slightly to maintain its horizontal position. Hunching over the small bowl she began to mutter and croon, and all the while Vetchling battled for breath. Martin sat silently, his head tipped back in contemplation, listening intently for any noise from Mallow upstairs.

'Aye, aye, the Blue Moon, as ever the time for making, the time for wishing. But nought is given without something being taken, and that's the thing. Old Violet knows. The taint is still there and our old magic holds strong, but 'tis blocked as ever by that toad.'

Martin glanced across at his aged mother, now rocking backwards and forwards, the chair creaking rhythmically. He'd been privy to her prophecies since boyhood and knew of her power. She could have been a truly great Wise Woman ...

'Martin!' she hissed suddenly, making him jerk in the chair. 'There's death ahead, death and danger! You must take care and you must act swift. I see a wolf with a serpent in his belly and you must beware! 'Tis as ever, that Old Heggy hindering me and mine at every turn! Why should Raven's brat always take what's ours? Why is her spawn ever above mine?'

'What must I do, Mother?' asked Martin, his narrow face intent. 'You know I want what is right and just.'

'Aye, my lad, and you must fight for it. Pah! I don't see nothing now – 'tis gone!'

She thrust the bowl of water at him and he rose to take it from her, placing it carefully on the scrubbed table. Vetchling stirred and moaned, and Martin ensured her blanket was still in place, despite the warmth of the evening. Neither Violet nor Vetchling had been persuaded to wash or change their clothes yet, and Martin was at a loss as to how this could be achieved. His aunt groaned and whimpered in her sleep.

'She needs more tincture, but 'tis almost gone,' said Violet sadly. 'I couldn't make no more this summer and now 'tis too late – the poppies have died.'

'Is there nothing else she can have in its place?'

'No, 'tis my poppy syrup she loves, for it makes her sleep and eases the pain.'

'Mother, I don't want to distress you, but maybe ... should we call in the doctor from the Hall? Perhaps she—'

'Don't you dare!' cried Violet, her filthy face darkening further. 'I don't want nobody poking about my sister in her last days!'

'Her last days?' said Martin. 'But ... do you mean—?'

'Aye, don't be a half-wit! Can't you hear how bad she is?' said Violet furiously. 'I done my best for her but her time is over now and the Dark Angel is nearby. Can't you feel him?'

'But there may be some medicine that—'

'NO! Stupid boy! There's a time for cure and there's a time for care, and our Vetchling has reached the end o' her days in this realm. We must let her go quietly, let the Dark Angel lead her soul into the Otherworld. We'll see her again, right enough. No interfering, Martin! And the same for me, when my time here is over too. Promise me that, boy!'

'I promise, Mother.'

'And now you get abroad, my lad, and take the mouse-wife with you. Make sure she brings more meat in the morning, mind.'

'I will, Mother. She'll be taking care of you every day now, so don't fret. And the boys will bring wood and water. We'll talk about a wash another time.'

'You might, I shan't!' she snapped, glaring at him. 'Now be off, but don't rest easy in your bed tonight. 'Tis the Blue Moon – see what's afoot on the Green. I feel ... something is there, something we should stop, but I know not what. He that we summoned is still with us, but now he ain't so strong and we need to give him strength. We must get 'un through this year.'

The beautiful moondancing on the hill was done. The moon magic had been drawn down again and danced into the spirals of Stonewylde, buried inside the sacred hill marked by the standing stone. Sylvie and Celandine both knelt in the grass, the little girl with her mother's arms around her. The hares had boldly approached to sit all around them, their ears laid down on their backs, gazing up at the glorious Blue Moon. She rode the clear skies in her silver chariot, large and bright, stealing all the starlight to make herself even brighter. Bluebell had fallen asleep in Yul's arms and he held her tight, gazing at his wife and eldest daughter through a blur of tears.

He thought back to that night of the Summer Solstice, the Dark Moon, when he'd wantonly destroyed the trust, so sacrosanct and inviolate, that held every true partnership together. Nothing could ever be the same again. He'd sacrifice anything that was his to give, in order to rewind the days and nights since that terrible betrayal. If only he could relive that night, but this time make the right choice and turn his back on Rainbow and her lure. Why had he succumbed to her? He'd asked himself this a million times since, and there was absolutely no answer that made sense. He'd known, the second he turned Skydancer's head towards the path leading down to the beach, that he was on a fatal, headlong plunge into self-destruction. He'd known that, and yet he'd still gone ahead and done it.

Tonight, for the first time in months, Sylvie had been so warm and loving that Yul felt maybe he had a real chance of winning her back. But what about his foul act of infidelity? He felt dirty and soiled and didn't want to taint her as well. Should he confess all and hope she'd forgive him? Or should he continue with this lie – pretend it had never happened, and hope that Rainbow had told nobody and would keep the secret for evermore.

The moon was high, and, thinking of Celandine still kneeling in the grass, he laid Bluebell down and went over to rouse Sylvie from her moongazy trance. She smiled up at him and he realised that she wasn't under the same kind of spell that she'd once been at the moonrise. Together they gathered their things and Yul carried Bluebell, whilst Celandine walked quietly by their side. They made their way down through the tussocks of grass, past the rocks and boulders into the field below, and through the archway of branches into the woods.

The moonlight was bright, finding chinks in the canopy of leaves where it peeped through and pooled onto the ground below. Celandine was enchanted and began to skip ahead on dainty feet. To both her parents she was a woodland faerie with the moonbeams dusting her silver curls and pale limbs. If Yul hadn't been carrying Bluebell, he'd have liked to take Sylvie in his arms and thank her for such a magical evening and such special children.

'Celandine's moongazy, isn't she, but not destructively so, as I was,' said Sylvie softly as they walked through the moon-dappled wood.

'Yes – perhaps because she's Stonewylde born and bred, rather than stifled in an urban nightmare as you were from birth,' he said. 'You seem a lot calmer now than when you were younger.'

'I am – I'm fully aware of everything going on. It's so much better.'

'You seem better in yourself anyway, health-wise,' he said. 'I know you always said you weren't ill, and I was wrong to go on about that, but honestly, Sylvie, you weren't looking very well for a while.'

'I was at low ebb and depressed, but that's gone now – thanks to Leveret.'

'Leveret? Why, what's she done?'

'She made me some special tincture that cures depression. I've been on it for a couple of months or so now and it's really done the trick. In fact I can probably stop taking it now.'

'But it is safe, isn't it? I mean it's—'

'Yul! Don't start fussing please – it's a lovely natural remedy, a beautiful golden tincture. It's as old as the hills and it's made from bright yellow summer flowers. It's cured my depression and stopped me feeling so tired and run down. Leveret's been making quite a lot of herbal remedies – you must go and see. She's set up in Mother Heggy's cottage – Clip's had it renovated for her. She's really good and she has a natural talent for healing.'

'I'm so out of touch with everything,' he said. 'I hardly know what's going on at Stonewylde any more, and certainly not what you're up to.'

'Well, let's think about a fresh start, shall we?' she said. 'We'll talk about it tomorrow maybe – or perhaps after Lammas when it's quieter. Things feel different now, and we all need to start again. Certainly you must mend your relationship with Leveret. She's such a lovely girl – we all adore her. Will you try?'

'Of course,' he said. 'You'll see what a different man I am now.'

Clip carried Hare's basket down the path from the Dolmen to the Hall as she was quite heavy now. Leveret took Clip's drum and her headdress, and was quiet on the way back. Her mind was still in the magical place where they'd journeyed, trying to make sense of what they'd experienced. So much of her journey had been in blackness, which was unusual. Raven had failed to explain why, other than telling her to learn to use her other senses as sight wasn't the only one, and a true seer had vision even in darkness. Leveret was slightly disappointed as she'd hoped for more insight at the Blue Moon. Clip seemed a little despondent too. He'd said something about making a sacrifice – killing the wolf and feeding the serpent – but Leveret got the feeling he didn't really understand what he'd been shown on the journey either.

When they got back to the tower, he handed the basket over to Leveret.

'Are you sure you don't want me to come up to Mother Heggy's cottage?' he asked. 'I could carry Hare and then leave you in peace?'

'That's really kind, thank you Clip, but I'd intended to get Magpie to help. I mentioned it to Marigold earlier and she was okay with it. If you are, of course?'

'Oh yes, Magpie's an excellent companion. I'll see you in the morning then. Bright blessings for the Blue Moon, my little Leveret.'

Unexpectedly he stooped and kissed her cheek before leaving her by the courtyard. Leveret took the heavy basket and her hare headdress and looked along the row of terraced cottages. A light burned in most of them, as it wasn't very late, and at Marigold's she found Magpie waiting. He beamed at her and waved good-bye to Marigold and Cherry who both sat knitting.

'I've put some sandwiches and a drink in his bag, Leveret,' said

Marigold. 'Have a blessed Blue Moon, and take care of our lad, won't you?'

As they walked up the long path towards Mother Heggy's cottage, Leveret reflected on the recent difference in everyone's attitudes towards her and Magpie's friendship. She recalled Maizie's outrage when she'd gone into the woods with him at the Moon Fullness less than a year ago. She remembered all the taunts and teasing in school at her championing him, when others bullied and mocked him. Yet here were their adopted carers – Clip and Marigold – letting them go off together completely unsupervised at the Moon Fullness. Leveret guessed it was because they now thought of her as the Shaman; normal rules didn't apply any more. She'd chosen the life of the celibate, so presumably nobody saw Magpie as a possible partner – he was now merely a friend. That was all she'd ever wanted him to be anyway.

The brilliant moon rinsed them in silver as they made their way to the ancient cottage. It stood dark and solid on the silvery grass and, as they approached, Leveret was delighted to see Crow roosting in his favourite spot, tucked in where the chimney met the thatch. As she opened the door, which, since casting the spell of protection, she no longer locked, he lifted his head from beneath his wing and gave a great *CAW!* He was an intelligent bird and had recently become very tame, helped by the titbits Leveret fed him. If she were at the tower he'd fly onto the crenellated roof loudly announcing his arrival, although he never ventured inside. Whenever she visited Mother Heggy's cottage he'd usually appear, and recently he'd begun to hop inside the cottage to join her. His favourite spot seemed to be perching on the back of the rocking chair, which made Leveret smile. He had to scrabble to hold on if the chair moved and it seemed such a funny thing for a crow to do.

They entered the cottage with its lovely aroma of dried herbs and wood-smoke, and as the air inside was altered by their presence, Leveret thought she heard a sigh. They released Hare from the basket and she hopped over to her favourite spot by the settle against the far wall. As Leveret lit a candle inside the lantern,

Crow strutted in through the open door, his white tail feather gleaming brightly. Magpie opened a drawer in the dresser and found his sketch pad and pencils.

'I shall sit quietly inside the pentagram, Maggie,' Leveret explained. 'I've already had a journey tonight, so this will be more of a quiet meditation. I'm still hoping to make contact with dear Mother Heggy somehow.'

Magpie nodded and smiled at her, settling himself down on his chair at the table.

'Shall we get out both Books of Shadows?' asked Leveret. 'You can make sure ours is all up to date with the illustrations, and I'd like to have the old one in the circle with me. Maybe it'll help summon Mother Heggy.'

Carefully she removed the ancient leather-bound book from its cloth and placed it inside the circle marked out on the stone floor. She set it all up as usual, with small objects representing the elements at the five points, and lit the sticks inside the little fire-cauldron in the centre. She placed Mother Heggy's sacred tools – the athame and gathering knife – on the old Book of Shadows, which formed an altar of sorts. There was no mead or cake, as she'd already had those with Clip, but Leveret had come to realise that all ritual was flexible, and it really didn't matter if she deviated from a ceremony. She knew her most effective experiences with magic had been when she'd completely abandoned the formal ways and followed her own instincts.

Magpie took the new Book of Shadows and opened it up, leafing through some of their entries. He was proud of his illustrations next to Leveret's writing, but he frowned at her untidiness. Now his reading and writing were progressing so well, he'd started to find some of her work a little sloppy. He lit his own lantern and pulled it close so he could see the Book more clearly. Taking up an ink pen, he began to tidy some of her script by over-laying it with his own careful, artistic writing.

Leveret sat in the circle ready to still herself. She pulled on the hare headdress, knowing that Mother Heggy would approve. Hare stood up in the corner, shook herself as a dog might, and lolloped over to join her. Leveret stroked the creature who climbed into her lap and settled down. Crow perched on the back of the rocking chair, his feet gripping the snarled wood, and blinked at her. Leveret sighed and threw a handful of herbs into the cauldron. Quietly she began to call on the elements and the forces of Stonewylde to enter her circle. She hoped with all her heart that tonight, Mother Heggy would finally join her.

Martin and his wife left the ramshackle cottage at the end of the lane and walked up the track towards the heart of the Village. Mallow carried a basket containing empty dishes and many dirty rags, needing to be boiled clean. Tomorrow she must bring down more soap and cloths, and she'd have to pick up a new scrubbing brush from the Village Store on her way past. Then she remembered it was Lammas in the morning. They'd all be up at the Lammas Field at dawn and celebrating throughout the day, with a ceremony in the Stone Circle at sunset; the Village Store would be closed tomorrow. She wondered if Martin would want her to spend Lammas cleaning the cottage or joining him at the festival; whatever he decided, Mallow knew she must take food to the two old women in the morning. She was exhausted tonight and longed for her bed. She was worried about how she'd keep their own cottage up to Martin's exacting standards if she were down at his mother's all day, every day, and she fervently hoped that he'd make allowances at home.

'You can miss the sunrise ceremony tomorrow,' he said abruptly, as if reading her thoughts. 'You need to be up very early to put our cottage to rights afore you leave for the Village, and you need to prepare our lunchtime picnic. I'll be in the Lammas Field o' course, for Swift will join the reapers this year. You can work at Mother's cottage until 'tis time for you to carry the picnic up to the field for us, and after that you'll return and continue your work at Mother's. You must attend the sunset ceremony in the Stone Circle of course, and put in an appearance at the feast and dance in the Great Barn afterwards. 'Twill be a long day, Mallow – do not let me down by slacking, will you?'

'No, Martin,' she replied. She hoped he might give her a little praise for her efforts today as she'd worked her fingers to the knuckle with all that scrubbing. The cottage was indescribably soiled, the residue of a lifetime's neglect, and many a time today she'd had to fight back nausea at the sheer filth that she'd been forced to deal with. Old Violet terrified her and always had done, but Martin's wrath terrified her more.

'Go back home now,' he said, 'and make sure my festival clothes are laid out ready for tomorrow. I'm staying in the Village a while longer. No dawdling along the way! Don't wait up for me – you should be asleep when I get back. Remember, I can always tell if you're pretending.'

As Martin and Mallow parted company in the Village, Sweyn and Jay were leaving by another path. Many couples were out on the Green tonight for the Moon Fullness, and many had gone elsewhere for some Blue Moon magic. Lammas was the traditional day for a boy to ask a girl officially to walk with him, and to exchange corn favours, ideally with both families' blessings. Tonight on the benches and cobbled area outside the Great Barn there was a great deal of giggling and preening amongst the younger members of the community in preparation for this.

Sweyn and Jay, however, were not interested in such things. They'd both drunk a great deal of cider in the Jack, and after relieving themselves copiously in a bush, they resumed their mission: to call on Mother Heggy's cottage.

'Will she be there?'

'Dunno, but if she ain't we'll still get inside the place and see what she's been up to.'

'What if Clip's with her?'

'We'll wish 'em bright blessings and be gone.'

'I still don't see why she gets a whole cottage to herself when there are families crowded in the Village,' said Jay. 'Don't seem right to me.'

'I know,' said Sweyn. 'That's what I thought when I heard

315

they'd re-thatched the place for her. I went up to have a look myself but ...'

He stopped at the memory of the unsuccessful visit, and involuntarily touched his forehead. It was still slightly tender to the touch but he'd reluctantly had it seen to by the doctor and was now on the mend. He'd conveniently forgotten that Leveret had shown concern; all he remembered was that she'd gained the upper hand when he'd attempted to visit the cottage. The thought of that abortive visit still made him angry; the magpie's slimy droppings had proved very difficult to clean off.

'Well, let's hope she is there so we can make her see how wrong it is to hog the place to herself.'

'Maybe she's going to set up home with Magpie!' sniggered Sweyn.

'Don't mention sodding Magpie!' said Jay harshly. 'I still can't believe Uncle Martin made me and Swift go up the crones' cottage the other day to sort out firewood and water and Magpie didn't have to! Ain't fair, that! And now the old boy says we have to go regular and do it.'

'Magpie should take his turn,' said Sweyn. 'Swift told me about it and he weren't happy neither. And he said you and him went up Quarrycleave with them models and photographers? What was all that about? I thought it were special to you, that place.'

'Yeah, 'twere Swift's fault. He told 'em about it and then they wanted me to show 'em as I'm meant to be the expert now. But it were a bloody disaster!'

'What happened?'

'There was a raven that dive-bombed everyone and pissed off Finn, who used to be Fennel when he were Hallfolk. One o' the girls – Goddess, they were skinny bitches, weren't they? – saw an adder and got hysterical, and then that Faun, she were showing off and she fell off a rock and hurt her leg. And Holly – Aitch – was upset about the dust. It were bloody stupid the whole thing.'

'Did you sort out where you're going to take a girl at the Moon Fullness? You said—'

'Yeah, I can see now how to get through the place and up to the Snake Stone. There's a way up to the top by all the boulders. It'd be tricky in the dark, but I reckon if it were a really bright moon or you had a torch, you could do it.'

'Should've gone tonight,' said Sweyn. 'It's bright enough tonight and no clouds at all.'

'Yeah, I didn't sort it for tonight. I need to plan it carefully to make it work. 'Tis better if I wait till the autumn anyway ...'

They'd finally reached the chalky path that led up towards the cottage. It was a ribbon of moonlight glowing white against the dull grey of the grass, snaking away up the hill. From here, the smell of the sea was stronger although they could hear no sound from it. In the heavy silence, as they stopped to catch their breath, they felt the eeriness of the night all around them. Both of them suddenly shivered, despite the warmth of the air and the heat from their exertion.

With slightly reluctant feet they continued up the path, going slower and slower. After a while, looming ahead of them, they saw the dark shape of the cottage with the paler thatch. The two small windows on either side of the door glowed softly. They stopped and gazed at it. Neither said a word, not wanting to admit to the feeling of dread that had seeped into their rather addled brains. As they stood there in the hush, the temperature suddenly seemed to drop. From behind them, a cold mist crept in and the bright moonlight became dim.

Alarmed, they both looked up and saw the moon rapidly disappearing behind a dark, swirling inkiness, the brilliant disc dulling and then fading as the light was blotted out. The mist eddied around their legs, damp and cold, and then it was all around them and they could see nothing at all. Neither had brought torches as the night had been perfectly clear, but even torches wouldn't have penetrated this thick fog.

'Bloody hell!' hissed Jay. 'That were quick!'

'We better go back,' said Sweyn. 'If we just go back down on the path we'll find our way, but we don't want to get lost up there, do we? Not with the cliffs close by.'

'Yeah, let's go back,' said Jay. 'We'll get her another time. It ain't worth risking our own necks just to give her a seeing to. Anyway, I already got other plans for her.'

So having convinced themselves of the foolhardiness of continuing in the sea mist, they abandoned their mission. Carefully they retraced their steps back down the pathway to the Village, leaving Leveret and Magpie undisturbed in Mother Heggy's cottage.

'The little mites are worn out,' said Maizie, as Yul and Sylvie came back downstairs, having tucked the girls into their beds in the cottage. 'And they've to be up early tomorrow morning too, for the Lammas sunrise in the field. Have you two both got your robes ready for the morning?'

She picked up the felt slippers she was working on and continued embroidering.

'Mine are laid out upstairs,' said Sylvie. 'I always love the Lammas robes. The headdress they've made me this year is as beautiful as ever, despite the awful weather.'

'Cherry said she'd make sure my robes are ready up at the Hall,' said Yul. 'She says she's got rid of all traces of the Aitch invasion, although I'm still sleeping in my office at the moment. It's as if there's still a whiff of Hallfolk in the rooms somehow.'

'Well, you know what I think on that subject,' said Sylvie. 'For me, there's always been a whiff of Hallfolk in there.'

Yul looked at her sadly.

'You really don't like those rooms, do you?'

'No! I always said—'

'Why don't the pair o' you take a turn around the Green?' suggested Maizie, looking up over her sewing. 'Seems to be a private conversation and you don't want me being a cuckoo, do you? And 'tis a beautiful night ...'

Grinning like a couple of liberated teenagers, Yul and Sylvie let themselves out of the cottage and back into the moon-silver night.

'Will you be warm enough?' Yul asked.

'I've got my shawl,' said Sylvie, and slipped her hand into his as they sauntered along the lane.

They gazed up at the sparkling dome above, whilst bats flickered around them in a frenzy of activity. A barn owl flew silently along the lane towards them like a great pale ghost, and veered off into the trees. And all the while, the Bright Lady cast her gaze over Stonewylde, peering into every nook and cranny, seeking out every dark corner.

They reached the Green where there were still people about. The Great Barn doors were open and a few people were inside, finishing off their preparations for the next day. The Jack in the Green was almost empty, but for a couple of men who sat over their game of dice. All the younger ones who'd been larking about on the benches had returned to the Hall, excited about the prospect of making it official the next day. A few older couples still strolled about and Yul and Sylvie joined them. Hand in hand they stepped into the ancient grove now known as the Village Green, where the Green Man magic was powerful and the Bright Lady danced for him in silver shoes.

Leveret came out of her reverie slowly. She wondered if she'd actually fallen asleep inside the pentagram as she felt that quite some time had passed. Hare was sleeping in her lap and the fire in the cauldron had burnt down to a few smouldering embers. The small candles marking the five points of the pentacle had gone out, and, looking across, she saw that Magpie was asleep. His folded arms cushioned his head on the table, whilst the crow had vanished, presumably through the door that still stood slightly ajar.

A little stiffly, Leveret rose from her cushion and stepped outside the circle, not bothering to dismiss any energy, as she could feel it had long gone. She carefully put Hare in her basket, and rolled out a heavy rug and blanket onto the floor next to the settle. Magpie would have to sleep on the rug as he was too tall to comfortably stretch out on the settle. Before she awoke him, Leveret stepped outside the cottage and stood gazing at the night. It was perfectly clear, the moon a brilliant white disc high in the sky, the sea a distant gleaming strip on the horizon. Leveret breathed deeply of the Blue Moon magic, her heart heavy.

She remembered nothing of her time in the circle. She recalled trying to reach Mother Heggy. She'd tried to picture the crone she'd seen in that brief vision in the Stone Circle back in January, when Magpie had taken her hand so desperately and shared with her what he'd been lucky enough to see. But Mother Heggy had not appeared to her tonight, nor sent any message or revelation. Leveret knew that the shadows that had shrouded Stonewylde for so many months were still there, blighting people's lives. She felt it her responsibility to help lead the community from the darkness, and yet darkness was all she'd seen tonight, both in the Dolmen and here in the cottage. Why wasn't Mother Heggy honouring Leveret with her presence? Didn't she approve of Leveret being the new Wise Woman?

With a sigh of sorrow, Leveret gazed up at the Blue Moon.

'Mother Heggy, please help,' she whispered. 'I want to do your bidding – please show me what to do.'

She returned to the cottage and closed the door. She roused the sleeping Magpie, who didn't wake up properly at all, and guided him over to lie down on the thick rug. She put a cushion under his head and covered him gently with a blanket, stroking his hair tenderly. She loved this boy so much and felt the deep connection between them that had always been there. It went beyond love and friendship – it was as if their souls belonged together, side by side, through eternity. He murmured in his sleep but no words came, and Leveret knew they never would. But this no longer mattered, for now he could read and write a little and he could still communicate with her in their special way.

'Sleep tight, dear Maggie,' she said softly, and went over to blow out the candle on the table. She glanced down at what he'd been drawing in their Book of Shadows whilst she slept in the circle. She was surprised and then amused to see he'd over-written her handwriting with his neater and better-formed lettering. Maybe she should get him a book on calligraphy, she thought, rather than simply concentrating on teaching him the basics of writing. He seemed to appreciate the artistry of fine lettering.

She leafed through the pages, turning the heavy parchment in the great book that Clip had bought for her. She saw the work they'd added yesterday, when she'd made a decoction for stomach gripes and a gargle for bleeding gums. The old folk at the Hall loved her remedies, and Hazel was happy to recommend them. Leveret noticed the list they'd made of the herbs gathered this evening, before she and Clip went up to the Dolmen, when the moon was waxing full. Magpie's spelling was definitely improving and he'd learnt how to use the pocket book of herbs and plants to check how to write a word. She was so very proud of him and the way he'd applied himself to learning. She'd always known he wasn't stupid; it was just language he had a problem with.

Leveret turned the last page, surprised that he'd added something after the Blue Moon harvest list. What else had he needed to draw? The sight that greeted her on the next pages made her heart leap in her chest and all the air burst from her lungs. Her throat constricted with the shock and her eyes filled with scalding tears.

Magpie had used his watercolour pencils and a big double page spread to draw a scene from this very cottage. The full moon shone in through the window, patterning the floor. A small figure wearing hare's fur on her head sat on the flagstones, a hare in her lap and five small candles burning around her on the circumference of the circle. She glowed with a magical aura, giving off a strange green light. In the rocking chair nearby sat a tiny woman, her face ancient and wrinkled. She wore a battered hat and boots, a shapeless old dress with a shawl wrapped around her. She was watching the girl in the circle, and in her gnarled hand she held the athame, whilst the crow with the white tail feather perched on the back of the chair.

Leveret shuddered as she looked at the fine detail in the drawing, a true record of what Magpie had witnessed that night. Then she looked at what he'd written in bold black ink at the bottom of the page. In his careful handwriting, the spelling obviously gleaned from the wildflower handbook, he'd written two words: *Prepare Wolfsbane.*

The moonlight gleamed through the tiny gaps in the heavy canopy, speckling the dry earth with flecks of silver. Where it touched Sylvie's flesh she glowed, as if sprinkled with tiny stars. Yul traced her smoothness with reverent fingertips.

'I love you so much,' he said softly. 'I wish we—'

She put her fingers across his mouth, not wanting to spoil the magic of the moment with words. She stroked his lips, running her fingers down his jaw and throat, seeking out that hollow she'd only been thinking about earlier. How had this happened? It had seemed so inevitable, once they'd entered the sacred circle of the clearing. The yew had drawn them both under its boughs, weaving its enchantment, igniting their passion all over again.

Sylvie thought that this must be one of the most perfect moments of her life – her beloved Yul back in her arms, a changed man who still adored her, but had recognised the mistakes he'd made. She knew that things would work out between them now and there'd be no going back to the awful state of estrangement. She sighed happily, pulling him down so she could kiss him again . . .

Yul felt himself drowning in a slurry-pit of guilt. If only he'd resisted temptation and remained faithful to this beautiful, innocent woman who would never betray him, never smash the trust between them, never destroy the perfect balance and understanding. He felt the breath catch in his throat in a silent sob of remorse . . .

Martin's face was contorted into a grimace of contempt. So – the bastard upstart and his whore were reunited, and now doing it under a tree, practically in public view. So much for everything falling into place. He felt bitterly disappointed. At Samhain when they'd summoned in the Stone Circle, and at Imbolc when his mother had sat in the Great Barn laughing at the travesty of Yul's leadership – then Martin had felt that all would end up right with the world.

But since then, nothing had happened to hasten the end of Yul's rule at Stonewylde. Hallfolk had returned but quickly departed, and Yul still held the position of magus. Yul's sister was being honoured as the next Wise Woman – not to mention Shaman – of Stonewylde, whilst Martin's poor mother starved in a ruined cottage on the fringe of the community. He himself must treat fools like Cherry and Marigold as equals, and kowtow to the likes of Sylvie. Her treatment of him when she'd discovered Holly and Fennel in the Hall still rankled. She'd spoken to him as one would a servant – he who had more right than Clip to be owner of Stonewylde.

Now Yul and Sylvie were reunited and the Dark Goddess knew where that would lead. Martin's mouth hardened into a thin line and his eyes narrowed as he watched them lying there, sated with their disgusting passion. He'd waited long enough; now was the time to make things happen. It was Lammas tomorrow, and Martin made a silent vow that by Samhain he would have destroyed the present regime. At Samhain it would be a year since he and the crones had performed that dark rite in the Stone Circle and called down the elemental forces, tearing open the veil to the Otherworld to summon the dead. He'd waited long enough for his mother's magic to take effect; the time had come to make it happen himself.

As Martin left the hushed shelter of the ancient yew and stepped back onto the Village Green, he felt himself hardening with resolve. Nothing would stop him overthrowing the bastard, destroying his wife and family, and ensuring that Stonewylde returned to its former glory, run by the leaders it deserved.

21

Maizie whisked the last apple-pie out of the massive range in the Great Barn's kitchen and passed it to a waiting woman to cut into slices. Scarlet from the heat of the kitchen and the exertion of organising food for so many people, she breathed a sigh of relief. Rosie came in to find her standing at the sink, flushed and sweaty.

'That's it, Mother,' she said, bustling over and putting an arm around her. 'This Harvest Festival is your last feast. At Samhain you'll be sitting out there and enjoying the food for the first time in years. You've done enough – there are plenty of us young 'uns to organise the festival feasts.'

'Are you putting me out to grass?' laughed Maizie, pouring herself a glass of water and gulping it down.

'Aye, I am!' said Rosie. 'I been helping you for many a year now and I know what needs doing. I'm taking over the organising and 'tis starting now! You go out there this minute, and sit down and eat something. When they start clearing the tables, you're to stay put. I'm in charge now!'

Feeling guiltily relieved to be ousted from her position as queen bee, Maizie untied her apron and went into the Barn. The excited noise from so many people chatting and eating at the long trestle tables rose to the rafters. She stood in the doorway for a minute or two watching the sight before her. It was now the Autumn Equinox and one of the worst harvests they'd had in many years. At the Lammas celebrations seven weeks ago, folk had been worried about the poor quality and yield of the cereal crop ready to be brought in. Then just two days after they'd symbolically reaped the Lammas field and stooked the sheaves prior to starting the harvesting proper, the rains had started. From having virtually no rain all spring and summer – since Imbolc in fact – the skies had opened dramatically and the rain had poured torrentially, almost without stopping, for a week. The weak stalks had collapsed under the driving rain and then the mildew had set in.

This Harvest Festival was no better, with a poor yield in the orchards, gardens and hedgerows. Everything had been stunted; too deprived of water to grow well and then subjected to rot when the August deluge began. It was sad and depressing, but Maizie had seen enough harvests to understand that the bounty of Mother Earth is never constant. Some years the harvest was overwhelming, but everything works in balance, and this dearth was only to be expected.

Her eyes roamed along the tables watching the folk she'd known all her life. She located Gefrin, sitting with Meadowsweet's kin and enjoying himself. What a difference in the lad! He was a proper man now, and looked so much better since he'd had a sweetheart to bring a smile to his face. Maizie liked Meadowsweet and approved of the alliance. The girl wasn't the brightest of lanterns but then neither was Gefrin, and she seemed to bring out the best in him. Her family lived and worked over the hills at the Tall Trees farm; a good, honest, old-fashioned farming family. As successive children were handfasted, Meadowsweet's father Holm built or converted a cottage for each one, aided by countless brothers, uncles and cousins. So should they become handfasted, which seemed likely, Gefrin would have a fine cottage to share with his goodwife and the support of her extended family. He'd been labouring there himself since leaving school and they seemed to like him well enough.

Maizie found Sweyn sitting with Jay and her spirits dropped. She didn't like her youngest son mixing with him, and nor did she like Sweyn's behaviour recently. He'd always been a bit rough and boisterous, reminding her more of Alwyn than any of her other children, but lately he'd become very aggressive. He was morose and bad-tempered for much of the time, and mixing with Jay could only make this worse. Maizie wished that he'd find himself a nice sweetheart and turn out like Gefrin. She could see Gregory and Geoffrey with their young families, both lovely men and good fathers, and Robin, Snowdrop and Edrun were further along the table wondering where Rosie had got to.

Maizie then located Leveret over in the corner sitting with Clip and Magpie. Despite her best efforts, she still couldn't really bring herself to like the boy. She remembered the old Magpie too well; the boy with the dripping nose and dull eyes who stank of soiled clothes and unwashed body. But she had to admit that the young man with such bright golden hair and gentle ways was a different person altogether, and he and Leveret were as inseparable as ever. If what Leveret said was true – that she would become the Wise Woman – then Maizie knew she'd stick to the old ways and wouldn't be handfasted. So Magpie would never be her son-in-law, and for that Maizie was silently grateful.

As she gazed at her youngest child, Maizie felt her heart melting with pride. She was still in the process of mending bridges with Leveret and they were establishing a new relationship. The girl was growing up and entirely independent of her. Maizie had to admit that she'd thrived under Clip's care. No longer waif-like and miserable, she was bright-eyed and sparkling, her small frame filled out into gentle curves, her hair a long tumble of dark curls. Her skin was tanned from so much time spent out of doors but she was much cleaner than before, and although still dressing like an ancestor, she was now more careful about her appearance.

Maizie and Leveret had begun to weave her special Wise Woman's robes from the very finest of flax, grown and retted this year. They'd agreed to have the robes completed for Imbolc when she'd be sixteen and an adult. It seemed fitting that she should officially take on her role then. Much as Maizie had used to sneer, she now had to admit that her little Leveret was perfect for the job of Wise Woman, young though she was. Leveret spent time most days with Hazel learning about medicine, and also with the elderly folk living in the Hall, who shared with her what they knew of the old lore.

Maizie still regretted that her daughter had turned her back on becoming a proper doctor, but she knew that folk spoke highly of Leveret's remedies and sought her out when they didn't want to bother Hazel. Several times Maizie had overheard people talking of her daughter's cures and healing, and this made her very proud. She'd even accepted that the girl used Old Heggy's cottage, although she'd yet to venture up there herself. Now, as Maizie watched her daughter in earnest conversation with Clip, she thanked the Goddess that it had all worked out so well after that trouble they'd had earlier in the year.

But then her gaze fell on her eldest child sitting next to his wife, both in their festival robes. Sylvie was talking to Hazel across the table but Yul sat silently, his face closed. He seemed to be miles away, and Maizie knew him well enough to understand the droop of his head and the scowl on his face. What on earth was the matter with the boy? What more did he want to make him happy? Maizie knew that the Blue Moon on Lammas Eve had marked a turning point for the pair of them. Since that night Sylvie had blossomed; the sparkle was back in her eyes and the spring in her step.

Maizie knew that she was keen to live with Yul again, for the two women had discussed it. Maizie loved having Sylvie and her granddaughters staying in the cottage, but it had only ever been a temporary arrangement. Sylvie was adamant she wouldn't go back to the grand apartments in the Hall; she wanted to live in a simple cottage. For some reason Yul was dragging his heels over this. Maizie had suggested they all live with her, which she'd have loved, but although Yul had stayed over a few times he'd declined her offer. Maizie simply couldn't understand why he hadn't jumped at the chance to be properly reunited with Sylvie and his girls. Looking at him now, she could see there was something really bothering him. Poor Yul – his life was never simple and her heart, as ever, went out to him.

'Leveret, I really don't like you working with this stuff,' said Clip. 'Do you know how lethal it is?'

He glared down at the chopped roots on the table, the exposed flesh white and innocent. Leveret was working on a piece of slate and using an old knife from Maizie's drawer, not wanting to contaminate her sacred knife.

'Of course I do,' she replied. 'That's why I'm wearing thick leather gloves and why I'll dispose of the knife and slate afterwards.'

'But why harvest it at all?'

'Because it was the one message I received from Mother Heggy at the Blue Moon. I've waited until autumn, as I read that's when the roots are most full of aconitine. That's the actual poison in Wolfsbane.'

'I think you've made a mistake,' said Clip. 'Mother Heggy would never tell you to harvest Wolfsbane. Why would she do that? Just preparing the concoction could kill you, let alone swallowing any of it.'

'It's not a concoction, it's a tincture. See the alcohol? I'm adding these chopped roots to the alcohol in this flask, and when it's steeped enough I'll transfer it to this vial. I've already labelled it and marked it *"Poison"*. Honestly, Clip, please don't treat me as if I were a fool. I'm well aware of just how lethal this is and I know there isn't an antidote.'

'Alright – I'm just concerned for your wellbeing. Are you absolutely sure Mother Heggy wanted you to prepare this? I find it hard to believe she'd direct you to poison anyone.'

Leveret shrugged. She'd wondered the same thing but the message in the Book of Shadows was unequivocal. She'd tried to question Magpie about it but communication that specific was difficult. He'd beamed when she'd asked about his lovely drawing of Mother Heggy and had pointed to the rocking chair and nodded. Clearly he'd seen the crone that night as Leveret sat inside the circle in a trance. But when she'd pointed to the entry below the picture – *"Prepare Wolfsbane"* – he'd merely looked puzzled.

But Leveret had enough faith in Mother Heggy to believe that she must do this, and it was bad luck that Clip had arrived right in the middle of it. He'd immediately recognised the distinctive Aconite flowers and leaves, which she'd also harvested to give the tuberous roots extra potency. She felt uncomfortable preparing something so lethal, not wanting to be like Old Violet with her poisons, but was sure there must be a good reason for it.

'Please, Leveret, promise me you'll keep this stuff hidden well away. Imagine if Celandine or Bluebell were to find it accidentally when they visit? Or if Hare were to find a morsel of the root?'

'That's why I didn't bring Hare up here today. When I've finished I'll sweep the floor and table very thoroughly and then scrub them. And of course I won't keep the tincture where I store my remedies. I'd planned on putting it in Mother Heggy's hidey-hole – you remember that secret shelf up inside the chimney? Nobody except me and Magpie knows about that place, and it'll be safe in there until I discover why she wanted me to make it.'

'Alright. But burn those gloves when you've finished, won't you?' He went over to the dresser along one wall and studied the rows of bottles, flasks and vials on display. 'You've been so busy this summer. You're gaining a really good reputation as a healer.'

'Thank you,' she smiled, carefully putting the finely chopped roots into the flask and covering them with alcohol. 'Although I haven't been able to cure your stomach ache, have I?'

'Your remedies have helped considerably,' he said. 'I'm very grateful.'

'Do you need any more yet? You should've run out by now.'

'I'll check when I get back to the tower but I think I'm alright for the time being. Why I came to see you here is because you had a visitor this morning – a girl called Meadowsweet who says she's walking with your brother Gefrin.'

'What did she want?'

'I don't know, but she's coming back this evening to see you and I promised her you'd be in. I hope that's alright.'

'Yes, I'd planned on studying tonight. The evenings have really drawn in lately, haven't they? You can feel autumn's here.'

'We need to talk about that. I'll be leaving soon and there are things we must sort out – my library, for instance.'

'Oh Clip! You know how I feel about you going.'

'I've vowed to be gone by Samhain, which gives me less than six weeks here. I'm feeling the wanderlust starting to kick in.'

'Have you decided where you're going?'

'No, not yet. I want to get all the loose ends tied up here first. I'm in the final stages of signing over Stonewylde into a charitable trust. Nobody knows of that except Sylvie, but I'll have to announce it soon as the Board of Trustees needs to be set up. Obviously it's the kind of the thing the Council of Elders would naturally take on. Then there are all my things in the tower, not to mention my books.'

Leveret looked at him sadly. She couldn't bear the thought of Stonewylde without Clip.

'You know that whatever you leave behind, I'll look after for you until your return, and if you need anything sent to you wherever you are, I'll arrange it. We haven't really discussed it, but I'm assuming you still want me to stay in the tower?'

'Definitely,' he nodded. 'I need to know all my things are being cared for by somebody who appreciates them. Cherry's had her beady eye on my collection of desiccated frogs for a long time.'

Mallow trudged along the lane towards the cottage at the end, no longer tumbledown and filthy. She carried a basket of food for Old Violet and her clean clothes, bending a little under the weight, as Martin had insisted she also take the bottles of mead and some of her new blackberry jam. The blackbirds were singing sweetly in the clear autumn morning but Mallow kept her head down as she hurried, as ever worrying about getting everything done in time.

She'd managed to clean the cottage from top to bottom now, and the place was almost unrecognisable. Martin had arranged for everything broken to be repaired, and now Old Violet also had a comfortable wicker chair on wheels in which Mallow could take her to the Village. After the passing on of Vetchling, the remaining sister had been completely distraught for several days and in that period, Martin had persuaded her to have a proper hot bath and change her clothes. She'd put up a fight but, soothed with a large dose of very strong mead, she'd eventually succumbed. Now it was Mallow's weekly chore to take her mother-in-law to the Bath House and wash her.

She visited every day after the most pressing work in her own home was completed, and made sure Violet was fed and comfortable. She found it really hard work to keep two cottages clean, especially where Martin was so very particular and came home every evening to give their cottage a thorough inspection. He usually managed to find at least one fault; if it wasn't a smudge of ash on the range, it was a speck of dust on a shelf or a crease in an ironed shirt. The consequences of these transgressions varied depending on his mood, and where Mallow was now also looking after his mother every single day and walking some distance to do so, it was almost impossible to maintain the standards Martin demanded. She tried so very hard to please him, but sometimes she felt he actually enjoyed finding faults and punishing her.

'You're late today!' Violet said querulously as Mallow let herself in.

'I'm sorry, Mother Violet,' said Mallow, keeping her head down. 'I got your mead here.'

'Aye, well I want my rabbit dinner so get that warmed,' said Violet. ''Tis lonely here without dear Vetch and I'm hungry.'

Whilst Mallow set about stoking up the range and putting the pot of stew on to heat, Violet managed to heave herself up and shuffled over to the basket where the mead sat. She was almost bent double and found all movement difficult. The upstairs rooms had been closed off as she couldn't manage the stairs, and she had a bed made up downstairs in the corner. Mallow had to empty her close stool daily, for a trip down to the earth-closet privy at the bottom of the long garden was completely beyond Violet's capabilities.

'Your Swift visited last night,' mumbled Violet. 'He chopped the wood for me and came in for a chat with his old granny.'

Mallow nodded, too scared of the crone to welcome conversation.

'He'll go far, that boy,' she continued. 'Fly the nest and won't come back.'

Mallow started to sweep the floor but Violet screeched at her to stop and fetch a glass of mead.

'But Mother Violet, 'tis very early for mead,' she began.

'Pah, what do you know? I miss my dear sister and I need comfort right enough. Why did she pass on to the Otherworld afore me? Ain't nothing worth hanging on for now I'm all alone. Used to be the three of us but now 'tis just me and I can't even brew a potion. I must suffer you scuttling around all day like a brown mouse come in from the field – 'tisn't how I want to live. Why did my Vetchling have to go?'

She sat rocking in distress, her knotted hands clutching at her shawl. Mallow felt a tremor of pity for her, remembering that awful morning in August. She'd arrived wet through in the pouring rain to continue her clean-up of the hovel, only to find Vetchling dead in her chair, the sickening battle for breath finally over. Violet had been asleep herself, an empty bottle of mead lying on the floor. After a terrible moment of horror, Mallow had run all the way back into the Village to the Great Barn and asked someone to phone up to the Hall for Martin. She'd never used a phone herself before. When Martin arrived, Mallow had fallen apart completely and he'd had to take her in hand quite severely. Violet had insisted on laying Vetchling out herself, but of course she couldn't manage it alone, so Mallow had had to assist, washing and dressing the filthy withered body as it lay on the table. Very few had attended the Passing On

332

ceremony at the yew, as Martin had let it be known Violet didn't want folk there.

Mallow dished up a bowl of rabbit stew and took it over to Violet on a tray. The crone sat there sucking it from the spoon with her toothless mouth, complaining bitterly that there weren't enough herbs in it for her liking, whilst Mallow took the chamber pot out from the close stool to empty in the earth closet. She hated it here, was terrified of her mother-in-law, and couldn't wipe the image of Vetchling's pitiful corpse from her memory. She'd been having nightmares ever since and Martin had been so angry when she woke up screaming that she'd been sent to sleep in Swift's old bedroom on her own, which scared her even more.

Starling had attended the Passing On ceremony alone, as Cledwyn had refused to come. Jay had walked by her side, amazed at the difference in his aunt. She'd lost a great deal of weight in the short months since leaving the cottage, and walked with her head down, her hair concealing her face. Jay had put her silence down to grief at losing her mother, and he tried to summon a sad expression as Vetchling had been his grandmother. Violet had been wheeled there in the chair and had been the one to light the pyre. Marigold had refused to let Magpie attend on the grounds that Vetchling had been a terrible grandmother to him and didn't deserve his mourning. Mallow was very glad that the whole episode was now over, but being given the role of Violet's carer was something she hated. Why, she wondered, couldn't they make the crone move up to the Hall?

Meadowsweet arrived at the tower and diffidently asked if she could talk to Leveret in private.

'I been wanting to thank you,' she said. 'Gefrin told me it was you as sorted out his skin and that's been the making of us.'

'I'm glad to hear it,' said Leveret, looking slightly askance at such shallowness.

'All them boils and suchlike always put me off him afore, but once I could see his face proper I realised he were a nice lad.

333

D'you know what I mean, Leveret? 'Tis like you can't see beyond something daft that's blocking the truth.'

Leveret nodded, knowing there was wisdom in this.

'And Gefrin told me how you'd talked to him about stuff and the way he treats people and I realised that you had a lot to do with us getting together at Lammas. We're really serious and I think we may be handfasted at Hare Moon.'

'That's very nice,' said Leveret. 'Congratulations.'

'So I bought you a gift to say thank you,' continued Meadowsweet. ''Tis outside by a tree.'

Intrigued, Leveret followed the older girl down the exterior staircase, across the lawn and over to where the parkland started. Tethered to an elm tree was a large grey puppy, lying on the ground with its nose on its paws and its eyes looking up mournfully. As they approached, its long tail thumped on the ground but its expression remained fearful. It was trembling from head to claw.

'A puppy?' gasped Leveret, her heart lurching with shock. 'Oh Meadowsweet – I can't have a puppy! I'd love to of course, but not in the tower. There isn't—'

'Father's going to drown him today. He were born wrong and he's got something that don't work in his back legs. I begged Father to let him live when he were born and he's a fair man – he said he'd give 'un a chance. But he's eight weeks old now and 'tis obvious he'll never make a working dog. Father won't have no pets – we got terriers and field-dogs and our barn cats, but every creature must work, and poor Shadow will never be able to run proper. He'll never herd the sheep or cows, nor catch rabbits or rats. No farm would want 'un. Today, Father said that's it, he's got to go now as he's weaned and needs feeding.'

Leveret felt a lump in her throat. Shadow. She looked down at him, a true Stonewylde farm dog with his long, grizzly-grey coat and half-cocked ears, his fanned tail that flickered hopefully as she gazed at him. His enormous brown eyes looked away as if in embarrassment at the position he'd put her in. She knelt and he wriggled closer to her, a bright pink tongue appearing to lick her hand politely. His fur was matted and he smelt of the farmyard.

'So what's wrong with his legs?'

'I don't rightly know. He were the runt o' the litter and his hind quarters were all twisted funny. I'd hoped they'd straighten out but they ain't. He can walk and he can trot along, but he's not fast. Father prides himself on our dogs – he's bred 'em careful and they're the best. But not little Shadow here.'

Somehow he'd managed to wriggle himself into Leveret's lap as she crouched and now she was being smothered with puppy love, impossible to resist.

'Well ... I guess Clip's leaving soon and I will be all alone in the tower. He must learn not to chew things ...'

'Oh he won't, Leveret! You'll see – our dogs are very clever and they learn quick. He's kind of always known he's for the mill pond – he's been such a good boy and tried to make hisself invisible and not be no trouble. I love him and when Gefrin said you'd take him in—'

'Gefrin? It was *his* idea?'

Meadowsweet nodded, tickling the puppy's round tummy.

'He said you were the softest person he knows. He said you'd look after an ant if 'twere injured.'

Leveret smiled and undid the piece of hemp rope that tied Shadow to the tree. He stood up, his back legs twisted indeed, and shook himself. Meadowsweet burst into tears and flung her arms around Leveret.

'Shadow is a special pup and 'tis fitting that the Shaman o' Stonewylde should be guarded by him. My old granny said you'll be pleased of 'un one day.'

Hazel removed the cuff from Sylvie's arm and noted down her blood pressure. She smiled, delighted to see how bonny Sylvie was looking.

'You're really in good shape,' she said. 'You've regained some weight, which is excellent, and everything seems to be as it should. I'll need to remove the old implant from your arm and then pop in your new one. We can do that tomorrow, if you're free?'

Sylvie nodded, pulling down her sleeve.

'I do feel a million times better than I did. My skin's improved and my hair, and I just feel bouncier and more my old self. I'd become so very depressed but now everything's looking up. I hope Yul and I will be living together again very soon.'

'That's marvellous news! So it's all going well between you now? All the old problems resolved?'

'To be honest, Hazel, it wasn't looking good at one point and I'd started to think that maybe we'd never get back together again. But it's funny – Holly and Fennel turning up like that almost seemed to trigger something between us. We became united again in our mutual dislike for them, and then on Lammas Eve at that Blue Moon ... Well, let's just say, the old moon magic worked its spell on us.'

'I'm so pleased for you both, Sylvie! I was going to ask if you wanted to wait with this new implant as it seemed a little unnecessary having that put in if you were in effect a single woman. But you'll need it now, I assume!'

'Yes, although we've still to sort out where we're going to live. That seems to be the stumbling block at the moment. I can't bear to live in those apartments and I really want to live in the Village in a simple cottage.'

'And Yul doesn't want that?'

'I'm not sure. It's been quite hard to talk to him lately. There's something bothering him but he hasn't told me yet, so I have no idea what it is. Though I'm sure it's nothing we can't sort out.'

'Okay, so we'll get the new implant put in tomorrow. I assume your last period was at the Dark Moon, so let me check. That would be September—'

'Actually I didn't have one then.'

'No? Are you out of synch now? It does happen, and I've noticed it more and more since Stonewylde women have been on these implants. So when was it?'

'Um ... I'm not sure. I missed September's and August's too. I remember being pleased because I wanted to come up here that day and I—'

'Sylvie, are you telling me you've missed two periods? You made love with Yul at the Blue Moon on Lammas Eve and you haven't had a period since?'

Sylvie stared at Hazel in shock.

'But ... no, surely not? You've always said the implants are virtually foolproof, Hazel.'

'They are! I know yours is due for replacing, but even so ... You're not on any other medication that could be affecting it, so—'

'Well, I have been taking Leveret's remedy for a few months now, but that's just a natural tonic. That wouldn't have affected a hormone implant, surely?'

Hazel had gone very still. Her kind brown eyes locked into Sylvie's pale grey ones and she sighed.

'What was this natural tonic? It wasn't by any chance—'

'Hypericum or St John's Wort, if you prefer. But it's just made from flowers!'

Hazel chuckled incredulously.

'That's one of the natural remedies known to affect hormonal contraception. Sylvie, we need to do a test. I think it's highly likely that you're pregnant.'

22

Yul gazed at the latest e-mail that had just pinged into his inbox. His heart thumped with despair and he felt like hurling the computer across the room. He must have uttered something because Harold looked up from his work.

'What was that, Yul? I didn't—'

'Nothing!' he growled.

With a shrug, Harold turned back to his screen, gazing at the columns in the spreadsheet.

'Are you looking at the Aitch report, Harold? How's it going?'

'Yes I am, and 'tis looking good. We're on target with everything and there don't seem to be no production problems.'

'When are we expecting to have finished the order?'

'By Yule at the latest, and possibly before. I reckon ... end of November if everyone continues to produce the goods as fast as they're doing now.'

'Good! Let's see if we can speed it up a bit and finish with the whole bloody thing even sooner.'

'Did you hear that the first magazine with the photos is out now? Most will be out next month, but there's one got 'em already in a big spread. 'Tis strange seeing our Stonewylde in a glossy magazine like that. Holly sent the—'

'I don't want to know!' cried Yul, his voice almost cracking. 'I really don't want to hear anything about it!'

Harold glanced across at him; Yul had been behaving very strangely lately.

'Sorry. But there's one thing I must ask. Holly – Aitch or whatever we're meant to call her – she sent me an e-mail asking if they can add to the order as the boots are—'

'Absolutely not!'

'Okay, I'll tell her no then. I just thought maybe—'

There was a tap on the door and Sylvie came in, her cheeks glowing and eyes dancing. Her silver hair wafted around her shoulders and fell to her waist, and Yul felt a jolt of love and desire for her all rolled into one.

'Sorry to disturb you hard-working chaps! Can you spare me a minute please, Yul? I've got a couple of things to tell you.'

It was still raining outside, the late September weather gloomy and dull, so they made their way into the library. This however was full of students, as was the grand sitting room; Miranda tended to utilise all the space possible. They found the Dining Hall being prepared for lunch, and the huge ballroom which nowadays sported sofas and chairs and a large screen for watching films, was occupied by some of the elderly folk from Hazel's wing.

'We could go into my study, but Harold's working in the next room, so if it's something private ...'

'It is. Um ...'

'Sylvie, this is ridiculous. Let's go up to our old rooms. There's loads of space there and you know how private they are.'

Reluctantly she followed him up the wide staircase, past the stained glass window. She glimpsed Martin further down the corridor and that triggered all sorts of memories. She approached the arched doorway into the sitting room with dread. Yul pushed open the heavy oak door and she felt a band of constriction tightening around her chest, stifling her breath. He held it open for her and as she walked in, Sylvie sensed something in the room hiding its face, scuttling into the murky corners. Never before, apart from that night at Samhain when she'd been here alone during the power-cut, had she felt such a powerful presence of other in the room.

Her skin erupted into goose-flesh and the hair on the back of her neck prickled. She was very pleased that Bluebell wasn't here as the little girl was so sensitive to atmosphere and this would have triggered her nightmares again. Sylvie looked around the room, glancing at the window seat, the huge fireplace, the sofas and occasional tables. This room held so many memories for her and most of them unpleasant. She tried to recall the good ones, but even those were tainted; sitting breast-feeding Celandine

– but then there'd be a sudden draught, or a book would fall off the shelf. Cuddled up on the sofa with Yul – but she'd get an overwhelming urge to look behind her. It hit her full force then – the rooms were truly haunted. She shuddered at the thought and vowed that whatever happened, she and the girls would never live here again.

They sat down in the window seat and Sylvie gazed outside at the grey, blowy day. Yul watched her, his heart breaking. If he didn't make a decision soon about Rainbow and her threats, he'd lose Sylvie forever. Should he just give in and allow Rainbow back for a visit? She'd been pestering him to agree to this for weeks, bombarding him with increasingly threatening e-mails, like the one that had just arrived. Or should he call Rainbow's bluff and refuse, running the risk of her telling Sylvie his dirty, guilty secret? She'd threatened that enough times and he knew she'd have no qualms about ruining their lives. The third option was to confess to Sylvie and throw himself on her mercy. For the first time in his life, Yul just couldn't decide what to do for the best.

'There are two things – important things – I wanted to tell you, Yul. The first is about my mother, and I want to ask a huge favour.'

Yul dragged his thoughts away from Rainbow and her black-mail and looked into his wife's beautiful face. Her skin was like the finest porcelain and her eyes grey pools of tranquillity. He tried to summon a smile for her and nodded encouragingly.

'It's a long story and I won't go into it all now, but my mum's mother is terminally ill and doesn't have long left. She's asked to see Mum to make her peace before she dies. She also wants to meet her grandchildren – me and Rufus – and her great-grand-children too.' She ignored Yul's look of amazement and contin-ued. 'Mum's decided she's definitely going, and she'd really like me and the girls and Rufus to be there too. I think perhaps she wants her mother to see just what she managed to achieve all on her own, despite being abandoned at such a tender age. I'd like to be there to support her – it's only for two nights – and

I wondered if you would please come with us? Going up to London, staying in a hotel, all the practical considerations of travel – it would be lovely if you could look after us and help. If you are agreeable to the girls coming along – which of course is your decision too – it would be great for them to have you there.'

She paused, trying to gauge his expression. He took her hands in his.

'If you want to do this for Miranda and you're absolutely sure, then of course I'll come along and help. It could be a nightmare – you and Miranda haven't been to London for so many years and Rufus and the girls have never left Stonewylde. Well, apart from Celandine and her ballet trip. So yes, I'd be happy to come.'

'Oh Yul! That's wonderful! I really want to be there for Mum. It'll be so difficult for her.'

'When is the trip?'

'We haven't arranged it yet, but the sooner the better. I think her mother doesn't have long now. Next week perhaps – the beginning of October? Oh Yul, this proves to me how much you've changed. Before, you would've argued and moaned and tried to bully me into staying here. This really means a lot to me.'

He reached across the window seat and took her in his arms, holding her tight. She clung to him in return, loving the strength and leanness of him. But over his shoulder, in the corner of the room near the dumb-waiter, something shifted slightly in the shadows. Suddenly a wisp of aroma threaded just out of range, taunting her with its elusiveness. She pulled back and stood up abruptly.

'What was the other thing you wanted to tell me?' he asked, gazing up at her with blazing eyes.

'Oh, never mind,' she said quickly, heading for the door. 'It can wait. It's not something I'm sure about yet anyway ... some other time. Sorry, Yul, but I need to get out of here.'

Faun and Rowan sat at the table, with the dishes cleared away and the sounds coming through from the kitchen of Rowan's mother washing up. Rowan's father sat in his chair by the fire, which he'd just lit as it was now October and the nights were becoming chilly. Rowan was tired after a long day in the Nursery and this was her reward; something she'd been looking forward to all evening.

Together they gazed at the cover of the glossy magazine. It had arrived today and had been brought down from the Gatehouse and delivered to Rowan just before the close of Nursery. They'd held back opening it, delaying the delicious moment until now, when they had ample time to savour the big spread about Aitch's new Earth Ethics autumn/winter collection. On the front cover was a thumbnail photo with the caption 'Where is Stonewylde?' and Faun tapped it.

'That's Minky, isn't it? She was definitely Finn's favourite model.'

'Shall we open it then?' asked Rowan.

Together they flicked through the pages until Faun squealed with delight. They pored over the pages, then abruptly Faun sat back in her chair and her lip quivered.

'I'm only in one of them and that's in the background!'

'Oh darling girl! But aren't you lovely in it? Look at your hair!'

'But look – it's stupid Minky here, and JoJo there, and both of them with that other girl – Sabrina. Look, Mother – Rufus is in practically EVERY photo! I don't believe it!'

And with that Faun burst into tears. Rowan's mother came scurrying out of the kitchen and her father stood up in alarm.

'What's wrong with our Faun?'

Rowan cradled the sobbing girl in her arms and shook her head at them.

'She's just a mite disappointed with the photos. She looks beautiful o' course, but she's only in one of 'em.'

'No! After all that excitement too! And our Faun were by far the prettiest of the lot!'

'Yes, but I'm too FAT! And I'm not tall enough and—'

'Don't talk rot!' said her grandfather. 'You're not fat at all, my girl. And you don't want to be any taller or you won't find yourself a husband.'

'I don't want a stupid husband!' cried Faun. 'I want to be a model!'

'There, there,' soothed Rowan. 'Don't cry, my baby. It's so bad for your eyes. Stop crying and we'll have another look and read what the article says.'

Eventually Faun calmed down and they looked again carefully, noting how Rufus did indeed grace every photo, and Kestrel and Lapwing were also in most, although more in the background.

'Finn really did like Rufus,' Faun said sadly. 'Just about the only thing that makes me pleased is that Betony and Skipper aren't in any more than me. That would be really awful. And when I think of the agony I suffered with my poor leg.'

'Oh you were such a brave girl!' said her grandmother. 'They should never have taken you up Quarrycleave! That place is—'

'This article is quite interesting,' said Rowan. 'There's an interview with Holly and she talks of how she grew up here. I remember she was a bossy little cow and o' course they all hated me, them Hallfolk girls, 'cos I was chosen as May Queen.'

'Oh Mother! You must have been so very beautiful!'

'Aye, Magus certainly thought so,' agreed her grandmother. 'We were so proud and honoured to have our girl favoured.'

'Was Dawn jealous too?' asked Faun. 'She was one of the Hallfolk girls, wasn't she?'

'I expect she was jealous 'cos they all loved Magus,' said Rowan. 'She was a bit quieter than most of them though, to be fair, and not as unkind. Dawn always were nicer than the other Hallfolk girls.'

'She's started to show,' remarked her mother. 'I noticed 'un when I took the buns into the Village School today. She's carrying high and we all know what that means.'

'It'll be an Imbolc baby,' said Rowan, 'if she did conceive at the Hare Moon on her handfasting night – though I think she reckons 'twas at Mead Moon a month later.'

'Aye,' chuckled her mother. ''Twould be better at Hare Moon though. Remember the old rhyme?

'When the hands are tied, kiss the bride,
When you jump the broom, kiss the groom,
When wrists be bound, lay on the ground,
When bluebells are thick, make it stick!'

'Oh Granny! That's so old-fashioned,' laughed Faun. She turned back to the photos again. 'Well, the only good thing is that there'll be a few more magazines like this and hopefully they'll show more of me in the others.'

'That's the spirit!' cried her grandfather.

''Tis true,' agreed Rowan. 'You're bound to be in more o' the shots in the other magazines. And Finn promised to send us some photos for your portfolio, didn't he?'

'Yes, and Rainbow promised I could sit for her next time she's here and she'd do a big painting of me! When's she coming back, I wonder?'

'To be honest, Faun, although o' course I want you to be a top model, I do think really your future is in acting. You're right, my darling – you're just too curvy and lovely to be one o' these stick-skinny models. You're more like a luscious and glamorous film star.'

'But how do I get to do that?' demanded Faun. 'How do any film people even know I exist, stuck here in Stonewylde?'

'We'll have to ask Rainbow when she's back. She said she'd return in the autumn and we'll ask her then. I think you'd have to go to acting school or somesuch thing, and we'd maybe have to live in the Outside World.'

'Really?' Faun's eyes gleamed at the thought of that. 'Oh yes, I want to go to acting school, Mother! Never mind about this silly modelling. I'll be a rich and famous film star instead!'

Clip sat by the fire and Shadow lay at his feet, his chin on Clip's slightly chewed felt slipper. Leveret brought over two cups of camomile tea and sat down on the sofa. Immediately Hare sat up in the new, larger wicker basket by the wall and loped over.

At present, she was slightly bigger than Shadow although that wouldn't be the case for much longer. After an initial bout of nipping and kicking, order had been established and Hare had permitted the puppy to join her in the basket just so long as he remembered his manners. He adored Hare and loved to cuddle up to her at every opportunity.

The greatest love of his life, though, was Leveret. He wouldn't let her out of his sight and had truly become her shadow. He guarded her fiercely, even initially growling at Clip when he came close. He was such a funny dog, always looking sheepish and guilty as if apologising for having survived his mill pond fate. His back legs would never be right, but Leveret had examined him carefully and could see he was in no pain at all. He was perfectly capable of walking, and his paws were enormous; he was going to be a big dog, despite being the runt. He had the usual intelligence of the Stonewylde grey sheepdogs, and combined with his mission to obey Leveret, this was quite formidable. His first meeting with Magpie had been a little fraught as each had been jealous of the other, but they'd settled down into mutual understanding and now got on fine.

'Are you sure you don't want to come with us to London?' asked Clip, sipping his tea. 'There are all sorts of things I could show you.'

'No thanks,' she replied. 'I've always said I don't want to leave Stonewylde, and besides, who'd look after Shadow and Hare?'.

'I'm sure Magpie would,' he said. 'But fair enough – it will be a busy trip anyway, so perhaps it's best you're not coming.'

'Is Yul alright about you joining them?'

'Yes,' chuckled Clip. 'Old habits die hard with Yul, and he almost forgot he's turned over a new leaf. But he could see it made sense for me to come along. I'd like to see Miranda's mother myself – as you know, all this happened because of that one dreadful act of mine. How she could've treated her poor daughter the way she did because of my wickedness is unbelievable. I'd like to explain to her, just to put the record straight. I also want to speak to the lawyer who's been involved.'

'Why? I don't understand.'

'Apparently he and Miranda have been corresponding by e-mail for a month or so, and she says he's one of the very top lawyers around. Her parents would of course only hire the best. I think he's due to retire soon, and I wanted to get his opinion on what we're doing here at Stonewylde. My own lawyer has done everything to form the charitable trust and we're ready now to appoint the Board of Trustees. I just wanted to get this chap of Miranda's – or rather, her mother's – to have a look at all the paperwork and make sure I haven't left any loopholes. That business with Holly and Fennel coming back recently got me worrying – I don't want any more Hallfolk coming here and thinking they've every right to. Once I sign Stonewylde over, it'll no longer be my or my heirs' property and I don't want any of that lot thinking they can take advantage.'

'I still don't see why you have to talk to another lawyer.'

'To check that it's all in order – I'm not sure I have complete faith in the local one I've been using. And Leveret, there's another reason I'm going to London with them, but you must promise me you'll tell nobody because I really don't want any fuss.'

'Yes of course I promise. What is it?'

'You know these silly stomach aches I've been getting for a while? I'm going to have it checked out before I leave. I've got an appointment with somebody good in London.'

'Oh Clip! I'm so pleased! I've been really worried about you.'

'I know. I don't want to go to Hazel and I don't want a fuss. I've been trying to ignore the pains and I think it's something like irritable bowel or just severe wind. I do hope it's not gallstones or anything like that. I was thinking that there's no point me going to the Amazon or the Outback and just as I'm about to go into trance with the local Shaman, doubling up in agony. But don't tell anyone, will you?'

'Of course I won't. So you're all going up there by train?'

'That's right, Yul, Sylvie and the girls, Miranda and Rufus and me. I'm actually quite looking forward to it. Apparently this lawyer has booked us all into a suite in a very posh hotel in Kensington, with no expense spared. I gather Miranda's parents were very wealthy, which makes the financial struggles she had to face even more appalling.'

'I'll miss you, Clip,' said Leveret, stroking Hare. 'But I suppose I'd better get used to it.'

'It's only for two nights – we'll be back before you know it. But yes, when we do get back I'm only here for another couple of weeks and then I'm off.'

'I can't bear the thought of it! But what about your stomach?'

'I'll have the diagnosis very quickly – that's one of the reasons I've chosen this particular consultant. If any treatment is needed, I can arrange for that en route to my exciting destination, wherever that may be.'

Leveret sighed heavily, and Shadow cocked his ears and looked up at her. He was her one consolation and she knew that when Clip had gone, Shadow would help ease her loneliness. Clip got up and disappeared downstairs into his room for a minute, to return carrying his black feather cloak. Shadow growled at it and got up for a suspicious sniff.

'I'd like to give you my raven cloak, Leveret,' he said. 'It seems especially fitting that you should have it, given your spirit guide.'

'Oh Clip!' said Leveret, touched beyond words. 'I feel so honoured! Thank you.'

She reached across and stroked the cloak, which was made of very fine black wool with hundreds of black feathers sewn on. She had no idea where it had come from for Clip had worn it for as long as she could remember.

'I can't think of anyone else who'd put it to as good use as you,' he said, 'except maybe Martin. And I really don't want him to have it.'

'No!' agreed Leveret, imagining how very sinister Martin would look in it. 'Martin's been really making me feel uncomfortable lately.'

'Has he? In what way?'

'It's the way he looks at me – as if he'd like to do me real harm. I find him quite frightening.'

Clip nodded.

'He's a strange man and I think he's becoming stranger. When Vetchling died I thought he'd move his mother into his cottage, but instead he sends his poor wife down there every single day. I thought the other day how worn out she looks.'

'It can't be easy being married to him either, can it? He's such a miserable person and lately he looks almost unhinged. Should we speak to my mother or Hazel about it? Perhaps his wife needs some help to care for Old Violet.'

Clip agreed with this, and hung the black cloak on a peg on the wall.

'Maybe you'd like to wear it when you next journey?' he said. 'It really is a very magical cloak, and it's taken me to other realms many a time.'

'I will, and you'll be with me in spirit if not in person. I'll keep Shadow well away from it too – he looks just a little too interested in all those feathers, doesn't he?'

Martin stood in the shadowy hall watching all the fuss created by the seven people preparing to leave and catch a train. They were oblivious of him, too wrapped up in their own worries about cases and clothes, tickets and toys. His eyes narrowed as he watched them, especially Clip, his cuckoo brother, the one who'd ousted him from his rightful place as their father Basil's heir. His mother had assured him that the owner of Stonewylde had taken her virginity before he'd taken Raven's. Nobody knew for sure exactly when Clip had been born; Raven and Old Heggy had hidden him away in the hovel for a while before his existence had been discovered. But Violet was adamant that Martin had come first and as eldest son, should have been the heir.

He couldn't wait until Samhain when Clip was leaving. Martin had all sorts of plans afoot, all types of contingencies covered, and was waiting to herald a new dawn for Stonewylde. He was determined to stop the rot and decay that had been rife since the murder of Magus all those years ago. Proper leadership was required, and a return to the old ways.

The seven despised people left and, later on, Martin went upstairs to check on his master's rooms. As he entered through the heavy door, he too was met with a presence, but unlike Sylvie, he greeted it warmly. The rooms were clean and polished and he'd had his goodwife place a bowl of flowers on the table. He checked the bathrooms were in order and the master bedroom made up with fresh linen. All was as it should be, the terrible mess made by that group of Outsiders brought in by Holly and Fennel now eradicated.

He returned through the connecting chambers to the sitting room, and as he passed by he caught a glimpse of silvery blond hair in the great mirror. He too could smell that distinctive aroma of Magus' scent and he paused for a moment to savour it. The scar on his temple throbbed; in a sudden explosion of fury he recalled that Winter Solstice when Clip had tricked him and had cracked him on the head with his Shaman's staff. Martin had vowed to burn the staff and stuff the ashes down Clip's throat; that desire was still there. He remembered Sylvie sitting in here in her scarlet cloak waiting to be rescued, whilst his poor master was lured to Quarrycleave and the serpent waiting for him at Snake Stone. So much treachery and betrayal! As for Harold, daring to lock him in here as he bled from his wound ... with another throb of hatred, Martin vowed that Harold too would meet his just end, along with all the others.

He hurried out of the rooms and downstairs, to pull on his coat and briskly make his way to see his mother. Samhain was fast approaching, the anniversary of when the summons had been made to the Otherworld. A year had almost passed since the veil had been rent aside and his master recalled from that shadowy place. Martin knew the lore that once a shade had been in this realm for a year and a day, it could not return to the Otherworld. It would once more take flesh, and he was ready to offer himself as host. Then the glorious days would begin again and the vermin would be cast out of the granary. He had made a list and was looking forward to working his way through it.

He entered Old Violet's cottage and found his mother dozing in her rocking chair, the fire crackling and a blanket tucked around her knees. He could smell the rabbit stew – all she cared to eat nowadays – keeping warm on the range. He wondered how she managed to dish it up herself and carry it to her chair in the evenings, for she was crippled and bent with arthritis. Mallow was here until early afternoon every day, but then returned to continue her duties in their own cottage. He decided to start sending her back down here every evening to serve his mother's supper and put her to bed. The nights were drawing in and he wanted her warm and safe. The extra walk all the way back down to the Village every evening during winter would upset Mallow no end as she was always complaining how tired she was. Martin smiled cruelly at this; he'd work her to the bone and it would serve her right, stupid, lazy chit that she was. Plenty more where she came from too, especially once the master was back for good.

'Your time is almost come,' Old Violet wheezed, watching the expressions flitting across her son's face. The firelight flickered and, as he turned to her, she could almost swear it was Basil himself. Silly fool he'd been – she'd soon dealt with him, once his brother Elm had been shown the moongazy delights he was missing. That Raven had met her match there, for Elm was a nasty piece o' work, right enough; Violet chuckled to herself. She'd never been one to let folk get in her way, although Heggy had outwitted her at every turn. But no matter – now she could help her son finally take his rightful place at Stonewylde. Samhain was the time, and 'twas fast approaching.

'When 'tis a mite closer, I must to do some baking,' she said. 'There's no dear sister nor feckless Starling to help no more, and I'll not have that mouse-wife squealing in my ear. You can help me, my boy. 'Twill be fitting and proper for you to help your old mother, the Wise Woman o' Stonewylde, bake the cakes for Samhain and the Dark Angel.'

*

Martin thoroughly enjoyed the following three days. Those whom he despised most were all away from Stonewylde together, for the first time ever. He would have liked to savour the experience more, but there was much to be done for the next phase of his plan. All too soon the driver who'd gone to collect them from the station returned, the large vehicle drawing up outside the porch. There was confusion and chaos as they tumbled out with their luggage and made their noisy entrance into the hall. Martin explained what he wanted and ushered the seven folk, all tired and bedraggled from London, up the great staircase towards Yul and Sylvie's apartments. He was very excited, twitching with nervous energy, and wouldn't brook any refusal.

''Tis a special surprise I arranged!' was all he'd say, and nobody liked to disappoint him.

The little girls were exhausted from their trip and the new and strange experiences they'd had, and the others weren't much better. Everyone had been longing for a quiet return to normality. Miranda in particular was emotionally drained, and had been looking forward to a peaceful cup of tea in her rooms. Rufus had much to think about, and had been anticipating a long session on the Internet researching his new dream, whilst Clip wanted to see Leveret and tell her all the latest developments. Yul and Sylvie had enjoyed the closeness of being together constantly over three days and two nights. They'd loved feeling like a couple again and their daughters had basked in the warmth and happiness of their parents' reunion.

But, despite their reluctance, they all trooped obligingly up the stairs and Martin paused at the threshold to the grand apartments. The light was already starting to fade in the overcast October afternoon and the corridor was shadowy. Bluebell's hand slipped into Sylvie's and she shivered. Martin turned and smiled at everyone, and Clip recoiled at the expression in the man's eyes as he spoke.

'Welcome back to Stonewylde!'

Martin threw open the door and they all went inside. The table lamps cast soft light around the room and a generous fire burnt brightly in the hearth. Clip was surprised to see people seated in there already: Maizie, Rowan and Faun. He wondered if this were some kind of Elders' meeting, although others such as Dawn, Cherry and Tom weren't there. Mallow hovered near the dumb waiter and when it pinged she jumped like a frog. As everyone found a seat, she brought a tea-tray over to the table and began to set out the cups for pouring. Everyone tried to ignore the rattling of cups on saucers as she did her best to steady her hands.

'For Goddess' sake, woman!' hissed Martin and she flinched at his tone.

'Do let me help,' said Sylvie quietly, leaning forward.

'No!' said Martin. 'Even she can manage to pour tea.'

Celandine and Bluebell, squashed between their parents on the sofa, exchanged looks of resignation at their plight. They'd been longing to run out and play on the Village Green after days of being cooped up.

'Did you have a lovely time?' Maizie asked them, feeling awkward sitting around like this. 'I missed you both and so did the chickens.'

'Yes, thank you, Granny Maizie. It was all very exciting.'

'Yes and our hotel had a television and a little fridge and air came out of a hole in the wall, but guess what – the windows didn't open and—'

'Enough tittle-tattle!' said Martin sternly. 'If you all have your tea and are sitting comfortable, I'll tell you why you're here.'

Bluebell buried her face in Sylvie's jacket as his wintry gaze swept the assembled group. Yul had been silent until now, bemused by Martin's authority but trying to be true to his new promise to Sylvie; from now on he'd be a member of the community and wouldn't dominate. But looking at the tired faces around him he had to intervene.

'We've had a very busy few days,' he said, 'and we all need to unwind, especially my daughters. So please make it quick, Martin.'

Martin glared at him and his thin face darkened.

'I'll take as long as I like, and no upstart—'

The arched door opened suddenly and Leveret walked in.

'Oh! Sorry – Swift just brought me a message to come here immediately. I ...'

'Come and sit down,' said Clip to the bewildered girl. 'Martin was just about to explain why we're all gathered here so mysteriously.'

'Aye, sit down and keep your mouth shut! I've brought you all here to show you once and for all that I can no longer stand back and watch the rot, the canker, the blight that has blackened Stonewylde for so many years. The time has come for me to—'

'The time has come for me to return.'

At the sound of the deep voice, everyone's heads swivelled towards the interconnecting door leading to the other rooms. Mouths fell open in shock at the sight of the blond hair and expensive suit.

'And how good it feels to be back at long last,' he continued.

'What the hell are *you* doing here?' Yul demanded furiously, trying to jump up from his place on the sofa. He was wedged in by Celandine who'd jerked with surprise, and Sylvie reached across the children and grabbed his arm to prevent him rising.

'No, Yul! Please, don't do anything ...'

Buzz walked across the room to the fireplace where all could see him. He stood with the flames dancing behind him and smiled at everyone, scanning the shocked faces.

'What the hell am I doing here? Good question. I could ask the same of many of you. These were my father's rooms, and I have every right to be in them. Thanks to Martin I've come back – only to find that Stonewylde has been run into the ground, ruined and laid waste. All the hard work and dedication my father poured into the estate has been wasted, squandered by poor leadership and lack of skill.'

'Absolutely not!' spluttered Clip. 'We've actually—'

'But no longer! I'm here now and—'

'You may be here now, but you won't be staying!' said Yul, shaking with suppressed rage. Sylvie still held his arm and could feel him tremble. 'I don't know why you think it acceptable to come back now, when you were banished and have never been invited back. But—'

'Oh, but I have been invited back,' said Buzz smoothly. 'Martin's invited me back, and he assures me there are many at Stonewylde who'd welcome a return to the old, proper regime.'

'Aye, the old regime!' cried Martin, capering across the room to stand next to Buzz. He was tall, thin and old, and looked particularly so next to the younger, stockier man. 'We're getting rid of the upstarts, the bastards and cuckoos! We're—'

'We're going to see a rightful shake-up,' said Buzz. 'I've come back with a great deal of money to put Stonewylde to rights again. I shall repair all the damage you've inflicted over the years, and once more swell the coffers and the granaries. My father left the running of his business to me, and now I've returned to put everything right. By all accounts, just in the nick of time.'

23

Marigold stared at Cherry and Tom in consternation as they faced one another in the kitchens.

'There's someone up there, that's for sure!' said Cherry. ''Tis not just our Yul and Sylvie and all them who came back today. Another car arrived earlier and 'tis parked now out o' sight round the back.'

'Aye, and the Gatehouse said Martin were up there waiting by the gates and told 'em to let the car in!' said Tom.

'But who was in the car?'

'We don't know! Its windows are all black and you can't see inside. But it must be someone Martin knows 'cos he got in the car hisself and came back down to the Hall with 'em, so the Gatehouse said.'

'But did nobody see who got out here?'

Cherry shook her head.

'Nobody saw them arrive and Martin must've sneaked 'em upstairs so quick! And then I had to send up a big tea tray.'

'I reckon 'tis Hallfolk back. And I reckon as there's so much o' this secrecy that 'tis Buzz this time around.'

'Oh Goddess! What shall we do?'

The three of them stood on the worn flagstones of the kitchens paralysed with indecision. Daylight was fading fast and Marigold turned the lights on.

'I think we should leastways get Edward up here – and be ready to go in and help if we're needed,' said Cherry.

'Aye – Yul and Clip are in there, and Miranda, Maizie and Sylvie. But why Rowan and Faun? And the children?'

'Well, Cherry – you and I are Elders,' said Tom. 'Shall we go up and see what's afoot? Martin's been acting very strange of late.'

'Aye that's true, but you can't just barge in there,' said Marigold. 'No, I think we should ask Edward to come just in case there's trouble. But even if 'tis Buzz back, he won't be staying.'

'Can you imagine Yul letting Buzz stay?' mused Cherry. 'He vowed to kill him once, and after what he said at the meeting that time, I don't reckon much has changed there.'

Inside the grand apartments, the atmosphere was as taut as a high-wire. Buzz still stood with his back to the fire smiling genially at the assembled group, whilst Martin fidgeted from foot to foot. Mallow huddled in the corner, and everyone else was seated.

'So, are you my half-brother then?' asked Faun, staring at the big blond man in the well-cut suit. 'Mother said I have a brother called Buzz.'

'That's right! It's a pleasure to meet you, Faun – how lovely to have such a beautiful sister.'

Faun dimpled prettily at this and wriggled in her chair.

'It's nice to have a brother who thinks that,' she said boldly. 'The other two don't.'

'Ah yes, and this must be Rufus?' Buzz turned his gaze to the boy who blushed scarlet through his freckles. 'A pleasure to meet you too.'

'Hold on a minute!' said Yul sharply. 'This isn't some bloody family reunion! You have no—'

'Actually it *is* a family reunion,' said Buzz, his pale blue eyes fixing on Yul with dislike. 'Faun's right – she's my sister and Rufus is my brother. I've never met them before, and that's partly why I've come here.'

'You may be Rufus' half-brother,' said Miranda, 'but we want nothing to do with you. You were sent away by your father

356

because you attempted to strangle my daughter, so don't try to pull the kindly brother act now.'

Buzz gazed at her, his smooth skin darkening slightly, but he maintained his expression of benign calm.

'Oh come, Miranda – that was all so many years ago! Surely we can all be forgiven for youthful folly? You of all people should be aware of how easy it is to make mistakes when young and passionate! Besides, I know she's forgiven me, haven't you, Sylvie?'

He turned his blue gaze on her, a smile playing on his small mouth, and Sylvie's cheeks stained an ugly red.

'The old regime you spoke of is well and truly dead,' she replied shakily. 'You're not welcome here.'

'Speak for yourself!' said Rowan. 'As far as I'm concerned, any true son o' Magus is welcome here!'

'What do you mean by that?' cried Maizie. 'Are you saying my Yul isn't Magus' true son? Because—'

'Please, everyone, stop!' said Clip. 'This isn't getting us anywhere. Buzz, I appreciate that Martin has invited you back and has perhaps given you a false idea of the situation here at Stonewylde. I can assure you it's not all doom and gloom, and it's—'

'Oh yes it is!' said Martin. 'The whole place is—'

'Martin, please! That's enough!'

'No 'tis not! You got no right to tell me what to do, son o' Raven! No right at all. My mother—'

Buzz laid a heavy hand on Martin's arm.

'Martin, perhaps this isn't the time for that right now – not yet. Maybe I can finish what I'm trying to explain to these good folk?'

Martin flushed but closed his mouth and looked down at his feet. Buzz smiled and his eyes fell on Celandine. He winked at her and she quickly looked away. Sylvie's breath caught in her throat and she felt Bluebell stiffen next to her.

'Buzz, I have no wish to be unpleasant,' said Clip, 'but you can see that your presence here is upsetting for many. You've come here without an invitation, despite whatever Martin says,

357

and it was wrong to sneak in when we were all away. That was underhand and—'

'Sneaking is *not* something I do!' said Buzz sharply. 'Any subterfuge involved was out of sheer necessity. I tried a direct approach earlier this year via your office boy. I've e-mailed and I've phoned, politely requesting a meeting. But I was rebuffed, refused, without even the decency of a proper hearing, and that's why I've had no choice but to resort to this unannounced visit.'

'You were refused because we didn't want you here and you can't stay now. We don't need you or your money, thank you.'

'That's not true, Clip, and you well know it,' said Buzz. 'I'm very aware of the situation here, perhaps better than you. Stonewylde is sinking fast and will soon go under. There are debts, bills to pay, and income is desperately needed. I have money and—'

'We don't *want* your bloody money!' shouted Yul, jerking against Sylvie's restraining hand and pushing it away impatiently. 'We don't *need*—'

'Ah, but you do need money,' said Buzz with an edge to his voice. 'I *do* wish you'd have the courtesy to let me speak. I've come a long way to be here and it would be polite to let me have my say.'

'Manners never were *your* strongest point!' said Yul.

'Nor yours! You've—'

'Enough of this!' said Clip. 'Buzz, why don't you come downstairs and perhaps you and I can discuss finances in private?'

'Very kind, but too late. My original offer of help was refused and now things have changed. So I've deliberately gathered you all together – with Martin's assistance of course – because I have things to say that you all need to hear.'

'Please, the children are tired and need to get back to the Village,' said Sylvie. 'I don't want them forced to sit here and listen to this any longer.'

She started to move but Buzz stepped forward as if he'd stop her, and held up a hand.

'Just give me five minutes and then anyone who wishes to leave may do so. Fair enough? Five minutes and no interruptions!'

'Mummy, I want to go!' whispered Bluebell. 'I don't like that man and I don't like it in here.'

But Clip nodded at Buzz.

'Five minutes then.'

Edward hurried into the kitchen bringing the rain and darkness with him. He pulled off his waterproofs and shook his grizzled mane of hair. He joined Cherry, Marigold and Tom seated at one end of the vast table running down the centre of the kitchens, noting their worried expressions.

'We ain't called Hart, Robin nor Greenbough,' said Tom. 'Nor Harold neither, though he's in the building somewhere. But we wondered if we ought to get Hazel and Dawn – what do you think, Edward?'

'How long have they all been up there?' asked Edward. 'And have you heard anything?'

Cherry shook her head.

'We've heard nought, but we've not been standing outside listening. They been up there a good half hour now, maybe a bit more.'

'We think 'tis Buzz in there and we just don't know ... will everyone be alright?' wondered Marigold.

'Aye, there's more of us than there is o' him!' chuckled Edward. 'And man to man, Yul's tougher than Buzz as we know from the past. I don't think we need to bother anyone else just yet. Far as we know, there's no trouble.'

'Just thinking o' these Hallfolk crawling all over the place again makes my blood boil!' said Cherry. 'As if they have every right to come back here! Yul won't stand for it, I know he won't!'

'Aye, sister, but Yul's hands are tied,' said Marigold. 'He's not in charge and 'tis a committee that runs Stonewylde. Yul may have to do as he's told.'

'Never!' said Edward. 'We're a part o' that committee too, and I'd not stand by and see Buzz or any o' them others suck away our lifeblood again.'

*

359

In Magus' grand chambers, the fire crackled in the momentary silence. As the last person to arrive, Leveret was sitting slightly on the outside. She watched the faces carefully and felt the awful tension in the room. So much emotion, and most of it negative and destructive. Her brother's face was dark and hollowed, and Leveret saw how his eyes glittered dangerously. She felt his control, the coiled energy and hatred held in abeyance, but all the more vicious for being kept in check. She noticed Yul's hands flex on his lap and understood what he'd like to do. Sylvie must have noticed too, for again she reached across the children and took his hand in hers. Together they formed a barrier of protection for the little girls – but also a restraint to prevent sudden action on his part.

Sylvie had turned very pale now, after that strange flush, and looked as if she might faint. Poor little Bluebell and Celandine – they were obviously terrified and had no idea of the history behind this hatred and rivalry that pulsed around them. Leveret herself had no memory of Buzz and all her knowledge of his behaviour and banishment was hearsay. But when she looked at him her skin prickled in an odd way, and she felt his evil and malice. He was a good looking man, well-built and well-groomed, his silvery blond hair fashionably styled, his face smooth and lightly tanned, his hands manicured. His features were small but even, his eyes robin's egg blue.

Leveret felt uncomfortable even looking at him, but his presence in the room was powerful and compelling. This was the cause of the terrible undercurrents, because Yul's presence at the opposite end of the spectrum was equally potent. The conflicting energy seemed almost to crackle in the air – strange to think they'd been fathered by the same man. Looking across at Maizie, Leveret wondered about Buzz's mother, who'd produced so different a son.

'I know that the coffers at Stonewylde are empty,' began Buzz. 'I've heard of the hardships the people have had to face, with overcrowding in the Village and cottages needing repairs. I've heard that the boilers, roofs and floors at the Hall are in dire need of maintenance or replacement. I know that this year's harvest has been abysmal. I've heard about the problems you've experienced with troublesome youngsters and then I gather your computer network was compromised, which led to serious consequences with the attempts you'd made to build up a mail-order business. Not to mention police involvement because of obscene spamming. It's a very sorry and pathetic state of—'

'How the hell do you—' cried Yul, but Buzz immediately blocked him with a sharply raised hand.

'No!' he barked, making several people jump. 'No interruptions!'

Leveret felt Yul's absolute fury but saw Sylvie's hand squeeze his, silently begging for no violence in front of the children. Buzz took a deep breath and continued in a smoother voice.

'It's been almost fourteen years since my father was killed. In that time, you've all coped very well considering the lack of leadership and direction. I know you've tried to do your best with some sort of committee to run the place, but many of those members are getting older and, to be frank, they lack experience in running anything greater than a kitchen or a farmyard, let alone such a vast and complex estate as Stonewylde. I feel for you all – you have my respect for what you've managed to achieve, and my sympathy for your present plight.'

'How kind!' muttered Clip, and Martin glared at him. He still hovered by Buzz like some kind of sidekick. Buzz seemed to notice this all of a sudden, and directed Martin to a chair near the door, as if appointing a footman to his rightful position.

'This is where I come in,' he said, with a smile as sincere as a politician's. 'Since my father's death I've played a major part in running his company. Once I'd graduated from university, I assumed control of the business. Not all of you would be aware of this, but in his lifetime Magus had built up a hugely successful organisation and was a very wealthy man. I've ensured that his company has gone from strength to strength and it's now worth a vast amount, as, of course, am I personally. So my reason for coming here now – *not* sneaking I assure you, but with necessary concealment due to the hostility I knew I'd encounter – is to make you, Clip, as owner of the estate, a proposition.'

'But—'

'Please – hear me out! In return for the opportunity to move back permanently to Stonewylde, along with my family and any other Hallfolk who wish to come, I'll pour all my personal wealth into the estate, as my father used to do. After a thorough inspection and appraisal, I'll replace the boilers and repair the roofs. I'll have new cottages built and a proper water supply installed, which won't be reliant on the spring that feeds the river. I'll put in a sewer system and electricity to every cottage, expanding the wind farm and solar panel systems. I'll replace the tractors and replenish the farming equipment, and invest in new and better livestock and agricultural systems. I'll continue the sterling work of educating the youngsters here – one of the few areas where I know my father failed – and will provide every Villager with a decent home and a decent living. In return I expect to have the Hall exclusively for my personal use and any guests I see fit to invite, and a full complement of staff handpicked by Martin.'

He paused and there was a stunned, shocked silence broken a moment later by Maizie, who laughed mockingly.

'You're as blind as your father were if you think for one minute we'd ever, *ever* go back to the bad old ways!'

Buzz regarded her for a moment, and then pointedly turned his back on her to address Clip.

'Of course I appreciate, Clip, that you may need an opportunity to think about my proposal.'

'Actually, I don't think—'

'And there's something else that we need to factor into this equation too,' said Buzz. 'I've only presented to you the bare bones of this wonderful opportunity, but naturally there are other considerations. You perhaps think that you enjoy a united front, a committee of equals where everything is run democratically? Apart from the odd outburst from Yul, who I gather likes to think of himself as the magus.'

Buzz paused here, ready to counteract any reaction. But Yul

kept very still and silent, and Leveret admired the steely self-discipline that refused to rise to Buzz's rather clumsy baiting.

'But in fact, you are far from equals here. There are three people apart from myself, who will one day also have access to Magus' great wealth. We four children were given equal shares in our father's Will.'

'What?' cried Miranda. 'What are you talking about? Magus died before Rufus – and Faun – were born!'

'So he did,' said Buzz. 'But he'd made a Will that summer, after they were conceived, and just before I left Stonewylde, in which he acknowledged both your and Rowan's unborn children as his heirs. Of course as minors they're not yet entitled to their shares in the company or their place on the Board, all of which are administered by a Trustee until they reach adulthood – in the Outside World sense. I too had to wait until such a time, as I was only sixteen when my father was killed.'

'But ... in that case, Yul must also be entitled to his quarter share,' said Sylvie. 'He reached adulthood not long after you, Buzz. Why hasn't he inherited yet? Surely—'

'Yul? Oh no, Sylvie – he wasn't mentioned in the Will. Despite all that happened, Magus never officially acknowledged Yul as his progeny.'

'What?' Now it was Maizie's turn to be astounded. 'But Magus *did* acknowledge Yul as his! At Samhain, in the Stone Circle! And he—'

'He may have verbally done so, but he did not alter his Will. He hated Yul until his death and didn't want Yul to inherit any of his wealth.'

There was a silence. Buzz turned round and threw a couple of logs onto the fire. He glanced up in the massive mirror above and regarded the slightly distorted reflection of the group of people, all their faces registering complete amazement.

'Are you saying that my Faun has inherited a lot of money?' asked Rowan slowly. 'She's rich from Magus' money because she's his daughter?'

'That's right,' said Buzz, turning back to face the room. 'Faun owns twenty-five per cent of the shares of Magus' company, as one of his four children. She can't touch them yet, not until she's eighteen, but she has a great deal of money accrued from the dividends that have been invested for her over the years. Following the original Trustee's retirement, I'm now the official Trustee for the minors, and I could arrange for some of this money to be released. Faun, you're a very rich girl!'

'But ... but you said four children, twenty-five per cent,' said Sylvie. 'And you said Yul wasn't acknowledged as Magus' child. I don't understand ... if you, Faun and Rufus are Magus' recognized heirs, who's the fourth child?'

Buzz smiled again, and this time he closely resembled a snake approaching its victim. His mouth was stretched wide but his eyes were cold with malice.

'Yes, I was shocked at this too. But really, it's not hard to believe. She ensnared my father when she was very young, which put paid to his relationship with my own poor mother. And then, despite being married to someone else, she did it all over again several years later! What a Village slut had to offer a man such as Magus is—'

'No need for that, young man,' said Maizie quietly, her cheeks crimson. She looked over at Leveret, whose heart had started to thump loudly in her chest. Maizie's deep grey eyes were full of shamed apology as she faced her white-faced daughter, who felt everything slide suddenly into perfect place. 'Leveret, my love – Magus were your father too.'

The four sitting at the table were interrupted by the arrival of a gang of youngsters spilling loudly into the kitchen.

'Get out!' screeched Cherry.

'But we've come for work detail!' protested a girl. 'We're down for doing food prep with Marigold.'

'And we're laying up with you, Cherry!' said another. 'It's all dark in the Dining Hall and we wondered where you'd got to.'

'Oh Sacred Mother!' exclaimed Marigold. 'I forgot all about dinner! I've got nothing on yet.'

She rose hastily and snatched her apron from the peg on the door. Cherry also sprung into action and shooed the group of students towards the Dining Hall.

'Right, you lot – cutlery on the tables, water jugs filled!'

Tom and Edward remained at the table as Marigold directed students towards the sinks to peel potatoes and others to prepare carrots and cabbage.

'What's to be done, eh?' muttered Tom. 'Old Greenbough were right – that Rainbow were the scout and here they all are, marching back in.'

'Never!' said Edward again. 'Things may be difficult at the moment but I'd rather that than have to doff my cap to anyone just 'cos they got pale hair! Look at my Kestrel away at university! I'm that proud o' the lad, and if Yul hadn't rid us o' Magus all them years ago, my Kes would be working alongside me on the farm. Nought wrong with that, o' course, but he has a choice now. I for one will never let them Hallfolk take over again, and I reckon all the folk will feel the same.'

Clip ushered everybody out of Magus' rooms, although Rowan and Faun elected to stay there and talk privately with Buzz. Everyone trooped out, shocked and upset. Clip murmured to Leveret and Maizie to go straight to the tower, saying that he'd join them soon. Sylvie and Yul were anxious to get the children down to the Village and ready for bed, and Miranda and Rufus wanted to discuss the incredible news of his inheritance. Clip stayed behind for a minute whilst Mallow scuttled over to clear away the tea things under Martin's watchful eye.

'Martin can serve you dinner up here,' Clip said to Buzz. 'You've given everyone plenty to think about, and as for humiliating Maizie and telling Leveret like that, in front of so many people ... We'll meet tomorrow morning in the Galleried Hall, and you can present your proposal to the Council of Elders. I would advise you though that it's highly unlikely that anyone – other than Rowan and Martin – will be interested.'

'I don't see why you're putting this to a committee,' said Buzz irritably. 'This is an offer I'm making to you personally, as the present owner of Stonewylde. It's not really anything to do with the others, and I'm not prepared to start negotiating with a bunch of Villagers, I can assure you.'

'I realise that,' said Clip. 'Which is why you'd never be welcome back here.'

'I might have known you'd be incapable of leading the community,' sneered Buzz. 'Still weak and vacillating, unable to stand up to people or make a decision. You haven't changed a jot in all these years, Clip.'

Clip merely smiled at this and headed for the door.

'And neither have you, Buzzard.'

Clip hurried through the Hall, down corridors, into the Galleried Hall, and to the entrance to the tower. The door was unlocked and he went through and climbed the spiral stone stairs. He could hear voices from the large room on the top floor and hesitated, not wishing to interrupt. But Shadow had heard him and growled, and Leveret called out for him to come up.

He entered the beautiful circular room, full of his precious things, to find that Leveret was building up the fire in the hearth whilst Maizie lit the oil lamps. They had electricity but usually preferred the softer, more natural light of the old fashioned lamps. Leveret put the kettle on the stove and invited her mother to sit on the sofa. Shadow sat at Maizie's feet, his tail thumping, and Hare tried to jump onto her lap.

'I'm not sure as I want the hare, thank you,' said Maizie, pushing the creature away and patting Shadow reluctantly. Traditionally Stonewylders didn't keep animals as pets and she felt awkward.

Clip sat in his chair and watched Leveret making tea for them all, understanding her need for busyness. Her face was closed and she was deep in thought, ignoring them both. Maizie sat in silence, her face miserable with shame, unsure how to begin. Then Leveret brought their cups over and sat down, regarding her mother steadily.

366

'Mother, this is a complete shock and I had no idea. But I've heard such dreadful things of Alwyn that it's a relief to know he's not my father. I'd rather have Magus' blood than the tanner's.'

Maizie nodded, her cheeks still rosy and her eyes a little too bright. Clip lent across and clasped her trembling hands in his.

'That was a terribly cruel way for Buzz to announce it to the world but nobody will think any the less of you, Maizie. As long as Leveret's alright, then don't feel upset. Sometimes secrets are better out.'

Maizie looked up at him gratefully and a glimmer of the pretty young girl who'd so captivated the young magus of Stonewylde was evident for a moment. Then she turned to her daughter, her lips quivering, and took a deep breath.

'Leveret, my dear ... you were always so special to me and now you know why – you were the living proof that Magus still loved me. May I tell you how it came about? You must never think you were conceived from lust or duty or by mistake. 'Twere out of love.'

'Would you rather I left you both?' asked Clip. 'This is very personal.'

'There's not a great deal to tell,' said Maizie, 'so unless Leveret minds you listening in, I don't.'

'Clip is the father I've never had,' said Leveret, 'and I love him dearly. So I don't mind him hearing anything.'

'Well, 'twere the Hare Moon,' said Maizie. 'Sweyn were a weanling, and Gefrin a toddler. I'd had them two as well as Rosie, Geoffrey and Gregory with Alwyn, and was well and truly fastened to the man. He knew o' course that Yul weren't his, but that were part of the arrangement – he'd treat the boy as his, and tell the world so. Magus wouldn't – couldn't – take Yul as his son on account o' that stupid prophecy of Old Heggy's.'

'It must have been difficult,' said Clip.

'Aye. I never loved Alwyn – never even liked him. He were a bully and a cruel man, and try as I may, I never could please him. But I loved my five little 'uns from him, especially my Rosie who were always such a sweet maid. What I couldn't take was

Yul's suffering and the way Magus turned a blind eye, but there were nought I could do other than try and keep Alwyn sweet. He were a greedy man, so I fed 'un well and were as good a wife as I could be, always hoping that if he were content, he'd leave my Yul alone.'

'Poor Mother,' said Leveret, stroking her hand.

'Well, everyone in the Village thought I'd got above myself that time when Magus were so enchanted with me. There were so many jealous girls and they all thought I'd got my comeuppance, being saddled with a brute such as Alwyn. Anyway, that May we'd had Beltane and o' course Magus were the Green Man and he had a young and pretty May Queen by his side. As ever I watched 'em with a smile on my face and a stone in my heart. Try as I might, I could never forget when he'd loved me so much that he'd ride down to the Village every night for me. I never forgot the promises he'd made, to be handfasted to me even though I were just a simple Village maid. I'd never healed from the wound that he'd cut deep inside when he abandoned me the night o' Yul's birth in the Stone Circle, as that old crone made her prophecy. My life were hard on account o' him, yet I still loved him.'

Maizie paused and Leveret edged closer to her on the sofa and laid her head on her mother's soft shoulder. Shadow looked up mournfully and laid his head on her knee, and Maizie sighed.

'Beltane had passed and then 'twas the night o' the Hare Moon. Magus came down to the Village to pick his girl. Alwyn were in the Jack, where he always were of an evening, and would be there for a long time yet. The woman in the cottage next door, Clarysage she were called, Goddess rest her soul, had offered to come in and sit with the little 'uns for me. I wanted to go to the woods and dig some ramson bulbs to make a new batch o' gripe water for Sweyn. He had terrible colic and were always grizzling. Any goodwife knows 'tis best picked at the Moon Fullness, so off I went with my basket and trowel. Well, 'twere a beautiful evening, still light, with the birds in full song, balmy and warm, all the buds bursting out. I were walking up the track leading into the woods and my heart were heavy. Alwyn were a swine at times and handy with his fists if I weren't careful. I seem to recall I were actually weeping as I walked along, looking at the bluebells and feeling the magic and wishing that my life weren't so hard. And suddenly, there were Magus riding towards me on Nightwing. The moon had yet to rise and 'twere twilight, and we were all alone on the path.'

She paused again, lost in her memories.

'And he got off that great beast, and scooped me up like I were a maid again and put me up on the saddle, and got on hisself behind me and off we went just like in the old days when I were a young girl without a care in the whole world. There was me, a handfasted woman with six – *six* – babes, and yet at that moment I felt like I were a maid again, all a-quiver. We rode up through the woods and up the hill to the top, to the great stone there. And we got off Nightwing and Magus laid me down on the grass, gentle and tender like it were my first time, and he kissed me. He kissed me as if all those years hadn't happened, and all those babies hadn't happened. And he made my heart whole again with that loving and yes, 'twere daft and foolish, but that didn't matter. I knew then that he'd never forgotten me and that somehow, I were still special to him.'

'Oh Mother – that's beautiful!'

'Aye, it were beautiful, right enough. Nothing like the conception of any of Alwyn's five, nor even Yul that Spring Equinox all them years ago. Your conception, Leveret, on the top o' that hill with the big pink Hare Moon a-rising and the magic o' Stonewylde all around us – that were the most beautiful conception a woman could wish for. And I knew I'd conceived that night. I felt it, a spiral o' new life inside me. There were hares all over the hill I recall, and I decided it 'twere a boy or girl, I'd call the babe Leveret. My little hare.'

Leveret felt the tears hot on her cheeks and buried her face in her mother's arm. Maizie stroked her hand and smiled.

'O' course, nought were to come of it. Life continued, and I had to make sure Alwyn bedded me soon after in case he decided to use his head and count the moons. He never suspected – nobody ever suspected. Except Sweyn – I think somehow that child knew. He always resented you, Leveret.'

She nodded at this, everything now making sense.

'But what about Magus, Mother? Did he know? Clearly he must have, to acknowledge me in his Will. Did you tell him?'

Maizie smiled again and chuckled.

'Just as I knew I'd conceived, so did he. *"Make a wish and make a child"* they do say, and I said the rhyme that night, whilst we still lay together as one. He kissed me and tried to stop my words, but they were out and he came a-riding down to the Village next Dark Moon to see if I were in the Great Barn along with all the others. And I were standing there by the Village Pump drawing water, and he said to me, "Oh, not in the Barn then, Maizie?" and I says "No, Magus, I'm not. Reckon that wish came true and my seventh is on its way!" and he smiled and wished me well and rode on. And all the old women at the pump told me how lucky I were to have a seventh and I said aye, I knew that right enough.'

After Maizie had left, Leveret and Clip sat in the softly lit room and pondered the strange events of that day. Leveret slipped down to the kitchen and collected their tray of supper, but she noticed Clip ate little.

'What did the consultant say?' she asked. 'With all these goings on, I'd completely forgotten about your appointment.'

'Oh, he reckons there's nothing to worry about,' said Clip airily, waving his fork. 'He's taken samples and done scans and so forth. He's going to let me know, but it's probably just some sort of irritable bowel, as I suspected, and I just need to watch my diet carefully.'

'Oh Clip, that's good news!' said Leveret. 'I've been so worried.'

'It's probably my own fault for all that fasting over the years,' he said. 'So make sure you always eat regularly and properly, Leveret. Fasting on the day of a journey is fine, but don't prolong it and neglect your body's needs, will you?'

'No, I'll be sensible. Clip, I want to ask your advice about this inheritance. I don't want money, you know that, though I'm happy for my mother's sake that Magus did acknowledge me. What I'd like to do, if you think it's alright, is give my share to Stonewylde. I'd like to put it towards all the things Buzz was talking about – the repairs and renovations. I don't want any of it personally and I'd like you to say that for me at the meeting tomorrow please.'

'That's really admirable, Leveret.'

'No it's not. I don't intend to ever leave Stonewylde, so what use is money to me? This way everyone will benefit.'

'That's a wonderful idea, and in the morning when I'm facing everyone in the Galleried Hall and Buzz is looking more and more like the predator he was named after, I shall surprise them all with your lovely, generous offer.'

Clip reached across and hugged her tight.

'You're my niece, my brother's child,' he said happily. 'But what you said earlier about me being a father to you – that touched my heart. Thank you, Leveret.'

24

Magpie and Leveret sat together at the table in Marigold and Cherry's cottage examining the newly-arrived book and pens lying on the scrubbed pine. Marigold was sitting in her armchair knitting, breakfasts long over and done with and lunch not yet on the horizon, but Cherry was at that moment on her way to the Galleried Hall to meet with the other Elders.

'See the different types of nibs on the pens, Maggie, and the different lines on the page here? And now look at this special lettering in the book. It—'

But he'd grabbed the book and was poring over it, his finger tracking the calligraphy on the page. He flicked through the pages of different script excitedly and looking up at Leveret, beamed his thanks to her.

'Can you do lettering like this, do you think? It takes some practice of course, but I know you've got the skills.'

Magpie filled the pens with ink, for he was accustomed to drawing-pens, and immediately set to. Very quickly he picked up the technique and was soon writing in beautiful and almost perfect script.

'You are so clever!' she exclaimed. 'Most people would take weeks to become as accomplished as that! Well done, Magpie!'

'Aye, he's a very clever boy, right enough,' said Marigold proudly. 'Last night when Cherry and I came in from the kitchens, he were sitting here reading a book – look, that book there with lots o' words in it. And he got up and he made us a nice cup

o' tea, and while we drank it he drew us a picture. It were beautiful – Magpie where've you put it, lad? I'm off now back to the
Hall but do show Leveret what you drew. We wondered if 'twere
of you, Leveret. She looks a bit like you.'

A little shyly, Magpie went upstairs and returned with his
sketchbook. He'd used watercolour pencils, which he liked for
speedy sketches, and as Leveret looked at the picture she felt
the hair on her arms rise. It was a beautiful picture of a standing stone, and on the clover-dappled grass lay a pretty young
woman with dark curls. Only her head and shoulders were visible in the picture, with one arm flung out in abandonment; her
eyes were closed and a smile played on her lips. All around her
sat hares in moongazy position, their ears laid back and their
big eyes gazing up at the huge, pink moon. Underneath, Magpie
had written "*the wish*".

Leveret looked at him in wonder. She took his hands and
gazed into his clear turquoise eyes, long-lashed and bright.

'How do you do it, Magpie? I understand what this is. But how
did you know?'

He simply smiled at her, his eyes now a little sad knowing he
could not explain. Leveret persisted.

'It was last night, wasn't it, while my mother was telling me
about how it happened and I was imagining how she must've
looked, all those years ago up at Hare Stone?'

He nodded eagerly.

'So how does it come to you? Do you get a picture in your
head of whatever I'm seeing or imagining?'

Again he nodded and squeezed her hands.

'Do you remember how you used to send me your thoughts, as
pictures? We haven't done that for a while – shall we try now?'

She closed her eyes and kept hold of his hands.

'Right, send me something then,' she said. 'Something a bit
magical.'

And there was an explosion of colour in her head, a kaleido-
scope of images so strong and vivid that she jolted backwards
and her eyes flew open wide.

'Is that what you see?' she gasped, looking at him in awe. 'I can't imagine what it's like being you, Magpie. Your world is pure magic.'

In the Galleried Hall, the meeting was in full swing. Clip sat in the carved wooden throne with the boars' heads for arm-rests, the circle of chairs around him. As he'd predicted, only Martin and Rowan wanted to accept Buzz's offer and the rest were adamant that they'd rather starve than take his money. Today Buzz was dressed more casually but still looked out of place amongst the simply dressed folk. He glared around the circle, his face tight with anger and disappointment.

'Dawn, surely you of all people can see the logic of what I'm proposing?'

'Why me of all people?' she asked. 'Because I used to be Hallfolk? All the more reason to reject a proposal to return to the bad old days. I'm infinitely happier as a Stonewylder with no social distinctions.'

'But those are just ideals! Equality may sound idyllic but we all know that people are different, and some of us are more capable of leading than others. How about you, Hazel? You've done so well, and with some investment you could have a first class medical centre here.'

Hazel had noticed Buzz's full mouthful of carefully maintained teeth, and guessed he'd had an implant to replace the tooth Yul had knocked out all those years ago. His nose was perfect and that too must have been surgically remodelled, for Yul had made a complete mess of it. But she guessed the real scars from Buzz's humiliating defeat went a great deal deeper, and this attempt to return as the great benefactor was all tied up with that.

'We already have a first class medical centre here.'

'But why not accept my generosity?'

'Precisely because it's that – *your* generosity!' said Miranda, and Hazel nodded.

'Why so much hostility?' he asked sadly, spreading his hands in bewildered supplication. 'All I'm trying to do is help.'

'The thing is, Buzz, we're not daft and we're all aware that you're just playing games. We don't want your help – we know it would come at too high a price,' said Miranda firmly. 'Why wait all these years to inform us that Leveret, Faun and Rufus are beneficiaries of Magus' Will?'

'There was no obligation to inform anyone,' he replied, 'and the original Trustee thought it better to wait.'

'You were just holding on until you had enough money personally to come back here and dazzle everyone with your wealth,' said Hazel. 'We want none of your business tactics and power struggles. Nor do we want a return to the 'us and them' regime, Hallfolk and Villagers. We're a simple but autonomous community and we intend to stay that way.'

Whilst the debate was going on in the Galleried Hall, Magpie had wandered into the kitchens for a drink before starting work in the Kitchen Garden. Leveret was visiting the elderly folk in their wing at the back of the Hall; she'd gleaned so much of the old knowledge and wisdom from them over the past months and enjoyed spending time there.

Marigold and Cherry had discussed cleaning the grand apartments where Buzz had slept, but decided to leave them be. Hopefully he wouldn't be staying beyond today and neither was prepared to do anything to make him comfortable. But they'd agreed it might be useful for Marigold to pop in there whilst everyone was in the Council of Elders meeting, just for a little look around. So when Magpie had finished his drink, Marigold took his arm and asked him to come with her as she was a little nervous of snooping about up there alone.

She felt very strange tip-toeing into the sitting room like a thief, with Magpie close behind. He'd never been in these chambers before and stood there awkwardly in the middle of the great room staring around in wonder. Marigold was tutting at every sign of Buzz's occupation, and then jumped out of her skin when the connecting door opened and Mallow crept through.

'Oh!' cried Mallow, dropping the tray she carried. It crashed to the ground and she immediately squatted down to pick up the crockery. Her hands shook and she raised a tearful face to Marigold, who bustled over to help collect up the mess of breakfast things.

'No need to cry!' clucked Marigold. 'Look, nothing's broke. 'Tis just a few crumbs and drops o' coffee, and we can clear it up in no time.'

Few people had much contact with Mallow, for she kept to herself in the cottage and didn't join the others for meals as Martin did. Cherry and Marigold's cottage was in the same row and they'd heard muffled sounds in the past but didn't like to pry. Now, looking closely at the small and terrified woman, Marigold felt a flood of sympathy.

'Thank you,' whispered Mallow, frantically picking up the remains of the breakfast. 'I were so shocked to see someone in here ...'

She tailed off, looking fearfully around her.

'Aye well, I just popped up to see if all were in order,' said Marigold. 'I didn't know you'd be seeing to Buzz.'

Mallow nodded, the heavy tray now re-laden, and stood up with it carefully.

'Martin told me to look after the Hallfolk,' she said. 'I'm just going to put this tray in the lift and then I must make his bed.'

Marigold gave the carpet a final wipe with the soiled napkin and heaved herself to her feet.

'Thank you, Marigold,' said Mallow. 'I were so spooked. I hate it in here, don't you? 'Tis frightening in these old rooms.'

'Frightening?'

Magpie had come over and nodded vigorously at this.

'Are you frightened, lad?'

He nodded and looked about fearfully.

'Get on with you!' said Marigold, clapping him on the back. 'There's nothing bad here, so don't be daft.'

She watched Mallow tread gingerly across the room under the weight of the tray and put it into the hatch.

'So I hear you're taking care of Old Violet, now Vetchling's passed on and Starling's taken off?'

Mallow nodded timidly, staring at the floor.

'That can't be easy – she's a nasty old piece o' work. Pardon my rudeness for I realise she's your mother by Martin, but she's not known for her soft tongue nor kind ways.'

'No,' said Mallow, glancing around furtively. 'She's ... she's wicked. Truly wicked, and I don't like going there. But I best be getting on, for I need to finish here and get down there quick or she'll be complaining and then Martin will get angry.'

'Pah!' said Marigold. 'If Martin don't—'

'What on earth is all this noise in here?' drawled a loud voice from behind the connecting door, and in walked Rainbow.

'Oh sweet Mother!' cried Marigold. 'Not another of 'em!'

'Watch your mouth, Marigold!' said Rainbow sharply.

'We didn't know *you* were back and all! Any more o' you nesting in here?'

'No there aren't! Magpie, it's lovely to see you again. How's the painting?'

'And you can keep your paws off my boy too! Come on, Magpie. Let's get back to the kitchens.'

'What a splendid idea!' said Rainbow, stretching languidly and shaking out her hair. 'I'll come down with you. Maybe you'd rustle me up something to eat? I'm starving. I seem to have over-slept and missed out on breakfast.'

Yul had been silent until now, knowing that if he spoke he would say too much. Sylvie sat next to him and he could feel her tension. The old Villagers amongst them bristled with dislike and indignation, whilst Harold twitched so much that Hazel grew quite concerned. Martin was silent too, clearly briefed to keep quiet today, and Rowan sat with her arms folded and a smug grin on her face, as if nothing that happened today was of any importance to her.

Only Clip seemed completely calm and unperturbed by Buzz's invasion into their territory, and Yul watched him speculatively.

He understood now that Clip's dreaminess in the past had perhaps been a smoke-screen; his father-in-law and uncle was not as daft as he appeared. Whilst in London on the recent visit, Yul had developed a reluctant respect for the older man. Six months ago Yul could never have sat here and let these events unfold without trying to intervene, but today he was able to take a back seat and watch, knowing that he wasn't the only one capable of controlling the situation.

'Look, I've come here in good faith to help,' said Buzz with only a hint of exasperation. 'I'm offering to put everything right with Stonewylde. Clip, why you've brought this proposal to the Council is beyond me as the decision is yours to make. Please – for once in your life, be strong and decisive! Stonewylde is yours. You own the place so you decide.'

Clip's pale grey eyes flicked round the circle and he noted Yul's dark, silent demeanour, which surprised him. Sylvie was pale and strained, her eyes scared. His gaze then rested on Buzz, large and uncomfortable in his chair and fighting the urge to shout at them all. Doubtless he bullied everyone he worked with and his civility was now wearing thin. Clip decided this had gone on long enough.

'Stonewylde is not mine, Buzz. Nobody owns Stonewylde – she owns us. We are merely her guardians, appointed to serve her. She takes from us what she needs to survive, and she gives back to us as she sees fit. She's Nature at its most fundamental, and *you* certainly don't have the means to put everything right with her. Stonewylde's needs go far deeper than material wealth, and what you have to offer isn't what she requires. Stonewylde is at present in shadow, in eclipse, but soon she'll be in glorious sunshine again. And it definitely won't be because you've splashed a bit of money about.'

'Oh, for Christ's sake!' yelled Buzz, shockingly loud in the ancient hall. 'Don't start with your bloody mystical bullshit now! You always were an old fool and—'

He stopped abruptly as Clip fixed him with a wolf-grey stare and pointed straight at him.

'*Be still!* You will never return to Stonewylde, Buzz, and nor will any of your kind. You are *never* to attempt a come-back again. The banishment that my brother Sol imposed still stands, and always will.'

Buzz sat looking as if he might explode, his pale blue eyes popping and bloodshot, but his mouth closed. Clip continued quietly.

'I shall be leaving at Samhain as I promised, and I've taken steps to ensure that the material and practical aspects of Stonewylde's needs are covered. I'm trusting in my shamanic insights that all will be well in the future with the other, spiritual aspects.'

There was a pause whilst everyone digested exactly what he'd said.

'Thank you, Clip,' said Yul. 'You've made us all feel protected from invasion, safe from the likes of Buzz and the other Hallfolk.'

Their eyes met and Clip inclined his head, acknowledging this huge step forward. But Martin jumped up from his seat and waved his arms around furiously, his thin face scarlet with fury.

'What have you done to Master Buzz, you evil, scheming sorcerer? Look at him! He can't speak! And he were wrong – Stonewylde isn't yours – Stonewylde is rightfully mine! I were born afore you and my mother said—'

'Your mother's the evil one!' cried Cherry. 'She's a wicked old hag and—'

'You, woman, will be one o' the first to go when—'

'Enough!' barked Clip. 'This is not the time for such talk. Buzz is silent, Martin, because he has nothing more to say that we wish to hear. And neither have you. Good folk, we have less than two weeks until Samhain, and I must tell you what will happen when I've left. I'm happy for Buzz to hear it so that he'll understand once and for all that Stonewylde does not need his money nor his presence.'

Everyone shifted in their seats, anxious to hear his words. Martin's mouth was clamped shut and Buzz remained red-faced but quiet, his furious gaze flashing around the circle of faces until it rested on Sylvie, who blanched even further. Clip wondered why she was quite so upset by him, especially now he'd been disarmed.

'Clip – about this business of you leaving at Samhain,' began Yul. 'I'm not sure if—'

'I have to go,' said Clip. 'My time here is done and I crave my freedom after so many years. I've set everything up to come into effect at my departure, and I'll tell you all about this. But first I have a message from Leveret about her inheritance. She wants to donate her money towards the upkeep of Stonewylde. She'll presumably be able to access her shares once she reaches eighteen, and in the meantime she'll use every penny she's accumulated to help Stonewylde with the repairs and things, and pay off some of the debts. She wants to give it for the common good of Stonewylders.'

There was a swell of approval at this news.

''Tis very good of the maid,' said Old Greenbough. 'So our troubles are over then?'

'Probably not completely, but it'll certainly help the current situation,' said Clip.

'Well, don't think Faun's giving her money to Stonewylde,' said Rowan, 'because she's not! I got an announcement to make too – we're going to stay with Buzz, and Faun will go to drama school in the Outside World and become a celebrity! Magus would've approved of that for his beautiful daughter.'

'I'm sure he would,' said Miranda drily. 'As for Rufus – he told me last night it's his ambition to be a doctor and he wants to go to medical school when he's older. He says he decided this a while ago and now he can use his money to fund that. Of course he wants to return to Stonewylde when he's qualified, to work with Hazel and Leveret. But he's only thirteen so it's all a long way off. And Clip has more to tell us, I believe, about the future plans for Stonewylde?'

'I certainly do. As I said earlier, it's too much for one person to own and run Stonewylde, and I wouldn't want to pass that burden on to my beloved daughter when I leave. She and I have discussed this and everything's now in place to turn Stonewylde into a charitable trust, run by a Board of Trustees. This'll come into effect the day after Samhain. It means that we get beneficial tax status and no one person is then responsible for running the place.'

Yul nodded slowly, seeing the advantages.

'Sylvie and I have talked it over,' Clip continued, 'and it's her dearest wish that Stonewylde should become a healing centre. We both feel the Green Magic is a restorative energy and should be used to heal. We want to turn Stonewylde into a place where both traditional and alternative remedies can be offered, and the Green Magic can be tapped into.'

There was an explosion of excitement about this, and Sylvie's eyes sought Clip's. He smiled at her, his thin, lined face illuminated with love.

'But there's more,' he continued. 'Yesterday, before we left London, I heard something really marvellous. You may recall the purpose of our visit, which we shared with you all before we left. It was a sad but successful visit, wasn't it, Miranda?'

Miranda nodded, still a little raw from the experience.

'Miranda's mother had made it very clear that Miranda wouldn't be inheriting their huge fortune because the whole lot had been legally tied up to go to charity. This was in the hands of their lawyers, and Miranda's been corresponding with Christopher, son of one of the original partners. We met him in London as it was his remit to look after us all. Yesterday, when we were packing up to leave, Christopher called me for a surprise meeting.'

Clip paused dramatically and smiled across at Miranda, who looked rather concerned.

'Despite his meanness towards his daughter, Miranda's father had been involved in fundraising all his life. Most of the money he left is at present invested, and he'd stipulated that the family's wealth was to be entirely donated to charity, and ideally to a hospital. Miranda's mother was to choose which one and write it into her Will, to come into effect on her death. Having met up with her daughter and other members of the family, she was very taken with all we told her of Stonewylde and Sylvie's healing. Later, she asked to see me in private and questioned me about the healing centre we're planning. I explained, and said it was all Sylvie's idea. Then Miranda's mother summoned Christopher and told him to arrange for the family's entire fortune to go to the charity we're setting up at Stonewylde, in Sylvie's name.'

There was complete silence as everyone tried to make sense of this news. Finally Sylvie spoke, a frown on her face.

'So ... so we don't need Buzz's money – or anyone's money? We'll have enough for everything we want to do at Stonewylde?'

'Exactly,' beamed Clip. 'Everything we need to start the healing centre, and much more besides. Your dream will come true, Sylvie!'

Leveret put in a few hours of study and then went to find Magpie, hoping they could go up to Mother Heggy's cottage together. He was working in the Art Room with David, who had a class of younger students there too. Magpie was in his own corner with a canvas before him, painting a seascape. Leveret could tell immediately that something had upset him, as his eyes were cloudy and his expression troubled. She watched him for a while, as he put tiny glints of light onto the peaks of water to make the green-blue sea in his picture come alive.

'What's wrong, Magpie?' she asked eventually.

He laid down his brush and took her hands, and she saw an image of Rainbow. The woman's eyes were exactly the colour he was using for his painting now.

'Rainbow's gone,' said Leveret, but he shook his head at this. Then she saw Rainbow clearly up in Yul's apartments, and sitting in the window seat behind her was the shade of a tall man with blond hair.

David came over and looked appraisingly at the painting.

'Did you hear Rainbow's back?' he asked Leveret. 'She was in here earlier, and she wants to take some of Magpie's work to show someone in London. She's trying to get him exhibited.'

'She can't!' snapped Leveret. 'I don't want her taking anything of Magpie's away. I don't trust her.'

David nodded in agreement.

'I know you're the best one for getting through to Magpie. Please, can you try to find out how he feels about it? I can't help but think she's only out to exploit him - I don't trust her either.'

The meeting in the Galleried Hall disbanded and everyone dispersed to discuss the exciting news. It was very difficult for the Elders to settle down to any work after such portentous events, and they were all keen to spread the news. Martin stomped down to see his mother in the Village in a complete rage, and luckily for her, Mallow was already back home so wasn't forced to bear the brunt of his bad temper.

The news that Stonewylde's financial problems were over and there was to be a special healing centre created when Clip left in two weeks' time, spread like heath-fire through the community. Yul and Sylvie stayed behind to have a word with Clip when everyone had left, and she threw her arms around her thin father and hugged him tight. When they finally released each other, Sylvie was in floods of tears.

'Don't cry, my darling girl,' said Clip softly. 'This is everything you dreamed of, isn't it? And it's your grandparents' chance to put right all their wrongs.'

'I know, I know,' she sobbed. 'It's just too good to be true! Oh Yul, isn't it wonderful?'

He'd hung back, not wishing to intrude, but came forward now and handed her a handkerchief.

'It's ... so unexpected. I'm finding it hard to take it in immediately. But yes, it is wonderful and I'm sure it's the right thing for Stonewylde. It certainly feels right.' He looked at Clip's grey careworn face and into his pale eyes. 'Clip, all that you said about Stonewylde – her needs, how we're only guardians and not owners – I'd never really understood that before. But now I feel enlightened and it's put me to shame. Some of my past behaviour—'

'We're all learning, Yul,' said Clip, patting his arm. 'We all do our best and hopefully we get there in the end. It wasn't till I saw Buzz in action today that I realised just how little like Magus you actually are. You're strong and you're a leader, but you're not in the same mould as Magus or Buzz. You've always acted with the best of intentions, not because you enjoy power for its own sake. I'm sorry if I've ever misjudged you in the past.'

Now Yul was a little bright-eyed with unshed tears, and unexpectedly, Clip opened his arms and took the young man into a heartfelt embrace, while Sylvie looked on in utter astonishment.

Later on, still feeling emotional and unable to settle to anything else, Sylvie and Yul decided to take the girls for a walk up to the Stone Circle. It was a lovely clear October afternoon with a couple of hours before twilight, and the leaves were well on the turn after such a dry summer. Bluebell was growing up and could now manage much longer walks than before, and because in the past Yul had always worked such long hours, they'd missed out on little family outings such as these. The four of them wrapped up in jackets, although the sun was shining, and set off out of the Village and up the track leading to the Long Walk.

The girls ran ahead excitedly, examining conkers and chestnuts and laughing at the squirrels' antics, whilst Yul and Sylvie strolled hand in hand.

'What a day!' said Yul. 'In fact, what a few days! So much excitement and everything turned on its head.'

'Oh yes,' agreed Sylvie. 'Everything has changed so fast. I feel quite exhausted by it all and I just want to catch my breath a bit.'

'Well, Buzz should be off any time now, and then we can all breathe a big sigh of relief,' said Yul.

'You were very good with him last night and this morning,' said Sylvie. 'I was so worried you'd thump him.'

Yul chuckled at this.

'Of course I wanted to! There were a few moments when it was a close thing, but really, it wouldn't have solved anything and

I'd have looked like some boy brawling in the street again. Clip handled him far better than I could have done.'

'He was wonderful, wasn't he?'

Yul agreed and they walked along in silence for a while, Sylvie wondering if Buzz had actually left yet. After the meeting, Clip had told him to have lunch, pack his stuff and be off as soon as possible. Buzz had nodded and swiftly left the Galleried Hall. Ever since his dramatic entrance the previous night in their old chambers, Sylvie had felt herself on the edge of a precipice, trying to put one foot in front of the other and not look down at the terrifying drop below. She'd been sure that Buzz was going to make some allusion to the ballet, especially when he'd winked at Celandine so conspiratorially. She was entirely blameless, but how awful it would look to have deceived Yul like that. But hopefully Buzz had now gone, and the moment of danger was past.

And as for her other secret ... she was dying to tell Yul about the tiny curled-up being inside her. They'd transgressed, but she didn't care; the thought of carrying his baby, conceived at the Blue Moon under their yew tree, was so magical that the two-children rule mattered nothing. Maybe she'd tell him today, in the Stone Circle. It was still early days but everything felt just right, and what a wonderful way to celebrate the events of the past few days.

The children raced up the Long Walk, russet leaves drifting down over their heads and crunchy beech mast underfoot. Soft golden sunlight streamed in shafts through the autumn leaves, and Yul glanced at Sylvie as they walked hand in hand. He felt deep inside that they'd finally reached a good place in their relationship and their marriage could start a new phase. The thought of Rainbow still filled him with guilt and dread, and he'd been terrified that Buzz might use it against him. But surely if he'd known about it, he'd have done so by now; Rainbow must have kept quiet after all. Yul decided the best option would be to bury the secret completely and just start again with Sylvie. They'd have to plan where to live as she clearly hated the beautiful apartments he loved so much, but that could all be part of their new beginning together.

The Stone Circle became visible through the stone portal and the girls paused at the threshold, well aware that thoughtlessly racing inside the huge, sunlit arena wasn't respectful. Bluebell took Celandine's hand and allowed her older sister to lead her inside. She scanned the area quickly, the stones even bigger to such a small person, and quickly located him. Today he stood leaning against one of the megaliths near the Altar Stone. He raised a hand to her and waved, and Bluebell swallowed and quickly looked away.

As she and Yul walked into the Circle, Sylvie thought for a second she saw someone already in there at the far end, but realised her mistake as her eyes adjusted to the brightness. The decorations of Autumn Equinox still graced every stone, and the girls started their usual autumn game of spotting the hidden dormice that Merewen always included for the children's amusement. Bluebell still held on tightly to her sister, but then Celandine shook her off and began a leaping, joyful dance in the centre, her hair flying and her arms outstretched. Bluebell rushed over and clung onto Yul, her thumb in her mouth, and he picked her up and kissed her.

'Come on, Suck-a-thumb! I thought you were going to stop that now you're five!'

They watched Celandine for a while as she improvised the most beautiful dance, honouring every stone and becoming an autumn leaf herself, just as she'd done at the previous Samhain in the Barn.

'She really is talented,' murmured Sylvie. 'It's not just moon-dancing – this is actual dancing genius. I wonder if she'll want to train and become a professional when she's older?'

'Maybe, and in that case we'll back her all the way,' said Yul, gazing at their child in wonder. 'And the same if she doesn't want to either. She can stay at Stonewylde and delight everyone here with her dance.'

'What do you want to do, Blue?' asked Sylvie, stroking the

younger child's curls as she clung like a bush-baby in Yul's arms.

'I want to be a mummy,' said Bluebell. 'And I want to write stories. Can I do both of those?'

'Of course you can,' laughed Yul. 'I haven't seen your hare story lately, have I? How's it coming on?'

'It's lovely!' said Bluebell, pulling away from his shoulder so she could see his face. 'Magpie's done some drawings for it and it's so pretty! Celandine's not doing writing much any more but I still am, and I got another one too about the Bluebell Faeries. I'll show you when we get home, Father.'

'That'll be wonderful,' he said, kissing her on the nose.

'You can really see Magpie's influence here in the Circle, can't you?' said Sylvie, wandering around and gazing up at the paintings. 'It's always looked beautiful, but since he's been involved the magic has somehow felt even stronger.'

'That's true,' said Yul. 'I must talk to Merewen before they start decorating for Samhain. I'm not sure if she'll remember that the Death Dance won't be held up here any more. I don't want the normal ghoulish motifs in our Stone Circle.'

'What did you have in mind then?'

'The crows and other black birds are fine,' he said. 'It's the skulls and images of death that I object to.'

'But Yul, it is the Festival of the Dead.'

'I know. But I prefer to think of it by its other name, the Festival of the Ancestors.'

'Are they holding the Death Dance down at the other yew this year?'

'I believe so. I think Clip's spoken to some of the older folk about it.'

'So will there be any kind of ceremony up here at all?'

'No, nothing. I've said we'll keep the bonfires and the labyrinth and wicker dome in the Village as usual. That works far better. This Circle, at Samhain, has far too many connotations and memories for me ...'

She squeezed his hand, thinking back to the previous Samhain and the terrible night when that storm had brewed up out of nowhere. It was the first time the awful scent and presence of Magus had become really apparent. Just remembering the experience she'd endured in the chambers, with no electricity and that great slash of lightning, made Sylvie's skin prickle. She snuggled up to his arm and closed her eyes.

'Yul, I really love you.'

'And I really love you, my beautiful Sylvie,' he said, stooping with Bluebell still in his arms to kiss her.

'There's something wonderful I want to tell—'

'Ah, very touching! What a perfect little family you are!'

They swung round to see Buzz coming through a gap in the stones. They froze whilst Celandine, dancing alone in the centre, stumbled and stopped. Buzz walked over to her, and Yul and Sylvie hurried towards them.

'I thought you'd left!' said Yul, heart pounding furiously.

'I'm about to go,' said Buzz, hatred veiling his face. 'But I thought I'd have one last look at the old Stone Circle.'

His gaze swept around, taking in the great stones, the faded paintings, the golden trees beyond. Sylvie found she was barely breathing and felt dizzy. She clutched on to Yul's arm and pulled Celandine in, so they formed a tight-knit little group. She couldn't look Buzz in the eye but she felt Yul next to her blazing with hostility, glaring aggressively at the intruder. Her heart thumped loudly too, but with dread. Buzz's next words confirmed her fears; why had she ever hoped he'd let her off the hook?

'What beautiful dancing, Celandine! You told me before that you loved to dance but I had no idea you were so talented.'

'What?' Yul snarled. 'What are you on about?'

'Oh, didn't Sylvie tell you?'

'Tell me what?'

'Or Celandine? Oh, Celandine, surely you told your daddy what a lovely time we spent together?'

'Buzz, leave her out of it!' cried Sylvie. 'Don't get the children involved.'

'Involved in what? What the hell's going on?' shouted Yul, his

388

face white and his eyes flashing fury. 'Sylvie, what is he talking about?'

He turned on her and she read in his expression not only his anger at Buzz, but his wounded pride at being made to look a fool like this. She hung her head and Celandine turned to face her father.

'It was when Mummy and I went to see the ballet. Buzz was there too and he bought me an ice-cream.'

'I don't believe this!' spat Yul. 'Why didn't you tell me?'

Buzz laughed, and Yul started to peel Bluebell off his chest, trying to loosen the grip of her arms and legs and set her on the ground.

'We knew you'd be cross,' said Celandine, 'so we thought we'd better not say anything.'

'Yul, please! He just turned up and—'

'That wasn't the only reason you didn't tell him, was it, Sylvie?'

Buzz's face too was pale, ready for action, but he smiled.

'Sylvie, what is he on about?' shouted Yul. 'I suggest you go now, Buzz, before I—'

He stopped and took a deep breath. His daughters both looked up at him with enormous round eyes and he took another lungful of air. Buzz laughed and began to back away, giving a little wave of farewell.

'I'll be off then. But Sylvie, don't forget to tell him everything, will you? We managed to conceal what we were up to in the theatre of course, but as for what happened at the nursing home all those years ago ...'

25

'No, Celandine, we're not going up to Hare Stone tonight,' said Sylvie. 'I'll take you to the Village Green if it's not too cold.'

The child looked at her mother, noting her pallor and dull eyes, and nodded.

'Do you think Father will come?' she asked quietly.

Sylvie merely shook her head.

'Was it my fault for telling him about the ballet?'

'No, of course not,' said Sylvie wearily. 'It's always best to tell the truth. We should have done that at the time instead of pretending it didn't happen. But Father's not cross with you, darling. He knows you were only doing what I told you to do.'

'Will it all get better again?' asked Celandine sadly. 'We were so happy and I thought we were all going to live together again.'

'I'm sure we are, but at the moment Father's too upset.'

'When we were all in the Stone Circle, I thought he was going to hurt Buzz,' said Celandine. 'It was horrible. Blue and I were really scared.'

'I know – I'm so sorry you had to see all that. Buzz was deliberately provoking him, but Father let Buzz walk away even though he wanted to be nasty back to him. That takes a lot of strength.'

'I suppose so,' said Celandine. 'Oh Mum, I wish we could all be together again up at Hare Stone! It was so wonderful before, all of us there with our picnic and feeling so joyful.'

'I know, and we will go up there together for the Moon Fullness again one day, maybe in the spring when it's warm. We'll sort this out and we'll all be happy soon. Poor Father – I can't tell you how bad I feel about it, Celandine.'

The little girl threw her slim arms around her mother's neck and kissed her pale face.

'When we dance for the Bright Lady tonight we'll ask her to help make it all better with moon magic, shall we, Mum?'

Leveret stood on the roof of the tower with Clip, gazing out at the golden trees all around. Shadow was by her side, remarkably calm and well-behaved for a puppy, and Hare lay in her arms like a long-eared baby. The autumn air was chill, fragrant with wood-smoke and the promise of winter ahead.

'Five more days,' she said sadly, standing close to the man beside her. 'I can't tell you how much I'll miss you.'

'I know, Leveret, and I feel the same. But please – let's look at this in a positive way. You can never truly be the Shaman whilst I'm still here and you need to grow into your new role. As for me – all I've ever wanted to do is be free of the coils of Stonewylde. I made a terrible mistake as a young man and when Sylvie came here, I behaved badly again. In life I think we're given chances to rectify our wrongs, but I failed, and consequently never gained the one thing I really wanted – the freedom to roam. Of course, a huge compensation this past year has been you coming into my life, a joy I'd never expected. But I feel finally that I've paid my dues for all past wrongs and can be free, so you must let me go with a happy heart.'

She nodded, stroking Hare's soft coat and trying not to cry.

'And tonight you want to be alone for the Moon Fullness?'

'Yes, Leveret – I'd like to spend my last one at Stonewylde up in the Dolmen alone, if you don't mind, especially as it's an eclipse. It seems fitting, given the name my mother and Old Heggy chose for me. Anyway, you love being in the cottage for the Moon Fullness, don't you?'

'Yes, I do,' she said quietly, her throat aching. 'But I thought ... the last one?'

'We'd neither of us get anywhere, would we? You'd be tearful and I'd be sad and guilty at making you tearful, and we'd never manage to journey. Better that we see this Hunter's Moon as a new beginning. I'm sure Mother Heggy will visit you as she did last month, especially as it's so close to Samhain.'

'What about Samhain? Will we spend that together?'

'I'm not sure. You know the Death Dance won't be taking place in the Stone Circle any more? I suppose I should offer my services at the Yew of Death, but what I'd really like to do is spend the evening in the Circle alone, taking leave of the ancestors there. Everyone else will be in the Village so it should be very special.'

'Maybe I could join you for that?' she asked hopefully. 'As a farewell ceremony before you leave the next morning?'

'What a good idea!' he said. 'Let's do that.'

Mallow lugged a great basket of logs towards the hearth, dragging them across the floor and leaving a trail of mess in her wake. Old Violet, rocking in her chair with a pipe in her gnarled hand, watched her malevolently. As Mallow staggered past she tried to stick out her boot but failed, and sat cursing and muttering.

'Was you speaking to me, Mother Violet?' asked Mallow, straightening her aching back.

'No I weren't, stupid girl,' she mumbled.

'You got a nice load o' logs chopped out there,' said Mallow. 'Was that my Swift's doing?'

'No, 'twere Jay's doing! Your Swift ain't been for days – can't be bothered no more. Jay's a good lad and he spent a fine evening with his old Great Aunt Violet. Gave him some tips and wrinkles, I did, and he's set up now – knows what's about.'

She chuckled hoarsely at this and clamped her gums around the stem of her pipe to draw the smoke deep into her lungs.

'Our Jay's all set up for Hunter's Moon, right enough,' she sputtered through the smoke. 'Old Violet knows, as ever. All is set and 'twill be my own boy's time soon. The wheel turns as ever, and 'tis almost a year and a day.'

'Yes, Mother Violet,' said Mallow, taking the broom to sweep up the mess she'd created.

'And you better watch your tail and all,' said Violet, hawking and aiming into the crackling fire. 'Dark Angel will be abroad soon enough, stalking and searching.'

Mallow's face registered terror and she hastily made the sign of the pentangle on her chest.

'Aye, the weeding out will soon begin, and not afore time!' said Violet, her evil chuckle hanging in the smoky air.

Miranda knocked on Yul's study door and went straight in, giving him no chance to refuse entry. He was at his desk staring at the computer screen, but didn't seem to be getting much work done. He looked up at her wearily.

'Time for a quick chat?' she asked, sitting down on the sofa. He sighed and joined her.

'Yes, especially now I no longer need worry about the money situation,' he said. 'Suddenly from having the whole thing to fret about, I've become a simple farm manager.'

'Hardly,' she said. 'There'll be a huge amount of co-ordination involved, won't there? Presumably you'll get someone professional in to do a proper survey of the building and repairs needed?'

He nodded unenthusiastically.

'Anyway, Christopher's phoned to say he's coming down. He'll oversee the charitable trust handover before Clip leaves on November 1st and he'll work with the local lawyer Clip's been using. They'll get the new Board of Trustees signed up and then Christopher can start proceedings for the funds to be assigned. It won't be instant; it could take quite some time, because of all the legal stuff.'

'But ... your mother hasn't passed on yet, has she?'

'No, but apparently my father set up many different funds and some are available now, so Christopher wants to get the ball rolling. Of course this money is purely for the healing centre, so although we can use it to renovate the Hall, we can't use it for stuff like general repairs to the Great Barn or the water supply to the Village, much as I'd like to.'

'The money Leveret's giving can do that.'

'Christopher's offered to advise us on Magus' Will too, if we want. It seems that Buzz is actually the Trustee for all three minors, and whilst Rowan might be happy for Faun's shares to be controlled by him, Maizie and I certainly don't want him in charge of our children's inheritances for any longer than necessary. Personal issues aside, it doesn't really seem ethical for him to control all the shares.'

'Christopher would be perfect for that – I liked him when we met in London,' said Yul. 'But can Leveret and Rufus afford to have him advise? I shouldn't imagine he comes cheap.'

Miranda smiled a little wistfully.

'I'm sure he'll offer us a good rate,' she said, 'given that he's probably earning huge fees from handling my parents' estate. I don't see why he can't do this as a favour, but I'll negotiate that. I'm glad you like him. He's a decent man, and he's been very kind and supportive in all this.'

'Okay, that'll be great then.'

'Are you alright for him to stay at Stonewylde as a guest? It seems a bit silly him staying Outside in a hotel and driving in every day, and it'd be nice for him to get a feel of the place.'

'It's Clip who decides that, but of course I'm happy for it.'

Miranda gazed at him, noting the droop of his head and the fatigue in his face.

'What's wrong, Yul? You've been down since Buzz's visit. Were you upset that you weren't one of Magus' beneficiaries? We could always ask Christopher about contesting the Will, if you wanted to go that route.'

'No,' said Yul, smiling wanly. 'To be frank, I wouldn't want his money anyway. It's different for Leveret, Faun and Rufus – and Buzz too of course – but Magus hated me and I wouldn't want to take his money. It would feel dirty to me, as if I'd gone back on my principles. I don't mean the others shouldn't take it, of course. It's just—'

'No, I understand and I'd feel exactly the same if he'd left me anything. But it is different for the other children, and I'm just glad that they're going to benefit. Rufus is so keen to study medicine one day, and I believe he's bright enough. The thought of him working here, with Hazel and Leveret, and maybe a team of other healers and doctors ... the whole thing is quite unbelievable really. But you're obviously unhappy. Sylvie confided in me about what happened the other day in the Stone Circle, when Buzz told you about turning up at the ballet. That was a terrible thing to do, but you mustn't let it get you down.'

'I know,' said Yul. 'I'm trying to just put it to one side but I can't. I feel ... I feel so betrayed that she and Buzz had a secret together that they kept for ages.'

'This reaction is exactly why he told you and you're behaving precisely as he wants! I know that recently you and Sylvie managed to patch things up. I'd hoped to see you moving back in together by now and I really can't see why you haven't. This latest thing from Buzz is nothing, yet he's managed to come between you. Sylvie was completely blameless. You mustn't treat her as if she's been unfaithful to you.'

Yul coloured at this but because he turned to the window, his mother-in-law failed to notice.

'I'll get over it, Miranda, really. I know it's stupid. It's just ... touched a nerve, I guess.'

For one moment he was almost tempted to tell her about Rainbow. He desperately felt the need to confide in someone and offload the guilt, and wished now that he'd told Sylvie long before. Or even on the day when Buzz had done his best to provoke him into some kind of adolescent behaviour – he should have come clean then, whilst she was looking so guilty. But the children had been there, crying and clinging, and how could he have told their beautiful mother that whilst she may have been the victim of Buzz's groping, he'd actually gone a great deal further than that with Rainbow? The nagging, gnawing knowledge was blighting everything, and he needed to deal with it. Yul resolved that he'd find Sylvie later and just tell her straight.

Hopefully, in view of the Buzz situation, she'd be understanding and maybe find it in her heart to forgive him. Telling her voluntarily would count in his favour, surely?

Marigold was up to her elbows in flour when Cherry hurried into the kitchens.

'Sister, you need to come quick and look at this.'

'Now? You can see—'

'This moment!'

Marigold cleaned herself hastily and followed her sister into the little office they'd always shared by the kitchens. On the table lay a screwed-up sheet of parchment paper, and Cherry eyed it with distaste.

'That – that's the thing you must see, Marigold.'

Marigold uncrumpled it, smoothing out the thick paper as best she could. It was a charcoal drawing and had become a little smudged with the rough handling, but despite the creases and smears, the subject was very clear. It was beautifully done, with bold, simple lines, and depicted a scene by the sea. On the long rock lay a naked woman, her hair spread out like seaweed. In her arms was a man, distinctive by the dark curly hair and the faint scars all over his back. It was signed *Rainbow*.

'What ...?'

Marigold's mouth hung open and her cheeks flushed. She wasn't often lost for words, but at this moment was incapable of forming any.

''Twere in the bedroom she slept in on this visit, up in their apartments in the children's old room,' said Cherry. 'She'd propped it against the mirror on the dressing table. And o' course, who should go in there first to change the bedding but that silly Primrose and Sorrel. Neither o' them girls would ever keep their mouths shut, would they? Both daft little gossips, the pair o' them. I were in the master bedroom where Buzz had slept and I heard 'em shrieking. 'Twere me as screwed it up, o'course.'

'Oh my sweet Goddess!' whispered Marigold. 'And do you think ... is it just a wish? Or something that happened?'

Cherry shook her head in sorrow.

'I'd like to say a wish, but 'tis too detailed, too real. I know the little vixen's an artist, but even so ... See those scars on his back? Yul don't show his back to many – always keeps it covered. So how does she know about that? 'Tis real, and I reckon it happened back in the summer.'

'Aye, couldn't have been this visit as 'tis much too cold for cavorting by the sea, and besides, I don't think Yul even knew she were here this time around. Not many saw her, tucked away up there with Buzz,' said Marigold. 'But what about Sylvie? D'you think she knows what her husband's been getting up to?'

Cherry shook her head.

'No I don't, and she mustn't hear about it from others! I told them girls to tell nobody, but I know they will. They was giggling and whispering and they've got no idea o' the mischief they could make. We got to find Sylvie and tell her afore she hears it from someone else.'

Sylvie had been searching for Leveret for ages, first looking in the tower and then the hospital wing, as well as the old folks' day room. She'd also looked in the Kitchen Gardens, where she knew Leveret spent time cultivating her herbs and medicinal plants, but found only Magpie there. He beamed at her and Sylvie greeted him warmly. She'd become fond of the strange boy, having seen how gentle and kind he was with her daughters. They loved him, not in the rough and tumble way that they climbed all over Rufus, but more respectfully, as if he were someone very special whom they were honoured to know. The illustrations he'd drawn in their little story books were exquisite, and what with the painting for her birthday too, Sylvie was amazed at the lad's talent.

'I don't suppose you know where Leveret is, do you, Magpie?' she asked, but when he nodded and pointed emphatically, she was still none the wiser.

She then bumped into Clip, wrapped up in a heavy cloak and

carrying a bag, just leaving to spend the rest of the day up at the Dolmen.

'She's popped up to Mother Heggy's cottage,' he said. 'She's coming back soon I think – she's spending Hunter's Moon up there tonight and wanted to get it all ready now. Magpie's going up too if you want him to take a message, but I'm pretty sure she's coming back down here first. She's only taking firewood and giving the place a clean at the moment, I believe.'

'She's such a busy girl,' said Sylvie. 'How does she fit in all her studies too? She's in her last year at school now, isn't she?'

Clip chuckled.

'Oh, she does it all, believe me. She works late into the night and always has her nose buried in a book. Sylvie ... when I've left, you will look out for her, won't you?'

'Of course I will.'

'She's very keen to stay in the tower and I'd like that too. She can take her meals in the Dining Hall and she'll be warm and comfortable, but I don't want her getting too solitary. I know she works with Hazel every day and with the old folk, and increasingly she spends more time cultivating, gathering and making her remedies, and Magpie's with her a lot. But she needs ordinary social company too, and family life. I know she thinks the world of her nieces, and you too. And I gather things are better between her and Yul now?'

Sylvie nodded at this.

'Yes definitely, and improving all the time, as is his relationship with Rufus. It's just me there's a problem with now.'

'Oh Sylvie – I thought it was all getting better?'

She stared out of the window, her grey eyes soft with longing.

'It was ... there's just been a misunderstanding, but I'm determined not to let it become a huge set-back. I wanted to speak to Leveret and ask her for some assistance; she's such a magical girl and so in harmony with everything here. I thought maybe she could help me. I'll go up to Mother Heggy's cottage and see if I can find her there.'

'I'm sure things will all work out,' said Clip. 'We'll have a chat tomorrow.'

Sylvie could see he was anxious to be on his way, so, avoiding everyone bustling around the Hall, she headed off for the ancient cottage near the cliffs.

Despite the coolness of the late October day, Cherry arrived breathless and sweating at Maizie's cottage. She'd hoped to find Sylvie in her office but it seemed she wasn't working there today, so the Village was her next destination. But Maizie, who'd just arrived back herself with the bread and a brace of rabbits for supper, had no idea where Sylvie might be. The girls were in Nursery and she could be anywhere.

'Come on in and have a cup o' tea anyway,' said Maizie, putting the kettle on the range. 'I were just having one myself afore I go into the garden to pull the vegetables for tonight. 'Tis not often I entertain you in my cottage, Cherry.'

But when she was shown the purpose of the visit, Maizie handed back the picture in dismay.

'Oh the stupid, stupid boy! What were he thinking of?'

'So you reckon it did happen then? 'Tis not just a drawing o' Rainbow's imagination and wishful longings?'

Maizie's plump face was crumpled with dismay as she shook her head.

'No – there's something in the drawing ... Rainbow's known Yul, you can tell just by looking at that. Somehow the picture shows it. Oh poor Sylvie! This will really cut her to the quick, and just when I were hoping all would be right between the pair o' them.'

'I wanted to tell her myself, gently like, afore any o' the tittle-tattles do. Them youngsters up the Hall – they got no idea and 'twould be terrible if she heard it from the likes o' them.'

'Aye, you're right there, Cherry, but best of all, Yul should tell her. 'Tis his duty, right enough. Why don't you give the drawing to him and let him search out the poor maid?'

*

Leveret had swept and dusted the place and filled the water jar from the nearby spring by the time Sylvie arrived at the cottage. Shadow growled menacingly as he heard someone on the track and moved closer to protect Leveret. She rested her hand on his shaggy head and he looked up at her with enormous, adoring eyes that were fast disappearing behind a great fringe of wiry fur.

'Look, it's Sylvie!' said Leveret. 'She's a friend.'

His tail wagged in welcome and he bounded forward to bestow his puppy greetings.

'Shadow! Gently!' cried Leveret and Sylvie laughed at his enthusiasm.

'He is gorgeous!' she said, trying to stroke him as he bounced around her legs in great excitement. 'What a lovely boy you are, Shadow! Leveret, do bring him down to the cottage soon, won't you? I'd like the girls to play with him. I wonder if there are any more puppies in the litter? I'd love to have one for Celandine and Bluebell.'

'I don't think so – these Stonewylde sheepdogs are bred very carefully and they're mostly spoken for before birth. If you stay living with Mother, I know she wouldn't want a dog in the house. In her mind, dogs are for herding sheep and cattle, or for taking out rabbiting or ratting, but not just for playing with and keeping as a pet. Maybe a kitten? She'd understand that a cat's useful for keeping the field-mice at bay.'

'I was hoping we wouldn't be living there much longer,' said Sylvie sadly. 'I'd thought we might get a cottage of our own together, but it all seems to have gone wrong again which is so ridiculous. I came to ask if you could ... I don't know ... try to focus on me and Yul tonight, at the Moon Fullness? It's almost as if there's some kind of curse on us. Every time things start to get better again, something else goes wrong. I know Yul and I belong together and I know Stonewylde needs us to be in harmony. But there's something blocking us and if there's anything magical that would help, please could you do it?'

Leveret smiled at her and nodded. She took Sylvie's hands in hers and closed her eyes. All around the sounds of the world receded as she entered the other place, somewhere full of shadows and mists and ...

'Oh Sylvie!' she exclaimed. 'A Beltane baby!'

Sylvie blanched and sat down on the chair quickly.

'Leveret, nobody knows about that except me and Hazel!'

Leveret's smile turned to a frown and she swayed slightly on her feet.

'But there's something else ... something dark and ... I don't know.'

She stared down at Sylvie in consternation, wondering again why she saw a little toad with golden eyes. This was the second time and she'd have to look up the symbolic significance of the toad.

'What? Not something bad about the baby is it?'

'No, no!' said Leveret hastily, realising that she must learn to guard her tongue more carefully. 'Nothing bad – I see a lovely little boy, just like Yul, dark-haired and laughing. That's all, so don't worry.'

At that moment the crow announced its arrival and hopped through the open door. Shadow went over for a tentative sniff, having been pecked on the nose too often to attempt anything more exuberant.

'I was going to tell Yul the other day, but then Buzz intervened and everything fell apart again. All I want is for us to be together. So if you could do anything for me tonight please?'

'I'll do my best,' promised Leveret. 'It's an eclipse tonight and I'll be in here, hopefully with Mother Heggy's spirit.'

'I've promised Celandine we'll dance on the Village Green, and Bluebell can stay home with Maizie. It's getting really cold at night-time now and I won't take her up to Hare Stone again until the spring. Though of course with this little one on the way ...' She patted her belly and smiled. 'I know we've broken the two-children rule and Hazel blames you, Leveret, but we—'

'*Me?* Why?'

'St. John's Wort – it can apparently affect hormonal contraception. Though the implant was at the end of its life anyway, so don't worry, it could've been that. And I'm so pleased about it! Hazel says it's almost definite I wouldn't suffer again with that psychosis I had after Bluebell's birth. And if you reckon it's a boy this time, everything will be different anyway. Oh Leveret – the thought of giving Yul a son!'

'I'm really sorry if it was my fault,' Leveret chuckled. 'I didn't realise that was a side effect, and I should've been more careful. But as long as you're happy ...'

'Oh yes! Now I must get back to the Village and get to work on some sewing. We're getting on really well with that Aitch stuff and I just want it all finished and done with.'

She rose and hugged Leveret, then patted Shadow's curly head.

'Goodbye, Leveret, and goodbye to you, Shadow and Crow.'

'Sylvie!'

She spun round to see Rowan and Faun approaching from the other path, trying to catch her up. Faun was dressed today in a jacket identical to the ones from the photo-shoot, and Sylvie noticed her felt hat was also from the collection.

'Oh hello, Rowan. You're looking very fashionable, Faun!'

Faun preened and flicked back her thick blonde hair with a satisfied smile.

'Aye, she's perfect for that Earth Ethics look with her beautiful colouring she got from her father. Well, Sylvie I just wanted to say how sorry I am – we all are.'

'Oh? I don't ...'

Sylvie looked at Rowan's lovely face, now gleeful with a strange look of spite, and felt a prickle of fear.

'It must be awful with everyone a-gossiping. Folk can be cruel.'

'I'm not sure ... what do you mean?'

'All the gossip! About Yul and Rainbow – 'tis shocking!'

'Yul and *Rainbow?* What? What are you talking about, Rowan?'

'Oh Mother!' cried Faun. 'She don't know yet! Nobody's told her!'

Faun covered her mouth with her hand and rolled her eyes in mock horror. Sylvie felt her tongue stick to the roof of her mouth and everything went slightly fuzzy around the edges. Rowan grabbed her arm and peered into her face.

'You gone very pale, Sylvie! Are you alright? Haven't you heard the news then? Your husband – they say he were making love with Rainbow all summer long behind your back! 'Tis terrible and we're so sorry for you. Aren't we, Faun?'

'Oh yes, we're so *very* sorry for you, Sylvie!'

26

'Rufus, run down to the Village, would you? Tell Maizie that Sylvie's with me and she'll be staying here tonight. She's a bit upset and I want her to have some space, away from the girls. Maybe Maizie would let you stay the night there? Take your toothbrush just in case she says yes.'

He pulled on his jacket and hurried out of the Tudor wing, using the private staircase leading to the outside door. Sylvie's old bedroom was his now and she'd arrived this way earlier, giving him a shock when she turned up with eyes almost shut with puffiness. He'd thought at first she was really ill – maybe one of the awful allergic reactions his mother had told him she used to get in the Outside World. Then he realised that she'd simply been crying very hard. He felt very sorry for her but was glad to escape, and the thought of staying the night in Maizie's cottage was exciting. He hoped she'd say yes – and maybe he could sleep in Yul's old bedroom? Rufus broke into a long-legged run as he cleared the corner of the wing and headed round towards the front of the Hall to join the main drive.

On the track leading down to the Village he bumped into Leveret, on her way back to the Hall. She smiled and he grinned back, blushing under his thatch of silky red hair. Knowing that Leveret was his sister made him very happy indeed, although neither of them had spoken much about it. He wanted to have a good talk with her at some point about becoming a doctor, knowing her interest in healing. He knew she spent a lot of time with Hazel and he hoped to do the same, although he suspected the doctor would say he was still too young.

'I'm off to see Maizie and the girls,' he said. 'Sylvie's with Mum in our rooms.'

'I've just come back from my mother and the girls in the Village,' she replied. 'They were wondering where Sylvie had got to.'

'She's upset about something,' he said, 'and that's why she's there.'

'Upset? I saw her earlier and she was fine. What's the matter?'

But Rufus only shrugged, having kept well out of the tearful discussion he'd heard vaguely through closed doors.

'I think Yul's done something wrong but I really don't know.'

'Oh well, I'm sure they'll sort it out. I've been on a wild goose chase,' said Leveret. 'It's really annoying – I'd just got back to the tower and there was a note saying my mother wanted to see me urgently. But when I got down to the Village she knew nothing about it! So I've been all the way down there for nothing, and now I must hurry to get to Mother Heggy's cottage in time for the moon rise. I'm just nipping back to the tower to collect my things and Shadow and Hare, and I hope Magpie's ready.'

'Have fun then,' said Rufus. 'Bright blessings!'

'And to you!' she replied. 'I like Hunter's Moon – and it's an eclipse tonight! Make sure you watch it, won't you? It's quite early I think – a couple of hours after sunset. I expect Celandine will love it, seeing as how she's moongazy. Look after her, won't you Rufus, if Sylvie's not there.'

'Yes I will, don't worry.'

They parted company and Leveret hurried to the tower, still cross that she'd wasted so much time on a false errand. Maizie had been very distracted but was adamant she'd never sent for her. Leveret climbed up the outside stairs, the quicker route than going into the Hall itself and through all the corridors, and let herself into the upstairs room. Of course Clip had left ages ago for the Dolmen, but it was strangely quiet. Hare looked up sleepily from the basket but Shadow was nowhere in sight.

With a groan, Leveret rushed down to the next floor, hoping the puppy hadn't got into Clip's room and chewed his felt slippers again. He had a thing about poor Clip's slippers. But the room was empty, so she hurried down to the ground level to her own room and the little library where they kept many of the books. She called Shadow, surprised he hadn't come bounding out already to knock her over with his boisterous welcome. Maybe he'd done something really naughty and was hiding under her bed. He'd done that once before when he'd chewed up something he shouldn't – and his guilt had been almost comical.

But Shadow was nowhere to be seen, and, feeling very puzzled, Leveret dashed back upstairs again. Where on earth could he be? She could have taken him with her to Maizie's when she got the message, but it was common knowledge that her mother didn't care for dogs and certainly wouldn't have him inside. Leveret often had to leave Shadow here on his own with Hare when she worked with Hazel and he was usually very good. She started to worry now, wondering if he'd somehow got out and run off somewhere.

It wasn't until she went back downstairs again to look more thoroughly for any sort of clue that she noticed the note lying on her pillow. Her heart leapt with relief, imagining someone had perhaps taken him out if he was howling, as he'd once done when she'd left him for too long. She snatched up the scrap of paper but her relief turned to shock, and then horror.

WALK UP THE TRACK TOWARDS THE GATEHOUSE.
DON'T TELL OR THE DOG WILL DIE.

Marigold was at that lull she reached every late afternoon when the food was prepared for supper but cooking hadn't yet commenced. Drying her hands and having checked the ovens were all hot, she pulled on her shawl and slipped out into the courtyard. It was a clear afternoon, the sun low in the sky and the temperature dropping. Only five days until Samhain, and if this weather continued the feasts could all be cooked outside on the bonfires. Every year Marigold prayed to the Goddess that it would be so.

She hurried along the cobbled courtyard towards her cottage further down the row. She wanted to check that Magpie had stocked up on firewood as she'd asked him to earlier, and also that he'd lit the fire. He was usually very good, but if he was busy drawing something – or lately, copying in the beautiful script he'd learnt – then sometimes he forgot and she came back to a cold cottage. She remembered he was off with Leveret tonight to Mother Heggy's cottage. Marigold didn't entirely approve of this, always worrying that they'd turn their ankles on the path or get lost in sea-mist and fall over the cliff-edge, but she admitted she was a terrible worry-wort and if she had her way, Magpie would never venture outside at all.

She passed Martin's cottage and heard the faint sound of crying coming from an upstairs window. Martin was in the Hall she knew, having seen him just now, and Swift would be with his friends in the dormitory or sitting room, so it must be Mallow. Marigold frowned; she was concerned for the poor little woman who was always so quiet and timid. She seemed to be wasting away to nothing recently and was constantly scuttling backwards and forwards to Old Violet's cottage, usually with a heavy basket. Marigold resolved to seek her out soon and try to help. It couldn't be easy being handfasted to Martin, who'd become even more unpleasant lately. Buzz's swift departure had upset him and he'd kept to himself ever since, when he wasn't barking out orders at everyone.

Letting herself into the cottage, Marigold saw that the fire was lit with the guard across. Magpie came clumping down the stairs and smiled at her.

'Are you off in a minute?' she asked. 'Make sure you wrap up nice and warm, won't you, Magpie?'

He nodded and then frowned, pulling her sleeve. He led her over to the table where his notebooks and pens were spread out.

'What is it? Have you done some more writing?'

407

But he picked up a piece of rag and unwrapped it, showing her the contents. It was a shrivelled-up brownish mushroom. He pointed to his mouth and shook his head vehemently, in the same moment that Marigold realised what it was.

'Oh no, Magpie! 'Tis what Leveret always said would happen! Were it from Jay?'

Magpie shrugged and pointed to the door.

'It were on the doorstep? Oh Mother, I thought all that nastiness were over and done with! 'Tis bound to be poisonous – good boy for not eating it. We should throw 'un in the fire!'

She snatched it from his hand, along with the rag, and yanking back the fireguard threw the lot into the flames.

'There, you're safe now. We'll sort this out tomorrow, my boy. I'm not having Jay start up again, not like last time with that rabbit. No, he won't do that again!'

She stopped as she saw the look on Magpie's face, and patted his arm kindly.

'Don't you worry, Magpie. 'Tis different this time around. You're safe here and so's Leveret. We won't stand no nonsense from that nasty Jay this time. When Leveret comes to get you, bring her round to me in the kitchens first so as I can tell her about this and warn her to be on her guard. D'you understand me?'

The heavy wicker cage used for transporting piglets lay in the lee of a high rock-face covered with swarming ivy. It was securely fastened with rope, and inside lay Shadow, nose on paws, trembling violently. In his fear, he'd brought up the enticing chunks of meat that he'd gulped down earlier, victim of his own puppy greed. He was hoarse from barking and yelping, and now merely whimpered from time to time. His ribs hurt where he'd been kicked hard and his paws were sore from trying to dig his way out of the sturdy cage. The temperature dropped as all around him the light began to fade from the sky. Shadow jumped at the loud *CRUK!* of a raven flying over the silent quarry, and lay shivering in abject misery.

He saw her before she saw him, hurrying up the track wrapped in her old cloak. She looked small and frightened, and he felt a throb of power; this had been a long time coming. She didn't notice the Landrover tucked away amongst trees, so he could stand there quite at ease in the dissolving light and watch her. He grinned to himself; so far, everything had gone perfectly to plan, just as Old Violet had promised it would. He was looking forward to the night ahead.

Then Leveret looked up, saw the shape of the vehicle and her mouth gaped in fear. She rushed forward towards him and Jay opened the driver's door and got in, slamming the door shut. She came round to his window, her face hollow, but he yelled at her through the glass.

'If you want the dog to live, get in the car.'

He saw her hesitation; she was terrified of being that close to him, but he gazed ahead stonily and after a second, she rushed around and yanked the passenger's door open. She stood outside, leaning in towards him, her face white.

'Are you stupid or what? I said, if you want the dog to live, get in the car.'

It felt good to have the upper hand over her. There was nothing she could do but comply. She climbed in but left the door open. He turned and glared at her and she pulled it shut.

'That's better. Don't piss me off tonight, Hare-brain, or you'll be very sorry. I ain't in the mood for any game-playing. Do as I say and the dog'll be alright. Mess me about and . . .'

She nodded, clamping her hands between her knees and that made him smile. He reached forward and turned the key in the ignition. She jumped like a startled bird and looked as if she'd try to escape, so he paused, with the engine running, and stared at her. Her frightened gaze met his, her eyes enormous, and he felt another pulse of pleasure.

'Do you want to leave? Or do you want the dog to live? It's your choice, Leveret.'

'Please, Jay, can you just—'

'If you speak again before I say you can, I'll stop the car and kick you out. Then you'll never see the dog again. Understood?'

She nodded and stared ahead, huddled up in the seat in terror. He slammed the car into gear and pulled away, joining the track and climbing up the slope that led away from the Village, away from the Hall, away from the safety of people.

Yul had taken himself off on foot, once the news of Sylvie's discovery had reached him. Miranda had rung through from her rooms to his office to warn him what had happened, and had told him in no uncertain terms to stay well away from Sylvie for the time being. His instinct was to ignore that and just barge his way into Miranda's rooms and demand to see his wife. The thing he'd dreaded most had happened, and although he couldn't now make that right, he could at least beg her forgiveness and try to explain himself.

But Miranda had sounded so very adamant that he was worried he'd only make things worse. He was far too upset to take poor Skydancer for another of those punishing rides; it really wasn't fair to make the stallion suffer too. Instead, he stumbled out of his office through the French windows and across the terrace and the lawns, with no idea where he was heading.

Not Hare Stone, he thought desperately; that would be too painful. And not the Stone Circle either, nor the Village Green. Then he knew where he must go, for it was the place of darkness and despair, the place where many years ago he'd almost succumbed to the Dark Angel in his suffering. Yul found his feet taking him up the steep path towards Mooncliffe.

Martin was in the library looking out and saw Yul's headlong flight across the grass. His thin mouth stretched into a smile. Not long to go now and the black-haired bastard would be overthrown. He knew that tonight, at Blood Moon, the sister would be dealt with. His mother, the true Wise Woman of Stonewylde, had told him all was now in motion and this time would not fail. And Samhain was so close! Martin's heart raced at the thought

410

of it and all they'd planned. His poor mother was too old and bent to take part directly in the ceremony, but nevertheless, it was all set and ready and she'd be there with him in spirit. One by one, the cuckoos would be cast out from the nest and the golden times would begin again.

He sighed heavily. These past years had been so difficult and, for a long time, hope seemed to have died. But last year's summoning at Samhain, thirteen years on, had been wildly successful, thanks to his mother's skill and power. It was a shame that his aunt had passed on and his cousin moved away, for there was nothing like the power raised by three women with the same intent in their hearts. The magic of those three together had been very strong. But never mind, for his mother was the one with the real ability and despite her feeble frame, her intent was as powerful as ever.

The sun had set as the Landrover reached Quarrycleave. Jay stopped the car at the foot of the quarry, the place where, many years before, his father had lived in a settlement of dirty caravans with a bunch of men who spoke a different language. All traces of this had long been removed, but, as Jay turned off the engine he had a sudden sense of the man he barely remembered; a very tall and frightening man with tattoos and piercings and a strange accent picked up from living in the Outside World.

Jay stared straight ahead out of the muddy windscreen as a succession of emotions surged in his heart. Sadness and regret at never having known his father. Anger at being cheated of such a hero, for Jay was proud of his father's infamous reputation. And determination that somebody would pay for all this by elevating Jay to his rightful position in Stonewylde society. His Great Aunt Violet had explained to him how it should be here – and how it would be, very soon. He had a job to do to help make this happen, and it was one that was no hardship to him at all. His task tonight was to rob Leveret of any chance of becoming Wise Woman, and he cracked his knuckles at the thought of the pleasure to come. This was something he relished; he'd been dreaming of it for a long time.

He turned to her and in the half-light his eyes gleamed. He hadn't bothered shaving, hadn't gone through all the stupid preparations he'd done last time he'd brought a girl up here. Back then he'd thought that perhaps being clean and smelling sweet would please a girl, soften her up and make her more amenable to his clumsy handling. But this evening he hadn't wasted time on any of that crap; he'd been at work all day and if he smelled of hard labour, that was her problem.

He reached into his breast pocket and pulled out a packet of cigarettes and matches. He'd saved these as a treat, along with the bottle of strong mead. He lit a cigarette, watching her flinch as he struck the match and made it flare into life. The first drag of the harsh cigarette felt so good as it hit his lungs, and Jay squirmed with pleasure. He fished out the little bottle of double-fermented mead and took a deep swig, gasping at its strength and the way his insides felt instantly liquid. He chuckled in the near darkness and felt her shrink into herself. Her terror was like a quaking shadow between them and Jay savoured every second of it.

'So, you want your little pup back, do you?' he said, his voice unexpectedly hoarse from the smoke and alcohol.

'Yes,' she whispered. 'Yes, I do. Please.'

'Well, he ain't harmed – not yet. Apart from a good kick.'

He waited for a reaction and felt her struggling to keep her words unspoken.

'He's a proper runt, ain't he? Bloody crippled, useless runt. I can see why Gefrin off-loaded him onto *you*. And stupid too – he came straight into my trap.'

'Is he ... is he alright?'

Jay laughed harshly and drank from the bottle again. The cigarette smoke filled the car as he'd kept the window shut, flicking the ash onto the dirty floor.

'He knows who's boss now, put it that way. He won't be standing up to me no more. But no, he ain't *seriously* injured.'

She was silent at this and he guessed that her fury was smothered by her fear, which made his lips twitch. She'd always been a gobby little bitch, squaring up to him against the odds, so this trembling silence showed just how scared she was.

'So, Leveret, the dog's life is in your hands. I don't give a shit about the animal, whether he lives or dies. I'd be happy to kick him to death. Or smash his skull open with a heavy rock. Or leave him to die slowly of thirst. Or give him some o' the poison I got here.'

She jerked in horror and he laid a heavy hand on her arm.

'But it don't make no odds to me, so this is the deal I'll do with you. If you do everything I tell you and don't make no fuss, no noise, no struggling – I'll let the dog live. I'll turn him free and I won't harm him. But if there's one wrong move from you, one step out of line, then I'll make you watch him die. Understood?'

'Yes,' she said in a strangled voice.

'Course, you might decide the pup's life ain't worth it,' he said, pulling out another cigarette. He lit it and inhaled deeply. 'You might decide that you just can't be a good girl for me after all – that what I want from you is too much. In that case, Leveret, do you know what will happen?'

'You'll kill Shadow,' she whispered.

'Yeah, I'll kill Shadow, and then I'll force you anyway. I won't care if you scream and struggle – there ain't nobody around to hear it anyway. I'll take what I want whether you like it or not. But it'll be so much easier for everyone if you don't fight me. Understood?'

'Yes.'

Maizie eyed her eldest granddaughter worriedly, noting the frantic way Celandine had started to pace around the cottage.

'For Goddess' sake, sit down, child!' she said.

'She can't help it, Granny Maizie,' said Bluebell, colouring in her picture at the table. 'It's the Moon Fullness tonight, and—'

'*Please*, Granny Maizie!' said Celandine. 'Mummy said we'd go onto the Village Green and I need to go there *now*!'

'I'll take her,' said Rufus, getting up from the armchair. 'I'll look after her, like Leveret said.'

'Oh did she now?' said Maizie sharply. 'Seems 'tis all decided. Well, I suppose if you wrap up warm enough, Celandine, and promise me you'll just have a quick dance around the Green ...'

'Oh *yes*, Granny Maizie, thank you!'

She was almost crying with relief and rushed to the door to grab her coat from the hook. Rufus found his jacket too and started to pull his boots on.

'And your boots, missy. You're not going out in shoes, not when 'tis Hunter's Moon and so close to winter now.'

'But she can't dance in boots, Granny!' said Bluebell, showing no inclination herself to go out into the chilly evening.

'I don't care about that,' said Maizie firmly. 'Warm boots or nothing. And not too long, Rufus.'

Yul stood on the cliff top gazing out to sea. He wore no coat but the cold didn't reach him. The sun had set though the moon had yet to rise, and he watched the dull water with a heavy heart. He hadn't been up here for so long, hating the place and all the bad memories it brought. But it was fitting tonight, and he almost savoured the melancholy and guilt dredged up by the sight of the round, pale disc of rock. Sylvie – his beloved moongazy girl, and the suffering she'd gone through here at the hands of Magus. He remembered her standing on the stone, her skin chased with the tiny silver threads of light, and the endless moon eggs he'd made her hold. He recalled her collapsing in agony and being forced to lie there whilst Magus leeched her moon magic, stealing her gift to feed his insatiable hunger.

And tonight Sylvie was still suffering and it was he who'd caused it by his betrayal. Miranda had said there'd been a picture left behind by Rainbow which was in Cherry's hands, but others had seen it too and everyone was talking of it. This must be the ultimate humiliation for Sylvie. He'd inflicted it on her as deliberately and cold-heartedly as Magus had once inflicted pain. He was no better than his father after all, and Sylvie would be infinitely better off without him; all he brought her was heartache. As he thought this, a sliver of the dark pink moon appeared above the horizon. It was as if someone had slashed at the fabric of the night sky and made it bleed.

In the Dolmen Clip had fallen into a deep trance whilst staring beyond the dancing flames of his fire. He was wrapped up well against the cold, with layers of woollens under his cloak, a warm felt hat on his head and lined boots on his feet. Even his hands were mittened. He'd been cold for a while now and guessed it was one of the effects of the medication he'd been prescribed. He felt so weary and his head bowed on his chest as the silver wolf led him into another realm, finally revealing to him what was to come and what must be done. In the dark sky, the Hunter's Moon rose in silence and an owl hooted as it passed over the ancient stone portal, entrance to another world.

Now that the time had come, Jay felt almost reluctant to leave the warmth of the Landrover cab. But he was sure the moon would be rising very soon, if it hadn't already – it was difficult to see from here. When he'd mentioned his plan to her the other evening, Old Violet had said that tonight during the eclipse, when the full moon was overshadowed, was the perfect time to ensure that Leveret would never fulfil her potential as Wise Woman. The crone had also said that he might get her with child. She wasn't sixteen for another four months and had no implant. Jay really liked the thought of getting uppity little Leveret knocked up. He imagined her walking around Stonewylde, his child growing in her belly and everyone shocked and amazed, and that gave him a surge of confidence. He felt very male and very powerful, and she was ripe for the plucking.

'Right then, Leveret, time for us to get on with it,' he said. He stuffed the cigarettes, matches and mead in his pocket and pulled the keys from the ignition. Then he remembered his earlier plan, and from his other pocket, pulled out the length of fine rope and turned on the dim light inside the vehicle.

'Hold out your wrists in front of you,' he said, and proceeded to bind them together, wrapping the rope around and noticing how her hands shook. He enjoyed the feeling of mastery it gave him, tethering her like a slave-girl. 'Just in case you make a break for it, you won't get far like this. Quarrycleave's dangerous and it'd be your neck you'd break, with your hands tied.'

She sat huddled, her head down, and Jay felt omnipotent. He got out of the car and came round to pull her out as she couldn't manage the door. As it slammed shut they heard a faint but frantic yelping begin. Leveret's head shot up, swivelling round to hear better.

'Shadow!' she cried.

'Yeah, noisy, ain't he?' laughed Jay.

'He ... he sounds so frightened! Please can we check he's alright?'

'No, we can't!'

'Please, Jay,' she whispered in a small voice, 'please—'

He took a swipe at her, catching her arm, and she almost fell.

'Yeah, and he'll be bloody dead if you don't shut up and do as you're told! Remember what I said, Hare-brain.'

He led the way and she followed, stumbling over the rough ground leading down into the open part of the horse-shoe shaped quarry. The closed end was the high cliffs of hewn rock and the entire interior consisted of half-worked rock-faces, canyons that ran between them, and in the more open parts, piles and piles of boulders and spoil. In the gloomy twilight he looked back at her impatiently and then cursed.

'Bugger! I forgot the torch. Stay there and don't move.'

Jay hurried back to the car knowing there was nowhere for her to run or hide, not with her hands tied and being miles away from anywhere safe. He grinned to himself as he grabbed the flashlight and made his way back to where she stood waiting, small and defenceless, her head bowed and hands bound. A thrill ran through Jay's body making him shudder in anticipation of the pleasure to come. The fiasco with Tansy receded and he knew that this time, he'd score the bullseye.

'Where are you off to now?' demanded Martin, grabbing Mallow's arm as she hurried along the courtyard past the kitchens. He'd appeared out of nowhere from the shadows and she gave a cry of alarm, dropping her basket.

'Stupid, clumsy woman!' he said, cuffing her as she stooped to pick it up.

'Nothing's broke,' she gabbled, 'and 'tis only some clean clothes for her and a jar o' butter.'

'You're visiting my mother?' he barked.

'Yes, Martin, like I do every evening,' she said, nodding eagerly. 'So's I can build up the fire and help her into bed after her supper.'

'But why are you going tonight? Are you a complete half-wit?'

'But ... but you said I must go every night, Martin. Every morning and every night you said, without fail.'

He located her skinny arm under her cloak and squeezed it hard, making her squeak with pain.

'And what night is it tonight?'

'Ooow ... 'tis ... 'tis Hunter's Moon, and—'

With a sharp twist of her flesh he let her go, and she staggered backwards, tears filling her eyes.

'Never disturb my mother at the Moon Fullness! Have you forgot she's the Wise Woman?' he spat, advancing on her again.

'No! No, Martin, I know she's the Wise Woman! I just thought ...'

'As ever, you thought wrong. I wonder what I did to deserve a stupid goodwife such as you, Mallow. My first wife were daft, but you're dafter, and you're not even pretty as she was. And you only gave me one child, which is a disgrace when our Magus were telling us to breed more labour for Stonewylde. Why did I ever saddle myself with a dull, plain mare such as you?'

Mallow stood snivelling now, her basket sitting on the cobbles as she cried into her hands. Martin's thin face twisted with malice as he looked down at her, but then he heard the kitchen door opening behind and he stepped forward to shield her from view. He picked up the basket and thrust it at her.

'Go home this minute,' he hissed, 'and take off your cloak and your boots and get up to the little back bedroom. Don't take a lantern – stand on the chair in the middle o' the room in the darkness. Do you understand? I expect to find you there when I return later, and remember I *always* know when you've disobeyed.'

She nodded, sobbing convulsively, and he jabbed her bony chest.

'If I find you've not done my bidding, there'll be trouble tonight. You've pushed me to the end of my patience, Mallow, and I'll stand for no more of it.'

The flashlight seemed to make the darkness deeper, and Leveret tried to place her feet carefully, as she could see nothing of where she trod. Jay illuminated the stacks of hewn stone, scored where the old chisels had cut in. The shadows danced as the harsh white light played on the rock, and the only sound was the puppy's terrified yelping in the distance. Several times Leveret stumbled and after a while, Jay held onto her arm. He didn't want her damaged before they'd even started. They made their way through the heart of the quarry but Jay was oblivious to the chill and terror of the place that started to seep into their bones. The sensation of death and menace that crept up from the ground to permeate everything didn't affect him. Nor did he sense the silent baying for blood that had started all around them.

He walked boldly through the corridors of stone, as might a young warrior with his looted prize. He yanked the dark-haired girl along, making no allowances for her fear nor the fact her wrists were bound. He was intent only on plunder and desecration, and felt his pulse quickening by the minute into a state of aroused excitement. The canyons rustled with glossy ivy and the full moon shone through the gaps overhead. Jay had planned where they were headed, for the Snake Stone was the hub of the place, the core of the quarry which drew everything to it.

Finally they reached the foot of the enormous column of

stone where the boulders were piled and great tiers of rock clustered, forming a way up to the top. Jay gave off a sharp and pungent odour as he'd worked himself into a sweat, and he perched against a boulder to catch his breath. Leveret stood before him in the darkness, shaking convulsively. He took out another cigarette and lit it, tipping his head skyward to savour the sensation of strong tobacco smoke hitting the back of his throat. He played the beam of the flashlight over Leveret, shining it on her cloak and the long dark curls that tumbled over her shoulders.

'What are you wearing under that?' he growled, and reached forward to pull back the material.

Instinctively she jerked away from his touch and with an oath he grabbed the front of her cloak and yanked her forward, almost pulling her off her feet.

'Bloody stand still, bitch!' he barked, and slowly and deliberately pushed the two sides of her heavy cloak back over her shoulders. 'I see you didn't dress yourself up for me!'

She wore an old woollen robe underneath, with a leather belt round her waist and sturdy boots on her feet. She looked like one of the Stonewylde ancestors and very different to the girls Jay had discovered in the Outside World. He was disappointed that she looked so dowdy, as if she'd done it deliberately to cheat him of the pleasure of feasting his eyes on her.

'If you'd been done up all pretty like at the Outsiders' Dance last Yule, I'd have let you keep your dress on,' he said. 'But as soon as we get up the top, you'll take that lot off and I'll have you naked.'

Leveret's head shot up and in the bright light, he saw the terror in her eyes. He chuckled and flicked the cigarette butt away. Pulling out the bottle of mead he took a long gulp and smacked his lips. Then he put the bottle away, and slowly and deliberately reached out to place his hand on her breast. Again she flinched, but this time didn't pull back, standing rigid and quaking. Smiling, he ran his hand over the softness of her, pulling and squeezing as a farmer might examine an animal.

'Nice little tits, Leveret,' he sneered. 'They're bigger than they was last time I had a feel.'

She said nothing and he felt her body shrink beneath his touch. He slid his hand across to examine her other breast, giving it the same rough treatment.

'That must've been ... ooh, 'twere that time we had old Magpie in the woods with the rabbit, and you tried to rescue him. Remember? And I chased you across the Green and pinned you down, and you were bloody rude to me. Remember? How things have changed. You won't be rude to me tonight, will you? Will you?'

'No,' she croaked.

'You'll say stuff like "Oh Jay, you're so good" and "Ooh Jay, do it again!"' He laughed hoarsely at this. 'And you'll be squirming underneath me, but for a different reason this time around. You're such a lucky girl doing it here for your first time, ain't you? Bet you never dreamt o' this. But I have and it's taken a bit o' planning to get it to happen tonight.'

With a final painful squeeze, he pulled his hand away and stood upright. He towered over her and felt a hard jolt of lust as he imagined how it would soon feel when he forced his way deep inside that small, soft body. The puppy's distant yelps had died down a little. With a grunt of anticipation, Jay spun Leveret around to face the way they must go to climb up to the top of Snake Stone.

Magpie entered the busy kitchen and located Marigold amongst the team of youngsters and adults. All were hard at work cooking for the large number of mouths that must be fed, and Marigold was far too busy to be interested in his attempts to communicate. Frowning, he made his way to the tower, but of course Leveret wasn't there and neither was Clip. He turned on the electric light at the bottom of the spiral stairs and peered into Leveret's bedroom, then went up the stairs and found Hare on the top floor. She climbed out of her basket and stretched, then hopped over to greet him. Magpie stroked her soft fur absently, gazing

420

around the shadowy room. He opened the door and stepped out onto the staircase leading to the roof.

Up there it was cold and dark, with the moon peering through the branches of the trees. Magpie stood gazing out, lost in contemplation as he stared at the Hunter's Moon. Suddenly the crow landed, appearing from nowhere in the darkness and settling on one of the crenellations. Opening its beak, it began to caw loudly and repeatedly. Magpie stared at it for a while but then returned indoors. He sat on the sofa in the cold room and Hare jumped onto his lap, laying down her ears and nuzzling his hand gently.

On the top of Snake Stone Jay stood tall; a king surveying his realm, his captured woman meek at his side. The brilliant white moon shone down on them, silvering their skin and eyes. Jay was out of breath from the strenuous climb and his heart pounded. He glanced down at Leveret.

'What time is the eclipse?' he asked but she shook her head, unable to speak.

He'd turned off the flashlight to see the scene by moonlight. Taking the bottle from his pocket again he drunk deeply, the heady mead feeling good inside him, then lit another cigarette.

'You can get undressed now, Leveret. Take everything off underneath, but you can keep the cloak on until I'm ready for you. See how kind I am?'

He untied the rope that bound her wrists – she couldn't escape him here unless she jumped. He chuckled, feeling the strangeness of the night pulsing through his veins, the wildness of the place drawing him in. As she silently obeyed him, he thought back to all the insults this girl had flung at him, all the times she'd turned her nose up as if he were repulsive, all the disdainful looks she'd cast his way. Somehow she'd always managed to make him feel stupid and ugly; he'd never thought this night would finally come.

He glanced down at her now that she was still again, standing small but straight-backed with the cloak wrapped around her. In

421

the silvery light he glimpsed her bare feet on the rock, and, at the thought of her nakedness under the cloak, he was suddenly alive with hot, dark desire. He almost chose to forget about the eclipse and take her now, hard and fast, spill her virginal blood on the white rock, spill his seed into her ripeness and seal her fate forever. But Old Violet had impressed upon him that if the magic were to be truly powerful, it was during the darkness of the eclipse that he must take the girl. So instead, he denied the primeval urge and turned back to gaze out over the shadows of the quarry waiting below.

The dog was quiet now and all was still as the hard white moon rose higher in the glittering sky. And then ... the eclipse began. Just a tiny edge of the moon disappeared, the merest dent in her round perfection. But this dent grew into a small bite, taken from the side, and slowly, slowly, the silver was eaten away. Jay watched in fascination, blood pumping hard through his body, mead fuelling his anticipation. The desire to break her pulsed harder and harder inside him – very soon he'd push her down onto the rock, pin her there and take her as brutally as he could. Up here at Quarrycleave, nobody would hear her if she screamed. And how he longed to make her scream – to know that he'd finally pierced her arrogance and her superiority and reduced her to nothing more than a receptacle for his thrusting pleasure.

He was aware of the silent girl by his side watching and waiting, counting the heartbeats until that moment when the Bright Lady was completely shadowed and perhaps even bloodied by the dark eclipse; in reality the Blood Moon as some still called her in October. Then he'd spoil the girl forever; taint her purity and plunder her magical gift. After that, she could never truly be the all-powerful Wise Woman of Stonewylde.

Jay felt a slight rustling movement by his side and sensed the folds of material brushing his arm and leg. He smiled – was she readying herself for him without being told? Was she removing her cloak to welcome him into her arms? Perhaps she wanted him after all, had felt a secret need for him all along. He gazed

422

up at the moon, now so dark crimson as to be almost gone, and then turned at last to the girl waiting by his side.

In absolute shock he gaped at what he saw, almost gagging on his own saliva. His eyes popped in horror at the thing that now stood beside him in the eclipsed darkness on the Snake Stone.

'*I shall go into a hare,*' it whispered, and he saw the long ears on her head standing tall and erect.

'*I shall go into a hare,*' it snarled, baring sharp teeth that gleamed in the moonlight.

'*I shall go into a hare!*' it screamed, and pale arms rose up and the cloak fell back and she was naked, a tiny perfect woman with the head of a hare and bright, feral eyes, and teeth so small and barbed. Her arms were held high; pointed, clawed wings that jutted above her, and she spun in frenzy, a flurry of fur and dark hair and blurred transformation in the eclipsed moonlight.

Jay screamed in terror as suddenly the girl was no more and in reality, a hare stood before him. A great hare standing up on her hind legs advanced on him with vicious paws that boxed him hard, beating off the violator. The wild creature was powerful and female and brooked no domination – she was *not* to be taken and would fight to the death. She pushed him, punched him inexorably to the edge, to the precipice where he teetered . . .

But as he fell, down, down like the silver-haired man before him only fourteen years ago; as he fell from Snake Stone like so many others before had fallen throughout the ages, down into the waiting maw, down into the jaws of the Beast below; as he fell – Jay grabbed at her. For why should she live and not him? He grabbed and she stumbled and in the darkness, as the Bright Lady was veiled, the Hare Woman of Stonewylde slipped. She fell and the thing waiting hungrily below for blood to be spilt – that thing was waiting for her too.

27

Yul was awoken the next morning by Magpie flinging open the door to the cottage and tramping inside in the darkness. Both were equally shocked to see the other, and almost immediately Magpie stumbled out again and disappeared. Yul sat up on the tiny narrow settle where he'd spent a cold, cramped night and tried to stretch his stiff limbs. He found matches and lit a lantern, and the tiny cottage flared into life in the brightness. He then lit the fire and put the kettle on to boil, having noticed a jar of homemade herbal tea placed nearby with a mug. Leveret had certainly made herself cosy here. He gazed at the rows and rows of carefully labelled jars and bottles on the dresser and the shelves, but his mind was elsewhere.

Last night had been a bad one, watching the eclipse alone at Mooncliffe. So many ghosts had haunted his reveries, but most of all Magus, who'd capered about on the great disc of stone laughing gleefully, taunting Yul for his stupidity. Yul had seriously considered jumping from the cliff-top and ending his pointless life. He knew that his act of betrayal was a marriage-breaker. Bad enough to be unfaithful to his beloved wife, but to have done so with Rainbow, at the Summer Solstice on Sylvie's birthday, and then for others to have seen a drawing of it ... She would never truly forgive him for this. She might try, in time, but Yul knew it could never again be the same between them. Something pure and magical had been smashed, and even the glue of forgiveness would never make it whole again.

The only thing that had stopped him plunging to his death last night was the thought of his daughters. He'd pictured their little faces, so serious and loving, as Magus had urged him to spill his brains on the jagged rocks far below. He couldn't make them suffer his suicide, so instead he must live apart from Sylvie for the rest of his life. That would be just punishment for his transgression. He'd stepped back from the brink, and then dear Mother Heggy had come to him just as the Bright Lady was emerging from her blood-red caul, and had led him down through the dead bracken to her cottage. He'd even heard her crow, perched on the rooftop above, calling to him as he'd pushed open the door and stumbled inside.

Yul had tripped over a jumble of things lying on the floor but had made it to the little settle against the wall, thrown himself down with a groan of anguish, and huddled under the blanket in the silvery blackness. Sleep had come eventually as the ancient rocking chair moved very slightly to and fro, and the ancient Wise Woman, who'd always loved him, watched over him in the darkness of the Hunter's Moon.

Magpie banged on the cottage door and then barged inside, causing Maizie to sit up in bed in alarm. Nobody called out so she quickly found her warm shawl, pushed her feet into her slippers and went downstairs, holding up her lantern to see who'd come into her cottage at this time of day. It was the hour before dawn and she'd been awake anyway, contemplating getting up to stoke the range and put the kettle on. She recalled that Sylvie wasn't there, but Rufus was asleep in Yul's old room whilst her little granddaughters slept in their room next to hers. It made Maizie's heart glad to have a cottage full of young 'uns again, and she'd planned on cooking them all a nice bit of bacon this morning, along with their eggs and toast.

She was bemused to see who had come crashing uninvited into her cottage.

'What do you want, Magpie? 'Tis very early to be disturbing folk like this.'

Of course the lad couldn't answer her, but hopped around the parlour in a state of distress, gesticulating wildly and tugging at her arm. She had no idea what was wrong with him and shrugged him off, calling up the stairs to Rufus and the girls to come and see if they could understand what was up with Magpie. They should be getting up soon for school and Nursery anyway.

It was Bluebell's idea to give Magpie pencil and paper, and he seized it gratefully, sitting down at the table with Rufus and the girls crowding around him to see what he produced. Maizie took herself off into the kitchen to make tea and start the breakfasts, still irritated at Magpie's lack of manners in arriving at such an hour.

He drew a fast sketch of Leveret, whom they recognised instantly. He nodded and tried to drag them out of the cottage but nobody understood.

'We can't visit Auntie Leveret now, Magpie!' said Celandine. 'It's too early and Granny's making our breakfast!'

But then they realised something was wrong, and by miming he explained she was in trouble and they must help. But where she was – how could he explain that? He had no concept of the distance involved though he knew it was a long way. He tried to mime, tried to explain, and eventually picked up the pencil and wrote "*cwri*". This elicited guesses about cows and fields, and Rufus, who'd heard of cowry shells, thought of the beach. But it was little Bluebell, a new writer herself, who cracked the code.

'Quarry!' she shrieked. 'She's at the quarry!'

Rufus proved himself to be calm and level-headed, throwing on his clothes and running up the lane with Magpie to the Great Barn, where there was a phone. He rang up to the Hall but nobody was in the main office where he'd hoped to find Yul. Martin answered another extension and was singularly unhelpful, saying Rufus was talking a load of nonsense. Next he tried his mother, who immediately told him to call Hazel on her extension if it seemed as though there might have been an accident. All the while that Rufus was trying to get help, Magpie hopped around frantically, nodding at Rufus' explanations on the phone and almost in tears with frustration.

After that things moved very fast indeed. Magpie's state of distress was taken seriously and Hazel swung into action. The boys and several others drove in borrowed work vehicles up to the quarry, pink and benign in the rising sun that washed the pale rock-faces clean of all guilt. But the rose-hued stone revealed the horror of the previous night as Jay was found broken and white in a great pool of dark, sticky blood, his body as smashed as the bottle inside his pocket.

The sound of a dog's desperate yelping echoed through the canyons of rock. It bounced off the cliff-face at the end where everyone gathered around Jay's mutilated corpse. Magpie was already traumatised by the car journey and terrified of the Place of Bones and Death, remembering his previous visit with Leveret. Beside himself with fear, he began to climb the great boulders in dangerous haste, a terrible keening noise bursting from his throat, and the others struggled to keep up with him. The swarming snakes carved all up the sides of the huge column of stone were bathed in the soft pink light that permeated the place. It should have been a beautiful sight, but everyone was frightened, and everyone dreaded what they'd discover next as they neared the platform above.

Leveret's body was found quite near the top of the stone pillar, wedged in a crevice between two great boulders. Magpie reached her first, noticing her cloak bundled up in the gap and a mess of sticks and grass displaced where she'd landed on what looked like a raven's nest. Her hare headdress was still in place and at first she looked as if she were merely curled up asleep. Her naked body was mostly covered by the warm cloak and there were no obvious signs of injury or blood.

Magpie tried to lift her to cover her bare limbs, but Hazel, not far below, shouted urgently for him not to move her at all. Too late, he'd cradled her head in his lap and the headdress slipped to reveal the trauma to her skull. He let out a great cry of anguish and, at that, her eyes opened in an unfocused gaze.

'Shadow,' she whispered, as her eyelids fluttered close again.

*

The news spread rapidly amongst the community, bringing Clip down from the Dolmen, Yul back from Mother Heggy's cottage, and Sylvie out from her retreat in Miranda's rooms. This was the day when Christopher was arriving to finalise the paperwork for the handover of the estate, and he was surprised to be greeted by such uproar. The helicopter had already swooped down from the sky like a great bird and air-lifted Leveret to hospital, where she remained unconscious but stable, with injury to her head and a broken wrist. The note about the dog was discovered and then Tansy reluctantly came forward to tell of her own ordeal at Quarrycleave; the course of events leading to Jay's gruesome death became obvious.

Maizie finally overcame her distaste for Magpie and engulfed the bewildered lad in a crushing embrace. It was understood by all that if he hadn't alerted everyone not only to Leveret's disappearance, but also to her whereabouts, she wouldn't have survived. Poor Shadow was lost without Leveret. Magpie and Clip did their best to console him, but the pup remained subdued and trembling. Hare also moped about the tower and the crow sat on the roof making such a noise that Clip had to scare him away. Clip had managed to rescue Leveret's headdress and he cleaned it up for her. He had a strong feeling it had played a part in protecting her the previous night. He did wonder why she'd taken it to the quarry in the first place, and guessed it must have been tucked away in the large pocket in her cloak, ready for the ritual he knew she'd planned in Mother Heggy's cottage.

Clip spent some time at the hospital with Leveret over the next couple of days. Maizie had felt unable to leave Stonewylde, once she'd been assured that her daughter was recovering and would soon be home. Yul popped in and Hazel was a constant visitor, but Leveret was unable to speak and was mostly asleep, so it made sense for everyone to wait and visit her when she came home to the Stonewylde hospital. Clip, however, maintained a vigil by her bedside as she drifted in and out of consciousness. Her head was bandaged and her wrist plastered, and she seemed very peaceful as she lay in the room surrounded by the paraphernalia of modern medicine. Clip was an incongruous addition in his sky-blue robe, with his silvery hair so long and unkempt. But the nurses soon realised he was harmless and were glad the poor child's father, as they believed him to be, was so devoted.

'I've come to take leave of you, Leveret,' he whispered to her, the night before Samhain. 'I've written you a letter and I'll leave it for you in the tower. When you're recovered you can read it and I hope then you'll understand my reasons for not waiting for your return. More than ever, I have to leave tomorrow at Samhain, as I've always said I shall. I'm so sorry that we can't say farewell properly and I hope you'll forgive me.'

She stirred slightly and her lips moved, but she couldn't surface, and Clip squeezed her hand.

'Don't worry, my dear, I know you can hear me. The doctors say you're in a severe state of shock after your fall, which is why you can't speak or wake up at the moment. But the CT scan shows brain damage is unlikely and Hazel says the team here are excellent, although she's itching to get you back to Stonewylde in her care. Rufus wants to nurse you, and your mother is beside herself wanting you home. Poor Magpie's missing you terribly, as are Shadow, Hare and Crow. And little Celandine and Bluebell send you their special love and kisses. So you need to get better soon – they're all waiting for you to come back home again.'

He raised her limp hand and held it against his whiskery cheek as he gazed at her, his wolf's eyes bright with tears.

'I shall miss you, Leveret, and I just hope you know how very much you mean to me. This past year spent in your company, watching you grow and learn, has been one of the very best of my life. I couldn't leave Stonewylde if it weren't for you. You've given me my freedom. You'll be a truly magical Shaman, far better and wiser than I ever was, and you have Mother Heggy watching over you too, helping you to fulfil your destiny as the Wise Woman of Stonewylde.'

Leveret stirred again, trying to move her head, and her hand twitched in a glimmer of movement. He had no idea of the darkness that seethed in her mind, the terror and trauma that banished all light and silenced her speech. Clip leant over to kiss her cheek, his tears spilling.

'Farewell, my little Leveret. I can't visit again before I leave as I have so many preparations to make, but you'll always be in my heart. I'll see you again one day – I don't know when – maybe as you said, in another realm when we're journeying. Make a speedy recovery because Stonewylde needs you.'

The crone drew angrily on her pipe, kicking out at the log that poked from the fire but unable to reach it with her foot. She muttered furiously to herself as she rocked in her chair, bemoaning her age and how her body had twisted and hunched in such a way that she could now barely stand, let alone go up to the Stone Circle to perform a ceremony.

''Twas only last year!' she champed, her gums gripping the clay pipe. 'Only last year I cast such powerful magic and summoned him back through the veil! Look at me now – nought but a shrivelled old stump!'

'Mother, your magic is as powerful as ever,' said Martin, sitting in Vetchling's chair and gazing into the flames. 'You're ever the Wise Woman, ever the one who can cast and summon and scry.'

'Aye, but she ain't tainted, that hare-girl!' spat Violet. 'She were meant to be spoiled, or better yet, the Beast might've had 'un with her maiden blood all spilt on Snake Stone. I thought Jay would take her and then perhaps the Beast would finish her off, or she'd be with child and no use. But I were wrong and I should've seen it a-coming!'

'No, Mother, your magic is still there.'

'Pah! No use smoothing me down,' she mumbled. 'Old Violet should've known, should've scried. I sent that boy up to Quarrycleave to his death, and he were one of us!'

'From what I heard, he were going to take her up there anyway,' said Martin. 'Swift says Jay had an itch for the ugly little maid long since and he'd always planned to force her, so don't you blame yourself for that. 'Tweren't your fault.'

'Well, nought must go wrong tomorrow night,' she said. 'All is prepared and all is set. I wish I'd be there too, for how can you do the work alone? Oh, when I think back to some o' the Samhains I spent in that Circle, with my dear sister working alongside o' me ...'

'Aye, Mother, and after tomorrow night, all will be well again, just as you always said.'

'But Heggy's magic still reaches out, beyond the grave,' said Old Violet sadly. ''Twere ever so. Every time I cast or I hex, she's there a-blocking me! That hare-girl – 'twere Heggy as saved her. Same with that moongazy Sylvie – Heggy's protection. Yul, all them years ago – 'twere Raven, there at Heggy's bidding. Magpie should be gone, useless brat, but oh no, he's too bright now to be fooled. And instead, 'tis our own loved ones who're taken. My Vetch, that daft Starling – as good as dead – and now Jay! And 'twere Heggy who had Jackdaw killed by her crow up at Mooncliffe all them years ago. Now 'tis just you and me left, son, against the whole lot of 'em.'

'Would you like a cup o' tea, Mother?' he asked.

'No I would not!' she spat. 'Give me a drop o' mead, and then we must once more go through the ceremony for tomorrow night. You must know it all perfect. And the cakes – they're ready for you to take, Martin. Oh, after tomorrow night, all will be well and then we'll show 'em all – my magic is the stronger, and Old Heggy and that slut Raven will be finished forever. My boy came first, and my boy *will* be master.'

'But this lawyer, Mother? What of this charity thing that Clip says will happen at Stonewylde? How can—'

'Pah, 'tis nought! Once Clip's gone tomorrow night, 'twill never happen, right enough. Don't you fear, my son. When our Magus has found flesh again and is truly amongst us in body, all that trouble will wither away, you mark my words. You and Magus together'll be stronger than anything, and Stonewylde will be ours once more.'

*

431

The Samhain celebrations in the Green Labyrinth on the Village Green, and in the Great Barn, were unusually subdued. The terrible event at Hunter's Moon in the quarry was still too fresh in folks' minds for them to relish a festival, even if it were one that honoured the dead. The Barn was decorated as usual and the children performed their dance and drama, but as she watched, Maizie was weighed down with sadness. She thought back to the previous year and the trouble she'd had with Leveret disappearing and then falling asleep in the Barn; she almost wept again at the thought of it. What she wouldn't give to have her little one safe and well in Stonewylde again. Hazel had told her that it would only be a couple more days and then Leveret could be transferred to the hospital at the Hall. Maizie planned to live in the hospital wing until she was healed, so she could care for her daughter personally.

Sylvie, dressed in her grey and black robes, watched the children perform their dance and felt her heart sitting like a fist of stone in her chest. This time last year she'd told Hazel how wonderful her love life was, the only blight being the way Yul wrapped her in cotton wool. Now she could hardly bear to be anywhere near him and certainly couldn't look him in the eye. She'd returned to Maizie's cottage after Leveret's awful accident because the girls were so upset and needed her there, but when Maizie had tentatively broached the subject of Rainbow and the sketch, Sylvie had refused to talk about it. The only way at present she could deal with the situation and hold her head up in public, knowing everyone was gossiping, was to glaze her eyes, walk tall and refuse to acknowledge any of it. So far that tactic had worked, as most people were worried about upsetting her further by mentioning it. She knew that Clip was leaving first thing in the morning and she needed to get through that ordeal before she could start to deal with the issue of Yul's infidelity.

Miranda watched her grandchildren dance and noticed her daughter's suffering, knowing that Sylvie's humiliation must cut her to the quick. She'd tried to talk it over but had been firmly rebuffed. So be it – all Miranda could do was support Sylvie if she faltered. Hopefully there'd be enough hard work setting up the Stonewylde healing centre to distract her in the months ahead. Perhaps once she'd got over the shock of Yul's adultery, she'd find it in her heart to forgive him and start again.

Clip headed down to the labyrinth marked out on the Village Green wearing his black-feathered cloak. He liked to wear this at Samhain and tomorrow when he was gone it would become Leveret's. He still had much to do in the tower, although he'd now written those difficult letters of farewell. He felt bad to be leaving not only Leveret, but Sylvie too, at such a traumatic time. But he also knew that despite appearances to the contrary, Sylvie was tough and determined like her mother, and would survive Yul's stupid betrayal. The healing centre would provide her with a true vocation, both setting up and then running it, and all the papers had now been signed. He was so glad he'd been able to make her wish come true.

Clip walked the winding and tortuous path of the labyrinth like everyone else, with a white skull mask over his face. He thought of the Green Magic of Stonewylde that pervaded the entire estate, but especially this Village Green. That serpent of energy and life-force spiralled beneath him and as he imagined it, the serpent in his belly flexed its coils. Clip writhed, wishing now that he'd taken his prescribed medicine that morning. He hated the thought of his senses being blunted but the pain was bad today; maybe he'd take it before leaving the tower for tonight's ritual in the Stone Circle. He left the labyrinth and, clutching his slip of yew, Clip walked for the last time along the track leading back to the Hall. Despite yearning for his freedom and knowing that he was about to attain it, his heart was sad and his step heavy at the prospect of all he'd leave behind.

After the teenagers' drama, Yul left the Village Green knowing he had a little time before sunset when the next ceremonies would begin. Then he'd lead the community in the labyrinth, although this time he'd not share any Green Magic, as it was to be saved for the new healing centre. It had been suggested at the last Elders' meeting to redirect all the energy back into the earth below to make Stonewylde stronger and more powerful. He'd had to stifle a smile as this had been decided – everyone acted as if he had a choice in the matter. Did none of them realise that the Green Magic went wherever it chose, and hadn't chosen him for some time now?

Yul had noticed his father-in-law leaving the Green earlier and guessed he was off to finish packing. He wanted a quiet and private farewell with the man he'd resented and sneered at for so many years. He found Clip on the top floor of the tower surrounded by piles of possessions all over the floor. A fire crackled in the hearth in a break with tradition, and it was cosy. Yul realised it was many years since he'd been up here – not since his early days with Sylvie when they were first handfasted.

It was still the Samhain fast, with no food until after sunset, but Clip made them both a cup of herbal tea. Shadow was out with Magpie and Rufus, but as soon as Yul sat on the battered sofa, Hare jumped up onto his lap.

'I hadn't realised you had a pet hare,' he said, stroking her soft fur and marvelling at her amber eyes.

'She's Leveret's, not mine. We found her newly-born and injured at the Spring Equinox. Leveret raised her.'

'She's beautiful! A very fitting companion for my little sister. I remember now – there was a hare at the Story Web.'

They sat in silence for a while sipping their tea, and then Yul sighed heavily.

'Clip, I've come here because ... because I wanted to say goodbye and to wish you well.'

'That's a kind gesture, especially as I know in the past you've found my presence at Stonewylde so difficult. But as of tomorrow you'll be free of me and my bumbling around!'

Yul frowned but then saw the twinkle in Clip's eye.

'I never thought I'd say it, but I'll miss you,' Yul admitted. 'In truth, I can't imagine Stonewylde without you.'

'Thank you,' said Clip. 'And Yul – I know things are bad at the moment, but they will get better. In the end, what seems at the time like life and death invariably turns out to be nothing of the sort. This present situation between you and Sylvie – it'll pass.'

Yul grimaced and stared into his tea.

'I wish that were so. But I have horrible feeling that this won't pass. Sylvie and I will never have what we once did.'

Clip paused and regarded his dark haired son-in-law steadily. He noted the fine lines around Yul's mouth and eyes, and the strain and sadness in their deep grey depths. He'd acted like a fool, but his love for Sylvie wasn't in doubt.

'You may be right. But everything comes to an end, and it could be that what you and Sylvie have yet to come will be even better. Think metamorphosis – how can the caterpillar ever imagine the glory of the butterfly, especially when it's in chrysalis form?'

Yul nodded slowly, regretting more than ever now the hostility he'd always felt towards the older, wiser man. Clip could have been a proper father to him if only he'd let him. He sighed again and Clip stood up, straightening with a wince.

'I still have much to do here if I'm to leave the place tidy, but there's something I'd like to do for you,' he said. 'It'll only take ten minutes and there's time before you must leave for the sunset ceremony so please, Yul, close your eyes and relax. This is something your father used to enjoy when he was worried or tense.'

Clip proceeded to play his gongs just for Yul, filling the tower with the shimmering, quavering, burnished metal sound. It reverberated in the circular space, making the air and the fabric of the building quiver with wave upon wave of resonance. Yul felt the vibrations – gentle at first but growing larger and stronger by the second – fill his body, enter his flesh and then his very core, putting everything right within him. All was soothed, all was calm, for there was room for nothing other than this ancient, visceral music. It finally reached the bloom, a crescendo of noise so powerful as to almost stop his breath. And then it ceased, and slowly, slowly the music faded as the vibrations from the trembling metal discs grew ever fainter. Yul opened his eyes as the final quivering note died away and looked Clip straight in the eye.

'Thank you,' he said softly. 'I do wish you weren't leaving, Clip. I do wish we'd been close.'

Once again, Clip donned his raven cloak and tugged on his warm felt-lined boots. He pulled on a dark felt hat that made him look like an Elizabethan magician and took up his bag and trusty ash staff. The room was now tidy and all in order for his departure later on. The letters he'd written stood propped over the fireplace. He left several large handfuls of hay for Hare and filled her water bowl, put the guard in the fire-place and took up the lantern to light his way to the Stone Circle. His eyes swept the peaceful room and he smiled; all was as it should be.

He arrived at the Stone Circle late, as the temperature was plummeting. The Death Dance wasn't taking place here tonight and yet tiny red jars marked out the way, little flames flickering inside them. The braziers by the stones held burning torches and a small bonfire burnt in place of the funeral pyre. Crows and ravens, some in flight and some at perch, were painted on every stone and he recognised Magpie's influence in the perfect design of wings, beaks and claws. The arena flickered with sinister flame and Clip's heart fluttered in his chest. He gripped his staff more firmly, peering in through the entrance to locate Martin within.

Dressed in his black cloak, Martin stood by the Altar Stone. He wore the bird mask that had so frightened Yul all those years ago, and his silvery hair was visible above it. He looked like a great piebald corvid, even moving with an aggressive strut. Clip stood watching him for some time. This man was supposedly his half-brother, both of them fathered by Basil. Magus and he, on the other hand, had shared Raven as their mother. Martin and Magus were only related as cousins, as their fathers had been brothers. It was all so complicated, but Clip had always been aware that he was the link between the two men, sharing a parent with each of them. Maybe that was why both had resented him so much, but not each other – there'd been no rivalry between the two of them.

Clip could hear Martin muttering and chanting and knew he was performing some kind of dark Samhain ritual. He shuddered, thinking of Old Violet and her evil ways. She was a powerful crone, and Clip recalled that time at the Winter Solstice, the night that Yul had defeated Magus, when he'd taken Sylvie up to Hare Stone for her moondance. He remembered how Violet had frozen him on the spot. Her magic was stronger than his, and this knowledge made what he must do next all the more frightening. He must not fail.

He took a deep breath and entered the arena, calling Samhain blessings to Martin. His brother spun around, the bird mask with its great beak truly terrifying, like the Plague Doctors of old. Clip walked towards the Altar Stone, skirting around the edge of the labyrinth so as not to cross it. Martin seemed upset at being discovered in his evil spell-casting, flapping his arms in dismay at the intrusion.

'I'm sorry to interrupt you, Martin,' said Clip amiably in a normal voice, as if they weren't alone in an ancient circle just before midnight at Samhain, with the paraphernalia of dark magic spread all over the place. 'I found the gift you left me earlier and I wanted to say thank you, and also goodbye. Can you spare me a minute?'

'No I can't! I'm right in the middle o' this. 'Tis difficult now.'

'I'm so sorry. But it was really kind of your mother to bake me those cakes. I wanted you to pass on my thanks as I just don't have time to visit her personally before I leave.'

'Ah yes, the cakes.'

'She knows I always loved them in Magus' day, of course.'

'Aye, she said you did. Have you … have you eaten one yet?'

Martin had pushed the mask back onto the top of his head, so the beak now pointed skyward. Dressed in their black cloaks, tall and thin with silver hair, they were remarkably similar.

'Well, the note you left said they were for my journey tonight at Samhain. But in view of my leaving and as you said recently, us being half-brothers, I thought maybe we could bury the hatchet and share a tot of mead and a ceremony cake together now. For old times' sake?'

'Aye, but I don't have any—'

'No, I've brought them with me, and some mead too. Perhaps it's time, as brothers, that you and I made our peace before I leave Stonewylde?'

Martin's mouth stretched into a ghoulish grin and he nodded.

'I'm finishing a ritual that my poor old mother wants me to perform tonight,' he said, his voice more good-natured than it had been for a long time. ''Twill be midnight soon and 'tis important I do this afore then. But after that, I'll gladly share the mead and cake.'

'Excellent. I'll just set up the things on the Altar to make it more of a formal sharing. Please – do carry on. I won't get in your way and I'd like to have a quiet moment myself with our ancestors.'

Clip laid his bag on the Altar Stone and took out the small tin of cakes and a bottle of mead. He also placed two old goblets and an embossed pewter plate on the great horizontal stone and then taking his staff, moved back into the shadows to watch. He knew that midnight was approaching and at that moment, in the turning of the wheel of the year, the veil between this realm and the Otherworld would be at its thinnest.

As Martin chanted with the athame pointing earthwards, the atmosphere within the Stone Circle changed. From just the two of them, there was suddenly a multitude, as if a huge crowd had arrived, bigger than any gathering ever held here at a festival. Clip glimpsed ranks and ranks of faces, shadowy and grey, thronging around the Circle and crowding into every slip of space. He heard a strange kind of sighing, like soft wind in the trees, and everything seemed to shift slightly. Over by a stone in the far reaches of the Circle, he thought he glimpsed a cloaked figure, blacker than shadow and darker than night.

Martin called out, his voice rising above the soughing of souls, and one appeared in the centre of the circle, brighter and more vibrant than all the other shades. He was almost complete, almost fully there; his hair was silvery blond like Martin's and Clip's. He was tall and well-muscled, and Martin stepped forward with open arms to embrace him, to welcome home a returning brother. And the bright shadow vanished into him; just disappeared. The moment passed and all the other shades began to fade. The mistiness became thicker as if a curtain was closing. Clip saw a snatch of Vetchling with Jay next to her, and both were laughing. He shuddered convulsively as the veil was pulled across again and the faces and whispers receded.

Clip approached the Altar Stone and with his back to Martin, opened the cake tin. That old, familiar scent greeted him, not smelt in a long time. He took two of the rather battered-looking cakes and placed them on the pewter plate, then uncorked the small bottle of mead and poured a good measure into each of the two goblets. Martin had sheathed his athame and pushed back the mask again; now he strode purposefully over to the Altar to join him, a new spring in his step.

'Blessings to you at Samhain, brother,' said Clip softly. 'Let us eat and drink together, share the fruits of the Goddess, and forget the ills of the past. We are bound by blood ties and tonight of all nights we should honour our shared ancestors.'

Watching him carefully with a gleam in his eye, Martin took one of the cakes and the goblet of mead that Clip proffered. He raised the goblet and his lips smiled.

'To our ancestors and the Dark Angel!' he said, as Clip popped the little cake in his mouth whole, as he'd always done, and began to chew. Unexpectedly, Martin reached across and took Clip's goblet from him, swapping it for his own.

'Apologies, brother, but you can never be too careful,' he said as they toasted each other. Both men drank deeply, savouring the sweet, powerful mead.

'Won't you eat your mother's cake?' Clip asked, and Martin shook his head with a handsome smile. His eyes were dark brown and his hair lustrous. His face had thickened and lost the thin, lined look of late. He'd found a new lease of life.

'No, it's not for me, the Death Cap,' he chuckled, and Clip stared in disbelief at the depth and richness of his velvet voice. 'Do have another one yourself. It won't make any difference now, and we know how you love those cakes.'

'No thanks,' said Clip. 'I find I don't have a taste for them nowadays.'

'Really? But I recall just how very fond you once were of them.'

A mist began to rise from the ground, curling around the tiny red lights, making everything seem ghostly and strange. Firelight flickered from the braziers and the painted birds fluttered as Clip glanced over to where the dark shadow lurked. It had moved forward along the coils of the labyrinth, closer to them. His brother noticed and chuckled again, a sinister sound in the silence of the Stone Circle.

'Well, Clip, it seems another has joined us. The Dark Angel knows that Samhain is the time of the Death Dance, whatever that black-haired bastard upstart decrees. The Angel has joined us and has come to take you with him tonight.'

'Yes, I rather feared he would,' said Clip. 'A little sooner than I'd hoped, but I'm ready. What's a few weeks anyway?'

'What do you mean? Don't you care? The cake was—'

'Of course I care. I care about my precious daughter and my beloved niece, and all the other good folk of Stonewylde. They deserve better than the likes of you. Old Violet's magic is powerful but only goes so far. She never understood the strongest power of all, and neither do you.'

His brother with the dark eyes and blond hair, the creature of shadow and moonlight, seemed to shimmer and waver back into the other care-worn brother and then out again. He stepped forward and grabbed Clip's raven-feathered cloak, his face white with fury. Behind him, Clip saw the winged shadow growing darker and nearer.

'What are you talking about, you fool? You've eaten Death Cap and you won't see the dawn. There's no antidote!'

'I know,' said Clip. 'And neither is there an antidote for what you've drunk. We'll none of us see the dawn.'

'*WHAT?*' The tall figure stumbled backwards, looking at his hands in disbelief. 'But ... but you drank it too! I took your goblet! I don't—'

'We drank from the same bottle,' said Clip. 'My goblet, your goblet – they were the same.'

'So you've poisoned yourself? No! You—'

'The serpent in my belly has poisoned me already,' said Clip. 'As I said, what's a few weeks? If it means that I take you – both of you – with me to the Otherworld and free Stonewylde of your evil?'

His brother stared at him in horror as realisation dawned. Again he stared at his hands and shook his head wildly.

'I have no sensation in my fingers!' he shouted. 'My mouth's burning!'

He clutched at his throat, and then leaning over, vomited onto the beaten earth.

'Don't worry,' said Clip, his mouth also tingling and the nausea taking hold. 'Wolfsbane is quick, not like Death Cap. We'll all three be taken by the Dark Angel within the hour.'

'Wolfsbane? No! I don't want to die!' bellowed his brother. 'How could you have tricked me like this?'

He lurched forward, kicking over the small red glass jars and flickering flames, and grabbed Clip wildly. He gasped for air, clawing at his face, then doubled up again in agony.

'My guts are turning inside out!' he cried and Clip held him in a tight embrace, the two silver heads and black cloaks joining as one.

'So are mine,' whispered Clip. 'The serpents in our bellies writhe and uncoil and flicker their forked tongues. Come, my brothers, it's time. The Dark Angel is close and my silver wolf awaits me.'

Together they sank to the ground by the Altar Stone in a dark, groaning heap as the black shadow moved in and hovered over them. Engulfing the three brothers in his deep, cold wings, the Dark Angel silently ushered them to the Otherworld.

28

It was the Dark Moon of December, falling towards the beginning of the month, and Leveret was on her way to the Great Barn with her mother. Maizie had tried to stop her going, but Leveret was determined to bring some normality back into her life.

'Oh look, here comes Sylvie! Why's she heading for the Hall? Doesn't she realise 'tis Dark Moon?' said Maizie, tugging at Leveret's cloak slightly to straighten it. 'She should've stayed down in the Village today.'

'Blessings!' said Sylvie, bending to pat Shadow's head. His tail flickered in greeting but he stood solemnly by Leveret's side, no longer the carefree pup he'd been before Hunter's Moon.

'Blessings, my dear,' said Maizie, kissing her daughter-in-law. 'Not joining us in the Barn?'

'No ... I have so much to do at the moment,' said Sylvie, 'I really can't spare the time. Now that all the stuff's been sent off to Aitch and our contract fulfilled, I don't feel it's strictly necessary. But it's good to see you going down there, Leveret.'

'Well, I don't want everyone gossiping and saying that Jay did get me after all,' said Leveret. 'Mother's done her best to stop me today, but I keep telling her that I really need to be up and about. I'm healed as well as I'll ever be, and it's time I began to live a normal life.'

'It can never be normal,' said Maizie sadly. 'Who'll look after you in that tower? I must be—'

'Mother, please! You know it's all arranged. Magpie will have the ground floor room where you are now, I'll stay in Clip's old bedroom in the middle, and I have Shadow too – you know how he looks after me. Between him and Magpie I'm smothered with care and attention. I'll go to the Dining Hall for my meals and Magpie can fetch me things on a tray from the kitchens if necessary. Please – I want you to go home to the Village now. I'm sure Sylvie and the girls need you back in the cottage, don't you, Sylvie?'

'Oh yes, yes we do!' she agreed quickly. 'I'm really struggling with the range, the chickens aren't happy without you – they've practically stopped laying – and you know how the girls love your cooking. I'm useless! Please come home, Maizie.'

'Well ... if you're both sure 'tis the best choice.'

'Yes!' cried Leveret and Sylvie in unison.

Leveret and Maizie continued on their way to the Village. Finally they entered the Barn, rosy cheeked from the cold December wind that whipped along the cobbles and sighed through the skeletal branches all around the Village Green. They were late arriving and most of the menstruating women were already there, sitting around knitting the special socks for Yule and making decorations and crafts for the festival. As they walked in, with Shadow close by Leveret's side, there was a moment of silence, then a great cheer rose to the rafters. Maizie burst into tears and Leveret stood uncertainly, suddenly scared but unable to move. Rosie came rushing over and enveloped her in a great hug, leading her little sister, with their mother in tow, over to a comfortable corner. Another woman brought them tea and sticky buns. One by one, during that morning, most of the people in the Great Barn came over to pay their respects to Leveret.

Shadow too was subject to a great deal of fuss and petting, and Meadowsweet in particular was delighted to see him.

'How he's grown! What a lovely boy he is. Oh Leveret, I can't tell you how glad I am you have 'un. He'll be such a help, won't he?'

'Yes, he will. Hazel was going to arrange for someone to train him, but I don't think he needs it. He already seems to understand what to do.'

'I told you he were clever, didn't I? Father's so proud that he's yours and not drowned.'

'Having my Shadow has made everything seem possible,' said Leveret simply. 'Without him, I don't think I'd feel half as positive.'

She stood up, and immediately Maizie heaved herself to her feet.

'No, Mother. I need to do this for myself. I'm only going to the privy and I'm a big girl now.'

Hesitantly, she turned towards the back of the Barn and began to walk towards the lavatories. Shadow was by her side, moving at her shuffling pace, nudging her gently. Women silently moved aside as Leveret's long blackthorn stick tapped carefully in front of her, and eventually she reached the door. She was shaking from fingertip to toe, knowing all eyes were on her, desperate not to trip over something and make a fool of herself. But she made it, and taking a deep breath, she told Shadow to sit and stay as she fumbled for the door handle.

That evening Maizie packed up all her things from the tower and returned to the Village, with promises from Hazel, Marigold, Cherry and Miranda that they'd check regularly on Leveret and make sure Magpie was looking after her properly. After her trip down to the Village, Leveret felt exhausted and unable to face the Dining Hall, so Hazel and Magpie between them brought supper trays to the tower, which Hazel stayed and shared with them.

She watched Leveret carefully eating the food that Magpie had cut up for her and praised him for his care, knowing it wasn't that long ago he'd been unable to use a knife and fork himself. He beamed at this, then added a log to the fire, ensuring the guard was in place afterwards.

'The boys have fixed up your intercom now, Leveret,' said

Hazel. 'You'll need to learn which button is which, but you'll be able to buzz me, the kitchens, Miranda's rooms and Yul's office if you need anything. I think you'll be fine – you're a brave girl.'

Leveret grimaced at this.

'Nothing brave about it really. I'm blind, that's all there is to it.'

'But you could've taken a lot longer to come to terms with it.'

'I have Magpie and Shadow – they're my eyes. I'm luckier than most.'

'Hardly lucky! That Jay—'

'Hazel, I could've died or been paralysed. Losing my sight seems a pretty lucky alternative to me.'

'Malik says he's coming to visit you soon. I know we've explained the prognosis for optic nerve damage and he's pretty sure that nothing more can be done, but—'

'Oh Hazel, you silly thing – it's not me that lovely doctor wants to visit! I'm just an excuse.'

Hazel was quite relieved that Leveret couldn't see her blush at this, and quickly changed the subject. They spoke of Leveret resuming her studies, particularly as Rufus was keen to work with her and willing to read aloud. They weren't sure if it would be successful, but it was a start.

'The main thing is that I continue all the things I promised Clip I'd do. I won't let him down, not after the sacrifice he made for us all.'

Her voice broke and she stopped, the pain of losing him too intense. Hazel sighed and squeezed Leveret's hand. Like everyone, she was still reeling from the shock of Clip's death less than six weeks ago. When his and Martin's bodies had been discovered in the Stone Circle the morning after Samhain, the entire community had gone into mourning. Clip had been well loved by almost everyone at Stonewylde. Leveret had been spared the horrific news for a couple of days, but as soon as she returned to Stonewylde from the hospital, she had to be told. Her reaction – on top of the news that she was highly unlikely ever to regain her sight – had been to retreat into herself. She refused to eat or talk for a while, remaining silent in her world of darkness and despair.

Sylvie had tried her best, but it was Yul who'd hauled her out of the slough of hopelessness. He'd sat with her and insisted on reading aloud the letter that Clip had left for her explaining his actions and saying goodbye. Until then she'd refused to let anyone touch it; she couldn't bear to hear what Clip had wanted to tell her. As Yul read falteringly the words intended for Leveret alone, his voice had broken, and he'd struggled to reach the end of the eloquent, loving farewell. Together they'd wept, holding each other tightly in a way they hadn't done since she was a small child. The letter was heart-breaking, all the more so because when Clip had written it just a few days after her accident at Quarrycleave, he'd had no idea that Leveret would never read it for herself.

It was now common knowledge that Clip, after finally visiting a consultant during the trip to London, had been diagnosed with advanced cancer. He had little time left and would never roam the world as he'd hoped. Clip had understood what was happening with Martin – he'd been shown this during his journey at the Hunter's Moon, but had suspected it much earlier. Unless Martin was stopped, Magus' spirit would be made flesh and the shadows at Stonewylde would become deeper and darker, engulfing the community in a long winter of tyranny.

Leveret could understand this, but what added to the pain of losing Clip was the knowledge that it was she who'd prepared the Wolfsbane that killed him. He'd mentioned this in the letter, saying how Mother Heggy had directed her to prepare it especially for him and for this purpose, knowing how fast-working and final the poison was. Yul spent a long time reassuring Leveret that it wasn't her fault, and preparing the Wolfsbane had not, as she feared, put the idea into Clip's head. She had simply followed Mother Heggy's bidding and made the whole thing quick and simple for him.

Yul too was deeply affected by the death. He'd been the last person to see Clip alive and he remembered the glorious gong playing. All the time he'd been with Clip in his tower, his uncle had known he was living his last hours, and yet he'd wanted to do something special for Yul. What finally made Leveret rouse herself out of her depression was Yul imploring her to resume her mantle of Shaman and Wise Woman, because that was what Clip had wished for above all else. He'd entrusted Leveret to continue caring for the folk and she mustn't betray that trust, else his death would have been in vain.

As Hazel watched Leveret, who, with no obvious damage to her eyes, looked so normal, she again felt a surge of respect for the young girl who was determined to honour her promises to Clip. What Leveret hadn't told anyone – for who could possibly understand? – was what had happened when she first came home to Stonewylde and Magpie had come to visit. He'd walked into her little room in the hospital wing, and the nurse and Maizie had left them alone for a moment of privacy. At the sight of her, bandaged around the head and with her wrist strapped up, Magpie had fallen to his knees by the bedside dissolving into the terrible sobs that overwhelmed him at times of great distress.

Leveret had struggled in her darkness to sit up and locate him, and found his arms and head resting on the bed as he knelt on the floor.

'Magpie, please! I'm alive and I'm not going to die, so you mustn't cry like this. You saved my life, dear Maggie, and now we'll always be together, you and me, just like I've always said we would be. You'll be my carer, won't you?'

He'd grabbed hold of her good hand, tears streaming down his cheeks and completely beside himself with emotion, and as they held hands, suddenly ... there'd been an explosion inside her head. She saw the bed with its pretty cover and the hospital room. She saw herself, small and very bruised, her head a funny colour where she'd been painted with antiseptic, stitches in her wounds, bandages wrapped around and some of her hair shaved. And in that moment she realised that she may have lost her own sight, but when she held his hand, she would always have Magpie's to share.

*

Three people were leaving Stonewylde to live in the Outside World, and they were going before Yule. At the Council of Elders meeting just before Owl Moon in November, Rowan had announced that she and Faun were moving to London, and were taking Swift with them. It transpired that Rowan had been in close touch via e-mail with Rainbow, Buzz and Holly, as had Swift and Martin.

It had been a difficult meeting, with two key members now absent and Sylvie acting as if she wished Yul weren't present either. By common consensus, the great carved chair had remained empty in honour of Clip's memory. Christopher, the lawyer, had sat in Martin's place and gently explained some of the intricacies of the new regime. The charity was now in existence and after Yule, surveys of the buildings and facilities would begin as a first step towards setting up the healing centre at Stonewylde. At Miranda's request, Christopher had also joined the Board of Trustees in an administrative role, for she knew the minutiae of the legal side of things were beyond most folk's understanding, herself included.

With Martin gone and everyone feeling the loss of Clip, it should have been a less confrontational meeting than usual. But Rowan had been rather aggressive when she made her announcement, and had refused Christopher's offer of advice about Faun's share of her father's company. She said that Buzz had it all in hand and she trusted him more than she trusted any friend of Miranda's. Faun was to attend a drama school and Rowan was very excited about this. Dawn was concerned about Rowan, knowing that for all her success at Stonewylde, she'd struggle in the Outside World.

Dawn feared it would all end badly, and mentioned this when she, Miranda and Sylvie met at a later date. The three women sat together in Sylvie's office. Dawn was heavily pregnant with the baby due between Imbolc and the Spring Equinox, and although she still taught at the Village School, nowadays she was more involved behind the scenes. Rowan leaving so suddenly would have a big impact on the Nursery and they needed to recruit someone to step into her shoes; nobody who currently worked there wanted the responsibility of leadership. David still had contacts in the Outside World and the interviewing process must begin soon; it was always difficult to find teachers who were not only talented but also in sympathy with the Stonewylde ethos. As a long term solution, Sylvie realised that it would be helpful to encourage more of their school-leavers into teaching careers.

'The point is, we can't stop her going,' said Miranda, still stung by Rowan's antagonism towards her. She'd never quite appreciated how deep it went.

'No, but she's like a child in a sweetshop,' said Dawn, who had more recent experience of living in the Outside World than they did. 'She thinks it's going to be wonderful, a dream come true, and it's not. We're so very sheltered here at Stonewylde, so cocooned from the harsh reality of life. Rowan simply won't cope. Neither will Princess Faun, I'm sure. The girl has totally unrealistic expectations.'

'I'm sure most of the thirteen year-old girls in her drama school will have similarly unrealistic expectations,' said Sylvie drily. 'I hate to say it, but really, there's nothing we can do to stop them and nor should we try. They have plenty of money, thanks to Magus' legacy. Let Buzz take care of them if they're determined to leave.'

'But what if he exploits them? Because of Christopher's intervention, Buzz has now lost control of the fifty per cent of Magus' company owned by Leveret and Rufus. But he's still controlling Faun's shares – what if he isn't honest with them and Faun ends up losing out?'

Both Miranda and Sylvie shrugged in an almost identical gesture. Neither of them would be sad to see the back of Rowan, who'd been very free with her taunts and sneers lately, as had Faun. Nor could Sylvie forget the glee with which Rowan had told her about Yul and Rainbow. Miranda and Sylvie weren't quite as magnanimous as Dawn, an exceptionally kind soul, but one who hadn't been on the receiving end of Rowan's spite herself.

'We must simply let them find out for themselves,' said Miranda firmly. 'The one I'm more concerned about is Swift.'

'Yes, he is a worry. Now that his father's dead, he's adamant he wants to live with Buzz and "be Hallfolk", as he puts it. He's found out about transferring to a college close to Buzz, and Buzz has said he can stay with his family. Apparently Holly and Fennel have said they'll give him work experience at Aitch, and if he does well at college and passes his exams, he can start a career with them.'

'That sounds perfect,' said Dawn.

'But why are they helping him like this? How does his mother feel about it? What if it all falls apart?' asked Sylvie.

'Then he can come back here,' said Miranda. 'I feel that unlike Rowan, and by default Faun, Swift is something of a victim in the present situation. He didn't choose for his father to go bad – nor to die in the Stone Circle. His mother's been totally traumatised by what's happened, and has no opinion whatsoever on anything – who can blame the boy for wanting to seize such an opportunity? I've always liked Swift – devious and two-faced though he can be – and I respect him for wanting to get away and start a new life for himself. I don't think we need have any worries about Swift, but we'll let him know he has a home here if he ever wants to come back.'

The three women agreed on this, and then started to discuss who could replace Rowan in the Nursery until a qualified teacher was found. Sylvie realised that, for the first time ever, she was helping to make important decisions without even considering what Yul would say or think. She smiled to herself, sensing that hard knot inside her gain another layer of reinforcement. Who needed a husband anyway?

Sylvie sat in her old spot on the window seat of the grand sitting room, having come in to assess its possibility as a reception room for the healing centre. It was early afternoon, a few days before the Winter Solstice, and the light filtering through the diamond-shaped panes of whorled glass in the leaded windows was grey and dull. No fire crackled in the huge Purbeck marble fireplace, no personal photos or ornaments now graced the antique furniture in this beautiful but lifeless room. All evidence of the most recent visitors had been scrupulously removed from the rooms which now held an expectant air as if waiting to see who would next take up residency.

No trace of Magus' ghost lingered. For the past year, Sylvie had almost taken for granted that constant underlying atmosphere of menace that had stalked her all over Stonewylde, and particularly in these chambers. But since Samhain, there'd been nothing. No lingering scent, no unexplained draughts, no glimpses of a shadow nor creak of a footstep. She'd never have contemplated coming in here alone like this a couple of months ago, as the haunting had become so bad. Yet today, her first visit since Clip's death, she found that Magus' ghost had been well and truly exorcised. Nor was there any chance of Martin creeping around like a wraith, as he'd always done in the past.

In the letter he'd left his daughter, Clip had explained about Magus and the summons from the Otherworld made at the previous Samhain. How he'd known about this she had no idea, but as Sylvie had read the letter through her tears, everything had fallen into place. She was desperately sad that her father had gone, but she also respected his decision to end his life before the final stages of the disease took hold. If only he'd been diagnosed earlier – that was what made her so very sad, especially as she realised that Clip had probably ignored or dismissed all the initial symptoms. It was as if he'd known that this was how his life must end, when his time in this world was up, and he'd allowed destiny to run its course.

She understood his reluctance to engage at the end with conventional treatment, given that the cancer had been far too advanced for any cure to be feasible. In the letter he'd said that he was, in effect, taking the easy way out by not enduring the final few weeks of pain, and hoped to spare everyone the ordeal of watching him die. He said that by taking Martin and Magus with him to the Otherworld, Stonewylde would be free forever from their malignant influence and taint. Today, sitting in this lair which had always scared her, Sylvie felt her father had certainly succeeded.

Her heart jumped at a sudden fluttering deep inside her. Sylvie placed a hand on her belly and smiled secretively. Was it too soon, or was that him quickening? She remembered that strange sensation so well; like a small frog hopping, or a butterfly fanning its wings. She'd managed so far to hide her pregnancy from everyone except Hazel and Leveret, who'd both found out, and her mother whom she'd confided in. They'd all promised not to tell anyone; somehow this helped. Whilst nobody else knew, she could just pretend to herself that everything was lovely and the baby would be born into a happy world where Yul need play no part. Once the news was out, Sylvie knew she'd have to deal with reality. Being so tall and slim, she'd managed to hide her growing waistline and small bump, with the aid of thick winter clothes and shawls.

Sylvie started again as the door opened and Yul came in. She glared at him as he strode across the room towards her.

'Sorry to barge in on you, but I heard you'd come in here and I thought ... maybe we could talk?'

Sylvie shrugged and turned away, gazing out at the wintry trees and sky. Since that awful moment on the day of the Hunter's Moon when she'd been gloatingly informed of her husband's infidelity, Sylvie had managed to avoid speaking to him. The horrific incident at Quarrycleave had superseded all other concerns, with Leveret in hospital in the Outside World, Jay's horrible death, and everyone's distress. Then, only a few days later there'd been the events of Samhain: the terrible double death in the Stone Circle. Her grief at the loss of her father had superseded everything. All this had dragged on for weeks, displacing the need to deal with Yul. The funerals had been difficult – Magus and then Clip had always conducted them in the past. Grieving himself, Yul had struggled to perform the simple ceremony at the Yew of Death.

He'd skulked about since then, knowing that he must face Sylvie and wanting to do so, but also almost glad of the excuses not to. His wife had developed the art of looking through him as if he wasn't there; yet for the sake of the girls, at least, some kind of arrangement must be reached. Yul sat tentatively beside Sylvie on the cushions of the window seat, careful to leave plenty of space between them. He really didn't know where to start and she wasn't helping.

'I'm glad it's working out with Christopher staying here for a while,' he began. 'He's so helpful, and certainly—'

'I'm not interested in making small talk with you,' she said. 'If you have something important to say, then say it. Otherwise go away.'

'I'm sorry,' he said. 'I won't ever be able to tell you just how sorry I am.'

'Sorry? About?'

He couldn't look her in the face.

'About Rainbow,' he said quietly. 'I'd like to tell you what happened but there hasn't really been a chance.'

'I don't want to know what happened,' she said coldly. 'Why on earth would I want to hear the details of your ... your adultery?'

'I ... I just wanted to make sure you were in possession of the facts,' he said. 'I'm not sure what you heard but I thought that—'

'It really doesn't matter to me,' she said. 'I heard about it from Rowan, who seemed to find it amusing, and certainly enjoyed telling me. The whole community knows about it and Rainbow's picture of the pair of you *in flagrante* on the rock has been much discussed. You've never denied having sex with Rainbow, so I assume it *did* happen. What more is there to say?'

She moved to stand up, but Yul clutched her arm, his eyes desperately seeking hers.

'Please, Sylvie! Let me explain!'

She shook off his hand as if it burned her, but remained seated.

'No! There's nothing to explain. It happened and that's enough!'

'But I want to tell you about how I—'

'I don't want to hear any whining excuses or pathetic justifications! What it boils down to is that you didn't love me enough to be true to me.'

'But I did! I loved you so much, and you—'

'Yul, you were unfaithful to me whilst she was staying here for those three months, and she left not long after the Summer Solstice. We made love on the eve of Lammas. *We* made love yet all the time you'd done this behind my back and never told me. You had all those weeks, months even, to tell me about it. All that time when you could've come clean – but you didn't. Instead, you lived a lie. We made love under our yew tree – it was so magical – and I truly believed that everything was going to work out between us. I was so happy! We went to London and had a lovely time together, only to find Buzz here when we came back. Oh, you must have been *so* scared he'd tell me about Rainbow! And before that, when Holly and Fennel came! You must have panicked that they too might expose your filthy secret! But they didn't. And then Buzz told you about the ballet incident.'

'Yes, and—'

'And because of that you backed off! You put me through hell, made me feel so *guilty* for not telling you about Buzz being there in the theatre next to me, and all the time ... all the time you'd actually *had sex* with someone else!'

Sylvie's voice had risen steadily to a shout. With cheeks flushed and eyes bright with angry tears, she jumped up and stood glaring down at him as if she could kill him.

'You had the bloody nerve to make *me* feel guilty when all along you were harbouring that dirty little secret! That's what really, *really* gets me more than anything. It's your hypocrisy. I can't bear it! I no longer have *any* respect for you and I will *not* be treated like this. You betrayed me, Yul. You betrayed our love and our magic together.'

Yul stood up too, a fixed and defeated expression on his face. He stared at the carpet, unable to meet her flashing, furious eyes.

'Sylvie ... I know. I can't bear it either. If it's—'

'So as far as I'm concerned, Yul, you can go to hell. Or the Otherworld or whatever you like to call it. You're dead to me. I don't wish you dead – there's been too much death – but as far as I'm concerned, you're not my husband and I don't love you. I want absolutely nothing more to do with you!'

'Sylvie, please! I'll do anything to make it better, *anything*!' he cried, suddenly inflamed by her cruel words. 'How can I show you just how wretched I feel about what I did? How can I make it better? What do you want me to do? I'd give my life—'

'Stop being melodramatic!'

'You want light? I'll set myself on fire! You want blood? I'll cut my veins! Whatever you want, absolutely *anything*—'

'Don't be so ridiculous! Light? Blood? Stupid dramatics – the only thing I want is for you to go away. I don't want to see your face. Every time I see you or hear your voice, it cuts deeper and hurts even more. So if you really want to make it better, keep away from me so I don't have to endure your presence. You fill me with disgust.'

His brief fire was doused at this and he hung his head in despair.

'But the girls?' he mumbled. 'I—'

'We'll live with Maizie in the Village, permanently – we love it there and she's happy with the arrangement. You can come down to see the children whenever you wish, but give me warning when you'll visit so I can make sure I'm not around.'

He nodded dumbly, inwardly writhing with remorse.

'As far as the Council is concerned,' she continued, 'Stonewylde doesn't need you to run it, despite your attempts to take over in the past. In fact you don't need to be part of it at all. Legally we're now a Board, and Christopher will ensure the Trustees run the estate properly. Edward's in charge of the farms, my mother leads the schools, I'm organising the new healing centre, and Leveret and Rufus' money will be channelled into repairing and building anything that can't be covered by my grandparents' endowments. I don't think there's really much of a role for you any more, is there? So you can give up your place on the Council and then I won't have to engage with you at all.'

'Sylvie! How can you do this?'

'Quite easily, actually. You're still the magus of course, and from now on I bow out of all the ceremonies. Leveret's the Shaman and the Wise Woman, and she can help you with the rituals. I won't make a fool of myself by standing next to you in costume for everyone to laugh at. I'm no longer your wife or your partner, Yul. I'll never forget what you've done and I'll *never* forgive you for it.'

At this, Yul slumped down onto the seat again and began to cry into his hands. His dark curls fell over his face and his shoulders heaved as raw sobs engulfed him.

'Please, Sylvie, I beg you! Please don't—'

But she turned away and headed for the door. She felt so dead inside that even the sight of his distress didn't touch her. As she yanked open the door, wanting only to escape his company, the baby leapt again in her womb as if in protest at her anger. But Sylvie marched down the wide staircase, grabbed her coat and hat from the cloakroom off the entrance hall, and set off down to the Village which she now thought of as home. As she hurried back to the comfort of Maizie's warm cottage, tears streamed down her face. But surely, she thought fiercely, brushing them away, they were only from the biting wind and nothing to do with the final break-up of her once beautiful marriage.

29

Rufus knocked on the door of the cottage, glad to see that today there was smoke coming from the chimney. Inside he found Yul sitting in the old rocking chair by the fire gazing into the flames. The crow with the white tail-feather roosted peacefully up in the rafters, head tucked under its wing. Yul looked up blearily at the boy who'd brought cold air and the real world into his cocoon of isolation.

'More provisions from Marigold,' Rufus said quietly, putting some of the food into the little meat-safe at the coldest end of the cottage. He noticed the remains of last night's meal still lying on the table; judging by the mess, the crow had pecked at most of it. An empty mead bottle also sat on the table, and in the corner the bedclothes were messed up in a heap on the hard settle. It was warm and reasonably cosy, but Yul wasn't looking too good.

Rufus refilled the water jar at the spring and scraped the remains of yesterday's food onto the hard ground outside for the foxes. He checked the firewood situation and saw it was getting low. Back in the flickering warmth of the cottage, he put the kettle on to boil.

'Did you bring more mead?' asked Yul, rousing himself from his reverie.

'No, sorry. I didn't think you'd need any more yet.'

'Well, I do. Make sure you bring more tomorrow, would you?'

Rufus nodded, making them both a mug of herbal tea. He

pulled the other chair over to the hearth and sat down next to Yul. Their legs, stretched out before them, were almost identical in length and this gave Rufus a burst of pleasure. He'd be fourteen at Imbolc and was proud to be nearly as tall as his brother already.

'Leveret asks whether you'll come to her Story Web tomorrow, for Yule?'

Yul shook his head, his face impassive. He hadn't shaved for a couple of days and was starting to look unkempt.

'Tell her I'm sorry but I just can't face everyone at the moment. It was bad enough at the Winter Solstice ceremony.'

Rufus nodded again, thinking back to the sadness of the proceedings in the Stone Circle. Yul had stood on the Altar Stone alone, as he usually did for the ceremony, wearing the sumptuous Solstice robes. But Clip, Martin and Sylvie were all missing from the ritual, which Yul had deliberately cut short by leaving out many of the chants. Others had helped with the mead and cakes but had somehow lacked Martin's solemnity. Sylvie had stood at the back with Maizie and the girls, and folk had nodded at this, understanding her reasons. Leveret had stayed in the tower on Hazel's insistence; she was having one of her bad days when her head hurt and limbs shook.

Rufus had felt so sorry for Yul, knowing he was doing his best whilst his heart was breaking. The boy vowed that at the next festival he'd help Yul, and later when he'd told Leveret about it all, she'd promised she would too. Afterwards, Yul hadn't bothered going back to the Great Barn for the celebrations. Instead he'd stumbled up to Mother Heggy's cottage, having found solace here at the Hunter's Moon. Somehow, Leveret had known where he was and when Rufus called on her in the tower, she'd told him to care for his brother while he needed it, for nobody else could do it. While filled with concern for Yul, Rufus couldn't believe his luck at being given such an opportunity.

The Barn, full of Yule decorations, was magical. Candles twinkled, evergreens hung from every point, and mistletoe was bunched in profusion. Everyone had gathered for the lighting of the Yule log, which always took place a few days after the Solstice at Yule. Leveret had arranged to do a Story Web after the log was lit. She was nervous and didn't really feel ready for such a demanding task, but she knew that something was needed to bring the folk back together again. Seven weeks on from Samhain, everyone was still in shock from the tragic events and their awful consequences. Folk were bemused by talk of the healing centre, and with Rowan, Faun and Swift having left, Stonewylde felt in turmoil. Everyone was confused and in need of solidarity.

Leveret had Magpie to assist her. She'd decided to keep the event very simple with no theatricals, and wasn't really sure what would happen. The folk gathered early and the place was packed; almost everyone in the community who was able to come did so, wanting to show their support for the young girl who'd been so cruelly robbed of her eyesight. Leveret wore a simple fine woollen robe of dark green, as befitted the festival. Her hair hadn't been cut since last Imbolc when she'd moved out of Maizie's cottage, and fell right down her back in a wild tumble of dark curls. On the stage was a small fire-cauldron to provide some aromatic smoke, and, unexpectedly, the carved chair from the Galleried Hall, with the boars' head arms. Nobody admitted to bringing this down, but there it was and it seemed fitting as the Shaman's chair.

When all was quiet, Leveret walked through the channel in the crowd, flanked by Magpie who carried the basket, and Shadow. She sat down in the ancient chair and, as she settled and calmed her wildly-beating heart, she was enveloped by something strange emanating from the wood itself. She knew, instinctively, that it was yew and so right for the occasion – the tree of rebirth and regeneration. In the deep silence, with all eyes upon them, Magpie carefully put Hare onto her lap. He then took up the hare headdress, made so lovingly by Clip, and placed it on her head. Leveret hadn't worn this since the time on Snake Stone; for a moment, she was back there with the brilliant white moon blazing down, her clothes lying at her feet and the knowledge in her heart that she'd embrace the Dark Angel rather than submit to Jay's intent.

Magpie threw a handful of herbs onto the fire and then moved out of sight. The lights were low and a single soft spotlight shone down on Leveret. She was once more the Hare Woman of Stonewylde as she sat straight-backed and rock-still in the aromatic smoke that swirled around her. Shadow lay at her feet and all eyes were fixed on this strange girl. Everyone wondered what story she'd tell them tonight, at Yule, when Herne the Hunter was loose in the forest and the sun had passed its lowest point at the Solstice.

'Folk of Stonewylde, gather round,' she began, her sightless eyes scanning the crowds. Everyone shivered, for it was as if she could see each one of them, and see not only their Yule finery and excited cheeks, but inside their hearts as well. Every person sat up a little straighter and stared a little more intently at the Hare Woman of Stonewylde as she began, slowly, to weave her story of the myths of midwinter magic.

She spoke of the hunt and the chase, the endless and ancient quest for survival in the face of cold and hunger. She spoke of tribes and firelight, caves and magic, of totem animals and shamanic powers. She told her people how it felt to be safe and warm inside whilst wolves howled in the snowstorm outside. She spoke of blood ties, of the bonds and loyalties of the tribe and how the folk of Stonewylde had stayed together, cared for one another and thereby become strong. She described the beautiful and abundant land around them with fresh spring water flowing into a river, clay and reeds for brick, pots and thatch, stone for cutting and woodland aplenty for firewood and building. She painted the picture of a land of fertile earth, sheltered from the harshest of weather by rolling hills and the soft sea breezes that blew in warm. It was a land where crops could grow and animals could thrive, so that the folk wanted for nothing. And when the tribe had grown so strong and healthy, with their elders living for many winters and becoming old and wise, and their babes surviving and growing into sturdy children who ate well and learned new skills – then the people wanted to give thanks to the Goddess who walked the sacred land. They wished to mark the places in their lands where they felt her magical energy the strongest.

A special place was built, and it took many winters and many generations of strong men before it was complete, although from the very first day when the ground had been cleared, it had become a sacred circle. Generations of Stonewylde folk had laboured and sweated and had given their best to build the circle and make it the most beautiful, most perfect arena in the entire land. They'd placed the great stones with precision, taking many measurements over the years to accurately mark the exact points in the turning wheel of the year where the sun would rise or set and where the moon would appear. When the great stones were finally in their proper places, they'd painted them with pictures and symbols to enhance their magic. They'd built hallowed fires inside the circle and had drummed and danced, feeling the spirals of magical, earth energy beneath their feet, knowing that truly they were blessed to live in such a place.

Others from weaker tribes Outside would visit Stonewylde bearing gifts, begging to be permitted to see the wondrous Stone Circle of legend, surrounded by sacred oak trees. They would creep in anticipation down the Long Walk leading to the magical arena, leaving their gifts on the stones that marked the way. They would enter the consecrated circle and gaze in awe and wonder at the massive painted stones, feel the immense throb of energy that danced in the place, and overwhelmed, they would fling themselves to the ground and embrace the living magic of the place.

Sometimes the Goddess of Stonewylde would bless them with her Green Magic, making them strong if they were in good health, and making them healthy if they were sick. She would fill them with her power, and so they became whole and healed. Slowly word spread throughout the lands and even across the seas, and people travelled to Stonewylde from far and wide. They came on pilgrimages to visit the sacred place that the folk had built. Some would also discover the magical places that weren't marked quite so obviously – the even older circle right here within the Village, and the hill where the hares loved to dance the moon spirals, the cave where the owls flew by and the wolves would howl. All these blessed places of Stonewylde became the stuff of legend, and folk journeyed far from other lands just to be there, to be permitted to stay a while and be healed.

Leveret paused here, and Magpie rose silently to take Hare from her lap. Leveret stood confidently, clasping Clip's ash staff in one hand and the leather collar around Shadow's neck in the other. The flickering firelight illuminated her golden-furred and long-eared headdress, and her dark green dress that flowed to the ground. Leveret began to step round the stage, and people forgot that she was blind because their Shaman had the true sight, and she would not falter or stumble. She paced the circle, the staff raised high and the grey dog by her side, and they felt her power and her wisdom.

'Folk of Stonewylde, we've seen difficult times. We've suffered losses and betrayals. But these things pass and we now move on to better, happier times. We are the same tribe as our ancestors. Their blood still flows in our veins. We are made of the same stuff as them, passed down through the ages to us today. We still hold the sacred land and the Goddess still walks here, blessing us with her bounty and her favour. We are honoured by her and now we must once again share her special magic with others who need it. We must once more let other folk who need to be healed come into our lands, be welcomed by our tribe, and be permitted to cast themselves on the sacred earth here and be made whole again.'

She stopped in the centre of the stage and raised the heavy staff towards the roof. Above her hung a great bough of mistletoe, moving slightly in the heat.

'Folk of Stonewylde – the shadows that blighted our land are receding. The darkness and evil I spoke of before, in this very place, are now gone. They were banished by our beloved Clip, by the sacrifice he made for us all at Samhain. The vipers have been cast out, and, as the returning sun grows stronger every day, so too will our community become strong again. Babies will be born, new people from other tribes will come amongst us and become our friends. They'll share their skills and bring us gifts, and in return we shall take them to our hearts and share with them the abundance that we have. Once more we will honour our elders and listen to their wisdom. We'll build up our Village again, make fine new dwellings for our young folk, and draw new water and new energy for our people. Our craftspeople will once more practise their skills with pride and joy and our farmers will be amazed at the fecundity of our herds and flocks, of our fields and crops. A golden age is coming to Stonewylde and we must embrace it with open arms!'

She paused and Magpie appeared, taking Clip's ash staff from her and handing her the Asklepian wand. She released Shadow, who sat back on his haunches and stared solemnly up at her. Leveret's fingers traced the carved snake on the rowan, feeling the magic of the ancient symbol of life and healing. Every person in the Great Barn was silent and spell-bound. She smiled, her sightless green gaze roaming the sea of faces and encompassing them all with a sweep of the wand.

'At Beltane this year, when the Green Man once more raises the sap and fertilises the White Maiden in the never-ending cycle of rebirth and growth, something magical will come to pass. When this comes about, my beloved tribe, you will know that your Shaman the Hare Woman has spoken true, and will always be here to guide you. Yule blessings to all! Bright blessings and be whole and healthy!'

Later, Maizie sat at the long table in the Barn in her element. It was the Yule feast, and the first one she'd actually sat down to enjoy since she was a girl. Rosie had taken on the organisational role, but unlike her mother, she proved adept at delegating, thus giving herself some time for enjoyment too. So it was that Maizie and many members of her brood sat down this evening together to enjoy the traditional feast, perhaps the greatest one of the whole year. The only ones missing were her eldest and her youngest.

Tom had arranged for a small pony and cart for Leveret's transport. She could and had walked the distance from the Hall to the Village and back, but she walked slowly and in the cold, this wasn't ideal. Tom wanted to drive her himself, so after her performance he took her back to the tower. She was exhausted by the Story Web and looked forward to curling up by the fire and relaxing in peace and quiet. She'd persuaded Magpie to stay in the Barn and have some fun, which he certainly deserved. Leveret had Hare in the basket on the seat beside her, whilst Shadow loped alongside the cart. She huddled in her cloak in the chill evening and longed for the warmth and security of the tower.

'I wish your brother could've heard you tonight,' Tom said. 'He'd have been proud o' you.'

'I wish he'd been there too,' said Leveret sadly.

'They say ... they say he's gone into his cave for a bit,' said Tom. 'Can't blame 'un really – these things can happen in marriage, but 'tis hard. He'll be back, no doubt about that. As you said in that story, all will be well again.'

Leveret sat silently in her darkness, knowing that despite her encouraging words that evening, it might not be quite so simple.

'Come and join us, do!' cried Maizie, scarlet-cheeked and a little merry from the sweet red-currant wine she so loved. 'Meadowsweet's a fine new member of our family, right enough!'

'I ain't a member quite yet,' said the girl in embarrassment, but everyone squeezed up on the bench to allow her in. She smiled at Gregory and Geoffrey and their goodwives and little ones, as well as Rosie, Robin and their two children. Sylvie sat at the table too, with Celandine and Bluebell who were enjoying being with their cousins and feeling glad to be part of such a large family. Sweyn and Gefrin had been talking, but as soon as Meadowsweet sat with them, Gefrin turned all his attention to her, his narrow face lighting up with pleasure.

'Ah, look at our Gefrin!' cooed Maizie, sitting opposite them. ''Tis plain he's in love.'

'More fool him,' muttered Sweyn morosely, his bull neck scarlet and the sweat dripping down his heavy face.

'Oh come on, you'll have a sweetheart afore you know it!' said Maizie. 'Then all o' my weanlings will be paired off.'

'Not all,' said Sweyn. 'Leveret isn't. And Yul's split up from his wife.'

'Sshh! They'll be back together by Imbolc, you mark my words! And as for our Leveret ... 'tis different for her. And she has Magpie, if you can count him. He certainly cares for her as much as any husband, that's for sure.'

Sweyn rolled his eyes at this.

'Come on, Mother – don't pretend you like him now. We all know how you've always felt about the half-wit. Just 'cos he's had a bath don't make him any brighter.'

Maizie frowned, not wanting any nastiness to spoil her happy evening. She turned her attention to Gefrin and Meadowsweet instead, ignoring Sweyn. He was only out of sorts because no girl was yet interested in him.

'What did you think of our Leveret's story tonight?' she asked, tucking into another helping of the delicious plum pudding topped with a good dollop of clotted cream. 'Weren't she truly stepping into dear old Clip's boots?'

'Aye,' said Meadowsweet happily. 'She's a magical girl and you must be so proud o' her. My father's glad she had Shadow, especially now she's blind.'

'That great dog is certainly a help,' agreed Maizie. 'Gefrin, you must've felt proud o' her tonight, boy?'

'Aye,' he nodded, keeping his eyes on his plate, his cheeks flushing in tell-tale uneasiness as Sweyn snorted beside him.

'Oh don't mind Gef!' laughed Meadowsweet, punching him playfully on the bicep. 'He just feels a mite ashamed o' the way he used to treat his little sister. He wishes he'd been a bit kinder to her now.'

465

'What do you mean by that?' said Maizie sharply. 'Why would he feel ashamed?'

'Oh, just the things he and Sweyn used to do. He told me all about it one night when he'd had a drop too much – about what they used to get up to. 'Twas cruel stuff, but our Gefrin's turned over a new leaf and he feels bad about it now.'

'No, you got that wrong, my girl,' said Maizie. 'Hasn't she, Gefrin? 'Tweren't nothing for him to feel bad about, Meadowsweet! Just a bit o' teasing and messing about like brothers do.'

'No, 'twere a lot more than that,' said Meadowsweet, not seeing Gefrin's expression of dismay. 'He and Sweyn tormented her all the time, he said, and never let up. When she were little they had a regular game to see how many times in one day they could make her cry. They hurt her a lot but they never left marks so's you'd find 'em out, and they was always thinking up new torments. Why, he told me they often used to force her into a poky little cupboard under the eaves and lock her inside in the darkness, poor little mite! And last year at Imbolc when she were the Bright Maiden, they even—'

'Meadowsweet!' cried Gefrin in desperation, his terrified glance taking in Maizie's expression across the table. 'You're talking a load o' swill! Why don't—'

'No I ain't!' she said crossly. 'Don't you start denying it now, Gefrin! You told me all about Imbolc and how you and Sweyn switched poor Leveret's breakfast cakes for them tainted ones from Old Violet, and how you—'

With a shriek of outrage Maizie jumped up, almost tipping over the long trestle table in her distress. Her glass went flying, the crimson liquid spilling in a shocking pool onto the white cloth. The blood had drained from her cheeks and her eyes blazed as she glared at her two youngest sons in round-mouthed horror. They both stared fixedly at their plates, but Maizie leant over the table and grabbed Sweyn's collar and a handful of Gefrin's hair, her face now flooded scarlet with rage. She could barely speak, yanking them hard from their seats as if they were small children rather than strapping young men.

'Outside!' she spat, her lips quivering. 'Outside, and I'll hear the truth from you both! Aye, and you too, Meadowsweet my girl. I want to hear everything!'

News came at the beginning of January of Miranda's mother's death, and she and Sylvie travelled up to London the day before the funeral. Christopher met them off their train and whisked them away to check into the smart hotel he'd booked for them. He was dining with them that evening but had to work in the afternoon, so they decided to do a little sight-seeing. On the way back from the art gallery, they paused at the entrance to a filthy tube station leading down into the bowels of the earth. Shaking their heads at the unwanted newspapers thrust at them, Miranda suddenly smiled.

'Let's not go back to the hotel this way,' she said. 'Come on, let's hop on the old bus we used to take and see the flat. If it's still there, of course.'

The crowded bus was dirty too and the seats smelled of filth and detritus. They sat together, mother and daughter, on the long, jolting ride, stifled by the stink of traffic, people and polluted air. Their eyes were assailed by buses, cars, hoardings, endless tatty shops and ugly buildings, and their ears rang with the relentless, jangling cacophony that was the London suburbs.

'I really can't bear it,' said Sylvie, huddled miserably in her seat, her senses shrivelling in despair. 'I'd forgotten how awful it all is – thank Goddess we moved to Stonewylde!'

At that moment, they recognised the desolate area and together peered out from the bus's dirty window. The old tower-block was still standing, now even more dilapidated than ever. They saw the grimy balconies with their battered plastic shields, some hung with grey washing even in January, others crammed with bikes and rusty appliances. They saw the graffiti-sprayed entrance, the grey cement stairwell that probably still stank of urine, the sheer bleak ugliness of it. They got off the bus and stood at the kerbside staring in horror at the soulless place where they'd lived for so many years. Litter blew across the expanse of dirty grass and dog mess; they gazed in disbelief at the alien wasteland that had once been their home.

'I can't imagine ...' said Sylvie, fighting the tears, 'I can't imagine how it felt, to bring up a child in such a place. As a mother I now understand that need to protect and nurture and make everything as special as you can ... how *appalling* it must've been for you to have no options, no chance of anything better for me despite your very best efforts. Mum – you were wonderful. Because I never, ever felt ...'

She stopped, and Miranda took her tall, beautiful daughter in her arms and held her tight.

'I can't tell you how very proud I am of you,' she whispered. 'My darling Sylvie, you're the best achievement I could ever have dreamt of.'

The funeral was large and grand, and Miranda was anxious not to be noticed by anyone. She concealed her deep auburn hair under an encompassing head-scarf, hid behind dark glasses like a celebrity and kept a very low profile. Nobody knew anything about Sylvie so wouldn't have recognised her. Miranda and Sylvie mouthed amens at the prayers and sang a few words to some of the scarcely remembered hymns. As her mother was committed to the earth, Miranda shed a few bitter tears for the woman she'd never really known, and the sadness of lost opportunities. She couldn't help but make a comparison between this rather sterile rite and Clip's recent heart-breaking funeral. She was glad when it was all over and they could escape to their hotel, avoiding the large reception where her parents' friends and acquaintances were heading in droves.

Sylvie was returning to Stonewylde that evening, not wanting to leave the girls for too long with Yul absent. It wasn't fair on Maizie, who'd had rather an upset at Yule over Sweyn and Gefrin, and had been seriously out of sorts ever since. Sylvie gathered that finally Gefrin had come clean and admitted to drugging Leveret at Imbolc when she was the Bright Maiden.

When Sylvie had heard that she'd felt vindicated; she'd always thought that Leveret's behaviour that day had been out of character. Remembering the terrible row she'd had with Yul over it, she smiled grimly, knowing she'd been right all along.

Miranda was staying on in London another couple of days at Christopher's request. Apparently there were papers to be signed and personal effects to be gone through, but Sylvie knew there was more to it than that. She'd teased her mother gently about this new love-interest in her life and Miranda had surprised her by being neither defensive nor coy. She'd looked Sylvie in the eye and admitted that she found herself increasingly attracted to the kindly lawyer, who was only ten years older than her and about to take early retirement from the family law firm.

'I really do like him,' she'd admitted. 'He's amusing, he's a gentleman and he makes me feel as if I'm someone special. But ... we're worlds apart and I can't see how there could be any future for us. I'm certainly not prepared to leave Stonewylde to be with him in London – not that he's asked me. And I can't see him retiring to Dorset. He has all sorts of plans apparently, none of which could involve being buried alive in the green hills of Wessex.'

'Well ... I don't know what to advise, but I would say he's been very good to us so far with all the help he's given, and he's certainly interested in our plans for the healing centre. I like him – there's a kindness about him, a twinkle in his eye – and the girls have taken to him as well. For what it's worth, Mum, you have my blessing.'

Sylvie hadn't booked her train and didn't want to leave too late. She said goodbye to her mother in the hotel suite, wishing her a lovely evening with Christopher, and carried her small overnight bag down to the lobby. The lift was smooth and perfumed and as she crossed the thickly carpeted floor heading for the revolving doors, Sylvie reflected on the difference between this luxurious experience of London and the one she and Miranda had endured all those years ago.

Just as the glass carousel ejected her onto the steps of the hotel and the liveried doorman stepped forward to take her bag and put her into a taxi, she came face to face with a tall, heavily-built blond man dashing up the monogrammed steps. He grabbed her arm and cried, 'Sylvie!' and she stared at him in disbelief, shaking off his hand.

'Madam?' asked the doorman. 'A taxi? Or ...'

'No, she doesn't want a taxi, thank you!' said Buzz. 'Sylvie, I—'

'Oh no you don't!' she cried. 'How dare you? I'm going home—'

He smiled and held up his hands disarmingly.

'I'm sorry – let me rephrase that. I've just learnt that you're here. I wanted to pop over and have tea with you and apologise for my intrusion last autumn. I also wanted to let you know how Swift's getting on. Please, Sylvie, I promise to be on my best behaviour, so do spare me fifteen minutes of your time. We can nip in here to the hotel's tea-room if you like. Please?'

More because she wanted to hear about Swift than anything else, Sylvie went back through the door again and, within minutes, she and Buzz were sitting in the elegant restaurant waiting for their pot of Lady Grey. He smiled at her quite charmingly.

'Thank you for agreeing to this. I'm sorry – I dashed over as soon as I read the obituary for your grandmother and saw the funeral was today. I hadn't realised you'd actually be leaving the same day. I very nearly missed you altogether.'

'How did you know where we were staying?'

He grinned sheepishly, his pale blue eyes begging indulgence.

'I got one of my office girls to ring the lawyer's office. You know how girls will gossip ...'

Sylvie scowled at this, ignoring his attempts to charm her and disliking him more than ever.

'Since Martin's death, it's been impossible to find out anything,' he admitted.

'So it was Martin who was your mole all along,' she said slowly. 'When—'

'Right from the very start, when I was sent away aged sixteen,'

470

he said. 'We always kept in touch on the phone and he'd tell me all the snippets of gossip. That's how I knew about your illness and being sent to the nursing home. Once Martin learnt how to use the Internet, we'd e-mail. And then Swift got involved too. He's a bright lad, that one. He's settled into his new college and he's a wonderful house-guest. My wife's very taken with him and the children love him. And he seems to be dealing with his bereavement well. He'll go far, I'm sure, but he's done with Stonewylde. He sees his future out here in the real world.'

'I'm glad for him,' said Sylvie. 'Please send him my best wishes. I'm sure he'll make a success of his life and it's good to know you're taking care of him. Do thank your wife from me, and all of us at Stonewylde.'

The tea arrived and Sylvie poured, feeling Buzz's eyes watching her like a hawk.

'I'm sorry to hear of all those horrible deaths – Jay, Martin and Clip, and Leveret's accident too,' he said. 'I'm particularly sorry, of course, for the loss of your father.'

Sylvie nodded and sipped her tea, wanting now only to be finished and off to the station. She couldn't believe she'd agreed to this; Buzz could have told her about Swift on the hotel steps.

'Sylvie, I realised something when I visited back in the autumn and it all went so horribly wrong … I made a mistake and I won't ever return to Stonewylde again. It's not the golden place I remember and I simply don't belong there any more.'

'*What?*'

'I know,' he smiled ruefully. 'I never thought I'd be saying that either. But it's true. I remember Stonewylde as a rich man's paradise. Magus was more than a father – he was a god to me. Since he sent me away all those years ago, I've spent my adult life dreaming and scheming about how I'd return one day, as the glorious new magus …'

He stopped and looked down at his hands, then up again to meet her eye.

'I think you've all actually done a pretty good job of running the place,' he said. 'And your Internet business – before the crash – was destined to be a success.'

'Was that—' she gasped.

''Fraid so! Martin constantly fed me information and allowed me access into the system. It wasn't hard to infect it with that bespoke virus. Poor Harold didn't know what he was letting in to the network. Harold's a good fellow, by the way – very loyal to Stonewylde in case you're wondering, and very bright for a bloody Villager!'

'I always thought Harold wasn't to blame,' mused Sylvie.

Buzz poured them both another cup and gazed around the smart room. Wealthy people sat making discreet conversation and indulging in that most civilised of pastimes, the taking of afternoon tea.

'What I really wanted to say to you, before you disappear again into the green depths of Stonewylde, is that I won't bother you any more, so don't worry about that. I realise I've messed things up between you and Yul with my remarks – deliberately, I admit – and also that Rainbow stuck the knife in too with that picture. She's a nasty bitch. She hadn't actually told any of us about what happened between her and Yul at the Summer Solstice. I guess she was angry about it, and—'

Sylvie felt her cheeks stinging at the mention of Rainbow and Yul, and the reference to the Solstice cut like a scalpel, as she hadn't known that snippet of information. But she stopped him there.

'Hold on – why was she angry? I don't understand.'

'Rainbow's a gorgeous woman and accustomed to men worshipping her, especially once they've had a taste of her. But she said that Yul used her simply as a means of venting his frustration and anger, and nothing more. He certainly didn't want her for herself and neither did he appreciate her charms. Afterwards he told her she disgusted him, which isn't the sort of post-coital conversation she's used to – it really infuriated her. She'd imagined that once she'd seduced him, they'd embark on a wild and passionate affair. But instead he threw her out of Stonewylde

472

and refused to allow her back. So she told us nothing about it – felt humiliated I guess.'

'So how do you know all this now?'

'When she heard I was planning a surprise visit in the autumn, she begged to be allowed to tag along too. Perhaps she wanted to exact some sort of revenge on Yul for treating her like that. She'd been pestering him to allow her back and he'd ignored her repeatedly. When we came to stay in the autumn, Rainbow and I had both hoped to remain at Stonewylde, obviously, but Clip put paid to that plan. She realised then that it was hopeless and we'd never be able to return. So she planted that picture out of spite, wanting to mess things up between you both. That's when she finally told me that she'd accomplished her mission to entrap Yul, but with only very limited success. Until then, none of us had known anything about it.'

'I see,' said Sylvie quietly. 'Well, leaving the drawing certainly was a spiteful thing to do.'

'I know, and I told her not to be a fool. As if he'd change his mind and want her after all! She is beautiful and bloody sexy too, but she's not a patch on you, Sylvie. Why on earth would Yul *ever* choose her over you? Who could settle for cheap fizz when they're accustomed to the finest champagne?'

'Buzz, please don't—'

'Don't worry, I won't come on strong. I can see what you and Yul have going together. I'd hoped all along that maybe it was just a teenage thing – that maybe your feelings for each other would've faded over the years. I'd thought maybe now I'd stand a chance of winning you. But as soon as I saw you together, I realised how wrong I'd been.'

Sylvie bit back her reply; the last thing she wanted was to give Buzz any encouragement.

'I do have a train to catch,' she said, 'but thank you for putting my mind at rest about any future attempts to return to Stonewylde. I'm glad you can see now that it's not the place for you.'

Buzz sighed and looked strangely deflated.

'Sylvie, if you ever change your mind about me ...'

She frowned at him and shook her head.

'I don't think so, Buzz. Let's leave it at that and part on polite and civilised terms, shall we?'

'But I'm still here, if you'd like to keep your options open. I may have given up on Stonewylde but I could never completely give up on you. With Leveret and Rufus' shares in the company, there'd be opportunities for you to legitimately visit London. And—'

She leant down to pick up her bag but Buzz placed his thick, warm hand over hers on the table. She stared at it.

'Sylvie, please don't go yet! I wanted—'

'Take your hand off me,' she said quietly.

'Oh, come on, Sylvie, I just—'

'TAKE YOUR HAND OFF ME!' she shouted in a piercing voice that brought the whole restaurant to abrupt, shocked silence.

Buzz flushed scarlet and his eyes darted around in embarrassment as he snatched his hand away. Calmly, as conversations slowly resumed and a waiter hurried over, Sylvie picked up her bag and gave him a tight smile.

'Good bye, Buzz. Bright blessings to you.'

Christopher ordered the wine and then sat back to admire the woman opposite him. Miranda had been out to buy some clothes, realising that her Stonewylde wear was inappropriate for a smart London restaurant. She looked very attractive in black velvet and chiffon, her deep red hair piled up with the silver at her temples only adding further elegance. She'd visited the hotel beauty salon to have her hair, nails and make-up done, and now felt like a young girl on a date, not a grandmother past her mid-forties. The wine was poured and Christopher raised his glass, his eyes drinking her in.

'Miranda, you're stunning,' he said, a small smile on his lips. 'The most beautiful woman in the room.'

Their first course arrived and they began to eat, discussing the events of the day and the large turnout at the funeral.

'Did you recognise anyone there?' he asked. 'You must have seen some of them before, when you were a girl.'

Miranda shook her head, savouring the smoked salmon and shrimp terrine and wafer thin bread. She loved the Stonewylde food but this was so refined compared to the hearty fare that Marigold provided.

'I never took much notice of any of them, either then or today,' she replied.

'There were several people present today who'd attended that charity ball,' he said quietly. She looked up into his wide-spaced, twinkly blue eyes that now seemed sad. 'The one where you came dressed as a fairy and were led off into the woods.'

'How—'

'I was there at the party too, Miranda,' he said. 'I wasn't sure if I should tell you, but it seems deceitful not to.'

She'd flushed but then turned pale. She took a sip of the expensive wine and stared at him.

'That's extraordinary!'

'I know. I remember it so clearly, although I must have been in my mid-twenties then. I was a newly-qualified lawyer and I went there with my father and grandfather who were both partners in the family law firm. They dragged me along saying I should attend this type of event for business contacts – we didn't have the term "networking" in those days – and I recall that I really didn't want to go. I thought I'd be bored silly.'

'What were you dressed as?' she asked incredulously.

'Believe it or not, a knight!' he chuckled. 'In plastic chain-mail with a great tabard and a ridiculous helmet. It was all they had left that fitted me in the fancy dress hire place. I remember seeing you standing there with your parents, looking so pretty in that pink fairy outfit. As children, my sisters had loved the Flower Fairies and you looked exactly like one of those, so fresh and delicate.'

'How bizarre,' she said, 'to think we almost met!'

'I actually spoke to Clip,' he said. 'We were both watching you, two young men amazed to discover such an unexpected jewel at such a dull middle-aged party, and I remarked on your beautiful hair. He said it was as red as the Harvest Moon, which would soon be rising. I've always remembered that because it seemed such a very odd thing to say.'

'Not for Clip, and not when you know Stonewylde!' Miranda laughed.

'Then we saw you leave your parents' side and go outside alone, onto the lawns. The chap in the feathered hawk mask said he was going to talk to you and I actually wished him good luck! My God, Miranda – if I'd only realised what he intended to do ...'

Miranda smiled up at the waiter as he took away her plate. She laid her hand on Christopher's where it rested on the table.

'He never intended to do anything,' she said softly, her eyes sad. 'Clip really wasn't like that. Magus yes, but not Clip. I can say this now that he's gone: he told me that he only made love – his words, not mine – once in his life, and it was on that night with me. He was just carried away by the sight of the Harvest Moon and the beauty and poetry of the moment. I remember his gentleness, his reverence ... And truthfully, much as it caused me many years of upset and hardship, I'd never wish it hadn't happened.'

Christopher gazed into her eyes and felt himself falling deeper and deeper.

'Well, I must say when I met him again this time round, Clip seemed like a decent and very wise chap.'

'He was – decent and wise sums him up perfectly. He gave me Sylvie, and consequently my whole life at Stonewylde, which then resulted in Rufus too. I'd never wish that away.'

'You haven't had an easy life, though. Now both your parents are deceased, I feel able to speak more freely, and I must say I've always been appalled at their treatment of you.'

Miranda stared into the candle-flame flickering between them.

'I can't say it didn't hurt. Bringing up Sylvie in such awful conditions – that was the worst thing. I always felt I was failing her, however hard I tried. When she was a girl, her allergies were terrible and she was so very sick. Her body reacted severely to so many things and more than once I was convinced she'd die. And then there was her behaviour at the full moon ... of course now we're at Stonewylde and I understand about moongaziness, it all makes sense.'

Christopher looked mildly embarrassed and she chuckled.

'I know, I know – that's how I felt at first. But really, it's as if Stonewylde was always calling to her, even as a child. She'd try to get out on the balcony of our flat at the full moon and I feared for her life. Once we were at Stonewylde and she discovered that great stone on the hill, everything fell into place. It was as if she'd finally found the place she belonged, the place that had always called to her.'

'But your son Rufus isn't like that?'

'No, he's practical and rather intellectual, as Magus was. Sylvie's like her father – mystical and gentle.' She took a sip of wine and shook her head. 'Honestly, it's the strangest thing you were at the ball too and it could have been you I met rather than Clip. Life is so peculiar, isn't it? I mean the twists and turns and how your destiny can hinge on one tiny thing.'

'Funnily enough that same night at the ball I met the woman I ended up marrying,' mused Christopher. 'She was dressed as a marionette of all things.'

'How strange! What happened? You've never really said ...'

'Not much to say. We met, similar backgrounds, liked each other, parental encouragement on both sides, conventional wedding, two children, expensive lifestyle, drifted apart, divorce.'

'How very tidy!'

'Well, perhaps not quite as bloodless as that, but it was all fairly amicable. The children are both grown up of course, though younger than Sylvie. She kept the house in the shires and I have the London flat.'

'And now you're about to retire? You don't seem old enough.'

The waiter bought their main course and Miranda closed her eyes in delight at the fragrant Thai curry and jasmine rice, something they never ate at Stonewylde.

'I can afford to go into semi-retirement at least,' he explained, 'and I'll keep my hand in at the family firm and oversee my daughter as she becomes a partner. But quality of life is what I really care about now, not climbing career ladders and making money. What I'd love is to live deep in the country, go walking every day and keep bees.'

'Really? You wouldn't get bored?'

'I also plan to write a crime thriller. I've always wanted to have a bash at that. But Miranda, without wishing to ... overstep the mark in any way, I'm keen to take my responsibilities as Administrator of the Board of Trustees at Stonewylde very seriously. It's a truly marvellous project, this healing centre, and I knew as soon as Clip told me of the plans that it was something I'd like to help with. So ... I wished to ask if you think there's any possibility of me retiring down to Stonewylde? Perhaps renting or buying a cottage in the grounds somewhere? I wouldn't want to tread on—'

'That's a wonderful idea!' said Miranda, her heart singing with sudden joy. 'You can use the library there – it's a good one – and we can walk together in the hills, and ... oh yes, I'm sure the Board will approve that, Christopher. I'd really *love* you to come to Stonewylde!'

'That's good,' he said, his eyes soft and very blue in the twinkling candlelight. Gently he took her hand and raised it to his lips. 'Because I rather think I've fallen for you, Miranda. You've abandoned the fairy wings I know, but for me, you'll always be the most beautiful girl in the room.'

30

As she stood in the queue at the Bakery, Mallow – for no obvious reason – snapped. She placed her basket on the floor and announced loudly that she was never setting foot inside Old Violet's cottage again. Those around her, wrapped up in thick coats and shawls against the bitter January wind that moaned outside, stared in amazement. The small woman, so like a field-mouse with her brown shawl, brown hair and brown eyes, began to scream quietly. Even in the midst of a breakdown in the Bakery, she was timid.

Hazel was called and Mallow was eventually sedated and put to bed in the hospital wing, where all manner of previous cruelties to her skinny little body were revealed. She needed rest and nurture more than anything, and permission, after the death of her tyrannical husband and the departure of her uncaring son, to start her life again. Nobody had quite appreciated what she'd endured visiting Old Violet twice a day, and she hadn't dared to end the visits even after Hunter's Moon when Martin died.

Maizie was asked to call on the dreaded cottage at the end of the lane and also visit Starling to see what could be done for the old woman. But Maizie really didn't feel able to cope, having suffered her own set-back since Meadowsweet's terrible revelation at Yule. Maizie's comfortable take on life had been redefined, and everything she'd held true about the unity of her family was shown to be a sham. The shock of this was exacerbated by her guilt, for it wasn't as if Leveret had kept quiet about it over the years. Since she'd learnt to talk, Leveret had tried to tell her mother of the abuse her brothers subjected her to on a daily basis. Maizie knew she was very firmly to blame for refusing to listen and turning a blind eye. And now, despite the girl's assurances of forgiveness, Maizie was in torment over her failure to protect her youngest child, whom she'd always loved so dearly.

So Sylvie offered to do the visits in Maizie's place, even though she was busy with Christopher and all the work taking place up at the Hall. A team specialising in the architectural refurbishment and renovation of old buildings was looking at ethical ways of bringing the place up to date and making it suitable for visitors who might not be mobile. But Sylvie knew she could spare an hour or so to do the calls and make a report, and she was keen to help poor Maizie who'd been so kind to her.

First she visited the cottage where Starling now lived with her new partner Cledwyn and his old mother. It wasn't a pleasant cottage – a far cry from Maizie's beautifully clean and welcoming place – and the sour smell that greeted her was matched by the sour face of the old woman. Although she'd only seen Alwyn a few times, and those many years ago, Sylvie immediately recognised this brawny lump of a woman as his mother. Her hair was white but still showed some signs of ginger, and her belligerent underbite and porcine face were unmistakeable. She was reluctant to let Sylvie in, clutching her shawl to her meaty bosom and glaring, but after a while Sylvie found herself seated in the cluttered parlour surrounded by heavy leather furniture and ugly wood carvings.

'Fancy getting a visit from the magus' goodwife herself!' she rasped. 'Not that any relation o' his is welcome here, not after what he done to my poor Alwyn. He never—'

'I'm sorry to hear that, but it was a long time ago and nothing to do with me. I've come to speak to Starling.'

'Our Starling's busy out the back, lazy sow that she is.'

'I'd like a word with her to see if she can help take care of Old Violet,' said Sylvie, fighting the urge to wrinkle her nose at the unpleasant smell of the place. She felt her skin crawling; the old cat who also glared so belligerently was probably infested with fleas.

'Starling!' bellowed the woman, making Sylvie jump. 'Get your arse in here now!'

When Starling appeared, Sylvie did a double take. Surely this wasn't the same squat and bellicose woman she'd last encountered at Imbolc, during Leveret's disgrace? The woman before her today was thin in a sagging sort of way, loose skin hanging in folds and her face a dreariness of lines and grime. Her long greasy hair had been shorn into an unstyled bob, as if someone had simply hacked around it with shears. Her eyes were dull and her hands sore, and even in this freezing weather her legs beneath the old skirt were bare, and mottled with chilblains and fleabites.

She stood there silent and awkward, refusing to meet Sylvie's eye.

'The magus' goodwife wants to know if you'll take care o' your old Auntie Violet,' said Cledwyn's mother. 'What do you say to that, girl?'

'I can't,' she mumbled. 'I live here now.'

'Speak up, girl! Stand up straight and speak clear!'

Starling straightened slightly and raised her face, meeting Sylvie's horrified gaze. Her nose was a little misshapen and one eye was puffy with old yellow bruising. She appeared to be missing most of her teeth too.

'I look after Cled and his ma,' she said, her voice hoarse.

'I see. But ... could Old Violet perhaps move in here? There's room I know, and that would free up her cottage. She'd still be part of—'

'Never!' cried the old woman, a fleck of spittle flying across the room. 'I ain't having that hag in my cottage! Let her rot for all we care, eh Starling?'

'Aye, let her rot,' echoed Starling dully.

At Old Violet's home, Sylvie was even more repulsed. The cottage itself wasn't too dirty, which was obviously down to Mallow's hard work, but the old woman was filthy and smelt like rotten fish. She was furious that Mallow hadn't called recently, and was cold and hungry. It was clear that she was incapable of looking after herself. The fire had gone out and there was no more wood, so Sylvie couldn't even build it up for her. There was no food in the place either and the old woman had soiled herself where she sat.

'You're cursed, you spawn o' Raven!' shrieked the crone, as she sensed Sylvie's pity. 'Your fly-blown father took my boy, my own Martin, and now they're all gone! All my dear ones taken from me, taken by the Dark Angel. Ain't one soul left to care for poor Old Violet.'

'I'm so sorry,' said Sylvie, avoiding mention of the Death Cap cakes that had been especially baked for Clip. 'I'll get you something to eat now and I'll arrange for you to be taken up to the Hall. You'll be warm and cared for there, and it'll—'

'I ain't going up the Hall!' cried Violet. She picked up the heavy stick propped against her chair and tried to hit Sylvie with it. She was so feeble and twisted that she could barely raise it from the ground, but the intent was there. Her eyes glowed in her whiskery, shrunken face as she looked daggers at Sylvie. 'You think your family's safe, don't you? Just you wait, you skinny white maggot! You'll be a-squirming afore I'm done. That babe in your belly, he'll never—'

'Don't you DARE curse my children, you evil witch!' cried Sylvie, clutching her hands protectively to her abdomen. 'You can insult me all you like but don't you dare threaten my family!'

'Oh aye, the worm turns now, don't it?' Old Violet cackled toothlessly, her eyes flashing malevolence. 'Think you're all set now, don't you? But that black-haired bastard husband will—'

'I'm going!' shouted Sylvie, putting her hands to her ears before she could hear any more. Old Violet terrified her and she wouldn't remain in such an evil place a moment longer, not with the precious new life inside her. 'They'll come down to get you today, whether you like it or not. There's nobody in the Village to care for you so you've no choice. Goodbye!'

She dashed out of the dark cottage almost in tears, the crone's mocking laughter in her ears.

'The taint's still there,' crooned the hag. She rocked gently in her chair, all alone but for her moonlit memories. 'Taint's still up there a-biding its time, and when the toad is gone, Old Violet's revenge will be sweet.'

Leveret was unable to travel any distance on foot because of the cold, but she was determined to address that in the spring. She'd practise walking with Shadow and her stick to all her favourite places: Mother Heggy's cottage, the Stone Circle, the Village and even the Dolmen and Hare Stone eventually, though the tracks to those places weren't so well defined. She was still learning to walk without the use of her eyes to guide her and it wasn't easy, but she could now move around the Hall reasonably well and was confident that when the growing season began, she'd manage the Kitchen Gardens fairly easily.

Magpie lived in the tower with her and she had many visitors each day, everyone contributing to her care. Even Gefrin had called, accompanied by Meadowsweet, and those words of apology he'd been unable to offer before now tumbled from his lips in a flood of self-recrimination and guilt. Sweyn apparently refused to come, but Leveret told Maizie that was fine. That the abuse had stopped was enough – she wasn't out to humiliate him and didn't want a forced apology.

'One day, Mother,' she said, her green eyes gazing faraway into the distance, 'Sweyn will have a little dark-haired daughter. He'll love her dearly and when he looks at her, he'll remember my childhood and his heart will be heavy. So don't force him to make amends because the time isn't yet right, and don't deny him your love either – he can't help how he is. It may take a few years but he'll be alright in the end.'

Maizie looked in complete awe at her blind daughter, blessed with such vision. And her heart was heavy too; for the hundredth time, she silently berated herself for the blighting of her girl's childhood.

The Wolf Moon of January was approaching, and Leveret felt she should honour it in the Stone Circle alone with Yul. He'd almost completely gone to ground in Mother Heggy's cottage and not many people had seen him since the Winter Solstice ceremony, when he'd entered the darkness of exile. Rufus continued to be his link with the community and the bond between the two brothers had grown strong.

The moon rise that night was early and Leveret was driven up to the Circle by Tom's son Fletch in the little pony and trap. She insisted that he drop her off where the avenue of stones began and go straight back to the Hall, as Yul would walk her home later. With her stick of blackthorn and faithful Shadow, she now carefully made her way up the Long Walk. That it was pitch black made no difference to Leveret, who only experienced light when she held Magpie's hand. She felt a moment's shiver of fear as she entered the prickling darkness of the Stone Circle. But, taking a deep breath, she pictured again that vision from the night of her Yule Story Web, when she'd seen just how the ancient folk had built and used the temple of megaliths. She was wrapped in many layers topped with her cloak, and even her feet were warm in their lined boots, but as she stepped across the iron-hard earth she felt the coldness of the January night on her cheeks.

As she slowly walked across it, Leveret knew that nobody else was here in the great arena. She sensed the massive stones standing sentinel all around her, watching the small person who'd come into their presence. She felt the spirals beneath her feet, a coiled labyrinth of energy, and imagined how it would be when the healing centre were open and folk from Outside could come here to draw on the magic. She reached the Altar Stone and stopped, turning around to lean against it. Shadow, always silent and always close, sat down and together they waited for Yul.

He was a long time coming and Leveret knew that the moon would soon be rising. What if he didn't come? Nobody would fetch her. But she had faith and tried to picture him hurrying along from Mother Heggy's cottage. In her mind, Yul was a tall and dark presence, deep and teeming with passion and life. She longed to be alone with him tonight, just the two of them together as they'd been when she was young. Yul had helped her when she'd struggled to make sense of her life after Clip's death; she hoped when the time came that she could help her brother similarly. However she understood that he needed this period of darkness now, just as some seeds need the coldness of winter to germinate. Yul was wild and he was of nature, and when the time was right he'd show green shoots and flourish again.

Leveret felt Shadow stiffen by her side and heard him give a low growl. She too could sense someone approaching – she couldn't hear or smell anyone, but she felt it very strongly. Then a voice called to her and she answered, and soon Yul had hurried across the Circle and hugged her tight, his cheeks icy but his breath warm.

'Sorry!' he breathed. 'I fell asleep and it was only the crow that woke me up. I wonder if we've missed it? There's thick cloud so I can't see.'

'No, we have a little while,' she said.

'Shall I light the fire?'

'Yes, let's get nice and warm.'

They hadn't seen each other for some weeks now, but Rufus had been a reliable go-between, and Leveret had requested that Yul bring fire. She'd brought some mead and cakes along with Mother Heggy's athame, and as Yul unpacked wood from his bag and deftly built a small fire near the Altar Stone, she unrolled a thick felt rug from her back-pack and laid out the things. She pulled on the hare headdress over her felt hat, becoming once more the Shaman. Soon they sat side by side on the rug, shoulders touching and backs against the long Altar Stone, as close to the crackling fire as possible. Leveret held the sacred dagger and Shadow lay close, nose on paws, watching Leveret unblinkingly. He didn't know Yul and was vigilant with everyone except Magpie, whom he loved almost as much as he loved Leveret.

'She's at the horizon,' Leveret said softly. 'As the Bright Lady rises, as the Wolf Moon of January comes into our sky, we think of our dear Clip. We think of his totem the silver wolf, and we imagine Stonewylde at a time when wolves roamed wild and free. We call on the spirit of wolf to join us tonight, to come into the Circle and be part of our Moon Fullness celebrations. We call on the spirit of Clip, now also roaming wild and free just as he always wanted, to come if he will and join us tonight. We call on our ancestors, if they will, to join us tonight.'

She paused and breathed deeply of the pure, cold air. She felt stirrings all around her, eddies of movement and wisps of sentience; the Stone Circle was alive and teeming with wild energy. Leveret pulled off a mitten and found Yul's bare hand, clutching it fiercely.

'Come with me, brother, to a land of myth and magic,' she whispered. 'Travel with me on my journey into other realms. See, my great black Raven awaits us and we must follow where he'll take us tonight, at the Wolf Moon. My brother, the only one in this wōrld to share my blood and my flesh, the only one who understands the darkness and the power. Now that we are bonded again, Stonewylde will grow strong and all will prosper. We share magical blood, from our ancestor Raven who had the stars dance and sparkle before her, and our father Solstice with his silver Hallfolk power and strength, and our mother Maizie with her Villager feet planted in sacred Stonewylde earth. While we lead Stonewylde together, there can be neither shadow nor blight. Come, my brother, come with me on the journey and we will meet with our ancestors tonight, at Wolf Moon.'

Much later on that night of the full moon, having escorted his little sister back to the tower, Yul slipped into the Hall to bathe and eat his fill of Marigold's larder, then returned to Mother Heggy's cottage. He wasn't yet ready to return to normality. Sylvie had rejected him and he loved her more than life itself; he simply couldn't function without her love. He wasn't needed anywhere at Stonewylde other than to perform the ceremonies, and as Imbolc was the festival of the female, Yul decided to remain where he was and leave them all to it. He was sure Leveret and Sylvie would manage the rituals without him.

Rufus was his saviour. The boy walked up to the cottage every day after school bringing food, drink, candles, firewood and occasionally clean clothes. He stayed a while to give Yul some company; his only other companionship was the white-tailed crow which pecked him if he fell asleep by the unguarded fire, and stole the food from his plate at every opportunity. Yul relished living as a recluse. He collected water from the spring, washing from a bowl and not shaving or changing his clothes often. Rufus bought him books of all description from the great library at Stonewylde, anything that caught his fancy, and Yul devoured them. He grew close to his younger brother, appreciating the boy's kindness and quiet sense of humour. When Rufus confided that his dearest wish in life – other than to be a doctor – was to ride with Yul, he promised one day not only to teach him but also to find him the perfect horse of his own. Together, Yul vowed, they'd ride out on Dragon's Back on their stallions with the wind in their manes and the rising sun in their eyes, just as Yul had dreamt of when he was a lad.

Rufus kept Yul up to date with all the Stonewylde news and he heard of the developments with the healing centre. The surveys were now complete and the reports being drawn up. The ancient boiler down in the basements was being replaced with an eco-efficient system that used a combination of natural energies, and work had already started on this. Rufus told Yul how Christopher had now moved down from London into Woodland Cottage and was very happy there. He was sure his mother was walking with Christopher – she spent a lot of time with him and was always brushing her hair and putting make-up on her eyelashes, and Rufus was happy about this. He loved to hear her laugh and sing, and it also meant that he was free to spend more time in the tower with Leveret and Magpie, or down in the Village with Maizie, Sylvie and the girls. From being a lonely single child living with his mother, he'd now gained an extended family that welcomed him to their hearths.

He continued to chop wood and draw water for Maizie, although she'd found another youngster to help as well, as Rufus now had so many responsibilities. Yul always listened very carefully to news of his wife and daughters and wished that Rufus noticed more of what was going on. There was some secret about Sylvie, Rufus said, because often she'd stop talking with Miranda or Maizie when he walked in. Yul wanted to know more about this but Rufus shrugged with a grin; women's stuff really didn't interest him. Apparently Sylvie was always busy at the Hall with her work for the healing centre, and they'd decided to use the grand apartments at the front of the Hall for the visitors' accommodation. There was talk of a lift being put in, and all the bedrooms and bathrooms along that corridor were being redesigned. Rufus said it was weird having Outsiders all over the place, although Christopher made sure lots of Stonewylde folk were involved with the work, and all materials wherever possible were sourced from Stonewylde.

Celandine was practising her special dance for Imbolc and would be wearing a beautiful new dress that Maizie was sewing for her. Miranda had bought her some new ballet shoes from the Outside World, and she and Christopher were soon taking Celandine to London to the Royal Ballet to see ... Rufus couldn't remember what. Bluebell was still writing her book about the hares, and Magpie had done lots of drawings for it. Christopher had promised to get it properly printed for them as he thought it was really good, and his friend who had an art gallery in Cornwall had agreed to arrange an exhibition of Magpie's best work in the summer. Apparently the prints of his that David had put on sale had attracted a lot of interest and had sold out immediately, bringing in quite a bit of money.

The doctor who'd taken such care of Leveret in the Outside World hospital had been visiting to check on her eyes and see if there were any signs of change to her optic nerve. Rufus was very much in awe of Dr Malik, as they all called him, although Malik was his first name. He had become Hazel's friend and they saw each other most weeks which suited Rufus fine. He'd mentioned his career ambitions and now the doctor always spoke to him, telling him about new cases and recommending websites and books. He was a good man, according to Rufus, and interested in helping with the healing centre when it was up and running, as Hazel couldn't manage it all.

Nasty Old Violet had been moved up to the Hall now, Rufus told Yul, which was the thing that most Stonewylders were gossiping about. She'd had to be heavily sedated and restrained, and even then she'd shrieked and cursed and attacked people, so they'd driven her up in a car rather than risk frightening a horse. Rufus said she was actually a very scary old woman and he kept well away since the time she'd spotted his red hair and launched into a vicious tirade against him. Everybody feared her, and Rufus had heard Dr Malik and Hazel discussing her medication and how best to "make her comfortable". Rufus explained to Yul that this meant how to keep her quiet so she didn't upset all the other old folk and the people who cared for them.

Imbolc came and went and Yul continued his lonely existence, reading voraciously and living vicariously. Rufus had stubbornly refused to bring him mead since that first night, and after a while Yul was glad of this; he recognised his own weaknesses and knew he could have sunk into drunken oblivion up here alone. As February turned to March and the daylight was brighter and lasted longer, Yul began to feel a change not only in the land-scape and wildlife all around, but in himself as well. He heard of the birth of Dawn and David's baby girl, whom Rufus informed him was called Beith.

'She's so sweet,' Rufus said enthusiastically, 'and so small. Hazel delivered her but she let Leveret help, because Dawn and David wanted the Wise Woman there as well as the doctor. Leveret told me all about it, and I'm so glad Hazel didn't ask me to assist!'

Beith, Rufus explained, was Druid for birch and meant "new

beginning", and as Rufus spoke, Yul started for the first time to think of new beginnings for himself.

On his next visit Rufus said that Leveret wanted to visit very soon. Yul realised he'd better clean up the cottage, which he knew Clip had had renovated especially for her. He spent the next day sweeping, dusting and scrubbing, and Rufus brought her up the following morning. It was a strange sight to see Leveret slowly climbing the hill, her blackthorn stick feeling the ground in front of her, and Shadow close by her side constantly nudging her onto the path. Rufus was right behind, laden as ever with a great bag of things for his brother. It occurred to Yul how very lucky he was to have this young pair of siblings who both cared for him so much.

'It's the Spring Equinox in a couple of days, Yul,' said Leveret, and he was amazed at the change in her, not having seen her since the Wolf Moon. She spoke with authority and was so calm and assured. There was a deep kindness and a new maturity about her, and she seemed to have adjusted well to her lack of sight. 'I need to have the use of this cottage again and you need to get back to where you belong. You got away with it at Imbolc, but you must lead the Equinox ceremonies. I'll be there by your side to assist. Did you realise I'm now an adult? You missed my Rite of Adulthood at Imbolc, but it was a lovely ceremony and my robes that Mother made are beautiful … apparently. Look, here's my pendant.'

She showed him the gleaming disc around her neck depicting the Huntress' Bow of Imbolc on one side and her totem, the raven, on the other. Yul stared at it and then at her face, uncharacteristically pale from being indoors all winter. Her eyes were as green and sparkling as ever; he found it hard to believe she couldn't see. Her hair was very long now and her teeth so sharp and white, and as she sat in the rocking chair, he suddenly remembered her thus as a little girl of six years old, when she'd solemnly declared that one day she'd be the Wise Woman of Stonewylde. Where had those years gone? She was now sixteen and he was thirty. Even now time was passing rapidly. He realised then that he'd spent almost three months up here in Mother Heggy's cottage, hiding away in his cave nursing his wounds. Wounds which, he discovered, appeared to have healed a little, for he no longer felt quite so desperate and raw.

'It's lovely, Leveret. I'm sorry I missed your ceremony.'

'That's alright – I understand. But it's time for you to come back now. Your little girls have missed you so much, and Sylvie needs you too.'

'I don't think so,' he said quietly, but Leveret chuckled.

'It's the Moon Fullness on the eve of the Equinox. Why don't you go up to Hare Stone for that? I'm pretty sure she'll be there alone – you both need to sort things out. You can't hide away forever and I think you'll find that she's more accepting now, and perhaps even ready to forgive you.'

'Really? Did she —'

'I'm not saying any more – it's up to you now, Yul. Find her at the Moon Fullness when you can be alone together, not in public with everyone watching. She has a surprise for you. But Yul, for Goddess' sake, come to the Hall and have a bath and shave first – from what Rufus has told me, you look like a wild and woolly hermit!'

Two days later on the afternoon of the Storm Moon, the day before he had to return to the community to conduct the Spring Equinox ceremony in the Stone Circle, Yul left Mother Heggy's cottage to slip down to the Hall. Anxious not to bump into anyone in his current state, Yul had pre-arranged with Rufus to nip up the back stairs to his little brother's bedroom and use their bathroom in the Tudor wing for a much needed bath. Rufus had organised shaving things and some of Yul's clean clothes to be waiting in his bedroom, and assured Yul that he and Miranda would be in school, so the rooms would be empty.

As Yul crept up the wooden stairs and through the arched door, he remembered stealing up here to visit Sylvie all those years ago. He recalled the sight of her lying like a marble effigy on her bed, after Magus had taken his fill of her moon magic. He remembered holding her tight, leaving flowers for her, begging Miranda for forgiveness after the episode in the woods when he'd held her captive in a tree cage ... all the memories flooded back. Yul sank to the narrow single bed that had once been Sylvie's and was now their brother's, and he wept.

He sat there for a long time, all his guilt and hurt and bewilderment flooding out with the hot, bitter tears. Then, when the pain had been washed away, he ran himself a bath and shaved off the beard, although his hair was still long and wild. He lay for ages in the hot water, steaming with aromatic Stonewylde rosemary oil. When he finally emerged, Yul looked at his hollow-cheeked reflection in the mirror and made himself a promise. He would do anything to win Sylvie back. He'd beg her forgiveness, he'd promise her the earth, and somehow he'd make it all happen. Without her he just didn't want to carry on; he must make her see that. He knew that in the past, he'd always stepped back immediately when she'd rebuffed him. This evening he must look deeper and swallow his pride if at first she rejected him. He simply *had* to be reunited with her.

There were still a couple of hours until sunset when he must go up to Hare Stone to find Sylvie. Not wanting to bump into people in the Hall, Yul decided to pay Christopher a visit. He'd liked the man when they'd met in London, and was grateful for all he was doing for Stonewylde and also for Leveret and Rufus and the legal aspects of their inheritance. Slipping from Rufus' room down the back stairs again, he hurried unseen across the side lawn and onto the path that led towards Woodland Cottage, where Sylvie and Miranda had first lived when they came to Stonewylde all those years ago.

Sylvie put away the bulky file of students and their career advice details, still preferring this to a computerised system. She knew she was old-fashioned, and Harold had kindly offered to set it all up for her online, but she just liked this better. There was a meeting later on with the renovation team which she'd said she might attend, although Christopher had told her not to worry if she'd rather go back to the Village. Sylvie considered this but knew that if she went home now, she'd only get caught up with the girls coming out of Nursery and then Celandine would start pestering again about the Moon Fullness tonight. Sylvie wanted to go up to Hare Stone alone to dance for the Goddess and think things through. So she decided to stay here until sunset and then go straight up there, knowing Rufus would take Celandine onto the Village Green as arranged. He was such a lovely boy – how grateful she was for his and Maizie's support in recent months.

She sighed deeply, rubbing her swollen belly. She was now well over thirty weeks pregnant, but amazingly had so far succeeded in hiding it from the community. She found that this time round she'd filled out all over and her bump itself wasn't enormous, so with loose layers of clothes and helped by her height, she'd somehow managed to avoid detection. Only Miranda, Maizie, Leveret and Hazel knew – she didn't count Old Violet – although she realised that soon she'd have to tell others, especially her daughters, who thought their mother was getting rather fat.

Sylvie wasn't sure why she was so reluctant to tell everyone. Obviously she'd broken the strict two-children rule which might upset some, but now that the population at Stonewylde was stable again she thought it time they relaxed that restriction anyway. She guessed the main reason was because Yul didn't yet know, and somehow it seemed wrong for everyone to know before him. But he'd been gone now since the Winter Solstice and, although Sylvie knew he'd been living alone up in Mother Heggy's cottage since then, she couldn't bring herself to visit him. Gradually, over the months, her anger and hurt had cooled and she found that she missed him more than she liked to admit. But so far this hadn't been enough to prompt her to seek him out, and she understood that he'd taken her at her word and wouldn't approach her.

Her hand slipped into her pocket and found the tiny hare that he'd carved from a piece of yew all those years ago, by way of an apology. That was after Holly had forced him into kissing her on the Village Green. Sylvie smiled, thinking how much it had upset her then, but how very trivial it seemed now. And what about Rainbow? The little boy that she carried inside her, the beautiful result of that reunion on Lammas Eve under the yew, was infinitely more important than his one moment of stupidity with Rainbow. She knew from Buzz that it hadn't been a long deceitful affair spanning the spring and summer, but a lone and instantly-regretted moment of folly. Was she going to punish not only Yul and herself, but Celandine, Bluebell and this little boy forever? Or could she now forgive and maybe ... forget? Could Yul's single misjudged act of infidelity with Rainbow one day seem almost as unimportant as that silly kiss with Holly?

The night before she'd come across the long-forgotten golden hare tucked away in a little box, and it had seemed like a sign. In the same box she'd also found the corn knot Yul had made for her at Lammas when they were both fifteen. She'd sat there with the little favour in her palm, the tiny silver bow still intact but the slip of yew now brown and desiccated. She'd felt her tears well and then spill as she recalled how he'd given it to her so shyly, so hopefully, and asked her to accept his favour and be his sweetheart. She remembered telling him she was the happiest girl at Stonewylde to be favoured by him, and how disappointed she'd been to have to hide the token away instead of pinning it above her heart for all to see.

What had happened to that innocent, blazing love? Had it vanished, or had it simply changed into a more adult, slow-burning love that must accommodate children, work, daily life, pressure and even temptation? Her love was still there, beneath the layers of heartache and recrimination, and last night as Sylvie had returned the love-token to its box, she'd decided to carry the precious golden hare around as a reminder of Yul's past contrition and her past forgiveness.

It was almost time for the meeting. Sylvie remembered how at lunch, Miranda had been complaining that she didn't have her glasses. She hadn't been able to find them that morning and had struggled to teach without them; she was worried she'd be unable to see the architect's costings properly. She was sure she'd left them at Christopher's cottage the evening before, and the three of them had shared a joke about old age and failing eye-sight before they'd suddenly realised that poor Leveret was nearby. Mortified, they'd hung their heads, and Sylvie had then promised to try and find the glasses before the meeting, as she had some free time that afternoon.

It was a lovely warm spring day, and although the trees were still mostly brown and leafless, the blackthorn was blossoming starburst-white and the fat sticky-buds on the horse-chestnuts were fit to burst. The weeping willows were the palest of lime-green, wafting their tresses like girls with new haircuts. Sylvie, wearing a loose pale blue dress and cardigan, and wrapped in her crocheted shawl, made her way from the Hall towards the path leading to Woodland Cottage. The birds were singing jubilantly, excited that spring had arrived and the days were getting longer. All around her they were pairing off, building nests, announcing their joy. Suddenly Sylvie felt an uplifting of her soul. The baby leapt too, giving a mighty kick; she rubbed her belly and told him to quieten down in there.

The woodland path was bordered with starry white wood anemones and brilliant yellow celandine, reminding her of when their first child had been born. She and Yul had been so very happy together then, so very excited as the new parents of such a darling little girl. At Imbolc this year, Celandine had been really disappointed that her father hadn't been there to see her special dance, and Sylvie had felt guilty because she knew why he'd stayed away. How happy the girls would be if they were all together again. Little Bluebell had been very quiet and serious lately and there was a sad chapter in her hare book which had made Sylvie cry, emotional as she was at the moment. Her fingers closed around the hare in her pocket as she made her way to the cottage.

Yul had arrived earlier and been disappointed that Christopher wasn't around. He realised he shouldn't have expected to find him in, as, from what Rufus had said, he was constantly busy coordinating all the new plans, improvements and building work. It seemed Christopher was a great asset to Stonewylde and nobody else could have organised the regeneration of the Hall quite so efficiently. Yul had had a quick look around the downstairs rooms of the cottage, which he hadn't visited for so long. After Sylvie and Miranda had moved out, it had been occupied for many years by an elderly couple. But the old man had recently passed on and his widow had moved up to the Hall, leaving it vacant. It was a lovely little place and Christopher was obviously very comfortable there. He'd made it cosy, bringing many books and personal possessions and Yul was glad he felt at home – it certainly seemed that he planned on staying a while.

Yul wondered about going up to Hare Stone now, but it was still early. Gazing out at the overgrown garden, Yul smiled to himself. That's what he'd do! He'd missed hard physical exercise for some time, as Skydancer had remained at the Hall. If Christopher were going to stay, he'd need to plant vegetables soon and tend the patch, and Yul could repay some of the lawyer's kindness by making a start now on the digging. Yul went outside, located the spade and hoe in the woodshed and set to work. Luckily he was wearing his old boots, but he could feel his clean shirt starting to stick to his skin. He didn't want to be dirty for Sylvie up at Hare Stone tonight, so he tugged off the shirt and hung it on a branch. He could have a quick wash in the cottage afterwards. Feeling much happier than he'd been for a very long time, he set to, driving the spade hard into the fertile earth and feeling the sun warm on his back.

Sylvie walked up the garden path under the pretty cherry blossom and recalled how it had fallen like confetti on her and Miranda when Magus had first brought them here fifteen years before. She recalled her emotions that day – excited but nervous, and brimming with a bubbling sense of disbelief at their good fortune. As she now let herself in at the front door, she stood savouring the peace of the place, the calm and the quaintness.

She remembered their first sight of this interior, coming straight from the cramped and ugly London flat. The dark, polished floorboards, handmade rugs, crooked white-washed walls – all had been so very alien and beautiful to them. Sylvie remembered too Miranda's shock at learning there was no electricity, bathroom or fitted kitchen.

She smiled to herself, and for a moment could almost hear Magus' deep voice saying how welcome they were to share everything at Stonewylde. Sylvie realised that this was the first time in ages that she'd thought of Magus fondly, not as an evil presence haunting her but as a strong man who'd changed their world with one act of kindness, and had probably saved her life too.

The breath caught in her throat at the thought of this. She crossed the sitting room to the dresser where she'd already spotted Miranda's glasses in their case, but her mind was still in the past. She recalled Magus' deep brown eyes, his lazy smile, his charm and warmth. For all his faults and all that had gone wrong, he'd been an amazing man blessed with boundless strength and energy; she knew that Yul had inherited all this from his father. She'd been so very happy that day when she'd first come here, and so very lucky too. She was still lucky and had far more than most people could ever dream of. She loved and was loved in return, she was healthy and strong, and she lived in the most beautiful place in the world, surrounded by people who made her life a joy. She had two adorable children with another one on the way, and ... she was married to a man like no other.

At that moment she looked out of the window into the back garden and there he was, her dark and secretive boy of fifteen years ago, digging the earth. His wild curls fell into his eyes and the sweat ran down his face as he plunged the spade deep into the waiting ground. The sinews in his arms strained, the muscles bulged, and his powerful torso rippled with the effort, glistening with sweat in the golden afternoon sunshine. He paused, one foot on the spade so his trousers pulled tight across his buttocks and thighs, and wiped his brow with the back of his hand leaving a smear of dirt. He looked up then and his deep smoky-grey eyes, slanted and long-lashed, met hers in one eternal, earth-stopping moment.

Sylvie's heart leapt and then she was outside, hurrying carefully down the brick path and he abandoned the spade and rushed towards her, his eyes ablaze and his arms open. They fell into each other's embrace as if they'd never known separation, as if the long months apart and all the difficulties between them had never been. They were both sobbing, trembling with emotion and passion, unable to say the words they wanted but knowing that it didn't matter anyway. Their hearts knew and never again would anything come between them.

Except ... Yul pulled back and looked at her in shock. Slowly he lifted the baggy cardigan that hung over her loose dress and his hand smoothed down the folds of material flat against the hard mound of her belly. He stared at it, open-mouthed, and then looked up into her eyes. She was radiant with joy as she saw disbelief, quickly followed by hope, flare in his eyes.

'Yes, Yul – he was conceived on Lammas Eve and—'

'At the Blue Moon?'

'That's right, and he's due at Beltane.'

He shook his head, unable to take in the news, his face suffused with happiness and tears coursing down his hot cheeks.

'If you agree, Yul, I'd like to call him Ioho – it's Celtic for Yew, the tree of regeneration.'

'And the place where he was conceived! Oh Sylvie, a magical son ...'

Yul took her again in a much gentler embrace this time, cradling her to his naked chest, his strong arms a ring of love and protection around this most magical and unique woman, the mother of his children, and his one, true love. His heart sang with wild and pure elation as the past torments crumbled into oblivion. Gazing up to the bright blue skies, he thanked the Goddess for giving him this chance to start again and make things right. He bent his dark head, his deep grey eyes burning with adoration, and kissed Sylvie deeply but tenderly. She felt his love and never-ending devotion and knew then that she need never, ever doubt him again.

'Well, my moongazy girl,' he laughed, his voice low and shaky with emotion, 'shall we go up to Hare Stone for some very gentle moondancing? But no leaving your shoes on the path this time!'

Sylvie smiled at him, brimming with love and tears, and recalling so very clearly that first moondance all those years ago. In her pocket, her fingers closed around the tiny carved hare and in that moment, she truly understood the interdependence of darkness and light.

31

Leveret lay on her back, the sun warming her eyelids, thinking of Clip. All around her the larks exalted spring, squealing their joy as they rose in a fluster of beating wings. Magpie too basked in the Spring Equinox sunshine as he sat with his back to Hare Stone gazing out over the landscape below. His eyes roamed, drinking in the beauty that he would transform into pure magic on a canvas, for he was alone in his gift of seeing the Goddess clearly as she lived and breathed in the landscape. The sun glinted on his bright butterscotch-gold hair and fair skin. Magpie had grown into a tall young man who walked with his head high and a ready smile on his handsome face. It was only when looking more deeply into his eyes, so brilliantly turquoise and flecked with gold, that something else was seen – a strange shifting of focus that was the key to Magpie's different reality, and also to his breathtaking talent. Some might call him simple; others called him genius. To Leveret, he was her very soul. They shared something more profound and timeless than conventional love. Since she had lost her sight, this bond had strengthened until they were as much in harmony as was possible for two people to be.

As she lay on the warm, slightly damp grass, Leveret's thoughts drifted from Clip back to the magnificent sunrise ceremony that morning. Yul had taken his rightful place on the Altar Stone to chant in the dawn, whilst the mad carousel of painted hares danced all around the stones in the great circle. Leveret had assisted him, wearing her new robes and the hare headdress, particularly appropriate for this of all festivals. With her Asklepian wand in hand and Hare at her heels, she too was now in her rightful place, beside her brother the magus. Rufus had nervously helped Sylvie serve the mead and cakes to the community. Although she couldn't see, Leveret felt the almost palpable happiness amongst folk in the sacred arena. Yul and Sylvie, the darkness and the brightness, were once again in harmony at this festival which celebrated the balance between the two. All was now right with the world.

Afterwards at the festive breakfast in the Great Barn, Yul had announced, to deafeningly enthusiastic cheers, both his return to the community and Sylvie's advanced pregnancy. It had felt more like a feast than a breakfast as the folk tucked into their crossed buns and hard-boiled eggs, and toasted the radiant couple with milk. Everyone was excited about the new baby and if there were any rumblings about this child being their third, these were quickly squashed by Sylvie's spontaneous announcement: couples were once again free to have larger families if they so wished. This brought even more thunderous applause, as the restriction had been unpopular in a community where children were seen as a celebration of life itself.

It was so noisy and boisterous in the Village that Leveret and Magpie had decided to spend the rest of the day at Hare Stone, and bring Hare for a special outing on her anniversary. Now she loped around nearby, cropping the turf, whilst Shadow bounded all over the hill in delight. He knew better than to disturb the other hares further down but enjoyed the freedom of the field and woodland below. Leveret savoured the sensation of heat on her eyelids, and her mind roamed as freely as Shadow roamed the hillside. Thinking of the happiness amongst the folk at the sunrise ceremony, she realised that Clip's sacrifice was beginning to bear fruit. Knowing that Sylvie and Yul had become reunited was the best news ever, and he'd have been so pleased about it.

She was delighted when, a little later in the lull after lunch, Yul and his family came slowly up the hill to join them. Rufus was there too, and Leveret thought back to that time in the Dining Hall when the shy boy – her half-brother, though they hadn't yet known it – had diffidently asked her to put in a good word for him with Yul. That made Leveret smile, as Rufus and Yul were now very close. It seemed that the shadows really had been banished, with Yul and Sylvie back together, the baby due soon, and everyone apparently happy. With Martin and Jay now in the Otherworld and Swift, Rowan and Faun gone to the Outside World, Gefrin a much kinder young man and Sweyn skulking around keeping his head down, Stonewylde was a different place. The only sadness was that Clip wasn't there to be part of it. Leveret felt his absence as strongly as the loss of her eyesight.

They all sat together on the short grass watching the girls run around on the hill, playing with Shadow. It was idyllic, an especially beautiful and warm Equinox. Sylvie sat propped against the great stone, her straw hat shielding her face, relieved that she could now relax and reveal her secret to the world after concealing it for so long. Yul stuck as close as possible, his eyes blazing love, his hand never far from hers. Neither could believe how elated and yet grounded they felt, like two halves of a puzzle that that been wrenched apart but were now slotted back together, as they should be. The air around them almost crackled with the force-field of their attraction.

After a while, they heard frantic barking further down the slope and Rufus and Magpie went off to investigate. The pair of them got on well, united in their desire to care for Leveret. Rufus accepted Magpie's strangeness and silence as entirely normal, and never found the one-way conversation awkward. Magpie, using sign language when necessary, was equally at ease with the younger boy and treated him as a friend.

Before long, Rufus came running back up the hill alone. Magpie and the children were nowhere in sight.

'I don't know what it is,' he panted, 'but Shadow's found something strange down there amongst the boulders.'

'What do you mean, strange?' asked Sylvie, jerking upright. 'Are the girls there? Is it safe?'

'Magpie's with them, don't worry,' said Rufus, his freckles disappearing into his hot, flushed skin. 'It's a kind of gap, like an entrance. Yul, do come and see what you think.'

A little reluctantly, Yul followed him downhill to the outcrop of rocks.

'Just you and me now, Leveret,' said Sylvie serenely. 'Isn't it lovely today, all of us together like this?'

'It's a dream come true,' agreed Leveret. 'I'm so happy you're reunited. I never understood it when I was younger, and to be honest I was horribly jealous, but you really are two halves of the same whole, aren't you?'

'Yes we are, and now it's hard to imagine why we stayed apart for so long. It all seems such an over-reaction. Not just the Rainbow incident, but before that, when I first moved down to the Village – a year ago today. I really can't see now why I wanted to get away from Yul. I can't imagine not wanting to be near him.'

'There was other stuff going on then,' said Leveret. 'Dark forces at work, and you and Yul were victims of that. But those shadows are banished now and the bright sunshine is blessing us all. Yul was obviously delighted to hear about the baby?'

'Oh yes,' sighed Sylvie, thinking of how he couldn't keep his hands off the bump. He'd tried to listen to the baby's heartbeat, placing his head on Sylvie's belly. He'd felt the movement as the baby twisted about, and had whispered a welcome to the son he'd never thought to have. 'And he loves the name Ioho! The little fellow's really squirming and kicking today – he didn't like me struggling up the hill. I don't suppose I'll be coming up here again much until he's born. There's only the Growing Moon in April and then it's Beltane. The Hare Moon's not till the middle of May this year and I'm sure he'll arrive before that. And Leveret, I'd really like you to be with me when it's my time – please?'

Leveret smiled at this, reaching out and groping for Sylvie, who quickly clasped her hand.

'If I can, I will. I'd love to help bring him into the world. I need to learn about delivering babies. Not being able to see means I'll never make a midwife alone, but I can certainly assist.'

'We'll have to time it just right then,' said Sylvie. 'I hope Yul's around and not out on the other side of Stonewylde when I go into labour. I'd like you both there when Hazel delivers the baby, and Maizie's keen to lend a hand if she can. She's so glad about Yul and me, and now the secret's out in the open she's told me she wants to make Ioho all sorts of new things. I've told her I'm happy to use baby clothes from the Village Store but somehow this little boy is extra special to her. And as for the girls . . .'

Leveret laughed.

'I bet they were excited to hear they'd soon be having a little brother.'

'Oh yes! Yul and I told them this morning, straight after the sunrise ceremony, before we told the folk at breakfast. We thought they should know first. They were beside themselves with excitement. This baby is going to be so loved.'

'He'll have all the love in the world,' said Leveret. 'And it sounds like they're coming back now.'

They all trooped up the steep slope and flung themselves down onto the grass. Shadow went straight to Leveret and flopped at her feet, giving her leg a quick lick. Hare was now lying in the shadow cast by the monolith and opened a bleary eye at their arrival.

'So, what was it?' asked Sylvie, feeling very drowsy in the heat. She was pleased to see her girls still wore their straw hats, and passed them a drink. 'I hope you two were sensible?'

'Of course, Mummy,' said Bluebell, snuggling happily against Sylvie and putting a hand on her mother's belly, which had become family property now that Ioho's existence was known. 'We had Magpie to look after us and he'd always make sure we were alright.'

'I think it may be the entrance to a chamber of some sort,' said Yul, settling on Sylvie's other side. 'There's a cleft between two of the boulders which was all stuffed up with earth and grass, but Shadow's been digging at it and actually, the gap's quite big.'

'Really? A chamber? Like a cave or something?' Leveret was fascinated.

'I'm not sure. We'd have to come back with tools and a torch,' said Yul. 'It looks natural, but it could perhaps be a chambered tomb.'

'But we mustn't go in there!' said Celandine, coaxing Hare onto her lap and stroking her gently. 'It's right where we found those adder skins, Auntie Leveret – remember? And you said there could be a nest?'

'A hibernaculum – yes, I remember the adder skins stuck on the thistles! A chambered tomb would be the perfect dry place to hibernate for winter.'

'If there is something ancient hidden down there inside the hill, it would explain why this stone is up here above, marking it. I've often wondered about that,' said Sylvie. 'So when you say a chambered tomb—'

'They're quite common,' said Yul. 'Rufus and I read about them recently, didn't we, Rufus? Nobody's sure if they were for burials or rituals, or maybe both. Often they're a natural cave in a hill that's been extended deeper, with stones placed around the entrance.'

'We shouldn't disturb it though,' said Rufus, 'if it really is a hollow hill.'

'A hollow hill?' said Bluebell in wonder. 'That sounds magic!'

'It is magic – I've read all about them. Some people call them faerie hills,' said Rufus, and Bluebell squeaked with joy.

'Do actual faeries live inside them? Oh Uncle Rufus, that is *so* wonderful! I've always had funny feelings about Hare Stone – remember, Mummy? I can write my next story about a hollow hill!'

'What about your hare story, darling?' asked Sylvie. 'I thought you were still writing that?'

'No ... I finished it at last. It was too sad and I had to make it end ... but now I'm happy again and I can start a whole new book!'

'You're such a clever girl, Blue,' said Yul proudly. 'Can I read your hare book now it's finished?'

'Of course, Father,' said Bluebell, climbing over Sylvie's legs to fling her arms around him and kiss his cheek. 'It's been waiting for you to come home to us and now you have! I missed you so much. Apart from baby Ioho, you coming back is the best, best thing in the whole world!'

Yul grinned as if he'd burst, but as they packed up their things a little later to go back down to the Village, he watched Celandine practising some elegant, long-legged leaps around the stone and felt a stab of sadness too. He'd lived apart from his daughters for a year now and had missed so much. As he helped Sylvie to her feet, steadying her as she swayed and planting a kiss on her slightly sun-burnt nose, Yul vowed that he'd never again be apart from any of them.

After the moongazing up here last night with Sylvie, he'd reluctantly returned to Mother Heggy's cottage to sleep fitfully, one last time, on the cramped settle. But tonight he was moving in with them all, back to his old cottage in the Village. It wasn't ideal, although Maizie seemed to think so, but he didn't care – if that's where they wanted to be, he'd fit in with their wishes. Maybe he was always born to be a Villager and should never have lived up in the grand Hall at all. He smiled to himself as he took Sylvie's hand and tucked it into the crook of his arm ready for the walk home; he was so looking forward to sleeping in the same bed as her, feeling her next to him all night long, waking up to her beautiful smile in the morning.

They walked back down the hill, Bluebell still very excited that it might be hollow and perhaps home to the little folk. As they reached the boulders, Sylvie remembered that time when she'd heard Magus' voice right here and had been so terrified. But Magus was gone for good, and she stopped to look into the dark space between two rocks. It was no more than a cleft and impossible to see how far back it went. She shivered suddenly

506

– there was something rather eerie about the black void leading into the hillside.

'Girls, you must never play around this area here,' she said. 'Because—'

'Never ever touch an adder!' chanted Bluebell. 'We know, Mummy!'

'I think it's disgusting!' said Celandine with a shudder, keeping well back. 'If there is a cave in there and it's full of tangled up snakes ... ugh! I'll have nightmares tonight I'm sure.'

Leveret could of course see nothing and gingerly reached out to examine the entrance. She snatched back her hand quickly; she'd known this place before, and started to see the strangest vision ... but today was bright and happy and she didn't want to spoil it with darkness. Magpie held on to Shadow, not letting him near the boulders at all, in case there were adders still hibernating inside. Then he clasped Leveret's hand and at once she couldn't help but see the dark cleft between the rocks, the enticing entrance to the Otherworld. And she knew then exactly what was inside the Hollow Hill and why the stone marked it above, on the summit.

It rained heavily for almost the whole of April, but everyone was delighted after the previous year's drought. The waiting earth gulped the water, parched and desperate, and the weather was mild. All month long the life-giving water poured from the skies, soft and warm, nurturing the land and causing the duck-pond on the Village Green to flood. It truly was the growing month, with the moisture and warmth encouraging every living thing to come out early. Yul resumed his father's April task and used the month to take stock. Stonewylde was transforming into a new place, a place of pilgrimage for the sick, but it also remained a self-sufficient, organic farming community. Yul realised that this was where he was most needed and he threw himself whole-heartedly into managing the estate. After his exiled months of physical idleness he felt the effects of the saddle as he travelled all over Stonewylde. True to his word,

507

he took Rufus along whenever possible and taught him to ride.

Work progressed inside the Hall overseen by Christopher, who was careful to allocate his deceased clients' funds wisely. He appointed Harold as project-manager which was just what the young man needed after his shame over Stonewylde.com. Harold was very good at this and all went smoothly. Martin would've been difficult and obstructive, hating the progress and changes; without his sour and negative presence, Harold found new self-confidence and proved himself adept at managing the day-to-day aspects of the enormous project. Cherry moaned in perpetual horror about the mess caused by the renovations, but Christopher did his best to charm her into acceptance by seeking her opinion on many issues. Marigold reluctantly agreed to a complete refurbishment for her ancient kitchens, on the understanding that gadgets were not required when there were so many pairs of hands available. Christopher had much to learn about the Stonewylde way and was forced on many occasions to modify his ideas, which he always did with good grace.

Sylvie completed her year's work giving careers advice to the students, and encouraged a large group of youngsters, soon to take their exams, to continue their education afterwards and study to become nurses and teachers. Both professions were needed in Stonewylde.

Many of the older folk decided to retire, having served the estate for most of their lives, and Old Greenbough and Tom were among these. There was a big reshuffle in the Village to organise accommodation and more of the elderly people were moved up to the Hall into their own wing. Here they were comfortably cared for and began to develop their own community, although Old Violet did her best to terrorise everyone at every opportunity.

A building programme was drawn up to provide more housing for young families, and everyone was encouraged to help build the cottages together, in the traditional way. There was a general air of positivity and a returning community spirit that filtered down even to the youngsters in school. Everyone started to pull together, determined to preserve the Stonewylde ethos in the face of so much change.

In Maizie's cottage, Yul and his family lived like true Villagers and had never been happier. Sylvie and Maizie re-negotiated the delicate balance between them, for the focus had shifted since Yul's return. He was now the man of the household, coming home every day after his stock-taking and work around the estate, to find an adoring wife, doting mother and excited daughters all waiting expectantly for him. Sylvie bloomed in a way not seen since her and Yul's early days together, before they went off to study in the Outside World and their subsequent handfasting. Despite her blonde hair, she'd become a traditional Villager right down to the old leather boots and wicker basket, and she loved every minute of it.

As her time approached, she bowed out of most of her duties at the Hall, knowing that the Board of Trustees were managing perfectly well without her. It would be at least six months and probably a full year until everything was ready to welcome the first patients to the healing centre, as the building works and upgrading of facilities required were extensive. Sylvie was excited at the prospect of her dream becoming reality, but for the immediate future all she really wanted was to focus on her husband and family. The baby inside grew rapidly and she accepted her restricted mobility with serenity. It was good to have Maizie there to run the household, enabling Sylvie to relax in the final stages of pregnancy and enjoy her husband's attentive devotion.

Yul had become a man she hadn't seen before. Her dark boy, eager and passionate, had never quite overcome his impetuosity and impatience. There'd always been an edge to him that demanded attention and insisted on having the upper hand. But now he'd lost the sharpness of immaturity and youthful arrogance, and become honed into something smooth and well-tempered, a man of gentleness and strength, humility and authority. No longer did he need to prove himself at every opportunity. He listened, he attended, he cared for not only his wife and little girls, but his wider family and the community around him. At the age of thirty he'd grown up, and Sylvie had never known such happiness and contentment. Life was so very sweet.

Beltane came and with it the Dark Moon, so the traditional gathering of women in the Barn didn't happen. Yul was a virile Green Man and Sylvie the beautiful May Queen, a role she really hadn't wanted. But she'd been persuaded to take it on one last time, as she'd be thirty this summer and perhaps too matronly after that. She was very heavily pregnant and the baby was due in about a week or so. She felt a little incongruous dressed in white, with a headdress of hawthorn-blossom and bluebells sitting on her long blonde hair. Yul kissed her doubts away and assured her that rather than a young girl on the cusp of womanhood, she was a radiant and true representation of blooming female fecundity.

The sun rose and Rufus up on the May Sister stone lit the Bel Fire. Yul received a dowsing of Green Magic such as he'd never before experienced, even in his wild youth. He felt himself lift slightly from the stone, his great wreath of oak leaves bristling with the energy that shot through him. Tears smudged the green paint as he thanked the Goddess for blessing him once again with her gift. Standing silently next to Leveret, Magpie watched and noted the very moving sight of the Green Man receiving the earth energy at Beltane sunrise. He planned to paint a companion to the moondance picture he'd done last year for Sylvie, which now hung on the massive staircase in the Hall for everyone to see and admire. He knew as he watched Yul that this was the perfect scene, and his differently-wired brain recorded every detail.

The Dance of the Staves, the Maidens' Maypole Dance and Naming of the Babies all took place in sunshine on the Village Green, for the heavy rains had ceased a couple of days before to give way to warmth and sunshine. When it came to Dawn's turn, she proudly handed little Beith over to Yul to announce her name. Sylvie gave Dawn a special hug as she presented her with Beith's Imbolc charm on a ribbon, marking the festival nearest to the baby's birth.

'I'm so happy for you, Dawn,' she whispered. 'Your little girl is all you'd ever dreamt of, isn't she?'

'Oh, she is! I'd never dared to hope for all of this and my life's complete. It's your turn next, Sylvie,' Dawn replied. 'Any day now!'

'The way I'm feeling at this moment, it could be today,' Sylvie laughed, for her back was really aching from the weight of her belly. After such a discreet start she'd grown enormous in the final weeks, and had now reached that stage where all she wanted was for the birth to be over and done with.

There were games all afternoon on the Green. Yul made Sylvie a little nest of rugs and cushions under a beech tree coming into leaf, so she could watch the proceedings in comfort. She looked lovely resting there in her white dress, silky hair falling around her bare shoulders like a bridal veil. Pregnancy suited her, filling out her hollows and sharpness and giving her a look of smooth ripeness. Magpie and Leveret came across the Green, Magpie taking her hand so Leveret too could enjoy the lovely image of Sylvie reclining under the beech tree.

Maizie came over to join them, finally feeling her old self again. She was so very happy to have her special boy back home in the bosom of the family and wanted nothing more than for Yul, Sylvie and all three children to remain with her in the cottage, where there was plenty of room for them all.

'You're ready to drop I reckon,' she said, running her hand wisely over Sylvie's rock hard belly. 'He's very still today and 'tis a sure sign he's gathering up his strength.'

'More like he just can't move any more,' laughed Sylvie. 'He's outgrown his accommodation.'

'What do you reckon, Leveret?' asked Maizie. 'Put your hand here and tell me what you think.'

She pulled Leveret's hand across and placed it on Sylvie's bump. Leveret's hand tingled and then she felt overwhelmed by the strange sensation of this child, this special one, making contact with her through Sylvie's stretched skin. She had a jolt of certainty that she and the little boy would be very close. He'd be such a huge part of her life – the child she could never have herself. He was a magus and would be great; he'd be loved by everyone and would bring joy and true prosperity to Stonewylde. *When the Green Man returns to Stonewylde, all will prosper* ... it was carved in yew in the Jack in the Green, and would be so. But before that ... Leveret snatched her hand away, not wanting to see.

'He seems to be doing fine in there,' she said, laughing shakily. 'He'll come when he's ready.'

He came at the sunset ceremony that evening in the Stone Circle. His father stood chanting on the Altar Stone as the great ball of fire slowly sank below the horizon. The folk of Stonewylde filled the Circle where the Bel Fire had burnt all day, where the laughing Green Men danced on the stones and the huge Lord of the Greenwood above the Altar gazed down. The drumbeats were loud and insistent, filling the arena with a great throbbing, and the May Queen's backache that had nagged and twinged all day suddenly became much, much sharper.

Sylvie stood near the Altar Stone next to Leveret, who was once more wearing her headdress and beautiful new robes. Drowned out by the massive noise of the drums, surrounded by the crush of people and shifting, pulsating energy, Sylvie gasped and then groaned. Her tiny sound was engulfed and nobody noticed as her eyes flashed wide-open in shock. She looked down and saw that her waters had broken, and liquid was pooling around her bare feet on the earth. The baby inside began to burrow his way out on a grinding, splitting wave of pain and again she groaned, long and loud, and clutched the Altar Stone for support. Down, down, he pushed and she pushed, just wanting out, riding the crescendo of pain. Beside her, the young Wise Woman somehow sensed it and took her arm, making her squat on the ground. Leveret knelt down on the earth beside her and felt between Sylvie's legs; she found the crown of the baby's head there already, on the threshold of birth.

'Oh Goddess, Sylvie, he's coming! HAZEL! Quick, Magpie! Get Hazel or Mother now this minute!' she shouted over the wild drumming.

Sylvie let out the cry, the primeval scream of the female giving birth, that same sound so unchanged throughout the ages and throughout the lands, and she pushed and pushed and he was coming, swimming, emerging, tunnelling, travelling and there! One huge final push and he was out and slippery and then another ache, and cramp, and twist, and push and there! – the afterbirth. Leveret all alone and blind had eased him, supported him, twisted him out and now she held him hot, greasy, slimy, bloody. Still wearing her hare headdress and laughing with joy, she held precious little Ioho as he took his first breath of Stonewylde air into his lungs. He yelled triumphantly across the great arena where all his folk were now standing, silent and rapt, the drums and dancing forgotten. Tenderly the Wise Woman presented him to Sylvie as she sat propped against the Altar Stone. She cradled him, bloody against her white dress, her silver-blonde hair falling onto his waxy body and veiling his folds of almost-purple flesh and night-black hair. She smiled at his loud, insistent bleats for attention: 'I'm here, I'm born, I'm arrived!'

Leveret delved in her robes and found Mother Heggy's sacred white-handled knife and, feeling along the length, gauging the distance carefully as Hazel had shown her, cut the cord so he was now of this world. Leveret raised her blind eyes to the skies, to the twilight where no moon would rise tonight for it was the Dark Moon. She called out into the awe-struck hush, thanking the Dark Goddess for this precious gift of new life, for Ioho of the Yew, this little boy born of the Green Man and the May Queen, the Magus and the Moongazy Maiden.

'Your Hare Woman has spoken true! I told you that at Beltane, when the Green Man raises the sap and fertilises the White Maiden in the never-ending cycle of rebirth and growth, something magical will come to pass! And behold – our own magical baby is come! He is here amongst us!'

As she cried out these words she felt it coming, sizzling around the hidden labyrinth, until it burst forth from the ground. The Green Magic enveloped Sylvie where she reclined, her white dress smeared and blotted with blood. She was doused with the green light; it raced through her and into Ioho and the new-born creature glowed with the bright energy. Sparks seemed to fly from him and he yelled in triumph, his tiny naked body rigid in a spasm of ecstasy. Then the green energy faded and there he was, an ordinary babe cradled in the arms of his tearful mother, and his father looking on with such love and joy he could've set the world alight. The folk stared in wonder at this auspicious beginning for such a child – conceived under the yew tree on the Village Green at the Blue Moon on Lammas Eve, born at the Dark Moon in the Stone Circle at Beltane. Was ever a child more blessed?

32

Bluebell stood under her favourite tree on the Village Green – a huge sweet-chestnut that produced long serrated leaves like kippers, and, in the autumn, green prickly hedgehogs full of fat brown chestnuts to roast. She wore her best dress, dyed with delicate rose madder and embroidered all over the bodice with white stars. Granny Maizie had done those, and had knitted her soft white lambswool cardigan too. Bluebell also wore a circlet of bluebells in her hair which made her feel especially magical, as they were her own flower. She was the Princess of the Bluebell Faeries, in her story at least.

It was warm and sunny, the day of Hare Moon and the day of the handfastings. Uncle Gefrin was being wed to Meadowsweet today, and Granny Maizie was very busy and excited. Her parents were also busy as they must perform the ceremony together, wearing special robes for the occasion. Celandine was to dance at the start of the ceremony all on her own in the circle. She wore a beautiful white dress that Granny Maizie had made for her at Imbolc, when Auntie Leveret had become an adult.

Bluebell could see her sister still practising nervously, jumping about like a long-legged faun on the grass. Baby Ioho was safely asleep in the Nursery for now, Auntie Leveret sitting with him while they got the Village Green and Barn ready. Auntie Leveret spent a lot of time with the baby, and Bluebell thought it was because she really wanted to be a mummy but knew she couldn't. Ioho was only two weeks old and might need another feed soon. Bluebell hoped so; she loved to sit all cuddled up to her mother whilst he suckled, sharing the closeness and that lovely smell of baby, mummy and milk all mixed up.

Her thumb crept up to her mouth and she guiltily enjoyed the comfort it brought. Nobody could see her here under her tree if she stood right back against the trunk. The jagged leaves were young and fresh and starting to provide more cover, useful if she wanted to be secret. Bluebell wondered if she should start trying to make her spell now, whilst everyone was so busy and hadn't yet noticed her absence. It must be done today, for something bad was going to happen.

Bluebell did the complicated thing where she had to go through the alphabet as fast as she could and make her eyes jump quickly along a row of something one by one – she chose the chestnut leaves today – but that didn't help. The nightmare last night had been the worst yet, so bad that she'd had to climb in with Celandine, even though her sister didn't like being disturbed again. She'd really wanted to creep into her parents' bed but she knew her father would be cross. Baby Ioho was sleeping in his new cradle made of magical yew with a crow carved on it, and if she woke him up there'd be worse trouble. So, in the darkness, with her heart pounding, she'd tried to do the alphabet thing because sometimes it helped and pushed the dark stuff away.

The nightmare last night had been different to the old ones from the Hall. All her dreams about the Moonlight Man had stopped now. Bluebell understood that Grandfather Clip had taken him away to the Otherworld and he couldn't come back ever again – nor could Martin, of whom she'd lived in abject terror for as long as she could remember. On the night of Samhain she'd seen Grandfather Clip in a dream. She'd seen him wrap the Moonlight Man and Martin in a great cloak of black raven feathers like a dark wing, and fly them away through the veil of smoke and cobwebs into the scary Otherworld. Her grandfather had turned as he passed through, and looking back he'd seen her standing there, small and alone, watching him.

He'd smiled at her and his mouth had made the words *"Farewell, Bluebell!"* which had always been a joke between them because it rhymed. She'd been so sad that he'd gone, but very happy that he'd taken the other two bad men with him. She'd thought then that everything – apart from Father being away from them and all on his own – would be happy. And when Father came back again at the Spring Equinox and they learned of Baby Ioho growing in Mummy's tummy, life was perfect. Until yesterday.

Bluebell squatted down with her back against the sharp lines and fissures of bark. She didn't care if her white cardigan got dirty, even if Granny Maizie would be really cross. Today was Hare Moon and something was going to happen, and she thought it was about Celandine. Her sister wasn't safe any more because something really bad and evil would be set free today; she knew this from the nightmare. Then it would be on the prowl – those words made her shudder with terror – all around Stonewylde. Sooner or later it would find its prey. And its prey might be Celandine.

Bluebell remembered watching one of the barn cats which lived in the huge, dusty Village Store. Granny Maizie had been waiting her turn to collect some provisions – salt and new embroidery needles – and Bluebell had wandered off round the back of some sacks of oats. In a patch of sunlight she'd seen the cat. She'd wanted to stroke it but its tail was lashing and its ears were flattened and suddenly it had leapt through the air and there'd been a terrible mad squeaking that had abruptly stopped. The tiny mouse had spilled its entrails as it twitched in death, and Bluebell had sobbed for the rest of the morning. Granny Maizie had said that hunting creatures had to catch their prey – it was their job. She said it was only natural, and that the cat had probably spent hours watching and waiting for the right moment to pounce. Bluebell had imagined the little mouse happily going about its business all morning, not knowing it was actually prey and shortly would die.

It terrified her that today something was out there hunting and would strike like a cat. But who was the prey? She'd thought long and hard about this. Baby Ioho was protected because Auntie Leveret held him a lot and that must help as she was magic, and he slept in the yew cradle that Father had made especially for him. Bluebell knew that she herself was safe because she did the alphabet thing all the time and she'd made more magic with her Bluebell Faerie book. Most people thought it was just a story but they didn't realise she and Magpie had hidden real magic in the pictures and words. So that left Celandine. Bluebell was almost sure, after what had happened yesterday at the Hall and then last night's terror, it was her big sister with her dancing feet and her long silver hair and moongazy dreaming who would be the prey.

Yesterday she'd gone up to the Hall with Mummy for Baby Ioho to be weighed and checked. In the hospital wing, Hazel had needed to talk privately with her mother so Bluebell had been sent outside to play on the wide stone terrace. Some old folk were sitting out there in a sheltered spot in the sun, and they spoke kindly to her and stroked her blonde curls. But when Bluebell trotted around a corner of the wing following a bright butterfly, she'd bumped straight into an old woman sitting all alone in a wicker chair on wheels.

It was Baba Yaga, straight from the fairy-tale that Grandfather Clip had told them. The crone was hunched into a twisted shape, her face so lined and shrivelled that she hardly looked human any more. Her mouth was sunken around her toothless gums and her nose hooked. Her eyes glowed with dark fire beneath jutting brows and she shot out a claw to grab Bluebell's arm in a hard, pinching grip.

'Raven-spawn!' she'd cried. 'Still she lives on!'

Bluebell had been too terrified to speak, trying to pull away from her iron grasp, but the old woman was strong and cackled at her attempts to escape.

'Old Violet knows, right enough! 'Tis not over till the Black Moon! The taint remains, waiting as ever, ready to prowl and search out its prey!'

'What's waiting to prowl?' whispered Bluebell, pulled in so

close to the old woman that she felt her stinking breath, warm and sour on her face.

'The toad will crawl from under his stone and you'll be the one to help me, Raven-whelp, with your pretty curls and blue eyes. You'll help Old Violet, won't you?'

Her other clawed hand came up to trace Bluebell's petal-soft cheek and the little girl shrank from her touch in horror.

'I ... I won't help you!'

The crone cackled at this and Bluebell saw clearly the long whiskers on her chin, the seamed and bristly skin around her cavernous mouth. Her eyes burned black and wicked as she scratched Bluebell's cheek with a sharp talon, from eye-socket to jaw.

'Ah, but you will, my pretty! See, Old Violet has marked you and now you're mine. You find that toad-bag and release my magic, and do it tomorrow so it's ready for Black Moon. The feet will dance no more on the tainted hill, for 'tis the snake in the stone that holds the moongazy power. Hares and barn owls – pah! The serpent o' Stonewylde is ever the stronger, and Old Violet's magic is ever greater than Raven's.'

Bluebell had frozen at these words, so scared that she wet herself. She began to cry, ashamed and terrified, and the hag released her cruel grip.

'Go now, maggot-spawn. Do my bidding and then you're free. And if you tell a soul ...'

With a grimace, she opened her mouth wide and poked out a sticky brown tongue. Her talons came up like pincers and she mimed pulling out her tongue.

'If you speak o' this, I'll have your tongue while you sleep!'

Kestrel watched the lovely handfasting ceremony with his arm around his girlfriend's waist.

'I think it's fabulous!' she sighed. 'I didn't know there were places like this! When I get married I want this sort of do.'

She widened her eyes at Kestrel but he only grinned.

'Don't look at me!' he laughed. 'You know I'm still nursing a broken heart and I'm not getting caught on the rebound. I just thought you'd be interested in seeing this ceremony, as you said you liked quaint old customs. Don't go telling everyone back on campus though or they'll all want to visit.'

They sauntered across the grass as the massive circle of people broke up and the newly-wed couples processed proudly into the Great Barn for the feast. The girl by Kestrel's side stared in dewy-eyed amazement at the two gorgeous people who'd led the ceremony. As they'd spoken the words to bind the couples who stood before them, they'd barely taken their eyes off each other. It was as if they'd been saying the vows to one another, regardless of the crowds looking on, wrapped up in their own love and solemn promises. They still stood hand in hand up on the dais and there was an almost visible aura shimmering around the pair of them. He was so dark and she so blonde, and in full view of the throng, they fell into each other's arms and kissed deeply.

'Oh look at them! It's so romantic!' she breathed. 'And their costumes ...'

'That's Yul and Sylvie,' he said. 'Good to see them properly back together again. They're looking pretty loved-up, I must say.'

He watched as Leveret walked towards the Barn, a great shaggy grey dog by her side and her arm through Rufus'. She looked completely normal but he'd heard the news.

'Hi Leveret!' he called, leaving the girlfriend as he hurried over to reach her. She turned her little face towards him, her green eyes clear and bright, her hair a mass of luxuriant dark curls that reached her waist. She wore a pretty buttercup-yellow dress today in honour of her brother's handfasting, and a circlet of flowers on her head.

'Kestrel!' she cried, her face breaking into a smile.

'How can—'

'I'd recognise your voice anywhere,' she said. 'Welcome back.'

'Just a flying day-visit from University,' he said. 'I'm ... I'm so sorry about ...'

'Me too,' she replied. 'But it could have been worse, and life goes on.'

'I just wanted to say … well, it's good to see you again. You look really lovely – I always said you'd be worth waiting for and I was right.'

'Thank you!' she beamed, blushing. 'I'm afraid it would be a long wait – another lifetime in fact – but that's made my day.'

His girlfriend had reached them and she stared at Rufus.

'I've seen you before!' she exclaimed. 'I remember your amazing hair, like conkers. You were in those magazines with Kes, weren't you? Another Aitch model – wow!'

Now Rufus blushed scarlet behind his mass of freckles, and Kestrel laughed.

'Fame at last, eh Rufus? Would you mind escorting my ladyfriend into the Barn so I can take this beautiful little maiden in on my arm? Last time we did this, Leveret, you were drugged up to the eyeballs – yes, I have heard! So let's do it properly one more time, shall we?'

The party made its way slowly through the woods, once again adrift in a lake of deepest violet-blue. Birds flitted through the trees, serenading the family group as they chatted happily, well-fed from the wedding feast and looking forward to watching the moon rise. Sylvie was tired and had almost bowed out of this, but she knew how keen Yul was to perform the little ceremony tonight. They hadn't done this for the girls and it was a custom that had died out at Stonewylde. But when Yul had overheard Old Greenbough talking about how, when he was a lad, they'd always presented new-borns to the Bright Lady, he knew it would be perfect for little Ioho. Sylvie had thought they'd do it publicly on the Village Green, but Yul had set his heart on Hare Stone, their special and very magical place at the Moon Fullness.

'Keep up, Bluebell!' she called, looking back to where the little girl trailed way behind the party. 'Are you tired? Come and hold my hand, or maybe Uncle Rufus will give you a piggy-back if you ask nicely.'

She was a little concerned about her younger daughter, who'd been quiet and miserable all day. She hoped it wasn't jealousy, but doubted it. Bluebell had never resented her older sister's gift of dance and the attention it brought, and she adored the baby. In fact she'd been very happy, trotting about on her sturdy little legs and singing at the top of her voice with her normal exuberance until yesterday. Sylvie recalled she'd been silent and strange on their way back from the Hall. Whilst Hazel had been doing the check-up, Bluebell had somehow managed to scratch her face and had wet herself, which was most unusual. Maybe she was coming down with something? Sylvie resolved to ask Leveret's advice.

Celandine skipped on ahead, anxious to get up the hill even though the sun was still shining. Sylvie smiled, recognising all the signs; she was definitely becoming more moongazy as she grew older. At least with the warm summer months ahead they could come up here every month. For the ceremony this evening they'd also brought along Miranda and Christopher, as well as Leveret, Maizie, Rufus and Magpie, and Yul carried Ioho strapped to his chest in a warm cocoon.

Sylvie couldn't recall ever feeling happier in her whole life. Yul had told her of Clip's wise words about metamorphosis and he'd been right – this new love between them was stronger and deeper than ever before, tempered into something finer by the separation, betrayal and pain of the past months. She loved Yul so very deeply and seeing him now with his tiny son made her heart ache with joy. She was still very emotional, only two weeks on from Ioho's dramatic arrival in the Stone Circle at Beltane, but she knew the dreadful illness she'd suffered after Bluebell's birth wouldn't strike this time. She felt strong and positive and was enjoying every minute of their beautiful new life together with their three children.

'Bluebell, do catch up!' she called again, stopping and waiting for the dawdling child.

As the Hare Moon rose, Yul stood with his back to the great stone and lifted his naked son to the sky. They all stood in a semi-circle facing the glorious moonrise as Yul raised the tiny baby to the deep blue heavens. Leveret had brought along Clip's old shamanic drum and she kept the beat, primeval and compelling, as Yul offered up his son in silence. The baby must've been cold and, privately, Sylvie worried about this. But she'd told herself just a few minutes in the warm evening wouldn't hurt, and at first Ioho didn't cry. His little limbs flailed the air, his hands in fists, and then he wailed but more as if in greeting to the golden moon than in complaint. It was a beautiful moment and touched the hearts of everyone present.

'I offer you my son, Bright Lady,' said Yul in his deep, soft voice. 'May he always honour the old ways, walking in harmony with you and the spirit of our land. May he serve the folk of Stonewylde well!'

At that Ioho began to yell and soon after, Leveret slowed and then stopped the drumbeats. Yul lowered him and swaddled him in a soft, warm shawl, kissing his little face with such tenderness that Sylvie felt the ready tears well up. He was a fine little boy with a mop of dark hair, and, although he seemed to have his father's handsome features, he'd inherited her pale skin and silvery-grey wolf eyes. The effect was stunning. Yul handed him over to Sylvie who sat down on the rug and leant against the stone, unbuttoning her bodice to reveal her full, tingling breast.

As Ioho suckled, the moon rose higher. In the silence, the barn owl floated noiselessly overhead to land on the stone above her. Christopher, his arm around Miranda, was moved to tears at the beauty of the occasion. Everyone was hushed as they watched the moon grow brighter and Celandine dance around them in leaping, whirling spirals, bringing down the moon magic into the waiting earth. Yul nudged Christopher and pointed out the hares that had crept up to join her, and he shook his grey head in disbelief at such a wondrous sight.

Further down the hill Bluebell and Magpie crouched by the boulders that marked the entrance into the hollow hill. Her heart thumped wildly and she muttered continuously under her breath, 'R,S,T,U,V...' They were searching the ground, difficult in the darkness even though the moon shone brightly above, and had been doing this for some time now. Bluebell was torn between worry about putting her hand on a viper, and terror at not being able to find the toad-bag. But she'd told herself that snakes slept at night time and the threat about the toad-bag was worse. She didn't even know what she was looking for exactly and she couldn't ask anyone in case Baba Yaga got her tongue.

It felt very strange down here by the boulders; completely different to the top of the hill. Bluebell was aware of the yawning gap between the two rocks, almost her height, but too narrow for even her small body to squeeze through – not that she'd have wanted to. If it were a Hollow Hill as Rufus had said, and there were faeries inside, Bluebell couldn't imagine them being good, pretty faeries like the ones in her stories. Good ones would never want to live inside a dark, secret cave with a nest of adders. These must be bad faeries, especially if that Baba Yaga crone knew about this place. Bluebell pictured them now in silver and black dresses covered in the zigzag viper pattern. Their papery wings were made of old snake-skins, and tiny black forked tongues flickered from their mouths. They hissed viciously at the prospect of their treasure, the wicked toad-bag, being stolen away by the Princess of the Bluebell Faeries.

Then she heard her mother calling her name in the moonlit darkness, panic in her voice, and her father's voice joined in. Magpie tugged at her sleeve; he wanted to go back up the hill to the stone and all the family up there. Bluebell felt the tears burst through her eyes because she simply HAD to find the toad-bag tonight. The crone has said she must find it and release the bad magic, but Bluebell had made up a plan. She'd find the nasty thing and she'd somehow get it back to the cottage and then she'd throw it into the range and burn it. She knew that burning was a way of destroying and purifying. So if she burnt it then the magic couldn't be released on the Hollow Hill like the crone had said. Her sister would be safe, and the dancing feet would continue and the hares and barn owl would be stronger than the serpent. But Magpie was pulling her, trying to make her return to her family, and she could hear lots of voices now, all calling her name. And then she felt Auntie Leveret calling her name inside her head in the way she sometimes did.

She heard people rushing down the hill and realised that Magpie was standing up waving at them all to get their attention, and she sobbed and sobbed, still on her hands and knees patting the ground, trying to locate the toad-bag in the silver moonlight. Her father arrived first and scooped her up almost roughly. He was a mixture of happy and angry and he hugged her so tightly she thought her body would pop and she kept saying that she was sorry but she was crying too much. Back up on top of the hill by the stone there was much relief and everyone asking what she'd been doing and feeling bad they hadn't noticed she'd gone missing. But then Auntie Leveret said that Magpie told her they'd been searching for a toad, and her voice sounded strange as if she were frightened too. Luckily nobody was cross with Magpie, and Mummy held her tightly on her lap where she sat up against the stone and kissed her face again and again and stroked her hair.

'Bluebell, it was very, very silly to disappear like that in the darkness. Why were you looking for a toad? We've got lots of toads in the garden at home, haven't we? Yul, please let's go back now. Celandine's finished dancing, I'm tired and I'm sure everyone else is.'

Granny Miranda was holding Baby Ioho, jigging him gently in her arms, and Auntie Leveret was talking quietly to Magpie, who was still upset that they'd done wrong by disappearing. Bluebell felt bad as it was her fault, not his, and he hadn't wanted to come. Celandine was standing very still gazing up at the blazing silver moon, her long hair glinting with moonbeams, and Rufus was talking to Christopher about hollow hills and chambered tombs. Granny Maizie was sitting on the grass in a dream, staring up at the Hare Moon, and there were silver tears glinting on her cheeks. Bluebell got up from her mother's lap and felt her heart thumping again in panic, because any minute now they'd all be trooping back down the hill and she wouldn't have found

525

the toad-bag and the taint would still be here, its dark magic prowling around, searching for its prey.

Then she noticed darling Shadow, pale in the moonlight, over behind the standing stone. He was pawing at the ground and Bluebell just knew ... she dashed over to where he snuffled at the earth and she dropped to her knees, ignoring the dog drool she'd normally have hated and his big messy paws. He'd turned over a flat stone embedded in the ground and there it was, in his mouth, but she pulled it away in case he chewed it up and died.

'Bluebell!' called her father sharply. 'Come back here now!'

She jumped up, her hand closing around the damp thing and its long cord. She must hide it fast and she didn't have a pocket so very quickly she pulled the cord over her head. She tried not to think of the dirt and Shadow's spit on it, nor the bad magic it contained, and pushed the little bag down inside her dress. All the way home on that long walk down the hill, past the scary boulders and the secret door to the Viper Faeries' nest, into the woods and then eventually on the track leading back to the Village, Bluebell held on tightly to her mother's hand and felt her feet skipping and her heart fluttering on little wings of joy. She had the wicked toad-bag! She'd saved her sister and she'd taken the bad magic away from the moondancing hill and as soon as she'd managed to burn it, everything would be alright. And that silly old Baba Yaga was wrong after all – Bluebell wasn't going to do her bidding and help her, despite the cruel mark on her cheek.

'I'm sure he'll have researched something about it,' said Sylvie. 'I did start reading all his notes years ago but somehow ...'

She and Rufus walked along a dusty, dark corridor to the tiny room that had once served Professor Siskin when he visited Stonewylde. Sylvie remembered how shocked she'd been at its meanness, and how she'd resolved to put him in a grand suite of rooms on his return. That was not to be, and in the ensuing chaotic months, and then years, after his demise, his belongings had remained in this little room, tucked away and forgotten in this distant wing of the Hall. His suitcase and laptop had been found in the Jack in the Green and then all his personal belongings had been sent back from Oxford – everything was now crammed in here.

'I never knew anything about this!' said Rufus. 'It's amazing – he was actually chronicling the history of Stonewylde?'

Sylvie nodded, opening the door to the musty room which was little better than a glorified cupboard. She felt a pang of sadness, recalling her dear little professor and his excitement about giving her the photo of Yul – the one Magus had ripped up in a paroxysm of rage. Coming in here with her brother brought it all back again. She could picture him perfectly with his wispy white hair and half-moon glasses, his velvet jacket and Panama hat, hopping about on small feet boring people with his old-fashioned homilies and scholarly enthusiasms.

'He was a highly respected historian, a professor at Oxford no less, and I'm sure he'd be delighted that one of his relations was taking an interest in his life's work. I'd always meant to do something with his notes, but somehow life got in the way. To be honest I wouldn't have done it justice. I had thought maybe one day Bluebell, with her love of story, might be interested. But if you're keen, that's marvellous! You're so clever, Rufus, and I know Professor Siskin would approve of you taking up the mantle. Although I thought you wanted to be a doctor?'

'Yes, yes I do! But I love history and archaeology too, and I find anything to do with Stonewylde fascinating. I'd love to know if there *is* a chambered tomb up in the hill at Hare Stone. It's so exciting, Sylvie! I've been reading up about them and if we actually had one here at Stonewylde ... I'll read Professor Siskin's research notes and if he does mention it, maybe we could excavate the tomb?'

'I don't know about that,' she said doubtfully. 'I really don't think we should start digging around Hare Stone.'

'No, no, not dig!' Rufus said excitedly, his dark brown eyes dancing. 'There's definitely a gap between those boulders and I've read about this – sometimes they'd roll a stone across the entrance to seal it up. They wanted to keep out any wild animals that might smell the body or the bones that had been laid inside. So we wouldn't have to dig at all – just shift the rock perhaps, and only a little bit to make the entrance large enough to squeeze inside.'

Sylvie smiled at his enthusiasm. He was as passionate as the dear old professor had been. If only he'd lived to see Stonewylde now, she thought. He'd have loved Rufus, and little Ioho too.

'Well, I'll leave you to it,' she said, with a final glance around the dark room. 'If you want to take anything back to your room, please feel free. I know you'll take care of it. This stuff has sat here since he died over fourteen years ago, and as I said, I'm sure he'd love the thought of you taking an interest. He was such a lovely man and you'd have got on well with him.'

'What's wrong, Leveret? You're looking peaky,' said Maizie, her gaze flicking around the circular room at the top of the tower.

Leveret shrugged, feeding fresh salad leaves to Hare who sat contentedly across her lap.

'I don't know ... something doesn't feel right, but I don't know what it is. I've tried everything I know but it seems that I'm not to be shown what lies ahead.'

'You look tired,' said Maizie.

'Yes, I've been sleeping badly, with horrible nightmares.'

'Nothing worse than that for putting a body out of sorts,' said Maizie, sitting herself down with a sigh. 'Our Bluebell's been having bad dreams too, waking up the whole household with her screaming every night.'

'Poor little Blue – that must be hard with Ioho too.'

'Aye, 'tis. She's jumpy as a frog, blinking and fretting and chanting her alphabet all the time, which is plain rude, and she's started bed-wetting too. I even caught her at the range the other day with the door wide open trying to set fire to something! She very near burned herself and she wouldn't tell me what she were up to. I don't know what's got into the child lately. I told Sylvie it sometimes upsets the older ones when a new babe comes along, but I'm not sure 'tis that . . .'

'Why doesn't she come here and stay with me for a bit?' suggested Leveret. 'We can keep each other company and maybe she'll tell me what's bothering her.'

'Violet, if you don't stop this we'll have to move you into a room even further away from everyone else,' said Hazel firmly. 'It's got to stop.'

The stream of invective that poured from the crone's mouth sickened her and she raised her eyebrows at the nurse standing by.

'Where's that maggot-spawn girl? Send her to me! I ain't got my scrying bowl no more and I need to know what's abroad!'

'I don't know what you're on about, I'm afraid,' said Hazel, glancing through the medical notes.

'Did she find the toad-bag?' screeched Violet. 'Stupid bitch-doctor – just answer me that! Old Heggy put 'un round the cuckoo maiden's neck to protect her and it burnt my hand – see? I still bear the marks to this very day and Heggy done that with her toad-bag!'

'Really?' said Hazel, nodding to the nurse preparing the syringe.

'Aye, the Moongazy Maiden wore the toad-bag and it were from that whore Raven, all crammed with magical charms o' protection! And it burnt me when I laid hands on her to cut out her tongue and I threw 'un off. But then I couldn't find it and all these years it's lain up there, spoiling my taint, keeping my spell at bay! 'Tis a powerful talisman, that old bag o' charms.'

She glared up at the nurse, who silently handed the syringe to the doctor. There was a little struggle as Hazel began to roll up her sleeve, revealing a stringy arm, the withered flesh hanging off in folds of crepe. Old Violet wriggled impatiently.

'Just keep still, please,' said Hazel soothingly.

'You ain't listening!' cried the old woman. 'Nobody listens to me no more and you'll all rue the day you packed me away here! That child, the curly one with blue eyes, she's a-doing my bidding right enough, afore the Black Moon.' She stopped, an evil grimace spreading over her face. 'And when the girl takes the toad-bag off the hill, Raven's protection is gone, finished ... my spoiling and my tainting will ...'

Her eyelids fluttered and her chin slumped to her chest. A rattly snore escaped her toothless gums.

'I think she's deteriorating,' said Hazel, handing back the empty syringe. 'She's talking complete nonsense now and she's vicious with her tongue. We'll up her medication a little – I don't want her ranting and raving like this again. It's really not fair on all the other old folk.'

'Yes, Hazel,' said the nurse. 'Old Violet terrifies me – all of us – and I agree with you. She's been getting much worse recently. We need to keep her nice and quiet for everyone's sake.'

Sylvie sat in Maizie's rocking chair day-dreaming, baby at her breast. She had the cottage to herself and was enjoying the brief spell of peace. Her gaze swept the familiar white-washed walls, the old oak floor-boards, the hearth with its besom tucked neatly into a corner. She was happy here, but earlier that morning as she and Yul lay in each other's arms watching the sunlight creep into the bedroom, they'd discussed the future and whether or not to remain in the cottage. He'd mentioned the new building programme in the Village and had asked if she'd like him to build a home for the family.

Sylvie had snuggled more deeply into the crook of his arm, warm and safe, her hair spilling across his chest. Ioho had finished his early morning feed and was tucked back in his crib, and nobody else was yet awake. Yul had kissed her tenderly, his fingers stroking her milky skin, his face nuzzling her hair.

'I could build us a beautiful cottage,' he'd said softly, 'and it would be yours to decide on, what you'd like, how you'd like it set up. The garden would be laid out exactly as we chose, with our own chickens and beehives, and even a pig if you wanted to be really traditional. And I'd make you a spinning wheel and a loom, and—'

Wriggling out of his embrace to reach his lips, she'd silenced him with a kiss. Then she'd pulled back a little so she could gaze at him, and she'd seen his love, his tenderness, his kindness, all burning so very brightly in those deep grey eyes. She'd bent to kiss him again, her lips tingling where they brushed the dark stubble on his jaw. His face was still hollowed, the cheekbones sharp, from when he'd been living in exile and loneliness after she'd sent him away. Her heart had jolted then at the thought of his absence. How had she ever not wanted him? All she longed for now was her beloved Yul constantly by her side. She resented every second he spent away from her, working on the estate.

'That all sounds lovely,' she'd said softly, 'but it'd be an awful lot of work for you, wouldn't it? Maybe for now we should just stay here and enjoy the time together. The girls missed you so much when we were living apart. Perhaps we could think about our own cottage next year, but enjoy this year first and stay with Maizie? I'm happy here and so are the children. Just so long as you don't mind? I mean, the memories of your awful childhood?'

Yul had held her gaze and she'd felt herself consumed by the blaze she saw within him.

'You've banished any unhappiness, any bad memories, for-ever,' he whispered. 'That was all in another life-time, it seems. I remember you visiting me here for the first time, after that Samhain when I almost died. Mother had made me up a bed in the parlour and you came in and held me tight ... I remember thinking then how I wished you lived here with me.'

Sylvie smiled at this.

'I remember that too!' she said. 'Leveret was a toddler and Maizie was a little embarrassed having me here, Hallfolk no less, but she was very welcoming. I recall thinking just how much I wanted to live here with you. Well ... if you're happy to stay, then let's do that, and think about our own cottage another time. We've got so much catching up to do, and I don't want you labouring from dawn to dusk when we could be spending that time together.'

With a gentle fingertip she traced a groove in his skin that ran down the side of his mouth, where his face creased when he smiled. He turned his head to kiss her finger and laughed.

'What – are you discovering my wrinkles already?'

'I love these laughter lines on you,' she said. 'I've noticed them starting round my eyes, but surely we're too young for wrinkles?'

'I'll love all yours,' he promised. 'When you're as shrivelled and dried up as last year's apples, I shall still love you. Can you imagine us as a little old couple in our cottage, you with your knitting and me with my whittling, and all our grandchildren around us?'

'I've only just given birth!' she laughed. 'Don't wish grand-children on me already!'

Yul had smiled and pulled her down again so their mouths met, and they'd kissed as the sun pushed further into the room and filled it with brightness and warmth. And now, sitting here in the rocking chair, Sylvie thought dreamily of Yul and wished he were here instead of poring over the records with Edward, looking at the yields and projected figures. She decided that this evening she'd make a start on weaving the new linen for the shirt she planned to make him. She was keen to show him her new skills and be a proper wife, in the old Stonewylde way. She thought of the cottage he'd offered and it was tempting, but living here with Maizie was comfortable and easy, and she was still learning how to be a goodwife.

Sylvie glanced down at Ioho, firmly attached to her and suck-ing strongly at her breast. She was so glad her milk was plentiful this time and that she was able to satisfy his hunger. He was such a good little boy, sleeping and feeding well. She was sur-prised to find that instead of being shut contentedly as he fed, his startling grey eyes with the darker rings around the pale irises were wide open and locked onto her face.

'Are you looking at me, you darling boy?' she said softly. 'Have you been watching Mummy's face as she day-dreams?'

His gaze was so intense, so knowing. She smiled down at him with adoration, a gentle finger nudging back the wisps of dark

hair on his forehead, already curling like his father's. His eyebrows were winged exactly like Yul's – he was such a beautiful
little boy. A tiny hand with perfect fingernails reached up and
curled trustingly around her finger. Ioho gripped her tightly as if
they'd never be parted.

'What's going to become of you, I wonder?' she whispered.
'You're destined for great things, I'm sure. A Green Boy growing
up surrounded by such magic and so much love. You've made
my life complete, little Ioho, and your father's too. We're so very
lucky you came to us.'

He continued to gaze up at her as she fed him her milk. Sylvie
felt sure that he was communicating with her, telling her how
much he loved her too, for his eyes never left hers. She sighed
contentedly, thanking the Goddess yet again for such happiness.
It was two days before the Black Moon, when their world would
be shattered like a great mirror dropped on the cobblestones.

33

They all climbed the hill heading towards the massive sentinel stone that stood at the very top, as it had done throughout
the ages. They were almost the same party that had come at Hare
Moon, except for Maizie, who was organising the women in the
Barn making summer hats, and Miranda and Christopher, who
were busy setting up his hive at Woodland Cottage. Yul and
Magpie carried the picnic, Shadow assisted Leveret, and Sylvie
carried the baby. The girls brought Ioho's blanket, a clean nappy
and his sunshade, and Rufus had a spade, lantern and a crow-
bar. Today Yul had promised that they'd try to move one of
the stones in front of the chamber and perhaps squeeze inside.
Professor Siskin's notes hadn't specifically said that there was a
chambered tomb on this hill, but he'd suspected there was one
somewhere on the estate, in keeping with all the other sacred
sites. Rufus was very excited that – with Shadow's help – it was
he who'd discovered it.

Bluebell held Leveret's hand as they reached the outcrop of
rocks and paused to get their breath. The little girl kicked at the
ground and her face was red from crying; she hadn't wanted
them to come here today and had had a screaming tantrum
back in the Village, and again in the woods just now. Yul had
become angry with her, which only made it worse. They could
have left her behind with Maizie or in the Nursery, but he'd
wanted to make it a family party and little Bluebell would have
been missed. He'd hoped she'd get over it, although looking at

her tearful face now, he wondered if he'd been right to force her to join them.

Leveret dropped to her knees and held Bluebell close, whispering in her ear.

'Tell me, Blue. You can tell me what's so bad.'

But the child shook her head obstinately and even poked her tongue out, although Leveret couldn't see that.

'I understand you found something bad up here, but you said you'd burnt it, didn't you? So whatever it was has gone now. Hasn't it?'

'I ... I thought it would go. I thought I could save the day. But it didn't work. It's on the prowl now and it's much worse than the Moonlight Man ever was.'

'But what is it? I know it's something to do with a toad because Magpie told me that night.'

'No! He couldn't have, because he can't talk!'

'I've had strange visions about a toad too, Bluebell. I didn't understand what it meant – *please* tell me what you found. This toad might be something important.'

'It ... it was only a dirty old pouch thing on a string and ... I didn't see any toad at all,' said Bluebell reluctantly. 'I thought if I burnt it ...'

The party were now moving away; the plan was to eat their picnic up by the stone first and then come down here later to try and shift the boulder.

'We're on the move, Leveret!' said Sylvie. 'Come on, Bluebell!'

'We'll catch up in a second,' said Leveret. 'Bluebell's just telling me something.'

'I'm not!' said Bluebell crossly. 'I just want us to go home! We shouldn't have come here today. Why is it the Black Moon? What's that?'

'Is that what's been worrying you? You should've said! It's a special Dark Moon and it doesn't happen very often. Like the Blue Moon is a magical full moon when it's the second one in a month, the Black Moon is when there's a second Dark Moon in a month.'

535

'I don't like the Dark Moon anyway,' said Bluebell, her voice catching. 'So the Black Moon will be even worse.'

'I know – most people feel like that,' said Leveret gently. 'Me and Yul – we've both always loved the Dark Moon and I think Ioho will be the same as he was born on one. But please don't worry, Blue. The Black Moon will be fine.'

'O, P, Q, R,' chanted Bluebell, her eyes jumping from one clump of grass to the next. 'S, T, U, V, W, X, Y, Z!'

The picnic was over and Sylvie shook the crumbs from the cloth. Leveret snoozed on the rug with Bluebell cuddled up, thumb in mouth, dozing in the crook of her arm. They were exhausted, and Sylvie gathered they'd had another disturbed night in the tower, where Bluebell had been staying for a few nights. Sylvie gazed down at her daughter and sister-in-law, both looking so peaceful now. The little girl's face was still puffy where she'd been crying again during the picnic, begging for them all to go back to the Village, much to everyone's annoyance. It was a relief she'd dropped off to sleep now in the warm May sunshine. Sylvie thought she must bring Bluebell home today as it really wasn't fair on poor Leveret or Magpie, expecting them to cope with her nightmares. It was a shame they'd started up again after being absent for so long. Other than Ioho's arrival, Sylvie couldn't understand what had triggered them.

Yul, Magpie and Rufus had walked back down the hill with the tools and lantern. Celandine had been persuaded to go with them to watch, but she'd returned almost immediately. She'd spotted a papery snake-skin down by the boulders and had shrieked in terror, running back in panic to where Sylvie, Leveret, Bluebell and the baby sat by Hare Stone. The adders were out of hibernation now, basking in the sun to warm their cold blood, the males fighting in their strange upright dance to win the female. Leveret had told them all this after Celandine had come back shuddering with dread at the thought of snakes nearby. Leveret had hoped to allay her fears but Celandine had said she was only making it worse, and she really couldn't bear to hear about the horrible things.

Celandine was still jittery and uncomfortable as she sat now with Sylvie, holding her brother in her arms and rocking him, for her own comfort as much as his. Her silvery blonde hair was almost as long as her mother's and fell in silky strands around her arms, her curls outgrown. She was becoming so tall now, her limbs as slender as a foal's, and in September she'd be leaving Nursery to start at the Village School. Sylvie found her really helpful with the baby. Celandine fussed over him like a little mother, helping to bath him, changing his nappies and keeping him amused. She was still a serious, thoughtful child; often she'd look up and Sylvie would see Yul in her smoky grey eyes.

In the bright sunshine they all wore straw hats, and Ioho wore an adorable bonnet to shade his little face. Earlier on, as everyone sat eating the picnic and chatting, they'd all laughed when Rufus had said he looked like a flower with big white petals. Today, at one month old, Ioho had given his first proper smile and Sylvie's heart had melted. She'd looked deep into her son's amazing wolf-grey eyes, so like the grandfather's he'd never know, and she'd poured out her love to him. He was so very special, so precious, and she felt truly blessed. Who'd ever have imagined this darling little boy coming into their lives and truly uniting their family? He was the alchemy of darkness and brightness made one, conceived at the Blue Moon and born at the Dark Moon, living proof of the harmony and balance between his parents. Gazing at the tiny boy, Sylvie felt that he was the reason she'd been brought to Stonewylde; a new life so magical and destined for such great things.

A sudden shadow passed overhead, momentarily darkening the brilliant sunlight, and Sylvie felt her skin prickle. She squinted up, trying to make out its cause, and glimpsed a large, pale bird soaring against the sunbeams, impossible to see clearly. It looked like a barn owl but must surely be a seagull or perhaps a buzzard? The heat was still intense but she shivered and thought suddenly of Yul and the boys down at the entrance to the tomb. A whisper of dread trickled through her, for she'd never felt entirely comfortable about opening up this hidden cave in the hillside. Were they alright? Had something terrible happened? The skin on her arms tingled and the fine hair stood on end; briskly she rubbed it and dismissed her silly fears. She reached across and picked up her bottle of water, taking a long draught as she must keep up her fluid intake, what with the heat and breast-feeding.

Then, with her baby cradled happily in her elder daughter's arms, and her younger daughter cuddled up to her sister-in-law, and all beautiful and right with her world, Sylvie moved the edge of the rug slightly. The viper coiled beneath it stretched forward in smooth slow-motion and stabbed its fangs deep into her ankle. She looked down in complete, paralysed disbelief. The great silver and black chevroned snake recoiled sharply, pulling back into itself, into a kinked double S. Then it slithered away silently out of sight behind the standing stone, away to a new, warm basking spot.

It hadn't really happened surely – had she just imagined it? Sylvie stared at the rug, then stared at her foot, which had started to swell. There were two puncture holes and her ankle hurt – and now her leg hurt and she sat back suddenly, the world tilting. But it would be alright of course. It was just an adder bite and she wasn't a baby or young child – thank Goddess it hadn't bitten Ioho, Bluebell or Celandine! Snake bites in England didn't kill healthy adults. Hazel had explained all this last summer – only a handful of recorded deaths in many years as very few people were allergic to the venom. Pain, discomfort, even bruising ... feeling unwell perhaps, but no more than that, and certainly nothing to make a fuss about. She mustn't frighten the children by screaming. She tried not to imagine the dark venom in her bloodstream, travelling up her leg, in her veins and arteries. Would it affect her milk? What a good job she'd just fed Ioho. She'd have to give him dried baby milk for the next feed just to be on the safe side, or ask Dawn or another nursing mother to feed him. Sylvie was surprised to find herself feeling a little breathless. It was just shock of course; she'd be fine. But then . . .

Her mouth was very dry and her breath rasped; she found it hard to swallow. She felt so dizzy and slumped down onto the rug, cradling her head in her arm, everything slightly unreal. Her three children and Leveret looked at peace in the bright sunshine, with the larks singing all around them, and the bees buzzing in the clover and the sky so vast and sweet, a perfect for-get-me-not blue. Forget-me-not, she thought wildly, as a pair of swallows flew high above in graceful union. A beautiful cobalt-blue butterfly with silver-studded wings danced towards her, the exact shade of Bluebell's eyes. Her heart was beating very fast in her chest and she tried to speak, to waken Leveret, to ask for someone to please sort this out because actually, it was all becoming a bit frightening . . .

The bright day began to darken. She felt so very lightheaded and the pain in her leg was sharp, throbbing. Her throat was tight and the breath wouldn't come. It just wouldn't come. She felt sick, so weak, she wanted Yul now. And then Bluebell began to scream and scream, her face scarlet. The peace was shattered and Leveret was shouting for help and the baby was howling and Celandine was clutching him but trying to hold her tight too, shouting 'Mummy! Mummy!' over and over.

And Yul was there at last and Sylvie smiled, knowing now she'd be safe, now it would all be alright. She felt his arms lifting her, cradling her, holding her tight and safe . . .

Magpie had made a nest for the children and all three sat safe and protected in his lap, wrapped in his arms as he rocked them, all crying, with their mouths round holes of horror like little fledglings waiting to be fed. Leveret was holding Sylvie's wrist, her fingers pushing down hard to feel the pulse, her dark curls tumbling forward. Rufus was at her swollen leg – she could see his gleaming hair – and Yul was all wild eyes and wide mouth and white face. He was shouting at Rufus to go and get Hazel NOW and to call the air ambulance and Rufus was crying too, saying he'd go but she was reacting so badly and so rapidly that she must be allergic to the venom and she was in anaphylactic shock and he'd run for help but ... but it was darker and getting very cold now and everything was sinking deeper and deeper and slower and slower.

'Sylvie, Sylvie!' sobbed Yul, rocking her, stroking the hair back from her face frantically. 'Sylvie, don't leave me! *Don't leave me!'*

She could hear her children calling her, her baby crying for her, but they were far away and she must be gone now, for it was too late. But she loved them all so very much and this was not – surely – real? Not the end of her magical life at Stonewylde? Not her fate, to die on the hill marked by Hare Stone, the place where she'd danced for the Bright Lady and brought down the moon magic to the waiting land? This was not how it should be?

'I'm sorry ...' she whispered, as suddenly truth blossomed and she saw deep inside, into the perfect, inexorable pattern that was life and destiny.

Yul craned his ear next to her mouth to catch her words, and she tried to kiss him.

'I'll never leave you,' she whispered. 'I'll always be here with you ...'

'Sylvie,' he choked, and she felt his tears falling hot on her face, felt his body shaking so violently with great sobs, with terror. 'Sylvie, my Sylvie ...'

'Don't send me to the Otherworld, Yul,' she gasped, her throat now almost closed. 'Don't let me burn.'

'No! No! Of course you won't—'

'I ... I must be here, Yul, for eternity, beneath the earth in this hill. I'll dance for you in the moonlight ...'

'I won't let you go!' he cried, desperately cradling her against his chest, crushing her to his heart. 'You're my life ...'

Leveret was gripping her hand and suddenly she felt Leveret's healing power and strength pouring into her, flooding in like a cool river and up through her arm, trying to douse the venom that pulsed through her system, trying so desperately to fight it ...

'Stay with us!' shouted Leveret. 'Stay, Sylvie!'

'Sylvie, please ...' sobbed Yul, 'please, my moongazy girl ...'

She wasn't burned at the Yew of Death, and nor was her presence at Stonewylde marked by a simple pebble. Her presence became Stonewylde, for this had always been her destiny. From that moment of conception, as the crimson Harvest Moon rose over the woods and her young faerie mother accepted the seed of life from the man in the hawk mask, this had awaited Sylvie. She had finally found the place where she belonged: in the womb of the Goddess, deep inside the earth at this sacred place marked so very long ago by the ancestors.

One morning at dawn, as the red sun rose over the hills and the light was soft and blush-pink, Sylvie was taken from the Great Barn. The folk of Stonewylde had been paying their respects since sunset the evening before, but now she was brought back ceremoniously to the place that had always called to her. She lay on a litter of woven wicker laced with flowers, and was carried carefully on many strong shoulders. Through the woods filled with late bluebells and birdsong they came, the early morning light streaming mistily through the new greenery. Under the arch of branches and into the field they stepped, to climb slowly up the hill to the outcrop of rocks.

The chambered tomb inside the hill became her resting place, as it had for others long, long ago. Inscribed all around the ancient chamber were triple hares, their ears linked, dancing inside their circles of eternity. There were spirals patterned everywhere, and scratched and painted onto the stone walls and ceiling were older, more primitive images. Deft outlines of hares leapt, and some gazed up at the full moon. And that most primeval of symbols was all over – the serpent uncoiling into S.

The folk of Stonewylde had prepared the cold chamber, filling it with flowers, greenery and blossom to make a bower for the queen of their tribe. The carved stone bier in the centre of the long-barrow had been decorated in her honour to create a soft bed of cushions and petals. The other small, dark chambers leading off into the depths of the hillside were left undisturbed, respecting the precious ones who'd been laid there many life-times ago.

A galaxy of tiny candles had been lit to welcome her and to banish darkness, until the stone chamber became a temple of soft, flickering light. Sylvie was dressed in finest white linen and her arms were crossed on her breast. Her silver hair was spread around her on the pillow, a circlet of flowers around her head. On her breast Yul placed the tiny golden hare carved of yew, and the love token he'd woven for her and tied with silver ribbon one Lammas, hoping to be her sweetheart. Trembling, he kissed her white lips and placed in her cold fingers a lock of his own hair, which she would hold for eternity. Everyone departed, leaving Yul alone with his beloved.

Those who'd come up the hill went down to the Village, down to the Hall, down to their normal, now-saddened lives. But Leveret took her little nieces up to the standing stone at the top. Today she wore her hare headdress and the mantle of Wise Woman and she held the children's hands as they guided her, one on each side, to the summit. The dew was a sparkling carpet of crystal prisms at their feet and as they stood, their shadows were huge in the low, golden sunlight of early morning.

'We three,' Leveret said softly, 'we three will always take care of Ioho and we'll take care of each other, and your father too. We are three special ones, each with magic at our fingertips and each with a different gift. We all have Raven's blood in our veins and we are now the three maidens who must guard and protect Stonewylde and all the folk here.'

Bluebell looked at their giant shadows and knew that they must be as strong as giants, and just as brave. Inside she felt the shard of sorrow turning everything to ice.

'I have made you each a charm-bag,' the young Wise Woman said. 'There's one for Ioho too, when he's big enough to wear such a thing.'

'What's inside them, Auntie Leveret?' whispered Celandine,

taking the tiny sealed leather pouch that hung on a cord.

'A lock of your mother's silver hair, a crescent-moon of her fingernail, an adder-stone and some herbs,' said Leveret.

'An adder-stone?' shuddered Celandine.

'It's an ancient magical protection,' said Leveret. 'The Glain Neidr – a special stone with a hole in it.'

'Not a toad?' muttered Bluebell, her heart numb with grief as she pulled the cord of the charm pouch over her head.

'No, Bluebell, not a toad. That was just Old Violet's name for a charm pouch.'

'But why didn't it save Mummy then?' cried Bluebell. 'I don't understand! I thought it was bad but you said—'

'Bluebell, you didn't do wrong. You did the best you could, just as we talked about. The toad-bag kept your mother safe for as long as she needed to be here with us. But now ... now she's in the Hollow Hill with all the magic and that's right. You played the part you had to, just as we all did. Nobody could stop what had to happen.'

The children felt the dewy ground beneath their feet and gazed at the golden orb in the pink sky, the curling mist that still clung to the trees below, the three long-legged shadows before them. They both held on to the strong hand that gripped theirs with such confidence and comfort, so the shadows were linked into one triple figure. Perhaps one day the world would seem right again, but it didn't today.

Yul sat with her all day, unheeding the passing hours, wanting never to leave her side. Overhead, above Hare Stone, the sun climbed in the blue sky and the shadow cast by the great marker stone moved around measuring the time, like a black finger pointing accusingly. All day Yul sat with his true-love in their final hours together. He yearned, as the minutes ticked by, second by relentless second, to slow the turning of the earth and delay that moment when darkness would come. But at last the long day and the vigil in the tomb were over. The tired sun began to sink towards the waiting folds of land.

At sunset her family came to say farewell; her three children and her two mothers, her brother Rufus and her sister Leveret. Silently, for too many tears had been shed during the days since the Black Moon, they entered the tomb. Yul sat, as if carved in stone, his curly head bowed. They brought fresh flowers which they placed about her on the soft white bed where she lay. They lit more candles and they took one final look. The baby didn't cry and the little girls were hushed, beyond sobbing now.

Sylvie looked serene and at peace in the resting place that had always been here, had always called to her, had always waited for her. Stonewylde had at last taken her back, into the womb, into the place of dancing feet and moonlight, the place of hares and eternity, the place of moon magic and coiled spirals deep in the earth. Here was the resting place for the Moongazy Maiden who must lie beneath the earth and weave her magic for Stonewylde. Sylvie was finally here, deep in the hill, where she belonged.

The desolate group took their leave of her, the little girls on either side of their father, who could barely breathe for sorrow. The boulder was rolled smoothly back into place – so much easier than anyone had expected – and the tomb was once again sealed. Silently, the family group returned to the Village on automatic feet, to the ordinary things of life that awaited them. The baby must be fed, the girls tucked into bed and the range stoked with logs. Yul must remember to take in breath and let it out, and to swallow food and water, and to look his children in the eye and give them some purpose for living. Though what that could be, he had no idea.

Once more the Hollow Hill held its secret treasure, marked by a great stone on the top where the barn owl sat and the hares danced and gazed at the moon. The earth turned and life went on, as it does. Darkness and brightness, death and life, the pattern continued and slowly, the wounds in their hearts healed. Slowly, gradually, there was once more laughter and life. The children were loved and cared for by their family and the folk of

Stonewylde, who all tried to cushion the awful, tragic absence of their mother.

For Yul it took much, much longer. Never again was life bright or sweet in the same way. For him, every single thing was shrouded in the ashen-grey veil of mourning and grief. At first, after she'd been entombed in the hill, he too entered the grave. Darkness came upon him – the darkness of pain and despair, of loss so sharp it shredded his heart and sliced his soul. He lived in hunger and bleakness, hiding his blackness deep where nobody could find him. He locked himself in his own tomb of misery from which there was no release, and could never be any release, for Sylvie was gone. Sylvie, his love and his life – without her there was nothing. Nobody could reach him and nobody could help.

But then, in time, he began to feel her pain and desolation. She howled at him in the wind and washed him with tears of rain. He started to feel her sorrow all around him; her sacrifice was as nothing if he were only to walk the path of despair. With her sorrow, he began to understand her words, whispered as she'd died in his arms on the hill top.

'I'll never leave you,' she'd whispered. 'I'll always be here with you ...'

Slowly, he started to understand. Life gradually awakened inside him after a winter of frozen death. The Green Magic began to bud and unfurl within him, shoots of new life began to grow. Finally, he emerged blinking and starved from his Underworld of misery to a bright spring of awakening.

Then he understood her words and he felt her presence everywhere. She had not passed on to the Otherworld. She had not left him – she had stayed, to walk Stonewylde with him at every step. He felt her feet beside his on the earth. Her soft breath was in the breeze that caressed his cheek. Her eyes sparkled in the dew, her strands of silvery hair were the cobwebs that trailed like spun silk in the branches. Her voice came to him on the wind, spoke his name, told of her undying love for him. He laid his head on her breast and felt her beneath him as he lay on the grass on the hillside. Everywhere he looked, everywhere he turned, she was there with him.

Sylvie was Stonewylde all around him – his life, his soul, his reason for existence. She was there for all time and she would never leave him. She was the Goddess who walked forever in silver beauty over the land of Stonewylde. She was with him always; joy had ended, sorrow would never end, but love would nurture him for eternity.

Finally, when the wheel had turned and time had passed, Yul understood the mystery. Everything in this life is but smoke and shadow. At the end, only the beauty of the land remains – the seasons, the skies, the moon and the sun, the stars that sparkle in the heavens. All that remains, at the end of desire, is the dance of life and the magic of the Goddess who is life itself.

Sylvie lived on forever in the landscape – she *was* the landscape. Many years ago she had come hoping to be healed, and now she would give healing. Her love and her magic were in this place for all time, to be shared by her people and her beloved. Sylvie and Stonewylde were one.

S lowly, silently, the moon rose over the chimneys of the Hall, blazing through the mullioned windows to form geometric patterns of moon shadow on the walls of unlit rooms. Inside the teeming building, the elderly folk in their wing gazed out and reminisced about younger, wilder days, and how the Moon Fullness had enchanted them. The patients in the Healing Centre were entranced by her bright glance. They spoke of folk tales and magic, convinced that here, surely, the full moon was somehow different. Others were stirred by her touch, for she was part of their heritage and in their blood, and with her came the bloom of ripeness. Youngsters felt their heartbeats quicken under her gaze, dreaming of secrets yet unknown. Up in the tower, the silent gongs trembled slightly at her fingertips, and a whisper of sound vibrated through the circular room.

She cleared the trees in the woodlands and hallowed the Village Green and the dancer who moved with such quicksilver grace. She blessed all who celebrated her in hidden places, entwined and enraptured under her dazzling luminosity. She shone onto the enormous roof of the Great Barn where folk gathered together for their evening of crafts and companionship, gladdening their hearts. She brushed the eaves of the Jack in the Green where old men sat drinking tankards of Stonewylde cider and rolling dice. She climbed high in the sky above the Stone Circle, sending her silver beams around the arena to sanctify every tall stone, bathing the labyrinth of Green Magic beneath the earth with her radiant and glorious energy.

The Bright Lady peered through the stone portals of the Dolmen to dust the hare-headed shaman who sat motionless by a fire, journeying through other realms. With paws of silver the grizzled dog lay close by, twitching in moon-blessed dreams. She skimmed above the white canyons of Quarrycleave, still failing to penetrate the darkness there, and danced light-footed over the white disc of stone up at Mooncliffe. She was everywhere at Stonewylde, walking the night on tiptoes of silver, trailing a path of moonbeams and starlight, bringing a gleam to the eye and turning tears to drops of crystal.

An owl hooted long and low from the dark woods. The man climbed the Hollow Hill to the standing stone at its summit and hunkered down, his back against the tall monolith as he gazed out at the distant sea. The silver moon danced over the landscape and glinted in his eyes. He gazed up at the dusty white rainbow arched across the black velvet sky; millions upon millions of sparkling stars, bright diamonds flung on the cloak of night. What was his pin-prick of pain to such a universe?

The hares gathered further down the hill in their timeless moon-dance. And he felt her come to him, as she'd promised, as she always did. She was here, all around him, beneath him, above him. Once again his Moongazy Girl spread her immortal wings and danced for him, caressing his skin with her cold silver touch.

The man shut his eyes and hugged his knees and felt his heart continue, still, to beat. Up here, by the stone on the hill, no one but his beloved could touch him. Up here, as her brightness once more found his darkness, no one could hear him cry.

Acknowledgements

And now, nine years after that magical experience in a labyrinth of autumn leaves which inspired me to start writing, the Stonewylde Series is finally finished.

These books have changed my life, and nine years on, everything is as different as it could possibly be. I can never adequately thank all the people who've helped make this happen. You know who you are, and I hope you also know how very grateful I am to you.

But in an attempt to acknowledge the support I've been given, I'd like to thank:

My three sons, George, Oliver and William (oh alright then – Max, Olly and Will) for their constant love and faith, and for putting up with the original obsession that turned their lives upside down while I wrote like one possessed. You were teenagers when I started and are now three young men who fill my heart with pride. Will helped edit this final book and a publisher should snap him up – he's brilliant. My foster daughter Kirsty came along after the initial books were drafted, and has been such a wonderful support to me ever since. I'm sure all my children will end up writing one day.

My original agent, Clare Pearson of Eddison Pearson, who was fantastic and edited the original three books so patiently and with no reward – thank you, Clare!

My agent for these five Stonewylde books, Piers Russell-Cobb of MediaFund Ltd, who has represented me so well and negotiated such a great deal with Malcolm Edwards of Gollancz (and has taken me to posh watering holes in London!).

The team at Gollancz and Orion including my talented, over-worked editor, Gillian Redfearn, the ever-efficient Charlie Panayiotou, Nina, Jen, Jo, Maggy, Jon and all the people behind the scenes who've helped put Stonewylde on the shelves. Also the Art Dept and Larry Rostant for creating the stunning covers. Thanks, everyone.

Rob Walster at Big Blu Design for his original artwork, and for putting together the Stonewylde logo.

All my lovely family, far and wide, and especially my step-father for originally lending me the money to self-publish the first books, and all my sisters for their support and encourage-ment. Extra thanks must go to Claire for her help with the Stonewylde logo and other beautiful art work, and Kim for her enthusiastic help with publicity.

My friends and ex-colleagues in Dorset who watched their school-teaching friend become a different person, but who all supported me so wonderfully from the start, and still do to this day.

The Hare Preservation Trust (*www.hare-preservation-trust.co.uk* or see my website) for the information used in this final book about raising orphaned leverets. This is a tiny charity who need support – it was thanks to a hare that I reconnected with nature and wrote Stonewylde.

Most heartfelt thanks go to the huge Stonewylde Community – that band of readers who've supported me and the books so enthusiastically. Some joined right back in the beginning, some only recently, but you're all a great bunch of people and have enriched my life. It's thanks to you that the Stonewylde books are finding success, and I'd never have believed readers could embrace a series of books in the way you have, and turn the whole concept into something so amazing. Thank you all for everything you do to help promote the books, and for the warmth and friendship you've given me and each other. You're a very special group of people and even though Stonewylde has now finished, our community certainly hasn't. If anyone reading this has not yet discovered the community, take a peek at *www.stonewylde.net* and you'll be amazed!

And at the end, there's Mr B, the one who's made my life perfect and my dreams come true. None of this would have happened without your rock-solid love and support, not to mention your wizardry with all things technical. For everything – thank you!

Now Stonewylde is done, but for us, the adventure continues. Where next, Mr B?